White Gold Wielder

Also by Stephen R. Donaldson
Published by Ballantine Books:

Book Three of The Second Chronicles of Thomas Covenant

White Gold Wielder

STEPHEN R. DONALDSON

A Del Rey Book

BALLANTINE BOOKS • NEW YORK

A Del Rey Book
Published by Ballantine Books

Manufactured in the United States of America

First Edition: April 1983

Library of Congress Cataloging in Publication Data

Donaldson, Stephen R.
      White gold wielder.
      (The Second chronicles of Thomas Covenant; book 3)
      "A Del Rey book."
      I. Title. II. Series: Donaldson, Stephen R. Second
chronicles of Thomas Covenant; book 3.
PS3554.O469W48   1983   813'.54   82–20640
ISBN 0–345–30307–5

1 2 3 4 5 6 7 8 9 10

To BRUCE L. BLACKIE—

without whose help. . . .

Contents

Contents

What Has Gone Before

THE WOUNDED LAND, Book One of The Second Chronicles of Thomas Covenant, describes the return of Thomas Covenant to the Land—a realm of magic and peril where, in the past, he fought a bitter battle against sin and madness, and prevailed. Using the power of wild magic, he overcame Lord Foul the Despiser, the Land's ancient enemy, thus winning peace for the Land and integrity for himself.

Ten years have passed for Covenant, years that represent many centuries in the life of the Land; Lord Foul has regained his strength. Confident that he will succeed in his efforts to gain possession of Covenant's white gold ring—the wild magic —Lord Foul summons Covenant to the Land. Covenant finds himself on Kevin's Watch, where once before Foul prophesied that Covenant would destroy the world. Now that prophecy is reaffirmed, but in a new and terrible way.

Accompanied by Linden Avery, a doctor who was unwittingly drawn to the Land with him, Covenant descends to the old village of Mithil Stonedown, where he first encounters the heinous force that the Despiser has unleashed: the Sunbane. The Sunbane is a corruption of the Law of Nature; it afflicts the Land with rain, drought, fertility, and pestilence in mad succession. It has already slain the old forests; as it intensifies it threatens to destroy every form of life. The people of the Land are driven to bloody sacrificial rites to appease the Sunbane for their own survival.

Seeing the extremity of their plight, Covenant begins a quest for an understanding of the Sunbane, and for a way to heal the Land. Guided by Sunder, a man from Mithil Stonedown, he and Linden fare northward toward Revelstone, where lives the Clave, the lore-masters who most clearly comprehend and use the Sunbane. But the travelers are pursued by Ravers, Lord Foul's ancient servants, whose purpose is to afflict Covenant with a strange venom that will eventually drive him mad with power.

Surviving the perils of the Sunbane and the attacks of venom, Covenant, Linden, and Sunder continue northward. As they near Andelain, a once-beautiful region in the center of the Land, they encounter another village, Crystal Stonedown, in which a woman named Hollian is being threatened by the Clave because of her power to foresee the Sunbane. The travelers rescue her, and she joins them on their quest.

She informs Covenant that Andelain, while still beautiful, has become a place of horror. Dismayed by this desecration, Covenant enters Andelain alone to confront the evil therein. He learns that Andelain is not a place of evil: rather, it has become a place of power where the Dead gather around a Forestal who defends the trees. Covenant soon meets this Forestal, who was once a man named Hile Troy, and several of his former friends—the Lords Mhoram and Elena, the Bloodguard Bannor, and the Giant Saltheart Foamfollower. The Forestal and the Dead give Covenant gifts of obscure knowledge and advice; and Foamfollower offers Covenant the companionship of a strange ebony creature named Vain, who was created by the ur-viles of the Demondim, and whose purpose is hidden.

With Vain behind him, Covenant seeks to rejoin his companions, who, in his absence, have been captured by the Clave. His search for them nearly costs him his life, first in the desperate village of Stonemight Woodhelven, then among the Sunbane victims of During Stonedown. However, with the aid of the Waynhim, he at last wins his way to Revelstone. There he meets Gibbon, the leader of the Clave, and learns that his friends have been imprisoned so that their blood can be used to manipulate the Sunbane.

Desperate to free his friends and to gain knowledge of Lord Foul's atrocity, Covenant submits to a soothtell, a ritual of blood in which much of the truth is revealed. His visions show him two crucial facts: that the source of the Sunbane lies in the destruction of the Staff of Law, a powerful tool that formerly supported the natural order; and that the Clave actually serves Lord Foul through the actions of the Raver that controls Gibbon.

Unleashing the wild magic, Covenant frees his friends from Revelstone; he then resolves to find the One Tree, from which the original Staff of Law was made, so that he can fashion a new one to use against the Sunbane.

In this purpose he is joined by Brinn, Cail, Ceer, and Hergrom: *Haruchai*, members of the race that spawned the Bloodguard. With Linden, Sunder, Hollian, and Vain, Covenant turns eastward toward the sea, hoping there to find the means to pursue his quest. On the way, he encounters a party of Giants who name themselves the Search. One of them, Cable Seadreamer, has had an Earth-Sight vision of the Sunbane, and they have come to the Land to combat the peril. Guiding the Search to Seareach and *Coercri*, the former home of the Giants in the Land, Covenant uses his knowledge of their ancestors to persuade them to commit their Giantship to the service of his quest for the One Tree.

Before his departure from the Land, Covenant performs a great act of absolution for the Dead of *Coercri*, the former Giants who were damned by the manner of their death at the hands of a Raver. He then sends Sunder and Hollian back to the Land, hoping they will be able to inspire the villages to resist the Clave, and prepares himself to begin the next stage of his quest.

The One Tree, Book Two of The Second Chronicles of Thomas Covenant, details that quest—the voyage of the Giantship Starfare's Gem in search of the One Tree.

From the first, the journey is beset by treachery. Linden discovers too late that a Raver has boarded the vessel. The Raver uses a pack of rats to attack Covenant, triggering a venomrelapse which increases his power. Delirious, Covenant fears that he will destroy his friends, so he seals himself off from help. Linden is able to save him only by attempting a superficial possession of his spirit.

As he recovers, the quest sails toward the land of the *Elohim*, a reclusive and mystic people who the Giants believe will be able to reveal the location of the One Tree. But when Covenant and his companions reach *Elemesnedene*, home of the *Elohim*, they are met with distrust and mystification rather than aid. The *Elohim* proclaim Linden the Sun-Sage, denigrate Covenant because he lacks her health-sense, and refuse to provide the location of the One Tree except by entering Covenant's mind to lay bare the knowledge hidden there by the Forestal in Andelain. As a result, the Giants learn how to find the One Tree; but Covenant's mind is lost.

Meanwhile, Vain is captured and imprisoned by the *Elohim*, who fears his presence. But when Linden leads the quest away from *Elemesnedene*, he manages to make his escape.

Aboard Starfare's Gem, the quest sets out for the One Tree. To their surprise, the companions are joined by an *Elohim*, Findail the Appointed, who has been sent by his people to promote their secret purposes and to guard against Vain. And Linden finds that she cannot heal Covenant's mind without taking full possession of him—an act which she considers evil.

Damaged by a terrible storm, Starfare's Gem is forced to seek supplies and repairs in the seaport of *Bhrathairealm*, the home of the *Bhrathair*, a people who have spent most of their history in a war against the feral Sandgorgons of the Great Desert. They are ruled by an ancient thaumaturge, Kasreyn of the Gyre, who covets Covenant's ring. Kasreyn attempts to free Covenant's mind so that Covenant can be compelled to release it to him. These initial efforts fail, so Kasreyn seeks to coerce Linden to obtain the ring for him by exposing the *Haruchai* to the violence of the Sandgorgons—slaying Hergrom, crippling Ceer—and imprisoning the entire company when they try to flee Kasreyn's castle, the Sandhold.

However, Linden turns Kasreyn's machinations against him. She takes the damage done to Covenant's mind upon herself, thus restoring him to consciousness and power in time to save the quest by mastering a Sandgorgon and bringing about Kasreyn's death. As the companions and Starfare's Gem escape *Bhrathairealm*, Ceer is slain. But Linden recovers from the loss of mind she absorbed from Covenant, and the quest continues.

When the companions reach the Isle of the One Tree, Cable Seadreamer strives to dissuade Covenant and Linden from their purpose; but his muteness prevents him from making his Earth-Sight understood. In the name of the *Haruchai* people, and for Covenant's sake, Brinn battles the Guardian of the One Tree to obtain access to the Isle. In the process he becomes the Guardian himself, and allows the company to descend into the deep cave which holds the One Tree.

There Seadreamer sacrifices his life to reveal the truth of Lord Foul's secret manipulations: Covenant has been made so powerful by venom that he can no longer raise wild magic without threatening the Arch of Time. In addition, the One Tree is guarded by the Worm of the World's End: any attempt to touch the Tree will rouse the Worm, and all the companions will be destroyed unless Covenant fights to protect them.

Seeing the trap, Linden calls Covenant back from battle. In turn, he tries to return her to their former world so that she can tend his mortally wounded body, but she causes his attempt to fail so that she can remain with him. In despair, the company retreats to Starfare's Gem without a new Staff of Law, while the Isle of the One Tree sinks into the sea.

Here begins *White Gold Wielder*, Book Three of The Second Chronicles of Thomas Covenant.

"To go wherever dreaming goes"

THE LAND

↑ Northron Climb

Outer Earth

North Plains

Far
Woodhelve

Landsverge
Stonedown

Westron
Mountains

Revelstone

Grimmerdhore
Forest

Guards
Gap

Maerl R.

White R.

Trothgard

Gray R.

Soulsease R.

Llurallin R.

Rill R.

Andelainia
Hills

Last Hills

Center Plains

During
Stonedo

Black River

Crysta
Stoned

South Plains

Melenkurion
Skyweir

Kevin'
Wat

Mithil R.

Rivenrock

Doom's
Retreat

Mithil
Stonedown

N

Cravenhaw

Doriendor
Corishev

Southron Wastes

From a map by **Lynn K. Plagge**

PART I

Retribution

ONE: The Master's Scar

AWKWARD without its midmast, Starfare's Gem turned heavily toward the north, putting its stern to the water clogged with sand and foam which marked the passing of the One Tree. In the rigging, Giants labored and fumbled at their tasks, driven from line to line by the hoarse goad of Sevinhand's commands, even though Seadreamer lay dead on the deck below them. The Anchormaster stood, lean and rue-bitten, on the wheeldeck and yelled up at them, his voice raw with suppressed pain. If any compliance lagged, the Storesmaster, Galewrath, seconded him, throwing her shout after his like a piece of ragged granite because all the Search had come to ruin and she did not know any other way to bear it. The *dromond* went north simply to put distance between itself and the deep grave of its hope.

But Grimmand Honninscrave, the Giantship's Master, huddled on the afterdeck with his brother in his arms and did not speak. His massive face, so strong against storms and perils, looked like a yielded fortification; his beard tangled the shadows as the sun declined toward setting. And beside him stood the First of the Search and Pitchwife as if they were lost without the Earth-Sight to guide them.

Findail the Appointed stood there also, wearing his old misery like a man who had always known what would happen at the Isle of the One Tree. Vain stood there with one heel of the former Staff of Law bound around his wooden wrist and his useless hand dangling. And Linden Avery stood there as well, torn between bereavements: outrage and sorrow for Seadreamer swimming in her eyes, need for Covenant aching in her limbs.

But Thomas Covenant had withdrawn to his cabin like a crippled animal going to ground; and he stayed there.

3

He was beaten. He had nothing left.

Harsh with revulsion, he lay in his hammock and stared at the ceiling. His chamber had been made for a Giant; it outsized him, just as his doom and the Despiser's manipulations had outsized him. The red sunset through the open port bloodied the ceiling until dusk came and leeched his sight away. But he had been blind all along, so truncated of perception that he had caught no glimpse of his true fate until Linden had cried it into his face:

This is what Foul wants!

That was how his former strengths and victories had been turned against him. He could not feel Cail standing guard outside his door like a man whose fidelity had been redeemed. Beyond the slow rolling of the Giantship's pace, the salt of futility in the air, the distant creak of rigging and report of canvas, he could not tell the difference between this cabin and the dungeon of the Sandhold or the betrayed depths of Revelstone. All stone was one to him, deaf to appeal or need, senseless. He might have destroyed the Earth in that crisis of power and venom, might have broken the Arch of Time as if he were indeed the Despiser's servant, if Linden had not stopped him.

And then he had failed at his one chance to save himself. Horrified by love and fear for her, he had allowed Linden to return to him, abandoning the stricken and dying body of his other life. Abandoning him to ruin, though she had not intended any ruin.

Brinn had said to him, *That is the grace which has been given to you, to bear what must be borne.* But it was a lie.

In darkness he lay and did not move, sleepless although he coveted slumber, yearned for any oblivion which would bring surcease. He went on staring upward as if he too were graven of dead stone, a reification of folly and broken dreams snared within the eternal ambit of his defeat. Anger and self-despite might have impelled him to seek out his old clothes, might have sent him up to the decks to bear the desolation of his friends. But those garments he had left in Linden's cabin as though for safe-keeping; and he could not go there. His love for her was too corrupt, had been too severely falsified by selfishness. Thus the one lie he had practiced against her from the beginning came back to damn him.

He had withheld one important fact from her, hoping like a coward that it would prove unnecessary—that his desire for her would be permissible in the end. But by the lie of with-holding he had accomplished nothing except her miscomprehension. Nothing except the Search's destitution and the Despiser's victory. He had let his need for her blind both of them.

No, it was worse than that. He did need her, had needed her so acutely that the poignance of it had shredded his defenses. But other needs had been at work as well: the need to be the Land's rescuer, to stand at the center of Lord Foul's evil and impose his own answer upon it; the need to demonstrate his mortal worth against all the bloodshed and pain which condemned him. He had become so wrapped up in his isolation and leprosy, so certain of them and what they meant, that they had grown indistinguishable from Despite.

Now he was beaten. He had nothing left for which he might sanely hope or strive.

He should have known better. The old man on Haven Farm had spoken to Linden rather than to him. The *Elohim* had greeted her as the Sun-Sage, him as the wrongness which imperilled the Earth. Even dead Elena in Andelain had said plainly that the healing of the Land was in Linden's hands rather than his. Yet he had rejected comprehension in favor of self-insistence. His need or arrogance had been too great to allow comprehension.

And still, with the destruction of everything he held precious laid squarely at his door, he would not have done otherwise—would not give up his ring, not surrender the meaning of his life either to Linden or to Findail. It was all that remained to him: to bear the blame if he could not achieve the victory. Failing everything else, he could still at least refuse to be spared.

So he lay in his hammock like a sacrifice, with the stone vessel spread out unreadably around him. Fettered by the iron of his failures, he did not move or try to move. The first night after the dark of the moon filled his eyes. In Andelain, High Lord Mhoram had warned, *He has said that you are his Enemy. Remember that he seeks always to mislead you.* It was true: he was the Despiser's servant rather than Enemy. Even his former victory had been turned against him. Sucking the wounded places of his heart, he returned the sightless stare of the dark and remained where he was.

He had no measure for the passage of time; but the night

was not far advanced when he heard a stiff, stretched voice rumble outside his door. It uttered words he was unable to distinguish. Yet Cail's reply was precise. "The doom of the Earth is upon his head," the *Haruchai* said. "Will you not pity him?"

Too weary for indignation or argument, Honninscrave responded, "Can you believe that I mean him harm?"

Then the door opened, and a lantern led the Master's tall bulk into the cabin.

The light seemed small against the irreducible night of the world; but it lit the chamber brightly enough to sting Covenant's eyes, like tears he had not shed. Still he did not turn his head away or cover his face. He went on staring numbly at the ceiling while Honninscrave set the lantern on the table.

The table was low for the size of the cabin. From the first day of the quest's voyage, the Giantish furniture had been replaced by a table and chairs better suited to Covenant's stature. As a result, the lantern threw the hammock's shadow above him. He seemed to lie in the echo of his own dark.

With a movement that made his sark sigh along the wall, Honninscrave lowered himself to the floor. After long moments of silence, his voice rose out of the wan light.

"My brother is dead." The knowledge still wrung him. "Having no other family since the passing of our mother and father, I loved him, and he is dead. The vision of his Earth-Sight gifted us with hope even as it blighted him with anguish, and now that hope is dead, and he will never be released. As did the Dead of The Grieve, he has gone out of life in horror. He will never be released. Cable Seadreamer my brother, bearer of Earth-Sight voiceless and valiant to his grave."

Covenant did not turn his head. But he blinked at the sting in his eyes until the shadow above him softened it. *The way of hope and doom,* he thought dumbly. *Lies open to you.* Perhaps for him that had been true. Perhaps if he had been honest with Linden, or had heeded the *Elohim*, the path of the One Tree might have held some hope. But what hope had there ever been for Seadreamer? Yet without hope the Giant had tried to take all the doom upon himself. And somehow at the last he had found his voice to shout a warning.

Roughly, Honninscrave said, "I beseeched of the Chosen that she speak to you, but she would not. When I purposed to come to you myself, she railed at me, demanding that I forbear. Has he not suffered sufficiently? she cried. Have you no mercy?" He paused briefly, and his voice lowered. "She bears herself bravely, the Chosen. No longer is she the woman of frailty and fright who quailed so before the lurker of the Sarangrave. But she also was bound to my brother by a kinship which rends her in her way." In spite of her refusal, he seemed to believe that she deserved his respect.

Then he went on, "But what have I to do with mercy or forbearance? They are too high for me. I know only that Cable Seadreamer is dead. He will never be released if you do not release him."

At that, Covenant flinched in surprise and pain. If *I* don't—? He was sick with venom and protest. How can *I* release him? If revelation and dismay and Linden had not driven restraint so deeply into him during his struggle against the aura of the Worm of the World's End, he would have burned the air for no other reason than because he was hurt and futile with power. How can I bear it?

But his restraint held. And Honninscrave looked preternaturally reduced as he sat on the floor against the wall, hugging his unanswered grief. The Giant was Covenant's friend. In that light, Honninscrave might have been an avatar of lost Saltheart Foamfollower, who had given Covenant everything. He still had enough compassion left to remain silent.

"Giantfriend," the Master said without lifting his head, "have you been given the tale of how Cable Seadreamer my brother came by his scar?"

His eyes were hidden beneath his heavy brows. His beard slumped on his chest. The shadow of the table's edge cut him off at the torso; but his hands were visible, gripping each other. The muscles of his forearms and shoulders were corded with fatigue and strain.

"The fault of it was mine," he breathed into the empty light. "The exuberance and folly of my youth marked him for all to see that I had been careless of him.

"He was my brother, and the younger by some years, though as the lives of Giants are reckoned the span between us was slight. Surely we were both well beyond the present number of your age, but still were we young, new to our manhood, and but recently prenticed to the sea-craft and the ships we loved. The Earth-Sight had not yet come upon him, and so there was naught between us beyond my few years and the foolishness which he outgrew more swiftly than I. He came early to his stature, and I ended his youth before its time.

"In those days, we practiced our new crafts in a small vessel which our people name a *tyrscull*—a stone craft near the measure of the longboats you have seen, with one sail, a swinging boom, and oars for use should the wind be lost or misplayed. With skill, a *tyrscull* may be mastered by one Giant alone, but two are customary. Thus Seadreamer and I worked and learned together. Our *tyrscull* we named Foamkite, and it was our heart's glee.

"Now among prentices it is no great wonder that we reveled in tests against each other, pitting and honing our skills with races and displays of every description. Most common of these was the running of a course within the great harbor of Home —far sufficiently from shore to be truly at sea, and yet within any swimmer's reach of land, should some prentice suffer capsize—a mishap which would have shamed us deeply, young as we were. And when we did not race we trained for races, seeking new means by which we might best our comrades.

"The course was simply marked. One point about which we swung was a buoy fixed for that purpose, but the other was a rimed and hoary rock that we named Salttooth for the sheer, sharp manner in which it rose to bite the air. Once or twice or many times around that course we ran our races, testing our ability to use the winds for turning as well as for speed."

Honninscrave's voice had softened somewhat: remembrance temporarily took him away from his distress. But his head remained bowed. And Covenant could not look away from him. Punctuated by the muffled sounds of the sea, the plain details of Honninscrave's story transfixed the atmosphere of the cabin.

"This course Seadreamer and I ran as often as any and more than most, for we were eager for the sea. Thus we came to stand well among those who vied for mastery. With this my brother was content. He had the true Giantish exhilaration and did not require victory for his joy. But in that I was less worthy of my people. Never did I cease to covet victory, or to seek out new means by which it might be attained.

"So it befell that one day I conceived a great thought which caused me to hug my breast in secret, and to hasten Seadreamer to Foamkite, that I might practice my thought and perfect it for racing. But that thought I did not share with him. It was grand, and I desired its wonder for myself. Not questioning what was in me, he came for the simple pleasure of the sea. Together, we ran Foamkite out to the buoy, then swung with all speed toward upthrust Salttooth.

"It was a day as grand as my thought." He spoke as if it were visible behind the shadows of the cabin. "Under the faultless sky blew a wind with a whetted edge which offered speed and hazard, cutting the wave-crests to white froth as it bore us ahead. Swiftly before us loomed Salttooth. In such a wind, the turning of a *tyrscull* requires true skill—a jeopardy even to competent prentices—and it was there that a race could be won or lost, for a poor tack might drive a small craft far from the course or overturn it altogether. But my thought was for that turning, and I was not daunted by the wind.

"Leaving Seadreamer to the tiller and the management of the boom, I bid him run in as nigh to Salttooth as he dared. All prentices knew such a course to be folly, for the turning would then bear us beyond our way. But I silenced my brother's protests and went to Foamkite's prow. Still preserving my secret, hiding my hands from his sight, I freed the anchor and readied its line."

Abruptly, the Master faltered, fell still. One fist lay knotted in his lap; the other twisted roughly into his beard, tugging it for courage. But after a moment, he drew a deep breath, then let the air hiss away through his teeth. He was a Giant and could not leave his story unfinished.

"Such was Seadreamer's skill that we passed hastening within an arm's span of Salttooth, though the wind heeled us sharply from the rock and any sideslip might have done Foamkite great harm. But his hand upon the wind was sure, and an instant later I enacted my intent. As we sped, I arose and cast the anchor upon the rock, snagging us there. Then I lashed the line.

"This was my thought for a turning too swift to be matched by any other *tryscull*, that our speed and the anchor and Salttooth should do the labor for us—though I was uncertain how the anchor might be unsnared when the turn was done. But I had not told Seadreamer my purpose." His voice had become a low rasp of bitterness in his throat. "He was fixed upon the need to pass Salttooth without mishap, and my act surprised him entirely. He half gained his feet, half started toward me as if I had gone mad. Then the line sprang-taut, and Foamkite came about with a violence which might have snapped the mast from its holes."

Again he stopped. The muscles of his shoulders bunched. When he resumed, he spoke so softly that Covenant barely heard him.

"Any child might have informed me what would transpire, but I had given no consideration to it. The boom wrenched across the stern of Foamkite with a force to sliver granite. And Seadreamer my brother had risen into its path.

"In that wind and my folly, I would not have known that he had fallen, had he not cried out as he was struck. But at his cry I turned to see him flung into the Sea.

"Ah, my brother!" A groan twisted his voice. "I dove for him, but he would have been lost had I not found the path of his blood in the water and followed it. Senseless he hung in my arms as I bore him to the surface.

"With the sea thus wind-slashed, I saw little of his injury but blood until I had borne him to Foamkite and wrested him aboard. But there his wound seemed so great that I believed his eyes had been crushed in his head, and for a time I became as mad as my intent had been. To this day, I know nothing of our return to the docks of Home. I did not regain myself until a healer spoke to me, compelling me to hear that my brother had not been blinded. Had the boom itself struck him, mayhap he would have been slain outright. But the impact was borne by a cable along the boom, taking him below the eyes and softening the blow somewhat."

Once more he fell still. His hands covered his face as if to stanch the flow of blood he remembered. Covenant watched him mutely. He had no courage for such stories, could not bear to have them thrust upon him. But Honninscrave was a Giant and a friend; and since the days of Foamfollower Covenant had not been able to close his heart. Though he was helpless and aggrieved, he remained silent and let Honninscrave do what he willed.

After a moment, the Master dropped his hands. Drawing a breath like a sigh, he said, "It is not the way of Giants to punish such folly as mine, though I would have found comfort in the justice of puishment. And Cable Seadreamer was a Giant among Giants. He did not blame the carelessness which marked his life forever." Then his tone stiffened. "But I do not forget. The fault is mine. Though I too am a Giant in my way, my ears have not found the joy to hear this story. And I have thought often that perhaps my fault is greater than it has appeared. The Earth-Sight is a mystery. None can say why it chooses one Giant rather than another. Perhaps it befell my brother because of some lingering hurt or alteration done him by the puissance of that blow. Even in their youth, Giants are not easily stricken senseless."

Suddenly Honninscrave looked upward; and his gaze struck foreboding into Covenant's maimed empathy. His eyes under his heavy brows were fierce with extremity, and the new-cut lines around them were as intense as scars. "Therefore have I come to you," he said slowly, as if he could not see Covenant quailing. "I desire a restitution which is not within my power to perform. My fault must be assuaged.

"It is the custom of our people to give our dead to the sea. But Cable Seadreamer my brother has met his end in horror, and it will not release him. He is like the Dead of The Grieve, damned to his anguish. If his spirit is not given its *caamora*"— for an instant, his voice broke—"he will haunt me while one stone of the Arch of Time remains standing upon another."

Then his gaze fell to the floor. "Yet there is no fire in all the world that I can raise to give him surcease. He is a Giant. Even in death, he is immune to flame."

At that, Covenant understood; and all his dreads came together in a rush: the apprehension which had crouched in him since Honninscrave had first said, *If you do not release him;* the terror of his doom, to destroy the Earth himself or to surrender it for destruction by ceding his ring to Lord Foul. The Despiser had said, *The ill that you deem most terrible is upon you. Of your own volition you will give the white gold into my hand.* Either that or bring down the Arch of Time. There was no way out. He was beaten. Because he had kept the truth from Linden, seeking to deny it. And Honninscrave asked—!

"You want me to cremate him?" Clenched fear made him harsh. "With my ring? Are you out of your mind?"

Honninscrave winced. "The Dead of The Grieve—" he began.

"No!" Covenant retorted. He had walked into a bonfire to

save them from their reiterated hell; but risks like that were too great for him now. He had already caused too much death. "After I sink the ship, I won't be able to *stop!*"

For a moment, even the sounds of the Sea fell still, shocked by his vehemence. The Giantship seemed to be losing headway. The light of the lantern flickered as if it were going out. Perhaps there were shouts like muffled lamentations in the distance. Covenant could not be sure. His senses were condemned to the surface of what they perceived. The rest of the *dromond* was hidden from him.

If the Master heard anything, he did not react to it. His head remained bowed. Moving heavily, like a man hurt in every limb, he climbed to his feet. Though the hammock hung high above the floor, he stood head and shoulders over the Unbeliever; and still he did not meet Covenant's glare. The light of the lantern was below and behind him as he took one step closer. His face was shadowed, dark and fatal.

In a wan and husky voice, he said, "Yes, Giantfriend." The epithet held a tinge of sarcasm. "I am gone from my mind. You are the ring-wielder, as the *Elohim* have said. Your power threatens the Earth. What import has the anguish of one or two Giants in such a plight? Forgive me."

Then Covenant wanted to cry out in earnest, torn like dead Kevin Landwaster between love and defeat. But loud feet had come running down the companionway outside his cabin, had already reached his door. The door sprang open without any protest from Cail. A crewmember thrust her head past the threshold.

"Master, you must come." Her voice was tight with alarm. "We are beset by *Nicor*."

TWO: Leper's Ground

HONNINSCRAVE left the cabin slowly, like a man responding by habit, unconscious of the urgency of the summons. Perhaps he no longer understood what was happening around him. Yet he did respond to the call of his ship.

When the Master reached the companionway, Cail closed the door behind him. The *Haruchai* seemed to know instinctively that Covenant would not follow Honninscrave.

Nicor! Covenant thought, and his heart labored. Those tremendous serpentlike sea-beasts were said to be the offspring of the Worm of the World's End. Starfare's Gem had passed through a region crowded with them near the Isle of the One Tree. They had been indifferent to the *dromond* then. But now? With the Isle gone and the Worm restive?

And what could one stone vessel do against so many of those prodigious creatures? What could Honninscrave do?

Yet the Unbeliever did not leave his hammock. He stared at the dark ceiling and did not move. He was beaten, defeated. He dared not take the risk of confronting the Giantship's peril. If Linden had not intervened at the One Tree, he would already have become another Kevin, enacting a Ritual of Desecration to surpass every other evil. The threat of the *Nicor* paled beside the danger he himself represented.

Deliberately, he sought to retreat into himself. He did not want to know what transpired outside his cabin. How could he endure the knowledge? He had said, *I'm sick of guilt*—but such protests had no meaning. His very blood had been corrupted by venom and culpability. Only the powerless were truly innocent, and he was not powerless. He was not even honest. The selfishness of his love had brought all this to pass.

13

Yet the lives at stake were the lives of his friends, and he could not close himself to the *dromond*'s jeopardy. Starfare's Gem rolled slightly in the water as if it had lost all headway. A period of shouts and running had followed Honninscrave's departure, but now the Giantship was silent. With Linden's senses, he would have been able to read what was happening through the stone itself; but he was blind and bereft, cut off from the essential spirit of the world. His numb hands clutched the edges of the hammock.

Time passed. He was a coward, and his dreads swarmed darkly about him as if they were born in the shadows above his head. He gripped himself with thoughts of ruin, held himself still with curses. But Honninscrave's face kept coming back to him: the beard like a growth of pain from his cheeks, the massive brow knuckled with misery, the hands straining. Covenant's friend. Like Foamfollower. *My brother has met his end in horror.* It was intolerable that such needs had to be refused. And now the *Nicor*—!

Even a beaten man could still feel pain. Roughly, he pulled himself into a sitting position. His voice was a croak of coercion and fear as he called out, "Cail!"

The door opened promptly, and Cail entered the cabin.

The healed wound of a Courser-spur marked his left arm from shoulder to elbow like the outward sign of his fidelity; but his visage remained as impassive as ever. "Ur-Lord?" he asked flatly. His dispassionate tone gave no hint that he was the last *Haruchai* left in Covenant's service.

Covenant stifled a groan. "What the hell's going on out there?"

In response, Cail's eyes shifted fractionally. But still his voice held no inflection. "I know not."

Until the previous night, when Brinn had left the quest to take up his role as *ak-Haru Kenaustin Ardenol*, Cail had never been alone in his chosen duty; and the mental interconnection of his people had kept him aware of what took place around him. But now he was alone. Brinn's defeat of the former Guardian of the One Tree had been a great victory for him personally, and for the *Haruchai* as a people; but it left Cail isolated in a way that no one who had not experienced such mind-sharing could measure. His blunt *I know not* silenced Covenant like an admission of frailty.

Cail— Covenant tried to say. He did not want to leave the

Haruchai in that loneliness. But Brinn had said, *Cail will accept my place in your service until the word of the Bloodguard Bannor has been carried to its end.* And no appeal or protest would sway Cail from the path Brinn had marked out for him. Covenant remembered Bannor too poignantly to believe that the *Haruchai* would ever judge themselves by any standards but their own.

Yet his distress remained. Even lepers and murderers were not immune to hurt. He fought down the thickness in his throat and said, "I want my old clothes. They're in her cabin."

Cail nodded as if he saw nothing strange in the request. As he left, he closed the door quietly after him.

Covenant lay back again and clenched his teeth. He did not want those clothes, did not want to return to the hungry and unassuaged life he had lived before he had found Linden's love. But how else could he leave his cabin? Those loathed and necessary garments represented the only honesty left to him. Any other apparel would be a lie.

However, when Cail returned he was not alone. Pitchwife entered the chamber ahead of him; and at once Covenant forgot the bundle Cail bore. The deformity which bent Pitchwife's spine, hunching his back and crippling his chest, made him unnaturally short for a Giant: his head did not reach the level of the hammock. But the irrepressibility of his twisted face gave him stature. He was alight with excitement as he limped forward to greet Covenant.

"Have I not said that she is well Chosen?" he began without preamble. "Never doubt it, Giantfriend! Mayhap this is but one wonder among many, for surely our voyage has been rife with marvels. Yet I do not dream to see it surpassed. Stone and Sea, Giantfriend! She has taught me to hope again."

Covenant stared in response, stung by an inchoate apprehension. What new role had Linden taken upon herself, when he still had not told her the truth?

Pitchwife's eyes softened. "But you do not comprehend—as how should you, who have not seen the Sea loom with *Nicor* under the stars, not heard the Chosen sing them to peace."

Still Covenant did not speak. He had no words for the complex admixture of his pride and relief and bitter loss. The woman he loved had saved the Giantship. And he, who had once defeated the Despiser in direct combat—he no longer signified.

Watching Covenant's face, Pitchwife sighed to himself. In a more subdued manner, he went on, "It was an act worthy of long telling, but I will briefen it. You have heard that the Giants are able to summon *Nicor* upon occasion. Such a summons we wrought on your behalf, when last the venom-sickness of the Raver possessed you." Covenant had no memory of the situation. He had been near death in delirium at the time. But he had been told about it. "Yet to the *Nicor* we do not speak. They lie beyond our gift of tongues. The sounds which may summon them we have learned from our generations upon the sea. But those sounds we make blindly, uncertain of their meaning. And a Giantship which enters a sea of *Nicor* in their wrath has scant need of summons."

A small smile quirked his mouth; but he did not stop. "It was Linden Avery the Chosen who found means to address them for our survival. Lacking the plain might of arm for her purpose, she called Galewrath Storesmaster with her and went below, down to the bottommost hull of the *dromond*. There through the stone she read the ire of the *Nicor*—and gave it answer. With her hands she clapped a rhythm which Galewrath echoed for her, pounding it with hammers upon the hull."

Then for a moment the Giant's enthusiasm resurged. "And she was heeded!" he crowed. "The *Nicor* parted about us, bearing their anger into the south. We have been left without scathe!" His hands gripped the edge of the hammock, rocked it as if to make Covenant hear him. "There is yet hope in the world. While we endure, and the Chosen and the Giantfriend remain among us, there is hope!"

But Pitchwife's claim was too direct. Covenant flinched from it. He had wronged too many people and had no hope left for himself. A part of him wanted to cry out in protest. Was that what he would have to do in the end? Give Linden his ring, the meaning of his life, when she had never seen the Land without the Sunbane and did not know how to love it? Weakly, he muttered, "Tell that to Honninscrave. He could use some hope."

At that, Pitchwife's eyes darkened. But he did not look away. "The Master has spoken of your refusal. I know not the good or ill of these matters, but the word of my heart is that you have done what you must—and that is well. Do not think me ungrieved by Seadreamer's fall—or the Master's hurt. Yet the hazard of your might is great. And who can say how the *Nicor* would answer such fire, though they have passed us by? None may judge the doom which lies upon you now. You have done well in your way."

Pitchwife's frank empathy made Covenant's eyes burn. He knew acutely that he had not done well. Pain like Honnin-scrave's should not be refused, never be refused. But the fear and the despair were still there, blocking everything. He could not even meet Pitchwife's gaze.

"Ah, Giantfriend," Pitchwife breathed at last. "You also are grieved beyond bearing. I know not how to solace you." Abruptly, he stooped, and one hand lifted a leather flask into the hammock. "If you find no ease in my tale of the Chosen, will you not at the least drink *diamondraught* and grant your flesh rest? Your own story remains to be told. Be not so harsh with yourself."

His words raised memories of dead Atiaran in Andelain. The mother of the woman he had raped and driven mad had said with severe compassion, *In punishing yourself, you come to merit punishment. This is Despite.* But Covenant did not want to think about Atiaran. *Find no ease*— Belatedly, he pictured Linden in the depths of the *dromond*, holding the survival of the Search in her hands. He could not hear the rhythm of her courage, but he saw her face. Framed by her wheaten hair, it was acute with concentration, knotted be-tween the brows, marked on either side of the mouth by the consequences of severity—and beautiful to him in every bone and line.

Humbled by what she had done to save the ship, he raised the flask to his lips and drank.

When he awoke, the cabin was full of afternoon sunshine, and the pungent taste of *diamondraught* lingered on his tongue. The Giantship was moving again. He remembered no dreams. The impression he bore with him out of slumber was one of blankness, a leper's numbness carried to its logical extreme. He wanted to roll over and never wake up again.

But as he glanced blearily around the sun-sharp cabin, he saw Linden sitting in one of the chairs beside the table.

She sat with her head bowed and her hands open in her lap, as if she had been waiting there for a long time. Her hair gleamed cleanly in the light, giving her the appearance of a woman who had emerged whole from an ordeal—refined, perhaps, but not reduced. With an inward moan, he recollected what the old man on Haven Farm had said to her. *There is also love in the world.* And in Andelain dead Elena, Covenant's daughter, had urged him, *Care for her, beloved, so that in the end she may heal us all.* The sight of her made his chest contract. He had lost her as well. He had nothing left.

Then she seemed to feel his gaze on her. She looked up at him, automatically brushing the tresses back from her face; and he saw that she was not unhurt. Her eyes were hollow and flagrant with fatigue; her cheeks were pallid; and the twinned lines running past her mouth from either side of her delicate nose looked like they had been left there by tears as well as time. A voiceless protest gathered in him. Had she been sitting here with him ever since the passing of the *Nicor*? When she needed so much rest?

But a moment after he met her gaze she rose to her feet. A knot of anxiety or anger marked her brows. Probing him with her health-sense, she stepped closer to the hammock. What she saw made her mouth severe.

"Is that it?" she demanded. "You've decided to give up?"

Mutely, Covenant flinched. Was his defeat so obvious?

At once, a look of regret changed her expression. She dropped her eyes, and her hands made an aimless half-gesture as if they were full of remembered failure. "I didn't mean that," she said. "That isn't what I came to say. I wasn't sure I should come at all. You've been so hurt—I wanted to give you more time."

Then she lifted her face to him again, and he saw her sense of purpose sharpen. She was here because she had her own ideas—about hope as well as about him. "But the First was going to come, and I thought I should do it for her." She gazed into him as if she sought a way to draw him down from his lonely bed. "She wants to know where we're going."

Where—? Covenant blinked pain at her. She had not withdrawn her question: she had simply rephrased it. *Where?* A spasm of grief gripped his heart. His doom was summed up in that one grim word. Where *could* he go? He was beaten. All his power had been turned against him. There was nowhere left for him to go—nothing left for him to do. For an instant, he feared he would break down in front of her, bereft even of the bare dignity of solitude.

She was saying, "We've got to go somewhere. The Sunbane is still there. Lord Foul is still there. We've lost the One Tree, but nothing else has changed. We can't just sail in circles for the rest of our lives." She might have been pleading with him, trying to make him see something that was already plain to her.

But he did not heed her. Almost without transition, his hurt became resentment. She was being cruel, whether she realized it or not. He had already betrayed everything he loved with his mistakes and failures and lies. How much more responsibility did she wish him to assume? Bitterly, he replied, "I hear you saved us from the *Nicor*. You don't need me."

His tone made her wince. "Don't *say* that!" she responded intensely. Her eyes were wide with awareness of what was happening to him. She could read every outcry of his wracked spirit. "*I* need you."

In response, he felt his despair plunging toward hysteria. It sounded like the glee of the Despiser, laughing in triumph. Perhaps he had gone so far down this road now that he *was* the Despiser, the perfect tool or avatar of Lord Foul's will. But Linden's expostulation jerked him back from the brink. It made her suddenly vivid to him—too vivid to be treated this way. She was his love, and he had already hurt her too much.

For a moment, the fall he had nearly taken left him reeling. Everything in the cabin seemed imprecise, overburdened with sunlight. He needed shadows and darkness in which to hide from all the things that surpassed him. But Linden still stood there as if she were the center around which his head whirled. Whether she spoke or remained silent, she was the one demand he could not refuse. Yet he was altogether unready to tell her the truth he had withheld. Her reaction would be the culmination of all his dismay. Instinctively, he groped for some way to anchor himself, some point of simple guilt or passion to which he might cling. Squinting into the sunshine, he asked thickly, "What did they do about Seadreamer?"

At that, Linden sagged in relief as though a crisis had been averted. Wanly, she answered, "Honninscrave wanted to cremate him. As if that were possible." Memories of suffering seemed to fray the words as she uttered them. "But the First ordered the Giants to bury him at sea. For a minute there, I thought Honninscrave was going to attack her. But then something inside him broke. It wasn't physical—but I felt it snap."

Her tone said that she had sensed that parting like a rupture in her own heart. "He bowed to her as if he didn't know what else to do with all that hurt. Then he went back to the wheeldeck. Back to doing his job." Her shoulders lifted in a pained shrug. "If you didn't look at his eyes, you wouldn't know he isn't as good as new. But he refused to help them give Seadreamer to the sea."

As she spoke, his eyes blurred. He was unable to see her clearly in all that light. Seadreamer should have been burned, should have been freed from his horror in a *caamora* of white fire. Yet the mere thought made Covenant's flesh itch darkly. He had become the thing he hated. Because of a lie. He had known—or should have known—what was going to happen to him. But his selfish love had kept the truth from her. He could not look at her. Through his teeth, he protested, "Why did you have to do that?"

"Do—?" Her health-sense did not make her prescient. How could she possibly know what he was talking about?

"You threw yourself in the fire." The explanation came arduously, squeezed out by grief and self-recrimination. It was not her fault. No one had the right to blame her. "I sent you away to try to save my life. I didn't know what else to do. For all I knew, it was already too late for anything else—the Worm was already awake, I'd already destroyed—" A clench of anguish closed this throat. For a moment, he could not say, I didn't know how else to save you. Then he swallowed convulsively and went on. "So I sent you away. And you threw yourself in the fire. I was linked to you. The magic tied us together. For the first time, my senses were open. And all I saw was you throwing yourself in the fire.

"Why did you force me to bring you back?"

In response, she flared as if he had struck a ragged nerve. "Because I couldn't help you the way you were!" Suddenly, she was shouting at him. "Your body was there, but *you* weren't! Without you, it was just so much dying meat! Even if I'd had you in a hospital—even if I could've given you transfusions and surgery right then—I could not have saved you!

"I needed you to come back with me. How else was I supposed to get your attention?"

Her pain made him look at her again; and the sight went through him like a crack through stone, following its flaws to the heart. She stood below him with her face hot and vivid in the light and her fists clenched, as intense and uncompromising as any woman he had ever dreamed. The fault was not hers, though surely she blamed herself. Therefore he could not shirk telling her the truth.

At one time, he had believed that he was sparing her by not speaking, that he was withholding information so that she would not be overwhelmed. Now he knew better. He had kept the truth to himself for the simple reason that he did not want it to be true. And by so doing he had falsified their relationship profoundly.

"I should've told you," he murmured in shame. "I tried to tell you everything else. But it hurt too much."

She glared at him as if she felt the presence of something horrible between them; but he did not look away.

"It's always been this way. Nothing here interrupts the physical continuity of the world we came from. What happens here is self-contained. It's always the same. I go into the Land hurt—possibly dying. A leper. And I'm healed. Twice my leprosy disappeared. I could *feel* again, as if my nerves—" His heart twisted at the memory—and at the poignant distress of Linden's stare. "But before I left the Land, something always happened to duplicate the shape I was in earlier. Sometimes my body was moved. I stopped bleeding—or got worse. But my physical condition was always exactly what it would've been if I'd never been to the Land. And I'm still a leper. Leprosy doesn't heal.

"So this time that knife hit me—and when we got to the Land I healed it with wild magic. The same way I healed those cuts the Clave gave me." They had slashed his wrists to gain blood for their soothtell; yet already the scars had faded, were nearly invisible. "But it doesn't make any difference. What happens here doesn't change what's going on there. All it does is change the way we feel about it."

After that, his shame was too great to hold her gaze. "That's why I didn't tell you about it. At first—right at the beginning —I thought you had enough to worry about. You would learn the truth soon enough. But after a while I changed. Then I didn't want you to know. I didn't think I had the right to ask you to love a dead man."

As he spoke, her shock boiled into anger. The moment he stopped, she demanded, "Do you mean to say that you've been planning to die all along?" Her voice was abruptly livid against the quiet background of the ship and the sea. "That you haven't even been *trying* to find a way to survive?"

"No!" In despair, he sought to defend himself. "Why do you think I wanted a new Staff of Law—needed it so badly? It was my only hope. To fight for the Land without risking wild magic. And to send you back. You're a doctor, aren't you? I wanted you to save me." But the anguish of her stare did not waver; and he could not meet it, could not pretend that what he had done was justified. "I've been trying," he pleaded. But no appeal was enough. "I didn't tell you because I wanted to love you for a while. That's all."

He heard her moving; and the fear that she would walk out of the cabin, turn her back on him forever, wrenched at him. But she was not leaving. She retreated to the chair, seated herself there as if something in her had broken. Her hands covered her face as she hunched forward, and her shoulders jerked. Yet she made no sound. At her mother's deathbed, she had learned to keep her weeping to herself. When she spoke, her voice shook.

"Why do I end up killing everybody I care about?"

Her grief hurt him like the raw acid of his guilt. This, too, was on his head. He wanted to descend from the hammock, go to her, take her in his arms; but he had forfeited that privilege. There was nothing he could do except fight back his own rue and protest, "It's not your fault. You tried. I should've told you. You would've saved me if you could."

The vehemence of her reaction took him by surprise. "*Stop* that!" she spat. "I've got eyes! A mind of my own! I'm not some innocent kid you can *protect*." The sun flashed on her face. "You've been lying down here ever since we came back aboard as if you were to blame for everything. But you're not. Foul set this up. He manipulated you into it. What're you trying to do now? Prove him *right*?"

"I can't help it!" he retorted, stung by the salt she rubbed into his futility. "Of course he's right. Who do you think he is? He's *me*. He's just an externalization of the part of me that despises. The part that—"

"*No.*" Her contradiction cut him off, though she did not shout. She had become too clenched and furious for shouting, too extreme to be denied. "He's not you. He's not the one who's going to die." She might have said, I'm the one who kills. The words were plain in every line of her visage. But her passion carried her past that recognition as if she could not bear it in any other way. "Everybody makes mistakes. But all you've done is try to fight for what you love. You have an answer. I don't." The heat of her assertion contained no self-pity. "I haven't had one since this thing started. I don't know the Land the way you do. I haven't got any power. All I've been able to do is follow you around." Her hands rose into fists. "If you're going to die, do something to make it count!"

Then like a quick touch of ice he realized that she had not come here to question him simply because the First desired a destination. *She wants to know where we're going.* Her father had killed himself and blamed her for it; and she had killed her mother with her own hands; and now his, Covenant's, death seemed as certain as the Desecration of the Earth. But those things served only to give her the purpose he had lost. She was wearing her old severity now—the same rigid self-punishment and determination with which she had defied him from the moment of their first meeting. Yet the fierce fire in her eyes was new. And he recognized it. It was the unanswered anger of her grief, and it swept all costs aside in its desire for battle.

You've decided to give up?

Her demand made his failure as acute as agony. He could have shouted, I don't have any choice! He *beat* me! There's nothing I can do!

But he knew better. He was a leper and knew better. Leprosy itself was defeat, complete and incurable. Yet even lepers had reasons to go on living. Atiaran had told him that it was the task of the living to give meaning to the sacrifices of the dead; but now he saw that the truth went further: to give meaning to his own death. And to the prices the people he loved had already paid.

In the name of Linden's harsh insistence, he sat up in the hammock and asked hoarsely, "What do you want?"

His response seemed to steady her. The bitter pressure of her loss eased somewhat. In a hard voice, she said, "I want you to go back to the Land. To Revelstone. And stop the Clave. Put out the Banefire." He drew a hissing breath at the sheer audacity of what she required; but she went on without heeding him, "If you do that, the Sunbane'll slow down. Maybe it'll even recede. That'll give us time to look for a better answer."

Then she surprised him again by faltering. She did not face him as she concluded, "Maybe I don't care about the Land the way you do. I was too scared to go into Andelain. I've never seen what it used to be like. But I know sickness when I see it. Even if I weren't a doctor, I'd have the Sunbane carved on me in places where I'll never be able to forget it. I want to do something about that. I don't have anything else. The only way I can fight is through you."

As she spoke, echoes of power capered in Covenant's veins. He heard what she was saying; but his fear took him back to the beginning. Stop the Clave? Put out the Banefire? In blunt alarm, he replied, "That'll be a lot of fun. What in hell makes you believe I can even think about things like that without endangering the Arch?"

She met him with a sour smile, humorless and certain. "Because you know how to restrain yourself now. I felt it—when you called back all that wild magic and used it to send me away. You're more dangerous now than you've ever been. To Lord Foul."

For a moment, he held the look she gave him. But then his eyes fell. No. It was still too much: he was not ready. The ruin of his life was hardly a day old. How was it possible to talk about fighting, when the Despiser had already defeated him? He had only one power, and it had been transformed by venom and falsehood into a graver threat than any Sunbane. What she wanted was madness. He did not have it in him.

Yet he had to make some reply. She had borne too many burdens for him. And he loved her. She had the right to place demands upon him.

So he groped in bitter shame for a way out, for something he might say or do which would at least postpone the necessity of decision. Still without meeting Linden's stare, he muttered sourly, "There're too many things I don't understand. I need to talk to Findail."

He thought that would deflect her. From the moment when the Appointed of the *Elohim* had first attached himself to the Search, he had never come or gone at any behest but that of his own secret wisdom or cunning. Yet if anyone possessed the knowledge to win free of this defeat, surely his people did.

And surely also he would not come here simply because the Unbeliever asked for him? Covenant would gain at least that much respite while Linden tried to persuade Findail.

But she did not hesitate—and did not leave the cabin. Turning to face the prow, she rasped the name of the Appointed stridently, as if she expected to be obeyed.

Almost at once, the sunlight seemed to condense against the wall; and Findail came flowing out of the stone into human form as though he had been waiting there for her call.

His appearance was unchanged: behind his creamy mantle and unkempt silver hair, within his bruised yellow eyes, he looked like an incarnation of all the world's misery, an image of every hurt and stress that did not touch his tranquil and self-absorbed people. Where they were deliberately graceful and comely, he was haggard and pain-carved. He appeared to be their antithesis and contradiction—a role which appalled him.

Yet something must have changed for him. Before the crisis of the One Tree, he would not have answered any summons. But his manner remained as distant and disapproving as ever. Though he nodded an acknowledgment to Linden, his voice held a note of reproof. "I hear you. Vehemence is not needful."

His tone made no impression on Linden. Bracing her fists on her hips, she addressed him as if he had not spoken. "This has gone on long enough," she said stiffly. "Now we need answers."

Findail did not glance at Covenant. In *Elemesnedene*, the *Elohim* had treated Covenant as if he were of no personal importance; and now the Appointed seemed to take that stance again. He asked Linden, "Is it the ring-wielder's intent to surrender his ring?"

At once, Covenant snapped, "No!" Refusals ran in him like echoes of old delirium. Never give him the ring. Never. It was all that remained to him.

"Then," Findail sighed, "I must answer as I may, hoping to persuade him from his folly."

Linden glanced up at Covenant, looking for his questions. But he was too close to his internal precipice: he could not think clearly. Too many people wanted him to surrender his ring. It was the only thing which still wedded him to life, made his choices matter. He did not respond to Linden's gaze.

Her eyes narrowed as she studied him, gauged his condition. Then, as if she were wrenching herself back from a desire
to comfort him, she turned away, faced Findail again.

"Why—?" She spoke with difficulty, wrestling words past
a knot in her chest. "I hardly know where to begin. There's so
much— Why did you people do it?" Abruptly, her voice became stronger, full of indignation she had never been able to
forget. "What in God's name did you think you were doing?
All he wanted was the location of the One Tree. You could've
given him a straight answer. But instead you locked him in
that silence of yours." They had imposed a stasis upon his
mind. If Linden had not risked herself to rescue him, he
would have remained an empty husk until he died, blank of
thought or desire. And the price she had paid for that rescue—! Her outrage pulled him into focus with her as she concluded, "You're responsible for this. How can you stand to
live with yourself?"

Findail's expression turned into a glower. As soon as she
stopped, he replied, "Does it appear to you that I am made
glad by the outcome of my Appointment? Is not my life at
hazard as much as yours? Yes, as much and more, for you will
depart when your time is ended, but I must remain and bear
the cost. The fault is not mine."

Linden started to protest; but the gathering sadness in his
tone halted her. "No, do not rail against me. I am the Appointed, and the burden of what you do falls to me.

"I do not deny that the path we chose was harsh to the
ring-wielder. But are you truly unable to see in this matter?
You are the Sun-Sage. He is not. Yet the wild magic which is
the crux of the Arch of Time is his to wield, not yours. There
lies the hand of evil upon the Earth—and also upon the *Elohim*, who are the Earth's Würd.

"You have said that we serve the evil which you name Lord
Foul the Despiser. That is untrue. If you mislike my word,
consider other knowledge. Would this Despiser have sent his
servant the Raver against you in the storm, when already a
servant such as myself stood among you? No. You cannot
credit it. Yet I must say to you openly that there is a shadow
upon the hearts of the *Elohim*. It is seen in this, that we were
able to conceive no path of salvation which would spare you.

"You have not forgotten that there were those among us
who did not wish to spare you.

"Surely it is plain that for us the easiest path lay in the simple wresting from him of the ring. With wild magic could we bid any Despite defiance. Then for beings such as we are it would be no great task to achieve the perfection of the Earth. Yet that we did not do. Some among us feared the arrogance of such power, when a shadow plainly lay upon our hearts. And some saw that the entire price of such an act would fall upon you alone. You would be lost to yourselves, deprived of meaning and value. Perhaps the meaning and value of the Earth would be diminished as well.

"Therefore we chose a harder path—to share with you the burden of redemption and the risk of doom. The ring-wielder we silenced, not to harm him, but to spare the Earth the ill of power without sight. As that silence preserved him from the malice of Kasreyn of the Gyre, so also would it have preserved him from the Despiser's intent at the One Tree. Thus the choice would have fallen to you in the end. His ring you might have taken unto yourself, thereby healing the breach between sight and power. Or perhaps you might have ceded the ring to me, empowering the *Elohim* to save the Earth after their fashion. Then would we have had no need to fear ourselves, for a power given is altogether different than one wrested away. But whatever your choice, there would have been hope. To accomplish such hope, the price of the ring-wielder's silence—and of my Appointment—appeared to be neither too great nor too ill.

"That you took from us. In the dungeon of the Sandhold, you chose the wrong which you name possession above the responsibility of sight, and the hope we strove to nurture was lost.

"Now I say to you that he must be persuaded to surrender his ring. If he does not, it is certain that he will destroy the Earth."

For a moment, Covenant reeled down the path of Findail's explanation. His balance was gone. To hear his own dread expressed so starkly, like a verdict! But when he turned toward Linden, he saw that she had been hit harder than he. Her face had gone pale. Her hands made small, fugitive movements at her sides. Her mouth tried to form a denial, but she had no strength for it. Confronted by the logic of her actions as Findail saw it, she was horrified. Once again, he placed her at the center, at the cusp of responsibility and blame. And

Covenant's earlier revelation was still too recent: she had not had time to absorb it. She had claimed fault for herself—but had not understood the extent to which she might be accused.

Ire for her stabilized him. Findail had no right to drop the whole weight of the Earth on her in this way. "It's not that simple," he began. He did not know the true name of his objection. But Linden faced him in mute appeal; and he did not let himself falter. "If Foul planned this all along, why did he go to the trouble?" That was not what he needed to ask. Yet he pursued it, hoping it would lead him to the right place. "Why didn't he just wake up the Worm himself?"

Findail's gaze held Linden. When her wide eyes went back to his, he replied, "This Despiser is not mad. Should he rouse the Worm himself, without the wild magic in his hand, would he not also be consumed in the destruction of the world?"

Covenant shrugged the argument aside, went on searching for the question he needed, the flaw in Findail's rationalizations. "Then why didn't you tell us sooner? Naturally you couldn't condescend to explain anything before she freed me." With all the sarcasm he could muster, he tried to force the Appointed to look at him, release Linden. "After what you people did, you knew she'd never give you my ring if she understood how much you want it. But later—before we got to the One Tree. Why didn't you tell us what kind of danger we were in?"

The *Elohim* sighed; but still he did not relinquish Linden. "Perhaps in that I erred," he said softly. "Yet I could not turn aside from hope. It was my hope that some access of wisdom or courage would inspire the ring-wielder to step back from the precipice of his intent."

Covenant continued groping. But now he saw that Linden had begun to rally. She shook her head, struggled internally for some way to refute or withstand Findail's accusation. Her mouth tightened: she looked like she was chewing curses. The sight lit a spark of encouragement in him, made him lean forward to aim his next challenge at the *Elohim*.

"That doesn't justify you," he grated. "You talk about silencing me as if that was the only decent alternative you had. But you know goddamn well it wasn't. For one thing, you could've done something about the venom that makes me so bloody dangerous."

Then Findail did look at Covenant. His yellow gaze

snapped upward with a fierceness which jolted Covenant. *"We dared not."* His quiet passion left trails of fire across Covenant's brain. "The doom of this age lies also upon me, but I dare not. Are we not the *Elohim*, the Würd of the Earth? Do we not read the truth in the very roots of the Rawedge Rim, in the shape of the mountainsides and in the snows which gild the winter peaks? You mock me at your peril. By means of his venom this Despiser attempts the destruction of the Arch of Time, and that is no little thing. But it pales beside the fate which would befall the Earth and all life upon the Earth, were there no venom within you. You conceive yourself to be a figure of power, but in the scale of worlds you are not. Had this Despiser's lust for the Illearth Stone not betrayed him, enhancing you beyond your mortal stature, you would not have stood against him so much as once. And he is wiser now, with the wisdom of old frustration, which some name madness.

"Lacking the venom, you would be too small to threaten him. If he did not seek you out for his own pleasure, you would wander the world without purpose, powerless against him. And the Sunbane would grow. It would *grow*, devouring every land and sea in turn until even *Elemesnedene* itself had fallen, and still it would grow, and there would be no halt to it. Seeing no blame for yourself, you would not surrender your ring. Therefore he would remain trapped within the Arch. But no other stricture would limit his victory. Even we, the *Elohim*, would in time be reduced to mere playthings for his mirth. While Time endured, the Desecration of the world would not end at all.

"Therefore," the Appointed articulated with careful intensity, "we bless the frustration or madness which inspired the gambit of this venom. Discontented in the prison of the Earth, the Despiser has risked his hope of freedom in the venom which gives you such might. It is our hope also. For now the blame is plain. Since you are blind in other ways, we must pray that guilt will drive you to the surrender which may save us."

The words went through Covenant like a shot. His arguments were punctured, made irrelevant. Findail admitted no alternative to submission except the Ritual of Desecration— the outright destruction of the Earth to spare it from Lord Foul's power. This was Kevin Landwaster's plight on a scale which staggered Covenant, appalled him to the marrow of his bones. If he did not give up his ring, how could he bear to do anything but ruin the world himself in order to foil the eternal Sunbane of the Despiser?

Yet he could not surrender his ring. The simple thought was immediately and intimately terrible to him. That metal circle meant too much: it contained every hard affirmation of life and love that he had ever wrested from the special cruelty of his loneliness, his leper's fate. The alternative was better. *Yes.* To destroy. Or to risk destroying in any kind of search for a different outcome.

His dilemma silenced him. In his previous confrontation with Lord Foul, he had found and used the quiet center of his vertigo, the still point of strength between the contradictions of his plight; but now there seemed to be no center, no place on which he could stand to affirm both the Earth and himself. And the necessity of choice was dreadful.

But Linden had taken hold of herself again. The conceptions which hurt her most were not the ones which pierced Covenant; and he had given her a chance to recover. The look she cast at him was brittle with stress; but it was alert once more, capable of reading his dismay. For an instant, empathy focused her gaze. Then she swung back toward the Appointed, and her voice bristled dangerously.

"That's just speculation. You're afraid you might lose your precious freedom, so you're trying to make him responsible for it. You still haven't told us the truth."

Findail faced her; and Covenant saw her flinch as if the *Elohim*'s eyes had burned her. But she did not stop.

"If you want us to believe you, tell us about Vain."

At that, Findail recoiled.

Immediately, she went after him. "First you imprisoned him, as if he was some kind of crime against you. And you tried to trick us about it, so we wouldn't know what you were doing. When he escaped, you tried to kill him. Then, when he and Seadreamer found you aboard the ship, you spoke to him." Her expression was a glower of memory. "You said, 'Whatever else you may do, *that* I will not suffer.' "

The Appointed started to reply; but she overrode him. "Later, you said, 'Only he whom you name Vain has it within him to expel me. I would give my soul that he should do so.'

And since then you've hardly been out of his sight—except when you decide to run away instead of helping us." She was unmistakably a woman who had learned something about courage. "You've been more interested in him than us from the beginning. Why don't you try explaining *that* for a change?"

She brandished her anger at the *Elohim*; and for a moment Covenant thought Findail would answer. But then his grief-ensnared visage tightened. In spite of its misery, his expression resembled the hauteur of Chant and Infelice as he said grimly, "Of the Demondim-spawn I will not speak."

"That's *right*," she shot back at him at once. "Of course you won't. If you did, you might give us a reason to do some hoping of our own. Then we might not roll over and play dead the way you want." She matched his glare; and in spite of all his power and knowledge she made him appear diminished and judged. Sourly, she muttered, "Oh, go on. Get out of here. You make my stomach hurt."

With a stiff shrug, Findail turned away. But before he could depart, Covenant interposed, "Just a minute." He felt half mad with fear and impossible decisions; but a fragment of lucidity had come to him, and he thought he saw another way in which he had been betrayed. Lena had told him that he was Berek Halfhand reborn. And the Lords he had known had believed that. What had gone wrong? "We couldn't get a branch of the One Tree. There was no way. But it's been done before. How did Berek do it?"

Findail paused at the wall, answered over his shoulder. "The Worm was not made restive by his approach, for he did not win his way with combat. In that age, the One Tree had no Guardian. It was he himself who gave the Tree its ward, setting the Guardian in place so that the vital wood of the world's life would not again be touched or broken."

Berek? Covenant was too astonished to watch the *Elohim* melt out of the cabin. Berek had set the Guardian? Why? The Lord-Fatherer had been described as both seer and prophet. Had he been shortsighted enough to believe that no one else would ever need to touch the One Tree? Or had he had some reason to ensure that there would never be a second Staff of Law?

Dizzy with implications, Covenant was momentarily un-

aware of the way Linden regarded him. But gradually he felt
her eyes on him. Her face was sharp with the demand she had
brought with her into his cabin—the demand of her need.
When he met her gaze, she said distinctly, "Your friends in
Andelain didn't think you were doomed. They gave you Vain
for a reason. What else did they do?"

"They talked to me," he replied as if she had invoked the
words out of him. "Mhoram said, 'When you have understood
the Land's need, you must depart the Land, for the thing you
seek is not within it. The one word of truth cannot be found
otherwise. But I give you this caution: do not be deceived by
the Land's need. The thing you seek is not what it appears to
be. In the end, you must return to the Land.' "

He had also said, *When you have come to the crux, and
have no other recourse, remember the paradox of white gold.
There is hope in contradiction.* But that Covenant did not
comprehend.

Linden nodded severely. "So what's it going to be? Are you
just going to lie here until your heart breaks? Or are you going to fight?"

Distraught by fear and despair, he could not find his way.
Perhaps an answer was possible, but he did not have it. Yet
what she wanted of him was certain; and because he loved her
he gave it to her as well as he was able.

"I don't know. But anything is better than this. Tell the
First we'll give it a try."

She nodded again. For a moment, her mouth moved as if
she wished to thank him in some way. But then the pressure
of her own bare grasp on resolution impelled her toward the
door.

"What about you?" he asked after her. He had sent her
away and did not know how to recall her. He had no right.
"What're you going to do?"

At the door, she looked back at him, and her eyes were
openly full of tears. "I'm going to wait." Her voice sounded as
forlorn as the cry of a kestrel—and as determined as an act
of valor. "My turn's coming."

As she left, her words seemed to remain in the sunlit cabin
like a verdict. Or a prophecy.

After she was gone, Covenant got out of the hammock and
dressed himself completely in his old clothes.

THREE: The Path to Pain

WHEN he went up on deck, the sun was setting beyond the western sea, and its light turned the water crimson—the color of disaster. Honninscrave had raised every span of canvas the spars could hold; and every sail was belly-full of wind as Starfare's Gem pounded forward a few points west of north. It should have been a brave sight. But the specific red of that sunset covered the canvas with fatality, gilded the lines until they looked like they were slick with blood. And the wind carried a precursive chill, hinting at the bitter cold of winter.

Yet Honninscrave strode the wheeldeck as if he could no longer be daunted by anything the sea brought to him. The air riffled his beard, and his eyes reflected occasional glints of fire from the west; but his commands were as precise as his mastery of the Giantship, and the rawness of his voice might have been caused by the strain of shouting over the wind rather than by the stress of the past two days. He was not Foamfollower after all. He had not been granted the *caamora* his spirit craved. But he was a Giant still, the Master of Starfare's Gem; and he had risen to his responsibilities.

With Cail beside him, Covenant went up to the wheeldeck. He wanted to find some way to apologize for having proven himself inadequate to the Master's need. But when he approached Honninscrave and the other two Giants with him, Sevinhand Anchormaster and a steersman holding Shipsheartthew, the caution in their eyes stopped Covenant. At first, he thought that they had become wary of him—that the danger he represented made them fearful in his presence. But then

Sevinhand said simply, "Giantfriend," and it was plain even to Covenant's superficial hearing that the Anchormaster's tone was one of shared sorrow rather than misgiving. Instead of apologizing, Covenant bowed his head in tacit recognition of his own unworth.

He wanted to stand there in silence until he had shored up enough self-respect to take another step back into the life of the Giantship. But after a moment Cail spoke. In spite of his characteristic *Haruchai* dispassion, his manner suggested that what he meant to say made him uncomfortable. Involuntarily, Covenant reflected that none of the *Haruchai* who had left the Land with him had come this far unscathed. Covenant did not know how the uncompromising extravagance of the *Haruchai* endured the role Brinn had assigned to Cail. What promise lay hidden in Brinn's statement that Cail would eventually be permitted to follow his heart?

But Cail did not speak of that. He did not address Covenant. Without preamble, he said, "Grimmand Honninscrave, in the name of my people I desire your pardon. When Brinn assayed himself against *ak-Haru Kenaustin Ardenol*—he who is the sovereign legend and dream of all the *Haruchai* among the mountains—it was not his intent to bring about the death of Cable Seadreamer your brother."

The Master winced: his cavernous eyes shot splinters of red at Cail. But almost at once he regained his deliberate poise. He glanced around the Giantship as if to assure himself that all was still well with it. Then he turned over his command to Sevinhand, drew Cail and Covenant with him to the port rail.

The setting sun gave his visage a tinge of sacrificial glory. Watching him, Covenant thought obscurely that the sun always set in the west—that a man who faced west would never see anything except decline, things going down, the last beauty before light and life went out.

After a moment, Honninscrave lifted his voice over the wet splashing of the shipside. "The Earth-Sight is not a thing which any Giant selects for himself. No choice is given. But we do not therefore seek to gainsay or eschew it. We believe —or have believed—" he said with a touch of bitterness, "that there is life as well as death in such mysteries. How then should there be any blame in what has happened?" Honninscrave spoke more to himself than to Covenant or Cail. "The

Earth-Sight came upon Cable Seadreamer my brother, and the hurt of his vision was plain to all. But the content of that hurt he could not tell. Mayhap his muteness was made necessary by the vision itself. Mayhap for him no denial of death was possible which would not also have been a denial of life. I know nothing of that. I know only that he could not speak his plight—and so he could not be saved. There is no blame for us in this." He spoke as though he believed what he was saying; but the loss knotted around his eyes contradicted him.

"His death places no burden upon us but the burden of hope." The sunset was fading from the west and from his face, translating his mien from crimson to the pallor of ashes. "We must hope that in the end we will find means to vindicate his passing. To vindicate," he repeated faintly, "and to comprehend." He did not look at his auditors. The dying of the light echoed out of his eyes. "I am grieved that I can conceive no hope."

He had earned the right to be left alone. But Covenant needed an answer. He and Foamfollower had talked about hope. Striving to keep his voice gentle in spite of his own stiff hurt, he asked, "Then why do you go on?"

For a long moment, Honninscrave remained still against the mounting dark as if he had not heard, could not be reached. But at last he said simply, "I am a Giant. The Master of Starfare's Gem, and sworn to the service of the First of the Search. That is preferable."

Preferable, Covenant thought with a mute pang. Mhoram might have said something like that. But Findail obviously did not believe it.

Yet Cail nodded as if Honninscrave's words were ones which even the extravagant *Haruchai* could accept. After all, Cail's people did not put much faith in hope. They staked themselves on success or failure—and accepted the outcome.

Covenant turned from the darkling sea, left the rail. He had no place among such people. He did not know what was preferable—and could not see enough success anywhere to make failure endurable. The decision he had made in Linden's name was just another kind of lie. Well, she had earned that pretense of conviction from him. But at some point any leper needed something more than discipline or even stubbornness to keep him alive. And he had too sorely falsified his relationship with her. He did not know what to do.

Around Starfare's Gem, the Giants had begun to light lanterns against the night. They illuminated the great wheel, the stairs down from the wheeldeck, the doorways to the underdecks and the galley. They hung from the fore- and aftermasts like instances of bravado, both emphasizing and disregarding the gap where the midmast should have been. They were nothing more than small oil lamps under the vast heavens, and yet they made the Giantship beautiful on the face of the deep. After a moment, Covenant found that he could bear to go looking for Linden.

But when he started forward from the wheeldeck, his attention was caught by Vain. The Demondim-spawn stood beyond the direct reach of the lanterns, on the precise spot where his feet had first touched stone after he had come aboard from the Isle of the One Tree; but his black silhouette was distinct against the fading horizon. As always, he remained blank to scrutiny, as though he knew that nothing could touch him.

Yet he had been touched. One iron heel of the old Staff of Law still clamped him where his wrist had been; but that hand dangled useless from the wooden limb which grew like a branch from his elbow. Covenant had no idea why Foamfollower had given him this product of the dark and historically malefic ur-viles. But now he was sure that Linden had been right—that no explanation which did not include the secret of the Demondim-spawn was complete enough to be trusted. When he moved on past Vain, he knew more clearly why he wanted to find her.

He came upon her near the foremast, some distance down the deck from the prow where Findail stood confronting the future like a figurehead. With her were the First, Pitchwife, and another Giant. As Covenant neared them, he recognized Mistweave, whose life Linden had saved at the risk of his own during his most recent venom-relapse. The three Giants greeted him with the same gentle caution Honninscrave and Sevinhand had evinced—the wariness of people who believed they were in the presence of a pain which transcended their own. But Linden seemed almost unconscious of his appearance. In the wan lantern-light, her face looked pallid, nearly haggard; and Covenant thought suddenly that she had not rested at all since before the quest had arrived at the Isle of the One Tree. The energy which had sustained her earlier had eroded away; her manner was febrile with exhaustion. For a moment, he was so conscious of her nearness to collapse that he failed to notice the fact that she, too, was wearing her old clothes—the checked flannel shirt, tough jeans, and sturdy shoes in which she had first entered the Land.

Though her choice was no different than his, the sight of it gave him an unexpected pang. Once again, he had been betrayed by his preterite instinct for hope. Unconsciously, he had dreamed that all the shocks and revelations of the past days would not alter her, not impell her to resume their former distance from each other. Fool! he snarled at himself. He could not escape her percipience. Down in his cabin, she had read what he was going to do before he had known it himself.

The First greeted him in a tone made brusque by the sternness of her own emotions; but her words showed that she also was sensitive to his plight. "Thomas Covenant, I believe that you have chosen well." If anything, the losses of the past days and the darkness of the evening seemed to augment her iron beauty. She was a Swordmain, trained to give battle to the peril of the world. As she spoke, one hand gripped her sword's hilt as if the blade were a vital part of what she was saying. "I have named you Giantfriend, and I am proud that I did so. Pitchwife my husband is wont to say that it is the meaning of our lives to hope. But I know not how to measure such things. I know only that battle is better than surrender. It is not for me to judge your paths in this matter—yet am I gladdened that you have chosen a path of combat." In the way of a warrior, she was trying to comfort him.

Her attempt touched him—and frightened him as well, for it suggested that once again he had committed himself to more than he could gauge. But he was given no chance to reply. For once, Pitchwife seemed impatient with what his wife was saying. As soon as she finished, he interposed, "Aye, and Linden Avery also is well Chosen, as I have said. But in this she does not choose well. Giantfriend, she will not rest." His exasperation was plain in his voice.

Linden grimaced. Covenant started to say, "Linden, you need—" But when she looked at him he stopped. Her gaze gathered up the darkness and held it against him.

"I don't have anywhere to go."

The stark bereavement of Linden's answer went through him like a cry. It meant too much: that her former world had been ruined for her by what she had learned; that like him she could not bear to return to her cabin—the cabin they had shared.

Somewhere in the distance, Pitchwife was saying, "To her have been offered the chambers of the *Haruchai*. But she replies that she fears to dream in such places. And Starfare's Gem holds no other private quarters."

Covenant understood that also without heeding it. Brinn had blamed her for Hergrom's death. And she had tried to kill Ceer. "Leave her alone," he said dully, as deaf to himself as to Pitchwife. "She'll rest when she's ready."

That was not what he wanted to say. He wanted to say, Forgive me. I don't know how to forgive myself. But the words were locked in his chest. They were impossible.

Because he had nothing else to offer her, he swallowed thickly and said, "You're right. My friends didn't expect me to be doomed. Foamfollower gave me Vain for a reason." Even that affirmation was difficult for him; but he forced it out. "What happened to his arm?"

She went on staring darkness at him as if he were the linchpin of her exhaustion. She sounded as misled as a sleepwalker as she responded, "Mistweave won't go away. He says he wants to take Cail's place."

Covenant peered at her, momentarily unable to comprehend. But then he remembered his own dismay when Brinn had insisted on serving him; and his heart twisted. *"Linden,"* he demanded, forlorn and harsh in his inability to help her, "tell me about Vain's arm." If he had dared, he would have taken hold of her. If he had had the right.

She shook her head; and lantern-light glanced like supplication out of her dry eyes. "I can't." She might have protested like a child, It hurts. "His arm's empty. When I close my eyes, it isn't even there. If you took all the life out of the One Tree —took it away so completely that the Tree never had any— never had any meaning at all—it would look like that. If he was actually alive—if he wasn't just a thing the ur-viles made —he'd be in terrible pain."

Slowly, she turned away as though she could no longer support his presence. When she moved off down the deck with Mistweave walking, deferential and stubborn, behind her, he understood that she also did not know how to forgive.

He thought then that surely his loss and need had become too much for him, that surely he was about to break down. But the First and Pitchwife were watching him with their concern poignant in their faces. They were his friends. And they needed him. Somehow, he held himself together.

Later, Mistweave sent word that Linden had found a place to sleep at last, huddled in a corner of the galley near the warmth of one of the great stoves. With that Covenant had to be content. Moving stiffly, he went back to his hammock and took the risk of nightmares. Dreams seemed to be the lesser danger.

But the next morning the wind was stronger.

It might have been a true sailors' wind—enough to shake the *dromond* out of its normal routine and make it stretch, not enough to pose any threat to the sea-craft of the crew. It kicked the crests of the waves into spume and spray, sent water crashing off the Giantship's granite prow, made the lines hum and the sails strain. The sides of the vessel moved so swiftly that their moire markings looked like flames crackling from the sea. In the rigging, some of the Giants laughed as they fisted the canvas from position to position, seeking the *dromond*'s best stance for speed. If its midmast had not been lost, Starfare's Gem would have flown like exuberance before the blow.

However, the day was dull with clouds and felt unnaturally cold. A south wind should have been warmer than this. It came straight from the place where the Isle had gone down, and it was as chill as the cavern of the One Tree. Without the sun to light it, the sea had a gray and viscid hue. Though he wore a robe over his clothes, Covenant hunched his shoulders and could not stop shivering.

Seeking reassurance, he went up to the wheeldeck, where Heft Galewrath commanded the *dromond*. But she greeted him with only a blunt nod. Her normally stolid demeanor held a kind of alert watchfulness that he had not seen in her before. For the first time since they had met, she seemed accessible to misgiving. Rather than trouble her with his trepidations, he returned to the afterdeck and moved forward, looking for someone who could be more easily questioned.

It's not that cold, he told himself. It's just wind. But still the chill cut at him. No matter how he hugged the robe about him, the wind found its way to his skin.

Instinctively, he went to the galley, looking for warmth and Linden.

He found her there, seated at one wall near the cheery bustle of the *dromond*'s two cooks, a husband and wife aptly named Seasauce and Hearthcoal. They had spent so much of their lives working over the great stoves that their faces had become perpetually ruddy. They looked like images of each other as they blustered about their tasks, moving with a disingenuous air of confusion which concealed the ease of their teamwork. When they went out on deck, heat overflowed from them; and in their constricted demesne they radiated like ovens. Yet Covenant's chill persisted.

Linden was awake, but still glazed with sleep. She had paid only a part of the debt of her weariness. Though she acknowledged Covenant, behind her eyes everything was masked in somnolence. He thought at once that he should not bother her with questions until she had rested more. But he was too cold for good intentions.

Hunkering down beside her, he asked, "What do you think of this wind?"

She yawned. "I think," she said distantly, "that Foul's in a hurry to get us back.

However, after another day's rest, Linden was able to look at the weather more percipiently. By then, Covenant had worn himself petulant with aimless anxiety. He felt repeatedly that he had lost the center of his life, that he could no longer hold himself from flying outward in all directions when the vertigo of his fear arose. Nothing had happened to suggest that the *dromond* was in danger: yet his inchoate conviction of peril remained. Snappishly, he asked Linden his question a second time.

But long sleep had brought her back to herself, and the gaze she turned toward him was capable of knowledge. She seemed to see without effort that his irritation was not directed at her. She placed a brief touch on his forearm like a promise that she would not forsake him. Then she went out to look at the wind.

After a moment's assessment, she declared that this blow

was not unnatural or ill, not something which the Despiser had whipped up for his own ends. Instead, it was a reaction to the fundamental convulsion which had pulled down the Isle of the One Tree. By that violence, the balances of the weather had been disturbed, outraged.

It was conceivable that Lord Foul had known this would happen. But she felt no evidence of his influence on the wind.

When Covenant relayed her verdict to Honninscrave, the Master shrugged, his thoughts hidden behind the buttress of his brows. "No matter," he muttered as if he were not listening to himself. "Should it worsen, Starfare's Gem must run before it. Part-masted as we are, I will not hazard resistance to the wind's path. There is no need. At present, we are borne but a scant span from our true way."

That should have satisfied Covenant. His experience of the sea was trivial compared to Honninscrave's. Yet the alarm in his guts refused to be eased. Like Galewrath, the Master conveyed an impression of concealed worry.

During the next two days, the wind became more serious.

Blowing with incessant vehemence a few points west of north, it cut into the sea like the share of a plow, whined across the decks of the *dromond* like the ache of its own chill. In spite of its speed, Starfare's Gem no longer appeared to be moving swiftly: the wind bore the water itself northward, and what little bowwave the prow raised was torn away at once. Clouds hugged the world from horizon to horizon. The sails looked gray and brittle as they heaved the heavy stone along.

And that night the cold began in earnest.

When Covenant scrambled shivering out of his hammock the next morning, he found a scum of ice in the washbasin which Cail had set out for him. Faint patches of frost licked the moire-granite as if they had soaked in through the walls. Passing Vain on his way to the warmth of the galley, he saw that the Demondim-spawn's black form was mottled with rime like leprosy.

Yet the Giants were busy about their tasks as always. Impervious to fire if not to pain, they were also proof against cold. Most of them labored in the rigging, fighting the frozen stiffness of the lines. For a moment while his eyes teared, Covenant saw them imprecisely and thought they were furling the sails. But then he saw clouds blowing off the canvas like

steam, and he realized that the Giants were beating the sails
to prevent the frost on them from building into ice. Ice might
have torn the canvas from the spars, crippling Starfare's Gem
when the *dromond*'s life depended upon its headway.

His breathing crusted in his beard as he let the wind thrust
him forward. Without Cail's help, he would have been unable
to wrestle open the galley door. Slivers of ice sprang from the
cracks and vanished inward as the *Haruchai* broke the seal
caused by the moisture of cooking. Riding a gust that swirled
stiffly through the galley, Covenant jumped the storm-sill
and nearly staggered at the concussion as the door slammed
behind him.

"Stone and Sea!" Hearthcoal barked in red-faced and harm-
less ire. "Are you fools, that you enter aft rather than forward
in this gale?" With a dripping ladle, she gestured fiercely at
the other seadoor. Behind her, Seasauce clanged shut his
stove's firebox indignantly. But a moment later, all vexation
forgotten, he handed Covenant a steaming flagon of diluted
diamondraught, and Hearthcoal scooped out a bowl of broth
for him from the immense stone pot she tended. Awkward
with self-consciousness, he sat down beside Linden against
one wall out of the way of the cooks and tried to draw some
warmth back into his bones.

In the days that followed, he spent most of his time there,
sharing with her the bearable clangor and heat of the galley.
In spite of his numbness, the cold was too fierce for him; and
for her it was worse because her senses were so vulnerable to
it. He made one more attempt to sleep in his cabin; but after
that he accepted a pallet like hers in the galley. The wind
mounted incrementally every day, and with it the air grew
steadily more frigid. Starfare's Gem was being hurled like a
jerrid toward the ice-gnawed heart of the north. When Giants
entered the galley seeking food or warmth, their clothing was
stiff with gray rime which left puddles of slush on the floor as
it melted. Ice clogged their beards and hair, and their eyes
were haggard. Covenant made occasional forays out on deck
to observe the state of the ship; but what he saw—the thick,
dire sea, the lowering wrack, the frozen knurs of spume which
were allowed to chew at the railings because the crew was
too hard-pressed to clear them away—always drove him back
to the galley with a gelid knot in his chest.

Once he went far enough forward to look at Findail. When he returned, his lips were raw with cold and curses. "That bastard doesn't even feel it," he muttered to no one in particular, although Pitchwife was there with Linden, Mistweave, the two cooks, and a few other Giants. "It goes right through him." He could not explain his indignation. It simply seemed unjust that the Appointed should be untouched by the plight of the *dromond*.

But Linden was not looking at him: her attention was fixed on Pitchwife as if she wanted to ask him something important. At first, however, she had no opportunity to interpose her question. Pitchwife was teasing Hearthcoal and Seasauce like a merry child and laughing at the concealed humor of their rebuffs. He had a Giant's tall spirit in his bent frame, and more than a Giant's capacity for mirth. His japing dissipated some of Covenant's acid mood.

At last Pitchwife wrung an involuntary laugh from the cooks; and with that he subsided near Covenant and Linden, the heat of the stoves gleaming on his forehead. Covenant was conscious of Linden's tautness as she mustered her inquiry. "Pitchwife, what're we getting into?"

The Giant looked at her with an air of surprise which might have been feigned.

"Nobody wants to talk about it," she pursued. "I've asked Galewrath and Sevinhand, but all they say is that Starfare's Gem can go on like this indefinitely. Even Mistweave thinks he can serve me by keeping his mouth shut." Mistweave peered studiously at the ceiling, pretending he did not hear what was said. "So I'm asking you. You've never held anything back from me." Her voice conveyed a complex vibration of strain. "What're we getting into?"

Outside the galley, the wind made a peculiar keening sound as it swept through the anchorholes. Frost snapped in the cracks of the doors. Pitchwife did not want to meet her gaze; but she held him. By degrees, his good cheer sloughed away; and the contrast made him appear older, eroded by an unuttered fear. For no clear reason, Covenant was reminded of a story Linden had told him in the days before the quest had reached *Elemesnedene*—the story of the role Pitchwife had played in the death of the First's father. He looked now like a man who had too many memories.

"Ah, Chosen," he sighed, "it is my apprehension that we
have been snared by the Dolewind which leads to the Soulbiter."

The Soulbiter.

Pitchwife called it an imprecise sea, not only because every
ship that found it did so in a different part of the world, but
also because every ship that won free of it again told a different tale. Some vessels met gales and reefs in the south; others,
stifling calms in the east; still others, rank and impenetrable
beds of sargasso in the west. In spite of this, however, the
Soulbiter was known for what it was; for no craft or crew
ever came back from it unscathed. And each of those ships
had been driven there by a Dolewind that blew too long without let or variation.

Linden argued for a while, vexed by the conflicting vague-
ness and certainty of Pitchwife's explanations. But Covenant
paid no heed to either of them. He had a name now for his
chill anxiety, and the knowledge gave him a queer comfort.
The Soulbiter. It was not Lord Foul's doing. Neither could it
be avoided. And the outcome of that sea might make all
other fears unnecessary. Very well. The galley was too warm;
but outside cried and groaned a cold which only Giants could
endure for any length of time. Eventually, even the din of the
cooks became soothing to him, and he passed out of trepidation into a kind of waking somnolence—a stupefied inner silence like an echo of the emptiness which the *Elohim* had
imposed upon him in *Elemesnedene*.

That silence comprised the only safety he had known in this
world. It was a leper's answer to despair, a state of detachment and passivity made complete by the deadness of every
nerve which should have conveyed import. The *Elohim* had
not invented it: they had simply incarnated in him the special
nature of his doom. To feel nothing and die.

Linden had once redeemed him from that fate. But now he
was beaten. He made decisions, not because he believed in
them, but because they were expected of him. He did not
have the heart to face the Soulbiter.

In the days that followed, he went through the ordinary
motions of being alive. He drank enough *diamondraught* to
account for his mute distance to the people who watched him.
He slept in the galley, took brief walks, acknowledged greet-

ings and conversations like a living man. But inwardly he was becoming untouchable. After years of discipline and defiance, of stubborn argument against the seduction of his illness, he gave the effort up.

And still Starfare's Gem plowed a straight furrow across the gray and gravid sea while the wind blew arctic outrage. Except for a few worn paths here and there, the decks were now clenched with ice, overgrown like an old ruin. Its sheer weight was enough to make the Giants nervous; but they could not spare time or strength to clear the crust away. There was too much water in the wind: the blow sheared too much spray off the battered waves. And that damp collected in the sails faster than it could be beaten clear. At intervals, one stretch of canvas or another became too heavy to hold. The wind rent it out of its shrouds. A hail of ice-slivers swept the decks; tattered scraps of sail were left flapping like broken hands from the spars. Then the Giants were forced to clew new canvas up the yards. Bereft of its midmast, the granite *dromond* needed all its sails or none.

Day after day, the shrill whine of the rigging and the groans of the stone became louder, more distressed. The sea looked like fluid ice, and Starfare's Gem was dragged forward against ever-increasing resistance. Yet the Giantship was stubborn. Its masts flexed and shivered, but did not shatter. Grinding its teeth against the gale, Starfare's Gem endured.

When the change came, it took everyone by surprise. Rest had restored the combative smolder to Linden's eyes, and she had been fretting for days against the maddening pressure of the blast and the constriction of the galley; but even she did not see what was coming. And the Giants had no warning at all.

At one moment, Starfare's Gem was riding the howl of the wind through the embittered heart of a cloud-dark night. At the next, the *dromond* pitched forward like a destrier with locked forelegs; and the gale was gone. The suddenness of the silence staggered the vessel like a detonation. There was no sound except the faint clink and crash of ice falling from the slack sails. Linden jerked her percipience from side to side, probing the ship, then she muttered in astonishment, "We've stopped. Just like that."

For an instant, no one moved. Then Mistweave strode to the forward door, kicked it out of its frost. Cold as pure as

absolute winter came flowing inward; but it had no wind behind it. The air across the Giantship was still.

Shouts sprang along the decks. In spite of his inward silence, Covenant followed Mistweave and Linden out into the
night.

The clouds were gone: the dark was as clear and sharp as
a knife-edge. Spots of light marked out the Giantship as the
crew lit more lanterns. Near the eastern horizon stood the
moon, yellow and doleful. It was nearly full, but appeared
to shed no illumination, cast no reflection onto the black and
secret face of the water. The stars littered the sky in every
direction, all their portents lost. Linden muttered to herself,
"What in hell—?" But she seemed unable to complete the
question.

Honninscrave and Pitchwife approached from opposite ends
of the ship. When the First joined them, Pitchwife said with
unconvincing nonchalance, "It appears that we are here."

Covenant felt too numb to be cold. But Linden was shivering violently beside him. In a bitten voice, she asked, "What
do we do now?"

"Do?" replied Honninscrave distantly. His visage was benighted, devoid of content. "This is the Soulbiter. We must
await its will." Plumes of steam came from his mouth as if his
spirit escaped him at every word.

Its will, Covenant thought dumbly. My will. Foul's will.
Nothing made any difference. Silence was safety. If he could
not have hope, he would accept numbness. Returning to the
galley, he curled up on his pallet and fell immediately asleep.

But the next morning he was awakened by the cold and the
quiet. The stoves put out no heat. Except for Cail, the galley
was deserted. Abandoned. Starfare's Gem lay as still as if he
and the *Haruchai* were the only people left aboard.

A pang went through him, threatening his defenses. Stiff
with sleep and chill, he fumbled erect. "Where—?" he asked
weakly. "Where did they go?"

Cail's reply was flat and pitiless. "They have gone to behold
the Soulbiter."

Covenant winced. He did not want to leave the confines of
the galley. He feared the return of sensation and pain and
responsibility. But Cail's expressionless stare was insistent. Cail
was one of the *Haruchai*, kindred to Brinn and Bannor. His

comrades Ceer and Hergrom had given their lives. He had the right to make demands. And his gaze was as plain as words.

It is enough. Now you must resume yourself.

Covenant did not want to go. But he adjusted his rumpled attire, made an effort to secure the silence closely about him. When Cail opened the door for him, he took a step over the storm-sill and walked blinking into the bright, frigid morning.

After so many days hidden behind the glower of the clouds, the sun alone would have been enough to blind him. But it was not alone. White cold glared around the ship. Light sprang at him from all sides; dazzles as piercing as spears volleyed about his head. His tears froze on his cheeks. When he raised his hands to rub the beads away, small patches of skin were torn from his face.

But slowly his sight cleared. He saw Giants lining the rails, their backs to him. Everyone on board stood at the forward railings somewhere, facing outward.

They were still, as quiet as the Sea and the sails hanging empty in their gear. But no hush could silence their expectant suspense. They were watching the Soulbiter. Waiting for it.

Then he recovered enough vision to discern the source of all the dazzling.

Motionless in the water, Starfare's Gem lay surrounded by a flotilla of icebergs.

Hundreds of them in every size and configuration. Some were mere small humps on the flat sea. Others raised jagged crests to the level of the *dromond*'s spars. And they were all formed of the same impeccable ice: ice as translucent and complete as glass, as hard-faced as diamonds; ice on which the morning broke, shattering light in all directions.

They were moving. Singly or in squadrons, they bore slowly down on the ship as they floated southward. A few came so close that a Giant could have reached them in one leap. Yet none of them struck the *dromond*.

Along the deep the flotilla drifted with a wonderous majesty, as bewitching as the cold. Most of the Giants stood as if they had been carved from a muddier ice. They scarcely breathed while their hands froze to the rails and the gleaming burned into their eyes. Covenant joined Linden near the First, Pitchwife, and Mistweave. Behind the raw red of cold in her face lay a blue pallor as if her blood had become as milky as

frost; but she had stopped shivering, paid no heed to the drops
of ice which formed on her parted lips. Pitchwife's constant
murmur did not interrupt the trance. Like everyone else, he
watched the ice pass stately by as if he were waiting for someone to speak. As if the sun-sharp wonder of this passage were
merely a prelude.

Covenant found that he, too, could not look away. Commanded by so much eye-piercing glister and beauty, he braced
his hands on one of the crossbeams of the railing and at once
lost the power of movement. He was calm now, prepared to
wait forever if necessary to hear what the cold was going to
utter.

Cail's voice reached him distantly. The *Haruchai* was saying, "Ur-Lord, this is not well. Chosen, hear me. It is not
well. You must come away." But his protest slowly ran out of
strength. He moved to stand beside Covenant and did not
speak again.

Covenant had no sense of time. Eventually the waiting
ended. A berg drifted past the line of spectators, showing
everyone a flat space like a platform in its side. And from that
space rose cries.

"A ship at last!"

"Help us!"

"In the name of pity!"

"We have been marooned!"

He seemed to hear the same shouts behind him also, from
the other side of the Giantship. But that strange detail made
no impression on him.

His eyes were the only part of him that moved. As the iceberg floated southward amid the slow procession, its flat side
passed directly below the watchers. And he saw figures emerge
from the pellucid ice—human figures. Three or four of them,
he could not be sure. The number was oddly imprecise. But
numbers did not matter. They were men, and their destitution
made his heart twist against its shackles.

They were hollow-eyed, gaunt, and piteous. Their hands,
maimed by frostbite, were wrapped in shreds torn from their
ragged clothing. Emaciation and hopelessness lined their
faces. Their cracked and splintered voices were hoarse with
despair.

"Marooned!" they cried like a memory of the wind.

"Mercy!"

But no one on the *dromond* moved.

"Help them." Linden's voice issued like a moan between her beaded lips. "Throw them a line. Somebody."

No one responded. Gripped by cold, volitionless, the watchers only stared as the iceberg drifted slowly by, bearing its frantic victims away. Gradually, the current took the marooned men out of hearing.

"In the name of God." Her tears formed a gleaming fan of ice under each eye.

Again Covenant's heart twisted. But he could not break free. His silence covered the sea.

Then another berg drew near. It lay like a plate on the unwavering face of the water. Beneath the surface, its bulk lightly touched the ship, scraped a groan from the hushed hull. For a moment, the plate caught the sun squarely, and its reflection rang like a knell. Yet Covenant was able to see through the glare.

Poised in the sun's image were people that he knew.

Hergrom. Ceer.

They stood braced as if they had their backs to the Sandwall. At first, they were unaware of the Giantship. But then they saw it. Ceer shouted a hail which fell without echo onto the decks of the *dromond*. Leaving Hergrom, he sprinted to the edge of the ice, waved his arms for assistance.

Then out of the light came a Sandgorgon. White against the untrammeled background of the ice, the beast charged toward Hergrom with murder outstretched in its mighty arms.

Tremors shook Cail. Strain made steam puff between his teeth. But the cold held him.

For an instant, the implacable structure of Ceer's face registered the fact that the Giantship was not going to help him. His gaze shivered in Covenant's chest like an accusation that could never be answered. Then he sped to Hergrom's defense.

The Sandgorgon struck with the force of a juggernaut. Cracks sprang through the ice. A flurry of blows scattered Hergrom's blood across the floe. Ceer's strength meant nothing to the beast.

And still no one moved. The Giants were ice themselves now, as frigid and brittle as the wilderland of the sea. Linden's weeping gasped in her throat. Droplets of blood ran from Covenant's palms as he tried to rip his hands from the railing. But the grasp of the cold could not be broken.

Ceer. *Hergrom.*

But the plate of ice slowly drifted away, and no one moved.

After that, the waiting seemed long for the first time since Covenant had fallen under the spell of the Soulbiter.

At last another hunk of ice floated near the Giantship. It was small, hardly a yard wide, its face barely above the water. It seemed too small to be the bringer of so much fear.

For a moment, his vision was smeared with light. He could see nothing past the bright assault of the sun's reflections. But then his eyes cleared.

On that little floe stood Cable Seadreamer. He faced the *dromond*, stared up at the watchers. His posture was erect; his arms were folded sternly over the gaping wound in the center of his chest. Above his scar, his eyes were full of terrible knowledge.

Stiffly, he nodded a greeting. "My people," he said in a voice as quiet and extreme as the cold, "you must succor me. This is the Soulbiter. Here suffer all the damned who have died in a false cause, unaided by those they sought to serve. If you will not reach out to me, I must stand here forever in my anguish, and the ice will not release me. Hear me, you whom I have loved to this cost. Is there no love left in you for me?"

"*Seadreamer*," Linden groaned. Honninscrave gave a cry that tore frozen flesh around his mouth, sent brief drops of blood into his beard. The First panted faintly, "No. I am the First of the Search. I will not endure it." But none of them moved. The cold had become irrefragable. Its victory was accomplished. Already Seadreamer was almost directly opposite Covenant's position. Soon he would pass amidships, and then he would be gone, and the people of Starfare's Gem would be left with nothing except abomination and rue and cold.

It was intolerable. Seadreamer had given his life to save Covenant from destroying the Earth. Prevented by muteness from sharing the Earth-Sight, he had placed his own flesh in the path of the world's doom, purchasing a reprieve for the people he loved. And Covenant had refused to grant him the simple decency of a *caamora*. It was too much.

In pain and dismay, Covenant moved. With a curse that
splintered the silence, he burned his hands off the rail. Wild
magic pulsed through him like the hot ichor of grief: white
fire burst out of his ring like rage. "We're going to lose him!"
he howled at the Giants. "Get a rope!"

An instant later, the First wrenched herself free. Her iron
voice rang across the Giantship: "No!"

Jerking toward the mooring of a nearby ratline, she
snatched up one of the belaying-pins. "Avaunt, demon!" she
yelled. "We will not hear you!"

Fierce with fury and revulsion, she hurled the pin straight
at Seadreamer.

The Giants gaped as her projectile flashed through him.

It struck a chip from the edge of the ice and skipped away
into the sea, splashing distinctly. At once, his form wavered.
He tried to speak again; but already he had dissolved into
mirage. The floe drifted emptily away toward the south.

While Covenant stared, the fire rushed out of him, quenched
again by the cold.

But an instant later the spell broke with an audible crackle
and shatter of ice. Linden lifted raw hands to her face, blinked
her cold-gouged eyes. Coughing and cursing, Honninscrave
reeled back from the rail. "Move, sluggards!" His shout scattered flecks of blood. "Ware the wind!" Relief and dismay were
etched in frost on different parts of Pitchwife's face.

Numbly, the other Giants turned from the vista of the Sea.
Some seemed unable to understand what had happened; others
struggled in mounting haste toward their stations. Seasauce and
Hearthcoal bustled back to the galley as if they were ashamed
of their prolonged absence. The First and Galewrath moved
among the slower crewmembers, shaking or manhandling them
into a semblance of alertness. Honninscrave strode grimly in
the direction of the wheeldeck.

A moment later, one of the sails rattled in its gear, sending
down a shower of frozen dust; and the first Giant to ascend the
ratlines gave a hoarse call:

"The south!"

A dark moil of clouds was already visible above the *dromond*'s taffrail. The gale was coming back.

Covenant wondered momentarily how Starfare's Gem would
be able to navigate through the flotilla of icebergs in such a
wind—or how the ice-laden sails would survive if the blast hit

too suddenly, too hard. But then he forgot everything else because Linden was fainting and he was too far away to reach
her. Mistweave barely caught her in time to keep her from
cracking her head open on the stone deck.

FOUR: Sea of Ice

THE first gusts hit the Giantship at an angle, heeling it
heavily to port. But then the main force of the wind came up
against the stern, and Starfare's Gem righted with a wrench
as the sails snapped and bellied and the blast tried to claw
them away. The *dromond* lay so massively in the viscid sea
that for a moment it seemed unable to move. The upper spars
screamed. Abruptly, Dawngreeter split from top to bottom,
and wind tore shrilling through the rent.

But then Starfare's Gem gathered its legs under it, thrust
forward, and the pressure eased. As the clouds came boiling
overhead, the Giantship took hold of itself and began to run.

In the first moments, Honninscrave and the steerswoman
were tested to their limits by the need to avoid collision with
the nearest bergs. Under these frigid conditions, any contact
might have burst the granite of the *dromond*'s flanks like dry
wood. But soon the flotilla began to thin ahead of the ship.
Starfare's Gem was coming to the end of the Soulbiter. The
wind continued to scale upward; but now the immediate danger receded. The *dromond* had been fashioned to withstand
such blasts.

But Covenant was oblivious to the ship and the wind: he
was fighting for Linden's life. Mistweave had carried her into
the galley, where the cooks labored to bring back the heat of
their stoves; but once the Giant had laid her down on her
pallet, Covenant shouldered him aside. Pitchwife followed

Cail into the galley and offered his help. Covenant ignored him. Cursing with methodical vehemence under his breath, he chaffed her wrists, rubbed her cheeks, and waited for the cooks to warm some water.

She was too pale. The movement of her chest was so slight that he could hardly believe it. Her skin had the texture of wax. It looked like it would peel away if he rubbed it too hard. He slapped and massaged her forearms, her shoulders, the sides of her neck with giddy desperation pounding in his temples. Between curses, he reiterated his demand for water.

"It will come," muttered Seasauce. His own impatience made him sound irate. "The stoves are cold. I have no theurgy to hasten fire."

"She isn't a Giant," Covenant responded without looking away from Linden. "It doesn't have to boil."

Pitchwife squatted at Linden's head, thrust a leather flask into Covenant's view. "Here is *diamondraught*."

Covenant did not pause; but he shifted his efforts down to her hips and legs, making room for Pitchwife.

Cupping one huge palm under her head, the Giant lifted her into a half-sitting posture. Carefully, he raised the mouth of his flask to her lips.

Liquid dribbled from the corners of her mouth. In dismay, Covenant saw that she was not swallowing. Her chest rose as she inhaled; but no gag-reflex prevented her from breathing the potent liquor.

At the sight, his mind went white with fire. The hysteria of venom and power coursed through his muscles—keen argent fretted with reminders of midnight and murder. He thrust Pitchwife away as if the Giant were a child.

But he dared not try to reach heat into Linden. Without any health-sense to guide him, he would be more likely to kill than warm her. Swallowing flame, he wrenched her onto her side, hit her once between the shoulder blades, twice, hoping to dislodge the fluid from her lungs. Then he pressed her to her back again, tilted her head as he had been taught, clasped shut her nose, and with his mouth over hers started breathing urgently down her throat.

Almost at once, effort and restraint made him dizzy. He no longer knew how to find the still point of strength in the center of his whirling fears. He had no power to save her life except the one he could not use.

"Giantfriend." Hearthcoal's voice came from a great distance. "Here is a stewpot able to hold her."

Covenant's head jerked up. For an instant, he gaped incomprehension at the cook. Then he rapped out, "Fill it!" and clamped his mouth back over Linden's.

A muffled thunder of water poured into the huge stone pot. Wind shrieked in the hawseholes, plucked juddering ululations from the shrouds. Around Covenant, the galley began to spin. Head up: inhale. Head down: exhale. He had no way to keep his balance except with fire. In another moment, he was going to erupt or lose consciousness, he did not know which.

Then Seasauce said, "It is ready." Pitchwife touched Covenant's shoulder. Scooping his arms under Linden, Covenant tried to unknot his cramped muscles, stand erect.

Starfare's Gem brunted through the crest of a wave and dove for the trough. Unable to steady himself, he pitched headlong toward the wall.

Hands caught him. Mistweave held him while Pitchwife pulled Linden from his embrace.

He was giddy and irresistible with fire. He jerked away from Mistweave, followed Pitchwife toward the stove on which sat the oblong stewpot. The floor seemed to yaw viciously, but he kept moving.

The stovetop was as high as his chin. He could see nothing of Linden past the pot's rim except a crown of hair as Seasauce held her head above water. But he no longer needed to see her. Pressing his forehead against the base of the stewpot, he spread his arms as far as possible along its sides. The guts of the stove were aflame; but that heat would take too long to warm so much stone and water. Closing his eyes against the ghoul-whirl of his vertigo, he let wild magic pour down his arms.

This he could do safely. He had learned enough control to keep his power from tearing havoc through the galley. And Linden was buffered from his imprecise touch. With white passion he girdled the pot. Then he narrowed his mind until nothing else impinged upon it and let the fire flow.

In that way, he turned his back on silence and numbness.

For a time, he was conscious only of the current of his power, squeezing heat into the stone but not breaking it, not tearing the fragile granite into rubble. Then suddenly he realized that he could hear Linden coughing. He looked up. She was invisible to him, hidden by the sides of the pot and the steam pluming thickly into the air. But she was coughing, clearing her lungs more strongly with every spasm. And a moment later one of her hands came out of the vapor to clutch at the lip of the pot.

"It is enough," Pitchwife was saying. "Giantfriend, it is enough. More heat will harm her."

Covenant nodded dumbly. With a deliberate effort, he released his power.

At once, he recoiled, struck by the vertigo and fear he had been holding at bay. But Pitchwife put an arm around him, kept him on his feet. As the spinning slowed, he was able to watch Seasauce lift Linden dripping from the water. She still looked as pallid and frail as a battered child; but her eyes were open, and her limbs reacted to the people around her. When Mistweave took her from the cook, she instinctively hugged his neck while he wrapped her in a blanket. Then Cail offered her Pitchwife's flask of *diamondraught*. Still shivering fiercely, she pulled the flask to her mouth. Gradually, two faint spots of color appeared on her cheeks.

Covenant turned away and hid his face against Pitchwife's malformed chest until his relief eased enough to be borne.

For a few moments while the *diamondraught* spread out within her, Linden remained conscious. Though she was so weak that she tottered, she got down from Mistweave's arms. With the blanket swaddled around her, she stripped off her wet clothing. Then her gaze hunted for Covenant's.

He met it as bravely as he could.

"Why—?" she asked huskily. Her voice quivered. "Why couldn't we help them?"

"It was the Soulbiter." Her question made his eyes blur. Her heart was still torn by what she had seen. "They were illusions. We were damned if we refused to help. Because of how we would've felt about ourselves. And damned if we tried. If we brought one of those things aboard." The Soulbiter, he thought as he strove to clear his vision. It was aptly named. "The only way out was to break the illusion."

She nodded faintly. She was fading into the embrace of the *diamondraught*. "It was like watching my parents." Her eyes closed. "If they were as brave as I wanted them to be." Her voice trailed toward silence. "If I let myself love them."

Then her knees folded. Mistweave lowered her gently to

her pallet, tucked more blankets around her. She was already asleep.

By increments, the galley recovered its accustomed warmth. Seasauce and Hearthcoal labored like titans to produce hot food for the hard-pressed crew. As Honninscrave became more confident of the *dromond*'s stance against the gale, he began sending Giants in small groups for aliment and rest: a steady stream of them passed through the galley. They entered with hoar in their hair and strain in their eyes. The same gaunt look of memory marked every face. But the taste of hot food and the comradely bluster of the cooks solaced them; and when they returned to their tasks they bore themselves with more of their wonted jaunty sea-love and courage. They had survived the Soulbiter. Valiantly, they went back to their battle with the bitter grue of the sea.

Covenant remained in the galley for a while to watch over Linden. Her slumber was so profound that he distrusted it instinctively. He expected her to slip back into the tallow pallor of frostbite. She looked so small, frail, and desirable lying there nearly under the feet of the Giants. But her form curled beneath the blankets brought back other memories as well; and eventually he found himself falling from relief and warmth into bereavement. She was the only woman he knew who understood his illness and still accepted him. Already, her stubborn commitment to him—and to the Land—had proved itself stronger than his despair. He yearned to put his arms around her, clasp her to him. But he did not have the right. And in her analystic sleep she did not need the loyalty of his attendance. To escape the ache of what he had lost, he sashed his robe tightly about him and went out into the keening wind.

Instantly, he stumbled into the swirl of a snowfall as thick as fog. It flurried against his face. Ice crunched under his boots. When he blinked his eyes clear, he saw pinpricks of light around the decks and up in the rigging. The snow veiled the day so completely that the Giants were compelled to use lanterns. The sight dismayed him. How could Honninscrave keep the Giantship running, headlong and blind in such a sea, when his crew was unable to tend the sails without lamps?

But the Master had no choice. While this wind held, the *dromond* could do nothing but grit its teeth and endure.

The matter was out of Covenant's hands. Braving the flung snow and the ice-knurled decks with Cail's support, he went looking for the First.

But when he found her in the cabin she shared with Pitchwife, he discovered that he did not know what to say. She was polishing her longsword, and her slow stroking movements had a quality of deliberate grimness which suggested that the survival of Starfare's Gem was out of her hands as well. She had broken the spell of the Soulbiter; she could do nothing now. For a long moment, they shared a hard stare of determination and helplessness. Then he turned away.

The snowfall continued. It clung to the air, and the wind whipped it forward, darkening the day as if the sky were clogged with ashes.

It brought with it a slight moderation of the temperature; and the fierceness of the blast was softened somewhat. But in reaction the seas grew more tempestuous. And they no longer followed the thrust of the gale. Other forces bent them out of the grasp of the storm, forcing Starfare's Gem to slog and claw its way across the grain of the current. Honninscrave shifted course as much as he dared to accommodate the seas; but the wind did not give him much latitude. As a result, the massive vessel pounded forward with a wild gait, a slewing pitch-and-yaw with a sickening pause on the wavetops while the *dromond* hung momentarily out of control, followed by a plunge which buried the stern to its taffrail in black water. Only the unfrightened demeanor of the Giants convinced Covenant that Starfare's Gem was not about to founder.

Shortly before sunset, the snow lifted, letting a little dirty yellow light lick briefly across the battered seas. At once, Honninscrave sent Giants into the tops to scan the horizons before the illumination failed. They reported no landfall in sight. Then a night blinded by clouds closed down over the Giantship, and Starfare's Gem went running into the pit of an unreadable dark.

In the galley, Covenant rode the storm with his back braced between one wall and the side of a stove and his gaze fixed on Linden. Blank to the vessel's staggering, she slept so peacefully that she reminded him of the Land before the onset of the Sunbane. She was a terrain which should never have been violated by bloodshed and hate, a place that deserved better. But the Land had men and women—however few—who had fought and would fight for its healing. And Linden was among them. Yet in the struggle against her own inner Sunbane she had no one but herself.

The night stretched out ahead of Starfare's Gem. After a meal and a cup of thinned *diamondraught*, Covenant tried to rest. Recumbent on his pallet, he let the seas flop him from side to side and strove to imagine that he was being cradled. Fitfully, he dozed his way into true sleep.

But almost at once he began to flounder. He was back in the Sandhold, in Kemper's Pitch, strapped motionless for torture. He had passed, untouched, through knives and fire; but now he was being hurled down into himself, thrown with the violence of greed toward the hard wall of his fate. Then, however, he had been saved by Hergrom; and now Hergrom was dead. There was no one to save him from the impact that broke everything, filled the air with the splintering thunder of a mountain being riven.

His skin slick with sweat, he awakened—and the sound went on. Starfare's Gem was shattering. Concussions yelled through the hull. His face pressed the wall. A chaos of crockery and utensils burst across the galley. He tried to thrust himself back; but the ship's momentum pinned him. Stone screams answered the wind—the sound of masts and spars splitting under the strain. The *dromond* had been driven into some kind of collision.

The next instant, Starfare's Gem heaved to a halt. Covenant rolled out into the broken litter dancing across the floor. Bruising his knees and hands on the shards, he lurched to his feet. Then a tremendous weight hammered down on the prow of the ship; and the floor tilted as if the Giantship were on its way to the depths. The afterdoor of the galley jumped from its mounts. Until Starfare's Gem stumbled back into a semblance of trim, Covenant had to cling to Cail and let the *Haruchai* uphold him.

The *dromond* seemed to be settling. Cries of breakage retorted along the wind. Outside the galley, the air was frantic with shouts; but over them all rose Honninscrave's stentorian howl:

"Pitchwife!"

Then Hearthcoal stirred in one corner; Seasauce shrugged the remains of a broken shelf off his back; and Covenant started to move. His first thought was for Linden; but a swift glance showed him that she was safe: still clasped in the sopor of *diamondraught*, she lay on her pallet with Mistweave braced protectively over her. Seeing Covenant's look, Mistweave gave a quick nod of reassurance. Without hesitation, Covenant surged to the ruptured door and charged out into the teeth of the wind.

He could see nothing: the night was as black as Vain. All the lanterns seemed to have been blown out. When he located a point of light hanging near Shipsheartthew, it showed him only that the wheeldeck had been abandoned. But shouts of command and desperation came from the direction of the prow. Gripping Cail's shoulder because he could not keep his footing on the ice, Covenant labored forward.

At first, he followed the sound of Honninscrave's bellow, the First's iron orders. Then lanterns began to appear as Giants called for light so that they could see their way amid the snarled wreckage which crowded the vessel's foredeck.

In a prodigious tangle of sundered canvas and gear, pulleys and lines, sprawled several thick stone beams—the two upper spars and a section of the foremast. The great trunk of the mast had been broken in half. One of the fallen spars was intact; the other lay in three jagged pieces. At every step, the Giants kicked through slivers of granite.

Four crewmembers were crumpled in the wreckage.

The lantern-light was so wan, cast so many shadows, that Covenant could not see if any of them were still alive.

The First had her sword in her fist. Wielding it as deftly as a dagger, she cut through shrouds and sails toward the nearest of the fallen Giants. Galewrath and several others attacked the same task with their knives.

Sevinhand started into the wreckage. Honninscrave called him back, sent him instead to muster hands at the pumps. Covenant felt the *dromond* sinking dangerously; but he had no time for that fear. Through the din, he shouted at Cail, "Get Linden!"

"She has consumed much *diamondraught*," the *Haruchai* replied. "She will not be lightly roused." His tone was impersonal.

"I don't care!" snapped Covenant. "We're going to need her!"

Whirling away, he flung himself in the wake of the First.

She was crouched beside a limp form. As Covenant reached her, she surged erect again. Her eyes echoed the lanterns hotly. Darkness lay along her blade like blood. "Come!" she rasped. "We can do nothing here." Her sword sliced into the piled canvas with a sound like a cry.

Covenant glanced at the Giant she had left. The crewmember was a young woman he remembered—a grinning sailor with a cheerful determination to be always in the forefront of any work or hazard. He recognized half her face: the rest had been crushed by the broken butt of the mast.

For a moment, the dark came over him. Bereft of light, he blundered into the wreckage and could not fight free. But then he felt venom rise like bile in his throat, felt worms of fire begin to crawl down his forearm; and the shock steadied him. He had nearly let the wild destruction slip. Cursing, he stumbled after the First again.

A stolid shout reported that Galewrath had found another of the injured Giants dead. Covenant forced himself to go faster, as if his haste might keep the other crewmembers alive. But the First had already left behind a third corpse, a man with an arm-long splinter of stone driven through the base of his throat. In a fever of suppressed fire, Covenant thrashed onward.

Galewrath and the First converged on the last Giant with Honninscrave and Covenant following closely.

The face of this Giant was less familiar to him. She had never been brought specifically to his notice. But that did not matter. He cared only that she was alive.

Her breath came in hoarse wet heaves: black fluid ran from the corner of her mouth, formed a pool under her head. The bulk of the one unsnapped spar lay across her chest, crushing her to the hard deck. Both her forearms were broken.

The First slapped her longsword into its scabbard. Together, she and Galewrath bent to the beam, tried to lift it.

But the huge spar was far too heavy for them. Its ends were trapped: one stretched under the fallen mast; the other was snared in a mountain of gear and canvas.

Galewrath went on straining at the beam as if she did not know how to admit defeat. But the First swung upright, and her voice rang out over the deck, demanding help.

Giants were already on their way. Several of them veered toward the mast, fought to clear it so that they could roll it off the spar; others slashed into the wreckage at the far end with their knives.

There was little time. The life was being squeezed out of the pinned Giant: it panted from her mouth in damp shallow gasps. Her face was intense with pain.

No! Covenant panted in response. *No.* Thrusting himself forward, he cried through the clamor, "Get back! I'm going to break this thing off her!"

He did not wait to see whether he was obeyed. Wrapping his arms as far as he could around the bole of the spar, he brought up white fire to tear the stone apart.

With a fierce yell, Honninscrave wrenched Covenant from the spar, shoved him away.

"Honninscrave—!" the First began.

"I must have this spar whole!" roared the Master. His beard jutted fury and aggrievement along his jaw. "Starfare's Gem cannot endure any sea with but one mast!" The plight of his ship consumed him. "If Pitchwife can mend this shaft by any amount, then I must have a spar to hold sail! He cannot remake the Giantship entire!"

For an instant, he and the First confronted each other furiously. Covenant fought to keep himself from howling.

Then a groan and thud of granite shook the deck as four or five Giants rolled the mast off the end of the spar.

At once, the First and Honninscrave sprang to work. With Galewrath and every Giant who could lay hand to the beam, they pitted their strength against the spar.

The long stone shaft lifted like an ordinary timber in their arms.

As the weight left her, the crushed crewmember let out a shredded moan and lost consciousness.

Immediately, Galewrath crouched under the yard to her. Clamping one hand under the woman's chin, the other at

the back of her head to minimize the risk of further injuring
a broken spine, the Storesmaster drew her comrade from
beneath the spar to a small clear space in the middle of the
wreckage.

Covenant gaped at them half-wittedly, trembling as if he
had been snatched from the brink of an act of desecration.

Swiftly, Galewrath examined the crushed woman. But the
fragmentary light of the lanterns made her appear tentative,
hampered by hesitation and uncertainty. She was the
dromond's healer and knew how to treat any hurt that she
could see; but she had no way to correct or even evaluate such
severe internal damage. And while she faltered, the woman
was slipping out of reach.

Covenant tried to say Linden's name. But at that moment
a group of Giants came through the shambles carrying
lanterns. Mistweave and Cail were among them. Mistweave
bore Linden.

She lay in his arms as if she were still asleep—as if the
diamondraught's hold over her could not be breached by any
desperation.

But when he set her on her feet, her eyes fluttered open.
Groggily, she ran her fingers through her hair, pulled it back
from her face. Shadows glazed her eyes; she looked like a
woman who was walking in her dreams. A yawn stretched
her mouth. She appeared unaware of the pain sprawling at
her feet.

Then abruptly she sank down beside the dying Giant as
though her knees had failed. She bowed her head, and her
hair swung forward to hide her face again.

Rigid with useless impatience, the First clenched her fists
on her hips. Galewrath glared back at the lamps. Honninscrave
turned away as if he could not bear the sight, began whispering commands. His tone made the crew obey with alacrity.

Linden remained bowed over the Giant as if she were
praying. The noise of the crew in the wreckage, the creaking
of the *dromond*'s granite, the muffled crackle of ice made
what she was saying inaudible. Then her voice came into
clearer focus.

"—but the spinal cord is all right. If you splint her back,
strap her down, the bones should mend."

Galewrath nodded stiffly, glowering as if she knew there
was more to be said.

The next moment, a tremor ran through Linden. Her head jerked up.

"Her heart's bleeding. A broken rib—" Her eyes cast a white blind stare into the dark.

Through her teeth, the First breathed, "Succor her, Chosen. She must not die. Three others have lost life this night. There must not be a fourth."

Linden went on staring. Her voice had a leaden sound, as though she were almost asleep again. "How? I could open her up, but she'd lose too much blood. And I don't have any sutures."

"*Chosen.*" The First knelt opposite Linden, took hold of her shoulders. "I know nothing of these 'sutures.' Your healing surpasses me altogether. I know only that she must die if you do not aid her swiftly."

In response, Linden gazed dully across the deck like a woman who had lost interest.

"Linden!" Covenant croaked at last. "*Try.*"

Her sight swam into focus on him, and he saw glints of light pass like motes of vision across the dark background of her eyes. "Come," she said faintly. "Come here."

All his muscles were wooden with suppressed dismay; but he forced himself to obey. Beside the dying Giant, he faced Linden. "What do you—?"

Her expression stopped him. Her features wore the look of dreams. Without a word, she reached out, caught his half-hand by the wrist, stretched his arm like a rod over the Giant's pain.

Before he could react, she frowned sharply; and a blare of violation ripped across his mind.

In a rush, fire poured from his ring. Wild magic threw back the night, washing the foredeck with incandescence.

He recoiled in shock rather than pain; her hold did not hurt him. Yet it bereft him of choice. Without warning, all his preconceptions were snatched apart. Everything changed. Once before, in the cavern of the One Tree, she had exerted his power for herself; but he had hardly dared consider the implications. Now her percipience had grown so acute that she could wield his ring without his bare volition. And it *was* a violation. Mhoram had said to him, *You are the white gold*. Wild magic had become a crucial part of his identity, and no one else had the right to use it, control it.

Yet he did not know how to resist her. Her grasp on what she was doing was impenetrable. Already she had set fire to the Giant's chest as if she intended to burn out the woman's heart.

Around the Giantship, every sound fell away, absorbed by fire. The First and Galewrath shaded their eyes against the blaze, watched the Chosen with mute astonishment. Linden's mouth formed mumbling shapes as she worked, but no words came. Her gaze was buried deep in the flames. Covenant could feel himself dying.

For one moment, the Giant writhed against his thighs. Then she took a heavy, shuddering breath; and the trickle of blood at the corner of her mouth stopped. Her chest rose more freely. In a short time, her eyes opened and stared at the sensation of being healed.

Linden dropped Covenant's wrist. At once, the fire vanished. Night clapped back over the *dromond*. For an instant, even the lanterns appeared to have gone out. He flinched back against a pile of ruined gear, his face full of darkness. He hardly heard the First muttering, "Stone and Sea!" over and over again, unable to voice her amazement in any other way. He was completely blind. His eyes adjusted quickly enough, picking shapes and shadows out of the lantern-glow; but that was only sight, not vision: it had no power or capacity for healing.

Before him, Linden lay across the torso of the Giant she had called back from death. She was already asleep.

From his position in the *dromond*'s prow, Findail studied her as if he expected a transformation to begin at any moment.

Blinking fiercely, Covenant fought to keep the hot grief down. After a moment, he descried Pitchwife near the First. The lamps made the malformed Giant's face haggard, his eyes red. He was breathing heavily, nearly exhausted. But his voice was calm as he said, "It is done. Starfare's Gem will not run with its wonted ease until it has been granted restoration by the shipwrights of Home. But I have wived the breaches. We will not go down."

"Run?" Honninscrave growled through his beard. "Have you beheld the foremast? Starfare's Gem will never run. In such hurt, I know not how to make it walk."

The First said something Covenant did not hear. Cail came toward him, offered a hand to help him to his feet. But he did not react to any of them. He was being torn out of himself by the roots.

Linden had a better right to his ring than he did.

When the cold seeped so far into him that he almost stopped shivering, he made his preterite way to the oven-thick atmosphere of the galley. Seated there with his back to one wall, he stared at nothing as if he were stupefied, unable to register what he beheld. All he saw was the gaunt, compulsory visage of his doom.

Outside, the Giants labored at the needs of the ship. For a long time, the muffled thud of the pumps rose from below-decks. The sails of the aftermast were clewed up to their yards to protect them from any resurgence of the now-diminished Dolewind. The stone of the foremast and its spars was cleared out of the wreckage and set aside. Anything that remained intact in the fallen gear and rigging was salvaged. Either Seasauce or Hearthcoal was away from the stoves constantly, carrying huge buckets of broth to the Giants to sustain them while they worked.

But nothing the crew could do changed the essential fact: the *dromond* was stuck and crippled. When dawn came, and Covenant went, hollow-eyed and spectral, to look at the Giantship's condition, he was dismayed by the severity of the damage. Aft of the midship housing, nothing had been hurt: the aftermast raised its arms like a tall tree to the blue depths and broken clouds of the sky. But forward Starfare's Gem looked as maimed as a derelict. Scant feet above the first yards, which had been stripped to the bone by the collapse of the upper members, the foremast ended in a ragged stump.

Covenant had no sea-craft, but he recognized that Honninscrave was right: without sails forward to balance the canvas aft, Starfare's Gem would never be able to navigate.

Aching within himself, he turned to find out what the vessel had struck.

At first, what he saw seemed incomprehensible. Starfare's Gem lay surrounded to the horizons by a vast flat wilderland of ice. Jagged hunks were crushed against the *dromond*'s sides; but the rest of the ice was unbroken. Its snow-blown surface appeared free of any channel which could have brought the Giantship to this place.

But when he shaded his gaze and peered southward, he discerned a narrow band of gray water beyond the ice. And, squinting so hard that his temples throbbed, he traced a line between the *dromond*'s stern and the open sea. There the ice was thinner. It was freezing back over the long furrow which Starfare's Gem had plowed into the floe.

The Giantship was trapped—locked here and helpless. With all three masts intact and a favoring wind, it could not have moved. It was stuck where it sat until spring came to its rescue. If this part of the world ever felt the touch of spring.

Damnation!

The ship's plight stung him like the gusts which came skirling off the ice. In the Land, the Clave was feeding the Banefire, stoking it with innocent blood to increase the Sunbane. No one remained to fight the na-Mhoram's depredations except Sunder and Hollian and perhaps a handful of *Haruchai*—if any of them were still alive. The quest for the One Tree had failed, extinguishing Covenant's sole hope. And now—!

Have mercy on me.

But he was a leper, and there was never any mercy for lepers. Despite did not forbear. He had reached the point where everything he did was wrong. Even his stubborn determination to cling to his ring, to bear the cost of his doom himself, was wrong. But he could not endure the alternative. The simple thought wrung a mute howl from the pit of his heart.

He had to do something, find some way to reaffirm himself. Passivity and silence were no longer viable. His despair itself compelled him. He *had* to. Linden had proved the *Elohim* right. With his ring she was able to heal. But he could not forget the taste of eager fire when he had warmed the stewpot to save her. *Had* to! He could not give it up.

His ring was all he had left.

He had become the most fundamental threat to everything he loved. But suddenly that was no longer enough to stop him. Deliberately, he set aside Linden's reasons—her wish to see him do what she believed she would do in his place, her desire to fight Lord Foul through him—and chose his own.

To show himself and his companions and the Despiser if necessary that he had the right.

Without looking away from the ice, he said to Cail, "Tell Honninscrave I want to talk to him. I want to talk to everybody—the First, Linden, Pitchwife. In his cabin."

When the *Haruchai* moved soundlessly away, Covenant hugged the scant protection of his robe and set himself to wait.

The idea of what he meant to do made his pulse beat like venom in his veins.

There was blue in the sky, the first blue he had seen for days. A crusty glitter reflected the sun. But the ice was not as smooth as the sunlight made it appear. Its surface was marked with sharp spines and ridges, mounds where floe-plates rubbed and depressions which ran from nowhere to nowhere. The ice was a wasteland, its desolation grieving in the cold, and it held his gaze like the outcome of his life. Once in winter he had fought his way through long leagues of snow and despair to confront the Despiser—and he had prevailed. But he knew now that he would never prevail in that way again.

He shrugged against the chill. So what? He would find some other way. Even if the attempt drove him mad. Madness was just a less predictable and scrupulous form of power. And he did not believe that either Lord Foul or Findail had told him the whole truth.

Yet he did not intend to surrender his scruples or go mad. His leprosy had trained him well for survival and affirmation against an impossible future. And Foamfollower had once said to him, *Service enables service.* Hope came from the power and value of what was served, not from the one who served it.

When Cail returned, Covenant felt that he was ready. Slowly, carefully, he turned from the sea and picked his way across the clogged stone toward one of the entryways to the underdecks.

Below, the door to Honninscrave's cabin was open; and beside it stood Mistweave. His face wore a conflicted expression. Covenant guessed that the Giant had undertaken more than he realized when he had assigned himself to Cail's former responsibility for Linden. How could he have foreseen that his dedication to her would require him to ignore the needs of the *dromond* and the labors of the crew? The dilemma made him look unsure of himself.

But Covenant did not have any relief to offer the Giant, and the door was open. Frowning at the pain all the people around him had to bear, he went into the Master's cabin, leaving Cail outside.

Honninscrave's quarters were austere: except for a few chairs sized for Giants, a huge seachest, and a deep bunk, its only furnishings were a long table cluttered with nautical instruments and charts and two lamps hanging in stone gimbals. Honninscrave stood at the far end of the table as if Covenant's arrival had interrupted him in the act of pacing. Sevinhand sat on the edge of the bunk, more melancholy than ever in his weariness. Near him was the Storesmaster, her shoulders touching the wall, no expression on her blunt features. The First and Pitchwife occupied two of the chairs. She held her back straight, her scabbarded blade across her thighs, as though refusing to admit how tired she was; but her husband was slumped with fatigue, emphasizing the deformation of his spine.

In one corner of the chamber, Linden sat cross-legged on the floor. Sleep made her eyes bleary: when she raised them to acknowledge Covenant, she seemed hardly able to see him. In the company of these Giants, she appeared tiny and misplaced. But the hue of her skin and the steadiness of her respiration showed that she had been essentially restored to health.

The air of the cabin felt tense, as if Covenant had entered the middle of an argument. None of the Giants except Pitchwife and Sevinhand were looking at him. But when he turned his unspoken question toward Pitchwife, the First's husband bowed his head and did not answer. And the lines of Sevinhand's old rue were too deep to be challenged.

Covenant was stretched taut beyond gentleness. In a raw, brusque voice, he demanded, "So what do you think we should do about it?"

Linden frowned as if his tone hurt her. Or perhaps she had already read the nature of his intent. Without lifting her head, she murmured, "That's what they've been arguing about."

Her explanation eased him somewhat. He had gone so far down the road of his fate that he instinctively expected every hostile or painful or simply difficult emotion to be directed at himself. But his question remained. "What choice have we got?"

At that, the muscles at the corners of Honninscrave's jaw clenched. Sevinhand rubbed his cheeks with his palms as if he sought to push back the sorrow. The First let a sigh breathe softly through her teeth. But no one answered.

Covenant pulled air into his lungs, gripped his courage in the insensate cold of his fists. "If you don't have any better ideas, I'm going to break us out of this ice."

Then every eye was on him, and a shock of apprehension recoiled through the cabin. Honninscrave's face gaped like a reopened wound. All the sleep vanished from Linden's orbs. The First surged to her feet. As harsh as iron, she demanded, "Will you hazard the Earth to no purpose?"

"Do you think your restraint is that good?" Linden added instantly. She, too, had come to her feet as if she wanted to meet Covenant's folly standing. "Or are you just looking for an excuse to throw power around?"

"Hell and blood!" Covenant barked. Had Findail taught everyone aboard the *dromond* to distrust him? "If you don't like it"—his scarred forearm itched avidly—"give me an alternative! Do you think I *like* being this dangerous?"

His outburst sent a grimace of chagrin across the First's face. Linden dropped her eyes. For a moment, Pitchwife's difficult breathing punctuated the silence. Then his wife said softly, "Your pardon, Giantfriend. I did not intend affront. But we are not without choice in this strait." She turned, and her gaze went like the point of a blade toward Honninscrave. "You will speak now, Master."

Honninscrave glared at her. But she was the First of the Search: no Giant would have refused to obey her when she used that tone. He complied slowly, uttering each word like a flat piece of stone. Yet as he answered his hands made truncated, fumbling movements among the charts and implements on the table, contradicting him.

"I am uncertain of our position. I have been granted scant opportunity for sightings since the cloud-wrack cleared. And this sea has been little frequented by our people. Our charts and knowledge are likewise uncertain." The First frowned a reprimand at his digression; but he did not falter. "Where knowledge is insufficient, all choices are hazardous.

"Yet it would appear that we lie now some four- or five-score leagues north and east of the coast which you name Seareach, home of the Unhomed and site of their destitute city and grave, *Coercri*, The Grieve." He articulated that name with a special distinctness, as if he would prefer to hear it sung. Then he outlined the alternative which the First had in mind: that Covenant and the leaders of the Search leave Starfare's Gem and strike westward across the ice until they found land, after which they could follow the coast into Seareach.

"Or," Linden interposed warily, studying Covenant as she spoke, "we could forget Seareach and head straight for Revelstone. I don't know the terrain, but it's bound to be quicker than detouring that far south."

"Aye." Honninscrave permitted himself a growl of disgust or trepidation. "Should this littoral lie within hope of our charts." Emotion rose in his voice, slipping out of his rigid grasp. "And should the ice remain intact and traversable to that coast. And should this winter hold—for we are somewhat southerly to have encountered such ice in the natural course of the seas, and it may thaw beneath us unseasonably." To keep himself from shouting, he ground out the words like shards of rock. "And should the northward reaches of the Land be not rugged or mountainous beyond all possibility of travel. *Then*—" He grabbed a mouthful of air, held it between his teeth. "Then, I say, our way is clear before us."

His distress was acute in the confinement of the cabin. But the First did not relent. "We hear you," she said sternly. "The choice is jeopardous. Complete your tale, Master."

Honninscrave could not look at her. "Ah, my tale," he grated. "It is no tale of mine. My brother is dead, and the *dromond* I cherish lies locked in ice and crippled. It is no tale of mine." Yet the First's authority held him. Clutching a chart in each fist like a weightless and insufficient cudgel, he directed his voice at Covenant.

"You have offered to sunder the ice. Very good. To Cable Seadreamer my brother who gave his life, you refused the fire of release. But in the name of your mad desire for battle you will attempt a league of ice. Very good. But I say to you that Starfare's Gem cannot sail. In this maimed state, no. And were the time taken to do what mending lies within our power—time which is so precious to you—and were a channel opened to the sea, then still would our plight remain, for the *dromond* is no longer proof against the stress of the seas. With a kind wind, perchance, we might make way toward Seareach. But any storm would hold us in its mercy. A score of days—or tenscore—might find us yet farther from our goal. Starfare's Gem"—he had to swallow heavily to force out the words—"is no longer fit to bear the Search."

"But—" Covenant began, then halted. For an instant, he was confused. Honninscrave's grief covered an anger which he could not utter and Covenant could not decipher. Why was the Master so bitter?

But suddenly the implications of Honninscrave's speech swept over Covenant like a breaker; and his comprehension tumbled down the riptide. Starfare's Gem could not sail. And the First wanted the Search to leave the Giantship, set out afoot toward the Land. He found himself facing her with a knot of cold clenched around his heart. Dismay was all that kept him from fury.

"Nearly forty Giants." Foamfollower's people, the kindred of the Unhomed. "You're talking about leaving them here to die."

She was a Swordmain, trained to battle and difficult choices. Her sternness as she returned Covenant's gaze looked as careless of costs as a weapon. But behind her eyes moved shadows like specters of pain.

"Aye." Honninscrave's voice scraped the air. "They must be left to die. Or they must accompany us, and Starfare's Gem itself must be left to die. And from that day forward, no one of us shall ever again set gaze upon the crags and harborage of Home. We have no means for the making of a new *dromond*. And our people know not where we are." He spoke softly, but every word left a weal across Covenant's mind.

It was intolerable. He was no sailor; he could bear to abandon the Giantship. But to leave nearly forty Giants behind without hope—or to strand them in the Land as the Unhomed had been stranded!

The First did not waver: she knew her duty and would not shirk it. Covenant swung away from her, confronted Hon-

ninscrave down the length of the table. Its height made the
Master appear tall and hurt beyond any mitigation. But
Covenant could not accept that outcome.

"If we leave the crew here. With the ship." He drove his
gaze up at the Giant until Honninscrave met it. "What will
they need? In order to have any chance at all?"

Honninscrave's head jerked in surprise. For a moment,
his mouth parted his beard incredulously, as though he half
believed he was being taunted. But then with a wrench he
mastered himself. "Stores we have in plenty." His eyes clung
to Covenant like an appeal: *Be not false to me in this.* "But
the plight of the Giantship remains. It must have all the
mending which Pitchwife may contrive. It must have time."

Time, Covenant thought. He had already been away from
the Land for more than sixty days—away from Revelstone
for closer to ninety. How many more people had the Clave
killed? But the only alternative was to leave Pitchwife behind
with the ship. And he would surely refuse. The First herself
might refuse. Stiffly, Covenant asked, "How much time?"

"Two days," replied Honninscrave. "Perhaps three. Much
pitch will be required. And the labor itself will be awkward
and arduous."

Damnation! Covenant breathed. Three days. But he did not
back down. He was a leper: he knew the folly of trying to
purchase the future by selling the present. Grimly, he turned
to Pitchwife.

Fatigue seemed to emphasize the Giant's deformities. His
back bent as if it had been damaged by the weight of his
limbs and head. But his eyes glittered, and his expression had
lifted. He looked at Covenant as though he knew what the
Unbeliever was about to say—and approved of it.

Covenant felt wooden with failure. He had come here
primed for fire; but all he had been able to offer his companions was a patience he did not possess. "Try to do it in
one," he muttered. Then he left the cabin so that he would
not have to endure the reactions of the Giants.

Pitchwife's voice followed him. "Stone and Sea!" the
Giant chuckled. "It is a small matter. What need have I of an
entire day?"

Glaring at nothing, Covenant quickened his pace.

But as he reached the ladder leading to the afterdeck,
Linden caught up with him. She gripped his arm as if some-

thing had changed between them. Her intent seriousness bore
no resemblance to her old severity, and her eyes were damp.
Her soft mouth, which he had kissed with such longing, wore
the shape of a plea.

Yet he had not forgiven himself; and after a moment she
dropped her hand. Her gaze retreated somewhat. When she
spoke, she sounded like a woman who did not know the
words she needed.

"You keep surprising me. I never know what to expect
from you. Just when I think you're too far gone to be reached,
you do something like that. Like what you did for Sunder
and Hollian." Abruptly, she stopped as if she were hurt by
the inadequacy of what she was saying.

Covenant wanted to cry out. His desire for her was too
acute to be suffered. He had already perverted whatever
authenticity he might have had with her. And she was a
healer. She had more right to his ring than he did. Self-
loathing made him harsh.

"Do you really think I just want to throw power around?
Is that your opinion of me?"

At that, she winced. Her expression turned inward like a
baffled wail. "No," she murmured. "No. I was just trying to
get your attention." Then her eyes reached toward him again.
"But you scared me. If you could see yourself—"

"If I could see myself," he rasped so that he would not put
his arms around her, "I'd probably puke."

Savagely, he flung himself up the ladder away from her.

But when he gained the open air and brittle cold of the
afterdeck, he had to knot his arms across his chest to hold
in the hurt.

While he ate his breakfast in the galley, trying to absorb
some of the stoves' warmth, he could hear the sounds of work
outside. At first, Sevinhand's voice and Galewrath's commanded alternately. He supervised the preparation of the
foredeck; she led the breaking of the ice and the ritual songs
for the burial of the three fallen crewmembers. But after a
while Pitchwife made himself heard over the scuffle of feet
and clatter of gear, the stiff hiss and thud of half-frozen
cable. When Covenant had collected what little courage he
had left, he went out to watch.

During the night, the crew had cleared and organized the

wreckage. Now they were busy readying the truncated foremast. Pitchwife was hunched over a large stone vat of his special pitch; but his eyes and voice followed the sailors as they rigged lines between the intact yard and the splintered end of the mast. Except for the necessary questions and instructions, the Giants were unusually quiet, disspirited. The Dolewind had held them for a long time; and since their encounter with the Soulbiter they had had no rest at all. Now their future had become as fragile and arduous as ice. Even Giants could not carry so much strain indefinitely.

But Covenant had never seen Pitchwife at work before. Grateful for any distraction, he studied Pitchwife with fascination as the First's husband completed his preparations. Consigning his vat to another Giant, he hoisted a slab of setrock in a sling over his shoulder, then went to the ropes and began pulling himself slowly up the foremast.

Below him, the crew set his vat of pitch into a net that they had rigged from a pulley fixed as high as possible on the mast. When he reached that height himself, supported now by line lashed under his arms and around the mast, two Giants hauled the vat up to him. His breath plumed crisply in the cold.

At once, he began his work. Scooping up gouts of pitch, he larded them into the jagged crown of the mast. The pitch seemed viscid, but he handled it deftly, fingering it down into the cracks and smoothing it on all sides until he had fashioned a flat butt for the broken stone. Then he reached back to his setrock, snapped a chip from one edge, and tapped the piece into the pitch.

Almost without transition, the pitch became stone, indistinguishable from the mast's granite.

Muttering his satisfaction, he followed his vat back down to the deck.

Sevinhand sent several Giants swarming up to the yard to undo everything which had been rigged to the mast. At the same time, other crewmembers began binding ropes around the ends of the intact spar and preparing new gear up on the yard.

Pitchwife ignored them, turned his attention to the fallen portion of the mast. It had broken into several pieces; but one section was as long as all the rest combined. With pitch and setrock, he formed both ends of this section into flat butts like the new cap of the foremast.

Covenant could not see what all this would accomplish. And his need for haste made him restless. After a time, he realized that he had not seen Galewrath since he had come out on deck. When the dead had been given to the sea, she had gone to some other task. In an effort to keep himself occupied—and to generate some warmth—he tugged his robe tighter and went looking for the Storesmaster.

He found her in her particular demesne, a warren of holds, watercests, and storage-lockers belowdecks amidships. The *dromond* carried a surprising amount of wood for use both as fuel for the stoves and as raw material for repairs or replacements which could not be readily achieved with stone at sea. Galewrath and three other Giants were at work in a square hold which served as the ship's carpentry.

They were making two large sleds.

These were rough constructs with high rails and rude planking. But they looked sturdy. And each was big enough to carry a Giant.

Two crewmembers glued and pegged the shells together while Galewrath and the other Giant labored at the more difficult chore of carving runners. With files, knives, and hand-adzes, they stripped the bark from beams as thick as Covenant's thigh, then slowly shaped the wood to carry weight over ice and snow as easily as possible. The floor was already thick with bark and curlings, and the air smelled of clean resin; but the task was far from finished.

In response to Covenant's question, Galewrath replied that to reach Revelstone Covenant and his company would need more supplies than they could bear on their backs. And the sleds would also transport Covenant and Linden when the terrain permitted the Giants to set a pace the humans could not match.

Once again, Covenant was wanly abashed by the providence of the people who sought to serve him. He had not been able to think farther ahead than the moment when he would leave Starfare's Gem; but the Giants were concerned about more than the stark question of their ship's survival. He would have died long ago if other people had not taken such care of him.

His route back toward the upper decks passed the Master's cabin. The door was shut; but from within he heard the First's voice, raised in vexation. She was urging Honninscrave to stay with the *dromond*.

The Master's answering silence was eloquent. As ashamed as an eavesdropper, Covenant hastened away to see what progress Pitchwife and Sevinhand had made.

When he gained the foredeck, the sun stood above the gap where the midmast should have been, and the deformed Giant's plans were taking shape. Covenant was almost able to guess his intent. Pitchwife had finished the long stone shaft on the deck; and he and Sevinhand were watching as the crew wrestled the one unbroken spar up onto the yard. There they stood the spar against the truncated mast and secured it with loop after loop of cable. For two-thirds of its length, the spar reached above the end of the mast. To the upraised tip had been affixed the pulley of a massive block-and-tackle.

Covenant eyed the lashings and the spar distrustfully. "Is that going to hold?"

Pitchwife shrugged as if his arms had become too heavy for him. His voice was husky with fatigue. "If it does not, the task cannot be accomplished in one day. The spar I can mend. But the mast we hope to raise must then be broken to smaller fragments which I may bear aloft and wive whole again." He sighed without looking at Covenant. "Pray this will hold. The prospect of *that* labor I do not relish."

Wearily, he fell silent.

When the tackle had been attached to one flat end of the mastshaft Pitchwife had prepared, eight or ten Giants lifted the shaft and positioned it below the yard so that the lines hung as straight as possible in order to minimize the sideward stress on the spar. Creaking in its pulleys, the tackle tightened.

Covenant held his breath unconsciously. That spar looked too slender to sustain the granite shaft. But as the ropes strained tighter and the end of the mast-piece lifted, nothing broke.

Then the shaft hung straight from the spar, brushing against the bole of the mast. As the Giants pulled slowly on the towline of the tackle, the shaft continued to rise.

When its butt reached the level of Covenant's head, Pitchwife coughed, "Hold!"

The Giants on the towline froze. The tackle groaned; the shaft settled slightly as the ropes stretched. But still nothing broke.

His hands full of pitch, the deformed Giant moved to the shaft and gently covered the butt with an even and heavy layer. Then he retreated to the other side of the mast. A rope dangled near him. When he had carefully cleaned his hands, he gripped it and let the Giants on the yard haul him upward.

Bracing himself once again within a loop of rope passed around the mast and his back, he labored foot by foot up toward the maimed stump. Alone above the yard, he looked strangely vulnerable; yet he forced himself upward by main strength. Finally he hung at the rim of the mast.

For a long moment, he did not move; and Covenant found himself panting as if he sought to breathe for the Giant, send Pitchwife strength. The First had come to the foredeck. Her gaze was clenched on her husband. If the spar snapped, only a miracle could save him from being ripped down by falling stone and flying tackle.

Then he signalled to the Giants below. Sevinhand whispered a command; the crew began to raise the shaft again.

Now the bowing of the spar was unmistakable. Covenant could hardly believe that it was still intact.

By wary degrees, the shaft was drawn upward. Soon its flat crown ascended above Pitchwife's head. Then its butt reached the level of his chest.

He looked too weak to support his own weight; but somehow he braced himself, reached out his arms to prevent the shaft from swinging over the end of the mast—from scraping off its layer of pitch or mating crookedly. The Giants fisted the lines tighter, raised the shaft another foot; then Sevinhand stopped them. Slowly, Pitchwife shifted his position, aligned the stone with the mast.

He gave an urgent gasp of readiness. Fervently careful, the Giants began to lower the shaft. Alone, he guided it downward.

The flat ends met. At once, he thumbed a sliver of setrock into place; and the line separating stone from stone vanished as if it had never existed. The First let relief hiss through her teeth. A raw cheer sprang from the Giants as they let the tackle go.

The mast stood. It was not as tall as the aftermast—but it was tall enough now to carry a second spar. And two spans of canvas forward might give the *dromond* the balance it needed to survive.

The task was not yet done: the spar had to be attached to the new foremast. But most of the afternoon remained, and the necessary repairs were clearly possible now. Two Giants swarmed upward and helped Pitchwife down to the yard, then lowered him to his jubilant comrades. The First greeted him with a hug which looked urgent enough to crack his spine. A jug of *diamondraught* appeared from somewhere and was pressed into his hands. He drank hugely, and another cheer was raised around him.

Weak with relief, Covenant watched them and let his gratitude for Pitchwife's safety and success wash over him.

A moment later, Pitchwife emerged from the crowd of Giants. He was made unsteady on his feet by exhaustion and sudden *diamondraught*; but he moved purposefully toward Covenant. He gave the Unbeliever a florid bow which nearly cost him his balance. Then he said, "I will rest now. But ere nightfall I will set the spar. That will complete the labor I can do for Starfare's Gem." The raw rims of his eyes and the sway of his stance were acute reminders that he had saved the *dromond* from sinking before this day's work began.

But he was not done. His voice softened as he added, "Giantfriend, I thank you that you accorded to me this opportunity to be of service to the Giantship."

Bright in the sunshine and the reflections of the ice, he turned away. Chuckling at the murmured jests and praise of the crew, he linked arms with the First and left the foredeck like a drunken hero. In spite of his deformed stature, he seemed as tall as any Giant.

The sight eased Covenant in a way that made his eyes burn. Gratitude loosened his tension. Pitchwife had proved his fear and anger unnecessary. As Sevinhand and his crew went back to work, stringing new tackle so that they could hoist the spar into place against the foremast, Covenant moved away in search of Linden. He wanted to show her what the Giant had accomplished. And to apologize for his earlier harshness.

He found her almost at once. She was in the galley, asleep
like a waif on her pallet. Her dreams made her frown with
the solemn concentration of a child; but she showed no sign
of awakening. She was still recuperating from the abusive
cold of the Soulbiter. He let her sleep.

The warmth of the galley reminded him of his own
chilled weariness. He stretched out on his pallet, intending
to rest for a while and then go back to watch the Giants. But
as soon as he closed his eyes, his fatigue arose and carried
him away.

Later, in a period of half-consciousness, he thought he
heard singing. At first, the songs were ones of gladness and
praise, of endurance against exigent seas and safe arrival
Home. But after a while the melodies began to grieve, and
the songs became ones of parting, of ships lost and kindred
sundered; and through them ran a sound like the crackle of
flames, the anguish of a *caamora*, auguring doom. Covenant
had attempted a *caamora* once, on the headrock of *Coercri*.
But that bonfire had not been violent enough to touch him:
in the night of the Unhomed's dismay, he had succored
everyone but himself. Now as he sank back into dreams he
thought perhaps a more absolute blaze was needed, a more
searching and destructive conflagration. And he knew where
to find that fire. He slept like a man who feared to face what
was coming.

But when he awakened at last, the idea was gone.

The way Seasauce and Hearthcoal bustled about their work
suggested that a new day had dawned. Abashed by sleep, he
fumbled himself into a sitting position, looked across at
Linden's pallet and saw that it was empty. She and Mistweave
were not in the galley. But Cail stood nearby, as impassive as
if impatience were unknown to him.

When Covenant looked at him, the *Haruchai* said, "You
are timely roused, ur-Lord. The night is past. Those who will
sojourn with you ready themselves for departure."

A pang went through Covenant. Ready, he thought. The
people around him did everything possible on his behalf; but
he was never ready. Struggling to his feet, he accepted the
bowl of porridge Hearthcoal offered him, ate as much as his
haste could stomach. Then he went to the door Cail held open
for him and stepped out into the sharp morning.

Again, ice-glare and sunlight stung his eyes, but he fought them into focus. After a glance at the new foremast, he picked his way across the frozen afterdeck toward the Giants thronging near the port rail.

Hails greeted him. The crew parted, admitting him to their midst. In a moment, he found himself at the edge of the deck with Linden and Mistweave, the First and Pitchwife, and Honninscrave.

Both Linden and Pitchwife looked stronger than they had the previous day, although she avoided Covenant's gaze as if she did not trust him. The First eyed the west with the keenness of a hawk. But Honninscrave appeared painfully unsolaced, as though he had spent the long night haunted by his conflicting duties.

A glance past the railing showed Covenant that Galewrath's sleds had already been set down on the ice. Both were heavily laden; but the sacks and bundles of supplies had been arranged to accommodate at least one passenger in each sled.

When she had acknowledged Covenant, the First turned to Sevinhand, Galewrath, and the rest of the Giants. "Now has the time of parting come upon us once more." Her voice rang crisply across the frigid air. "The hazard is great, for no longer stands Cable Seadreamer's Earth-Sight at the helm of the Search. Yet do we pursue our sworn purpose—and for that reason I do not fear. We are mortal, and the visage of failure is heinous to us. But we are not required to succeed. It is required of us only that we hold fast in every gale and let come what may. On all the seas of the world, there are none better for this work than you who remain with Starfare's Gem. How then should I be afraid?

"This only do I charge you: when the ice uncloses, come after us. Sail to that littoral which you know, to Seareach and brave *Coercri*, The Grieve. If there we fail to meet you or send word, then the Search falls to you. Do what you must— and do not fear. While one valiant heart yet defends the Earth, evil can never triumph utterly."

Then she stopped, looked down at Pitchwife as if she were surprised by her own words. For answer, he gave her a gleam of pure pleasure. Sevinhand's eyes reflected hints of the cunning skill which had saved Starfare's Gem from the warships of the *Bhrathair*. Galewrath glowered stolidly at the future as though it had no power to daunt her. Weary and imperilled though they were, the crewmembers held up their heads and let their pride shine. Covenant suddenly did not know how he could bear to leave them.

But he had to. The First started down the ladder with Pitchwife behind her; and Covenant had no choice. They were not responsible for the Earth's peril; but their lives were at stake as much as his. When Cail offered him the ladder, he gestured the *Haruchai* ahead to catch him if he fell. Then he stooped through the railing, set his numb feet into the rungs, and fought his vertigo and his cold bones downward.

The ice felt as dead as the nerves of his soles, and in the shadow of the Giantship the breeze was as sharp as the sea; but he strode and slipped across the treacherous surface to one of the sleds. Linden followed him, her hair fluttering like the banner of her determination. Then came Mistweave, still stubborn in his resolve to serve the Chosen.

Honninscrave was last. He seemed hardly able to refrain from giving Galewrath and Sevinhand a host of unnecessary final instructions. But after a moment of silence like a mute cry he wrenched himself away from his ship and joined the company.

Abruptly, several Giants shifted out of Vain's way as he approached the rail. He vaulted over the side, landed lightly on the ice, and at once resumed his characteristic immobility, his black orbs gazing at nothing.

A shadow glided out of the air: Findail melted back into his human form near Vain as if he and the Demondim-spawn belonged to each other.

Obeying the First's murmured instructions, Covenant climbed into one of the sleds, sat down among the supplies. Linden settled herself in the other sled. Honninscrave and Mistweave picked up the leads, harnessed themselves into the lines. The First and Pitchwife went to the fore. Cail stood between the sleds; Vain and Findail brought up the rear.

Runners crunched against the ice as Covenant and his companions left the Giantship in search of hope.

Sixty-three days had passed since they had said farewell to Sunder and Hollian and Seareach. They were at least eighteenscore leagues from Revelstone.

FIVE: Landward

THE First set a rapid pace. Steam panted from Honninscrave's and Mistweave's lungs as they hauled the sleds along;
but they did not hang back. All the Giants were eager to get
out of sight of the *dromond*, to put behind them their crippled
vessel and imperilled people. The runners of the sleds pounded
through hollows in the ice, hit and slewed across pressure-
ridges. Covenant and Linden were tossed ungently from side
to side among the supplies. But Linden clung to the rails, made
no protest. And Covenant wanted every stride of speed the
Giants could attain. The Land and Lord Foul had taught him
many things; but he had never learned how to leave behind
friends who needed him. Hunching down into the heavy robes
and blankets he had been given, he kept his face turned blear-
eyed and cold-bitten toward the west and let Honninscrave
draw him at a hungry trot into the white wilderland.

Yet at last the thought of what he was doing impelled him
to look back toward the *dromond*. Stark in the distance
beyond Vain and Findail, the vessel shrank as if it were being
slowly swallowed by the bleak floe; and the sight of its
abandonment stuck in his throat. But then he descried the
pennon flying from the aftermast. Sevinhand must have raised
it as a salute to the departing company. Vivid with color and
jaunty in the wind, it captured for a moment the spirit of
Starfare's Gem like a promise of valor and endurance. When
Covenant's vision became too blurred to make out the Giantship any longer, he was able to face forward again and let
the stone vessel go.

Linden studied him across the gap between their sleds; but
he had nothing to say to her which would support being

82

shouted over the hard scrunching of the runners, the rhythmic thud of the Giants' feet and the gasp of their breathing. Once again he was being borne toward his goal and his fear, not by any effort of his own, but by the exertions of people who cared about him. At every crisis along his way, it was the same: for all his passion and power, he would have come to nothing without help. And what recompense did he make for that help? Only pain and peril and at least one lie; nothing more. But that was not something which his sore heart could cry out under these conditions, under the bitter blue of the sky and the gazes of his companions.

They were traveling due west. When they had left the vantage of Starfare's Gem, a strip of open water had still been visible against the southern horizon; and they could be certain that the closer they went to the sea the less reliable the floe would become. Under the circumstances, Covenant only hoped that they would not be forced northward to find a safe passage.

The First had pushed several paces ahead of her companions to watch for flaws and fissures in the frozen expanse. Behind her trotted Pitchwife. Though he bore no burden except his own deformation, his gait betrayed that he was already being pressed to his limits. By comparison, Mistweave and Honninscrave appeared able to sustain this speed for days, dragging the heavy sleds behind them and never faltering. And Cail was one of the *Haruchai*, born to ice and arduous survival. Only the vapor that plumed from his nostrils and the white crystals which formed along his cheeks showed that he was breathing more deeply than usual.

As for Vain and Findail, they moved as though the long trek ahead meant nothing to them. Vain's wooden forearm dangled uselessly from his elbow, but in every other way he remained the structurally immaculate enigma which the ur-viles had created for their own secret reasons. And the Appointed had long since demonstrated his conclusive immunity to any physical peril or stress.

Around them, the plain of ice seemed featureless and devoid of any content except cold to the edges of the world. The sun came down hard on the white floe, making the ice glare, forcing Covenant to squint until his temples throbbed. And the cold soaked into him through every fold and clasp of his coverings. The beat of the Giants' feet and the expulsion of their breath marked out the frigid silence. The sled jostled him incessantly against a bundle of firewood packed beside him. Grimly, he hugged his blankets and huddled into himself.

The First's fall took him by surprise. She was nothing more than a gray blur across his disfocused stare as she stepped into a fissure.

Scattering snow, she plunged heavily forward. Her chest struck the rim of the break. For an instant, she scrabbled frantically at the edge, then dropped out of sight.

Pitchwife was four or five strides behind her; but immediately he dove after her, skidding headlong to snatch at her disappearing arms.

He was too late. And he could not stop himself. In a flurry of limbs and snow, he toppled after his wife.

Slewing over the slick surface, Honninscrave and Mistweave wheeled the sleds to a halt. The one bearing Linden was nearly overturned; but Cail caught it, slammed it back onto its runners.

Covenant pitched out of his sled, landed on the ice, lurched to his feet. Ahead of him, the Master and Mistweave wrestled at the bindings which harnessed them to their burdens. Findail and Vain had stopped; but Cail was already halfway to the fissure.

Covenant and the Giants reached the rim together, with Linden a scant step behind them. Cail stood there gazing downward as if he had forgotten urgency.

The First and Pitchwife hung a few feet below the edge. The fissure was only a little wider than her shoulders, and she had clamped herself between the walls, holding her position by main strength. Pitchwife's arms clasped her hips; he dangled awkwardly between her thighs.

Below his feet, the snow which had fallen into the fissure became gray slush as the sea absorbed it.

He jerked a glance upward. "Stone and Sea!" he gasped. "Make haste!"

But the Master and Mistweave were not slow. Honninscrave threw himself flat on the ice with his head and shoulders over the rim. Mistweave braced the Master's legs; and Honninscrave reached down to take hold of the First.

In a moment, she scrambled out of the fissure, towing Pitchwife after her.

Her stern visage showed no reaction; but Pitchwife was
breathing hard, and his gnarled hands trembled. "Stone and
Sea!" he panted again. "I am a Giant and love an eventful
journey. But such happenings are not altogether to my taste."
Then a chuckle of relief came steaming between his bared
teeth. "Also I am somewhat abashed. I sought to rescue my
wife, yet it was she who caught my own fall."

The First rested a hand lightly on his shoulder. "Mayhap
if you were less impetuous in your rescuing." But as she
turned to Honninscrave, her voice stiffened. "Master, it is
my thought that we must bend our way somewhat northward.
This ice is not safe."

"Aye," he growled. Ever since he had been forced to the
realization that the company would have to leave Starfare's
Gem, he had not been able to stifle the undertone of bitterness
in his voice. "But that way is longer, and we are in haste.
Northward the ice will be not so easily traveled. And this
north is perilous, as you know."

The First nodded reluctantly. After a moment, she let out
a long sigh and straightened her back. "Very well," she said.
"Let us attempt the west again."

When no one mved, she gestured Covenant and Linden
back to the sleds.

Linden turned to walk beside Covenant. Her face was red
with cold and severe with concentration. In a flat, quiet voice,
she asked, "Why is this north perilous?"

He shook his head. "I don't know." The scars on his right
forearm itched in reaction to the First's fall and the suggestion
of other hazards. "I've never been north of Revelstone and
Coercri." He did not want to think about nameless dangers.
The cold was already too much for him. And he could not
figure out how the company was going to get across the
fissure.

But that problem was simply solved. While he and Linden
climbed into their sleds, the First and Pitchwife leaped the
gap. Then Honninscrave and Mistweave drew the sleds to
the rim of the crack. There Covenant saw that the sleds were
long enough to span the fissure. Honninscrave and Mistweave
pushed them out over the gap; the First and Pitchwife pulled
them across. When the rest of the company had passed the
crack, Honninscrave and Mistweave slipped their arms into
the harnesses again, and the First went on her way westward.

Now she set a slower pace, in part for caution and in part to accommodate Pitchwife's weariness. Still her speed was greater than any Covenant could have matched afoot. The ice seemed to rush jolting and skidding under the runners of the sled. But whenever she saw something she distrusted, she dropped to a walk and probed ahead with her longsword until she was sure that the ground was safe.

For the rest of the morning, her care proved unnecessary. But shortly after the company had paused for a brief meal and a few warming swallows of *diamondraught*, the point of her sword bit into the crust, and several hundred feet of packed snow along a thin line to the north and south fell from sight. This fissure also was easily crossed; but when the companions gained the far side, the First faced Honninscrave again and said, "It is too much. This ice grows fragile beneath us."

The Master breathed a curse through his frosted beard. Yet he did not demur when the leader of the Search turned toward the northwest and thicker ice.

For most of the afternoon, the floe remained flat, snowbrushed, and unreliable. From time to time, Covenant sensed that the surface was sloping upward; but the brightness of the sun on the white landscape made him unsure of what he saw. Although he sipped *diamondraught* at intervals, the cold sank deeper into his bones. His face felt like beaten metal. Gradually, he drifted into reveries of conflagration. Whenever he became drowsy with liquor and chill, he found himself half dreaming wild magic as if it were lovely and desirable— flame sufficient to tear down Kemper's Pitch; passion powerful enough to contend with the Worm of the World's End; venom capable of subsuming everything in its delirium. That fire was vital and seductive—and as necessary as blood. He would never be able to give it up.

But such dreams led him to places where he did not want to go. To the scream which had nearly torn out his heart when Linden had told him the truth of the venom and the Worm. And to that other fire which lay hidden at the roots of his need—to the *caamora* which he had always failed to find, though his soul depended on it.

Urgent with alarm, he repeatedly fought his way back from the brink of true sleep. And the last time he did so, he

was surprised to see that the north was no longer blank.
The First's path angled toward a ridge of tremendous ice-
chunks. Piled into the sky, they reached out for the horizons,
east and west. Although the sun was near setting, it was far
down in the south and did not blind him, but rather shone
full and faintly pink on the ridge, making the ice appear as
unbreachable as a glacier.

Here the First turned toward the west again, keeping as
close to the base of the ridge as possible without sacrificing
a clear route for the sleds. But in her way boulders and
monoliths lay like menhirs where they had rolled or fallen
from the violence which had riven the ice. She was forced
to slow her pace again as the difficulty of the terrain increased.
Nevertheless her goal had been achieved. The surface which
supported that ridge was unlikely to crack or crumble under
the pressure of the company's passage.

As the sun sank, vermilion and fatal, into the west, the
travelers halted for the night. Pitchwife slumped to the ice
and sat there with his head in his hands, too tired even to
talk. Covenant and Linden climbed stiffly from their sleds and
walked back and forth, rubbing their arms and stamping their
feet, while Mistweave and Honninscrave made camp. Honninscrave unpacked sections of heavily tarred canvas to use
as groundsheets, then laid more blankets. Mistweave un-
loaded Linden's sled until he had uncovered a large flat
rectangle of stone. This he set out as a base on which to
build a fire, so that melting ice would not wet the wood. To
no one in particular, the First announced her estimate that
the company had come more than twenty leagues. Then she
fell silent.

When Mistweave had a crisp blaze going, Pitchwife
struggled to his feet, rubbed the frost from his face, and
went to do the cooking. As he worked, he muttered in-
distinctly to himself as if the sound of some voice—his own
if no one else's—were necessary to his courage. Shortly, he
had produced a thick stew for his companions. But still the
pall of the waste hung over them, and no one spoke.

After supper, Pitchwife went to sleep almost at once,
hugging his groundsheet about him. The First sat sternly
beside the fire and toyed with the fagots as though she did
not want to reconsider her decisions. As determined as ever
to emulate the devotion of the *Haruchai*, Mistweave joined

Cail standing watch over the company. And Honninscrave stared at nothing, met no one's eyes. His orbs were hidden under the weight of his brows, and his face looked drawn and gaunt.

Linden paced tensely near the fire as if she wanted to talk to someone. But Covenant was absorbed by his visceral yearning for the heat of white flame. The effort of denial left him nothing to say. The silence became as cold and lonely as the ice. After a time, he gathered his blankets and followed Pitchwife's example, wrapping himself tightly in his ground-sheet.

He thought he would be able to sleep, if only because the cold was so persuasive. But Linden made her bed near his, and soon he felt her watching him as if she sought to fathom his isolation. When he opened his eyes, he saw the look of intention in her fire-lit face.

Her gaze was focused on him like an appeal; but the words she murmured softly took him by surprise.

"I never even learned her name."

Covenant raised his head, blinked his incomprehension at her.

"That Giant," she explained, "the one who was hurt when the foremast broke." The one she had healed with his ring. "I never found out who she was. I've been doing that all my life. Treating people as if they were pieces of sick or damaged meat instead of actual individuals. I thought I was a doctor, but it was only the disease or the hurt I cared about. Only the fight against death. Not the person."

He gave her the best answer he had. "Is that bad?" He recognized the attitude she described. "You aren't God. You can't help people because of who they are. You can only help them because they're hurt and they need you." Deliberately, he concluded, "Otherwise you would've let Mistweave die."

"Covenant." Now her tone was aimed at him as squarely as her gaze. "At some point, you're going to have to deal with me. With who I am. We've been lovers. I've never stopped loving you. It hurts that you lied to me—that you let me believe something that wasn't true. Let me believe we had a future together. But I haven't stopped loving you." Low flames from the campfire glistened out of the dampness in her eyes. Yet she was resolutely unemotional, sparing him her recrimination or sorrow. "I think the only reason you loved me was because I was hurt. You loved me because of my parents. Not because of who I am."

Abruptly, she rolled onto her back, covered her face with her hands. Need muffled the self-control of her whisper. "Maybe that kind of love is wonderful and altruistic. I don't know. But it isn't enough."

Covenant looked at her, at the hands clasped over her pain and the hair curling around her ear, and thought, Have to deal with you. Have to. But he could not. He did not know how. Since the loss of the One Tree, their positions had been reversed. Now it was she who knew what she wanted, he who was lost.

Above him, the stars glittered out their long bereavement. But for them also he did not know what to do.

When he awakened in the early dawn, he discovered that Honninscrave was gone.

A wind had come up. Accumulated snow gusted away over the half-buried remains of the campfire as Covenant thrashed out of his blankets and groundsheet. The First, Pitchwife, and Linden were still asleep. Mistweave lay felled in his canvas cover as if during the night his desire to match Cail had suffered a defeat. Only Cail, the Demondim-spawn, and Findail were on their feet.

Covenant turned to Cail. "Where—?"

In response, Cail nodded upward.

Quickly, Covenant scanned the massive chaos of the ridge. For a moment, he missed the place Cail had indicated. But then his gaze leaped to the highest point above the camp; and there he saw Honninscrave.

The Master sat atop a small tor of ice with his back to the south and the company. The wind tumbled down off the crest into Covenant's face, bearing with it a faint smell of smoke.

Blood and damnation! Grimly, Covenant demanded, "What in hell does he think he's doing?" But he already knew the answer. Cail's reply only confirmed it.

"Some while since, he arose and assayed the ice, promising a prompt return. With him he bore wood and a fire-pot such as the Giants use."

Caamora. Honninscrave was trying to burn away his grief.

At the sound of Cail's voice, the First looked up from her

bed, an inquiry in her eyes. Covenant found suddenly that he could not open his throat. Mutely, he directed the First's gaze up at Honninscrave.

When she saw the Master, she rasped a curse and sprang to her feet. Awakening Pitchwife with a slap of her hand, she asked Covenant and Cail how long Honninscrave had been gone.

Inflexibly, the *Haruchai* repeated what he had told Covenant.

"Stone and Sea!" she snarled as Pitchwife and then Linden arose to join her. "Has he forgotten his own words? This north is perilous."

Pitchwife squinted apprehensively up at Honninscrave; but his words were reassuring. "The Master is a Giant. He is equal to the peril. And his heart has found no relief from Cable Seadreamer's end. Perchance in this way he will gain peace."

The First glared at him. But she did not call Honninscrave down from his perch.

Eyes glazed with sleep and vision, Linden gazed up at the Master and said nothing.

Shortly, Honninscrave rose to his feet. Passing beyond the crest, he found his way downward. Soon he emerged from a nearby valley and came woodenly toward the company.

His hands swung at his sides. As he neared the camp, Covenant saw that they had been scoured raw by fire.

When he reached his companions, he stopped, raised his hands before him like a gesture of a futility. His gaze was shrouded. His fingers were essentially undamaged; but the aftereffects of his pain were vivid. Linden hugged her own hands under her arms in instinctive empathy.

The First's voice was uncharacteristically gentle. "Is it well with you, Grimmand Honninscrave?"

He shook his head in simple bafflement. "It does not suffice. Naught suffices. It burns in my breast—and will not burn out."

Then as if the will which held him upright had broken he dropped to his knees and thrust his hands into a drift of snow. Tattered wisps of steam rose around his wrists.

Dumb with helpless concern, the Giants stood around him. Linden bit her lips. The wind drew a cold scud across the ice, and the air was sharp with rue. Covenant's eyes blurred and ran. In self-defense there were many things for which he could claim he was not culpable; but Seadreamer's death was not among them.

At last, the First spoke. "Come, Master," she breathed thickly. "Arise and be about your work. We must hope or die."

Hope or die. Kneeling on the frozen waste, Honninscrave looked like he had lost his way between those choices. But then slowly he gathered his legs under him, stretched his tall frame erect. His eyes had hardened, and his visage was rigid and ominous. For a moment, he stood still, let all the company witness the manner in which he bore himself. Then without a word he went and began to break camp.

Covenant caught a glimpse of the distress in Linden's gaze. But when she met his look of inquiry, she shook her head, unable to articulate what she had perceived in Honninscrave.

Together, they followed the Master's example.

While Honninscrave packed the canvas and bedding, Mistweave set out a cold breakfast. His red-rimmed eyes and weary demeanor held a cast of abashment: he was a Giant and had not expected Cail's endurance to be greater than his. Now he appeared determined to work harder in compensation—and in support of Honninscrave. While Covenant, Linden, and the other Giants ate, Mistweave toiled about the camp, readying everything for departure.

As Covenant and Linden settled into their sleds, bundled themselves against the mounting edge of the wind, the First addressed Honninscrave once more. She spoke softly, and the wind frayed away the sound of her voice.

"From the vantage of your *caamora*, saw you any sign?"

His new hardness made his reply sound oddly brutal: "None."

He and Mistweave shrugged themselves into the lines of the sleds. The First and Pitchwife went ahead. With Cail between the sleds and Vain and Findail in the rear, the company set off.

Their progress was not as swift as it had been the previous day. The increased difficulty of the terrain was complicated by the air pouring and gusting down from the ridge. Fistsful of ice crystals rattled against the wood of the sleds, stung the faces of the travelers. White plumes and devils danced among the company. The edges of the landscape ached in the wind. *Diamondraught* and food formed a core of sustenance within him, but failed to spread any warmth into his limbs. He did not know how long he could hold out against the alluring and fatal somnolence of the cold.

The next time he rubbed the ice from his lashes and raised his head, he found that he had not held out. Half the morning was gone. Unwittingly, he had drifted into the passive stupor by which winter and leprosy snared their victims.

Linden was sitting upright in her sled. Her head shifted tensely from side to side as if she were searching. For a groggy instant, Covenant thought that she was using her senses to probe the safety of the ice. But then she wrenched forward, and her voice snapped over the waste:

"Stop!"

Echoes rode eerily back along the wind: Stop! Stop! But ice and cold changed the tone of her shout, made it sound as forlorn as a cry raised from the Soulbiter.

At once, the First turned to meet the sleds.

They halted immediately below a pile of broken ice like the rubble of a tremendous fortress reduced by siege. Megalithic blocks and shards towered and loomed as if they were leaning to fall on the company.

Linden scrambled out of her sled. Before anyone could ask her what she wanted, she coughed, "It's getting colder."

The First and Pitchwife glanced at each other. Covenant moved to stand beside Linden, though he did not comprehend her. After a moment, the First said, "Colder, Chosen? We do not feel it."

"I don't mean the winter," Linden began at once, urgent to be understood. "It's not the same." Then she caught herself, straightened her shoulders. Slowly and sharply, she said, "You don't feel it—but I tell you it's there. It's making the air colder. Not ice. Not wind. Not winter. Something else." Her lips were blue and trembling. "Something dangerous."

And this north is perilous, Covenant thought dully, as if the chill made him stupid. What kind of peril? But when he opened his mouth, no words came.

Honninscrave's head jerked up. Pitchwife's eyes glared white in his misshaped face.

At the same instant, the First barked, *"Arghule!"* and sprang at Covenant and Linden.

Thrusting them toward the sleds, she shouted, "We must flee!" Then she wheeled to scan the region.

Covenant lost his footing, skidded into Cail's grasp. The *Haruchai* flipped him unceremoniously onto his sled. Linden vaulted to her place. At once, Honninscrave and Mistweave heaved the sleds forward as quickly as the slick surface allowed.

Before they had taken three strides, the ice a stone's throw ahead rose up and came toward them.

The moving shape was as wide as the height of a Giant, as thick as the reach of Covenant's arms. Short legs bore it forward with deceptive speed. Dark gaps around its edge looked like maws.

Cold radiated from it like a shout.

The First slid to a halt, planted herself in the path of the creature. *"Arghule!"* she cried again. "Avoid!"

Pitchwife's answering yell snatched her around. His arm flailed a gesture toward the ridge. *"Arghuleh!"*

Two more creatures like the first had detached themselves from the rubble and were rushing toward the company.

In the south appeared a fourth.

Together, they emitted cold as fierce as the cruel heart of winter.

For an instant, the First froze. Her protest carried lornly across the wind. "But the *arghuleh* do not act thus."

Abruptly, Findail melted into a hawk and flew away.

Honninscrave roared a command: "Westward!" He was the Master of Starfare's Gem, trained for emergencies. With a wrench that threw Covenant backward, he hauled his sled into motion. "We must break past!"

Mistweave followed. As he labored for speed, he called over his shoulder to Linden, "Do not fear! We are Giants, proof against cold!"

The next moment, the *arghuleh* attacked.

The creature approaching the First stopped. At Pitchwife's warning shout, she whirled to face the *arghule*. But it did not advance. Instead, it waved one of its legs.

From the arc of the gesture, the air suddenly condensed into a web of ice.

Expanding and thickening as it moved, the web sailed toward the First like a hunter's net. Before it reached her, it grew huge and heavy enough to snare even a Giant.

At the same time, the *arghule* coming from the south halted, settled itself as though it were burrowing into the waste. Then violence boomed beneath it: ice shattered in all directions. And a crack sprang through the surface, ran like lightning toward the company. In the space between one heartbeat and another, the crack became as wide as the sleds.

It passed directly under Vain. The Demondim-spawn disappeared so quickly that Covenant did not see him fall.

Instinctively, Covenant turned to look toward the other two *arghuleh.*

They were almost close enough to launch their assaults.

The sled lurched as Honninscrave accelerated. Covenant faced again toward the First.

The web of ice was dropping over her head.

Pitchwife struggled toward her. But his feet could not hold the treacherous surface. Cail sped lightly past him as if the *Haruchai* were as surefooted as a Ranyhyn.

The First defended herself without her sword. As the web descended, she chopped at it with her left arm.

It broke in a blizzard of splinters that caught the light like instant chiaroscuro and then rattled faintly away along the wind.

But her arm came down encased by translucent ice. It covered her limb halfway to the shoulder, immobilized her elbow and hand. Fiercely, she hammered at the sheath with her right fist. But the ice clung to her like iron.

The sleds gained momentum. Nearing the First, Honninscrave and Mistweave veered to the side in an effort to bypass the *arghule.* The crack which had swallowed Vain faded toward the north. Findail was nowhere to be seen. Linden clutched the rail of her sled, a soundless cry stretched over her face.

Cail dashed past the First to challenge her assailant.

As one, she and Pitchwife shouted after him, *"No!"*

He ignored them. Straight at the creature he aimed his *Haruchai* strength.

Before he could strike, the *arghule* bobbed as if it were bowing. Instantly, a great hand of ice slapped down on him out of the empty air. It pounded him flat, snatched him under the bulk of the creature.

Covenant fought to stand in the slewing sled. Cail's fall went through him like an auger. The landscape was as white and ruined as wild magic. When his heart beat again, he was translated into fire. Power drove down through him, anchored him. Flame as hot as a furnace, as vicious as venom, cocked back his half-fist to hurl destruction at the *arghule*.

There a web flung by one of the trailing creatures caught him. The two *arghuleh* from the north had changed direction to pursue the company; then one of them had stopped to attack. The snare did not entirely reach him. But its leading edge struck the right side of his head, licked for an instant over his shoulder, snapped on his upraised fist.

Wild magic pulverized the ice: nothing was left to encase him. But an immense force of cold slammed straight into his brain.

Instantly, paralysis locked itself around him.

He saw what was happening; every event registered on him. But he was stunned and helpless, lost in a feral chill.

While Honninscrave and Mistweave fought the sleds sideward to avoid the *arghule*, the First sprang to Cail's aid with Pitchwife behind her. The creature sought to retreat; but she moved too swiftly. Bracing itself, it repeated the bow which had captured Cail.

Her left arm was useless to her, but she ignored the handicap. Fury and need impelled her. As the *arghule* raised its ice, she put her whole body into one blow and struck the creature squarely with all the Giantish might of her good fist.

The *arghule* shattered under the impact. The boom of its destruction echoed off the towering ridge.

Amid volleying thunder, the sleds rushed past the First. She whirled to face the pursuing *arghuleh*.

Pitchwife dove wildly into the remains of the creature. For an instant, he threw chunks and chips aside. Then he emerged, wearing frost and ice-powder as though even in death the *arghule* nearly had the capacity to freeze him. In his arms, he bore Cail.

From head to foot, the *Haruchai* was sheathed like the First's left arm in pure ice, bound rigid as if he were frozen past all redemption. Carrying him urgently, Pitchwife sped after the sleds.

The First snatched up a white shard, hurled it at the *arghuleh* to make them hesitate. Then she followed the company.

In response, the creatures squatted against the ice; and

cracks like cries of frustration and hunger shot through the floe, gaping jaggedly after the travelers. For a moment, the First had to skid and dodge across a ground that was falling apart under her. Then she missed her footing, fell and rolled out of the path of the attack. The cracks searched on for the company; but the sleds were nearly out of range.

The First regained her feet. Soon she, too, was beyond the reach of the *arghuleh*.

Covenant saw her come running up behind Pitchwife, clap him encouragingly on the shoulder. Pitchwife panted in great raw gasps as he strove to sustain his pace. The misshaping of his back made him appear to huddle protectively over Cail. Cail's scar was unnaturally distinct, amplified by the translucence of his casing. He was the last of the *Haruchai* who had promised themselves to Covenant. And Covenant still could not break the cold which clenched his mind. All hope of fire was gone.

Linden was shouting to the First, "We've got to stop! Cail needs help! *You* need help!"

Honninscrave and Mistweave did not slacken their pace. The First returned, "Should the *arghuleh* again draw nigh, will you perceive them?"

"Yes!" Linden shot back. "Now that I know what they are!" Her tone was hard, certain. "We've got to stop! I don't know how long he can stay alive like that!"

The First nodded. "Master!" she barked. "We must halt!"

At once, Honninscrave and Mistweave shortened their strides, let the sleds drag themselves to a standstill.

Pitchwife managed a few more steps, then stumbled to his knees in a low bowl of snow. The wind whipped flurries around him. His breathing rattled hoarsely as he hunched over Cail, hugging the *Haruchai* as if he sought to warm Cail with his own life.

Linden leaped from her sled before it stopped moving, caught her balance and hastened to Pitchwife's side. But Covenant remained frozen while Honninscrave and Mistweave drew the sleds around to Pitchwife, Cail, Linden, and the First.

Vain stood there as well. Covenant had not seen the Demondim-spawn arrive, did not know how he had escaped. Bits of ice clung to his tattered apparel, but his black form was unscathed. He did not breathe, and his midnight eyes were focused on nothing.

Pitchwife set Cail down. Linden knelt beside the *Haruchai*, searched him with her eyes, then touched her fingers to his case. At once, pain hissed between her teeth. When she snatched back her hands, her fingertips left small patches of skin on the ice. Bright in the sunlight, red droplets oozed from her torn flesh. "Damn it!" she rasped, more frightened and angry than hurt, "that's *cold*." Raising her head to the First, she shivered, "You obviously know something about these *arghuleh*. Do you know how to treat this?"

In reply, the First drew her falchion. Gripping it above her head, she brought its hilt down hard on the crust which locked her left arm. The ice broke and fell away, leaving her limb free, the skin undamaged. Stiffly, she flexed her hand and wrist. A wince touched her face, but she changed it to a scowl.

"See you? We are Giants—proof against cold as against fire. Requiring no other unction, we have learned none." Her glare suggested that she deemed this ignorance to be a kind of failure.

But Linden had no time for failure. "We can't do that to him," she muttered, thinking aloud. "We'd break half his bones." She peered closely at Cail to confirm her perceptions. "He's still alive—but he won't last long." Red-tipped, her fingers moved as if she had already forgotten their hurt. "We need fire."

Then she looked toward Covenant.

At the sight of him, her eyes went wide with shock and fear. She had not realized that he had been hit by the cold of the *arghuleh*.

It felt like a numb nail driven through the side of his head, impaling his mind painlessly. And it was slowly working its way deeper. His left eye had gone blind. Most of the nerves of his left side were as dead as leprosy. He wanted to cry out for help, but no longer knew how.

From out of nowhere, Findail appeared. Regaining his abused human shape, he placed himself at the fringes of the company and fixed his attention on Linden.

Ice muffled whatever she was saying. Covenant could not bear it: he did not want to die like this. Mad protests surged through him. All winter was his enemy; every league and ridge of the floe was an attack against him. From the pit of his dismay, he brought up flame and venom as if he meant to rid the Earth of all cold forever, tear Time from its foundations in order to shear away the gelid death which locked his brain.

But then there was another presence in him. It was alien and severe, desperate with alarm—and yet he found it strangely comforting. He struggled instinctively when it took his flame from him; but the cold and his impercipience made his strivings pointless. And the intrusion—an external identity which somehow inhabited his mind as if he had let down all his defenses—gave him warmth in return: the warmth of its own strict desire for him and the heat of his fire combined. For a moment, he thought he knew that other presence, recognized it intimately. Then the world turned into white magic and passion; and the cold fled.

A few heartbeats later, his eyes squeezed back into focus, and he found himself on his hands and knees. Linden had withdrawn from him, leaving behind an ache of absence as if she had opened a door which enabled him to see how empty his heart was without her. Dull bereavement throbbed in his right forearm; but his ring still hung on the last finger of his half-hand. The wind sent chills ruffling through his clothes. The sun shone as if the desecration of the Sunbane would never be healed. He had failed again. And proved once more that she—

This time she had simply reached into him and taken possession.

There was no difference between that and what Lord Foul had done to Joan. What he was doing to the Land. No difference except the difference between Linden herself and the Despiser. And Gibbon-Raver had promised that she would destroy the Earth.

She had the power to fulfill that prophecy now. She could take it whenever she wanted it.

Urgent grief came over him—grief for both of them, for himself in his doomed inefficacy, for her in her dire plight. He feared he would weep aloud. But then the wind's flat rush was punctuated by hoarse, hard breathing; and that sound restored his awareness of his companions.

The ice which had held the *Haruchai* was gone, and Cail

was coming back to life the hard way—fighting for every breath, wresting each inhalation with bared teeth from the near-death of cold. Even the *merewives* had not so nearly slain him. But Linden had restored him to the verge of survival. As Covenant watched, Cail carried himself the rest of the distance.

Honninscrave, Mistweave, and the First studied Cail and Linden and Covenant with concern and appreciation mixed together in their faces. Pitchwife had mastered his own gasping enough to grin like a grimace. But Linden had eyes only for Covenant.

She was wan with dismay at what she had done. From the first, her loathing for possession had been even greater than his; yet the necessity of it was thrust upon her time and again. She was forced to evil by the fundamental commitments which had made her a physician. And how was she forced? he asked himself. By her lack of power. If she were given his ring, as the *Elohim* desired, she would be saved the peril of this damnation.

He could not do it. Anything else; he would do anything else. But not this. More than once, she had challenged his protective instincts, protested his desire to spare her. But how could he have explained that everything else—every other attempt at protection or preservation—was nothing more than an effort to pay for this one refusal? To give her something in compensation for what he would not give.

Now he did it again. Ice-gnawed and frost-burned though he was—leprous, poisoned, and beaten—he wrenched his courage to its feet and faced her squarely. Swallowing grief, he said thickly, "I hope I didn't hurt anybody."

It was not much. But for the time being it was enough. Her distress softened as if he had made a gesture of forgiveness. A crooked smile took the severity from her lips. Blinking at sudden tears, she murmured, "You're hard to handle. The first time I saw you"—he remembered the moment as well as she did: he had slammed his door in her face—"I knew you were going to give me trouble."

The love in her voice made him groan because he could not go to her and put his arms around her. Not as long as he refused to make the one sacrifice she truly needed.

At her back, Mistweave had unpacked a pouch of *diamondraught*. When he handed it to her, she forced her

attention away from Covenant and knelt to Cail. Between
heaving respirations, the *Haruchai* took several sips of the
tonic liquor.

After that his condition improved rapidly. While his companions shared the pouch, he recovered enough strength to
sit up, then to regain his feet. In spite of its flatness, his
expression seemed oddly abashed. His pride did not know how
to sustain the fact of defeat. But after his experience with
the seduction of the *merewives*, he appeared to place less
importance on his self-esteem. Or perhaps Brinn's promise—
that Cail would eventually be free to follow his heart—had
somehow altered the characteristic *Haruchai* determination
to succeed or die. In a moment, Cail's visage was as devoid
of inflection as ever. When he indicated that he was ready to
travel again, his word carried conviction.

No one demurred. At a wry glance from Pitchwife, however, the First announced that the company would eat a meal
before going on. Cail appeared to think that such a delay was
unnecessary; yet he accepted the opportunity for more rest.

While the companions ate, Linden remained tense. She
consumed her rations as if she were chewing fears and
speculations, trying to find her way through them. But when
she spoke, her question showed that she had found, not an
answer, but a distraction. She asked the First, "How much do
you know about those *arghuleh?*"

"Our knowledge is scant," replied the Swordmain. She
seemed unsure of the direction of Linden's inquiry. "Upon
rare occasion, Giants have encountered *arghuleh*. And there
are tales which concern them. But together such stories and
encounters yield little."

"Then why did you risk it?" Linden pursued. "Why did we
come this far north?"

Now the First understood. "Mayhap I erred," she said in
an uncompromising tone. "The southern ice was uncertain,
and I sought safer passage. The hazard of the *arghuleh* I
accepted because we are Giants, not readily slain or harmed
by cold. It was my thought that four Giants would suffice to
ward you.

"Moreover," she went on more harshly, "I was misled in
my knowledge.

"Folly," she muttered to herself. "Knowledge is chimera,
for beyond it ever lies other knowledge, and the incomplete-

ness of what is known renders the knowing false. It was our knowledge that *arghuleh* do not act thus.

"They are savage creatures, as dire of hate as the winter in which they thrive. And their hate is not solely for the beasts and beings of blood and warmth which form their prey. It is also for their own kind. In the tales we have heard and the experience of our people, it is plain that the surest defense against the assault of one *arghule* is the assault of a second, for they will prefer each other's deaths above any other.

"Therefore," the First growled, "did I believe this north to be the lesser peril. Against any *arghule* four Giants must surely be counted a sufficient company. I did not know," she concluded, "that despite all likelihood and nature they had set aside their confirmed animosity to act in concert."

Linden stared across the waste. Honninscrave watched the knot of his hands as if he feared it would not hold. After a moment, Covenant cleared his throat and asked, "Why?" In the Land, the Law of nature was being steadily corrupted by the Sunbane. Had Lord Foul's influence reached this far? "Why would they change?"

"I know not," the First said sourly. "I would have believed the substance of Stone and Sea to be more easily altered than the hate of the *arghuleh*."

Covenant groaned inwardly. He was still hundreds of leagues from Revelstone; and yet his fears were harrying him forward as if he and his companions had already entered the ambit of the Despiser's malice.

Abruptly, Linden leapt to her feet, faced the east. She gauged the distance, then rasped, "They're coming. I thought they'd give up. Apparently cooperation isn't the only new trick they've learned."

Honninscrave spat a Giantish obscenity. The First gestured him and Mistweave toward the sleds, then helped Pitchwife upright. Quickly, the Master and Mistweave packed and reloaded the supplies. Covenant was cursing to himself. He wanted a chance to talk to Linden privately. But he followed her tense example and climbed back into his sled.

The First took the lead. In an effort to outdistance the pursuit, she set the best pace Pitchwife could maintain, pushing him to his already-worn limits. Yet Cail trotted between Covenant and Linden as if he were fully recovered.

Vain and Findail brought up the rear together, shadowing each other across the wind-cut wilderness.

That night, the company obtained little rest, though Pitchwife needed it urgently. Shortly after moonrise, Cail's native caution impelled him to rouse Linden; and when she had tasted the air, she sent the company scrambling for the sleds.

The moon was only three days past its full, and the sky remained clear. The First was able to find a path with relative ease. But she was held back by Pitchwife's exhaustion. He could not move faster than a walk without her support. And in an effort to shore up his strength, he had consumed so much *diamondraught* that he was not entirely sober. At intervals, he began to sing lugubriously under his breath, as though he were lunatic with fatigue. Somehow, the companions kept a safe distance between themselves and the *arghuleh*. But they were unable to increase their lead.

And when the sun rose over the wasted ice, they found themselves in worse trouble. They were coming to the end of the floe. During the night, they had entered a region where the ice to the south became progressively more broken as hunks snapped off and drifted away. Ahead of the First, the west became impassable. And beyond a wide area where icebergs were being spawned lay open water. She had no choice but to force her way up into the ragged ridge which separated the arctic glacier from the crumbling sheet of the floe.

There Covenant thought that she would abandon the sleds. He and Linden climbed out to make their way on foot; but that did not sufficiently lighten the loads Honninscrave and Mistweave were pulling. Yet none of the Giants faltered. Forging into a narrow valley which breached the ridge, they began to struggle toward the north and west, as if in spite of the exhaustion they now shared with Pitchwife they had not begun to be daunted. Covenant marveled at their hardiness; but he could do nothing to help them except strive to follow without needing help himself.

That task threatened to surpass him. Cold and lack of sleep sapped his strength. His numb feet were as clumsy as cripples. Several times, he had to catch himself on a sled so that he would not fall back down the valley. But Honninscrave or Mistweave bore the added burden without complaint until Covenant could regain his footing.

For some distance, the First's route seemed inspired or fortuitous. As the valley rose into the glacier, bending crookedly back and forth between north and west, its bottom remained passable. The companions were able to keep moving.

Then they gained the upper face of the glacier and their path grew easier. Here the ice was as rugged as a battleground —pressure-splintered and wind-tooled into high fantastic shapes, riddled with fissures, marked by strange channels and hollows of erosion—and the company had to wend still farther north to find a path. Yet with care the First was able to pick a passage which did not require much strength. And as the companions left the area of the glacier's rim, they were able to head once again almost directly westward.

Giddy with weariness and cold and the ice-glare of the sun, Covenant stumbled on after the sleds. A pace or two to his side, Linden was in little better condition. *Diamondraught* and exertion could not keep the faint, fatal hint of blue from her lips; and her face looked as pallid as bone. But her clenched alertness and the stubborn thrust of her strides showed that she was not yet ready to fall.

For more than a league, with the air rasping his lungs and fear at his back, Covenant followed the lead of the Giants. Somehow, he did not collapse.

But then everything changed. The First's route was neither inspired nor fortuitous: it was impossible. Balanced unsteadily on locked knees, his heart trembling, Covenant looked out from the edge of the cliff where the company had stopped. There was nothing below him but the bare, black sea.

Without forewarning, the company had reached the western edge of the glacier.

Off to the left was the jagged ridge which separated the main ice-mass from the lower floe. But elsewhere lay nothing but the endless north and the cliff and the rue-bitten sea.

Covenant did not know how to bear it. Vertigo blew up at him like a wind from the precipice, and his knees folded.

Pitchwife caught him. "No," the deformed Giant coughed. His voice seemed to snag and strangle deep in his throat. "Do not despair. Has this winter made you blind?" Rough

with fatigue, he jerked Covenant upright. "Look before you.
It needs not the eyes of a Giant to behold this hope."

Hope, Covenant sighed into the silence of his whirling
head. Ah, God. I'd hope if I knew how.

But Pitchwife's stiff grasp compelled him. Groping for
balance, he opened his eyes to the cold.

For a moment, they would not focus. But then he found
the will to force his gaze clear.

There he saw it: distinct and unattainable across half a
league of the fatal sea, a thin strip of land.

It stretched out of sight to north and south.

"As I have said," Honninscrave muttered, "our charts hold
no certain knowledge of this region. But mayhap it is the
coast of the Land which lies before us."

Something like a madman's laughter rose in Covenant's
chest. "Well, good for us." The Despiser would certainly be
laughing. "At least now we can look at where we want to go
while we're freezing to death or being eaten by *arghuleh*."
He held the mirth back because he feared it would turn to
weeping.

"Covenant!" Linden said sharply—a protest of empathy or
apprehension.

He did not look at her. He did not look at any of them.
He hardly listened to himself. "Do you call this hope?"

"We are Giants," the First responded. Her voice held an
odd note of brisk purpose. "Dire though this strait appears,
we will wrest life from it."

Mutely, Honninscrave stripped off his sark, packed it into
one of the bundles on his sled. Mistweave dug out a long coil
of heavy rope, then followed the Master's example.

Covenant stared at them. Linden panted, "Do you mean—?"
Her eyes flared wildly. "We won't last eight seconds in water
that cold!"

The First cast a gauging look down the cliff. As she studied
the drop, she responded, "Then our care must suffice to ward
you."

Abruptly, she turned back to the company. Indicating
Honninscrave's sled, she asked Cail, "Does this weight and
the Giantfriend's surpass your strength?"

Cail's flat mien suggested disdain for the question as he
shook his head.

"The ice affords scant footing," she warned.

He regarded her expressionlessly. "I will be secure."

She gave him a firm nod. She had learned to trust the *Haruchai*. Returning to the rim, she said, "Then let us not delay. The *arghuleh* must not come upon us here."

A prescient nausea knotting his guts, Covenant watched Honninscrave tie one end of the rope to the rear of his sled. The Giant's bare back and shoulders steamed in the sharp air, but he did not appear to feel the cold.

Before Covenant could try to stop her, the First sat down on the edge, braced herself, and dropped out of sight. Linden's gasp followed her away.

Fighting dizziness, he crouched to the ice and crept forward until he could look downward.

He arrived in time to see the First hit heavily into the sea. For an instant, white froth marked the water as if she were gone for good. Then she splashed back to the surface, waved a salute up at the company.

Now he noticed that the cliff was not sheer. Though it was too smooth to be climbed, it angled slightly outward from rim to base. And it was no more than two hundred feet high. Honninscrave's rope looked long enough to reach the water.

From the edge, Pitchwife grimaced down at his wife. "Desire me good fortune," he murmured. Weariness ached in his tone. "I am ill-made for such valors." Yet he did not falter. In a moment, he was at the First's side, and she held him strongly above the surface.

No one spoke. Covenant locked his teeth as if any word might unleash the panic crowding through him. Linden hugged herself and stared at nothing. Honninscrave and Mistweave were busy lashing their supplies more securely to the sleds. When they were done, the Master went straight to the cliff; but Mistweave paused beside Linden to reassure her. Gently, he touched her shoulder, smiled like a reminder of the way she had saved his life. Then he followed Honninscrave.

Covenant and Linden were left on the glacier with Cail, Vain, and the Appointed.

Gripping the rope, Cail nodded Covenant toward the sled.

Oh, hell! Covenant groaned. Vertigo squirmed through him. What if his hold failed? And what made the Giants think these sleds would float? But he had no choice. The *arghuleh* must be drawing nearer. And he had to reach the Land somehow, had to get to Revelstone. There was no other way.

The Giants had already committed themselves. For a moment, he turned toward Linden. But she had drawn down into herself, was striving to master her own trepidation.

Woodenly, he climbed into the sled.

As Covenant settled himself, tried to seal his numb fingers to the rails, brace his legs among the bundles, Cail looped his rope around Vain's ankles. Then he knotted the heavy line in both fists and set his back to the sled, began pushing it toward the cliff.

When the sled nosed over the edge, Linden panted, "Hold tight," as though she had just noticed what was happening. Covenant bit down on the inside of his cheek so hard that blood smeared his lips, stained the frost in his beard.

Slowly, Cail let the weight at the end of the rope pull him toward Vain again.

Vain had not moved a muscle: he seemed oblivious to the line hauling across the backs of his ankles. Reaching the Demondim-spawn, Cail stopped himself against Vain's black shins.

Without a tremor, the *Haruchai* lowered Covenant and the sled hand over hand down the face of the cliff.

Covenant chewed blood for a moment to control his fear; but soon the worst was over. His dizziness receded. Wedged among the supplies, he was in no danger of falling. Cail paid out the line with steady care. The rope cut small chunks out of the lip of the cliff; but Covenant hardly felt them hit. A shout of encouragement rose from Pitchwife. The dark sea looked as viscid as a malign chrism, but the four Giants swam in it as if it were only water. Pitchwife needed the First's support, but Honninscrave and Mistweave sculled themselves easily.

Honninscrave had placed himself in the path of the sled.

As its tip entered the water, he dodged below it and took the runners onto his shoulders. Rocking while he groped for a point of balance, the sled gradually became level. Then he steadied the runners, and Covenant found that the Master was carrying him.

Mistweave untied the rope so that Cail could draw it back up. Then Honninscrave started away from the wall of ice. The First said something to Covenant, but the lapping of the low waves muffled her voice.

Covenant hardly dared turn his head for fear of upsetting

Honninscrave's balance; but peripherally he watched Linden's descent. The thought that Vain might move hurt his chest. He felt faint with relief as the second sled came safely onto Mistweave's shoulders.

At a shout from the First, Cail dropped the rope, then slid down the ice-face to join the company.

Instinctively, Covenant fixed his attention like yearning on the low line of shore half a league away. The distance seemed too great. He did not know where Honninscrave and Mistweave would get the strength to bear the sleds so far. At any moment, the frigid hunger of the sea would surely drag them down.

Yet they struggled onward, though that crossing appeared cruel and interminable beyond endurance. The First upheld Pitchwife and did not weaken. Cail swam between the sleds, steadied them whenever Honninscrave or Mistweave wavered. If the seas had risen against them, they would have died. But the water and the current remained indifferent, too cold to notice such stark affrontery. In the name of the Search and Covenant Giantfriend and Linden Avery the Chosen, the Giants endured.

And they prevailed.

That night, the company camped on the hard shingle of the shore as if it were a haven.

SIX: Winter in Combat

FOR the first time since he had left the galley of Starfare's Gem, Covenant thought his bones might thaw. On this coast, the warmer currents which kept the sea free of ice moderated the winter's severity. The shingle was hard but not glacial. Clouds muffled the heavens, obscuring the lonely chill

of the stars. Mistweave's fire—tended by Cail because all the
Giants were too weary to fend off sleep—spread a benison
around the camp. Wrapped in his blankets, Covenant slept as
if he were at peace. And when he began to awaken in the stiff
gloom of the northern dawn, he would have been content to
simply eat a meal and then go back to sleep. The company
deserved at least one day of rest. The Giants had a right to it.

But as the dawn brightened, he forgot about rest. The
sunrise was hidden behind ranks of clouds, but it gave enough
light to reveal the broad mass of the glacier the company had
left behind. For a moment, the gray air made him uncertain
of what he was seeing. Then he became sure.

In the water, a spit of ice was growing out from the cliff—
from the same point at which the quest had left the glacier.
It was wide enough to be solid. And it was aimed like a
spear at the company's camp.

With an inward groan, he called the First. She joined him,
stood staring out at the ice for a long moment. Uselessly, he
hoped that her Giantish sight would contradict his unspoken
explanation. But it did not. "It appears," she said slowly,
"that the *arghuleh* remain intent upon us."

Damnation! Splinters of ice stuck in Covenant's memory.
Harshly, he asked, "How much time have we got?"

"I know not when they commenced this span," she replied.
"To gauge their speed is difficult. But I will be surprised to
behold them gain this shore ere the morrow."

He went on cursing for a while. But anger was as pointless
as hope. None of the companions objected as they repacked
the sleds for departure; the necessity was obvious. Linden
looked worn by the continuing strain of the journey, uncertain
of her courage. But the Giants had shed the worst of their
exhaustion. The light of attention and humor in Pitchwife's
eyes showed that he had begun to recover his essential spirit.
In spite of his repeated failures to match Cail, Mistweave bore
himself with an air of pride, as if he were looking forward
to the songs his people would sing about the feats of the
company. And the Master appeared to welcome the prospect
of the trek ahead as an anodyne for the immedicable gall of
his thoughts.

Covenant did not know how Vain and Findail had crossed
the water. But Vain's black blankness and the *Elohim*'s

Appointed's pain remained unaltered, dismissing the need for any explanation.

The company was still intact as it left the shore, started southwestward up the low sloping shingle to the uneven line of hills which edged the coast.

While the ground remained bare, Covenant and Linden walked beside Cail and the sleds. Though he was not in good shape, Covenant was glad for the chance to carry his own weight without having to fight the terrain. And he wanted to talk to Linden. He hoped she would tell him how she was doing. He had no ability to evaluate her condition for himself.

But beyond the hills lay a long, low plain; and there heavy snow began to fall. In moments, it obscured the horizons, wrapped isolation around the travelers, collected quickly at their feet. Soon it was thick enough to bear the sleds. The First urged Covenant and Linden to ride so that she would be free to amend her pace. Aided by her keen eyesight and her instinctive sense of terrain, she led her companions through the thick snowfall as if the way were familiar to her.

Toward midafternoon, the snow stopped, leaving the travelers alone in a featureless white expanse. Again, the First increased her pace, thrusting herself through the drifts at a speed which no other people could have matched afoot. Only the Ranyhyn, Covenant mused. Only Ranyhyn could have borne him with comparable alacrity to meet his doom. But the thought of the great horses gave him a pang. He remembered them as beasts of beautiful fidelity, one of the treasures of the Land. But they had been forced to flee the malison of the Sunbane. Perhaps they would never return. They might never get the chance.

That possibility brought him back to anger, reminded him that he was on his way to put an end to the Clave and the Banefire which served the Sunbane. He began to think about his purpose more clearly. He could not hope to take Revelstone by surprise. Lord Foul surely knew that the Unbeliever would come back to the Land, counted on Covenant's return for the fulfillment of his designs. But it was possible that neither the Despiser nor his Ravers understood how much damage Covenant intended to do along the way.

That had been Linden's idea. *Stop the Clave. Put out the Banefire. Some infections have to be cut out.* But he accepted it now, accepted it deep in the venom and marrow of his power. It gave him a use for his anger. And it offered him a chance to make the arduous and unfaltering service of the Giants mean something.

When he thought about such things, his right forearm itched avidly, and darkness rose in his gorge. For the first time since he had agreed to make the attempt, he was eager to reach Revelstone.

Two days later, the company still had not come to the end of the snow-cloaked plain.

Neither Linden's health-sense nor the Giants' sight had caught any glimpse of the *arghuleh*. Yet none of the companions doubted that they were being hunted. A nameless foreboding seemed to harry the sleds. Perhaps it arose from the sheer wide desolation of the plain, empty and barren. Or perhaps the whole company was infected by the rawness of Linden's nerves. She studied the winter—scented the air, scrutinized the clouds, tasted the snow—as though it had been given birth by strange forces, some of them unnatural; and yet she could not put words to the uneasiness of what she perceived. Somewhere in this wasteland, an obscure disaster foregathered. But she had no idea what it was.

The next day, however, mountains became visible to the east and south. And the day after that, the company rose up out of the plain, winding through low, rumpled foothills and valleys toward the ice-gnawed heights above them.

This range was not especially tall or harsh. Its peaks were old, and millennia of winter had worn them down. By sunset, the companions had gained a thousand feet of elevation, and the foothills and the plain were hidden behind them.

The following day, they were slowed to a crawl. While Covenant and Linden struggled through the snow on foot, the company worked from side to side up a rough, steep slope which disappeared into the gravid clouds and seemed to go on without end. But that ascent gave them another two thousand feet of altitude; and when it was over, they found themselves in a region that resembled rolling hills rather than true mountains. Time and cold had crumbled the crests which had once dominated this land; erosion had filled in the valleys. The First let the company camp early that night;

but the next morning she was brisk with hope for good progress.

"Unless we're completely lost," Covenant announced, "this should be the Northron Climbs." The simple familiarity of that name lifted his heart. He hardly dared believe he was right. "If it is, then eventually we're going to hit Landsdrop." Running generally northwestward through the Northron Climbs, the great cliff of Landsdrop formed the boundary between the Lower Land and the Upper.

But it also marked the border of the Sunbane; for the Sunbane arose and went west across the Upper Land from Lord Foul's covert in the depths of Mount Thunder, which straddled the midpoint of Landsdrop. When the company reached the cliff, they would cross back into the Despiser's power. Unless the Sunbane had not yet spread so far north.

However, Linden was not listening to Covenant. Her eyes studied the west as if she were obsessed with thoughts of disaster. Her voice conveyed an odd echo of memory as she murmured, "It's getting colder."

He felt a pang of fear. "It's the elevation," he argued. "We're a lot higher up than we were."

"Maybe." She seemed deaf to his apprehension. "I can't tell." She ran her fingers through her hair, tried to shake her perceptions into some semblance of clarity. "We're too far south for so much winter."

Remembering the way Lord Foul had once imposed winter on the Land in defiance of all natural Law, Covenant gritted his teeth and thought about fire.

For Linden was right: even his truncated senses could not mistake the deepening chill. Though there was no wind, the temperature seemed to plummet around him. During the course of the day, the snow became crusted and glazed. The air had a whetted edge that cut at his lungs. Whenever snow fell, it came down like thrown sand.

Once the surface had hardened enough to bear the Giants, their work became easier. They no longer needed to force a path through the thigh-deep freeze. As a consequence, their pace improved markedly. Yet the cold was bitter and penetrating. Covenant felt brittle with frost and incapacity, caught between ice and fire. When the company stopped for the night, he found that his blankets had frozen about him

like cerements. He had to squirm out of them as if he
were emerging from a cocoon in which nothing had been
transformed.

Pitchwife gave him a wry grin. "You are well protected,
Giantfriend." The words came in gouts of steam as if the
very sound of his voice had begun to freeze. "Ice itself is
also a ward from the cold."

But Covenant was looking at Linden. Her visage was raw,
and her lips trembled. "It's not possible," she said faintly.
"There can't be that many of them in the whole world."

No one had to ask her what she meant. After a moment,
the First breathed, "Is your perception of them certain,
Chosen?"

Linden nodded. The corners of her eyes were marked with
frost. "They're bringing this winter down with them."

In spite of the fire Mistweave built, Covenant felt that his
heart itself was freezing.

After that, the weather became too cold for snow. For a
day and a night, heavily laden clouds glowered overhead,
clogging the sky and the horizons. And then the sky turned
clear. The sleds bounced and slewed over the frozen surface
as if it were a new form of granite.

The First and Pitchwife no longer led the company.
Instead, they ranged away to the north to watch for *arghuleh*.
The previous night, she had suggested that they turn southward in order to flee the peril. But Covenant had refused. His
imprecise knowledge of the Land's geography indicated that
if the company went south they might not be able to avoid
Sarangrave Flat. So the travelers continued toward Revelstone;
and the First and Pitchwife kept what watch they could.

Shortly after noon, with the sun glaring balefully off the
packed white landscape and the still air as keen as a scourge,
the company entered a region where ragged heads and
splintered torsos of rock thrust thickly through the snow-pack,
raising their white-crowned caps and bitter sides like menhirs
in all directions. Honninscrave and Mistweave had to pick a
twisting way between the cromlechs, some of which stood
within a Giant's arm-span of each other; and the First and
Pitchwife were forced to draw closer to the company so that
they would not lose sight of the sleds.

Among the companions, Linden sat as tense as a scream

and muttered over and over again, "They're here. Jesus God. They're here."

But when the attack came, they had no warning of it. Linden's senses were foundering, overwhelmed by the sheer numbers and intensity of the cold. She was unable to pick specific dangers out of the general peril. And Pitchwife and the First were watching the north. The assault came from the south.

The company had entered a region which the *arghuleh* already controlled.

Honninscrave and Mistweave were striding through the center of a rude ring of tall stones, Mistweave on the Master's left, when two low hillocks across the circle rose to their feet. Maws clacking hungrily, the creatures shot forward a short distance, then stopped. One spun an instant web of ice which sprang at Mistweave's head; the other waited to give pursuit when the companions broke and ran.

Covenant's shout and Honninscrave's call rang out together. Impossibly surefooted on the iced snow, Mistweave and the Master leaped into a sprint. The jerk threw Covenant back in the sled. He grappled for the left railing, fought to pull himself upright. The First's answer echoed back; but she and Pitchwife were out of reach beyond the menhirs.

Then Linden's sled crashed against Covenant's. The impact almost pitched him out onto the snow.

Mistweave's burst of speed had taken him out from under the ice-web. But Linden was directly in its path. Heaving on the ropes, he tried to swing her aside. But Covenant's sled was in the way.

The next instant, the net came down on the lines and front of Linden's sled. Immediately, it froze. The lines became ice. When Mistweave hauled on them again, they snapped like icicles. Linden's head cracked forward, and she crumpled.

Cail had been between the sleds in his accustomed position. As the Giants had started into a run, he had run also, keeping himself between Covenant and the *arghuleh*. So even his *Haruchai* reflexes had not been enough to protect him as Mistweave had slewed Linden's sled to the side. Leaping to avoid the collision, he had come down squarely under the web.

His speed saved him from the full grasp of that ice. But

the net caught his left arm, binding him by the elbow to the sled.

Honninscrave had already pulled Covenant past Linden. Covenant had no time to shout for the Master to stop: the *arghule* was poised to launch another web. Venom seemed to slam through his forearm. With wild magic clenched in his half-fist, he swung to hurl power in Linden's defense.

In that instant, another *arghule* leaped from atop the nearest boulder and landed on Honninscrave. It bore him to the ground, buried him under sudden ice. Covenant's sled overturned. He sprawled to the crust practically within reach of the beast.

But his fear was fixed on Linden; he hardly comprehended his own peril. His head reeled. Shedding frost and snow in a flurry like a small explosion, a precursor of the blast within him, he surged to his feet.

Stark and lorn against the bare white, she still sat in her trapped sled. She was not moving. The rapacious cold of the *arghuleh* overloaded her nerves, cast her back into her atavistic, immobilizing panic. For an instant, she bore no resemblance to the woman he had learned to love. Rather, she looked like Joan. At once, the inextricable venom/passion of his power thronged through him, and he became ready to tear down the very cromlechs and rive the whole region if necessary to protect her.

But Mistweave was in his way.

The Giant had not moved from the spot where he had stumbled to a halt. His head jerked from side to side as his attention snapped frantically between Linden's plight and Honninscrave's. Linden had once saved his life. He had left Starfare's Gem to take Cail's place at her side. Yet Honninscrave was the Master. Caught between irreconcilable exigencies, Mistweave could not choose. Helplessly, he blocked Covenant from the *arghuleh* behind him.

"*Move!*" Fury and cold ripped the cry from Covenant's throat.

But Mistweave was aware of nothing except the choice he was unable to make. He did not move.

Over his right shoulder arced a second web. Gaining size and thickness as it sailed, it spread toward Linden. Its chill left a trail of frost across Covenant's sight.

Cail had not been able to free his left arm. But he saw the

net coming like all the failures of the *Haruchai*—Hergrom's slaughter and Ceer's death and the siren song of the *merewives* encapsulated in one peril—and he drew himself up as if he were the last of his people left alive, the last man sworn to succeed or die. His thews bunched, strained, stood out like bone—and his arm broke loose, still encased in a hunk of ice as big as a Giant's head.

Swinging that chunk like a mace, he leaped above Linden and shattered the web before it reached her.

She gaped through the spray of splinters as if she had gone blind.

Before Covenant could react, the second *arghule* behind Mistweave reared up and ripped the Giant down under its frigid bulk.

Then the First landed like the plunge of a hawk on the beast holding Honninscrave. Pitchwife dashed around one of the boulders toward Linden and Cail. And Covenant let out a tearing howl of power that blasted the first *arghule* to pieces in one sharp bolt like a rave of lightning.

From somewhere nearby, Findail gave a thin cry:

"Fool!"

Over her shoulder, the Swordmain panted, "We are hunted!" Hammering and heaving at the ice, she fought to pull Honninscrave free. "The *arghuleh* are many! A great many!" Honninscrave lay among the ruins of the beast as if it had succeeded at smothering him. But as the First man-handled him upright, a harsh shudder ran through him. All at once, he took his own weight, staggered to his feet.

"We must flee!" she cried.

Covenant was too far gone to heed her. Linden was safe, at least momentarily. Pitchwife had already snapped the ice from Cail's arm; and the two of them could ward her for a little while. Tall and bright with fire, he stalked toward the beast still struggling to subdue Mistweave. Whatever force or change had overcome the native hate of the *arghuleh* had also left them blind to fear or self-preservation. The creature did not cease its attack on Mistweave until Covenant burned its life to water.

In his passion, he wanted to turn and shout until the menhirs trembled, Come on! Come and get me! The scars on his forearm shone like fangs. I'll kill you all! They had dared to assail Linden.

But she had come back to herself now, had found her way out of her old paralysis. She was running toward him; and she was saying, crying, "No! That's enough! You've done enough. Don't let go!"

He tried to hear her. Her face was sharp with urgency; and she came toward him as if she meant to throw herself into his arms. He had to hear her. There was too much at stake.

But he could not. Behind her were more *arghuleh*.

Pitchwife had rushed to help Mistweave. Cail was at Linden's side. Fighting to draw the sleds after them, the First and a dazed Honninscrave scrambled to form a cordon around Covenant and Linden. Findail had disappeared. Only Vain stood motionless.

And from every side at once charged the vicious ice-beasts, crowding between the monoliths, a score of them, twoscore, as if each of them wanted to be the first to feast on warm flesh. As if they had come in answer to Covenant's call. Enough of them to devour even Giants. Without wild magic, none of the company except Vain had any chance to survive.

Something like an avid chuckle spattered across the background of Covenant's mind. In his own way, he was hungry for violence, fervid for a chance to stuff his helplessness back down the Despiser's throat. Thrusting Linden behind him, he went out to meet his attackers.

His companions did not protest. They had no other hope.

Bastards! he panted at the *arghuleh*. They were all around him, but he could barely see them. His brain had gone black with venom. Come and get me!

Abruptly, the First shouted something—a call of warning or surprise. Covenant did not hear the words; but the iron in her voice made him turn to see what she had seen.

Then plain shock stopped him.

From the south side of the ring, gray shapes smaller than he was appeared among the *arghuleh*. They were roughly human in form, although their arms and legs were oddly proportioned. But their unclad bodies were hairless; their pointed ears sat high on the sides of their bald skulls. And they had no eyes. Wide flat nostrils marked their faces above their slitted mouths.

Barking in a strange tongue, they danced swiftly around the *arghuleh*. Each of them carried a short, slim piece of black metal like a wand which splashed a vitriolic fluid at the ice-beasts.

That liquid threw the *arghuleh* into confusion. It burned them, broke sections off their backs, chewed down into their bodies. Clattering in pain, they forgot their prey, thrashed and writhed blindly in all directions. Some of them collided with the cromlechs, lost larger sections of themselves, died. But others, reacting with desperate instinct, covered themselves with their own ice and were able to stanch their wounds.

Softly, as if at last even he had become capable of surprise, Cail murmured, "Waynhim. The old tellers speak of such creatures."

Covenant recognized them. Like the ur-viles, they were the artificial creations of the Demondim. But they had dedicated themselves and their weird lore to pursuits which did not serve the Despiser. During Covenant's trek toward Revelstone, a band of Waynhim had saved him from a venom-relapse and death. But that had occurred hundreds of leagues to the south.

Swiftly, the creatures girdled the company, dashing the fluid of their power at the *arghuleh*.

Then Covenant heard his name called by an unexpected voice. Turning, he saw a man emerge between the southward rocks. "Thomas Covenant!" the man shouted once more. "Come! Flee! We are unready for this battle!"

A man whose soft brown eyes, human face, and loss-learned kindness had once given Covenant a taste of both mercy and hope. A man who had been rescued by the Waynhim when the na-Mhoram's *Grim* had destroyed his home, During Stonedown. A man who served these creatures and understood them and loved them.

Hamako.

Covenant tried to shout, run forward. But he failed. The first instant of recognition was followed by a hot rush of pain as the implications of this encounter reached him. There was no reason why Hamako and this Waynhim *rhysh* should be so far from home—no reason which was not terrible.

But the plight of the company demanded speed, decision. More *arghuleh* were arriving from the north. And more of those which had been damaged were discovering the expedient of using their ice to heal themselves. When Cail caught him by the arm, Covenant allowed himself to be impelled toward Hamako.

Linden trotted at his side. Her face was set with purpose now. Perhaps she had identified Hamako and the Waynhim from Covenant's descriptions of them. Or perhaps her percipience told her all she needed to know. When Covenant seemed to lag, she grasped his other arm and helped Cail draw him forward.

The Giants followed, pulling the sleds. Vain broke into a run to catch up with the company. Behind them, the Waynhim retreated from the greater numbers of the *arghuleh*.

In a moment, they reached Hamako. He greeted Covenant with a quick smile. "Well met, ring-wielder," he said. "You are an unlooked-for benison in this waste." Then at once he added, "Come!" and swung away from the ring. Flanked by Waynhim, he ran into the maze of the menhirs.

Covenant's numb feet and heavy boots found no purchase on the snow-pack. Repeatedly, he slipped and stumbled as he tried to dodge after Hamako among the rocks. But Cail gripped his arm, upheld him. Linden moved with small quick strides which enabled her to keep her footing.

At the rear of the company, several Waynhim fought a delaying action against the *arghuleh*. But abruptly the ice-beasts gave up the chase as if they had been called back—as if whatever force commanded them did not want to risk sending them into ambush. Shortly, one of the gray, Demondim-made creatures spoke to Hamako; and he slowed his pace.

Covenant pushed forward to the man's side. Burning with memory and dread, he wanted to shout, Well met like hell! What in blood and damnation are you *doing* here? But he owed Hamako too much past and present gratitude. Instead, he panted, "Your timing's getting better. How did you know we needed you?"

Hamako grimaced at Covenant's reference to their previous meeting, when his *rhysh* had arrived too late to aid the ring-wielder. But he replied as if he understood the spirit of Covenant's gibe, "We did not.

"The tale of your departure from the Land is told among the Waynhim." He grinned momentarily. "To such cunning watchers as they are, your passage from Revelstone to the Lower Land and Seareach was as plain as fire." Swinging around another boulder into a broad avenue among the stones, he continued, "But we knew naught of your return. Our watch was set rather upon these *arghuleh*, that come massed from the north in defiance of all Law, seeking ruin. Witnessing them gather here, we sought to discover their purpose. Thus at last we saw you. Well that we did so—and that our numbers sufficed to aid you. The mustering-place of the *rhysh* is not greatly distant"—he gestured ahead—"but distant enough to leave you unsuccored in your need."

Listening hard, Covenant grappled with his questions. But there were too many of them. And the cold bit into his lungs at every breath. With an effort of will, he concentrated on keeping his legs moving and schooled himself to wait.

Then the group left the region of jumbled monoliths and entered a wide, white plain that ended half a league away in an escarpment which cut directly across the vista of the south. Eddies of wind skirled up and down the base of the escarpment, raising loose snow like dervishes; and Hamako headed toward them as if they were the signposts of a sanctuary.

When Covenant arrived, weak-kneed and gasping for air, at the rock-strewn foot of the sheer rise, he was too tired to be surprised by the discovery that the snow-devils were indeed markers or sentinels of an eldritch kind. The Waynhim called out in their barking tongue; and the eddies obeyed, moving to stand like hallucinated columns on either side of a line that led right into the face of the escarpment. There, without transition, an entrance appeared. It was wide enough to admit the company, but too low to let the Giants enter upright; and it opened into a tunnel warmly lit by flaming iron censers.

Smiling a welcome, Hamako said, "This is the mustering-place of the Waynhim, their *rhyshyshim*. Enter without fear, for here the ring-wielder is acknowledged, and the foes of the Land are withheld. In these times, there is no true safety anywhere. But here you will find reliable sanctuary for one more day—until the gathered *rhysh* come finally to their purpose. To me it has been granted to speak for all Waynhim that share this Weird. Enter and be welcome."

In response, the First bowed formally. "We do so gladly. Already your aid has been a boon which we are baffled to repay. In sharing counsel and stories and safety, we hope to make what return we may."

Hamako bowed in turn: his eyes gleamed pleasure at her courtesy. Then he led the company down into the tunnel.

When Vain and the last of the Waynhim had passed inward, the entrance disappeared, again without transition, leaving in its place blunt, raw rock that sealed the company into the firelight and blissful warmth of the *rhyshyshim*.

At first, Covenant hardly noticed that Findail had rejoined them. But the Appointed was there as if Vain's side were a post he had never deserted. His appearance drew a brief, muted chittering from the Waynhim; but then they ignored him as if he were simply a shadow of the black Demondim-spawn.

For a few moments, the tunnel was full of the wooden scraping of the sleds' runners. But when the companions reached a bulge in the passage like a rude antechamber, Hamako instructed the Giants to leave the sleds there.

As the warmth healed Covenant's sore respiration, he thought that now Hamako would begin to ask the expected questions. But the man and the Waynhim bore themselves as if they had come to the end of all questions. Looking at Hamako more closely, Covenant saw things which had been absent or less pronounced during their previous encounter—resignation, resolve, a kind of peace. Hamako looked like a man who had passed through a long grief and been annealed.

With a small jolt, Covenant realized that Hamako was not dressed for winter. Only the worn swath of leather around his hips made him less naked than the Waynhim. In vague fear, Covenant wondered if the Stonedownor had truly become Waynhim himself? What did such a transformation mean?

And what in hell was this *rhysh* doing here?

His companions had less reason for apprehension. Pitchwife moved as if the Waynhim had restored his sense of adventure, his capacity for excitement. His eyes watched everything, eager for marvels. Warm air and the prospect of safety softened the First's iron sternness, and she walked with her hand lightly on her husband's shoulder, willing to accept whatever she saw. Honninscrave's thoughts were hidden beneath the concealment of his brows. And Mistweave—

At the sight of Mistweave's face, Covenant winced. Too much had happened too swiftly. He had nearly forgotten the tormented moment of Mistweave's indecision. But the Giant's visage bore the marks of that failure like toolwork at the corners of his eyes, down the sides of his mouth—marks cut into the bone of his self-esteem. His gaze turned away from Covenant's in shame.

Damn it to hell! Covenant rasped to himself. Is every one of us doomed?

Perhaps they all were. Linden walked at his side without looking at him, her mien pale and strict with the characteristic severity which he had learned to interpret as fear. Fear of herself—of her inherited capacity for panic and horror, which had proved once again that it could paralyze her despite every commitment or affirmation she made. Perhaps her reaction to the ambush of the *arghuleh* had restored her belief that she, too, was doomed.

It was unjust. She judged that her whole life had been a form of flight, an expression of moral panic. But in that she was wrong. Her past sins did not invalidate her present desire for good. If they did, then Covenant himself was damned as well as doomed, and Lord Foul's triumph was already assured.

Covenant was familiar with despair. He accepted it in himself. But he could not bear it in the people he loved. They deserved better.

Then Hamako's branching way through the rock turned a corner to enter a sizable cavern like a meeting-hall; and Covenant's attention was pulled out of its galled channel.

The space was large and high enough to have held the entire crew of Starfare's Gem; but its rough walls and surfaces testified that the Waynhim had not been using it long. Yet it was comfortably well-lit. Many braziers flamed around the walls, shedding kind heat as well as illumination. For a moment, Covenant found himself wondering obliquely why the Waynhim bothered to provide light at all, since they had no eyes. Did the fires aid their lore in some fashion? Or did they draw a simple solace from the heat or scent of the flames? Certainly the former habitation of Hamako's *rhysh* had been bright with warmth and firelight.

But Covenant could not remember that place and remain calm. And he had never seen so many Waynhim before: at least threescore of them slept on the bare stone, worked together around black metal pots as if they were preparing *vitrim* or invocations, or quietly waited for what they might learn about the people Hamako had brought. *Rhysh* was the Waynhim word for a community; and Covenant had been told that each community usually numbered between one-

and twoscore Waynhim who shared a specific interpretation of their racial Weird, their native definition of identity and reason for existence. This Weird, he remembered, belonged to both the Waynhim and the ur-viles, but was read in vastly different ways. So he was looking at at least two *rhysh*. And Hamako had implied that there were more. More communities which had been ripped from home and service by the same terrible necessity that had brought Hamako's *rhysh* here?

Covenant groaned as he accompanied Hamako into the center of the cavern.

There the Stonedownor addressed the company again. "I know that the purpose which impels you toward the Land is urgent," he said in his gentle and pain-familiar voice. "But some little time you can spare among us. The horde of the *arghuleh* is unruly and advances with no great speed. We offer you sustenance, safety, and rest as well as inquiries"— he looked squarely at Covenant—"and perhaps also answers." That suggestion gave another twist to Covenant's tension. He remembered clearly the question Hamako had refused to answer for him. But Hamako had not paused. He was asking, "Will you consent to delay your way a while?"

The First glanced at Covenant. But Covenant had no intention of leaving until he knew more. "Hamako," he said grimly, "why are you here?"

The loss and resolution behind Hamako's eyes showed that he understood. But he postponed his reply by inviting the company to sit with him on the floor. Then he offered around bowls of the dark, musty *vitrim* liquid which looked like vitriol and yet gave nourishment like a distillation of *aliantha*. And when the companions had satisfied their initial hunger and weariness, he spoke as if he had deliberately missed Covenant's meaning.

"Ring-wielder," he said, "with four other *rhysh* we have come to give battle to the *arghuleh*."

"Battle?" Covenant demanded sharply. He had always known the Waynhim as creatures of peace.

"Yes." Hamako had traveled a journey to this place which could not be measured in leagues. "That is our intent."

Covenant started to expostulate. Hamako stopped him with a firm gesture. "Though the Waynhim serve peace," he said carefully, "they have risen to combat when their Weird required it of them. Thomas Covenant. I have spoken to you concerning that Weird. The Waynhim are made creatures. They have not the justification of birth for their existence, but only the imperfect lores and choices of the Demondim. And from this trunk grow no boughs but two—the way of the ur-viles, who loathe what they are and seek forever power and knowledge to become what they are not, and the way of the Waynhim, who strive to give value to what they are through service to what they are not, to the birth by Law and beauty of the life of the Land. This you know."

Yes. I know. But Covenant's throat closed as he recalled the manner in which Hamako's *rhysh* had formerly served its Weird.

"Also you know," the Stonedownor went on, "that in the time of the great High Lord Mhoram, and of your own last battle against the Despiser, Waynhim saw and accepted the need to wage violence in defense of the Land. It was their foray which opened the path by which the High Lord procured the survival of Revelstone." His gaze held Covenant's though Covenant could hardly match him. "Therefore do not accuse us that we have risen to violence again. It is not fault in the Waynhim. It is grief."

And still he forestalled Covenant's protest, did not answer Covenant's fundamental question. "The Sunbane and the Despiser's malign intent rouse the dark forces of the Earth. Though they act by their own will, they serve his design of destruction. And such a force has come among the *arghuleh*, mastering their native savagery and sending them like the hand of winter against the Land. We know not the name of that might. It is hidden from the insight of the Waynhim. But we see it. And we have gathered in this *rhyshyshim* to oppose it."

"How?" the First interposed. "How will you oppose it?" When Hamako turned toward her, she said, "I ask pardon if I intrude on that which does not concern me. But you have given us the gift of our lives, and we have not returned the bare courtesy of our names and knowledge." Briefly, she introduced her companions. Then she continued, "I am the First of the Search—a Swordmain of the Giants. Battle is my craft and my purpose." Her countenance was sharp in the firelight. "I would share counsel with you concerning this combat."

Hamako nodded. But his reply suggested politeness rather than any hope for help or guidance—the politeness of a man who had looked at his fate and approved of it.

"In the name of these *rhysh*, I thank you. Our intent is simple. Many of the Waynhim are now abroad, harrying the *arghuleh* to lure them hither. In this they succeed. That massed horde we will meet on the outer plain upon the morrow. There the Waynhim will concert their might and strike inward among the ice-beasts, seeking the dark heart of the force which rules them. If we discover that heart—and are equal to its destruction—then will the *arghuleh* be scattered, becoming once more their own prey.

"If we fail—" The Stonedownor shrugged. There was no fear in his face. "We will at least weaken that horde sorely ere we die."

The First was faster than Covenant. "Hamako," she said, "I like this not. It is a tactic of desperation. It offers no second hope in event of first failure."

But Hamako did not waver. "Giant, we are desperate. At our backs lies naught but the Sunbane, and against that ill we are powerless. Wherefore should we desire any second hope? All else has been rent from us. It is enough to strike this blow as best we may."

The First had no answer for him. Slowly, his gaze left her, returned to Covenant. His brown eyes seemed as soft as weeping—and yet too hard to be daunted. "Because I have been twice bereft," he said in that kind and unbreachable voice, "I have been granted to stand at the forefront, forging the puissance of five *rhysh* with my mortal hands."

Then Covenant saw that now at last he would be allowed to ask his true question; and for an instant his courage failed. How could he bear to hear what had happened to Hamako? Such extravagant human valor came from several sources—and one of them was despair.

But Hamako's eyes held no flinch of self-pity. Covenant's companions were watching him, sensitive to the importance of what lay between him and Hamako. Even Mistweave and Honninscrave showed concern; and Linden's visage ached as if Hamako's rue were poignant to her. With a wrench of will, Covenant denied his fear.

"You still haven't told me." Strain made his tone harsh. "All this is fine. I even understand it." He was intimately familiar with desperation. In the warmth of the cavern, he had begun to sweat. "But why in the name of every good and beautiful thing you've ever done in your life are you here at all? Even the threat of that many *arghuleh* can't compare with what you were doing before."

The bare memory filled his throat with inextricable wonder and sorrow.

Lord Foul had already destroyed virtually all the natural life of the Land. Only Andelain remained, preserved against corruption by Caer-Caveral's power. Everything else that grew by Law or love from seed or egg or birth had been perverted.

Everything except that which Hamako's *rhysh* had kept alive.

In a cavern which was huge on the scale of lone human beings, but still paltry when measured by the destitution of the Land, the Waynhim had nurtured a garden that contained every kind of grass, shrub, flower, and tree, vine, grain, and vegetable they had been able to find and sustain. And in another cave, in a warren of pens and dens, they had saved as many species of animal as their lore and skill allowed.

It was an incomparable expression of faith in the future, of hope for the time when the Sunbane would be healed and the Land might be dependent upon this one tiny pocket of natural life for its renewal.

And it was gone. From the moment when he had recognized Hamako, Covenant had known the truth. Why else were the Waynhim here, instead of tending to their chosen work?

Useless rage cramped his chest, and his courage felt as brittle as dead bone, as he waited for Hamako's response.

It was slow in coming; but even now the Stonedownor did not waver. "It is as you have feared," he said softly. "We were driven from our place, and the work of our lives was destroyed." Then for the first time his voice gave a hint of anger. "Yet you have not feared enough. That ruin did not befall us alone. Across all the Land, every *rhysh* was beaten from its place and its work. The Waynhim gathered here are all that remain of their race. There will be no more."

At that, Covenant wanted to cry out, plead, protest, No! Not again! Was not the genocide of the Unhomed enough? How could the Land sustain another such loss?

But Hamako seemed to see Covenant's thoughts in his aghast face. "You err, ring-wielder," said the Stonedownor grimly. "Against Ravers and the Despiser, we were fore-warned and defended. And Lord Foul had no cause to fear us. We were too paltry to give him threat. No. It was the ur-viles, the black and birthless kindred of the Waynhim, that wrought our ruin from *rhysh* to *rhysh* across the Land."

Wrought our ruin. Our ruin across the Land. Covenant was no longer looking at Hamako. He could not. All that beauty. Gone to grief where all dreams go. If he met those soft, brown, irreparable eyes, he would surely begin to weep.

"Their assault was enabled to succeed because we did not expect it—for had not ur-vile and Waynhim lived in truce during all the millennia of their existence?—and because they have studied destruction as the Waynhim have not." Slowly, the edge of his tone was blunted. "We were fortunate in our way. Many of us were slain—among them some that you have known. *Vraith, dhurng, ghramin*." He spoke the names as if he knew how they would strike Covenant; for those were Waynhim who had given their blood so that he could reach Revelstone in time to rescue Linden, Sunder, and Hollian. "But many escaped. Other *rhysh* were butchered entirely.

"Those Waynhim that survived wandered without purpose until they encountered others to form new *rhysh*, for a Waynhim without community is a lorn thing, deprived of meaning. And therefore," he concluded, "we are desperate in all sooth. We are the last. After us there will be no more."

"But why?" Covenant asked his knotted hands and the blurred light, his voice as thick as blood in his throat. "Why did they attack—? After all those centuries?"

"Because—" Hamako replied; and now he did falter, caught by the pain behind his resolve. "Because we gave you shelter—and with you that making of the ur-viles which they name Vain."

Covenant's head jerked up, eyes afire with protests. This crime at least should not be laid to his charge, though instinctively he believed it. He had never learned how to repudiate any accusation. But at once Hamako said, "Ah, no, Thomas Covenant. Your pardon. I have led you to miscom-prehend me." His voice resumed the impenetrable gentleness of a man who had lost too much. "The fault was neither yours nor ours. Even at Lord Foul's command the ur-viles would not have wrought such harm upon us for merely sheltering you and any companion. Do not think it. Their rage had another source."

"What was it?" Covenant breathed. "What in hell happened?"

Hamako shrugged at the sheer simplicity of the answer. "It was their conviction that you gained from us an explanation of Vain Demondim-spawn's purpose."

"But I didn't!" objected Covenant. "You wouldn't tell me."

The Waynhim had commanded Hamako to silence. He had only replied, *Were I to reveal the purpose of this Demondim-spawn, that revelation could well prevent the accomplishment of his purpose.* And, *That purpose is greatly desirable.*

Now he sighed. "Yes. But how could our refusal be conveyed to the ur-viles? Their loathing permitted them no understanding of our Weird. And they did not inquire of us what we had done. In our place, they would not have scrupled to utter falsehood. Therefore they could not have believed any reply we gave. So they brought down retribution upon us, compelled by the passion of their desire that the secret of this Vain not be untimely revealed."

And Vain stood behind the seated company as if he were deaf or impervious. The dead wood of his right forearm dangled from his elbow; but his useless hand was still undamaged, immaculate. As beautifully sculpted as a mockery of Covenant's flawed being.

But Hamako did not flinch or quail again, though his somber gaze now held a dusky hue of fear.

"Thomas Covenant," he said, his voice so soft that it barely carried across the circle of the company. "Ring-wielder." His home, During Stonedown, had been destroyed by the na-Mhoram's *Grim;* but the Waynhim had given him a new home with them. And then that new home had been destroyed, ravaged for something the *rhysh* had not done. *Twice bereft.* "Will you ask once more? Will you inquire of me here the purpose of this black Demondim-spawn?"

At that, Linden sat up straighter, bit her lips to hold back the question. The First tensed, anticipating explanations. Pitchwife's eyes sparkled like hope; even Mistweave stirred from his gloom. Cail cocked one dispassionate eyebrow.

But Covenant sat like Honninscrave, his emotions tangled by Hamako's apprehension. He understood the Stonedownor, knew what Hamako's indirect offer meant. The Waynhim no longer trusted their former refusal—were no longer able to credit the unmalice of the ur-viles' intent. The violence of their ruin had shaken them fundamentally. And yet their basic perceptions remained. The trepidation in Hamako's visage showed that he had learned to dread the implications of both speaking and not speaking.

He was asking Covenant to take the responsibility of decision from him.

He and his *rhysh* had come here to die. Fiercely, with all the attention of the company on him, Covenant forced himself to say, "No."

His gaze burned as he confronted Hamako across the rude stone. "You've already refused once." Within himself, he swore bitterly at the necessity which compelled him to reject everything that might help or ease or guide him. But he did not shrink from it. "I trust you."

Linden gave him a glare of exasperation. Pitchwife's face widened in surprise. But Hamako's rue-worn features softened with undisguised relief.

Later, while Covenant's companions rested or slept in the warmth of the cavern, Hamako took the Unbeliever aside for a private conversation. Gently, Hamako urged Covenant to depart before the coming battle. Night was upon the Northron Climbs, the night before the dark of the moon; but a Waynhim could be spared to guide the company up the escarpment toward the relative safety of Landsdrop. The quest would be able to travel without any immediate fear of the *arghuleh*.

Covenant refused brusquely. "You've done too much for me already. I'm not going to leave you like this."

Hamako peered into Covenant's clenched glower. After a moment, the Stonedownor breathed. "Ah, Thomas Covenant. Will you hazard the wild magic to aid us?"

Covenant's reply was blunt. "Not if I can help it." If he had heeded the venom coursing in him, the itch of his scarred forearm, he would already have gone out to meet the *arghuleh* alone. "But my friends aren't exactly useless." And I don't intend to watch you die for nothing.

He knew he had no right to make such promises. The meaning of Hamako's life, of the lives of the gathered Waynhim, was not his to preserve or sacrifice. But he was who he was. How could he refuse to aid the people who needed him?

Scowling at unresolved contradictions, he studied the creatures. With their eyeless faces, gaping nostrils, and limbs made for running on all fours, they looked more like beasts or monsters than members of a noble race that had given its entire history to the service of the Land. But long ago one of them had been indirectly responsible for his second summons to the Land. Savagely maimed and in hideous pain, that Waynhim had been released from the Despiser's clutches to bait a trap. It had reached the Lords and told them that Lord Foul's armies were ready to march. Therefore High Lord Elena had made the decision to call Covenant. Thus the Despiser had arranged for Covenant's return. And the logic of that return had led ineluctably to Elena's end, the breaking of the Law of Death, and the destruction of the Staff of Law.

Now the last of the Waynhim people stood on the verge of ruin.

A long time passed before Covenant was able to sleep. He saw all too clearly what Lord Foul might hope to gain from the plight of the Waynhim.

But when his grasp on consciousness frayed away, the *vitrim* he had consumed carried him into deep rest; and he slept until the activity around him became constant and exigent. Raising his head, he found that the cavern was full of Waynhim—at least twice as many as he had seen earlier. The bleary look in Linden's face showed that she had just awakened; but the four Giants were up and moving tensely among the Waynhim.

Pitchwife came over to Linden and Covenant. "You have slept well, my friends," he said, chuckling as if he were inured to the expectancy which filled the air. "Stone and Sea! this *vitrim* is a hale beverage. A touch of its savor commingled with our *diamondraught* would gladden even the dullest palate. Life be praised, I have at last found the role which will make my name forever sung among the Giants. Behold!" With a flourish, he indicated his belt, which was behung on all sides with leather *vitrim*-skins. "It will be my dear task to bear this roborant to my people, that they may profit from its potency in the blending of a new liquor. And that unsurpassable draught will be named *pitchbrew* for all the Earth to adore."

He laughed. "Then will my fame outmeasure even that of great Bahgoon himself!"

The misshapen Giant's banter drew a smile from Linden. But Covenant had climbed out of sleep into the same mood with which the peril of the Waynhim had first afflicted him. Frowning at Pitchwife's humor, he demanded, "What's going on?"

The Giant sobered rapidly. "Ah, Giantfriend," he sighed, "you have slept long and long. Noon has come to the wasteland, and the Waynhim are gathered to prepare for battle. Although the *arghuleh* advance slowly, they are now within sight of this covert. I conceive that the outcome of their conflict will be determined ere sunset."

Covenant swore to himself. He did not want the crisis to be so near at hand.

Linden was facing him. In her controlled, professional voice, she said, "There's still time."

"Time to get out of here?" he returned sourly. "Let them go out there and probably get butchered as a race without so much as one sympathetic witness to at least grieve? Forget it."

Her eyes flared. "That isn't what I meant." Anger sharpened the lines of her face. "I don't like deserting people any more than you do. Maybe I don't have your *background*"—she snarled the word—"but I can still *see* what Hamako and the Waynhim are worth. You know me better than that." Then she took a deep breath, steadied herself. Still glaring at him, she said, "What I meant was, there's still time to ask them about Vain."

Covenant felt like a knotted thunderhead, livid and incapable of release. Her pointed jibe about his background underscored the extent to which he had falsified their relationship. From the time of their first meeting on Haven Farm, he had withheld things from her, arguing that she did not have the background to understand them. And this was the result. Everything he said to or heard from the woman he loved became gall.

But he could not afford release. Lord Foul was probably already gloating at the possibility that he, Covenant, might unleash wild magic to aid the Waynhim. Grimly, he stifled his desire to make some acerbic retort. Instead, he replied, "No. I don't want to hear it from Hamako. I don't want to let Findail off the hook."

Deliberately, he turned toward the Appointed. But Findail met him with the same trammeled and impenetrable rue with which he had rebuffed every challenge or appeal. More to answer Linden than to attack Findail, Covenant concluded, "I'm waiting for this bloody *Elohim* to discover the honesty if not the simple decency to start telling the truth."

Findail's yellow eyes darkened; but he said nothing.

Linden looked back and forth between Covenant and the Appointed. Then she nodded. Speaking as if Findail were not present, she said, "I hope he makes up his mind soon. I don't like the idea of having to face the Clave when they still know more about Vain than we do."

Grateful for at least that much acceptance from her, Covenant tried to smile. But he achieved only a grimace.

The Waynhim were milling around the cavern, moving as if each of them wanted to speak to every one else before the crisis; and their low, barking voices thickened the atmosphere. But the Giants were no longer among them. Honninscrave leaned against one wall, detached and lonely, his head bowed. Pitchwife had remained with Covenant, Linden, and Cail. And the First and Mistweave stood together near the opposite side of the space. Mistweave's stance was one of pleading; but the First met whatever he said angrily. When he beseeched her further, her reply cracked over the noise of the Waynhim.

"You are mortal, Giant. Such choices are harsh to any who must make them. But failure is only failure. It is not unworth. You are sworn and dedicate to the Search, if not to the Chosen, and I will not release you."

Sternly, she left his plain dismay, marched through the throng toward the rest of her companions. When she reached them, she answered their mute questions by saying, "He is shamed." She looked at Linden. "His life you saved when Covenant Giantfriend's was at risk. Now he deems that his indecision in your need is unpardonable. He asks to be given to the Waynhim, that he may seek expiation in their battle." Unnecessarily, she added, "I have refused him."

Linden muttered a curse. "I didn't ask him to serve me. He doesn't need—"

Abruptly, she cried, "Honninscrave! Don't!" But the Master did not heed her. Fury clenched in his fists, he strode toward Mistweave as though he meant to punish the Giant's distress.

Linden started after him; the First stopped her. In silence, they watched as Honninscrave stalked up to his crewmember. Confronting Mistweave, the Master stabbed one massive finger at the Giant's sore heart as if he knew the exact location of Mistweave's bafflement. His jaws chewed excoriations; but the interchanges of the Waynhim covered his voice.

Softly, the First said, "He is the Master. It is enough for me that he has found room in his own pain for Mistweave. He will do no true harm to one who has served him aboard Starfare's Gem."

Linden nodded. But her mouth was tight with frustration and empathy, and she did not take her eyes off Mistweave.

At first, Mistweave flinched from what Honninscrave was saying. Then a hot belligerence rose up in him, and he raised one fist like a threat. But Honninscrave caught hold of Mistweave's arm and snatched it down, thrust his jutting beard into Mistweave's face. After a moment, Mistweave acquiesced. His eyes did not lose their heat; but he accepted the stricture Honninscrave placed upon him. Slowly, the ire faded from the Master's stance.

Covenant let a sigh through his teeth.

Then Hamako appeared among the Waynhim, came toward the company. His gaze was bright in the light of the braziers. His movements hinted at fever or anticipation. In his hands he bore a long scimitar that looked like it had been fashioned of old bone. Without preamble, he said, "The time has come. The *arghuleh* draw nigh. We must issue forth to give combat. What will you do? You must not remain here. There is no other egress, and if the entrance is sealed you will be ensnared."

The First started to reply; but Covenant forestalled her. Venom nagged at the skin of his forearm. "We'll follow you out," he said roughly. "We're going to watch until we figure out the best way to help." To the protest in Hamako's mien, he added, "Stop worrying about us. We've survived worse. If everything else goes to hell and damnation, we'll find some way to escape."

A grin momentarily softened Hamako's tension. "Thomas Covenant," he said in a voice like a salute, "I would that we had met in kinder times." Then he raised his scimitar, turned on his heel, and started toward the throat of the cavern.

Bearing curved, bony daggers like smaller versions of Hamako's blade, all the Waynhim followed him as if they had chosen him to lead them to their doom.

They numbered nearly two hundred, but they needed only a few moments to march out of the cavern, leaving the company behind in the undiminished firelight.

Honninscrave and Mistweave came to join their companions. The First looked at Covenant and Linden, then at the other Giants. None of them demurred. Linden's face was pale, but she held herself firm. Pitchwife's features worked as if he could not find the right jest to ease his tension. In their separate ways, the First, Mistweave, and Honninscrave looked as unbreachable as Cail.

Covenant nodded bitterly. Together, he and his friends turned their backs on warmth and safety, went out to meet the winter.

In the tunnel, he felt the temperature begin to drop almost immediately. The change made no difference to his numb fingers and feet; but he sashed his robe tight as if in that way he might be able to protect his courage. Past the branchings of the passage he followed the Waynhim until the company reached the rude antechamber where the sleds were. Mutely, Honninscrave and Mistweave took the lines. Their breath had begun to steam. Firelight transmuted the wisps of vapor to gold.

The entrance to the *rhyshyshim* was open; and cold came streaming inward, hungry to extinguish this hidden pocket of comfort. Deep in Covenant's guts, shivers mounted. His robe had previously kept him alive, if not warm; but now it seemed an insignificant defense against the frozen winter. When he looked at Linden, she answered as if his thoughts were palpable to her:

"I don't know how many. Enough."

Then the entrance loomed ahead. Now the air blew keenly into Covenant's face, tugging at his beard, drawing tears from his eyes. A dark pressure gathered in his veins. But he ducked his head and went on. With his companions, he strode through the opening onto the rocky ground at the foot of the escarpment.

The plain was sharp with sunlight. From a fathomless sky, the midafternoon sun burned across the white waste. The air felt strangely brittle, as if it were about to break under its own weight. Stiff snow crunched beneath Covenant's boots. For a moment, the cold seemed as bright as fire. He had to fight to keep wild magic from leaking past his restraint.

When his sight cleared, he saw that the whirling snow-devils which had marked and guarded the *rhyshyshim* were gone. The Waynhim had no more need of them.

Barking softly to each other, the creatures surged together into the compact and characteristic wedge which both they and the ur-viles used to concentrate and wield their combined force. Hamako stood at the apex of the formation. When it was complete and the invocations had been made, he would hold the lore and power of five *rhysh* in the blade of his scimitar. As long as they did not break ranks, the Waynhim along the sides of the wedge would be able to strike individual blows; but Hamako's might would be two hundred strong.

Every moment, the battle drew closer. Looking northward, Covenant found that he could barely see the region of monoliths beyond the massed advance of the *arghuleh*.

Ponderous and fatal, they came forward—a slow rush of white gleaming over the snow and ice. Already, their feral clatter was audible above the voices of the Waynhim. It echoed like shattering off the face of the escarpment. The horde did not appear to greatly outnumber the Waynhim; but the far larger bulk and savagery of the *arghuleh* made their force seem overwhelming.

The company still had time to flee. But no one suggested flight. The First stood, stern and ready, with one hand resting on the hilt of her longsword. Glints reflected out of Honninscrave's eyes as if he were eager to strike any blow which might make his grief useful. Pitchwife's expression was more wary and uncertain; he was no warrior. But Mistweave bore himself as though he saw his chance for restitution coming and had been commanded to ignore it. Only Cail watched the advancing horde with dispassion, unmoved alike by the valor of the Waynhim and the peril of the company. Perhaps he saw nothing especially courageous in what the *rhysh* were doing. Perhaps to his *Haruchai* mind such extravagant risk was simply reasonable.

Covenant struggled to speak. The cold seemed to freeze the words in his throat. "I want to help them. If they need it. But I don't know how." To the First, he said, "Don't go out there unless the wedge starts to break. I've seen this kind of fighting before." He had seen ur-viles slash into the Celebration of Spring to devour the Wraiths of Andelain—and had been powerless against that black wedge. "As long as their formation holds, they aren't beaten." Then he turned to Linden.

Her expression stopped him. Her face was fixed, pale with cold, toward the *arghuleh*, and her eyes looked as livid as injuries. For one dire moment, he feared she had fallen again into her particular panic. But then her gaze snapped toward him. It was battered but not cowed. "I don't know," she said tightly. "He's right. There's some force out there. Something that keeps them together. But I can't tell what it is."

Covenant swallowed a knot of dread. "Keep trying," he murmured. "I don't want these Waynhim to end up like the Unhomed." Damned as well as doomed.

She did not reply; but her nod conveyed a fierce resolve as she turned back to the *arghuleh*.

They were dangerously close now. A score of them led the advance, and their mass was nearly that many deep. Though they were beasts of hate that preyed on everything, they had become as organized as a conscious army. Steadily, they gathered speed to hurl themselves upon the Waynhim.

In response, the Waynhim raised a chant into the chill. Together, they barked a raw, irrhythmic invocation which sprang back at them from the escarpment and resounded across the flat. And a moment later a black light shone from the apex of the wedge. Hamako flourished his scimitar. Its blade had become as ebon as Demondim vitriol. It emitted midnight as if it were ablaze with death.

At the same time, all the smaller blades of the Waynhim turned black and began to drip a hot fluid which steamed and sizzled in the snow.

Without knowing what he was doing, Covenant retreated. The frigid air had become a thrumming shout of power, soundless in spite of the chant which summoned it; and that puissance called out to him. His yearning for fire battered at the walls he had built around it; the scars on his forearm burned poisonously. He took a few steps backward. But he could not put any distance between himself and his desire to strike. Instinctively, he fumbled his way to the only protection he could find: a jagged rock that stood half his height near the entrance to the *rhyshyshim*. Yet he did not crouch or cower there. His numb hands gripped the argute stone in the same way that his eyes clung to the Waynhim and the *arghuleh*; and within himself he pleaded, No. Not again.

He had not been required to watch the actual destruction of the Unhomed.

Then Hamako gave a shout like a huzzah; and the wedge started forward. Moving as one, the Waynhim went out to the foe they had chosen for their last service.

Hushed amid the vicious advance of the ice-beasts, the long hoarse chant of the Waynhim, the echoes breaking up and down the escarpment, Covenant and his companions watched as the wedge drove in among the *arghuleh*.

For a moment, its thrust was so successful that the outcome appeared foregone. The *rhysh* poured their power into Hamako: he cut an irresistible swath for the wedge to follow. And as individuals the Waynhim slashed their ice-corroding fluid in all directions. *Arghuleh* snapped apart, fell back, blundered against each other.

Screaming from their many maws, they swarmed around the wedge, trying to engulf it, crush it among them. But that only brought the third side of the wedge into the fray. And Hamako's scimitar rang like a hammer on the ice, sent shards and limbs flying from side to side with every blow. He had aimed the wedge toward an especially large beast at the rear of the mass, an *arghule* that seemed to have been formed by one creature crouching atop another; and with each step he drew closer to that target.

The *arghuleh* were savage, impervious to fear. Webs and snares were flung across the wedge. Booming cracks riddled the snow-pack. But black liquid burned the nets to tatters. Falling chunks bruised the Waynhim, but did not weaken their formation. And the hard ground under the snow rendered the cracks ineffective.

Covenant leaned against his braced hands, half frozen there, hardly daring to credit what he saw. Low shouts of encouragement broke from the First; and her sword was in her hands. Avid with hope, Pitchwife peered into the fray as if he expected victory at any moment, expected the very winter to break and flee.

Then, without warning, everything changed.

The *arghuleh* were virtually mindless, but the force which ruled them was not. It was sentient and cunning. And it had learned a lesson from the way the Waynhim had rescued the company earlier.

Abruptly, the horde altered its tactics. In a sudden flurry

like an explosion of white which almost obscured the battle, all the beasts raised their ice at once. But now that ice was not directed at the wedge. Instead, it covered every *arghule* that had been hurt, broken, or even killed by the Waynhim.

Ice slapped against every gout of vitriol, smothered the black fluid, effaced it, healed the wounds.

Ice bandaged every limb and body that Hamako had hacked or shattered, restoring crippled creatures to wholeness with terrible celerity.

Ice gathered together the fragments of the slain, fused them anew, poured life back into them.

The Waynhim had not stopped fighting for an instant. But already half their work had been undone. The *arghuleh* revitalized each other faster than they were damaged.

More and more of them were freed to attack in other ways.

Unable to rend the wedge with their webs, they began to form a wall of ice around it as if they meant to encyst it until its power gave out through sheer weariness.

Covenant stared in horror. The Waynhim were clearly unprepared for this counterattack. Hamako whirled his blade, flaring desperation around him. Three times he pounded an *arghule* into pieces no larger than his fist; and each time a web snatched the pieces together, restored them, sent the beast at him again. Wildly he sprang forward to assail the web itself. But in so doing he broke contact with the wedge. Instantly, his scimitar relapsed to bone: it splintered when he struck. He would have fallen himself; but hands reached out from the wedge and jerked him back into position.

And there was nothing Covenant could do. The Giants were calling to him, beseeching him for some command. The First shouted imprecations he did not hear. But there was nothing he could do.

Except unleash the wild magic.

Venom thudded in his temples. The wild magic, unquenchable and argent. Every thought of it, every memory, every ache of hunger and yearning was as shrill and frantic as Linden's fervid cry: *You're going to break the Arch of Time! This is what Foul wants!* Desecration filled each pulse and wail of his heart. He could not call up that much power and still pretend to control it.

But Hamako would be killed. It was as distinct as the declining sunlight on the white plain. The Waynhim would be slaughtered like the people of the Land to feed the lust of evil. That same man and those Waynhim had brought Covenant back from delirium once—and had shown him that there was still beauty in the world. The winter of their destruction would never end.

Because of the venom. Its scars still burned, as bright as Lord Foul's eyes, in the flesh of his right forearm, impelling him to power. The Sunbane warped Law, birthed abominations; but Covenant might bring Time itself to chaos.

At no great distance from him, the wedge no longer battled offensively. It struggled simply to stay alive. Several Waynhim had fallen in bonds of ice they could not break. More would die soon as the *arghuleh* raised their wall. Hamako remained on his feet, but had no weapon, no way to wield the might of the wedge. He was thrust into the center of the formation, and a Waynhim took his place, fighting with all the fluid force its small blade could channel.

"Giantfriend!" the First yelled. *"Covenant!"*

The wedge was dying; and the Giants dared not act, for fear that they would place themselves in the way of Covenant's fire.

Because of the venom—sick fury pounding like desire between the bones of his forearm. He had been made so powerful that he was powerless. His desperation demanded blood.

Slipping back his sleeve, he gripped his right wrist with his left hand to increase his leverage, then hacked his scarred forearm at the sharpest edges of the rock. His flesh ground against the jagged projections. Red slicked the stone, spattered the snow, froze in the cold. He ignored it. The Clave had cut his wrists to gain power for the soothtell which had guided and misled him. Deliberately, he mangled his forearm, striving by pain to conceive an alternative to venom, struggling to cut the fang-marks out of his soul.

Then Linden hit him. The blow knocked him back. Flagrant with urgency and concern, she caught her fists in his robe, shook him like a child, raged at him.

"Listen to me!" she flamed as if she knew he could hardly hear her, could not see anything except the blood he had left on the rock. "It's like the Kemper! Like Kasreyn!" Back and forth she heaved him, trying to wrestle him into focus on her. "Like his son! The *arghuleh* have something like his *son!*"

At that, clarity struck Covenant so hard that he nearly fell.

The Kemper's son. Oh my God.

The *croyel*.

Before the thought was finished, he had broken Linden's grasp and was running toward the Giants.

The *croyel*!—the succubus from the dark places of the Earth which Kasreyn had borne on his back, and with which he had bargained for his arts and his preternaturally prolonged life. And out there was an *arghule* which looked like one ice-beast crouched on another. That creature had contracted with the *croyel* for the power to unite its kind and wage winter wherever it willed.

Findail must have known. He must have understood what force opposed the Waynhim. Yet he had said nothing.

But Covenant had no time to spend on the mendacity of the *Elohim*. Reaching the First, he shouted, "Call them back! Make them retreat! They can't win this way!" His arm scattered blood. "We've got to tell them about the *croyel*!"

She reacted as if he had unleashed her. Whirling, she gave one command that snatched the Giants to her side; and together they charged into the fray.

Covenant watched them go in fear and hope. Still furious for him, Linden came to his side. Taking rough hold of his right wrist, she forced him to bend his elbow and clamp it tightly to slow the bleeding. Then she watched with him in silence.

With momentum, weight, and muscle, the four Giants crashed in among the *arghuleh*. The First swung her long-sword like a bludgeon, risking its metal against the gelid beasts. Honninscrave and Mistweave fought as hugely as titans. Pitchwife scrambled after them, doing everything he could to guard their backs. And as they battled, they shouted Covenant's call in the roynish tongue of the Waynhim.

The reaction of the wedge was almost immediate. Suddenly, all the Waynhim pivoted to the left; and that corner of the formation became their apex. Sweeping Hamako along, they drove for the breach the Giants had made in the attack.

The *arghuleh* were slow to understand what was happening. The wedge was half free of the fray before the ice-beasts turned to try to prevent the retreat.

Pitchwife went down under two *arghuleh*. Honninscrave and Mistweave sprang to his aid like sledgehammers, yanked him out of the wreckage. A net took hold of the First. The leader of the wedge scored it to shreds. Frenetically, the Waynhim and the Giants struggled toward Covenant.

They were not swift enough to outrun the *arghuleh*. In moments, they would be engulfed again.

But the Waynhim had understood the Giants. Abruptly, the wedge parted, spilling Hamako and a score of companions in Covenant's direction. Then the *rhysh* reclosed their formation and attacked again.

With the help of the Giants, the wedge held back the *arghuleh* while Hamako and his comrades sped toward Covenant and Linden.

Covenant started shouting at Hamako before the Stonedownor neared him; but Hamako stopped a short distance away, silenced Covenant with a gesture. "You have done your part, ring-wielder," he panted as his people gathered about him. "The name of the *croyel* is known among the Waynhim." He had to raise his voice: the creatures were chanting a new invocation. "We lacked only the knowledge that the force confronting us was indeed *croyel*." An invocation Covenant had heard before. "What must be done is clear. Come no closer."

As if to enforce his warning, Hamako drew a stone dirk from his belt.

Recognition stung through Covenant. He was familiar with that knife. Or one just like it. It went with the invocation. He tried to call out, Don't! But the protest failed in his mouth. Perhaps Hamako was right. Perhaps only such desperate measures could hope to save the embattled *rhysh*.

With one swift movement, the Stonedownor drew a long incision across the veins on the back of his hand.

The cut did not bleed. At once, he handed the dirk to a Waynhim. Quickly, it sliced the length of its palm, then passed the knife to its neighbor. Taking hold of Hamako's hand, the Waynhim pressed its cut to his. While the invocation swelled, the two of them stood there, joined by blood.

When the Waynhim stepped back, Hamako's eyes were acute with power.

In this same way, his *rhysh* had given Covenant the strength to run without rest across the whole expanse of the Center Plains in pursuit of Linden, Sunder, and Hollian. But that great feat had been accomplished with the vitality of only eight Waynhim; and Covenant had barely been able to con-

tain so much might. There were twenty creatures ranged
around Hamako.

The second had already completed its gift.

One by one, his adopted people cut themselves for him,
pressed their blood into him. And each infusion gave him a
surge of energy which threatened to burst his mortal bounds.

It was too much. How could one human being hope to
hold that much power within the vessel of ordinary thew and
tissue? Watching, Covenant feared that Hamako would not
survive.

Then he remembered the annealed grief and determination
he had seen in Hamako's eyes; and he knew the Stonedownor
did not mean to survive.

Ten Waynhim had given their gift. Hamako's skin had begun to burn like tinder in the freezing air. But he did not
pull back, and his companions did not stop.

At his back, the battle was going badly. Covenant's attention had been fixed on Hamako: he had not seen how the
arghuleh had contrived to split the wedge. But the formation
was in two pieces now, each struggling to focus its halved
strength, each unable to break through the ice to rejoin the
other. More Waynhim had fallen; more were falling. Ice
crusted the Giants so heavily that they seemed hardly able to
move. They fought heroically; but they were no match for
beasts which could be brought back from death. Soon sheer
fatigue would overcome them, and they would be lost for good
and all.

"Go!" Covenant panted to Cail. Icicles of blood splintered
from his elbow when he moved his arm. "Help them!"

But the *Haruchai* did not obey. In spite of the ancient
friendship between the Giants and his people, his face betrayed no flicker of concern. His promise of service had been
made to Covenant rather than to the First; and Brinn had
commanded him to his place.

Hellfire! Covenant raged. But his ire was directed at himself. He could tear his flesh until it fell from the bones; but
he could not find his way out of the snare Lord Foul had set
for him.

Fifteen Waynhim had given blood to Hamako. Sixteen.
Now the Stonedownor's radiance was so bright that it seemed
to tug involuntary fire from Covenant's ring. The effort of
withholding it reft him of balance and vision. Pieces of mid-

night wheeled through him. He did not see the end of the Waynhim gift, could not witness the manner in which Hamako bore it.

But as that power withdrew toward the *arghuleh*, Covenant straightened his legs, pushed himself out of Cail's grasp, and sent his gaze like a cry after the Stonedownor.

Half naked in the low sunlight and the tremendous cold, Hamako shone like a cynosure as he flashed through the ice-beasts. The sheer intensity of his form melted the nearest attackers as if a furnace had come among them. From place to place within the fray he sped, clearing a space around the Giants, opening the way for the Waynhim to reform their wedge; and behind him billowed dense clouds of vapor which obscured him and the battle, made everything uncertain.

Then Linden shouted, "There!"

All the steam burned away, denaturing so fiercely that the ice seemed to become air without transition and the scene of the combat was as vivid as the waste. Scores of *arghuleh* still threw themselves madly against the wedge. But they had stopped using their ice to support each other. And some of them were attacking their fellows, tearing into each other as if the purpose which had united them a moment ago had been forgotten.

Beyond the chaos, Hamako stood atop the leader of the *arghuleh*. He had vaulted up onto the high back of the strangely doubled beast and planted himself there, pitting his power squarely against the creature and its *croyel*.

The beast did not attempt to topple him, bring him within reach of its limbs and maws. And he struck no blows. Their struggle was simple: fire against ice, white heat against white cold. He shone like a piece of the clean sun; the *arghule* glared bitter chill. Motionless, they aimed what they had become at each other; and the entire plain rang and blazed to the pitch of their contest.

The strain of so much quintessential force was too much for Hamako's mortal flesh to sustain. In desperate pain, he began to melt like a tree under the desert avatar of the Sunbane. His legs slumped; the skin of his limbs spilled away; his features blurred. A cry that had no shape stretched his mouth.

But while his heart beat he was still alive—tempered to his purpose and indomitable. The focus of his given heat did not waver for an instant. All the losses he had suffered, all the loves which had been taken from him came together here; and he refused defeat. In spite of the ruin which sloughed away his flesh, he raised his arms, brandished them like sodden sticks at the wide sky.

And the double creature under him melted as well. Both *arghule* and *croyel* collapsed into water and slush until their deaths were inseparable from his—one stained pool slowly freezing on the faceless plain.

With an almost audible snap, the unnatural cold broke. Most of the *arghuleh* went on trying to kill each other until the *rhysh* drove them away; but the power they had brought with them was gone.

Linden was sobbing openly, though all her life she had taught herself to keep her grief silent. "Why?" she protested through her tears. "Why did they let him do it?"

Covenant knew why. Because Hamako had been twice bereft, when no man or woman or Waynhim should have had to endure such loss so much as once.

As the sun went down in red and rue beyond the western line of the escarpment, Covenant closed his eyes, hugged his bloody arm to his chest, and listened to the lamentation of the Waynhim rising into the dusk.

SEVEN: Physician's Plight

THOUGH the night was moonless, the company resumed its journey shortly after the Waynhim had finished caring for their dead. The Giants were unwilling to submit to their weariness; and the pain Covenant shared with Linden made him loath to remain anywhere near the place of Hamako's end. While Mistweave prepared a meal, Linden treated

Covenant's arm, washing it with *vitrim*, wrapping it in firm bandages. Then she required him to drink more *diamondraught* than he wanted. As a result, he could hardly keep himself awake as the company left the region of the last *rhyshyshim*. While several Waynhim guided the Giants up the escarpment, he strove against sleep. He knew what his dreams were going to be.

For a time, the hurt in his forearm helped him. But once the Giants had said their long, heart-felt farewells to the Waynhim, and had settled into a steady gait, striding south-westward as swiftly as the dim starlight permitted, he found that even pain was not enough to preserve him from night-mares.

In the middle of the night, he wrenched himself out of a vision of Hamako which had made him sweat anguish. With renewed fervor, he fought the effect of the *diamondraught*.

"I was wrong," he said to the empty dark. Perhaps no one heard him over the muffled sound of the runners in the snow. He did not want anyone to hear him. He was not speaking to be heard. He only wanted to fight off sleep, stay away from dreams. "I should've listened to Mhoram."

The memory was like a dream: it had the strange imma-nence of dreaming. But he clung to it because it was more tolerable than Hamako's death.

When High Lord Mhoram had tried to summon him to the Land for the last battle against Lord Foul, he, Covenant, had resisted the call. In his own world, a small girl had just been bitten by a timber-rattler—a lost child who needed his help. He had refused Mhoram and the Land in order to aid that girl.

And Mhoram had replied, *Unbeliever, I release you. You turn from us to save life in your own world. We will not be undone by such motives. And if darkness should fall upon us, still the beauty of the Land endures—for you will not forget. Go in Peace.*

"I should've understood," Covenant went on, addressing no one but the cold stars. "I should've given Seadreamer some kind of *caamora*. Should've found some way to save Hamako. Forget the risk. Mhoram took a terrible risk when he let me go. But anything worth saving won't be destroyed by choices like that."

He did not blame himself. He was simply trying to hold

back nightmares of fire. But he was human and weary, and only the blankets wrapped around him held any warmth at all. Eventually, his dreams returned.

He could not shake the image of Hamako's strange immolation.

Without hope, he slept until sunrise. When he opened his eyes, he found that he was stretched out, not in the sled, but in blankets on the snow-packed ground. His companions were with him, though only Cail, Pitchwife, Vain, and Findail were awake. Pitchwife stirred the fagots of a small fire, watching the flames as if his heart were somewhere else.

Above him loomed a ragged cliff, perhaps two hundred feet high. The sun had not yet reached him; but it shone squarely on the bouldered wall, giving the stones a faint red hue like a reminder that beyond them lay the Sunbane.

While Covenant slept, the company had camped at the foot of Landsdrop.

Still groggy with *diamondraught*, he climbed out of his blankets, cradling his pain-stiff arm inside his robe next to the scar in the center of his chest. Pitchwife glanced at him absently, then returned his gaze to the fire. For the first time in many long days of exposure, no ice crusted the twisting lines of his visage. Though Covenant's breath steamed as if his life were escaping from him, he was conscious that the winter had become oddly bearable—preferable to what lay ahead. The small fire was enough to steady him.

Left dumb by dreams and memories, Covenant stood beside the deformed Giant. He found an oblique comfort in Pitchwife's morose silence. Surely Cail's flat mien contained no comfort. The *Haruchai* were capable of grief and admiration and remorse; but Cail kept whatever he felt hidden. And in their opposite ways Vain and Findail represented the antithesis of comfort. Vain's makers had nearly exterminated the Waynhim. And Findail's yellow eyes were miserable with the knowledge he refused to share.

He could have told Hamako's *rhysh* about the *croyel*. Perhaps that would not have altered Covenant's plight—or Hamako's. But it would have saved lives.

Yet when Covenant looked at the *Elohim,* he felt no desire to demand explanations. He understood Findail's refusal to do anything which might relieve the pressure of his, Covenant's, culpability. The pressure to surrender his ring.

He did not need explanations. Not yet. He needed vision, percipience. He wanted to ask the Appointed, Do you think she's up to it? Is she that strong?

However, he already knew the answer. She was not that strong. But she was growing toward strength as if it were her birthright. Only her preterite self-contradictions held her back—that paralysis which gripped her when she was caught between the horror of what her father had done to her and the horror of what she had done to her mother, between her fundamental passions for and against death. And she had a better right to the wild magic than he did. Because she could see.

Around him, his companions began to stir. The First sat up suddenly, her sword in her hands: she had been dreaming of battle. As he rose stiffly to his feet, Honninscrave's eyes looked strangely like Hamako's, as if he had learned something grim and sustaining from the example of the Stone-downor. Mistweave shambled upright like an image of confusion, a man baffled by his own emotions. The release and clarity of fighting the *arghuleh* had met some of his needs, but had not restored his sense of himself.

When Linden awoke, her gaze was raw and aggrieved, as if she had spent half the night unable to stanch her tears.

Covenant's heart went out to her, but he did not know how to say so. The previous evening, she had tended his mangled arm with a ferocity which he recognized as love. But the intensity of his self-repudiation had isolated them from each other. And now he could not forget that her right was better than his. That his accumulating falseness corrupted everything he did or wanted to do.

He had never learned how to give up.

His nightmares insisted that he needed the fire he feared.

Mistweave moved woodenly about the task of preparing breakfast; but abruptly Pitchwife stopped him. Without a word, the crippled Giant rose to his feet. His manner commanded the attention of the company. For a moment, he remained motionless and rigid, his eyes damp in the sunrise. Then, hoarsely, he began to sing. His melody was a Giantish plainsong, and his stretched and fraying voice drew a faint echo from the cliff of Landsdrop, an added resonance, so that he seemed to be singing for all his companions as well as for himself.

"My heart has rooms that sigh with dust
    And ashes in the hearth.
They must be cleaned and blown away
    By daylight's breath.
But I cannot essay the task,
For even dust to me is dear;
For dust and ashes still recall,
    My love was here.

"I know not how to say Farewell,
    When Farewell is the word
That stays alone for me to say
    Or will be heard.
But I cannot speak out that word
Or ever let my loved one go:
How can I bear it that these rooms
    Are empty so?

"I sit among the dust and hope
    That dust will cover me.
I stir the ashes in the hearth,
    Though cold they be.
I cannot bear to close the door,
To seal my loneliness away
While dust and ashes yet remain
    Of my love's day."

When he was done, the First hugged him hard; and Mist-weave looked like he had been eased. Linden glanced at Covenant, bit her lips to keep them from trembling. But Honninscrave's eyes remained shrouded, and his jaws chewed gall as though Farewell were not the only word he could not bring himself to utter.

Covenant understood. Seadreamer had given his life as bravely as Hamako, but no victory had been gained to make his death endurable. And no *caamora* had been granted to accord him peace.

The Unbeliever was bitterly afraid that his own death would have more in common with Seadreamer's than with Hamako's.

While the companions ate a meal and repacked the sleds, Covenant tried to imagine how they would be able to find

their way up the harsh cliff. Here Landsdrop was not as imposing as it was nearer the center of the Land, where a
thousand feet and more of steep rock separated the Lower
Land from the Upper, Sarangrave Flat from Andelain—and
where Mount Thunder crouched like a titan, presiding darkly
over the rift. But still the cliff appeared impassable.

But the eyesight of the Giants had already discovered an
answer. They towed the sleds southward; and in less than a
league they reached a place where the rim of the precipice
had collapsed, sending a wide scallop of earth down fanlike
across its base. This slope was manageable, though Covenant
and Linden had to ascend on foot while the Giants carried
the sleds. Before the morning was half gone, the company
stood among the snows of the Upper Land.

Covenant scanned the terrain apprehensively, expecting at
any moment to hear Linden announce that she could see the
Sunbane rising before them. But beyond Landsdrop lay only
more winter and a high ridge of mountains which blocked
the west and south.

These appeared to be as tall and arduous as the Westron
Mountains. However, the Giants were undaunted, wise in the
ways of peaks and valleys. Though the rest of the day was
spent winding up into the thin air of the heights, Covenant
and Linden were able to remain in their sleds, and the company made good progress.

But the next day the way was harder, steeper, cramped
with boulders and old ice; and wind came slashing off the
crags to blind the eyes, confuse the path. Covenant clung to
the back of the sled and trudged after Honninscrave. His
right arm throbbed as if the cold were gnawing at it; his
numb hands had no strength. Yet *vitrim* and *diamondraught*
were healing him faster than he would have believed possible;
and the desire not to burden his companions kept him on
his feet.

He lost all sense of progress; the ridge seemed to tower
above him. Whenever he tried to breathe deeply, the air
sawed at his lungs. He felt frail and useless and immeasurably
far from Revelstone. Still he endured. The specific disciplines
of his leprosy had been lost long ago; but their spirit remained to him—the dogged and meticulous insistence on
survival which took no account of the distance ahead or the

pain already suffered. When the onset of evening finally forced the company to halt, he was still on his feet.

The following day was worse. The air became as cold as the malice of the *arghuleh*. Wind flayed like outrage down the narrow coombs which gave the company passage. Time and again, Cail had to help either Covenant or Linden, or was needed to assist the sleds. But he seemed to flourish in this thin air. The Giants fought and hauled their way upward as if they were prepared to measure themselves against any terrain. And Linden stayed with them somehow—as stubborn as Covenant, and in an odd way tougher. Her face was as pale as the snow among the protruding rocks; cold glazed her eyes like frost. Yet she persevered.

And that night the company camped in the lower end of a pass between peaks ranging dramatically toward the heavens. Beyond the far mouth of the pass were no more mountains high enough to catch the sunset.

The companions had to struggle to keep their fire alight long enough to prepare a meal: the wind keening through the pass tore at the brands. Without a makeshift windbreak of blankets, no fire would have been possible at all. But the Giants did their best, contrived both to warm some food and to heat the water Linden needed for Covenant's arm. When she unwrapped his bandages, he was surprised to see that his self-inflicted wounds were nearly well. After she had washed the slight infection which remained, she applied another light bandage to protect his arm from being chafed.

Grateful for her touch, her concern, her endurance—for more things than he could name in that wind—he tried to thank her with his eyes. But she kept her gaze averted, and her movements were abrupt and troubled. When she spoke, she sounded as forlorn as the peaks.

"We're getting close to it. This—" She made a gesture that seemed to indicate the wind. "It's unnatural. A reaction to something on the other side." The lines of her face stiffened into a scowl. "If you want my guess, I'd say there's been a desert sun for two days now."

She stopped. Tensely, Covenant waited for her to go on. From the first, the Sunbane had been a torment to her. The added dimension of her senses exposed her unmercifully to the outrage of that evil, to the alternating drought and suppuration of the world, the burning of the deserts and the screaming of the trees. Gibbon had prophesied that the true destruction of the Earth would be on her head rather than Covenant's—that she would be driven by her very health-sense to commit every desecration the Despiser required. And then the Raver had touched her, poured his malice like distilled corruption into her vulnerable flesh; and the horror of that violation had reduced her to a paralysis as deep as catatonia for two days.

When she had come out of it, after Covenant had rescued her from the hold of Revelstone, she had turned her back entirely on the resource of her percipience. She had begged him to spare her, as he had tried to spare Joan. And she had not begun to recover until she had been taught that her health-sense was also open to beauty, that when it exposed her to ill it also empowered her to heal.

She was a different woman now; he was humbled by the thought of how far she had come. But the test of the Sunbane remained before her. He did not know what was in her heart; but he knew as well as she did that she would soon be compelled to carry a burden which had already proved too heavy for her once.

A burden which would never have befallen her a second time if he had not allowed her to believe the lie that they had a future together.

Firelight and the day's exertions made her face ruddy against the background of the night. Her long-untended hair fluttered on either side of her head. In her eyes, the reflection of the wind-whipped flames capered. She looked like a woman whose features would not obey her, refused to resume the particular severity which had marked her life. She was returning to the place and the peril that had taught her to think of herself as evil.

Evil and doomed.

"I never told you," she murmured at last. "I just wanted to forget about it. We got so far away from the Land—even Gibbon's threats started to seem unreal. But now—" For a moment, her gaze followed the wind. "I can't stop thinking about it."

After the extremity of the things she had already related to him, Covenant was dismayed that more remained to be told. But he held himself as steady as he could, did not let his regard for her waver.

"That night." An ache crept into her voice. "The first night we were on Starfare's Gem. Before I finally figured out we had a Raver aboard. And that rat bit you." He remembered: that bite had triggered a venom-relapse which had nearly destroyed the quest and the Search and the *dromond* before she found a way to penetrate it and treat him. "I had the most terrible nightmare."

Softly, she described the dream. They had been in the woods behind Haven Farm; and he had taken Joan's place at the mercy of Lord Foul's misled band of fanatics; and she, Linden, had gone running down the hillside to save him. But never in all her life had she been able to stop the violence which had driven the knife into his chest. And from the wound had gushed more blood than she had ever seen. It had welled out of him as if a world had been slain with that one blow. As if the thrust of the knife had stabbed the very heart of the Land.

She had been altogether unable to stanch it. She had nearly drowned in the attempt.

The memory left her aghast in the unsteady light; but now she did not stop. She had been gnawing her questions for a long time and knew with frightening precision what she wanted to ask. Looking straight into Covenant's consternation, she said, "On Kevin's Watch, you told me there were two different explanations. External and internal. Like the difference between surgery and medicine. The internal one was that we're sharing a dream. 'Tied into the same unconscious process,' you said.

"That fits. If we're dreaming, then naturally any healing that happens here is just an illusion. It couldn't have any effect on the bodies we left behind—on our physical continuity back where we came from.

"But what does it mean when you have a nightmare in a dream? Isn't that some kind of prophecy?"

Her directness surprised him. She had surpassed him; he could not follow without groping. His own dreams— Quickly, he scrambled to protest, "Nothing's that simple." But then he had to pause. An awkward moment passed before he found a countering argument.

"You had that dream under the influence of a Raver. You dreamed what it made you feel. Lord Foul's prophecy—not yours. It doesn't change anything."

Linden was no longer looking at him. She had bowed her head, braced her forehead in her palms; but her hands did not hide the silent tears streaming down her cheeks. "That was before I knew anything about power." With an honesty that dismayed him, she exposed the root of her distress. "I could've saved Hamako. I could've saved them all. You were so close to erupting. I could've taken your wild magic and torn out that *croyel*'s heart. *I'm* no danger to the Arch of Time. None of them had to die."

Dread burned like shame across his face. He knew she spoke the truth. Her health-sense was still growing. Soon she would become capable of anything. He swallowed a groan. "Why didn't you?"

"I was watching *you*!" she flung back at him in sudden anguish. "Watching you tear your arm apart. I couldn't think about anything else."

The sight of her pain enabled him to take hold of himself, fight down his instinctive panic. He could not afford to be afraid. She needed something better from him.

"I'm glad you didn't," he said. "Never mind what it would've done to me. I'm glad you didn't for his sake." Thinking of her mother, he added deliberately, "You let him achieve the meaning of his own life."

At that, her head jerked up; her gaze knifed at him. "He *died*!" she hissed like an imprecation too fierce and personal to be shouted. "He saved your life at least twice, and he spent his own life serving the Land you claim to care so much about, and the people that adopted him were nearly wiped off the face of the Earth, and he *died*!"

Covenant did not flinch. He was ready now for anything she might hurl at him. His own nightmares were worse than this. And he would have given his soul for the ability to match Hamako. "I'm not glad he died. I'm glad he found an answer."

For a long moment, her glare held. But then slowly the anger frayed out of her face. At last, her eyes fell. Thickly, she murmured, "I'm sorry. I just don't understand. Killing people is wrong." The memory of her mother was present to her as it was to Covenant. "But dear Christ! Saving them has got to be better than letting them die."

"Linden." She clearly did not want him to say anything else. She had raised the fundamental question of her life and needed to answer it herself. But he could not let the matter drop. With all the gentleness he had in him, he said, "Hamako didn't want to be saved. For the opposite reason that your father didn't want to be saved. And he won."

"I know," she muttered. "I know. I just don't understand it." As if to keep him from speaking again, she left the fire, went to get her blankets.

He looked around at the mute, attentive faces of the Giants. But they had no other wisdom to offer him. He wanted intensely to be saved himself; but no one would be able to do that for him unless he surrendered his ring. He was beginning to think that his death would be welcome when it came.

A short time later, the fire blew out. Mistweave tried to light it again and failed. But when Covenant finally went to sleep, he dreamed that the blaze had become violent enough to consume him.

During the night, the wind died. The dawn was as clear as crystal; and the crags shone in the high, thin air as if no taint could reach them. A mood of impossible hope came over the companions as they labored toward the far end of the pass.

Under other circumstances, the view from that eminence would have delighted them. Sunlight flashed through the pass to illuminate the range as it tumbled downward in a dramatic succession of snow-bright crests and saw-backed arêtes, mighty heads fronting the heavens and spines sprawling toward lower ground. And beyond the bare foothills all the way to the southwestern horizon lay the high North Plains which led to Revelstone.

But where the sun hit the Plains they looked as brown and battered as a desert.

That in itself would not have wrenched the Giants to silence, raised Linden's hands to her mouth, stifled Covenant's breathing; for at this time of year the region below them might be naturally dry. But as soon as the sun touched the denuded waste, a green fur began to spread across it. Distance made teeming shoots and sprouts look like an unconscionably rapid pelt.

With a curse, Covenant wheeled to scan the sun. But he

could see no sign of the corona which should have accompanied the sudden verdure.

"We're under the fringe," said Linden tonelessly. "I told you about that—the last time we crossed Landsdrop. We won't see the aura until later."

Covenant had not forgotten her explanation. The Sunbane was a corruption of Earthpower, and it arose from the ground, from the deep roots of Mount Thunder where Lord Foul now made his home. But it was focused or triggered by the sun and manifested itself visibly there, in the characteristic penumbra of its phases and the power for perversion of its initial contact.

Thickly, he grated to his companions, "We'll need stone for protection. It's the first touch that does the damage." He and Linden had been preserved by the alien leather of their footwear. The *Haruchai* and Vain had already shown that they were immune. Findail needed no advice on how to care for himself. But the Giants— Covenant could not bear that they might be at risk. "From now on—every day. We've got to have stone under us when the sun comes up."

The First nodded mutely. She and her people were still staring at the green mantle which thickened at every moment across the distant plains.

That sight made Covenant long for Sunder and Hollian. The Graveler of Mithil Stonedown had left his home and people to serve as Covenant's guide through the perils of the Sunbane; and his obdurate skill and providence, his self-doubting courage, had kept Covenant and Linden alive. And Hollian's eh-Brand ability to foretell the phases of the Sunbane had been invaluable. Though he had Giants with him now, and Linden's strength, Covenant felt entirely unready to face the Sunbane without the support of his former companions.

And he wanted to know what had happened to them. He had sent them from Seareach because they had believed that they had no clear role in the quest for the One Tree, no place among such mighty beings as Giants—and because he had loathed to leave the Clave uncontested during the unpredictable period of his absence. So he had given them the *krill* of Loric, the powerful blade which he had raised from Glimmermere. And he had laid upon them the charge of mustering resistance among the villages against the bloody requirements of the Clave. Accompanied only by Stell and Harn, armed with nothing more than their own knives, the *krill*, Sunder's *orcrest* stone and Hollian's *lianar* wand, and encouraged by the thin hope that they might eventually gain the aid of more *Haruchai*, the two lone Stonedownors had gone in sunlight and poignant valor to hazard their lives against the forces which ruled the Land.

That memory outweighed any amount of unreadiness. The distant preternatural green swelling below him brought back the past with renewed vividness. Sunder and Hollian were his friends. He had come this far in the name of Revelstone and the Clave; but now he wanted keenly to rejoin the two Stonedownors.

Rejoin or avenge.

"Come on," he rasped to his companions. "Let's get down there."

The First gave him a measuring glance, as though she half distrusted the constant hardening of his attitude. But she was not a woman who hung back. With a stern nod, she sent him and Linden to the sleds. Then she turned and started down the steep, snowbound slope as if she, too, could not wait to confront the ill that had brought the Search here.

Heaving Covenant's sled into motion, Honninscrave let out a cry like a challenge and went plunging after the Swordmain.

In the course of that one day, the company passed down out of the mountains, came to the foothills and the end of the snow. Careening at a mad pace which could only have been controlled by Giants, they sped from slope to slope, pausing only when the First needed to consider her best route. She seemed determined to regain the time lost by the arduous ascent of the range. Before noon, a band of green—the color of chrysoprase and Daphin's eyes—closed around the sun like a garrote. But Covenant could not look at it. He was nearly blind with vertigo. He was barely able to cling to the rails of the sled and hold the contents of his stomach down.

Then the ice and snow of the heights failed on the verge of a moiling chaos of vegetation which had already grown high enough to appear impenetrable. His head still reeling, Covenant considered himself fortunate that dusk prevented the First from tackling the verdure immediately. But the Swordmain was not insensitive to the nausea in his face—or the aggravated ache in Linden's. While Mistweave and Honninscrave prepared a camp, she passed a flask of *diamondraught* to the two humans, then left them alone to try to recover themselves.

The liquor settled Covenant's guts, but could not soften the wide, white outrage and dread of Linden's stare. At intervals during the evening, Pitchwife and the First addressed comments to her; but her replies were monosyllabic and distant. The crouching vegetation spoke a language that only she could hear, consuming her attention. Unconscious of being watched, she chewed her lips as if she had lost her old severity and did not know how to recapture it.

Her huddled posture—thighs pressed against her chest, arms hugged around her shins, chin braced on her knees—reminded him of a time many days ago, a time when they had begun traveling together, and she had nearly broken under the pressure of her first fertile sun. She had quailed into herself, protesting, *I can't shut it out. It's too personal. I don't believe in evil.*

She believed in evil now; but that only made the sensory assault of the Sunbane more intimate and unanswerable—as heinous as murder and as immedicable as leprosy.

He tried to stay awake with her, offering her the support of his silent companionship. But she was still taut and unslumberous when the mortal pull of his dreams took him away. He went to sleep thinking that if he had possessed anything akin to her percipience the Land would not be in such danger— and she would not be so alone.

Visions he could neither face nor shun seemed to protract the night; yet dawn and Cail's rousing touch came too early. He awoke with a jerk and found himself staring at the dense growth. His companions were already up. While Pitchwife and Mistweave prepared a meal, and Honninscrave dismantled the sleds, the First studied the choked terrain, clenching a tuneless hum between her teeth. A gap among the peaks sent an early shaft of light onto the vegetation directly in front of the camp. The sun would touch the company soon.

Covenant's skin crawled as he watched the verdure writhe and grow. The contrast between the places where the sun hit and where it did not only made the effect more eerie and ominous. In the stony soil among the foothills, there were no trees. But the hardy, twisted shrubs were already as tall as trees; thistles and other weeds crowded the ground between the trunks; huge slabs of lichen clung to the rocks like scabs. And everything the sun touched grew so rapidly that it seemed animate—a form of helpless flesh tortured mercilessly toward the sky. He had forgotten how horrific the Sunbane truly was. He dreaded the moment when he would have to descend into that lush green anguish.

Then the sunlight fell through the gap onto the company.

At the last moment, the First, Honninscrave, and Pitchwife had found rocks on which to stand. Under Mistweave's feet lay the stone with which he had formerly shielded his camp-fires from ice and snow.

Distantly, Linden nodded at the caution of the Giants. "Cail's got something you don't," she murmured. "You need the protection." But Vain and Findail required no defense; and Covenant and Linden had their footwear. Together, they faced the onset of the sun.

As it first crested the gap, the sun appeared normal. For that reason, at least this much of the foothills remained free of vegetation. Yet the company stayed motionless, suspended and silent in an anticipation like dread. And before their eyes the sun changed. A green aura closed around it, altering the light. Even the strip of bare ground between the end of the snow and the beginning of the vegetation took on an emerald timbre.

Because of the winter which still held the mountains, the air was not warm. But Covenant found that he was sweating.

Grimly, Linden turned her back on the sun. The Giants went to their tasks. Vain's constant, black, ambiguous smile betrayed no reaction. But Findail's pain-marked face looked more aggrieved than ever. Covenant thought he saw the *Elohim*'s hands trembling.

Shortly after the company had eaten, Honninscrave finished reducing the sleds to firewood. He and Mistweave packed their supplies into huge bundles for themselves and smaller ones for Pitchwife and the First. Soon Covenant's companions were prepared to commence the day's journey.

"Giantfriend," the First asked sternly, "is there peril for us here other than that which we have all witnessed?"

Peril, he thought dumbly. If the Riders of the Clave don't

come this far north. And nothing else has changed. "Not under this sun," he replied with sweat in his voice. "But if we stand still too long, we'll have trouble moving again."

The Swordmain nodded. "That is plain."

Drawing her blade, she took two long steps down the hillside and began hacking tall thistles out of her way.

Honninscrave followed her. With his bulk and muscle, he widened her path for the rest of the company.

Covenant compelled himself to take his position at Pitchwife's back. Cail followed between the Unbeliever and Linden. Then came Mistweave, with Vain and Findail inseparably behind him.

In that formation, the failed quest for the One Tree met the atrocity of the Sunbane.

For the morning and part of the afternoon, they managed a surprising pace. Monstrous scrub brush and weeds gave way to stands of immense, raw bracken clotted with clumps of grass; and every added degree of the sun's arc made each frond and leaf and stem yearn more desperately upward, as frantic as the damned. Yet the First and Honninscrave forged ahead as fast as Covenant and Linden could comfortably walk. The air became warmer, noticeably more humid, as the snows and elevation of the mountains were left behind. Although Covenant had added his robe to Pitchwife's bundle, he perspired constantly. But his days in the range had toughened him somewhat; he was able to keep the pace.

But toward midafternoon the company entered a region like a surreal madland. Juniper trees as contorted as ghouls sprawled thickly against each other, strangled by the prodigious vines which festooned them like the web of a gargantuan and insane spider. And between the vine stems and tree trunks the ground was profuse with lurid orchids that smelled like poison. The First struck one fierce blow against the nearest vine, then snatched back her green-slick blade to see if she had damaged it: the stem was as hard as ironwood. Around her, the trees and vines rustled like execration. In order to advance at all, the companions had to clamber and squirm awkwardly among the hindrances.

Night caught them in the middle of the region, with no stone in sight and scarcely enough space for them to lay their blankets between the trunks. But when Cail roused the company the next morning, they found that he had somehow contrived to collect sufficient small rocks to protect two of the Giants. And the stone which Mistweave still carried could hold two more. Thus warded, they braced themselves to meet the sun.

When its first touch filtered insidiously down through the choked trees, Covenant flinched; and Linden jerked a hand to her mouth to stifle a gasp.

They could see only pieces of the sun's aura. But those pieces were red. The color of pestilence.

"Two days!" Covenant spat to keep himself from groaning. "It's getting worse."

The First stared at him. Bitterly, he explained that the Sunbane had formerly moved in a cycle of three days. Any shortening of that period meant that its power was increasing. And *that* meant— But he could not say such things aloud. The hurt of them went too deep. It meant that Sunder and Hollian had failed. Or that the na-Mhoram had found a source of blood as large as his malice. Or that Lord Foul was now confident of victory, and therefore the Clave no longer made any pretense of holding back the Sunbane.

Glowering, the First absorbed Covenant's answer. After a moment, she asked carefully, "May it be that this is but a variation—that the essential period remains unaltered?"

That was possible. He remembered one sun of two days. But when he turned to Linden for her opinion, she was not looking at him. Her hand had not come down from her mouth. Her teeth were closed on the knuckle of her index finger, and a drop of blood marked her chin.

"Linden." He grabbed at her wrist, yanked her hand away.

Her dismay slapped at him. "The sun of pestilence." Her voice came twisted and harsh from her knotted throat. "Have you forgotten what it's like? We don't have any *voure*."

At that, a new fear stung Covenant. *Voure* was the pungent sap of a certain plant—a sap that warded off the insects which thrived under a red sun. And more: it was also an antidote for the Sunbane-sickness. That pestilential disease could attack through any kind of exposed cut or injury. "Hellfire," he breathed. Then snapped, "Get a bandage on that finger!" His arm was healed enough to be safe; but this sun might prove the small marks on her knuckle fatal.

Around him, steam rolled like a miasma. Wherever the light

touched the vines and trunks, their bark opened and began to ooze. The steam stank of decomposition.

Nameless insects started to whine like augers through the mounting stench. Suddenly, Covenant caught up with Linden's apprehension. In addition to everything else, she had realized before he did that even a Giant might sicken and fail from breathing too much of that vapor—or from being bitten by too many of those insects.

She had not moved. Her eyes appeared glazed and inward, as if she could not move. Small red beads formed around her knuckle and dropped to the dirt.

Fierce with exasperation and alarm, Covenant snarled at her, "By hell! I said, get a bandage on that *finger*. And *think* of something. We're in big trouble."

She flinched. "No," she whispered. The delicacy of her features seemed to crumble. "No. You don't understand. You don't feel it. It was never this—I can't remember—" She swallowed heavily to keep herself from crying out. Then her tone became flat and dead. "You don't feel it. It's hideous. You can't fight it."

Wisps of steam passed in front of her face as if she, too, had begun to rot.

Urgently, Covenant grabbed her shoulders, ground his numb fingers into her. "Maybe I can't. But you can. You're the Sun-Sage. What do you think you're *here* for?"

The Sun-Sage. *Elohim* had given her that title. For an instant, her gaze became wild; and he feared he had torn the thin fabric of her sanity. But then her eyes focused on him with an emotional impact that made him wince. Abruptly, she was alabaster and adamantine in his grasp. "Let go of me," she articulated distinctly. "You don't give enough to have the right."

He pleaded with her mutely, but she did not relent. When he dropped his arms and stepped back, she turned away as if she were dismissing him from her life.

To the First, she said, "Get some green wood. Branches or whatever you can find." She sounded oddly hard and brittle, not to be touched. "Soak the ends in *vitrim* and light them. The smoke should give us some protection."

The First cocked an eyebrow at the tension between Covenant and Linden. But the Giants did not hesitate: they were acquainted with Linden's health-sense. In moments, they had wrenched several boughs the size of brands from nearby trees. Pitchwife muttered mournfully at the idea of using his precious *vitrim* for such a purpose, but he handed one of his pouches to the First readily enough. Shortly, the four Giants and Cail held flaming branches that guttered and spat with enough smoke to palliate the reek of rot. Outsized flying insects hummed angrily around the area, then shot off in search of other prey.

When the supplies had been repacked, the First turned to Linden for instructions, tacitly recognizing the change which had taken place in the Chosen. Covenant was Giantfriend and ring-wielder; but it was Linden's percipience upon which the company depended now for survival.

Without a glance at Covenant, Linden nodded. Then she took Pitchwife's place behind the First and Honninscrave; and the company started moving.

Beclouded with smoke and rot, they struggled on through the wild region. Under the particular corruption of the sun's scarlet aura, vines which had been too hard for the First's sword were now marked with swellings that burst and sores that ran. Fetor and borers took hold of some of the trees, ate out their hearts. Others lost wide strips of bark, exposing bald wood fatally veined with termites. The narcoleptic sweetness of the orchids penetrated the acrid smoke from time to time. Covenant felt that he was laboring through the fruition of what Lord Foul had striven to achieve ten years and three and a half millennia ago—the desecration of all of the Land's health to leprosy. Here the Despiser emerged in the throes of victory. The beauty of Land and Law had been broken. With smoke in his eyes and revulsion in his guts, images of gangrene and pain on all sides, Covenant found himself praying for a sun of only two days.

Yet the red sun produced one benefit: the rotting of the wood allowed the First to begin cutting a path once more. The company was able to improve its pace. And finally the juniper wildland opened into an area of tall, thick grass as corrupt and cloying as a tarpit. The First called a halt for a brief meal and a few swallows of *diamondraught*.

Covenant needed the liquor, but he could hardly eat. His gaze refused to leave the swelling of Linden's bitten finger.

Sunbane-sickness, he thought miserably. She had suffered from it once before. Sunder and Hollian, who were familiar with such sickness, had believed that she would die. He would never forget the look of her as she had lain helpless in the grip of convulsions as flagrant as his nightmares. Only her health-sense and *voure* had saved her.

That memory compelled him to risk her ire. More harshly than he intended, he began, "I thought I told you—"

"And I told you," she retorted, "to leave me alone. I don't need you to mother me."

But he faced her squarely, forced her to recognize his concern. After a moment, her belligerence failed. Frowning, she turned her head away. "You don't have to worry about it," she sighed. "I know what I'm doing. It helps me concentrate."

"Helps—?" He did not know how to understand her.

"Sunder was right," she responded. "This is the worst—the sun of pestilence. It sucks at me—or soaks into me. I don't know how to describe it. I become it. It becomes me." The simple act of putting her plight into words made her shudder. Deliberately, she raised her hand, studied her hurt finger. "The pain. The way it scares me. It helps make the distinction. It keeps me separate."

Covenant nodded. What else could he do? Her vulnerability had become terrible to him. Huskily, he said, "Don't let it get too bad." Then he made another attempt to force food down into his knotted stomach.

The rest of the day was atrocious. And the next day was worse. But early in the evening, amid the screaming of numberless cicadas and the piercing frustration of huge, smoke-daunted mosquitoes, the company reached a region of hills where wide boulders still protruded from the surrounding morass of moss and ground ivy. That proved to be a fortuitous camping place; for when the sun rose again, it was wreathed in dusty brown.

After only two days.

The elevation of the rocks protected the travelers from the effect of the desert sun on the putrifying vegetation.

Everything that the fertile sun had produced and the sun of pestilence had blighted might as well have been made of wax. The brown-clad sun melted it all, reduced every form of plant fiber, every kind of sap or juice, every monstrous insect to a necrotic gray sludge. The few bushes in the area slumped like overheated candles; moss and ivy sprawled into spilth that formed turbid pools in the low places of the terrain; the bugs of dawn fell like clotted drops of rain. Then the sludge denatured as if the desert sun drank it away.

Long before midmorning, every slope and hollow and span of ground had been burned to naked ruin and dust.

For the Giants, that process was more horrible than anything else they had seen. Until now, only the scale of the Sunbane's power had been staggering. Verdure grew naturally, and insects and rot could be included in the normal range of experience. But nothing had prepared Covenant's companions for the quick and entire destruction of so much prodigious vegetation and pestilence.

Staring about her, the First breathed, "Ah, Cable Seadreamer! There is no cause for wonder that you lacked voice to utter such visions. The wonder is that you endured to bear them at all—and that you bore them in loneliness."

Pitchwife clung to her as if he were reeling inwardly. Open nausea showed in Mistweave's face. He had learned to doubt himself, and now the things he could no longer trust covered all the world. But Honninscrave's deep eyes flamed hotly— the eyes of a man who knew now beyond question that he was on the right path.

Grimly, Linden demanded a knife from Pitchwife. For a moment, he could not answer her. But at last the First stirred, turned from the harsh vista of the waste; and her husband turned with her.

Dazedly, Pitchwife gave Linden his blade. She used its tip to lance her infected finger. With *vitrim*, she cleansed the wound thoroughly, then bound it in a light bandage. When she was done, she lifted her head; and her gaze was as intense as Honninscrave's. Like him, she now appeared eager to go forward.

Or like High Lord Elena, who had been driven by inextricable abhorrence and love, and by lust for power, to the mad act of breaking the Law of Death. After only three days under the Sunbane, Linden appeared capable of such things.

Soon the company started southwestward again across a wasteland which had become little more than an anvil for the fierce brutality of the sun.

It brought back more of the past to Covenant. Heat-haze as thick as hallucination and dust bleached to the color of dismay made his memories vivid. He and Linden had been summoned to Kevin's Watch during a day of rain; but that night Sunder's father, Nassic, had been murdered, and the next day had arisen a desert sun—and Covenant and Linden had encountered a Raver amid the hostility of Mithil Stonedown.

Many of the consequences had fallen squarely upon Sunder's shoulders. As the Stonedown's Graveler, he had already been required to shed the lives of his own wife and son so that their blood would serve the village. And then the Raver's actions had cost him his father, had compelled him to sacrifice his friend, Marid, to the Sunbane, and had faced him with the necessity of bleeding his mother to death. Such things had driven him to flee his duty for the sake of the Unbeliever and the Chosen—and for his own sake, so that he would be spared the responsibility of more killing.

Yet during that same desert sun Covenant's life had also been changed radically. The corruption of that sun had made Marid monstrous enough to inflict the Despiser's malice. Out in the wasteland of the South Plains, Marid had nailed venom between the bones of Covenant's forearm, crucifying him to the fate Lord Foul had prepared for him.

The fate of fire. In a nightmare of wild magic, his own terrible love and grief tore down the world.

The sun would not let him think of anything else. The company had adequate supplies of water, *diamondraught*, and food; and when the haze took on the attributes of vertigo, leeched the strength out of Covenant's legs, Honninscrave carried him. Foamfollower had done the same for him more than once, bearing him along the way of hope and doom. But now there was only haze and vertigo and despair—and the remorseless hammer-blow of the sun.

That phase of the Sunbane also lasted for only two days. But it was succeeded by another manifestation of pestilence.

The red-tinged heat was less severe. The stricken Plains contained nothing which could rot. And here the insect life was confined to creatures that made their homes in the ground. Yet this sun was arduous and bitter after its own fashion. It brought neither moisture nor shade up out of the waste. And before it ended, the travelers began to encounter stag beetles and scorpions as big as wolves among the low hills. But the First's sword kept such threats at bay. And whenever Honninscrave and Mistweave took on the added weight of Covenant and Linden, the company made good speed.

In spite of their native hardiness, the Giants were growing weary, worn down by dust and heat and distance. But after the second day of pestilence came a sun of rain. Standing on stone to meet the dawn, the companions felt a new coolness against their faces as the sun rose ringed in blue like a concentration of the sky's deep azure. Then, almost immediately, black clouds began to pile westward.

Covenant's heart lifted at the thought of rain. But as the wind stiffened, plucking insistently at his unclean hair and beard, he remembered how difficult it was to travel under such a sun. He turned to the First. "We're going to need rope." The wind hummed in his ears. "So we don't lose each other."

Linden was staring toward the southwest as if the idea of Revelstone consumed all her thoughts. Distantly, she said, "The rain isn't dangerous. But there's going to be so much of it."

The First glared at the clouds, nodded. Mistweave unslung his bundles and dug out a length of line.

The rope was too heavy to be tied around Covenant and Linden without hampering them. As the first raindrops hit, heavy as pebbles, the Swordmain knotted the line to her own waist, then strung it back through the formation of the company to Mistweave, who anchored it.

For a moment, she scanned the terrain to fix her bearings in her mind. Then she started into the darkening storm.

As loud as a rabble, the rain rushed out of the east. The clouds spanned the horizons, blocking the last light. Gloom fell like water into Covenant's eyes. Already, he could barely discern the First at the head of the company. Pitchwife's misshapen outlines were blurred. The wind leaned against Covenant's left shoulder. His boots began to slip under him. Without transition, soil as desiccated as centuries of desert changed to mud and clay. Instant pools spread across the ground. The downpour became as heavy as cudgels. Blindly, he clung to the rope.

It led into a blank abyss of rain. The world was reduced to this mad drenching lash and roar, this battering cold. He should have retrieved his robe before the rain started: his T-shirt was meaningless against the torrents. How could there be so much water, when for days the North Plains and all the Land had been desperately athirst? Only Pitchwife's shape remained before him, badly smudged but still solid— the only solid thing left except the rope. When he tried to look around toward Cail, Mistweave, Vain, and Findail, the storm hit him full in the face. It was a doomland he wandered because he had failed to find any answer to his dreams.

Eventually, even Pitchwife was gone. The staggering downpour dragged every vestige of light and vision out of the air. His hands numb with leprosy and cold, Covenant could only be sure of the rope by clamping it under his elbow, leaning his weight on it. Long after he had begun to believe that the ordeal should be given up, that the company should find some shelter and simply huddle there while the storm lasted, the line went on drawing him forward.

But then, as suddenly as the summons which had changed his life, a pressure jerked back on the rope, hauled it to a stop; and he nearly fell. While he stumbled for balance, the line went slack.

Before he recovered, something heavy blundered against him, knocked him into the mire.

The storm had a strange timbre, as if people were shouting around him.

Almost at once, huge hands took hold of him, heaved him to his feet. A Giant: Pitchwife. He was pushed a few steps toward the rear of the formation, then gripped to a halt.

The rain was at his back. He saw three people in front of him. They all looked like Cail.

One of them caught his arm, put a mouth to his ear. Cail's voice reached him dimly through the roar.

"Here are Durris and Fole of the *Haruchai*! They have come with others of our people to oppose the Clave!"

Rain pounded at Covenant; wind reeled through him. "Where's Sunder?" he cried. "Where's Hollian?"

Blurred in the fury of the torrents, two more figures became discernible. One of them seemed to hold out an object toward Covenant.

From it, a white light sprang through the storm, piercing the darkness. Incandescence shone from a clear gem which had been forged into a long dagger, at the cross where blade and hilt came together. Its heat sizzled the rain; but the light itself burned as if no rain could touch it.

The *krill* of Loric.

It illuminated all the faces around Covenant: Cail and his kinfolk, Durris and Fole; Mistweave flanked by Vain and Findail; Pitchwife; the First and Honninscrave crowding forward with Linden between them. And the two people who had brought the *krill*.

Sunder, son of Nassic, Graveler from Mithil Stonedown.

Hollian Amith-daughter, eh-Brand.

EIGHT: The Defenders of the Land

THE torrents came down like thunder. The rain was full of voices Covenant could not hear. Sunder's lips moved, made no sound. Hollian blinked at the water streaming her face as if she did not know whether to laugh or weep. Covenant wanted to go to them, throw his arms around them in sheer relief that they were alive; but the light of the *krill* held him back. He did not know what it meant. The venom in his forearm ached to take hold of it and burn.

Cail spoke directly into Covenant's ear again. "The Graveler asks if your quest has succeeded!"

At that, Covenant covered his face, pressed the ring's imminent heat against the bones of his skull. The rain was too much for him; suppressed weeping knotted his chest. He had been so eager to find Sunder and Hollian safe that he had never considered what the ruin of the quest would mean to them.

The First's hearing was keener than his. Sunder's query had reached her. She focused her voice to answer him through the roar. "The quest has failed!" The words were raw with

strain. "Cable Seadreamer is slain! We have come seeking
another hope!"

The full shout of Sunder's reply was barely audible. "You
will find none here!"

Then the light receded: the Graveler had turned away.
Holding the *krill* high to guide the company, he moved off
into the storm.

Covenant dropped his hands like a cry he could not utter.

For an instant, no one followed Sunder. Silhouetted against
the *krill*'s shining, Hollian stood before Covenant and Linden.
He hardly saw what she was doing as she came to him, gave
him a tight hug of welcome. Before he was able to respond,
she left him to embrace Linden.

Yet her brief gesture helped him pull himself together. It
felt like an act of forgiveness—or an affirmation that his return and Linden's were more important than hope. When
Cail urged him after the light, he pushed his numb limbs into
motion.

They were in a low place between hills. Gathered water
reached almost to his knees. But its current ran in the direction he was going, and Cail bore him up. The *Haruchai*
seemed more certain than ever. It must have been the mental
communion of his people which had drawn Durris and Fole,
with the Stonedownors behind them, toward the company.
And now Cail was no longer alone. Mud and streams and
rain could not make him miss his footing. He supported
Covenant like a figure of granite.

Covenant had lost all sense of his companions; but he was
not concerned. He trusted the other *Haruchai* as he trusted
Cail. Directing his attention to the struggle for movement,
he followed Sunder as quickly as his imbalance and fatigue
allowed.

The way seemed long and harsh in the clutches of the
storm. At last, however, he and Cail neared an impression of
rock and saw Sunder's *krill*-light reflecting wetly off the edges
of a wide entrance to a cave. Sunder went directly in, used
the argent heat of the *krill* to set a ready pile of wood afire.
Then he rewrapped the blade and tucked it away within his
leather jerkin.

The flames were dimmer than the *krill*, but they spread
illumination around a larger area, revealing bundles of wood

and bedding stacked against the walls. The Stonedownors and *Haruchai* had already established a camp here.

The cave was high but shallow, hardly more than a depression in the side of a hill. The angle of the ceiling's overhang let rainwater run inward and drizzle to the floor, with the result that the cave was damp and the fire, not easily kept alight. But even that relative shelter was a balm to Covenant's battered nerves. He stood over the flames and tried to rub the dead chill out of his skin, watching Sunder while the company arrived to join him.

Durris brought the four Giants. Fole guided Linden as if he had already arrogated to himself Mistweave's chosen place at her side. Vain and Findail came of their own accord, though they did not move far enough into the cave to avoid the lashing rain. And Hollian was accompanied by Harn, the *Haruchai* who had taken the eh-Brand under his care in the days when Covenant had rescued them from the hold of Revelstone and the Banefire.

Covenant stared at him. When Sunder and Hollian had left Seareach to begin their mission against the Clave, Harn had gone with them. But not alone: they had also been accompanied by Stell, the *Haruchai* who had watched over Sunder.

Where was Stell?

No, more than that; worse than that. Where were the men and women of the Land, the villagers Sunder and Hollian had gone to muster? And where were the rest of the *Haruchai*? After the heinous slaughter which the Clave had wrought upon the people, why had only Durris and Fole been sent to give battle?

You will find none here.

Had the na-Mhoram already won?

Gaping at Sunder across the guttering fire, Covenant moved his jaw, but no words came. In the cover of the cave, the storm was muffled but incessant—fierce and hungry as a great beast. And Sunder was changed. In spite of all the blood his role as the Graveler of Mithil Stonedown had forced him to shed, he had never looked like a man who knew how to kill. But he did now.

When Covenant had first met him, the Stonedownor's youthful features had been strangely confused and conflicted by the unresolved demands of his duty. His father had taught him that the world was not what the Riders claimed it to be —a punishment for human offense—and so he had never learned to accept or forgive the acts which the rule of the Clave and the stricture of the Sunbane required him to commit. Unacknowledged revulsion had marked his forehead; his eyes had been worn dull by accumulated remorse; his teeth had ground together, chewing the bitter gristle of his irreconciliation. But now he appeared as honed and whetted as the poniard he had once used to take the lives of the people he loved. His eyes gleamed like daggers in the firelight. And all his movements were tense with coiled anger—a savage and baffled rage that he could not utter.

His visage held no welcome. The First had told him that the quest had failed. Yet his manner suggested that his tautness was not directed at the Unbeliever—that even bare relief and pleasure had become impossible to articulate.

In dismay, Covenant looked to Hollian for an explanation.

The eh-Brand also showed the marks of her recent life. Her leather shift was tattered in places, poorly mended. Her arms and legs exposed the thinness of scant rations and constant danger. Yet she formed a particular contrast to Sunder.

They were both of sturdy Stonedownor stock, dark-haired and short, though she was younger than he. But her background had been entirely different than his. Until the shock which had cost her her home in Crystal Stonedown—the crisis of the Rider's demand for her life, and of her rescue by Covenant, Linden, and Sunder—she had been the most prized member of her community. As an eh-Brand, able to foretell the phases of the Sunbane, she had given her people a precious advantage. Her past had contained little of the self-doubt and bereavement which had filled Sunder's days. And that difference was more striking now. She was luminous rather than angry—as warm of welcome as he was rigid. If the glances she cast at the Graveler had not been so full of endearment, Covenant might have thought that the two Stonedownors had become strangers to each other.

But the black hair that flew like raven wings about her shoulders when she moved had not changed. It still gave her an aspect of fatality, a suggestion of doom.

In shame, Covenant found that he did not know what to say to her either. She and Sunder were too vivid to him;

they mattered too much. *You will find none here.* With a perception as acute as intuition, he saw that they were not at all strangers to each other. Sunder was so tight and bitter precisely because of the way Hollian glowed; and her luminescence came from the same root as his pain. But that insight did not give Covenant any words he could bear to say.

Where was Stell?

Where were the people of the Land? And the *Haruchai*? And what had happened to the Stonedownors?

The First tried to bridge the awkward silence with Giantish courtesy. In the past, the role of spokesman in such situations had belonged to Honninscrave; but he had lost heart for it.

"Stone and Sea!" she began. "It gladdens me to greet you again, Sunder Graveler and Hollian eh-Brand. When we parted, I hardly dared dream that we would meet again. It is—"

Linden's abrupt whisper stopped the First. She had been staring intensely at Hollian; and her exclamation stilled the gathering, bore clearly through the thick barrage of the rain.

"Covenant. She's pregnant."

Oh my God.

Hollian's slim shape showed nothing. But hardly ninety days had passed since the Stonedownors had left Seareach. Linden's assertion carried instant conviction; her percipience would not be mistaken about such a thing.

The sudden weight of understanding forced him to the floor. His legs refused to support the revelation. *Pregnant.*

That was why Hollian glowed and Sunder raged. She was glad of it because she loved him. And because he loved her, he was appalled. The quest for the One Tree had failed. The purpose for which Covenant had sent the Stonedownors back to the Upper Land had failed. And Sunder had already been compelled to kill one wife and child. He had nowhere left to turn.

"Oh, Sunder." Covenant was not certain that he spoke aloud. Eyes streaming, he bowed his head. It should have been covered with ashes and execration. "Forgive me. I'm so sorry."

"Is the fault yours then that the quest has failed?" asked Sunder. He sounded as severe as hate. "Have you brought us to this pass, that my own failure has opened the last door of doom?"

Yes, Covenant replied—aloud or silent, it made no difference.

"Then hear me, ur-Lord." Sunder's voice came closer. Now it was occluded with grief. "Unbeliever and white gold wielder. Illender and Prover of Life." His hands gripped Covenant's shoulders. "Hear me."

Covenant looked up, fighting for self-control. The Graveler crouched before him. Sunder's eyes were blurred; beads of wet firelight coursed his hard jaws.

"When first you persuaded me from my home and duty in Mithil Stonedown," he said thickly, "I demanded of you that you should not betray me. You impelled me on a mad search of the desert sun for my friend Marid, whom you could not save—and you refused me the use of my blood to aid you—and you required of me that I eat *aliantha* which I knew to be poison—and so I beseeched of you something greater than fidelity. I pleaded of you meaning for my life— and for the death of Nassic my father. And still you were not done, for you wrested Hollian Amith-daughter from her peril in Crystal Stonedown as if it were your desire that I should love her. And when we fell together into the hands of the Clave, you redeemed us from that hold, restored our lives.

"And *still* you were not done. When you had taught us to behold the Clave's evil, you turned your back on that crime, though it cried out for retribution in the face of all the Land. There you betrayed me, ur-Lord. The meaning of which I was in such need you set aside. In its place, you gave me only a task that surpassed my strength."

That was true. In blood-loss and folly and passion, Covenant had made himself responsible for the truth he had required Sunder to accept. And then he had failed. What was that, if not betrayal? Sunder's accusations made him bleed rue and tears.

But Sunder also was not done. "Therefore," he went on hoarsely, "it is my right that you should hear me. Ur-Lord and Unbeliever, white gold wielder," he said as if he were addressing the hot streaks that stained Covenant's face, "you have betrayed me—and I am glad that you have come. Though you come without hope, you are the one hope that I have known. You have it in your hands to create or deny whatever truth you will, and I desire to serve you. While you remain, I will accept neither despair nor doom. There is neither betrayal nor failure while you endure to me. And if the truth you teach must be lost at last, I will be consoled that my love and I were not asked to bear that loss alone.

"Covenant, hear me," he insisted. "No words suffice. I am glad that you have come."

Mutely, Covenant put his arms around Sunder's neck and hugged him.

The crying of his heart was also a promise. This time I won't turn my back. I'm going to tear those bastards down.

He remained there until the Graveler's answering clasp had comforted him.

Then Pitchwife broke the silence by clearing his throat; and Linden said in a voice husky with empathy, "It's about time. I thought you two were *never* going to start talking to each other." She was standing beside Hollian as if they had momentarily become sisters.

Covenant loosened his hold; but for a moment longer he did not release the Graveler. Swallowing heavily, he murmured, "Mhoram used to say things like that. You're starting to resemble him. As long as the Land can still produce people like you. And Hollian." Recollections of the long-dead Lord made him blink fiercely to clear his sight. "Foul thinks all he has to do is break the Arch of Time and rip the world apart. But he's wrong. Beauty isn't that easily destroyed." Recalling a song that Lena had sung to him when she was still a girl and he was new to the Land, he quoted softly, " 'The soul in which the flower grows survives.' "

With a crooked smile, Sunder rose to his feet. Covenant joined him, and the two of them faced their companions. To the First, Sunder said, "Pardon my unwelcome. The news of your quest smote me sorely. But you have come far across the unknown places of the Earth in pain and peril, and we are well met. The Land has need of you—and to you we may be of use." Formally, he introduced Durris and Fole in case the Giants had not caught their names earlier. Then he concluded, "Our food is scanty, but we ask that you share it with us."

The First replied by presenting Mistweave to the Stonedownors. They already knew Vain; and Findail she ignored as if he had ceased to impinge upon her awareness. After a glance around the shallow, wet cave, she said, "It would appear that we are better supplied for sharing. Graveler, how great is our distance from this Revelstone the Giantfriend seeks?"

"A journey of five days," Sunder responded, "or of three, if we require no stealth to ward us from the notice of the Clave."

"Then," stated the First, "we are stocked to the verge of bounty. And you are in need of bounty." She looked deliberately at Hollian's thinness. "Let us celebrate this meeting and this shelter with sustenance."

She unslung her pack; and the other Giants followed her example. Honninscrave and Mistweave started to prepare a meal. Pitchwife tried to stretch some of the kinks out of his back. The rain continued to hammer relentlessly onto the hillside, and water ran down the slanted ceiling, formed puddles and rivulets on the floor. Yet the relative dryness and warmth of the shelter were a consolation. Covenant had heard somewhere that exposure to an incessant rain could drive people mad. Rubbing his numb fingers through his beard, he watched his companions and tried to muster the courage for questions.

The First and Pitchwife remained stubbornly themselves in spite of rain and weariness and discouragement. While she waited for food, she took out her huge longsword, began to dry it meticulously; and he went to reminisce with Sunder, describing their previous meeting and adventures in Sarangrave Flat with irrepressible humor. Mistweave, however, was still doubtful, hesitant. At one point, he appeared unable to choose which pouch of staples he should open, confused by that simple decision until Honninscrave growled at him. Neither time nor the blows he had struck against the *arghuleh* had healed his self-distrust, and its cracks were spreading.

And the Master seemed to grow increasingly unGiantlike. He showed a startling lack of enthusiasm for his reunion with the Stonedownors, for the company of more *Haruchai* —even for the prospect of food. His movements were duties he performed simply to pass the time until he reached his goal, had a chance to achieve his purpose. Covenant did not know what that purpose was; but the thought of what it might be sent a chill through him. Honninscrave looked like a man who was determined to rejoin his brother at any cost.

Covenant wanted to demand some explanation; but there

was no privacy available. Setting the matter aside, he looked around the rest of the gathering.

Linden had taken Hollian to a dryer place against one wall and was examining the eh-Brand with her senses, testing the health and growth of the child Hollian carried. The noise of the rain covered their quiet voices. But then Linden announced firmly, "It's a boy." Hollian's dark eyes turned toward Sunder and shone.

Vain and Findail had not moved. Vain appeared insensate to the water that beaded on his black skin, dripped from his tattered tunic. And even direct rain could not touch the Appointed: it passed through him as if his reality were of a different kind altogether.

Near the edge of the cave, the *Haruchai* stood in a loose group. Durris and Fole watched the storm; Cail and Harn faced inward. If they were mentally sharing their separate stories, their flat expressions gave no sign of the exchange.

Like Bloodguard, Covenant thought. Each of them seemed to know by direct inspiration what any of the others knew. The only difference was that these *Haruchai* were not immune to time. But perhaps that only made them less willing to compromise.

He was suddenly sure that he did not want to be served by them anymore. He did not want to be served at all. The commitments people made to him were too costly. He was on his way to doom; he should have been traveling alone. Yet here were five more people whose lives would be hazarded with his. Six, counting Hollian's child, who had no say in the matter.

And what had happened to the other *Haruchai*—to those that had surely come like Fole and Durris to oppose the Clave?

And why had Sunder and Hollian failed?

When the food was ready, he sat down among his companions near the fire with his back to the cave wall and his guts tight. The act of eating both postponed and brought closer the time for questions.

Shortly, Hollian passed around a leather pouch. When Covenant drank from it, he tasted *metheglin*, the thick, cloying mead brewed by the villagers of the Land.

Implications snapped at him. His head jerked up. "Then you *didn't* fail."

Sunder scowled as if Covenant's expostulation pained him; but Hollian met the statement squarely. "Not altogether." Her mouth smiled, but her eyes were somber. "In no Stonedown or Woodhelven did we fail altogether—in no village but one."

Covenant set the pouch down carefully in front of him. His shoulders were trembling. He had to concentrate severely to keep his hands and voice steady. "Tell me." All the eyes of the travelers were on Sunder and Hollian. "Tell me what happened."

Sunder threw down the hunk of bread he had been chewing. "Failure is not a word to be trusted," he began harshly. His gaze avoided Covenant, Linden, the Giants, nailed itself to the embers of the fire. "It may mean one thing or another. We have failed—and we have not."

"Graveler," Pitchwife interposed softly. "It is said among our people that joy is in the ears that hear, not in the mouth that speaks. The quest for the One Tree has brought to us many aghast and heart-cruel tales, and we have not always heard them well. Yet are we here—sorely scathed, it may be"—he glanced at Honninscrave—"but not wholly daunted. Do not scruple to grant us a part in your hurt."

For a moment, Sunder covered his face as if he were weeping again. But when he dropped his hands, his fundamental gall was bright in his eyes.

"Hear me, then," he said stiffly. "Departing Seareach, we bore with us the *krill* of Loric and the ur-Lord's trust. In my heart were hope and purpose, and I had learned a new love when all the old were dead." All slain: his father by murder, his mother by necessity, his wife and son by his own hand. "Therefore I believed that we would be believed when we spoke our message of defiance among the villages.

"From The Grieve, we wended north as well as west, seeking a way to the Upper Land which would not expose us to the lurker of Sarangrave Flat." And that part of the journey had been a pleasure, for they were alone together except for Stell and Harn; and Seareach from its coast to its high hills and the surviving remnant of Giant Woods had never been touched by the Sunbane. Uncertainty had clouded their earlier traversal of this region; but now they saw it as a beautiful land in the height of its fall glory, tasted the transforming savor of woodlands and animals, birds and flowers. The Clave taught that the Land had been created as a place of punishment, a gallow-fells, for human evil. But Covenant had repudiated that teaching; and in Seareach for the first time Sunder and Hollian began to comprehend what the Unbeliever meant.

So their purpose against the Clave grew clearer; and at last they dared the northern reaches of the Sarangrave in order to begin their work without more delay.

Climbing Landsdrop, they reentered the pale of the Sunbane.

The task of finding villages was not easy. They had no maps and were unacquainted with the scope of the Land. But eventually the farsighted *Haruchai* spotted a Rider; and that red-robed woman unwittingly led the travelers to their first destination—a small Woodhelven crouched in a gully among old hills.

"Far Woodhelven did not entirely welcome us," muttered the Graveler sourly.

"The Rider took from them their youngest and their best," Hollian explained. "And not in the former manner. Always the Clave has exercised caution in its demands, for if the people were decimated where would the Riders turn for blood? But with the foreshortening of the Sunbane such husbandry was set aside. Riders accosted each village with doubled and trebled frequency, requiring every life that their Coursers might bear."

"Deprived of the *Haruchai* which you redeemed," Sunder added to Covenant, "the Riders turned from their accustomed harvestry to outright ravage. If the tales we have heard do not mislead us, this ravage commenced at the time of our seaward passage from the Upper Land into Sarangrave Flat. The na-Mhoram read us in the *rukh* which I then bore, and he knew you were gone into a peril from which you could not strike at him." The Graveler spoke as if he knew how Covenant would take this news—how Covenant would blame himself for not giving battle to the Clave earlier. "Therefore what need had he for any caution?"

Covenant flinched inwardly; but he clung to what the Stonedownors were saying, forced himself to hear it.

"When we entered Far Woodhelven," the eh-Brand went on, "they were reduced to elders and invalids and bitterness. How should they have welcomed us? They saw us only as blood with which they might purchase a period of survival."

Sunder glared into the fire, his eyes as hard as polished stones. "That violence I forestalled. Using the *krill* of Loric and the *orcrest* Sunstone, I raised water and *ussusimiel* without bloodshed under a desert sun. Such power was an astonishment to them. Thus when I had done they were ready to hear whatever words we might speak against the Clave. But what meaning could our speech have to them? What opposition remained possible to the remnant of their village? They were too much reduced to do aught but huddle in their homes and strive for bare life. We did not altogether fail," he rasped, "but I know no other name for that which we accomplished."

Hollian put a gentle hand on his arm. The rain roared on outside the cave. Water trickled constantly past Covenant's legs. But he ignored the wet, closed his mind to the fierce and useless regret rising like venom from the pit of his stomach. Later he would let himself feel the sheer dismay of what he had unleashed upon the Land. Right now he needed to listen.

"One thing we gained from Far Woodhelven," the eh-Brand continued. "They gave us knowledge of a Stonedown lying to the west. We were not required to make search for the opportunity to attempt our purpose a second time."

"Oh, forsooth!" Sunder snarled. Bafflement and rage mounted within him. "That knowledge they gave us. Such knowledge is easily ceded. From that day to this, we have not been required to make any search. The failure of each village has led us onward. As we passed ever westward, nearer to Revelstone, each Woodhelven and Stonedown became more arduous of suasion, for the greater proximity of the na-Mhoram's Keep taught a greater fear. Yet always the gifts of *krill* and Sunstone and *lianar* obtained for us some measure of welcome. But those folk no longer possessed blood enough to sustain their fear—and so also they lacked blood for resistance. Their only answer to our gifts and words was their knowledge of other villages.

"Thomas Covenant," he said suddenly, "this is bile to me— but I would not be misheard. Betimes from village to village we happened upon a man or a woman young and hale enough to have offered other aid—and yet unwilling. We encountered folk for whom it was inconceivable that any man or woman might love the Land. Upon occasion our lives were attempted, for what dying people would not covet the powers we bore? Then only the prowess of the *Haruchai* preserved us. Yet in the main we were given no other gift because no other gift was possible. I have learned a great bitterness which I know not how to sweet—but the blame of it does not fall upon the people of the Land. I would not have believed that the bare life of any village could suffer so much loss and still endure."

For a moment, he fell silent; and the battering sound of the rain ran through the cave. He had placed his hand over Hollian's; the force of his grip corded the backs of his knuckles. He was no taller than Linden, but his stature could not be measured by size. To Covenant, he appeared as thwarted and dangerous as Berek Halfhand had been on the slopes of Mount Thunder, when the ancient hero and Lord-Fatherer had at last set his hand to the Earthpower.

The silence was like the muffled barrage of the storm. The Clave had already shed a heinous amount of blood—yet too many lives remained at stake, and Covenant did not know how to protect them. Needing support, he looked toward Linden. But she did not notice his gaze. Her head was up, her eyes keen, as if she were scenting the air, tracing a tension or peril he could not discern.

He glanced at the Giants. But Honninscrave's orbs were hidden beneath the clenched fist of his brows; and Mistweave, Pitchwife, and the First were fixed on the Stonedownors.

At the mouth of the cave, Cail raised one arm as though in spite of his native dispassion he wished to make a gesture of protest. But then he lowered his hand back to his side.

Abruptly, Sunder began speaking again. "Only one village did not accord to us even that chimera of a gift—and it was the last." His voice was knotted and rough. "From it we have lately come, retracing our way because we had no more hope.

"Our path from village to village led us westward in a crescent-line, so that we passed to the east of Revelstone wending toward the north—toward a place which named itself Landsverge Stonedown. The Woodhelven giving us that knowledge lay perilously nigh the Keep of the na-Mhoram, but Landsverge Stonedown was nigher—and therefore we feared its fear of the Clave would be too great to be countered. Yet when we gained the village, we learned that it would never suffer such fear again."

He paused, then growled, "It was altogether empty of life.

The Riders had gutted it entirely, borne every beating heart away to feed the Banefire. Not one child or cripple remained to be consumed by the Sunbane."

After that, he stopped—gripped himself still as if he would not be able to say another word without howling.

Hollian gave him a sad hug. "We knew not where to turn," she said, "so we returned eastward. It was our thought that we must avoid the grasp of the Clave and await you—for surely the Unbeliever and white gold wielder would not fail of his quest"—her tone was candid, but free of sarcasm or accusation—"and when he came he would come from the east. In that, at least, we were blessed. Far sooner than we had dared desire, the *Haruchai* became cognizant of your presence and guided us together." A moment later, she added, "We have been blessed also in the *Haruchai*."

Linden was no longer facing the loose circle of her companions. She had turned toward Cail and his people; and the lines of her back were tight, insistent. But still she said nothing.

Covenant forced himself to ignore her. The Stonedownors were not done. Apprehension made his tone as trenchant as anger. "How did you meet Durris and Fole?" He could no longer suppress his quivering. "What happened to Stell?"

At that, a spasm passed over Sunder's face. When the answer came, it came from the eh-Brand.

"Thomas Covenant," she said, speaking directly to him as if at that moment nothing else mattered, "you have twice redeemed me from the malice of the Clave. And though you reft me of my home in Crystal Stonedown, where I was acknowledged and desired, you have given me a purpose and a love to repair that loss. I do not wish to cause you hurt."

She glanced at Sunder, then continued, "But this tale also must be told. It is needful." Stiffening herself to the necessity, she said, "When we passed to the east of Revelstone—tending toward the north—we encountered a band of some score *Haruchai*. With fourscore more of their people, they had come to make answer to the depredations of the Clave. And when they had heard our story, they understood why the people of the Land had not arisen in resistance. Therefore they set themselves a task—to form a cordon around Revelstone, a barrier that would prevent the passage of any Rider. Thus they thought to oppose the Clave—and to starve the Banefire—while they also awaited your return.

"Yet four of them elected to join the purpose of our search. Durris and Fole, whom you see, and also Bern and Toril"—her throat closed momentarily—"who are gone—as Stell is gone. For our ignorance betrayed us.

"It was known to all that the Clave possesses power to dominate minds. By that means were the *Haruchai* ensnared in the past. But none among us knew how great the power had grown. As we traversed the proximity of Revelstone, Bern, Toril, and Stell scouted some distance westward to ensure our safety. We were yet a day's journey from the Keep, and not Harn, Durris, nor Fole met any harm. But the slightly greater nearness of the others bared them to the Clave's touch—and to its dominion. Setting aside all caution, they left us to answer that coercion.

"Sensing what had transpired—the utter loss of mind and will—Harn, Durris, and Fole could not give chase, lest they also fall under the na-Mhoram's sway. But Sunder and I—" The memory made her falter, but she did not permit herself to stop. "We gave pursuit. And we gave battle, striving with *krill*-fire and force to break the hold of the Clave—though in so doing we surely made our presence known to the na-Mhoram, forewarning him of us—and perhaps also of you. Mayhap we would have opposed Stell and his companions to the very gates of Revelstone. We were desperate and fevered. But at the last we halted." She swallowed convulsively. "For we saw that Bern, Stell, and Toril were not alone. From around the region came a score and more of the *Haruchai*—all ensnared, all walking mindless and deaf toward the knife and the Banefire." Tears filled her eyes. "And at that sight," she went on as if she were ashamed, "we were broken. We fled because naught else remained for us to do.

"During the night," she finished softly, "Gibbon na-Mhoram reached out to us and attempted mastery of the *krill*'s white gem. But Sunder my love kept the light clean." Then her tone hardened. "If the na-Mhoram remains in any way accessible to fear, I conceive he has been somewhat daunted—for surely Sunder gave him to believe that the ur-Lord was already returned."

But Covenant hardly heard her conclusion. He was foun-

dering in the visions her words evoked: the immedicable stupor
of the *Haruchai*; the frenzy of the Stonedownors as they had
pleaded, opposed, struggled, driving themselves almost into
the jaws of the Clave and still failing to save their comrades;
the glee or apprehension implicit in Gibbon's efforts to con-
quer the *krill*. His brain reeled with images of the enormous
consequences of his earlier refusal to fight the Clave. Among
the Dead in Andelain, Bannor had said to him, *Redeem my*
people. Their plight is an abomination. And he had thought
himself successful when he had broken open the hold of
Revelstone, set the *Haruchai* free. But he had not succeeded,
had not. He had let the Riders and the na-Mhoram live to
do again every evil thing they had done before; and the Sunbane had risen to a period of two days on the blood of
ravaged villages and helpless *Haruchai*.

Yet Linden's sharp protest pierced him, snatched him out
of himself. An instinct deeper than panic or shame wrenched
him to his feet and sent him after her as she scrambled
toward Cail and Harn.

But she was too slow, had divined the meaning of their
tension too late. With appalling suddenness, Harn struck Cail
a blow that knocked him out into the force of the rain.

Sunder, Hollian, and the Giants sprang upright behind
Covenant. One running stride ahead of him, Linden was
caught by Fole and heaved aside. An instant later, Durris'
arm slammed like an iron bar across Covenant's chest. He
stumbled back against the First.

She held him. He hung in her grasp, gasping for breath
while small suns of pain staggered around his sight.

Veiled by torrents, Cail and Harn were barely visible. In
mud that should have made footing impossible, rain that
should have blinded them, they battled with the precise
abandon of madmen.

Furiously, Linden yelled, "Stop it! Are you out of your
minds?"

Without inflection, Durris replied, "You miscomprehend."
He and Fole stood poised to block any intervention. "This
must be done. It is the way of our people."

Covenant strove for air. Stiffly, the First demanded an
explanation.

Durris' dispassion was implacable. He did not even glance

at the fierce struggle being waged through the rain. "In this fashion, we test each other and resolve doubt."

Cail appeared to be at a disadvantage, unable to match the sheer conviction of Harn's attack. He kept his feet, countered Harn's blows with a skill which seemed inconceivable in that downpour; but he was always on the defensive.

"Cail has spoken to us concerning *ak-Haru Kenaustin Ardenol*. He was companion to the victor, and we desire to measure our worth against his."

A sudden feint unbalanced Cail, enabling Harn to slash his feet from under him; but he recovered with a tumbling roll-and-kick.

"Also it has been said that Brinn and Cail betrayed their chosen fidelity to the seduction of the *merewives*. Cail seeks to demonstrate that the lure of their seduction would have surpassed any *Haruchai* in his place."

Cail and Harn were evenly matched in ability and strength. But Harn had watched his kindred lose their wills and walk into the jaws of the Clave: he struck with the force of repudiation. And Cail had succumbed to the *merewives*, learned to judge himself. Brinn's victory over the Guardian of the One Tree had led to Cable Seadreamer's death. A flurry of punches staggered Cail. As he reeled, a heavy two-fisted blow drove his face into the mire.

Cail!

Covenant grabbed a shuddering breath and twisted out of the First's hands. Fire flashed in his mind, alternately white and black. Flames spread up his right forearm as if his flesh were tinder. He gathered a shout that would stop the *Haruchai*, stun them where they stood.

But Durris went on inflexibly, "Also we desire to grieve for Hergrom and Ceer—and for those whose blood has gone to the Banefire."

Without warning, he spun away from the company, leaped lithe and feral into the rain toward Cail and Harn. Fole was at his side. Together, they attacked.

Then Sunder cried at Covenant, "Do not!" He caught Covenant's arm, braved fire to halt the imminent eruption. "If the na-Mhoram is conscious of the *krill* in my hands, how much more clearly will your power call out to him?"

Covenant started to yell, I don't care! Let him try to stop

me! But Fole and Durris had not hurled themselves solely upon Cail. They were assailing each other and Harn as well; and Cail had risen from the mud to plunge into the general melee. Blows hammered impartially in all directions.

We desire to grieve. Slowly, the fire ran out of Covenant. Ah, hell, he sighed. Have mercy on me. He had no right to question what the *Haruchai* were doing. He had too much experience with the violence of his own grief.

Linden studied the combatants intently. Her face showed a physician's alarm at the possibility of injury. But Sunder met Covenant's gaze and nodded mute comprehension.

As abruptly as it had begun, the fighting stopped. The four *Haruchai* returned stoically to the shelter of the cave. They were all bruised and hurt, though none as sorely as Cail. But his visage concealed defeat, and his people wore no aspect of triumph.

He faced Covenant squarely. "It is agreed that I am unworthy." Slow blood trickled from a cut on his lip, a gash over one cheekbone. "My place at your side is not taken from me, for it was accorded by *ak-Haru Kenaustin Ardenol.* But I am required to acknowledge that the honor of such a place does not become me. Fole will ward the Chosen." After a fraction of hesitation, he added, "Other matters have not been resolved."

"Oh, Cail!" Linden groaned. Covenant spat a curse that was covered by the First's swearing and Pitchwife's expostulation. But there was nothing any of them could do. The *Haruchai* had passed judgment, and they were as untouchable as Bloodguard.

Muttering direly to himself, Covenant hugged his arms over his heart and retreated to the simple comfort of the fire.

After a moment, Sunder and Hollian joined him. They stood nearby in silence until he raised his head. Then, in a softer voice, as if his own plight had been humbled by astonishment, Sunder said, "You have much to tell us, ur-Lord."

"Stop calling me that," Covenant growled. His mouth was full of gall. Ur-Lord was the title the *Haruchai* typically used for him. "There haven't been any Lords worth mentioning for three thousand years."

But he could not refuse to give the Stonedownors the story of his failed quest.

* * *

The task of narration was shared by Linden, the First, and Pitchwife. Sunder and Hollian gaped at the tale of the *Elohim* and Findail, of the way in which Covenant had been silenced; but they had no words for their incomprehension. When the companions began to speak of Cable Seadreamer, Honninscrave rose abruptly and stalked out into the rain; but he returned shortly, looking as sharp and doomed as a boulder gnawed by the sempiternal hunger of the sea. His voice rising in grief at loss and celebration of valor, Pitchwife described the crisis of the One Tree. Then the First related the sailing of Starfare's Gem into the bitten cold of the north. She explained the company's harsh decision to abandon the *dromond*; and the stern iron of her voice made the things she said seem more bearable.

It fell to Covenant to speak of Hamako and the Waynhim, of the company's reentry into the Sunbane. And when he was finished, the violence of the storm had become less.

The rain was fading toward sunset. As the downpour receded to a drizzle, the clouds broke open in the east and followed the sun away, exposing the Land to a night as clear and cold as the stars. A moon with a look of rue on its face swelled toward its full.

The fire seemed brighter now as dark deepened outside the cave. Sunder stirred the embers while he considered what he had heard. Then he addressed Covenant again, and the flames glinted like eagerness in his eyes. "Is it truly your intent to assail the Clave? To bring the Banefire to an end?"

Covenant nodded, scowling.

Sunder glanced at Hollian, then back to Covenant. "I need not say that we will accompany you. We have been thwarted beyond endurance. Even Hollian's child—" For a moment, he faltered in confusion, murmured, "My son," as if he had just realized the truth. But then he resumed firmly, "Even he is not too precious to be hazarded in such a cause."

Covenant started to retort, No, you're wrong. You're all too precious. You're the future of the Land. If it has a future. But the Graveler had come too far to be denied. And Covenant had lost the right or the arrogance to try to withhold the consequences of their own lives from the people he loved.

He took a deep breath, held it to steady himself. The force of Durris' arm had left a pain in his chest that would not go away. But Sunder did not ask the question he feared, did not say, How can you think to confront the might of Revelstone, when your power threatens the very foundation of the Earth? Instead, the Graveler inquired, "What will become of the *Haruchai*?"

That question, too, was severe; but Covenant could face it. Slowly, he let the pent air out of his lungs. "If I succeed, they'll be all right." Nightmares of fire had annealed him to his purpose. "If I fail, there won't be much left to worry about."

Sunder nodded, looked away. Carefully, he asked, "Thomas Covenant, will you accept the *krill* from me?"

More abruptly than he intended, Covenant snapped, "No." When he had first given away Loric's blade, Linden had asked him why he no longer needed it. He had replied, *I'm already too dangerous.* But he had not known then how deep the danger ran. "You're going to need it." To fight with if he failed.

Or if he succeeded.

That was the worst gall, the true root of despair—that even a complete victory over the Clave would accomplish nothing. It would not restore the Law, not heal the Land, not renew the people of the Land. And beyond all question it would not cast down the Despiser. The best Covenant could hope for was a postponement of his doom. And that was as good as no hope at all.

Yet he had been living with despair for so long now that it only confirmed his resolve. He had become like Kevin Landwaster, incapable of turning back, of reconsidering what he meant to do. The sole difference was that Covenant already knew he was going to die.

He preferred that to the death of the Land.

But he did not say such things to his companions. He did not want to give the impression that he blamed Linden for her inability to aid his dying body in the woods behind Haven Farm. And he did not wish to quench the Stonedownors' nascent belief that they had one more chance to make what they had undergone meaningful. Despair belonged to the lone heart, and he kept it to himself. Lord Foul had corrupted everything else—had turned to ill even the affirmative rejection of hate which had once led Covenant to withhold his hand from the Clave. But Sunder and Hollian had been restored to him. Some of the *Haruchai* and the Giants could still be saved. Linden might yet be returned safely to her natural world. He had become ready to bear it.

When Honninscrave left the cave again to pace out his tension under the unpitying stars, Covenant followed him.

The night was cold and poignant, the warmth of the earth drenched away by the long rain. Apparently unconscious of Covenant, Honninscrave climbed the nearest hillside until he gained a vantage from which he could study the southwestern horizon. His lonely bulk was silhouetted against the impenetrable sky. He held himself as rigid as the fetters in Kasreyn's dungeon; but the manacles on him now were more irrefragable than iron. From far back in his throat came small whimpering noises like flakes of grief.

Yet he must have known that Covenant was there. After a moment, he began to speak.

"This is the world which my brother purchased with his soul." His voice sounded like cold, numb hands rubbing each other to no avail. "Seeing that the touch of your power upon the One Tree would surely rouse the Worm, he went to his death to prevent you. And this is the result. The Sunbane waxes, perpetrating atrocity. The human valor of the Stonedownors is baffled. The certainty of the *Haruchai* is thwarted. And against such evils you are rendered futile, bound by the newborn doom to which Cable Seadreamer served as midwife. Do you consider such a world worthy of life? I do not."

For a time, Covenant remained silent. He was thinking that he was not the right person to hear Honninscrave's hurt. His own despair was too complete. His plight was constricted by madness and fire on all sides; and the noose was growing tighter. Yet he could not let the need in Honninscrave's question pass without attempting an answer. The Giant was his friend. And he had his own losses to consider. He needed a reply as sorely as Honninscrave did.

Slowly, he said, "I talked to Foamfollower about hope once." That memory was as vivid as healthy sunshine. "He said it doesn't come from us. It doesn't depend on us. It comes from the worth and power of what we serve." Without flinching, Foamfollower had claimed that his service was to Covenant. When Covenant had protested, *It's all a mistake,* Foamfollower had responded, *Then are you so surprised to learn that I have been thinking about hope?*

But Honninscrave had a different objection. "Aye, verily?"

he growled. He did not glance at Covenant. "And where now under all the Sunbane lies the 'worth and power' that you serve?"

"In you," Covenant snapped back, too vexed by pain to be gentle. "In Sunder and Hollian. In the *Haruchai*." He did not add, In Andelain. Honninscrave had never seen that last flower of the Land's loveliness. And he could not bring himself to say, In me. Instead, he continued, "When Foamfollower and I were together, I didn't have any power. I had the ring—but I didn't know how to use it. And I was trying to do exactly what Foul wanted. I was going to Foul's Creche. Walking right into the trap. Foamfollower helped me anyway." The Giant had surrendered himself to agony in order to carry Covenant across the fierce lava of Hotash Slay. "Not because there was anything special or worthy or powerful about me, but simply because I was human and Foul was breaking my heart. That gave Foamfollower all the hope he needed."

In the process, Covenant had caused the Giant's death. Only the restraint he had learned in the cavern of the One Tree kept him from crying, Don't talk to me about despair! I'm going to destroy the world and there's nothing I can do about it! I need something better from you! Only that restraint—and the tall dark shape of the Master as he stood against the stars, torn by loss and as dear as life.

But then Honninscrave turned as if he had heard the words Covenant had not uttered. His moon-gilt stance took on a curious kindness. Softly, he said, "You are the Giantfriend, and I thank you that there is yet room in your heart for me. No just blame attaches to you for Seadreamer's death—nor for the refusal of *caamora* with which by necessity you sealed his end. But I do not desire hope. I desire to *see*. I covet the vision which taught my brother to accept damnation in the name of what he witnessed."

Quietly, he walked down from the hilltop, leaving Covenant exposed to the emptiness of the night.

In the cold silence, Covenant tried to confront his plight, wrestled for an escape from the logic of Lord Foul's manipulations. Revelstone was perhaps only three days away. But the wild magic had been poisoned, and venom colored all his dreams. He contained no more hope than the black gulf of the heavens, where the Worm of the World's End had already fed. Honninscrave's difficult grace did not feel like forgiveness. It felt as arduous as a grindstone, whetting the dark to a new sharpness. And he was alone.

Not because he lacked friends. In spite of the Land's destitution, it had blessed him with more friendship than he had ever known. No, he was alone because of his ring. Because no one else possessed this extreme power to ruin the Earth. And because he no longer had any right to it at all.

That was the crux, the conflict he could not resolve or avoid; and it seemed to cripple his sense of himself, taking his identity away. What did he have to offer the Land except wild magic and his stubborn passion? What else was he worth to his friends?—or to Linden, who would have to carry the burden as soon as he set it down? From the beginning, his life here had been one of folly and pain, sin and ill; and only wild magic had enabled him to make expiation. And now the Clave had reduced the village to relics. It had ensnared the *Haruchai* once more. The Sunbane had attained a period of two days. Seadreamer and Hergrom and Ceer and Hamako were dead. If he surrenderd his ring now, as Findail and doom urged, how would he ever again be able to bear the weight of his own actions?

We are foemen, you and I, enemies to the end. But the end will be yours, Unbeliever, not mine. At the last there will be but one choice for you, and you will make it in all despair. Of your own volition you will give the white gold into my hand.

Covenant had no answer. In Andelain among the Dead, Mhoram had warned, *He has said to you that you are his Enemy. Remember that he seeks always to mislead you.* But Covenant had no idea what the former High Lord meant.

Around him, a dismay which no amount of moonlight could palliate gripped the hills. Unconsciously, he had sunk to the ground under the glinting accusation of the stars. Findail had said like the Despiser, *He must be persuaded to surrender his ring. If he does not, it is certain that he will destroy the Earth.* Covenant huddled into himself. He needed desperately to cry out and could not—needed to hurl outrage and frenzy at the blind sky and was blocked from any release by the staggering peril of his power. He had fallen into the Despiser's trap, and there was no way out.

When he heard feet ascending the hill behind him, he

covered his face to keep himself from pleading abjectly for help.

He could not read the particular emanations of his companions. He did not know who was approaching him. Vaguely, he expected Sunder or Pitchwife. But the voice which sighed his name like an ache of pity or appeal was Linden's.

He lurched erect to meet her, though he had no courage for her concern, which he had not earned.

The moon sheened her hair as if it were clean and lovely. But her features were in shadow; only the tone of her voice revealed her mood. She spoke as if she knew how close he was to breaking.

As softly as a prayer, she breathed, "Let me try."

At that, something in him did break. "*Let* you?" he fumed suddenly. He had no other way to hold back his grief. "I can hardly *prevent* you. If you're so all-fired bloody eager to be responsible for the world, you don't need *my* permission. You don't even need the physical ring. You can use it from there. All you have to do is *possess* me."

"Stop," she murmured like an echo of supplication, "stop." But his love for her had become anguish, and he could not call it back.

"It won't even be a new experience for you. It'll be just like what you did to your mother. The only difference is that I'll still be alive when you're done."

Then he wrenched himself to a halt, gasping with the force of his desire to retract his jibe, silence it before it reached her.

She raised her fists in the moonlight, and he thought she was going to start railing at him. But she did not. Her percipience must have made the nature of his distress painfully clear to her. For a long moment, she held up her arms as if she were measuring the distance a blow would have to travel to strike him. Then she lowered her hands. In a flat, impersonal tone that she had not used toward him for a long time, she said, "That isn't what I meant."

"I know." Her detachment hurt him more than rage. He was certain now that she would be able to make him weep if she wished. "I'm sorry." His contrition sounded paltry in the sharp night, but he had nothing else to offer her. "I've come all this way, but I might as well have stayed in the cavern of the One Tree. I don't know how to face it."

"Then let somebody try to help you." She did not soften;

but she refrained from attacking him. "If not for yourself, do it for me. I'm right on the edge already. It is all I can do," she articulated carefully, "to just look at the Sunbane and stay sane. When I see you suffering, I can't keep my grip.

"As long as I don't have any power, there's nothing I can do about Lord Foul. Or the Sunbane. So you're the only reason I've got. Like it or not. I'm here because of you. I'm fighting to stay in one piece because of you. I want to *do* something"—her fists rose again like a shout, but her voice remained flat—"for this world—or against Foul—because of you. If you go on like this, I'll crack." Abruptly, her control frayed, and pain welled up in her words like blood in a wound. "I need you to at least stop looking so much like my goddamn father."

Her father, Covenant thought mutely. A man of such self-pity that he had cut his wrists and blamed her for it. *You never loved me anyway.* And from that atrocity had come the darkness which had maimed her life—the black moods, the violence she had enacted against her mother, the susceptibility to evil. Her instances of paralysis. Her attempt on Ceer's life.

Her protest wrung Covenant's heart. It showed him with stunning vividness how little he could afford to fail her. Any other hurt or dread was preferable. Instinctively, he made a new promise—another commitment to match all the others he had broken or kept.

"I don't know the answer," he said, keeping himself quiet in fear that she would perceive how his life depended on what he was saying. "I don't know what I need. But I know what to do about the Clave." He did not tell her what his nightmares had taught him. He did not dare. "When we're done there, I'll know more. One way or the other."

She took him at his word. She had a severe need to trust him. If she did not, she would be forced to treat him as if he were as lost as her parents; and that alternative was plainly appalling to her. Nodding to herself, she folded her arms under her breasts and left the hilltop, went back to the shelter and scant warmth of the cave.

Covenant stayed out in the dark alone for a while longer. But he did not break.

NINE: March to Crisis

BEFORE dawn, the new company ate breakfast, re-packed their supplies, and climbed the nearest hillside to await the sun with stone underfoot. Covenant watched the east gauntly, half fearing that the Sunbane might already have accelerated to a cycle of only one day. But as the sun crested the horizon, the air set blue about it like a corona, giving the still sodden and gray landscape a touch of azure like a hint of glory—as if, Covenant thought dourly, the Sunbane in any hands but Foul's would have been a thing of beauty. But then blackness began to seethe westward; and the light on the hills dimmed. The first fingers of the wind teased at Covenant's beard, mocking him.

Sunder turned to him. The Graveler's eyes were as hard as pebbles as he took out the wrapped bundle of the *krill*. His voice carried harshly across the wind. "Unbeliever, what is your will? When first you gave the *krill* into my hand, you counseled that I make use of it as I would a *rukh*—that I attune myself to it and bend its power to my purpose. This I have done. It was my love who taught me"—he glanced at Hollian—"but I have learned the lesson with all my strength." He had come a long way and was determined not to be found wanting. "Therefore I am able to ease our way—to hasten our journey. But in so doing I will restore us un-questionably to the Clave's knowledge, and Gibbon na-Mhoram will be forewarned against us." Stiffly, he repeated, "What is your will?"

Covenant debated momentarily with himself. If Gibbon were forewarned, he might kill more of his prisoners to stoke the Banefire. But it was possible that he was already

192

aware of the danger. Sunder had suggested as much the previous day. If Covenant traveled cautiously, he might simply give the na-Mhoram more time for preparation.

Covenant's shoulders hunched to strangle his trepidation. "Use the *krill*," he muttered. "I've already lost too much time."

The Graveler nodded as if he had expected no other reply.

From his jerkin, he took out his Sunstone.

It was a type of rock which the Land's former masters of stonelore had named *orcrest*. It was half the size of his fist, irregularly shaped but smooth; and its surface gave a strange impression of translucence without transparency, opening into a dimension where nothing but itself existed.

Deftly, Sunder flipped the cloth from the *krill*'s gem, letting bright argent blaze into the rain-thick gloom. Then he brought the Sunstone and that gem into contact with each other.

At once, a shaft of vermeil power from the *orcrest* shot straight toward the hidden heart of the sun. Sizzling furiously, the beam pierced the drizzle and the thunderheads to tap the force of the Sunbane directly. And the *krill* shone forth as if its light could cast back the rain.

In a snarl of torrents and heavy thunder, the storm swept over the hilltop. The strait red shaft of the *orcrest* seemed to call down lightning like an affront to the heavens. But Sunder stood without flinching, unscathed by any fire.

On the company, no rain fell. Wind slashed the region; thunder crashed; lightning ran like screams across the dark. But Sunder's power formed a pocket in the storm, a zone free of violence.

He was doing what the Clave had always done, using the Sunbane to serve his own ends. But his exertion cost no blood. No one had been shed to make him strong.

That difference sufficed for Covenant. With a grim gesture, he urged his companions into motion.

Quickly, they ranged themselves around Sunder. With Hollian to guide him, the Graveler turned toward the southwest. Holding his *orcrest* and the *krill* clasped together so that they flamed like a challenge, he started in the direction of Revelstone. His protection moved with him, covering all the company.

By slow degrees, a crimson hue crept into the brightness of the *krill*, tinging the light as if the core of the gem had begun to bleed; and long glints of silver streaked the shaft of Sunbane-fire. But Sunder shifted his hands, separated the two powers slightly to keep them pure. As he did so, his zone contracted somewhat, but not enough to hamper the company's progress.

They were scourged by wind. Mud clogged their strides, made every step treacherous. Streams frothing down the hillsides beat against their legs, joined each other to form small rivers and tried to sweep the travelers away. Time and again, Covenant would have fallen without Cail's support. Linden clung severely to Fole's shoulder. All the world had been reduced to a thunderous wall of water—an impenetrable downpour lit by vermeil and argent, scored by lightning. No one tried to speak; only the Giants would have been able to make themselves heard. Yet Sunder's protection enabled the company to move faster than the Sunbane had ever permitted.

Sometime during the day, two gray, blurred shapes appeared like incarnations of the storm and entered the rainless pocket, presented themselves to Covenant. They were *Haruchai*. When he had acknowledged them, they joined his companions without a word.

The intensity with which Linden regarded Sunder told Covenant something he already knew: the Graveler's mastery of two such disparate periapts was a horrendous strain on him. Yet he was a Stonedownor. The native toughness of his people had been conditioned by generations of survival under the ordeal of the Sunbane. And his sense of purpose was clear. When the day's journey finally ended, and he let his fires fall, he appeared so weary that he could hardly stand— but he was no more defeated by fatigue than Covenant, who had done nothing except labor through nearly ten leagues of mire and water. Not for the first time, Covenant thought that the Graveler was more than he deserved.

As the wind whipped the clouds away to the west, the company made camp in an open plain which reminded Covenant of the strict terrain near Revelstone. In a bygone age, that region had been made fruitful by the diligence of its farmers and cattleherds—and by the beneficent power of the Lords. Now everything was painfully altered. He felt that he was on the verge of the Clave's immediate demesne —that the company was about to enter the ambit of the na-Mhoram's Keep.

Nervously, he asked Hollian what the next day's sun would be. In response, she took out her slim *lianar* wand. Its polished surface gleamed like the ancient woods of the Land as she held it up in the light of the campfire.

Like Sunder's left forearm, her right palm was laced with old scars—the cuts from which she had drawn blood for her foretellings. But she no longer had any need of blood. Sunder smiled and handed her the wrapped *krill*. She uncovered it only enough to let one white beam into the night. Then, reverently, like a woman who had never learned anything but respect for her own abilities, she touched her *lianar* to the light.

And flame grew like a plant from the wood. Delicate shoots waved into the air; buds of filigree fire bloomed; leaves curled and opened. Without harming her or the wood, flame spread around her like a growth of mystery.

It was as green and tangy as springtime and new apples.

At the sight, Covenant's nerves tightened involuntarily.

Hollian did not need to explain to him and Linden what her fire meant. They had witnessed it several times in the past. But for the benefit of the watching, wide-eyed Giants, she said quietly, "The morrow will bring a fertile sun."

Covenant glanced at Linden. But she was studying the *Haruchai*, scrutinizing them for any sign of peril. However, Sunder had said that Gibbon's grasp extended only a day's journey beyond the gates of Revelstone; and when Linden at last met Covenant's gaze she shook her head mutely.

Two more days, he thought. One until that Raver can reach us. Unless he decides to try his *Grim* again. *The ill that you deem most terrible.* That night, nightmares stretched him until he believed he would surely snap. They had all become one virulent vision, and in it his fire was as black as venom.

In the pre-green gloom of dawn, another pair of *Haruchai* arrived to join the company. Their faces were as stony and magisterial as the mountains where they lived; and yet Covenant received the dismaying impression that they had come to him in fear. Not fear of death, but of what the Clave could make them do.

Their plight is an abomination. He accepted them. But that was not enough. Bannor had commanded him to redeem them.

When the sun rose, it tinged the stark bare landscape a sick hue that reminded him of the Illearth Stone.

Six days had passed since the desert sun had melted every vestige of vegetation off the Upper Land. As a result, all the plain was a wilderness. But the ground was so water-soaked that it steamed wherever the sun touched it; and the steam seemed to raise fine sprouts of heather and bracken with the suddenness of panic. Where the dirt lay in shadow, it remained as barren as naked bones; but elsewhere the uncoiling green stems grew desperately, flogged by the Sunbane and fed by two days of rain. In moments, the brush had reached the height of Covenant's shins. If he stood still much longer, he might not be able to move at all.

But ahead of him, the Westron Mountains thrust their ragged snowcaps above the horizon. And one promontory of the range lay in a direct line with Sunder's path. Perhaps Revelstone was already visible to the greater sight of the Giants.

If it were, they said nothing about it. Pitchwife watched the preternatural heath with a look of nausea. Mistweave's doubt had assumed an aspect of belligerence, as if he resented the way Fole had supplanted him at Linden's side—and yet believed that he could not justify himself. The First hefted her longsword, estimating her strength against the vegetation. Only Honninscrave studied the southwest eagerly; but his clenched visage revealed nothing except an echo of his earlier judgment: *This is the world which my brother purchased with his soul. Do you consider such a world worthy of life?*

However, the First was not required to cut the company's way. Sunder used his Sunstone and the *krill* as the Riders used their *rukhs*, employing the Sunbane to force open a path. With vermeil fire and white light, the Graveler crushed flat the growth ahead of the company, plowed a way through it. Unhindered by torrents and streams and mire, the travelers were able to increase the previous day's pace.

Before the heather and bracken grew so tall that they blocked Covenant's view of the mountains, he glimpsed a red beam like Sunder's standing from the promontory toward the sun. With an inward shiver, he recognized it. To be visible from that distance, it would have to be tremendous.

The shaft of the Banefire.

Then the writhing brush effaced all the southwest from sight.

For a time, the tight apprehension of that glimpse occupied all his attention. The Banefire. It seemed to dwarf him. He had seen it once, devouring blood with a staggering heat and ferocity that had filled the high cavity of the sacred enclosure. Even at the level where the Readers had tended the *master-rukh*, that conflagration had hit him with an incinerating force, burning his thoughts to ashes. The simple memory of it made him flinch. He could hardly believe that even rampant wild magic would be a match for it. The conflict between such powers would be fierce enough to shatter mountains. And the Arch of Time? He did not know the answer.

But by midmorning Sunder began to stumble; and Covenant's attention was wrenched outward. The Graveler used his periapts as if together they formed a special kind of *rukh*; but they did not. The *rukhs* of the Riders drew their true strength straight from the *master-rukh* and the Banefire, and so each Rider needed only enough personal exertion to keep open a channel of power to Revelstone; the Banefire did the rest. But Sunder wielded the Sunbane and the *krill* directly.

The effort was exhausting him.

Linden read his condition at a glance. "Give him *diamondraught*," she muttered stiffly. Her rigid resistance to the ill of the vegetation made her sound distant, impersonal. "And carry him. He'll be all right. If we take care of him." After a moment, she added, "He's stubborn enough to stand it."

Sunder smiled at her wanly. Pallor lay beneath the shade of his skin; but as he sipped the Giantish liquor he grew markedly stronger. Yet he did not protest when Honninscrave hoisted him into the air. Sitting with his back against the Master's chest, his legs bent over the Giant's arms, he raised his powers again; and the company resumed its trek.

Shortly after noon, two more *Haruchai* joined Covenant, bringing to ten the number of their people ranged protectively on either side of him and his companions.

He saluted them strictly; but their presence only made him more afraid. He did not know how to defend them from Gibbon.

And his fear increased as Sunder grew weaker. Even with Sunstone and *krill*, the Graveler was only one lone man.

While the obstacles swarming in front of him were simply bracken and heather, he was able to furrow them as effectively as any Rider. But then the soil changed: the terrain became a jungle of mad rhododendron, jacaranda, and honeysuckle. Through that tangle he could not force his way with anything like the direct accuracy which the Banefire made possible. He had to grope for the line of least resistance; and the jungle closed behind the travelers as if they were lost.

The sun had fallen near the Westron Mountains, and the light had become little more than a filtered gloom, when Linden and Hollian gasped simultaneously, "Sunder!"

Honninscrave jerked to a halt. The First wheeled to stare at the Graveler. Covenant's throat constricted with panic as he scrambled forward at Linden's back.

The Master set Sunder down as the company crowded around them. At once, Sunder's knees buckled. His arms shook with a wild ague.

Covenant squeezed between the First and Pitchwife to confront the Graveler. Recognition whitened Hollian's face, made her raven hair look as stark as a dirge. Linden's eyes flicked back and forth between the Sunstone and the *krill*.

The vermeil shaft springing from his *orcrest* toward the setting sun had a frayed and charred appearance, as if it were being consumed by a hotter fire. And in the core of the *krill*'s clear gem burned a hard knot of blackness like a canker.

"The na-Mhoram attempts to take him!" Hollian panted desperately. "How can he save himself, when he is so sorely weary?"

Sunder's eyes were fixed on something he could no longer see. New lines marked his ashen face, cut by the acid sweat that slicked his skin. Tremors knotted in his muscles. His expression was as naked and appalled as a seizure.

"Put them down!" Linden snapped at him, pitching her voice to pierce his fixation. "Let go! Don't let him do this to you!"

The corners of Sunder's jaw bulged dangerously. With a groan as if he were breaking his own arm, he forced down the Sunstone, dropped it to the ground. Instantly, its crimson beam vanished: the *orcrest* relapsed to elusive translucence.

But the blackness at the center of the *krill* swelled and became stronger.

Grimly, Sunder clinched his free hand around the blade's wrappings. Heat shone from the metal. Bowing his head, he held the *krill* in a grip like fever and fought to throw off the Clave's touch—fought with the same human and indefeasible abandon by which he had once nearly convinced Gibbon that Covenant was dead.

Linden was shouting, "Sunder! Stop! It's killing you!" But the Graveler did not heed her.

Covenant put out his half-hand. Fire spattered from his ring as if the simple proximity of Gibbon's power made the silver-white band unquenchable.

Findail's protest rang across the jungle. Covenant ignored it. Sunder was his friend, and he had already failed too often. Perhaps he was not ready to test himself against the Clave and the Banefire. Perhaps he would never be ready. But he did not hesitate. Deliberately, he took hold of the *krill*. With the strength of fire, he lifted the blade from Sunder's grasp as if the Graveler's muscles had become sand.

But when he closed wild magic around the *krill*, all his flame went black.

Midnight conflagration as hungry as hate burst among the company, tore through the trees. A rage of darkness raved out of him as if at last the venom had triumphed, had become the whole truth of his power.

For an instant, he quailed. Then Linden's wild cry reached him.

Savage with extremity, he ripped his fire out of the air, flung it down like a tapestry from the walls of his mind. The *krill* slipped between his numb fingers, stuck point first in the desecrated soil.

Before he could move, react, breathe, try to contain the horror clanging in his heart like the carillon of despair, a heavy blow was struck behind him; and Cail reeled through the brush.

Another blow: a fist like stone. Covenant pitched forward, slammed against the rough trunk of a rhododendron, and sprawled on his back, gasping as if all the air had been taken out of the world. Glints of sunset came through the leaves like emerald stars, spun dizzily across his vision.

Around him, fighting pounded among the trees. But it made no sound. His hearing was gone. Linden's stretched shout was mute; the First's strenuous anger had no voice.

Galvanized by frenzy, Hollian dragged Sunder bodily out of the way of the battle. She passed in front of Covenant, blocked his view for a moment. But nothing could block the bright, breathless vertigo that wheeled through him, as compulsory and damning as the aura of the Worm.

Cail and the Giants were locked in combat with Harn, Durris, and the rest of the *Haruchai*.

The movements of the attackers were curiously sluggish, imprecise. They did not appear to be in control of themselves. But they struck with the full force of their native strength— blows so hard that even the Giants were staggered. Pitchwife went down under the automatic might of Fole and another *Haruchai*. Swinging the flat of her falchion, the First struggled to her husband's aid. Honninscrave leveled one of the *Haruchai* with each fist. Cail's people no longer had the balance or alertness to avoid his massive punches. But the attackers came back to their feet as if they were inured to pain and assailed him again. Mistwave bearhugged one *Haruchai*, knocked another away with a kick. But the *Haruchai* struck him a blow in the face that made his head crack backward, loosened his grasp.

Moving as stiffly as a man in a *geas*, Harn pursued Cail through the battle. Cail eluded him easily; but Harn did not relent. He looked as mindless as Durris, Fole, and the others.

They had been mastered by the Clave.

Slowly, the vertigo spinning across Covenant's sight came into focus; and he found himself staring at the *krill*. It stood in the dirt like a small cross scant feet from his face. Though fighting hit and tumbled everywhere, no one touched Loric's eldritch blade.

Its gem shone with a clear, clean argence; no taint marred the pure depths of the jewel.

Gibbon's attempt on it had been a feint—a way of distracting the company until he could take hold of all the *Haruchai*.

All except Cail.

With the dreamy detachment of anoxia, Covenant wondered why Cail was immune.

Abruptly, the knotting of his muscles eased. He jerked air into his lungs, biting raw hunks of it past the stunned paroxysm which had kept him from breathing; and sound began to leech back into the jungle—the slash of foliage, the grunt and impact of effort. For a moment, there were no voices; the battle was fought in bitter muteness. But then, as if from a great distance, he heard Linden call out, "Cail! The *merewives*! You got away from them!"

Covenant heaved himself up from the ground in time to see Cail's reaction.

With the suddenness of a panther, Cail pounced on Harn. Harn was too torpid to counter effectively. Ducking under Harn's blunt blows, Cail knocked him off balance, then grabbed him by the shoulder and hip, snatched him into the air. Harn lacked the bare self-command to twist aside as Cail plunged him toward a knee raised and braced to break his back.

Yet at the last instant Harn did twist aside. When Brinn and Cail had been caught in the trance of the *merewives*, Linden had threatened to snap Brinn's arm; and that particular peril had restored him to himself. Harn wrenched out of Cail's grasp, came to his feet facing his kinsman.

For a moment, they gazed at each other impassively, as if nothing had happened. Then Harn nodded. He and Cail sprang to the aid of the Giants.

Still coughing for air, Covenant propped himself against a tree and watched the rest of the fight.

It did not last long. When Cail and Harn had broken Fole and Durris free of Gibbon's hold, the four of them were soon able to rescue the remaining six.

Pitchwife and Mistweave picked their battered bodies out of the brush. The First glared sharply about her, holding her sword ready. Honninscrave folded his arms over his chest to contain the startling force of his own rage. But the *Haruchai* ignored the Giants. They turned away to face each other, speaking mind-to-mind with the silent dispassion of their people. In spite of what had just happened, they did not appear daunted or dismayed.

When their converse was over, Cail looked at the Giants and Linden, then met Covenant squarely. He did not apologize. His people were *Haruchai*, and the offense to their rectitude went too deep for mere contrition. In a voice entirely devoid of inflection, free of any hint of justification or regret, he said, "It is agreed that such unworth as mine has its uses. Whatever restitution you command we will undertake. But we will not again fall from ourselves in this way."

Covenant did not know what to say. He had known the *Haruchai* for a long time, and the Bloodguard before them; yet he was still astonished by the extravagance of their judgments. And he was certain that he would not be able to bear being served by such people much longer. The simple desire to be deserving of them would make him wild.

How was it possible that his white fire had become so black in so little time?

Pitchwife murmured something like a jest under his breath, then grimaced when no one responded. Honninscrave had become too bleak for mirth. In his frustrated desire to prove himself to himself, Mistweave had forgotten laughter. And the First was not mollified by Cail's speech. The *Haruchai* had aroused her battle instinct; and her face was like her blade, whetted for fighting.

Because the sun was setting and Sunder was exhausted, she commanded the Master and Mistweave to prepare a camp and a meal. Yet the decision to rest did not abate her tension. Dourly, she stalked around the area, hacking back the brush to form a relatively clear space for the camp.

Covenant stood and watched her. The blow he had received made everything inside him fragile. Even his truncated senses were not blind to her sore, stern vexation.

Linden would not come near him. She stayed as far away from him as the First's clearing permitted, avoiding him as if to lessen as much as possible his impact on her percipience.

The glances that Hollian cast toward him over Sunder's shoulder were argute with fright and uncertainty in the deepening twilight. Only Vain, Findail, and the *Haruchai* behaved as if they did not care.

Covenant started to cover his face, then lowered his hands again. Their numbness had become repugnant to him. His features felt stiff and breakable. His beard smelled of sweat; his whole body smelled, he was unclean and rank from head to foot. He feared that his voice would crack; but he forced himself to use it.

"All right. Say it. Somebody."

The First delivered a fierce cut that severed a honeysuckle stem as thick as her forearm, then wheeled toward him. The tip of her blade pointed accusations at him.

Linden winced at the First's anger, but did not intervene.

"Giantfriend," the leader of the Search rasped as if the name hurt her mouth. "We have beheld a great ill. Is it truly your intent to utter this dark fire against the Clave?"

She towered over Covenant, and the light of Mistweave's campfire made her appear dominant and necessary. He felt too brittle to reply. Once he had tried to cut the venom out of his forearm on a ragged edge of rock. Those faint scars spread like fretwork around the fundamental marks of Marid's fangs. But now he knew better. Carefully, he said, "He will not do that to me and get away with it."

The First did not waver. "And what of the Earth?"

Her tone made his eyes burn, but not with tears. Every word of his answer was as distinct as a coal. "A long time ago," with the blood of half-mindless Cavewights on his head, "I swore I was never going to kill again. But that hasn't stopped me." With both hands, he had driven a knife into the chest of the man who had slain Lena; and that blow had come back to damn him. He had no idea how many *Bhrathair* had died in the collapse of Kemper's Pitch. "The last time I was there, I killed twenty-one of them." Twenty-one men and women, most of whom did not know that their lives were evil. "I'm sick of guilt. If you think I'm going to do anything that will destroy the Arch of Time, you had better try to stop me now."

At that, her eyes narrowed as if she were considering the implications of running her blade through his throat. Hollian and Linden stared; and Sunder tried to brace himself to go to Covenant's aid. But the First, too, was the Unbeliever's friend. She had given him the title he valued most. Abruptly, the challenge of her sword dropped. "No, Giantfriend," she sighed. "We have come too far. I trust you or nothing."

Roughly, she sheathed her longsword and turned away.

Firelight gleamed in the wet streaks of Linden's concern and relief. After a moment, she came over to Covenant. She did not meet his gaze. But she put one hand briefly on his right forearm like a recognition that he was not like her father.

While that touch lasted, he ached to take hold of her hand and raise it to his lips. But he did not move. He believed that if he did he would surely shatter. And every promise he had made would be lost.

* * *

The next day, the fruits of the verdant sun were worse. They clogged the ground with the teeming, intractable frenzy of a sea in storm. And Sunder's weariness went too deep to be cured by one night of *diamondraught*-induced sleep, one swallow of the rare and potent roborant Pitchwife created by combining his liquor with *vitrim*. But the Clave made no more efforts to take control of the *krill* or the *Haruchai*. The shade of the trees held some of the underbrush to bearable proportions. No *Grim* or other attack came riding out of Revelstone to bar the way. And the travelers had made such good progress during the past two days that they did not need to hurry now. None of them doubted that the Keep of the na-Mhoram was within reach. At infrequent intervals, the distortion of the jungle provided a glimpse of the southwestern sky; and then all the companions could see the hot, feral shaft of the Banefire burning toward the sun like an immedicable scald in the green-hued air.

Every glimpse turned Linden's taut, delicate features a shade paler. Memory and emanations of power assaulted her vulnerable senses. She had once been Gibbon-Raver's prisoner in Revelstone, and his touch had raised the darkness coiled around the roots of her soul to the stature of all night. Yet she did not falter. She had aimed the company to this place by the strength of her own will, had wrested this promise from Covenant when he had been immobile with despair. In spite of her unresolved hunger and loathing for power, she did not let herself hang back.

The Stonedownors also held themselves firm. They had a score to settle with the Clave, a tally that stretched from the hold of Revelstone and the ruin of the villages down to the Sunbane-shaped foundations of their lives. Whenever Sunder's need for rest became severe, Hollian took the *orcrest* and *krill* herself, though she was unskilled at that work and the path she made was not as clear as his. The silent caterwaul and torment of the vegetation blocked the ground at every step; but the company found a way through it.

And as the sun began to sag toward the high ridge of the Westron Mountains—still distant to the south and west beyond the region which had once been named Trothgard, but near at hand in the east-jutting promontory of the range— the companions reached the verge of the jungle below the rocky and barren foothills of the high Keep.

Halting in the last shelter of the trees, they looked up at their destination.

Revelstone: once the proud bastion and bourne of the ancient, Land-serving Lords; now the home of the na-Mhoram and the Clave.

Here, at the apex of the promontory, the peaks dropped to form an upland plateau pointing east and sweeping north. All the walls of the plateau were sheer, as effective as battlements; and in the center of the upland lay Glimmermere, the eldritch tarn with its waters untouched by the Sunbane until they cascaded down Furl Falls in the long south face of the promontory and passed beyond the sources of their potency. But the Keep itself stood to the east of Glimmermere and Furl Falls. The Unhomed had wrought the city of the Lords into the eastward wedge of the plateau, filling that outcrop of the Earth's hard gutrock with habitations and defenses.

Directly above the company stood the watchtower, the tip of the wedge. Shorter than the plateau, its upper shaft rose free of the main Keep bulking behind it; but its lower half was sealed by walls of native stone to the rest of the wedge. In that way, Revelstone's sole entrance was guarded. Long ago, massive gates in the southeast curve of the watchtower's base had protected a passage under the tower—a tunnel which gave admittance only to the closed courtyard between the tower and the main Keep, where stood a second set of gates. During the last war, the siege of Revelstone had broken the outer gates, leaving them in rubble. But Covenant knew from experience that the inner gates still held, warding the Clave with their imponderable thickness and weight.

Above the abutment over its opening, the round shaft of the watchtower was marked with battlements and embrasures to the crenellated rim of its crown. They were irregular and unpredictable, shaped to suit the tower's internal convolutions. Yet the face of the watchtower was as simple as child's work compared to the dramatic complexity of the walls of the main Keep. For a surprising distance into the plateau, the sheer cliffs had been crafted by the Unhomed—written with balconies and buttresses, parapets and walkways, and punctuated with windows of every description, embrasures on the lower levels, oriels and shaded coigns higher up—a prolific and apparently spontaneous multiplication of detail that always gave Covenant an impression of underlying structure,

meaning which only Giants could read. The faint green sunset
danced and sheened on the south face, confusing his human
ability to grasp the organization of something so tall, grand,
and timeless.

But even his superficial senses felt the tremendous power
of the Banefire's beam as it struck sunward from athwart the
great Keep. With one stroke, that red force transgressed all
his memories of grandeur and glory, changed the proud
habitation of the Lords to a place of malefic peril. When he
had approached Revelstone so many days ago to rescue
Linden, Sunder, and Hollian, he had been haunted by grief
for the Giants and Lords and beauty the Land had lost. But
now the knot of his chosen rage was pulled too tight to admit
sorrow.

He intended to tear that place down if necessary to root out
the Clave—and the bare thought that he might be forced to
damage Revelstone made him savage.

Yet when he looked at his companions, saw the rapt faces
of the Giants, his anger loosened slightly. The Keep had the
power to entrance them. Pitchwife's mien was wide with the
glee of appreciation; the First's eyes shone pride at the handi-
work of her long-dead people; Mistweave gazed upward
hungrily, all dismay forgotten for a time. Even Honninscrave
had momentarily lost his air of doom, as though he knew
intuitively that Revelstone would give him a chance to make
restitution.

Conflicting passions rose in Covenant's throat. Thickly, he
asked, "Can you read it? Do you know what it means? I've
been here three times"—four counting the brief translation
during which he had refused Mhoram's summons—"but no
one's ever been able to tell me what it means."

For a moment, none of the Giants answered. They could
not step back from the wonder of the Keep. They had seen
Coercri in Seareach and marveled at it; but for them Revelstone was transcendent. Watching them, Covenant knew with
a sudden pang that now they would never turn back—that
no conceivable suasion would induce them to set their Search
and their private purposes aside, to leave the Sunbane and
Lord Foul to him. The Sunbane had eroded them in fundamental ways, gnawing at their ability to believe that their
Search might actually succeed. What could Giants do to aid a

Land in which nature itself had become the source of horror? But the sight of Revelstone restored them to themselves. They would never give up their determination to fight.

Unless Covenant found his own answer soon, he would not be able to save them.

Swallowing heavily, Pitchwife murmured, "No words. There are none. Your scant human tongue is void—" Tears spread through the creases of his face, mapping his emotion.

But the First said for him, "All tongues, Giantfriend. All tongues lack such language. There is that in the granite glory of the world's heart which may not be uttered with words. All other expression must be dumb when the pure stone speaks. And here that speech has been made manifest. Ah, my heart!" Her voice rose as if she wanted to both sing and keen. But for her also no words were adequate. Softly, she concluded, "The Giants of the Land were taught much by their loss of Home. I am humbled before them."

For a moment, Covenant could not respond. But then a memory came back to him—a recollection of the formal salutation that the people of Revelstone had formerly given to the Giants. *Hail and welcome, inheritor of Land's loyalty. Welcome whole or hurt, in boon or bane—ask or give. To any requiring name we will not fail.* In a husky voice, he breathed:

> "Giant-troth Revelstone, ancient ward—
> Heart and door of Earthfriend's main:
> Preserve the true with Power's sword,
> Thou ages-Keeper, mountain-reign."

At that, the First turned toward him; and for an instant her face was concentrated with weeping as if he had touched her deep Giantish love of stone. Almost immediately she recovered her sternness—but not before he had seen how absolutely she was ready now to serve him. Gruffly, she said, "Thomas Covenant, I have titled you Giantfriend, but it is not enough. You are the Earthfriend. No other name suffices."

Then she went and put her arms around her husband.

But Covenant groaned to himself, *Earthfriend. God help me!* That title belonged to Berek Halfhand, who had fashioned the Staff of Law and founded the Council of Lords. It did not become a man who carried the destruction of the Arch of

Time in his envenomed hands. The man who had brought to ruin all Berek's accomplishments.

He glared back up at the Keep. The sun had begun to set behind the Westron Mountains, and its light in his eyes hampered his sight; but he discerned no sign that the watchtower was occupied. He had received the same impression the last time he had been here—and had distrusted it then as he did now. Though the outer gates were broken, the tower could still serve as a vital part of the Keep's defenses. He would have to be prepared for battle the moment he set foot in that tunnel. If the Clave did not seek to attack him before then.

His shoulders hunching like anticipations of brutality, he turned away from the Keep and retreated a short distance into the vegetation to an area of rocks where the company could camp for the night.

Shortly, his companions gathered around him. The Giants left their delighted study of Revelstone to clear the ground, start a fire, and prepare food. Sunder and Hollian cast repeated glances like wincing toward the Keep, where the ill of their lives had its center, and where they had once nearly been slain; but they sat with Covenant as if he were a source of courage. The *Haruchai* arranged themselves protectively around the region. Findail stood like a shadow at the edge of the growing firelight.

Linden's disquiet was palpable. Vexation creased her brows; her gaze searched the twilight warily. Covenant guessed that she was feeling the nearness of the Raver; and he did not know how to comfort her. During all the Land's struggles against Despite, no one had ever found a way to slay a Raver. While Lord Foul endured, his servants clung to life. The Forestal of Garroting Deep, Caer-Caveral's creator and former master, had demonstrated that Herem or Sheol or Jehannum might be sorely hurt or reduced if the bodies they occupied were killed and they were not allowed to flee. But only the body died; the Raver's spirit survived. Covenant could not believe that the Land would ever be free of Gibbon's possessor. And he did not know what else to offer that might ease Linden.

But then she named the immediate cause of her unease; and it was not the na-Mhoram. Turning to Covenant, she said unexpectedly, "Vain's gone."

Taken aback, he blinked at her for a moment. Then he surged to his feet, scanned the camp and the surrounding jungle.

The Demondim-spawn was nowhere in sight.

Covenant wheeled toward Cail. Flatly, the *Haruchai* said, "He has halted a stone's throw distant." He nodded back the way the company had come. "At intervals we have watched him, but he does not move. Is it your wish that he should be warded?"

Covenant shook his head, groping for comprehension. When he and Vain had approached Revelstone looking for Linden, Sunder, and Hollian, the Clave had tried to keep Vain out—and had hurt him in the process. Yet he had contrived his way into the Keep, found the heels of the Staff of Law. But after that he had obeyed the Riders as if he feared what they could do to him. Was that it? Having obtained what he wanted from Revelstone, he now kept his distance so that the Clave would not be able to damage him again?

But how was it possible that the Demondim-spawn could be harmed at all, when the Sunbane did not affect him and even *Grim*-fire simply rolled off his black skin?

"It's because of what he is," Linden murmured as though Covenant's question were tangible in the air. They had discussed the matter at other times; and she had suggested that perhaps the Clave knew more about Vain than the company did. But now she had a different answer. "He's a being of pure structure. Nothing but structure—like a skeleton without any muscle or blood or life. Rigidness personified. Anything that isn't focused straight at him can't touch him." Slowly, as if she were unconscious of what she was doing, she turned toward Revelstone, lifted her face to the lightless Keep. "But that's what the Sunbane does. What the Clave does. They corrupt Law—disrupt structure. Desecrate order. If they tried hard enough"—she was glowering as if she could see Gibbon waiting in his malice and his glee—"they could take him apart completely, and there wouldn't be enough of him left to so much as remember why he was made in the first place. No wonder he doesn't want to come any closer."

Covenant held his breath, hoping that she would go on—that in this mood of perception or prophecy she would name the purpose for which Vain had been created. But she did not.

By degrees, she lowered her gaze. "Damn that bastard any-way," she muttered softly. "Damn him to hell."

He echoed her in silence. Vain was such an enigma that Covenant continually forgot him—forgot how vital he was, to the hidden machinations of the *Elohim* if not to the safety of the Earth. But here Findail had not hesitated to leave the Demondim-spawn's side; and his anguished yellow eyes showed no interest in anything except the hazard of Covenant's fire. Covenant felt a prescient itch run through his forearm. Wincing, he addressed Cail.

"Don't bother. He'll take care of himself. He always has." Then he went sourly back to his seat near the fire.

The companions remained still as they ate supper, chewing their separate thoughts with their food. But when they were done, the First faced Covenant across the smoking blaze and made a gesture of readiness. "Now, Earthfriend." Her tone reminded him of a polished blade, eager for use. "Let us speak of this proud and dire Keep."

Covenant met her gaze and grimaced in an effort to hold his personal extremity beyond the range of Linden's percipi-ence.

"It is a doughty work," the First said firmly. "In it the Unhomed wrought surpassingly well. Its gates have been broken by a puissance that challenges conception—but if I have not been misled, there are gates again beyond the tower. And surely you have seen that the walls will not be scaled. We would be slain in the attempt. The Clave is potent, and we are few. Earthfriend," she concluded as if she were pre-pared to trust whatever explanation he gave, "how do you purpose to assail this donjon?"

In response, he scowled grimly. He had been expecting that question—and dreading it. If he tried to answer it as if he were sane, his resolve might snap like a rotten bone. His friends would be appalled. And perhaps they would try to stop him. Even if they did not, he felt as certain as death that their dismay would be too much for him.

Yet some reply was required of him. Too many lives depended on what he meant to do. Stalling for courage, he looked toward Hollian. His voice caught in his throat as he asked, "What kind of sun are we going to have tomorrow?"

Dark hair framed her mien, and her face itself was smudged with the dirt of long travel; yet by some trick of the firelight—or of her nature—she appeared impossibly clear, her countenance unmuddied by doubt or despair. Her movements were deft and untroubled as she accepted the *krill* from Sunder, took out her *lianar*, and invoked the delicate flame of her foretelling.

After a moment, fire bloomed from her wand. Its color was the dusty hue of the desert sun.

Covenant nodded to himself. A desert sun. By chance or design, he had been granted the phase of the Sunbane he would have chosen for his purpose. On the strength of that small grace, he was able to face the First again.

"Before we risk anything else, I'm going to challenge Gibbon. Try to get him to fight me personally. I don't think he'll do it," though surely the Raver would covet the white ring for itself and might therefore be willing to defy its master's will, "but if he does, I can break the Clave's back without hurting anybody else." Even though Gibbon held the whole force of the Banefire; Covenant was ready for that as well.

But the First was not content. "And if he does not?" she asked promptly. "If he remains within his fastness and dares us to harm him?"

Abruptly, Covenant lurched to his feet. Linden's gaze followed him with a flare of alarm as she caught a hint of what drove him; but he did not let her speak. Pieces of moonlight filtered through the dense leaves; and beyond the trees the moon was full—stretched to bursting with promises he could not keep. Above him, the walls and battlements of Revelstone held the silver light as if they were still beautiful. He could not bear it.

Though he was choking, he rasped out, "I'll think of something." Then he fled the camp, went blundering through the brush until he reached its verge on the foothills.

The great Keep towered there, as silent and moon-ridden as a cairn for all the dreams it had once contained. No illumination of life showed from it anywhere. He wanted to cry out at it, What have they done to you? But he knew the stone would not hear him. It was deaf to him, blind to its own desecration—as helpless against evil as the Earth itself. The thought that he might hurt it made him tremble.

Cail attended him like an avatar of the night's stillness. Because he had passed the limit of what he could endure, he turned to the *Haruchai* and whispered hoarsely, "I'm going to sleep here. I want to be alone. Don't let any of them near me."

He did not sleep. He spent the night staring up at the city as though it were the last barrier between his hot grief and Lord Foul's triumph. Several times, he heard his friends approach him through the brush. Each time, Cail turned them away. Linden protested his refusal, but could not breach it.

That solitary and intimate fidelity enabled Covenant to hang on until dawn.

He saw the light first on the main Keep's rim beyond the parapets of the watchtower, while the shaft of the Banefire shot toward the east. This daybreak had the hue of deserts, and the sun gave the high gray stone a brown tinge. Once again, Hollian had foretold the Sunbane accurately. As he levered his strain-sore and weary bones upright, he thought of the eh-Brand with an odd pang. Married by the child she bore, she and Sunder had grown steadily closer to each other —and Covenant did not know how to heal the wound between himself and Linden.

Behind him, he heard Linden accost Cail a second time. When the *Haruchai* denied her again, she snapped in exasperation, "He's got to eat. He's still at least that human." Her voice sounded ragged, as if she also had not slept. Perhaps the air around Revelstone was too full of the taste of Ravers to permit her to sleep. Gibbon had shown her the part of herself which had arisen in hunger to take her mother's life. Yet now, in this fatal place, she was thinking of Covenant rather than of herself. She would have forgiven him long ago—if he had ever given her the chance.

Stiffly, as if all his muscles had been calcified by the night and his long despair, he started up the hill toward Revelstone.

He could not face Linden now, feared to let her look at him almost as much as he feared the massive granite threat of the Keep. Concealment was no longer possible for him; and he dreaded how she would react to what she saw.

The light was on the watchtower, coloring it like a wilderland and dropping rapidly toward the foothills. At the edges of his vision on either side, he saw the treetops start to melt; but the center of his sight was filled by the tower. Its embrasures and abutments were empty, and the darkness behind them made them look like eyes from which the light of life had been extinguished. Light of life and desecration, he thought vaguely, as if he were too weak with inanition and fear to be troubled by contradictions. He knew how to deal with them: he had found that answer in the thronehall of Foul's Creche, when the impossibility of believing the Land true and the impossibility of believing it false had forced him to take his stand on the still point of strength at the center of his vertiginous plight. But such comprehension was of no use to him now. All the anger had gone out of him during the night; and he ascended toward the gaping mouth of Revelstone like a husk for burning.

Yet the apparent desertion of the city made him uneasy. Was it possible that the Clave had fled—that his mere approach had driven the Riders into hiding? No. The virulence of the Banefire's beam gave no indication that it had been left untended. And Lord Foul would not have permitted any withdrawal. What better victory for the Despiser than that Covenant should bring down the Arch in conflict with the Clave?

Lord Foul had said, *At the last there will be but one choice for you, and you will make it in all despair.* He had promised that, and he had laughed.

Something that might have been power stirred in Covenant. His hands curled into fists, and he went on upward.

The sun laid his shadow on the bare dirt in front of him. Its heat gripped the back of his neck, searching for the fiber of his will in the same way that it would reduce all the Upper Land's monstrous verdure to gray sludge and desert. He seemed to see himself spread out for sacrifice on the ground —exposed for the second time to a blow as murderous as the knife which had pierced his chest, stabbed the hope out of his life. An itch like a faint scurry of vermin spread up his right forearm. Unconsciously, he quickened his pace.

Then he reached the level ground at the base of the tower, and the tunnel stood open before him among its ruined gates. The passage was as dark as a grave until it met the dim illumination reflecting into the courtyard from the face of the main Keep. Dimly, he saw the inner gates at the far side of the court. They were sealed against him.

Involuntarily, he looked back down toward the place where his companions had camped. At first the sun was in his eyes, and he could descry nothing except the eviscerated gray muck which stretched out to the horizons like a sea as the Sunbane denatured life from the terrain. But when he shaded his sight, he saw the company.

His friends stood in a cluster just beyond the edge of the sludge. The First and two *Haruchai* were restraining Honninscrave. Pitchwife held Linden back.

Covenant swung around in pain to face the tunnel again.

He did not enter it. He was familiar with the windows in its ceiling which allowed the Keep's defenders to attack anyone who walked that throat. And he did not raise his voice. He was instinctively certain now that Revelstone was listening acutely, in stealth and covert fear. He sounded small against the dusty air, the great city and the growing desert as he spoke.

"I've come for you, Gibbon. For you. If you come out, I'll let the rest of the Riders live." Echoes mocked him from the tunnel, then subsided. "If you don't, I'll take this place apart to find you.

"You know I can do it. I could've done it the last time— and I'm stronger now." *You are more dangerous now than you've ever been.* "Foul doesn't think you can beat me. He's using you to make me beat myself. But I don't care about that anymore. Either way, you're going to die. Come out and get it over with."

The words seemed to fail before they reached the end of the passage. Revelstone loomed above him like the corpse of a city which had been slain ages ago. The pressure of the sun drew a line of bitter sweat down his spine.

And a figure appeared in the tunnel. Black against the reflection of the courtyard, it moved outward. Its feet struck soft echoes of crepitation from the stone.

Covenant tried to swallow—and could not. The desert sun had him by the throat.

A pair of hot pains transfixed his forearm. The scars gleamed like fangs. An invisible darkness flowed out of the passage toward him, covering his fire with the pall of venom. The sound of steps swelled.

Then sandaled feet and the fringe of a red robe broached the sunshine; and Covenant went momentarily faint with the knowledge that his first gambit had failed. Light ran swiftly up the lines of the stark scarlet fabric to the black chasuble which formalized the robe. Hands appeared, empty of the characteristic *rukh*, the black iron rod like a scepter with an open triangle fixed atop it, which a Rider should have held. Yet this was surely a Rider. Not Gibbon: the na-Mhoram wore black. He carried a crozier as tall as himself. The habitual beatitude or boredom of his round visage was punctured only by the red bale of his eyes. The man who came out to meet Covenant was not Gibbon.

A Rider, then. He appeared thick of torso, though his ankles and wrists were thin, and his bearded cheeks had been worn almost to gauntness by audacity or fear. Wisps of wild hair clung like fanaticism to his balding skull. His eyes had a glazed aspect.

He held his palms open before him as if to demonstrate that he had come unarmed.

Covenant wrestled down his weakness, fought a little moisture into his throat so that he could speak. In a tone that should have warned the Rider, he said, "Don't waste my time. I want Gibbon."

"Halfhand, I greet you," the man replied. His voice was steady, but it suggested the shrillness of panic. "Gibbon na-Mhoram is entirely cognizant of you and will waste neither time nor life in your name. What is your purpose here?"

Impressions of danger crawled between Covenant's shoulderblades. His mouth was full of the copper taste of fear. The Rider's trunk appeared unnaturally thick; and his robe seemed to move slightly of its own accord as if the cloth were seething. Covenant's scars began to burn like rats gnawing at his flesh. He hardly heard himself reply, "This has gone on too long. You make the whole world stink. I'm going to put a stop to it."

The Rider bared his teeth—a grin that failed. His gaze did not focus on Covenant. "Then I must tell you that the na-Mhoram does not desire speech with you. His word has been given to me to speak, if you will hear it."

Covenant started to ask, What word is that? But the question never reached utterance. With both hands, the Rider un-belted the sash of his robe. In prescient dread, Covenant watched the Rider open his raiment to the sun.

From the line of his shoulders to the flex of his knees, his entire body was covered with wasps.

Great yellow wasps, as big as Covenant's thumb.

When the light touched them, they began to snarl.

For one hideous moment, they writhed where they were;

and the Rider wore them as if he were one of the Sunbane-warped, made savage and abominable by corruption. Then the swarm launched itself at Covenant.

In that instant, the world went black. Venom crashed against his heart like the blow of a sledgehammer.

Black fire; black poison; black ruin. The flame raging from his ring should have been as pure and argent as the metal from which it sprang; but it was not, *was not*. It was an abyss that yawned around him, a gulf striding through the air and the ground and the Keep to consume them, swallow the world and leave no trace. And every effort he made to turn the dark fire white, force it back to the clean pitch of its true nature, only raised the blaze higher, widened the void. Swiftly, it became as huge as the hillside, hungry for ruin.

Linden was not shouting at him. If she had torn her heart with screams, he would not have been able to hear her. She was too far away, and the gathering cataclysm of his power filled all his senses. Yet he heard her in his mind—heard her as she had once cried to him across the Worm's aura and the white ring's eruption, *This is what Foul wants!*—felt the remembered grasp of her arms as she had striven to wrest him back from doom. If he let his conflagration swell, they would all die, she and the others he loved and the Land he treasured, all of them ripped out of life and meaning by blackness.

The strain of self-mastery pushed him far beyond himself. He was driven to a stretched and tenuous desperation from which he would never be able to turn back—a hard, wild exigency that he would have to see through to its conclusion for good or ill, ravage or restitution. But the simple knowledge that he would not be able to turn back and did not mean to try enabled him to strangle the destruction pouring from him.

Abruptly, his vision cleared—and he had not been stung. Thousands of small, charred bodies still smoked on the bare ground. Not one of the wasps was left to threaten him.

The Rider remained standing with his mouth open and his eyes white, miraculously unscathed and astonished.

Covenant felt no triumph: he had gone too far for triumph. But he was certain of himself now, at least for the moment. To the Rider, he said, "Tell Gibbon he had his chance." His voice held neither doubt nor mercy. "Now I'm coming in after him."

Slowly, the astonishment drained from the man's face. His

frenzy and glee seemed to collapse as if he had suffered a relapse of mortality. Yet he remained a Rider of the Clave, and he knew his enemy. All the Land had been taught to believe that Covenant was a betrayer. The man looked human and frail, reduced by failure; but he did not recant his faith.

"You surpass me, Halfhand." His voice shook. "You have learned to wield—and to restrain. But you have come to havoc the long service of our lives, and we will not permit you. Look to your power, for it will not aid you against us."

Turning as if he were still able to dismiss Covenant from consideration, he followed the echoes of his feet back into the tunnel under the watchtower.

Covenant watched him go and cursed the mendacity which enabled Lord Foul to take such men and women, people of native courage and dedication, and convince them that the depredations of the Clave were virtuous. Revelstone was full of individuals who believed themselves responsible for the survival of the Land. And they would be the first to die. The Despiser would sacrifice them before hazarding his truer servants.

Yet even for them Covenant could not stop now. The fire still raved within him. He had not quenched it. He had only internalized it, sealed its fury inside himself. If he did not act on it, it would break out with redoubled vehemence, and he would never be able to contain it again.

Violence taut in his muscles, he started stiffly down the hillside toward his friends.

They began the ascent to meet him. Anxiously, they studied the way he moved as if they had seen him emerge from the teeth of hell and could hardly believe it.

Before he reached them, he heard the flat thunder of hooves.

He did not stop: he was wound to his purpose and unbreachable. But he looked back up at Revelstone over his shoulder.

Between the broken gates came Riders mounted on Coursers, half a dozen of them pounding in full career down the slope. The Sunbane-bred Coursers were large enough to carry four or five ordinary men and woman, would have been large enough to support Giants. They had malicious eyes, the faces and fangs of sabertooths, shaggy pelts, and poisoned spurs at the back of each ankle. And the Riders held their *rukhs* high and bright with flame as they charged. Together they rushed downward as if they believed they could sweep the company off the hillside.

Yet for all their fury and speed they looked more like a charade than a true assault. The Banefire made them dangerous; but they were only six, and they were hurling themselves against ten *Haruchai*, four Giants, the Appointed of the *Elohim*, and four humans whose strength had not yet been fully measured. Covenant himself had already killed— Deliberately, he left the charge to his companions and walked on.

Behind him, the Coursers suddenly went wild.

Sunder had snatched out his Sunstone and the *krill*; but now he did not draw his power from the sun. Instead, he tapped the huge beam of the Banefire. And he was acquainted with Coursers. At one time, he had learned to use a *rukh* in order to master a group of the beasts; he knew how to command them. Fierce red flarings shot back and forth through the *krill*'s white light as he threw his force at the attack; but he did not falter.

The impact of his countervailing instructions struck chaos into the Coursers. Two of them fell trying to lunge in several directions simultaneously. A third stumbled over them. The others attacked the fallen, tried to kill them.

Reft of control, the Riders sprawled to the hard ground. One was crushed under the massive body of a Courser. Another received a dangerous spur slash. She cried out to her comrades for help; but they were already in flight back toward the Keep, bearing the broken Rider for his blood. Weakly, she struggled after them.

Sunder ordered the Coursers out into the desert so that the Clave would not be able to use them again. But two of them squealed with pain when they tried to obey: they had broken legs. Gripping her falchion in both fists, the First stalked up to the maimed beasts and slew them.

Then Sunder, Linden, and Pitchwife approached Covenant.

The Graveler was panting heavily. "Gibbon does not put forth his full strength. I am not the equal of six Riders." Yet there was a grim pride in his tone. At last he had struck an effective blow against the Clave.

"He's trying to provoke you," Linden warned. "You almost didn't pull back in time. You've got to be careful." Fear of Ravers twisted her face into a scowl.

"Earthfriend," breathed Pitchwife, "what will you do?

There is a madness upon Grimmand Honninscrave. We will not be long able to withhold him."

But Covenant made no reply. His legs were trembling now, and he could not stop what he was doing or turn aside. He headed toward a blunt boulder jutting from the lower slope of the foothill. When he reached it, he struggled up onto its crown, defying the way the wide landscape below and about him sucked at his balance. All his limbs felt leaden with suppressed devastation. From horizon to horizon, the desert sun had almost finished its work. In the low places of the terrain lay ponds of sludge which had once been trees and brush and vines, but every slope and rise was burned to dust and death. The thought that he would have to damage Revelstone was intolerable. Sheer grief and self-loathing would break him if he set his hand to that stone. Yet the necessity was inescapable. The Clave and the Banefire could not be permitted to go on. His heart quivered at the conflict of his fears—fear of harming the Keep and of not harming it, fear of himself, of the risk he meant to take; his desire to avoid killing and his need to protect his friends. But he had already chosen his path. Now he started down it.

Trembling as if he were on the verge of deflagration, he spoke the name he had been hoarding to himself ever since he had begun to understand the implications of what he meant to do.

The name of a Sandgorgon.

"Nom."

TEN: The Banefire

CLEARLY through the sudden shock of the company, he heard Linden gasp. There was no wind, nothing to soften the arid pressure of the sun. Below him, the terrain was falling into the paradoxical purity of desecration. The cleanliness of extermination. No wonder fire was so hard to resist. His balance seemed to spin out of him into the flat brown sky. He had not eaten or slept since the previous day. Perhaps it was inanition which made the horizons cant to one side as if they were about to sail away. Inanition or despair.

But Pitchwife and Cail caught him, lowered him from the boulder; and Linden came to him in a blur of vertigo. He had never been good at heights. He knew that she was saying his name, yet he felt unable to hear her. Her face was impossible to focus. She should have been protesting, *A Sandgorgon? Are you out of your mind? What makes you think you can control it?* But she was not. Her hands gripped his shoulders roughly, then flinched away. This time, her gasp was like a cry. "You—!" she began. But the words would not come. "Oh, Covenant!"

The First's voice cut through the wild reel of the hills. "What harms him?" All his friends were crowded around him and spinning. He saw Mhoram and Foamfollower, Bannor and Elena—and Caer-Caveral—all there as if they deserved better from him. "What has transpired to harm him?" They had met him in Andelain and given him everything they dared; and this was the result. He was caught on a wheel that had no center. "Chosen, you must speak!"

"He's on fire." Linden's tone was wet with tears. "The venom's on fire. We'd already be dead, but he's holding it inside. As long as he can. Until it eats its way out."

The First cursed, then snapped a command that Covenant failed to hear. A moment later, Pitchwife's heat-impervious hands lifted a bowl of *diamondraught* to Covenant's mouth.

Its potent smell stung his nostrils with panic. *Diamondraught* would restore him. Perhaps it would restore his self-mastery as well. Or it might fuel the blaze of his suppressed power. He could not take the chance.

Somehow, he slowed the spin. Clarity was possible. He could not afford to fail. And he would not have to hang on long; only until he reached the culmination of his nightmares. It was possible. When he was certain of the faces hovering around him, he said as if he were suffocating, "Not *diamondraught. Metheglin.*"

The First glared doubt at him; but Linden nodded. "He's

right," she said in a rush. "He has to keep his balance. Between strength and weakness. *Diamondraught* is too strong."

People were moving: Hollian and Mistweave went away, came back at once with a pouch of the Land's thick mead. That Covenant drank, sparingly at first, then more deeply as he felt his grasp on the conflagration hold. By degrees, the vertigo frayed out of him. His friends were present and stable. The ground became solid again. The sun rang in his eyes, clanged against his temples, like Lord Foul's silent laughter; and his face streamed with the sweat of desperation. But as the *metheglin* steadied him, he found that he was at least able to bear the heat.

With Pitchwife's help, he gained his feet. Squinting, he turned to the east and thrust his gaze out into the shimmering desert.

"Will it come?" the First asked no one in particular. "The wide seas intervene, and they are no slight barrier."

"Kasreyn said it would." Linden bit her lips to control her apprehension, then continued, "He said, 'Distance has no meaning to such power.'" Covenant remembered that. *The Sandgorgons answer their release swiftly.* That was how Hergrom had been killed. But Covenant had already summoned Nom once at Linden's instigation; and he had not been slain. And Nom had not gone back to Sandgorgons Doom. Therefore why should the beast answer him now? He had no reason for such a wild hope—no reason at all except the fact that Nom had bowed to him when he had refrained from killing it.

But the east was empty, and the haze closed against him like a curtain. Even the eyes of the Giants discerned no sign of an answer.

Abruptly, Cail's uninflected voice broke the silence.

"Ur-Lord, behold."

With one arm, he pointed up the hillside toward Revelstone.

For an instant, Covenant believed that the *Haruchai* wanted him to observe the immense hot vermeil shaft of the Banefire. With sun-echoes burning white and brown across his sight, he thought the sizzling beam looked stronger now, as though Gibbon-Raver were feeding it furiously to arm the Clave for combat. Killing the captured villagers and *Haruchai* as fast

as their blood could be poured onto the floor of the sacred
enclosure where the Banefire burned.

At the idea, the spots flaring against the backs of his eyes
turned black. His restraint slipped. The fang-marks on his
forearm hurt as if they had been reopened.

But then he saw the Riders at the base of the tower. Four
of them: two holding up their *rukhs* to master a *Haruchai*
they had brought with them; two equipped with knives and
buckets.

They intended to shed their mind-bound prisoner in full
view of Covenant and the company.

Covenant let out a shout that made the air throb. But at
the same time he fought for control, thinking, No. No. He's
trying to provoke me. The blackness in him writhed. He
refused it until it subsided.

"Honninscrave." The First sounded almost casual, as if
the sight of atrocities made her calm. "Mistweave. It is my
thought that we need not permit this."

Half the *Haruchai* had started upward at a sprint. She made
no effort to call them back. Stooping to the dirt, she picked
up a rock larger than her palm; and in the same motion she
hurled it at the Riders.

Striking the wall behind them, it burst in a shower of
splinters that slashed at them like knives.

Instantly, Honninscrave and Mistweave followed the First's
example. Their casts were so accurate that one of the Riders
had a leg smashed, another was ripped by a hail of rebounding fragments. Their companions were compelled to
release the *Haruchai* so that they could use their *rukhs* to
defend themselves.

While the four Riders retreated into the tunnel, their
captive turned on them. Suddenly free of their coercion, he
slew the injured men. Then he pivoted disdainfully on his
heel and strode down the slope to meet his people. He was
bleeding from several cuts inflicted by sharp pieces of stone,
but he bore himself as if he were unscathed.

Covenant hated killing. He had chosen his path in an effort
to spare as many lives as possible. But as he watched the
released *Haruchai* walking toward him like pure and utter
dispassion, a dire grin twisted the corners of his mouth. In
that moment, he became more dangerous to Gibbon and
the Clave than any host of warriors or powers.

When he looked toward the east again, he saw a plume of dust rising through the haze.

He did not doubt what it was. Nothing but a Sandgorgon could travel with enough swift strength to raise that much dust.

Mutely, Linden moved to his side as if she wanted to take his arm and cling to it for support. But the dark peril he radiated kept her from touching him.

Mistweave watched the dust with growing amazement. Pitchwife muttered inanely to himself, making pointless jests that seemed to ease his trepidation. The First grinned like a scimitar. Of the Giants, only Honninscrave did not study the beast's approach. He stood with his head bowed and his arms manacled across his chest as if throwing stones at the Riders had whetted his hunger for violence.

Unexpectedly, Findail spoke. He sounded weary and mascerated, worn thin by the prolonged burden of his responsibility; but some of the bitterness was gone from his voice. "Ring-wielder," he said, "your purpose here is abominable and should be set aside. Those who hold the Earth in their hands have no justification for vengeance. Yet you have found a wise way to the accomplishment of your ends. I implore that you entrust them to this beast. You little comprehend what you have summoned."

Covenant ignored the *Elohim*. Linden glanced at the Appointed. Sunder and Hollian gazed at him in confusion. But none of the companions spoke.

Nom had become visible at the arrow-point of the advancing dust.

Albino against the desiccated waste, the beast approached at a startling pace. Its size was not commensurate with its might: it was only a few hands taller than Covenant, only a little more thickly built than the *Haruchai*; yet given time and concentrated attention and freedom it was capable of reducing the entire gutrock wedge of Revelstone to wreckage. It had a strange gait, suited to deserts: its knees were back-bent like a bird's to utilize the full thrust of the wide pads of its feet. Lacking hands, its arms were formed like battering rams.

And it had no face. Nothing defined its hairless head except the faint ridges of its skull under its hide and two covered slits like gills on either side.

Even to Covenant's unpenetrating sight, the Sandgorgon

looked as pure and uncontestable as a force of nature—a hurricane bound into one savage form and avid for a place to strike.

It came running as if it meant to hurl itself at him.

But at the last it stopped in a thick nimbus of dust, confronted him across a scant stretch of bare dirt. For a moment, it trembled as it had trembled when he had defeated it in direct combat and it had not known how to hold back its elemental fury even to save its own life. Service was an alien concept to its brute mind; violence made more sense. Sweat blurred the edges of his vision as he watched the beast quiver for decision. Involuntarily, he held his breath. A few small flames slipped past his control and licked at his forearm until he beat them back.

Nom's trembling mounted—and abruptly subsided. Lowering itself to the ground, the beast placed its forehead in the dirt at Covenant's feet.

Slowly, he let pent air leak away through his teeth. A muffled sigh of relief passed through the company. Linden covered her face momentarily, then thrust her fingers through her hair as if she were trying to pull courage up out of her alarm.

"Nom," he said, and his voice shook. "Thanks for coming."

He did not know to what extent the beast was able to understand him; but it surged erect by unfolding its knees and stood waiting before him.

He did not let himself hesitate. The bond which held Nom was fragile. And he could feel venom gnawing in him like acid. His purpose was as clear to him as the soothtell which had sent him on his futile quest for the One Tree. Turning to his companions, he addressed them as a group.

"I want you to stay here." Gritting his will, he strove to suppress the tremors which made his tone harsh. "Leave it to Nom and me. Between us, we're already too much for the job." And I can't bear to lose any of you.

He had no right to say such things. Every member of the company had earned a place in this hazard. But when he considered what might happen to them, he burned to spare them.

"I'll need Linden," he went on before anyone could protest. "Gibbon's going to try to hide from me. I won't be able to locate the Raver without her." The mere thought hurt him; he knew how deeply she dreaded Ravers. "And I'll take Cail and Fole. To guard our backs." Even that concession made him want to rage. But Linden might need the protection. "The rest of you just wait. If I fail, you'll have to do it for me."

Unable to face what his friends wanted to say, the pained indignation in their eyes, the expostulations rising from their hearts, he impelled Linden into motion with his hand on the small of her back. A gesture called Nom to his side. Striding stiffly past the people who had served him with their lives and deserved better than this, he started up the slope toward Revelstone.

Then for a moment he came so close to tears that his courage nearly broke. Not one of his companions obeyed. Without a word, they arranged themselves for battle and followed him.

Under her breath, Linden murmured, "I understand. You think it all depends on you. Why should people as good as they are have to suffer and maybe get killed for it? And I'm so scared—" Her face was pale and drawn and urgent. "But you have got to stop trying to make other people's decisions for them."

He did not reply. Keeping his attention fixed on the open tunnel under the watchtower, he forced his power-clogged muscles to bear him steadily upward. But now he feared that he was already defeated. He had too much to lose. His friends were accompanying him into his nightmares as if he were worthy of them. Because he had to do something, no matter how insufficient or useless it might be, he moved closer to Cail and whispered, "This is enough. Bannor said you'd serve me. Brinn told you to take his place. But I don't need this kind of service anymore. I'm too far gone. What I need is hope."

"Ur-Lord?" the *Haruchai* responded softly.

"The Land needs a future. Even if I win. The Giants'll go Home. You'll go about your business. But if anything happens to Sunder or Hollian—" The idea appalled him. "I want you to take care of them. All of you. No matter what." He was prepared to endanger even Linden for this. "The Land has got to have a future."

"We hear you." Cail's tone did not betray whether he was relieved, moved, or offended. "If the need arises, we will remember your words."

With that Covenant had to be content.

Nom had moved somewhat ahead of him, thrusting toward the great Keep as if it triggered a racial memory of the Sandwall which the *Bhrathair* had raised to oppose the Sandgorgons in the years before Kasreyn had bound them to their Doom. The beast's arms swung in anticipation. Grimly, Covenant quickened his pace.

In that way, with Linden beside him, two Stonedownors and four Giants behind him, and eleven *Haruchai* nearby, Thomas Covenant went to pit himself against the Clave and the Banefire.

There was no reaction from Revelstone. Perhaps the na-Mhoram did not know what a Sandgorgon was, wanted to see what it would do before he attempted to provoke Covenant again. Or perhaps he had given up provocation in order to prepare his defenses. Perhaps the Raver had found a small worm of fear at the bottom of his malice. Covenant liked that idea. What the Clave and the Banefire had done to the Land could not be forgiven. The way in which this Raver had transformed to ill the ancient and honorable Council of Lords could not be forgiven. And for Gibbon's attack on Linden, Covenant would accept no atonement except the cleansing of the Keep.

Those who hold the Earth in their hands have no justification for vengeance.

Like hell, Covenant gritted. Like hell they don't.

But when he reached the base of the watchtower, he commanded Nom to halt and paused to consider the tunnel. The sun was high enough now to make the inner courtyard bright; but that only deepened the obscurity of the passage. The windows of the tower gaped as if the rooms behind them were abandoned. A silence like the cryptic stillness of the dead hung over the city. There was no wind—no sign of life except the stark hot shaft of the Banefire. Between the two slain Coursers, dead wasps littered the ground. The Riders had taken their own fallen with them for the sake of the blood. But red splotches marked the rocks in front of the tower as if to tell Covenant that he had come to the right place.

He turned to Linden. Her taut pallor frightened him, but he could no longer afford to spare her. "The tower," he said as the company stopped behind him. "I need to know if it's empty."

The movement of her head as she looked upward seemed fatally slow, as if her old paralysis had its hand on her again. The last time she was here, Gibbon's touch had reduced her to near catatonia. *The principal doom of the Land is upon your shoulders. Through eyes and ears and touch, you are made to be what the Despiser requires.* Once she had pleaded with Covenant, *You've got to get me out of here. Before they make me kill you.*

But she did not plead now or seek to shirk the consequences of her choices. Her voice sounded dull and stunned; yet she accepted Covenant's demands. "It's hard," she murmured. "Hard to see past the Banefire. It wants me—wants to throw me at the sun. Throw me at the sun forever." Fear glazed her eyes as if that cast had already begun. "It's hard to see anything else." However, a moment later she frowned. Her gaze sharpened. "But Gibbon isn't there. Not there. He's still in the main Keep. And I don't feel anything else." When she looked at Covenant again, she appeared as severe as she had at their first meeting. "I don't think they've ever used the tower."

A surge of relief started up in Covenant, but he fought it down. He could not afford that either. It blunted his control, let hints of blackness leak through his mind. Striving to match her, he muttered, "Then let's go."

With Nom and Linden, Cail and Fole, he walked into the tunnel; and his companions followed him like echoes.

As he traversed the passage, he instinctively hunched his shoulders, bracing himself against the attack he still expected from the ceiling of the tunnel. But no attack came. Linden had read the tower accurately. Soon he stood in the courtyard. The sun shone before him on the high, buttressed face of the Keep and on the massive inner gates.

Those stone slabs were notched and beveled and balanced so that they could open outward smoothly and marry exactly when they closed. They were heavy enough to rebuff any force of which their makers had been able to conceive. And they were shut, interlocking with each other like teeth. The lines where they hinged and met were barely distinguishable.

"I have said it," the First breathed behind Covenant. "The Unhomed wrought surpassingly well in this place."

She was right; the gates looked ready to stand forever.

Suddenly, Covenant became urgent for haste. If he did not
find an answer soon, he would go up like tinder and oil. The
sun had not yet reached midmorning; and the shaft of the
Banefire stood poised above him like a scythe titanic and
bloody enough to reap all the life of the world. Sunder's hands
clutched the *krill* and his *orcrest*, holding them ready; but he
looked strangely daunted by the great Keep, by what it
meant and contained. For the first time in the ordeal of the
Search, Pitchwife seemed vulnerable to panic, capable of
flight. Linden's skin was the color of ashes. But Honninscrave
held his fists clinched at his sides as if he knew he was close
to the reasons for Seadreamer's death and did not mean to
wait for them much longer.

Covenant groaned to himself. He should have begun his
attack last night, while most of his friends slept. He was sick
of guilt.

With a fervid sweep of his arm, he sent Nom at the gates.

The Sandgorgon seemed to understand instinctively. In
three strides, it reached full speed.

Hurtling forward like a juggernaut, it crashed headlong
against the juncture of the clenched slabs.

The impact boomed across the courtyard, thudded in Covenant's lungs, rebounded like a cannonade from the tower.
The stones underfoot shivered; a vibration like a wail ran
through the abutments. The spot Nom struck was crushed and
dented as if it were formed of wood.

But the gates stood.

The beast stepped back as if it were astonished. It turned
its head like a question toward Covenant. But an instant later
it rose up in the native savagery of all Sandgorgons and began
to beat at the gates with the staggering might of its arms.

Slowly at first, then more and more rapidly, the beast
struck, one sledgehammer arm and then the other in accelerating sequence, harder and faster, harder and faster, until
the courtyard was full of thunder and the stone yowled distress. Covenant was responsible for that—and still the gates
held, bore the battery. Chips and splinters spat in all directions; granite teeth screamed against each other; the flagstones
of the court seemed to ripple and dance. Still the gates held.

To herself, Linden whimpered as if she could feel every
blow in her frangible bones.

Covenant started to shout for Nom to stop. He did not un-

derstand what the Sandgorgon was doing. The sight of such
an attack would have rent Mhoram's heart.

But an instant later he heard the rhythm of Nom's blows
more clearly, heard how that pulse meshed with the gutrock's
protesting retorts and cries; and he understood. The Sandgorgon had set up a resonance in the gates, and each impact increased the frequency and amplitude of the vibrations. If the
beast did not falter, the slabs might be driven to tear themselves apart.

Abruptly, red fire poured down off the abutment immediately above the gates. Riders appeared brandishing their
rukhs: four or five of them. Wielding the Banefire together,
they were more mighty than an equal number of individuals;
and they shaped a concerted blast to thrust Nom back from
the gates.

But Covenant was ready for them. He had been expecting
something like this, and his power was hungry for utterance,
for any release that would ease the strain within him. Meticulous with desperation, he put out wild magic to defend the
Sandgorgon.

His force was a sickening mixture of blackness and argence,
mottled and leprous. But it was force nonetheless, fire capable
of riving the heavens. It covered the Riders, melted their *rukhs*
to slag, then pitched them back into the Keep with their robes
aflame.

Nom went on hammering at the gates in a transport of destructive ecstasy as if it had finally met an obstacle worthy
of it.

Honninscrave quivered to hurl himself forward; but the
First restrained him. He obeyed her like a man who would
soon be beyond reach of any command.

Then Nom struck a final blow—struck so swiftly that Covenant did not see how the blow was delivered. He saw only the
small still fraction of time as the gates passed from endurance
to rupture. They stood—and the change came upon them like
the last inward suck of air before the blast of a hurricane—
and then they were gone, ripped apart in a wrench of detonation with fragments whining like agony in all directions and
stone-powder billowing so thickly that Nom disappeared and
the broken mouth of Revelstone was obscured.

Slowly, the high, wide portal became visible through the
dust. It was large enough for Coursers, suitable for Giants.

But the Sandgorgon did not reappear. Covenant's stunned ears were unable to pick out the slap of Nom's feet as the beast charged alone into the stone city.

"Oh my God," Linden muttered over and over again, "oh my God." Pitchwife breathed, "Stone and Sea!" as if he had never seen a Sandgorgon at work before. Hollian's eyes were full of fear. But Sunder had been taught violence and killing by the Clave, had never learned to love Revelstone: his face was bright with eagerness.

Half deafened by the pain of the stone, Covenant entered the Keep because now he had no choice left but to go forward or die. And he did not know what Nom would do to the city. At a wooden run, he crossed the courtyard and passed through the dust into Revelstone as if he were casting the die of his fate.

Instantly, his companions arranged themselves for battle and followed him. He was only one stride ahead of Cail, two ahead of the First, Linden, and Honninscrave, as he broached the huge forehall of the na-Mhoram's Keep.

It was as dark as a pit.

He knew that hall; it was the size of a cavern. It had been formed by Giants to provide a mustering-space for the forces of the former Lords. But the sun angled only a short distance into the broken entrance; and some trick of the high stone seemed to absorb the light; and there was no other illumination.

Too late, he understood that the forehall had been prepared to meet him.

With a crash, heavy wooden barriers slammed shut across the entryway. Sudden midnight echoed around the company.

Instinctively, Covenant started to release a blaze from his ring. Then he yanked it back. His fire was entirely black now, as corrupt as poison. It shed no more light than the scream that swelled against his self-control, threatening to tear his throat and split Revelstone asunder.

For an instant like a seizure, no one moved or spoke. The things they could not see seemed to paralyze even the First and the *Haruchai*. Then Linden panted, "Sunder." Her voice shook wildly; she sounded like a madwoman. "Use the *krill*. Use it now."

Covenant tried to swing toward her. What is it? What do

you see? But his imprecise ears missed her position in the dark.
He was peering straight at Sunder when the *krill* sent a peal
of vivid white ringing across the cavern.

He had no defense as Hollian's shrill cry echoed after the
light:

"The na-Mhoram's *Grim*!"

Argent dazzled him. The *Grim*! He could not think or see.
Such a sending had attacked the company once before; and
under an open sky it had killed Memla na-Mhoram-in, had
nearly slain Linden and Cail. In the enclosed space of the
forehall—

And it would damage Revelstone severely. He had seen the
remains of a village which had fallen under the *Grim*: During
Stonedown, Hamako's birthplace. The acid force of the na-
Mhoram's curse had eaten the entire habitation to rubble.

Covenant wheeled to face the peril; but still he could not
see. His companions scrambled around him. For one mad
instant, he believed they were fleeing. But then Cail took hold
of his arm, ignoring the pain of suppressed fire; and he heard
the First's stern voice. "Mistweave, we must have more light.
Chosen, instruct us. How may this force be combatted?"

From somewhere beyond his blindness, Covenant heard
Linden reply, "Not with your sword." The ague in her voice
blurred the words; she had to fight to make them comprehensible. "We've got to quench it. Or give it something else to
burn."

Covenant's vision cleared in time to see the black hot thunderhead of the *Grim* rolling toward the company just below
the cavern's ceiling.

Confined by the forehall, it appeared monstrously powerful.

Nom was nowhere to be seen; but Covenant's knees felt
vibrations through the floor as if the Sandgorgon were attacking the Keep's inner chambers. Or as if Revelstone itself
feared what Gibbon had unleashed.

From the entryway came the noise of belabored wood as
Mistweave sought to break down the barrier which sealed the
hall. But it had been fashioned with all the stoutness the
Clave could devise. It creaked and cracked at Mistweave's
blows, but did not break.

When the boiling thunderhead was directly over the company, it shattered with a tremendous and silent concussion that would have flattened Covenant if Cail had not upheld him.

In that instant, the *Grim* became stark black flakes that floated murderously downward, bitter as chips of stone and corrosive as vitriol. The thick *Grim*-fall spanned the company.

Covenant wanted to raise fire to defend his friends. He believed he had no choice; venom and fear urged him to believe he had no choice. But he knew with a terrible certainty that if he unleashed the wild magic now he might never be able to call it back. All his other desperate needs would be lost. Loathing himself, he watched and did nothing as the dire flakes settled toward him and the people he loved.

Fole and another *Haruchai* impelled Linden to the nearest wall, as far as possible from the center of the *Grim*-fall. Harn tugged at Hollian, but she refused to leave Sunder. Cail was ready to dodge—ready to carry Covenant if necessary. The First and Honninscrave braced themselves to pit their Giantish immunity to fire against the flakes. Findail had disappeared as if he could sense Covenant's restraint and cared about nothing else.

Glaring in the *krill*-light, the flakes wafted slowly downward.

And Sunder stood to meet them.

From his *orcrest* he drew a red shaft of Sunbane-fire and started burning the black bits out of the air.

His beam consumed every flake it touched. With astonishing courage or abandon, he faced the entire *Grim* himself. But the bits were falling by the thousands. They were too much for him. He could not even clear the air above his own head to protect himself and Hollian.

Then Pitchwife joined him. Incongruously crippled and valiant, the Giant also attacked the *Grim*, using as his only weapon the pouches of *vitrim* he had borne with him from Hamako's *rhyshyshim*. One after another, he emptied them by spraying *vitrim* at the flakes.

Each flake the liquid touched became ash and drifted harmlessly away.

His visage wore a grimace of grief at the loss of his carefully-hoarded Waynhim roborant; but while it lasted he used it with deliberate extravagance.

Honninscrave slapped at the first flake which neared his

head, then gave an involuntary cry as the black corrosive ate into his palm. The *Grim* had been conceived to destroy stone, and no mortal flesh was proof against it.

Around Covenant, the cavern started to reel. The irreconcilable desperation of his plight was driving him mad.

But at that instant a huge splintering crashed through the air; and the wooden barricade went down under Mistweave's attack. More light washed into the forehall, improving the ability of the *Haruchai* to dodge the *Grim*. And wood followed the light. Fiercely, Mistweave tore the barrier beam from timber and flung the pieces toward the company.

Haruchai intercepted the smaller fragments, used them as cudgels to batter *Grim*-flakes from the air. But the First, Honninscrave, and then Pitchwife snatched up the main timbers. At once, wood whirled around the company. The First swung a beam as tall as herself as if it were a flail. Honninscrave swept flakes away from Sunder and Hollian. Pitchwife pounced to Linden's defense with an enormous club in each fist.

The *Grim* destroyed the wood almost instantly. Each flake tore the weapon which touched it to charcoal. But the broken barricade had been huge; and Mistweave attacked it with the fury of a demon, sending a constant rush of fragments skidding across the floor to the hands of the company.

Honninscrave took another flake on his shoulder and nearly screamed; yet he went on fighting as if he were back in the cave of the One Tree and still had a chance to save his brother.

Three of the *Haruchai* threw Linden from place to place like a child. In that way they were able to keep her out of the path of the *Grim*-fall more effectively than if one of them had tried to carry her. But their own movements were hampered. Two of them had already suffered burns; and as Covenant watched, a black bit seemed to shatter Fole's left leg. He balanced himself on his right as if pain had no meaning and caught Linden when she was tossed to him.

Around the cavern, flakes began to strike the floor and detonate, ripping holes the size of Giant-hands in the smooth stone. Acrid smoke intensified the air as if the granite were smoldering.

Durris, Harn, and two more *Haruchai* whipped brands and staves around the Stonedownors. Sunder lashed a frenzy of red power at the *Grim*. The First and Honninscrave labored like berserkers, spending wood as rapidly as Mistweave fed it to them. Pitchwife followed his wife's example, protected her back with boards and timbers. He still had one pouch of *vitrim* left.

And Cail bounded and ducked through the drifting peril with Covenant slung over his shoulder like a sack of grain.

Covenant could not catch his breath to shout. Cail's shoulder forced the air from his lungs. But he had to make himself heard somehow. "Sunder," he gasped. "Sunder."

By intuition or inspiration, the *Haruchai* understood him. With a strength and agility that defied the thickening *Grim*-fall, he bore Covenant toward the Graveler.

An instant later, Covenant was whirled to his feet beside Sunder. Vertigo squalled around him; he had no balance. His hands were too numb to feel the fire mounting in him at every moment. If he could have seen Sunder's face, he would have cried out, for it was stretched and frantic with exhaustion. But the light of the *krill* blazed at Covenant's eyes. In the chaos of the cavern, that untrammeled brightness was the only point on which he could anchor himself.

The company had already survived miraculously long. But the *Grim* seemed to have no end, and soon even Giants and *Haruchai* would have to fall. This sending was far worse than the other one Covenant had experienced because it was enclosed—and because it was being fed directly by the Banefire. Through the stamp of feet and the burst of fires, he heard Linden cursing the pain of the people who kept her alive—people she could not help even though she suffered their hurts like acid on her own flesh. He had nowhere else to turn except to the *krill*.

Plunging toward Sunder, he got both hands on Loric's blade. He did not feel the edges cut into his fingers, did not see the blood. He feared that his weight would topple Sunder; but somehow Sunder braced himself against the collision, managed to hold Covenant upright for a moment.

That moment was long enough. Before he fell tangled in the Graveler's arms, Covenant sent one heart-rending blast of wild magic and risk through the gem of the *krill*.

His power was as black as the *Grim* now. But his desire was pure; and it struck the *krill* with such suddenness that the gem was not tainted by it. And from that gem, light rang like a piece of the clean sun. Its brightness seemed to tear asunder the veil of Revelstone's gloom, lay bare the essential skeleton of the granite. Light shone through both flesh and stone, swept all shadow and obscurity away, made clear the farthest corners of the forehall, the heights of the vaulted ceiling. If his eyes had been equal to the argence, in that instant he would have seen the deep heart of the great Keep and Gibbon already fleeing to the place where he had chosen to hide himself. But Covenant was blind to such things. His forehead was butted against Sunder's shoulder and he was falling.

When he rolled himself off Sunder's panting chest, groped through dizziness to regain his feet, the moment of his power had passed. The cavern was lit only by the sun's reflection from the entrance and the *krill*'s normal shining. His companions stood at various distances from him; but while his head spun he seemed to have no idea who they were.

But the *Grim* was gone. The black flakes had been swept away. And still he retained his grip on the wild magic.

He could not make the stone under him stop whirling. Helplessly, he clung to the first *Haruchai* who came to him. The numbness of his hands and feet had spread to his other senses. His mind had gone deaf. He heard nothing but the rumble of distant thunder, as if the sun outside Revelstone had become a sun of rain.

His thoughts spun. Where was Nom? There were villagers in the hold—and *Haruchai*. Unless the Clave had killed them already? Gibbon had to be somewhere. What would he do next? The venom made Covenant vicious, and the sheer effort of containing so much ignited violence took his sanity away. He thought he was speaking aloud, but his teeth were clenched and immobile. Why doesn't somebody tell that damn thunder to shut up so I can hear myself?

But the thunder did not stop; and the people around him fought their weariness and injuries to ready themselves. Dimly, he heard the First's battlecry as she swept out her sword.

Then the darkness at the end of the forehall came toward him, and he saw that the Riders had unleashed their Coursers at the company.

Need cleared his head a little. The *Haruchai* holding him pushed him away, and other hands took him. He found himself near Linden at the rear of the company, with only Mist-

weave between them and the entrance. All the *Haruchai*
around them were injured. Those who were not had gone with
the First and Honninscrave to meet the charge of the Coursers. Sunder and Hollian stood alone in the center of the hall.
She supported him while he strove urgently to interfere with
the Clave's command over the beasts. But exhaustion weakened him, and the Banefire was too near. He could not blunt
the assault.

At least a score of the fierce Coursers rushed forward,
borne by the stone thunder of their hooves.

The *Haruchai* protecting Covenant and Linden were severely wounded. Fole stood with his left foot resting in a pool
of his own blood. Harn had a deep burn on one hip. The other
four *Haruchai* there were nearly maimed by various hurts.
The air still reeked of *Grim*-flakes and pain.

The beasts struck with a scream of animal fury; and Covenant wanted to shriek with them because it was too much and
he was no closer to his goal and the fingers of his will were
slipping moment by moment from their hold on the world's
ruin.

One heartbeat later, the scream arose again behind him like
an echo. Riding his vertigo, he turned in time to see Mistweave go down under the hooves of four more Coursers.

The Giant had remained at the entrance to guard the company's rear. But he had been watching the battle, the plight
of his companions. The return of the beasts which Sunder had
scattered earlier took him by surprise. They reared behind
him, pounded him to the stone. Then they thudded past him
inward, their feral red eyes flaming like sparks of the Banefire.

Covenant could not resist as Harn and two more *Haruchai*
thrust him toward one wall, interposed themselves between
him and the Coursers. Fole and the rest bore Linden to the
opposite wall so that the attack would be divided. Wounded
and extravagant *Haruchai* faced the huge savagery of the
Sunbane-shaped mounts.

You bastard! Covenant cried at Gibbon as if he were weeping. You bloody bastard! Because he had nothing else left, he
braced himself on venom and readied his fire so that no more
Haruchai would have to die for him.

But once again he had underestimated them. Two of the
Coursers veered toward Linden; two came for him. And Harn

hobbled out to meet them. He was between Covenant and the
beasts. Covenant could not strike at them. He had to watch
as Harn pitched headlong to the stone directly under the
hooves of the leading Courser.

Pitched and rolled, and came up under the beast's belly
with its left fetlock gripped in both hands.

Unable to halt, the Courser plunged to the stone. The fall
simultaneously crushed its knee and drove its poisonous spur
up into its barrel.

Squealing, it thrashed away from him. Its fangs slashed the
air. But it could not rise with its leg broken, and the poison
was already at work.

Near the entrance, Mistweave struggled to lever himself to
his feet. But one of his arms sprawled at an unconscionable
angle, and the other seemed too weak to lift him.

As the first Courser fell, the second charged toward Covenant. Then it braked with all four legs to keep itself from
crashing into the wall. It looked as immense as thunder as it
reared to bring its hooves and spurs down on Covenant and
his defenders.

The Ranyhyn also had reared to him, and he felt unable to
move. Instinctively, he submitted himself to his dizziness. It
unbalanced him, so that he stumbled away to the right.

Each forehoof as it hammered down was caught by one of
the *Haruchai*.

Covenant did not know their names; but they stood under
the impact of the hooves as if their flesh were granite. One of
them had been burned on the arm and could not keep his
grip; he was forced to slip the hoof past his shoulder to avoid
the spur. But his comrade held and twisted until the other
spur snapped off in his hands.

Instantly, he drove the spur like a spike into the base of the
Courser's neck.

Then the floor came up and kicked Covenant in the chest.
At once, he was able to see everything. But there was no air
in his lungs, and he had forgotten how to control his limbs.
Even the fire within him was momentarily stunned.

The uninjured *Haruchai* were taking their toll on the beasts
pounding in the far end of the hall. Honninscrave swung his
fists like bludgeons, matching his bulk and extremity against
the size and strength of the Coursers. Pitchwife struck and
struck as if he had temporarily become a warrior like his

wife. But the First surpassed them all. She had been trained for combat, and her longsword leaped from thrust to thrust as if it were weightless in her iron hands, slaying Coursers on all sides.

Only one of the beasts got past her and her companions to hurl itself at Sunder and Hollian.

The Graveler tried to step forward; but Hollian stopped him. She took the *orcrest* and *krill* from him, held them high as she faced the Courser. Red fire and white light blazed out of her hands, daunting the beast so that it turned aside.

There Cail caught up with it and dispatched it as if it were not many times larger than he.

But the *Haruchai* guarding Linden were not so successful. Hampered by their wounds, they could not match the feats of their people. Fole attempted what Harn had done; but his leg failed him, and the Courser pulled from his grasp. It plowed into another *Haruchai*, slammed the man against the wall with such force that Covenant seemed to see Hergrom being crushed by a Sandgorgon in the impact. The third *Haruchai* thrust Linden away an instant before a hoof clipped the side of his head. His knees folded, and he sagged to the floor. Covenant had never seen one of the *Haruchai* fall like that.

Fole started after Linden; but a kick caught him by the shoulder, knocked him aside.

Then both Coursers reared over Linden.

Her face was clear in the reflected light from the courtyard. Covenant expected to see panic, paralysis, horror; and he gulped for air, struggled to put out power fast enough to aid her. But her visage showed no fear. It was argute with concentration: her eyes stabbed up at the beasts. Every line of her features was as precise as a command.

And the Coursers faltered. For an instant, they did not plunge at her. Somehow with no power to support her she drove her percipience into their minds, confused them.

Their minds were brutish, and the Banefire was strong. She could not hold them for more than an instant. But that was enough.

Before they recovered, Mistweave crashed into them like a battering ram.

He had once left Linden in peril of her life because he had not been able to choose between her and Honninscrave; and that failure had haunted him ever since. But now he saw his chance to make restitution—and did not mean to let any mortal pain or weakness stop him. Ignoring his hurts, he threw himself to Linden's rescue.

His right arm flopped at his side, but his left was still strong. His initial charge knocked both Coursers back. One of them fell onto its side; and he followed it at once, struck it a blow which made its head rebound with a sickening thud from the hard stone, its body quiver and lie still.

Wheeling, he met the second Courser as it rose to pound down on him. His good hand caught it by the gullet; his fingers ground inward to strangle the beast.

Its fangs gaped for his face. Its eyes flared insanely. Its forehooves slashed at his shoulders, tearing him with its spurs; blood streamed down his sides. But Linden had saved his life when he had been more deeply injured than this—and he had failed her. He would not do so again.

He held the beast until Fole and the other *Haruchai* came to his aid. They grabbed its forelegs, turned its spurs against itself. In a moment, the Courser was dead. Mistweave dropped it heavily to the floor.

His muscles began to tremble as the poison worked its way into him.

Then the fighting was over. Gasps and silence echoed from the far end of the forehall. Grimly, Covenant gained his feet to stumble desperately toward Linden and Mistweave.

She had not been harmed. Mistweave and the *Haruchai* had taken all the hurt onto themselves. Her eyes ran as if the wounds of her friends had been etched on her heart. Yet the shape of her mouth and the angles of her cheeks were sharp with wrath. She looked like a woman who would never be paralyzed again. If she had spoken, she might have said, Just let him try. Just let that butchering sonofabitch try.

Before Covenant could summon any words, the First reached his side.

She was panting with exultation. Her eyes were bright, and her blade dripped thick blood. But she did not talk of such things. When she addressed him, she took him by surprise.

"The Master is gone," she said through her teeth. "He pursues his purpose inward. I know not what he seeks—but I fear that he will find it."

Behind her, Pitchwife retched for air as if his exertions had
torn the tissues of his cramped lungs. Mistweave shivered toward convulsions as Courser-poison spread into him. Sunder's
face was gray with exhaustion; Hollian had to hold him to
keep him on his feet. Six of the *Haruchai* had been burned by
the *Grim* and nearly crippled; one was in Mistweave's plight,
gouged by a spur during the battle. Findail had vanished. Linden looked as bitter as acid.

And Honninscrave was gone. Nom was gone. Seeking their
individual conceptions of ruin in the heart of Revelstone.

Too many lives. Too much pain. And Covenant was no
closer to his goal than the entrance-hall of the na-Mhoram's
Keep.

That tears it, he thought dumbly. That is absolutely enough.
I will not take any more of this.

"Linden," he said thickly. His voice was hoarse with fire.
"Tell Pitchwife how to treat these people."

For an instant, her eyes widened. He feared that she would
demur. She was a physician: seven *Haruchai* and Mistweave
needed her sorely. But then she seemed to understand him.
The Land also required healing. And she had wounds of her
own which demanded care.

Turning to Pitchwife, she said, "You've got some *vitrim*
left." In spite of the Banefire, her senses had become explicit,
immune to bafflement. "Use it on the burns. Give *diamondraught* to everybody who's hurt." Then she gazed squarely
back at Covenant. "Mistweave's arm can wait. But *voure* is
the only thing I know of that'll help against the poison."

He did not hesitate; he had no hesitation left. "Cail," he
said, "you know Revelstone. And you know *voure*." The distilled sap which the Clave used to ward off the effects of the
sun of pestilence had once saved Cail's life. "Tell your people
to find some." There were only four *Haruchai* uninjured.
"And tell them to take Sunder and Hollian with them." Hollian was experienced with *voure*. "For God's sake, keep them
safe."

Without waiting for a response, he swung toward the First.

"What you ought to do is secure our retreat." His tone
thickened like blood. He had told all his companions to stay
out of Revelstone, and none of them obeyed. But they would
obey him now. He would not accept refusal. "But it's too late

for that. I want you to go after Honninscrave. Find him somehow. Don't let him do it—whatever it is."

Then he faced Cail again. "I don't need to be protected. Not
anymore. But if there's anybody left in the hold," any villagers
or *Haruchai* the Clave had not yet shed, "they need help.
Break in there somehow. Get them out. Before they're fed to
the Banefire.

"Linden and I are going after Gibbon."

None of his companions protested. He was impossible to
refuse. He held the world in his hands, and his skin seemed to
be wearing thinner, so that the black power gnawing in him
showed more and more clearly. His cut fingers dripped blood;
but the wound gave him no pain. When Linden indicated the
far end of the forehall, he went in that direction with her,
leaving behind him all the needs and problems for which he
lacked both strength and time. Leaving behind especially Sunder and Hollian, on whom the future depended; but also the
First and Pitchwife, who were dear to him; Mistweave on the
verge of convulsions; the proven *Haruchai*; leaving them behind, not as encumbrances, but as people who were too precious to be risked. Linden also he would have left behind, but
he needed her to guide him—and to support him. He was hag-
ridden by vertigo. The reports of their steps rustled like dry
leaves as they moved; and he felt that he was going to the
place where all things withered. But he did not look back or
turn aside.

When they passed out of the cavern into the mazing,
Giant-planned ways of the great Keep, they were suddenly
attacked by a small band of Riders. But the proximity of
rukh-fire triggered his ring. The Riders were swept away in a
wash of midnight.

The dark was complete for a short distance. Ahead, however, the normal lights of the city burned, torches smoking in
sconces along the walls. No fires of the Lords had ever
smoked: their flames had not harmed the essential wood. The
Clave kept its passage lit so that Gibbon could move his forces
from place to place; but these halls were empty. They echoed
like crypts. Much beauty had died here, been undone by time
or malice.

Behind him, Covenant heard the sounds of renewed combat; and his shoulders flinched.

"They can take care of themselves," Linden gritted, holding her fear for her friends between her teeth. "This way."

Covenant stayed with her as she turned toward a side passage and started down a long sequence of stairs toward the roots of Revelstone.

Her perception of the Raver made no mistakes. Not uncertainty, but only her ignorance of the Keep, caused her to take occasional corridors or turnings which did not lead toward her goal. At intervals, Riders appeared from nowhere to attack and retreat again as if they raised their fire for no other reason than to mark Covenant's progress through the Keep. They posed no danger in themselves; his defenses were instantaneous and thorough. But each onslaught accentuated his dizziness, weakened his control. His ability to suppress the black raving frayed. He had to lean on Linden as if she were one of the *Haruchai*.

Always the path she chose tended downward; and after a while he felt a sick conviction that he knew where she was going—where Gibbon had decided to hazard his fate. The place where any violence would do the most damage. His forearm throbbed as if it had been freshly bitten. Then Linden opened a small, heavy door in a chamber which had once been a meeting hall, with curtains on its walls; and a long twisting stairwell gaped below them. Now he was sure. Night gyred up out of the depths; he thought that he would fall. But he did not. She upheld him. Only his nightmares gathered around him as they made the long descent toward the place where Gibbon meant to break him.

Abruptly, she stopped, wheeled to look upward. A man came down the stairs, as noiseless as wings. In a moment, the *Haruchai* reached them.

Cail.

He faced Covenant. Haste did not heighten his respiration; disobedience did not abash him. "Ur-Lord," he said, "I bring word of what transpires above."

Covenant blinked at the *Haruchai*; but the nauseous whirl of his vision blurred everything.

"It is fortunate that *voure* was readily found. The company is now sorely beleaguered. That battle is one to wring the heart"—he spoke as if he had no heart—"for it is fought in large part by those who should not give battle. Among the few Riders are many others who merely serve the Clave and Revelstone. They are cooks and herders, artisans and scullions, tenders of hearth and Courser. They have no skill for this work, and it is a shameful thing to slay them. Yet they will not be halted or daunted. A possession is upon them. They accept naught but their own slaughter. Felling them, Pitchwife weeps as no *Haruchai* has ever wept." Cail spoke flatly; but Linden's grasp on Covenant's arm conveyed a visceral tremor of the emotion Cail projected.

"*Voure* and *vitrim* enable the company for defense," he went on. "And the hold has been opened. There were found Stell and some few other *Haruchai*, though no villagers. They have gone to the support of the company. The Graveler and the eh-Brand are well. But of neither the First nor the Master have we seen sign."

Then he stopped. He did not ask permission to remain with Covenant; his stance showed that he had no intention of leaving.

Because Covenant said nothing, Linden breathed for him, "Thanks. Thanks for coming." Her voice ached on behalf of the innocent men and women who were Gibbon's victims— and of her companions, who had no choice.

But Covenant had passed beyond the details of pain and loss into a state of utter purpose, of unanodyned grief and quintessential fury. *Felling them, Pitchwife weeps as no* Haruchai *has ever wept*. That must be true; Cail would not lie. But it was only one more drop in an ocean eating away the very shores of Time. The ocean of Lord Foul's cruelty. Such things could not be permitted to continue.

Lifting himself out of vertigo and Linden's grasp, the Unbeliever started downward again.

She called his name, but he did not answer. With Cail at her side, she came hastening after him.

The way was not long now. Soon he reached the bottom of the stairwell, halted in front of a blank wall that he remembered—a wall with an invisible door which he had seen only once before and never been asked to open. He did not know how to open it. But that did not matter. What mattered was that Gibbon had chosen this place, *this place*, for his battleground. Simple dismay added a twist which nearly snapped the knot of Covenant's self-command.

But he was not required to breach the door for himself. It opened inward at Gibbon's word, admitting Covenant, Linden, and Cail to one of the greatest treasures of the old Lords.

To the Hall of Gifts.

After all these centuries, it was still intact. The air was tanged with smoke because the torches Gibbon had set for himself created light by destruction. And that kind of light could not do justice to the wonder of the high cavern. But everything Covenant saw was still intact.

The legacy of the Lords to a future which despised them.

The makers of Revelstone had wrought little in this spacious cave. They had given it a smooth floor, but had not touched the native stone of its walls, the rough columns which rose tremendously to support the ceiling and the rest of the Keep. Yet that lack of finish suited the purpose for which the Hall had been conceived. The rude surfaces everywhere displayed the best work of the finest artists and craftspeople of the ancient Land.

Tapestries and paintings behung the walls, defying the decay of centuries—preserved by some skill of the artists or quality of the Hall's atmosphere. Stands between the columns held large sculptures and carvings. Small pieces rested on wooden shelves cunningly attached to the stone. Many different fabrics were displayed; but all the other works were made of either wood or stone, the two fundamental materials which the Land had once revered. The Hall contained no metal of any description.

Covenant had not forgotten this place, never forgotten it; but he thought now that he had forgotten its pricelessness. It seemed to bring everything back to him in a rush, every treasured or abhorred memory: Lena and Atiaran, love and rape; Mhoram's hazardous and indefeasible compassion; the unscrupulous lore of ur-viles; Kevin in his despair; Ranyhyn as proud as wind; Ramen as stubborn as earth. And Giants, Giants on all sides, Giants wonderously depicted with their fealty and grief and grandeur wreathed about them as if the tapestries and stoneworks and carvings were numinous with eternity. Here the people of the Land had shown what they could do when they were given peace.

And it was here, in this place of destructible beauty and heritage, that Gibbon-Raver had chosen to challenge Covenant for the survival of the Earth.

Moving unconsciously inward, as if he were blind to the brink of madness gaping at his feet, Covenant went to meet the na-Mhoram.

Stark in his black robe and scarlet chasuble, with his iron crozier held ready and his red eyes bright, Gibbon stood on a mosaic which swirled through the center of the floor. Covenant had not seen that mosaic before; it must have been set at a later time. It was formed of small stone chips the color of *aliantha* and agony; and it portrayed Kevin Landwaster at the Ritual of Desecration. Unlike most of the works around it, it conveyed no sense of underlying affirmation. Instead, it expressed Kevin's lurid and extreme pain as if that were a source of satisfaction.

Gibbon had taken his position over the Landwaster's heart.

At the edge of the mosaic, Honninscrave knelt in the stone.

Covenant's entrance into the Hall of Gifts did not make the Giant look up, though his head was the only part of himself he could have moved. By some cunning of Gibbon-Raver's power, Honninscrave had been fused into the floor. Kneeling, he had sunk into it to the middle of his thighs and forearms as though it were quicksand. Then it had solidified around him, imprisoning him absolutely.

His eyes stared in despair at the failure of his life. Loss scarred his face with memories of Seadreamer and Starfare's Gem.

And the na-Mhoram laughed.

"See you, Unbeliever?" His voice was crimson and eager. "No Unbelief will redeem you now. I will spare you only if you grovel."

In response, Cail sprang past Covenant toward Gibbon as if he thought he could shatter the Raver.

But Gibbon was ready. His fist tightened on his crozier; fire spread from the open triangle at its tip.

An involuntary scream tore through Honninscrave.

Cail leaped to a halt, stood almost trembling a few feet from the na-Mhoram.

"I know you, *Haruchai*," the Raver breathed softly, savagely. "The groveler you serve will not assail me—he values the relics of his dead past and fears to harm them. He values the lost Earth. But you have not the folly of that scruple. Yet you remain a fool. You will not require me to crush the life of this mad Giant who sought to confront me, deeming me as paltry as himself."

Cail turned on his heel, strode back to Covenant's side. His visage held no expression. But sweat beaded on his temples, and the muscles at the corners of his eyes squeezed and released like the labor of his heart.

Linden tried to curse, but the words came out like wincing. Instinctively, she had placed herself half behind Covenant.

"Hear you?" Gibbon went on, raising his voice so that it contaminated every corner of the great Hall. "You are all fools, and you will not lift finger or flame against me. You will do naught but grovel at my whim or die. You are beaten, Unbeliever. You fear to destroy that which you love. Your love is cowardice, and you are beaten."

Covenant's throat closed as if he were choking on smoke.

"And *you*, Linden Avery." His raw contempt filled the air. "Knowing my touch, you have yet dared me again. And this you name victory to yourself, thinking that such folly expiates your rooted evil. You conceive that we have misesteemed you, that you have put aside Despite. But your belief is anile. You have not yet tasted the depths of your Desecration.

"Hear you all?" he cried suddenly, exalted by malice. "You are damned beyond description, and I will feast upon your souls!"

Torn between outrage and visceral horror, Linden made whimpering noises between her teeth. She had come this far because she loved Covenant and loathed evil; but Gibbon appalled her in every nerve and fiber of her being. Her face was as pale as a gravestone; her eyes stared like wounds. Covenant had gone numb to everything else; but he was still aware of her. He knew what was happening to her. She was being ripped apart by her desire for the power to crush Gibbon— to extirpate him as if he were the part of herself she most hated.

If she did that, if she took hold of Covenant's fire and wielded it for herself, she would be lost. The inheritance of her parents would overcome her. Destroying Gibbon, she would shape herself in his image, affirm the blackness which had twisted her life.

That at least Covenant could spare her. And the moment had come. He was caught in the throes of a rupture so funda-

mental and puissant that it might tear Time asunder. If he did
not act now, his control would be gone.

Deliberately, desperately, he started forward as if he did
not realize that he had gone past the brink.

At once, Gibbon lifted his crozier higher, gripped it more
tightly. His eyes spat red. "Bethink you, Unbeliever!" he
snapped. "You know not what you do! Consider your hands."

Involuntarily, Covenant looked down at them, at the *krill*-
cuts across the insides of his fingers.

His severed flesh gaped, exposing bone. But the cuts were
not bleeding. Instead, they oozed an essence of leprosy and
venom. The very fluid in his veins had become corruption.

Yet he was prepared for this. His chosen path had brought
him here. It was foretold by dreams. And he had already
caused the shattering of Revelstone's gates, already brought
immeasurable damage into the Keep. More harm would not
alter his doom.

The scars on his forearm shone black fury. Like poison and
flame, he strode onto the mosaic toward Gibbon.

"Fool!" the na-Mhoram cried. A grimace of fear betrayed
his face. "You cannot oppose me! The Banefire surpasses you!
And if it does not, I will possess your Linden Avery. Will you
slay her also?"

Covenant heard Gibbon. He understood the threat. But he
did not stop.

Suddenly, the Raver sent a blast of fire toward Honninscrave; and Covenant erupted to protect the Master.

Erupted as if his heart could no longer contain the magma
of his power.

Flame as dark and fathomless as an abyss shouted across
the glittering surface of the mosaic, rebounded among the
pillars, echoed off the high ceiling. Soulless force ripped Gibbon's blast from the air, scattered it in tatters, rose on and on
with a deafening vehemence, trumpeting for the Raver's life.
His hands lifted in front of him with the palms outward like
an appeal for peace; but from his sliced fingers wild magic
streamed, venomous and fatal. All his flesh had turned black;
his bones were ebon and diseased. The only pure things about
him were the stark circle of his ring and the quality of his
passion.

The na-Mhoram retreated a step or two, held up his crozier

with vermeil frenzy wailing from its triangle. Fire hot enough
to incinerate stone crashed at Covenant. The concentrated
ferocity of the Banefire seemed to scorch straight into his
vitals. But he went forward through it.

That Gibbon had slaughtered the people of the Land to
feed the Banefire and the Sunbane. That he had taught rites
of bloodshed to those who survived, so that they slew each
other in order to live. That he had filled Revelstone itself with
such pollution. *Blast and counter-blast, Honninscrave struggling uselessly again, Cail hauling Linden out of the terrible
concussion of powers with screams in her eyes too acute for
paralysis and precious artifacts falling like fagots.* That he had
torn the forehall with *Grim*-fire and had sent his innocent
servants to compel their own butchery from the company.
That he had so appalled Linden that she believed the legacy
of her parents. That he had brought his violence *here*, requiring Covenant to spend the Land's treasured past as tinder.

Gibbon's crozier channeled so much might from the Banefire, so much force and rage, that Covenant nearly wept at the
ruin it wrought, the price it exacted from him. Under his
boots, the colored pieces of the mosaic caught fire, became as
brilliant and incandescent as prophecy. He trod an image of
the Landwaster's heart as if that were where his own path led.

Erect and benighted in the core of his infernal power, he
tried to advance on the na-Mhoram.

And failed.

Air and light ceased to exist. Every precious thing near
his blaze burned away. The nearby columns began to melt:
the floor of the Hall rippled on the verge of dissolution. More
force than ever before in his life coursed from him and
slammed at Gibbon. The essential fabric of the Earth's existence trembled as if the last wind had begun to blow.

Yet he failed.

Lord Foul had planned well, prepared well. Gibbon-Raver
was cornered and could not flee, and so he did not falter. And
the Banefire was too strong. Centuries of bloodshed had produced their intended fruit; and Gibbon fed it to Covenant,
thrust it morsel by bitter morsel between his unwilling teeth.
The Banefire was not stronger than he was; it was simply
stronger than he dared to be. Strong enough to withstand any
assault which did not also crumble the Arch of Time.

At the taste of that knowledge, Covenant felt his death closing around him, and his despair grew wild. For a long moment with red fury blazing at him like the sun, he wanted to cry out, scream, howl so that the heavens would hear him, *No! NO!*

Hear him and fall.

But before the weaving of the world could tear, he found he knew that answer also. *To bear what must be borne.* After all, it was endurable—if he chose to go that far, and the choice was not taken from him. Certainly it would be expensive. It would cost him everything. But was that not preferable to a Ritual of Desecration which would make Kevin's look like an act of petty spite? Was it not?

After a time, he said softly, Yes. And again, Yes. Accepting it fully for the first time. *You are the wild magic.* Yes.

With the last ragged fragments of his will, he pulled himself back from the brink of cataclysm. He could not quench the blackness—and if he did not quench it soon, it would kill him. The venom was eating away his life. But not yet. His face was stretched and mortal with unutterable pain; but he had accepted it. Turning away from Gibbon, he walked off the mosaic.

As he looked toward Linden and Cail to beg their forgiveness, Nom burst into the Hall of Gifts with the First in fierce pursuit.

She wrenched to a halt when she saw the wreckage of the Hall, the extent of Covenant's desperation; then she went swiftly to join Cail and Linden. But the Sandgorgon shot toward the na-Mhoram as if the beast at last had located its perfect prey.

Flashing past Covenant, pounding across the mosaic, Nom crashed into the red heart of Gibbon's power.

And was catapulted away over Honninscrave's head like a flung child. Even a Sandgorgon was a small thing to pit against the force of the Banefire.

But Nom understood frustration and fury, effort and destruction. It did not understand fear or defeat. Surely the beast recognized the sheer transcendence of Gibbon's might. But Nom did not therefore desist or flee. Instead, it attacked in another way.

With both arms, it hit the floor so hard that the entire center of the Hall bucked and spattered like a sheet of water.

The mosaic cracked across its face, lifted in pieces, fell apart.

Shrieking rage, Gibbon staggered to regain his balance, then cocked back his crozier to deliver a blast which would fry Nom's flesh from its bones.

But he was maddened by strain and death-lust, and his blow required a moment's preparation. He did not see the chief result of Nom's attack.

That blow sent a fracture from wall to wall—a split which passed directly through the place where Honninscrave knelt in the stone. His bonds were shattered as if that had been Nom's intent.

With a roar, Honninscrave charged the na-Mhoram.

Gibbon was too intensely focused on Nom, too precariously poised. He could not react in time. His human flesh had no defense as Honninscrave struck him a blow which seemed to crush his bones. His crozier clattered across the floor, rang against the base of a column, and lay still, deprived of fire.

The First cried Honninscrave's name; but her voice appeared to make no sound in the stunned Hall.

For a moment, Honninscrave remained hunched and panting over Gibbon's corpse. Covenant had time for one clear thought: You can't kill a Raver that way. You can only kill the body.

Then the Master turned toward his companions; and Covenant nearly broke. He did not need Linden's percipience to see what had happened, did not need to hear her anguished whisper. He had witnessed such horrors before. And Honninscrave's plight was plain.

He stood as if he were still himself. His fists clenched as if he knew what he was doing. But his face was flowing like an hallucination, melting back and forth between savage glee and settled grim resolve. He was Grimmand Honninscrave, the Master of Starfare's Gem. And he was *samadhi* Sheol, the Raver that had led the Clave in Gibbon's body.

At war with each other.

The entire battle was internal. Red flared into his eyes and glazed away. Grins bared his teeth, were fought back. Snarling laughter choked in his throat. When he spoke, his voice cracked and seized under the strain.

"Thomas Covenant."

At once, his voice scaled upward out of control, crying, "Madman! Madman!"

He forced it down again. "Earthfriend. Hear me." The effort seemed to tear the muscles of his face. Helpless with power, Covenant watched in fever as Honninscrave wrestled for possession of his soul. Through his teeth, the Giant articulated like a death-gasp, "Heed the bidding of your despair. It must be done."

At once, several piercing shrieks burst from him—the Raver's staccato anguish, or Honninscrave's. "Help him," Linden panted. "Help him. Dear God." But there was nothing anybody could do. She alone had the capacity to interfere in such a struggle—and if she made the attempt, Covenant meant to stop her. If *samadhi* Sheol sprang from Honninscrave to her, it would have access to the wild magic through her.

Retching for air, Honninscrave gained the mastery.

"You must slay me." The words bled from his lips, but they were distinct and certain. His face turned murderous, then regained its familiar lines. "I will contain this Raver while you slay me. In that way, it also will be slain. And I will be at peace."

Sheol writhed for freedom; but Honninscrave held.

"I beg of you."

Covenant let out a groan of fire, but it went nowhere near the Giant. The First gripped her sword in both fists until her arms trembled; but her tears blinded her, and she could not move. Cail folded his arms across his chest as if he were deaf.

Linden was savage with suppressed weeping. "Give me a knife. Somebody give me a knife. Oh God damn you all to hell. *Honninscrave*." But she had no knife, and her revulsion would not let her go any closer to the Raver.

Yet Honninscrave was answered.

By Nom, the Sandgorgon of the Great Desert.

The beast waited a moment for the others to act, as if it understood that they all had to pass through this crisis and be changed. Then it padded over to Honninscrave, its strange knees tense with strength. He watched it come while the Raver in him gibbered and yowled. But he was the Master now in a way which surpassed *samadhi* Sheol, and his control did not slip.

Slowly, almost gently, Nom placed its arms around his

waist. For an instant, his eyes gazed toward his companions
and yearned as if he wished to say farewell—wished poignantly at the last that he had found some way to go on living.
Then, with a wrench as unexpected as an act of kindness, the
Sandgorgon crumpled him to the floor.

As if he were not in tears, Covenant thought dumbly, You
can't kill a Raver that way. But he was not sure anymore.
There were mysteries in the world which even Lord Foul
could not corrupt.

Linden gave a gasp as if her own bones had broken. When
she raised her head, her eyes were bright and hungry for the
power to exact retribution.

Stiffly, the First started toward the body of her friend.

Before she reached him, Nom turned; and Cail said as if
even his native dispassion were not proof against surprise,
"The Sandgorgon speaks."

Covenant could not clear his sight. All his peripheral vision
was gone, blackened by imminent combustion.

"It speaks in the manner of the *Haruchai*." Faint lines of
perplexity marked the space between Cail's brows. "Its speech
is alien—yet comprehensible."

His companions stared at him.

"It says that it has rent the Raver. It does not say slain. The
word is 'to rend.' The Raver has been rent. And the shreds of
its being Nom has consumed." With an effort, Cail smoothed
the frown from his forehead. "Thus has the Sandgorgon
gained the capacity for such speech."

Then the *Haruchai* faced Covenant. "Nom gives you thanks,
ur-Lord."

Thanks. Covenant grieved. He had let Honninscrave die.
Had failed to defeat Gibbon. He did not deserve thanks. And
he had no time. All his time had been used up. It was too
late for sorrow. His skin had a dark, sick underhue; his sense
of himself was fraying away. A gale of blackness rose in him,
and it demanded an answer. The answer he had learned in
nightmares. From Linden and the First and Cail and Nom and
fallen Honninscrave he turned away as if he were alone and
walked like a mounting flicker of fire out of the Hall of Gifts.

But when he put his feet to the stairs, a hand closed around
his mind, and he stopped. Another will imposed itself on his,
taking his choices from him.

Please, it said. *Please don't.*

Though he had no health-sense and was hardly sane, he recognized Linden's grasp. She was possessing him with her percipience.

Don't do this to yourself.

Through the link between them, he knew that she was weeping wildly. But behind her pain shone a fervid passion. She would not permit him to end in this way. Not allow him to go willingly out of her life.

I can't let you.

He understood her. How could he not? She was too vulnerable to everything. She saw that his control was almost gone. And his purpose must have been transparent to her; his desperation was too extreme to elude her discernment. She was trying to save him.

You mean too much.

But this was not salvation: it was doom. She had misinterpreted his need for her. What could she hope to do with him when his madness had become irremediable? And how would she be able to face the Despiser with the consequences of possession chained about her soul?

He did not try to fight her with fire. He refused to risk harming her. Instead, he remembered the imposed silence of the *Elohim* and the delirium of venom. In the past, either defense had sufficed to daunt her. Now he raised them together, sought deliberately to close the doors of his mind, shut her out.

She was stronger than ever. She had learned much, accepted much. She was acquainted with him in ways too intimate to be measured. She was crying hotly for him, and her desire sprang from the roots of her life. She clinched her will to his with a white grip and would not let him go.

To shut her out was hard, atrociously hard. He had to seal off half of himself as well as all of her, silence his own deep yearning. But she still did not comprehend him. She still feared that he was driven by the same self-pity grown to malice which had corrupted her father. And she had been too badly hurt by the horror of Gibbon's power and Honninscrave's death to be clear about what she was doing. At last he was able to close the door, to leave her behind as he started up the stairs again.

Lorn and aggrieved, her cry rose after him:
"I love you!"

It made him waver for a moment. But then he steadied himself and went on.

Borne by a swelling flood of black fire, he made his way toward the sacred enclosure. Twice he encountered bands of Riders who opposed him frenetically, as if they could sense his purpose. But he had become untouchable and was able to ignore them. Instinct and memory guided him to the base of the huge cavity in the heart of Revelstone where the Banefire burned.

It was here that the former inhabitants of the city had come together to share their communal dedication to the Land. Within its sheer cylinder were balconies where the people had stood to hear the Lords speak from the dais below them. But that dais was gone now, replaced by a pit from which the Banefire licked blood for food.

At the nearest doorway he stopped. Findail stood there waiting for him.

The yellowish anguish of the Appointed's eyes had not changed. His face was a wasteland of fear and old pain. But the anger with which he had so often denounced Covenant was gone. In its place, the *Elohim* emitted simple rue. Softly, he said, "You are going to your death, ring-wielder. I comprehend you now. It is a valiant hazard. I cannot answer for its outcome—and I know not how I will prove worthy of you. But I will not leave you."

That touched Covenant as the *rukhs* of the Riders had not. It gave him the strength to go on into the sacred enclosure.

There the Banefire met him, howling like the furnace of the sun. Its flames raged as high as the upper balconies where the immense iron triangle of the *master-rukh* now rested, channeling the power of the Sunbane to the Clave. Its heat seemed to char his face instantly, sear his lungs, cinder the frail life of his flesh and rave through him into the last foundation of his will. The fang-marks on his forearm burned like glee. Yet he did not halt or hesitate. He had set his feet to this path of his own volition: he accepted it completely. Pausing only to bring down the *master-rukh* in molten rain so that the surviving Riders would be cut off from their strength, he moved into the inferno.

That is the grace which has been given to you.

A small clear space like hope opened in his heart as he followed his dreams into the Banefire.

To bear what must be borne.

After a time, the blackness in him burned white.

PART II

Apotheosis

ELEVEN: Aftermath

HELD upright and active only by the fierce pressure of her need, Linden Avery walked numbly down through the ways of Revelstone, following the mounting stream of water inward. She had just left Nom on the upland plateau, where the Sandgorgon tended the channel it had brunted through sheer rock and dead soil from the outflow of Glimmermere to the upper entrance of the Keep; and the tarn's untainted waters now ran past her along a path prepared for it by the First, Pitchwife, and a few *Haruchai.*

Pure in spite of the harsh ages of the Sunbane, those waters shone blue against the desert of the late afternoon sun until they began to tumble like rapids into Revelstone. Then torchlight glinted across their splashing rush so that they looked like the glee of mountains as they washed passages, turned at closed doors and new barricades, rolled whitely down stairways. The Giants were adept at stone, and they read the inner language of the Keep. The route they had designed led with surprising convolution and efficiency to Linden's goal.

It was an open door at the base of the sacred enclosure, where the Banefire still burned as if Thomas Covenant had never stood within its heart and screamed against the heavens.

In rage and despair she had conceived this means of quenching the Clave's power. When Covenant had turned away from the Hall of Gifts and his friends, she had seen where he was going; and she had understood him—or thought she understood. He meant to put an end to his life, so that he would no longer be a threat to what he loved. Like her father, possessed by self-pity. But, standing so near to Gibbon-Raver,

she had learned that her own former visceral desire for death
was in truth a black passion for power, for immunity from all
death forever. And the way that blackness worked upon her
and grew showed her that no one could submit to such hunger
without becoming a servant of the Despiser. Covenant's intended immolation would only seal his soul to Lord Foul.

Therefore she had tried to stop him.

Yet somehow he had remained strong enough to deny her.
In spite of his apparently suicidal abjection, he had refused
her completely. It made her wild.

In the Hall, the First had fallen deep into the grief of
Giants. Nom had begun to belabor a great grave for Honninscrave, as if the gift the Master had given Revelstone and
the Land belonged there. Cail had looked at Linden, expecting
her to go now to aid the rest of the company, care for the
wounded. But she had left them all in order to pursue Covenant to his doom. Perhaps she had believed that she would
yet find a way to make him heed her. Or perhaps she had simply been unable to give him up.

His agony within the Banefire had nearly broken her. But it
had also given her a focus for her despair. She had sent out
a mental cry which had brought Nom and Cail running to her
with the First between them. At the sight of what Covenant
was doing, the First's visage had turned gray with defeat. But
when Linden had explained how the Banefire could be extinguished, the First had come instantly back to herself. Sending
Cail to rally their companions, she had sped away with Nom
to find the upland plateau and Glimmermere.

Linden had stayed with Covenant.

Stayed with him and felt the excoriation of his soul until
at last his envenomed power burned clean, and he came walking back out of the Banefire as if he were deaf and blind
and newborn, unable in the aftermath of his anguish to acknowledge her presence or even know that she was there, that
through her vulnerable senses she had now shared everything
with him except his death.

And as he had moved sightlessly past her toward some
place or fate which she could no longer guess, her heart had
turned to bitterness and dust, leaving her as desolate as the
demesne of the Sunbane. She had thought that her passion was
directed at him, at his rejection of her, his folly, his desperate
doom: but when she saw him emerge from the Banefire and

pass by her, she knew better. She had been appalled at herself—at the immedicable wrong of what she had tried to do to him. Despite her horror of possession, her revulsion for the dark ill which Lord Foul had practiced on Joan and the Land, her clear conviction that no one had the right to master others, suppress them, rule them in that way, she had reacted to Covenant's need and determination as if she were a Raver. She had tried to save him by taking away his identity.

There was no excuse. Even if he had died in the Banefire, or brought down the Arch of Time, her attempt would have been fundamentally evil—a crime of the spirit beside which her physical murder of her mother paled.

Then for a moment she had believed that she had no choice but to take his place in the Banefire—to let that savage blaze rip away her offenses so that Covenant and her friends and the Land would no longer be in danger from her. Gibbon-Raver had said, *The principal doom of the Land is upon your shoulders.* And, *You have not yet tasted the depths of your Desecration.* If her life had been shaped by a miscomprehended lust for power, then let it end now, as it deserved. There was no one nearby to stop her.

But then she had become aware of Findail. She had not seen him earlier. He seemed to have appeared in answer to her need. He had stood there before her, his face a hatchment of rue and strain; and his yellow eyes had ached as if they were familiar with the heart of the Banefire.

"Sun-Sage," he had breathed softly, "I know not how to dissuade you. I do not desire your death—though mayhap I would be spared much thereby. Yet consider the ring-wielder. What hope will remain for him if you are gone? How will he then refuse the recourse of the Earth's ruin?"

Hope? she had thought. I almost took away his ability to even know what hope is. Yet she had not protested. Bowing her head as if Findail had reprimanded her, she had turned away from the sacred enclosure. After all, she had no right to go where Covenant had gone. Instead, she had begun trying to find her way through the unfamiliar passages of Revelstone toward the upland plateau.

Before long, Durris had joined her. Reporting that the resistance of the Clave had ended, and that the *Haruchai* had already set about fulfilling her commands, he had guided her up to the afternoon sunlight and the stream of Glimmermere.

She had found the First and Nom together. Following the
First's instructions, Nom was bludgeoning a channel out of
the raw rock. The beast obeyed her as if it knew what she
wanted, understood everything she said—as if it had been
tamed. Yet the Sandgorgon did not appear tame as it tore into
the ground, shaping a watercourse with swift, exuberant ferocity. Soon the channel would be ready, and the clear waters
of Glimmermere could be diverted from Furl Falls.

Leaving Nom to Linden, the First went back into Revelstone to help the rest of the company. Shortly she sent another
Haruchai upland to say that the hurts of *Grim*-fire and Courser-poison were responding to *voure*, *vitrim*, and *diamondraught*. Even Mistweave was out of danger. Yet there were
many injured men and women who required Linden's personal
attention.

But Linden did not leave the Sandgorgon until the channel
was open and water ran eagerly down into the city and Nom
had convinced her that it could be trusted not to attack the
Keep once more. That trust came slowly: she did not know to
what extent the rending of the Raver had changed Nom's essential wildness. But Nom came to her when she spoke. It
obeyed her as if it both understood and approved of her orders. Finally she lifted herself out of her desert enough to ask
the Sandgorgon what it would do if she left it alone. At once,
it went and began improving the channel so that the water
flowed more freely.

Then she was satisfied. And she did not like the openness
of the plateau. The wasted landscape on all sides was too
much for her. She seemed to feel the desert sun shining
straight into her, confirming her as a place of perpetual dust.
She needed constriction, limitation—walls and requirements
of a more human scale—specific tasks that would help her
hold herself together. Leaving the Sandgorgon to go about its
work in its own way, she followed the water back into Revelstone.

Now the rapid chattering torchlight-spangled current drew
her in the direction of the Banefire.

Durris remained beside her; but she was hardly aware of
him. She sensed all the *Haruchai* as if they were simply a part
of Revelstone, a manifestation of the Keep's old granite. With
the little strength she still possessed, she focused her percipience forward, toward the fierce moil of steam where the Bane-

fire fought against extinction. For a time, the elemental passion of that conflict was so intense that she could not see the outcome. But then she heard more clearly the chuckling eagerness with which Glimmermere's stream sped along its stone route; and she knew the Banefire would eventually fail.

In that way, the upland tarn proved itself a thing of hope.

But hope seemed to have no meaning anymore. Linden had never deluded herself with the belief that the quenching of the Banefire would alter or weaken the Sunbane. Ages of bloodshed had only fed the Sunbane, only accelerated its possession of the Land, not caused it or controlled it.

When Covenant had fallen into despair after the loss of the One Tree, she had virtually coerced him to accept the end of the Clave's power as an important and necessary goal. She had demanded commitments from him, ignoring the foreknowledge of his death as if it signified nothing and could be set aside, crying at him, *If you're going to die, do something to make it count!* But even then she had known that the Sunbane would still go on gnawing its way inexorably into the heart of the Earth. Yet she had required this decision of him because she needed a concrete purpose, a discipline as tangible as surgery on which she could anchor herself against the dark. And because anything had been preferable to his despair.

But when she had wrested that promise from him, he had asked, *What're you going to do?* And she had replied, *I'm going to wait,* as if she had known what she was saying. *My turn's coming.* But she had not known how truly she spoke— not until Gibbon had said to her, *You have not yet tasted the depths of your Desecration,* and she had reacted by trying to possess the one decent love of her life.

Her turn was coming, all right. She could see it before her as vividly as the savage red steam venting like shrieks from all the doors of the sacred enclosure. *Driven to commit all destruction.* The desert sun lay within her as it lay upon the Land; soon the Sunbane would have its way with her altogether. Then she would indeed be a kind of Sun-Sage, as the *Elohim* avowed—but not in the way they meant.

An old habit which might once have been a form of self-respect caused her to thrust her hands into her hair to straighten it. But its uncleanness made her wince. Randomly, she thought that she should have gone to Glimmermere for a bath, made at least that much effort to cleanse—or perhaps merely disguise—the grime of her sins. But the idea was foolish, and she dismissed it. Her sins were not ones which could be washed away, even by water as quintessentially pure as Glimmermere's. And while the Banefire still burned, and the company still needed care, she could not waste time on herself.

Then she reached the wet fringes of the steam. The Banefire's heat seemed to condense on her face, muffling her perceptions; but after a moment she located the First and Pitchwife. They were not far away. Soon they emerged from the crimson vapor as if Glimmermere's effect upon the Banefire restored them to life.

Pitchwife bore the marks of battle and killing. His grotesque face was twisted with weariness and remembered hurt. It looked like the visage of a man who had forgotten the possibility of mirth. Yet he stood at his wife's side; and the sight tightened Linden's throat. *Weeps as no* Haruchai *has ever wept.* Oh, Pitchwife, she breathed to him mutely. I'm sorry.

The First was in better shape. The grief of Honninscrave's end remained in her eyes; but with Pitchwife beside her she knew how to bear it. And she was a Swordmain, trained for combat. The company had achieved a significant victory. To that extent, the Search she led had already been vindicated.

Somehow, they managed to greet Linden with smiles. They were Giants, and she was important to them. But a dry desert wind blew through her because she could not match them. She did not deserve such friends.

Without preamble, the First gestured toward the sacred enclosure. "It is a bold conception, Chosen, and worthy of pride. With mounting swiftness it accomplishes that which even the Earthfriend in his power—" But then she stopped, looked more closely at Linden. Abruptly, her own rue rose up in her, and her eyes welled tears. "Ah, Chosen," she breathed. "The fault is not yours. You are mortal, as I am—and our foe is malign beyond endurance. You must not—"

Linden interrupted the First bitterly. "I tried to possess him. Like a Raver. I almost destroyed both of us."

At that, the Giant hardened. "No." Her tone became incisive. "It skills nothing to impugn yourself. There is need of you. The wounded are gathered in the forehall. They must be tended." She swallowed a memory of pain, then went on, "Mistweave labors among them, though he is no less hurt.

He will not rest." Facing Linden squarely, the First concluded, "It is your work he does."

I know, Linden sighed. I know. Her eyes blurred and ran
as if they had no connection to the arid loss in her heart.

With that for recognition and thanks, she let Durris guide
her toward the forehall.

The sheer carnage there smote her as she entered the great
hall. The *Grim* had done severe damage to the floor, tearing
chunks from it like lumps of flesh. Dead Coursers sprawled in
pools of their own blood. A number of the *Haruchai* had been
hurt as badly as Mistweave; one of them was dead. Riders lay
here and there across the floor, scarlet-robed and contorted,
frantic with death. But worse than anything else were the
hacked and broken bodies of those who should never have
been sent into battle: cooks and cleaners, herders and gather-
ers, the innocent servants of the Clave. Among the litter of
their inadequate weapons, their cleavers, pitchforks, scythes,
clubs, they were scattered like the wreckage which their masters had already wrought upon the villages of the Land.

Now Linden could not stanch her tears—and did not try.
Through the blur, she spoke to Durris, sent him and several
other *Haruchai* in search of splints, bindings, a sharp knife,
hot water, and all the *metheglin* they could find to augment
the company's scant *vitrim* and dwindling *diamondraught*.
Then, using percipience instead of sight to direct her, she went
looking for Mistweave.

He was at work among the fallen of the Clave as if he were
a physician—or could become one by simply refusing to let
so much hurt and need lie untended. First he separated the
dead from those who might yet be saved. Then he made the
living as comfortable as possible, covered their wounds with
bandages torn from the raiment of the dead. His aura reached
out to her as though he, too, were weeping; and she seemed
to hear his very thoughts: This one also I slew. Her I broke.
Him I crippled. These I took from life in the name of service.

She felt his distress keenly. Self-distrust had driven him to
a kind of hunger for violence, for any exertion or blow which
might earn back his own esteem. Now he found himself in the
place to which such logic led—a place that stank like an
abattoir.

In response, something fierce came unexpectedly out of the
wilderness of Linden's heart. He had not halted his labor to

greet her. She caught him by the arm, by the sark, pulled at him until he bent over her and she was able to clinch her frail strength around his neck. Instinctively, he lifted her from the floor in spite of his broken arm; and she whispered at him as if she were gasping, "You saved my life. When I couldn't save myself. And no *Haruchai* could save me. You're not responsible for this. The Clave made them attack you. You didn't have any choice." Mistweave. "You couldn't just let them kill you." Mistweave, help me. All you did was fight. I tried to *possess* him.

He's gone, and I'll never get him back.

For a moment, Mistweave's muscles knotted with grief. But then slowly his grip loosened, and he lowered her gently to her feet. "Chosen," he said as if he had understood her, "it will be a benison to me if you will tend my arm. The pain is considerable."

Considerable, Linden thought. Sweet Christ, have mercy. Mistweave's admission was an appalling understatement. His right elbow had been crushed, and whenever he moved the splinters ground against each other. Yet he had spent the entire day in motion, first fighting for the company, then doing everything he could to help the injured. And the only claim he made for himself was that the pain was considerable.

He gave her more help than she deserved.

When Durris and his people brought her the things she had requested, she told him to build a fire to clean the knife and keep the water hot. Then while the sun set outside and night grew deep over the city, she opened up Mistweave's elbow and put the bones back together.

That intricate and demanding task made her feel frayed to the snapping point, worn thin by shared pain. But she did not stop when it was finished. Her work was just beginning. After she had splinted and strapped Mistweave's arm, she turned to the injuries of the *Haruchai*, to Fole's leg and Harn's hip and all the other wounds dealt out by the *Grim* and the Coursers, the Riders and the people of Revelstone. Fole's hurt reminded her of Ceer's—the leg crushed by a Sandgorgon and never decently treated—and so she immersed herself in the damage as if restitution could be made in that way, by taking the cost of broken bones and torn flesh upon herself. And after that she began to tend as best she could the Riders and servants of the Clave.

Later, through the riven gates at the end of the forehall, she felt midnight rise like the moon above the Keep. The reek of spilled and drying blood filled the air. Men and women cried out as if they expected retribution when she touched them. But still she went weary and unappeased about her chosen work. It was the only answer she had ever found for herself until she had met Covenant. Now it was the only answer she had left.

Yes. It was specific and clean. It had meaning, value; the pain of it was worth bearing. Yes. And it held her in one piece.

As if for the first time: Yes.

She had never faced so many wounds at once, so much bloodshed. But after all, the number of men and women, old and young, who had been able to survive their hurts this long was finite. The consequences of the battle were not like the Sunbane, endless and immedicable. She had nearly finished everything she knew how to ask of herself when Cail came to her and announced that the ur-Lord wished to see her.

She was too tired to feel the true shock of the summons. Even now she could see Covenant standing in the Banefire until his blackness burned away as if he had taken hold of that evil blaze and somehow made it holy. His image filled all the back of her mind. But she was exhausted and had no more fear.

Carefully, she completed what she was doing. As she worked, she spoke to Durris. "When the Banefire goes out, tell Nom to turn the stream back where it belongs. Then I want the dead cleaned out of here. Tell Nom to bury them outside the gates." They deserved at least that decency. "You and your people take care of these." She gestured toward the people arrayed around her in their sufferings and bandages. "The Land's going to need them." She understood poignantly Covenant's assertion that Sunder and Hollian were the Land's future. Freed from the rule of the Clave, these wounded men and women might help serve the same purpose.

Durris and Cail blinked at her, their faces flat in the incomplete torchlight. They were *Haruchai*, disdainful of injury and failure—not healers. And what reason did they have to obey her? Their commitment was to Covenant, not to her. With Brinn, Cail had once denounced her as a minion of Corruption.

But the *Haruchai* were not unaffected by their part in the Land's plight. The *merewives* and the Clave had taught them their limitations. And Brinn's victory over the Guardian of the One Tree had done much to open the way for Cable Seadreamer's death and the Despiser's manipulations. In a strange way, the *Haruchai* had been humbled. When Linden looked up at Cail, he said as if he were still unmoved, "It will be done. You are Linden Avery the Chosen. It will be done."

Sighing to herself, she did what she could for the last of the wounded—watched him die because she was only one woman and had not reached him in time. Then she straightened her stiff knees and went with Cail out of the forehall.

As she turned, she glimpsed a perfect ebony figure standing at the verge of the light near the gates. Vain had returned. Somehow, he had recognized the end of the Clave and known that he could safely rejoin the company. But Linden was past questioning anything the Demondim-spawn did. She lost sight of him as she entered the passages beyond the forehall; and at once she forgot him.

Cail guided her deep into a part of Revelstone which was new to her. The movement and confusion of the past day had left her sense of direction so bewildered that she had no idea where she was in relation to the Hall of Gifts; and she could barely discern the sacred enclosure in the distance as the Banefire declined toward extinction. But when she and Cail reached a hall that led like a tunnel toward the source of a weird silver illumination, she guessed their destination.

The hall ended in a wide, round court. Around the walls were doorways at intervals, most of them shut. Above the doors up to the high ceiling of the cavity were coigns which allowed other levels of the Keep to communicate with this place. But she recognized the court because the polished granite of its floor was split from wall to wall with one sharp crack, and the floor itself shone with an essential argence like Covenant's ring. He had damaged and lit that stone in the excess of his power when he had emerged from the soothtell of the Clave. Here had been revealed to him enough of the truth to send him on his quest for the One Tree—but only enough to ensure the outcome Lord Foul intended. In spite of her exhaustion, Linden shivered, wondering how much more had been revealed to him now.

But then she saw him standing in one of the doorways; and

all other questions vanished. Her eyes were full of silver; she felt she could hardly see him as he dismissed Cail, came out into the light to meet her.

Mute with shame and longing, she fought the inadequacy of her vision and strove to annele her sore heart with the simple sight of him.

Luminous in silver and tears, he stood before her. All the details were gone, blinded by the pure glow of the floor, his pure presence. She saw only that he carried himself as if he had not come to berate her. She wanted to say in a rush before she lost her sight altogether, Oh, Covenant, I'm so sorry, I was wrong, I didn't understand, forgive me, hold me, *Covenant*. But the words would not come. Even now, she read him with the nerves of her body; her percipience tasted the timbre of his emanations. And the astonishment of what she perceived stopped her throat.

He was there before her, clean in every limb and line, and strong with the same stubborn will and affirmation which had made him irrefusable to her from the beginning. Alive in spite of the Banefire; gentle toward her regardless of what she had tried to do to him. But something was gone from him. Something was changed. For a moment while she tried to comprehend the difference, she believed that he was no longer a leper.

Blinking furiously, she cleared her vision.

His cheeks and neck were bare, free of the unruly beard which had made him look as hieratic and driven as a prophet. The particular scraped hue of his skin told her that he had not used wild magic to burn his whiskers away: he had shaved himself with some kind of blade. With a blade instead of fire, as if the gesture had a special meaning for him. An act of preparation or acquiescence. But physically that change was only superficial.

The fundamental alteration was internal. Her first guess had been wrong; she saw now that his leprosy persisted. His fingers and palms and the soles of his feet were numb. The disease still rested, quiescent, in his tissues. Yet something was gone from him. Something important had been transformed or eradicated.

"Linden." He spoke as if her name sufficed for him—as if he had called her here simply so that he could say her name to her.

But he was not simple in any way. His contradictions remained, defining him beneath the surface. Yet he had become new and pure and clean. It was as if his doubt were gone—as if the self-judgments and -repudiation which had tormented him had been reborn as certainty, clarity, acceptance in the Banefire.

It was as if he had managed to rid himself of the Despiser's venom.

"Is it—?" she began amazedly. "How did you—?" But the light around him seemed to throng with staggering implications, and she could not complete the question.

In response, he smiled at her—and for one stunned instant his smile seemed to be the same one he had given Joan when he had exchanged his life for hers, giving himself up to Lord Foul's malice so that she would be free. A smile of such valor and rue that Linden had nearly cried out at the sight of it.

But then the angles of his face shifted, and his expression became bearable again. Quietly, he said, "Do you mind if we get out of this light? I'm not exactly proud of it." With his half-hand, he gestured toward the doorway from which he had emerged.

The cuts on his fingers had been healed.

And there were no scars on his forearm. The marks of Marid's fangs and of the injuries he had inflicted on himself had become whole flesh.

Dumbly, she went where he pointed. She did not know what had happened to him.

Beyond the door, she found herself in a small suite of rooms clearly designed to be someone's private living quarters. They were illuminated on a more human scale by several oil lamps and furnished with stone chairs and a table in the forechamber, a bare bed in one back room and empty pantry shelves in another. The suite had been unused for an inestimably long time, but the ventilation and granite of Revelstone had kept it clean. Covenant must have set the lamps himself—or asked the *Haruchai* to provide them.

The center of the table had been strangely gouged, as though a knife had been driven into it like a sharp stick into clay.

"Mhoram lived here," Covenant explained. "This is where I talked to him when I finally started to believe that he was my friend—that he was capable of being my friend after everything I'd done." He spoke without gall, as if he had reconciled himself to the memory. "He told me about the necessity of freedom."

Those words seemed to have a new resonance for him; but almost immediately he shrugged them aside. Indicating the wound in the tabletop, he said, "I did that. With the *krill*. Elena tried to give it to me. She wanted me to use it against Lord Foul. So I stabbed it into the table and left it there where nobody else could take it out. Like a promise that I was going to do the same thing to the Land." He tried to smile again; but this time the effort twisted his face like a grimace. "I did that even before I knew Elena was my daughter. But he was still able to be my friend." For a moment, his voice sounded chipped and battered; yet he stood tall and straight with his back to the open door and the silver lumination as if he had become unbreakable. "He must've removed the *krill* when he came into his power."

Across the table, he faced her. His eyes were gaunt with knowledge, but they remained clear. "It's not gone," he said softly. "I tried to get rid of it, but I couldn't."

"Then what—?" She was lost before him, astonished by what he had become. He was more than ever the man she loved—and yet she did not know him, could not put one plain question into words.

He sighed, dropped his gaze briefly, then looked up at her again. "I guess you could say it's been fused. I don't know how else to describe it. It's been burned into me so deeply that there's no distinction. I'm like an alloy—venom and wild magic and ordinary skin and bones melted together until they're all one. All the same. I'll never be free of it."

As he spoke, she saw that he was right. He gave her the words to see that he was right. Fused. An alloy. Like white gold itself, a blend of metals. And her heart gave a leap of elation within her.

"Then you can control it!" she said rapidly, so rapidly that she did not know what she was about to say until she said it. "You're not at Foul's mercy anymore!" Oh, *beloved.* "You can beat him!"

At that, sudden pain darkened his visage. She jerked to a halt, unable to grasp how she had hurt him. When he did not reply, she took hold of her confusion, forced it to be still. As carefully as she could, she said, "I don't understand. I can't. You've got to tell me what's going on."

"I know," he breathed. "I know." But now his attention was fixed on the gouged center of the table as if no power had ever been able to lift the knife out of his own heart; and she feared that she had lost him.

After a moment, he said, "I used to say I was sick of guilt. But not anymore." He took a deep breath to steady himself. "It's not a sickness anymore. I *am* guilt. I'll never use power again."

She started to protest; but his certainty stopped her. With an effort, she held herself mute as he began to quote an old song.

"There is wild magic graven in every rock,
contained for white gold to unleash or control—
gold, rare metal, not born of the Land,
nor ruled, limited, subdued
by the Law with which the Land was created—
but keystone rather, pivot, crux
for the anarchy out of which Time was made:
wild magic restrained in every particle of life,
and unleashed or controlled by gold
because that power is the anchor of the arch of life
that spans and masters Time."

She listened to him intently, striving for comprehension. But at the same time her mind bifurcated, and she found herself remembering Dr. Berenford. He had tried to tell her about Covenant by describing one of Covenant's novels. According to the older doctor, the book argued *that innocence is a wonderful thing except for the fact that it's impotent. Guilt is power. Only the damned can be saved.* The memory seemed to hint at the nature of Covenant's new certainty.

Was that it? Did he no longer doubt that he was damned?

He paused, then repeated, "Keystone. The Arch of Time is held together at the apex by wild magic. And the Arch is what gives the Earth a place in which to exist. It's what imprisons Foul. That's why he wants my ring. To break Time so he can escape.

"But nothing's that simple anymore. The wild magic has been fused into me. I *am* wild magic. In a sense, I've become the keystone of the Arch. Or I will be—if I let what I am loose. If I ever try to use power.

"But that's not all. If it were, I could stand it. I'd be willing to be the Arch forever, if Foul could be beaten that way. But I'm not just wild magic. I'm venom, too. Lord Foul's venom. Can you imagine what the Earth would be like if venom was the keystone? If everything in the world, every particle of life, was founded on venom as well as wild magic? That would be as bad as the Sunbane." Slowly, he lifted his head, met Linden with a glance that seemed to pierce her. "I won't do it."

She felt helpless to reach him; but she could not stop trying. She heard the truth as he described it; he had named the change in himself for her. In the Banefire he had made himself as impotent as innocence. The power to resist Despite, the *reason* of his life, had been burned out of him. Aching for him, she asked, "Then what? What will you do?"

His lips drew taut, baring his teeth; for an instant, he appeared starkly afraid. But no fear marked his voice. "When I saw Elena in Andelain, she told me where to find Foul. In Mount Thunder—a place inside the Wightwarrens called Kiril Threndor. I'm going to pay him a little visit."

"He'll kill you!" Linden cried, immediately aghast. "If you can't defend yourself, he'll just kill you and it'll all be wasted," everything he had suffered, venom-relapses, the loss of Seadreamer and Honninscrave, of Ceer, Hergrom, and Brinn, the silence of the *Elohim*, his *caamora* for the Unhomed of Seareach, the tearing agony and fusion of the Banefire. "*Wasted!* What kind of answer is *that?*"

But his certainty was unshaken. To her horror, he smiled at her again. Until it softened, his expression wrung her out of herself, made her want to scream at him as if he had become a Raver. Yet it did soften. When he spoke, he sounded neither desperate nor doomed, but only gentle and indefeasibly resigned.

"There are a few things Foul doesn't understand. I'm going to explain them to him."

Gentle, yes, and resigned; but also annealed, fused to the hard metal of his purpose. *Explain* them to him? she thought wildly. But in his mouth the words did not sound like folly. They sounded as settled and necessary as the fundament of the Earth.

However, he was not untouched by her consternation. More urgently, as if he also wanted to bridge the gulf between them, he said, "Linden, think about it. Foul can't break the Arch without breaking me first. Do you really think he can do that? After what I've been through?"

She could not reply. She was sinking in a vision of his death—of his body back in the woods behind Haven Farm pulsing its last weak life onto the indifferent stone. The old man whose life she had saved before she had ever met Covenant had said to her like a promise, *You will not fail, however he may assail you. There is also love in the world.* But she had already failed when she had let Covenant be struck by that knife, let him go on dying. All love was gone.

But he was not done with her. He was leaning on the table now, supporting himself with his locked arms to look at her more closely; and the silver glow of the floor behind him limned his intent posture, made him luminous. Yet the yellow lamplight seemed human and needy as it shone on his face, features she must have loved from the beginning—the mouth as strict as a commandment, the cheeks lined with difficulties, the hair graying as if its color were the ash left by his hot mind. The kindness he conveyed was the conflicted empathy and desire of a man who was never gentle with himself. And he still wanted something from her. In spite of what she had tried to do to him. Before he spoke, she knew that he had come to his reason for summoning her here—and for selecting this particular place, the room of a compassionate, dangerous, and perhaps wise man who had once been his friend.

In a husky voice, he asked, "What about you? What're you going to do?"

He had asked her that once before. But her previous response now seemed hopelessly inadequate. She raised her hands to her hair, then pushed them back down to her side. The touch of her unclean tresses felt so unlovely, impossible to love, that it brought her close to tears. "I don't know," she said. "I don't know what my choices are."

For a moment, his certitude faded. He faced her, not because he was sure, but because he was afraid. "You could stay here," he said as if the words hurt him. "The lore of the old Lords is still here. Most of it, anyway. Maybe the Giants could translate it for you. You might find a way out of this mess for yourself. A way back." He swallowed at an emotion that leaked like panic past his resolve. Almost whispering, he added, "Or you could come with me."

Come with—? Her percipience flared toward him, trying to read the spirit behind what he said. What was he afraid of? Did he dread her companionship, fear the responsibility and grief of having her with him? Or was he dismayed to go on without her?

Her legs were weak with exhaustion and desire, but she did not let herself sit down. A helpless tremor ran through her. "What do you want me to do?"

He looked like he would have given anything to be able to turn his head away; yet his gaze held. Even now, he did not quail from what he feared.

"I want what you want. I want you to find something that gives you hope. I want you to come into your power. I want you to stop believing that you're evil—that your mother and father are the whole truth about you. I want you to understand why you were chosen to be here." His visage pleaded at her through the lamplight. "I want you to have *reasons*."

She still did not comprehend his apprehension. But he had given her an opportunity she coveted fervidly, and she was determined to take it at any cost. Her voice was thick with a kind of weeping she had suppressed for most of her life; but she no longer cared how much frailty or need she exposed. All the severity and detachment to which she had trained herself had fled, and she did not try to hail them back. Trembling fiercely to herself, she uttered her avowal.

"I don't want hope. I don't want power. I don't care if I never go back. Let Foul do his worst—and to hell with him. I don't even care if you're going to die." That was true. Death was later: he was now. "I'm a doctor, not a magician. I can't save you unless you go back with me—and if you offered me that, I wouldn't take it. What's happening here is too important. It's too important to *me*." And that also was true; she had learned it among the wounded in the forehall of the Keep. "All I want is a living love. For as long as I can get it." Defying her weakness, she stood erect before him in the lamplight as if she were ablaze. "I want you."

At that, he bowed his head at last; and the relief which flooded from him was so palpable that she could practically embrace it. When he looked up again, he was smiling with love—a smile which belonged to her and no one else. Tears streaked his face as he went to the door and closed it, shutting out the consequences of wild magic and venom. Then from the doorway he said thickly, "I wish I could've believed you were going to say that. I would've told Cail to bring us some blankets."

But the safe gutrock of Revelstone enclosed them with solace, and they did not need blankets.

TWELVE: Those Who Part

THEY did not sleep at all that night. Linden knew that Covenant had not slept the previous night, on the verge of the jungle outside Revelstone; she had been awake herself, watching the stretched desperation of his aura with her percipience because Cail had refused to let her approach the ur-Lord. But the memory no longer troubled her; in Covenant's place, she might have done the same thing. Yet that exigent loneliness only made this night more precious—too precious to be spent in sleep. She had not been in his arms since the crisis of the One Tree; and now she sought to impress every touch and line of him onto her hungry nerves.

If he had wanted sleep himself, she would have been loath to let him go. But he had resumed his certainty as if it could take the place of rest; and his desire for her was as poignant as an act of grace. From time to time, she felt him smiling the smile that belonged solely to her; and once he wept as if his tears were the same as hers. But they did not sleep.

At the fringes of her health-sense, she was aware of the great Keep around her. She felt Cail's protective presence outside the door. She knew when the Banefire went out at last, quenched by the sovereign waters of Glimmermere. And as the abused stone of the sacred enclosure cooled, the entire city let out a long granite sigh which seemed to breathe like relief through every wall and floor. Finally she felt the distant flow of the lake stop as Nom restored the stream to its original channel. For the remainder of this one night, at least, Revelstone had become a place of peace.

Before dawn, however, Covenant arose from Mhoram's intimate bed. As he dressed, he urged Linden to do the same. She complied without question. The communion between them was more important than questions. And she read him clearly, knew that what he had in mind pleased him. That was enough for her. Shrugging her limbs back into the vague discomfort of her grimy clothes, she accepted the clasp of his numb hand and climbed with him through the quiet Keep to the upland plateau.

At Revelstone's egress, they left Cail behind to watch over their privacy. Then, with a happy haste in his strides, Covenant led her west and north around the curve of the plateau toward the eldritch tarn which she had used against the Banefire without ever having seen it.

Toward Glimmermere, where Mhoram had hidden the *krill* of Loric for the Land's future. Where sprang the only water outside Andelain Earthpowerful enough to resist the Sunbane. And where, Linden now remembered, Covenant had once gone to be told that his dreams were true.

She felt he was taking her to the source of his most personal hope.

From the east, a wash of gray spread out to veil the stars, harbingering dawn. A league or two away in the west, the Mountains strode off toward the heavens; but the hills of the upland were not rugged. In ages past, their grasses and fields had been rich enough to feed all the city at need. Now, however, the ground was barren under Linden's sensitive feet; and some of her weariness, a hint of her wastelanded mood, returned to her, leeching through her soles. The sound of the water, running unseen past her toward Furl Falls, seemed to have a hushed and uncertain note, as if in some way the outcome of the Earth were precariously balanced and fragile about her. While the Sunbane stalked the Land, she remembered that Covenant's explanation of his new purpose made no sense.

There are a few things Foul doesn't understand. I'm going to explain them to him.

No one but a man who had survived an immersion in the Banefire could have said those words as if they were not insane.

But the dry coolness of the night still lingered on the plateau; and his plain anticipation made doubt seem irrelevant, at least for the present. Northward among the hills he led her, angling away from the cliffs and toward the stream. Moments before the sun broached the horizon, he took her past the crest of a high hill; and she found herself looking down at the pure tarn of Glimmermere.

It lay as if it were polished with its face open to the wide sky. In spite of the current flowing from it, its surface was unruffled, as flat and smooth as burnished metal. It was fed by deep springs which did not stir or disturb it. Most of the water reflected the fading gray of the heavens; but around the rims of the tarn were imaged the hills which held it, and to the west could be seen the Westron Mountains, blurred by dusk and yet somehow precise, as faithfully displayed as in a mirror. She felt that if she watched those waters long enough she would see all the world rendered in them.

All the world except herself. To her surprise, the lake held no echo of her. It reflected Covenant at her side; but her it did not heed. The sky showed through her as if she were too mortal or insignificant to attract Glimmermere's attention.

"Covenant—?" she began in vague dismay. "What—?" But he gestured her to silence, smiled at her as if the imminent morning made her beautiful. Half running, he went down the slope to the tarn's edge. There he pulled off his T-shirt, removed his boots and pants. For an instant, he looked back up at her, waved his arm to call her after him. Then he dove out into Glimmermere. His pale flesh pierced the water like a flash of joy as he swam toward the center of the lake.

She followed half involuntarily, both moved and frightened by what she saw. But then her heart lifted, and she began to hurry. The ripples of his dive spread across the surface like promises. The lake took hold of her senses as if it were potent enough to transform her. Her whole body ached with a sudden longing for cleanliness. Out in the lake, Covenant broke water and gave a holla of pleasure that carried back from the hills. Quickly, she unbuttoned her shirt, kicked her shoes away, stripped off her pants, and went after him.

Instantly, a cold shock flamed across her skin as if the

water meant to burn the grime and pain from her. She burst back to the surface, gasping with a hurt that felt like ecstasy. Glimmermere's chill purity lit all her nerves.

Her hair straggled across her face. She thrust the tresses aside and saw Covenant swimming underwater toward her. The clarity of the lake made him appear at once close enough to touch and too far away to ever be equalled.

The sight burned her like the water's chill. She could see him—but not herself. Looking down at her body, she saw only the reflection of the sky and the hills. Her physical substance seemed to terminate at the waterline. When she raised her hand, it was plainly visible—yet her forearm and elbow beneath the surface were invisible. She saw only Covenant as he took hold of her legs and tugged her down to him.

Yet when her head was underwater and she opened her eyes, her limbs and torso reappeared as if she had crossed a plane of translation into another kind of existence.

His face rose before her. He kissed her happily, then swung around behind her as they bobbed back upward. Breaking water, he took a deep breath before he bore her down again. But this time as they sank he gripped her head in his hands, began to scrub her scalp and hair. And the keen cold water washed the dirt and oil away like an atonement.

She twisted in his grasp, returned his kiss. Then she pushed him away and regained the surface to gulp air as if it were the concentrated elixir of pleasure.

At once, he appeared before her, cleared his face with a jerk of his head, and gazed at her with a light like laughter in his eyes.

"You—!" she panted, almost laughing herself. "You've got to tell me." She wanted to put her arms around him; but then she would not be able to speak. "It's wonderful!" Above her, the tops of the western hills were lit by the desert sun, and that shining danced across the tarn. "How come I disappear and you don't?"

"I already told you!" he replied, splashing water at her. "Wild magic and venom. The keystone of the Arch." Swimming in this lake, he could say even those words without diminishing her gladness. "The first time I was here, I couldn't see myself either. You're *normal!*" His voice rose exuberantly. "Glimmermere *recognizes* me!"

Then she did fling her arms about his neck; and they sank

280 White Gold Wielder

together into the embrace of the tarn. Intuitively, for the first time, she understood his hope. She did not know what it meant, had no way to estimate its implications. But she felt it shining in him like the fiery water; and she saw that his certainty was not the confidence of despair. Or not entirely. Venom and wild magic: despair and hope. The Banefire had fused them together in him and made them clean.

No, it was not true to say that she understood it. But she recognized it, as Glimmermere did. And she hugged and kissed him fervently—splashed water at him and giggled like a girl—shared the eldritch lake with him until at last the cold required her to climb out onto a sheet of rock along one edge and accept the warmth of the desert sun.

That heat sobered her rapidly. As Glimmermere evaporated from her sensitive skin, she felt the Sunbane again. Its touch sank into her like Gibbon's, drawing trails of desecration along her bones. After all, the quenching of the Banefire had not significantly weakened or even hampered Lord Foul's corruption. The Land's plight remained, unaltered by Covenant's certitude or her own grateful cleansing. Viscerally unwilling to lie naked under the desert sun, she retrieved her clothes and Covenant's, dressed herself while he watched as if he were still hungry for her. But slowly his own high spirits faded. When he had resumed his clothing, she saw that he was ready for the questions he must have known she would ask.

"Covenant," she said softly, striving for a tone that would make him sure of her, "I don't understand. After what I tried to do to you, I don't exactly have the right to make demands." But he dismissed her attempted possession with a shrug and a grimace; so she let it go. "And anyway I trust you. But I just don't understand why you want to go face Foul. Even if he can't break you, he'll hurt you terribly. If you can't use your power, how can you possibly fight him?"

He did not flinch. But she saw him take a few mental steps backward as if his answer required an inordinate amount of care. His emanations became studied, complex. He might have been searching for the best way to tell her a lie. Yet when he began to speak, she heard no falsehood in him; her percipience would have screamed at the sound of falsehood. His care was the caution of a man who did not want to cause any more pain.

"I'm not sure. I don't think I can fight him at all. But I keep asking myself, how can he fight me?

"You remember Kasreyn." A wry quirk twisted the corner of his mouth. "How could you forget? Well, he talked quite a bit while he was trying to break me out of that silence. He told me that he used pure materials and pure arts, but he couldn't create anything pure. 'In a flawed world purity cannot endure. Thus within each of my works I must perforce place one small flaw, else there would be no work at all.' That was why he wanted my ring. He said, 'It's imperfection is the very paradox of which the Earth is made, and with it a master may form perfect works and fear nothing.' If you look at it that way, an alloy is an imperfect metal."

As he spoke, he turned from her slowly, not to avoid her gaze, but to look at the fundamental reassurance of his reflection in the tarn. "Well, I'm a kind of alloy. Foul has made me exactly what he wants—what he needs. A tool he can use to perfect his freedom. And destroy the Earth in the process.

"But the question is my freedom, not his. We've talked about the necessity of freedom. I've said over and over again that he can't use a tool to get what he wants. If he's going to win, he has to do it through the choices of his victims. I've said that." He glanced at her as if he feared how she might react. "I believed it. But I'm not sure it's true anymore. I think alloys transcend the normal strictures. If I really am nothing more than a tool now, Foul can use me any way he wants, and there won't be anything we can do about it."

Then he faced her again, cocked his fists on his hips. "But *that* I don't believe. I don't believe I'm anybody's tool. And I don't think Foul can win through the kinds of choices any of us has been making. The *kind* of choice is crucial. The Land wasn't destroyed when I refused Mhoram's summons for the sake of a snakebit kid. It isn't going to be destroyed just because Foul forced me to choose between my own safety and Joan's. And the opposite is true, too. If I'm the perfect tool to bring down the Arch of Time, then I'm also the perfect tool to preserve it. Foul can't win unless I choose to let him."

His surety was so clear that Linden almost believed him. Yet within herself she winced because she knew he might be wrong. He had indeed spoken often of the importance of freedom. But the *Elohim* did not see the world's peril in those terms. They feared for the Earth because Sun-Sage and ring-wielder were not one—because he had no percipience to guide his choices and she had no power to make her choices count. And if he had not yet seen the full truth of Lord Foul's machinations, he might choose wrongly despite his lucid determination.

But she did not tell him what she was thinking. She would have to find her own answer to the trepidation of the *Elohim*. And her fear was for him rather than for herself. As long as he loved her, she would be able to remain with him. And as long as she was with him, she would have the chance to use her health-sense on his behalf. That was all she asked: the opportunity to try to help him, redeem the harm of her past mistakes and failures. Then if he and the Land and the Earth were lost, she would have no one to blame but herself.

The responsibility frightened her. It implied an acknowledgment of the role the *Elohim* had assigned to her, an acceptance of the risk of Gibbon's malign promise, *You are being forged.* But there had been other promises also. Covenant had avowed that he would never cede his ring to the Despiser. And the old man on Haven Farm had said, *You will not fail, however he may assail you.* For the first time, she took comfort in those words.

Covenant was looking at her intently, waiting for her response. After a moment, she pursued the thread of his explanation.

"So he can't break you. And you can't fight him. What good is a stalemate?"

At that, he smiled harshly. But his reply took a different direction than she had expected. "When I saw Mhoram in Andelain"—his tone was as direct as courage—"he tried to warn me. He said, 'It boots nothing to avoid his snares, for they are ever beset with other snares, and life and death are too intimately intergrown to be severed from each other. When you have come to the crux, and have no other recourse, remember the paradox of white gold. There is hope in contradiction.'" By degrees, his expression softened, became more like the one for which she was insatiable. "I don't think there's going to be any stalemate."

She returned his smile as best as she could, trying to

emulate him in the same way that he strove to match the ancient Lord who had befriended him.

She hoped he would take her in his arms again. She wanted that, regardless of the Sunbane. She could bear the violation of the desert sun for the sake of his embrace. But as they gazed at each other, she heard a faint, strange sound wafting over the upland hills—a high run of notes, as poignant as the tone of a flute. But it conveyed no discernible melody. It might have been the wind singing among the barren rocks.

Covenant jerked up his head, scanned the hillsides. "The last time I heard a flute up here—" He had been with Elena; and the music of a flute had presaged the coming of the man who had told him that his dreams were true.

But this sound was not music. It cracked on a shrill note and fell silent. When it began again, it was clearly a flute— and clearly being played by someone who did not know how. Its lack of melody was caused by simple ineptitude.

It came from the direction of Revelstone.

The tone cracked again; and Covenant winced humorously. "Whoever's playing that thing needs help," he muttered. "And we ought to go back anyway. I want to settle things and get started today."

Linden nodded. She would have been content to spend a few days resting in Revelstone; but she was willing to do whatever he wanted. And she would be able to enjoy her scrubbed skin and clean hair better in the Keep, protected from the Sunbane. She took his hand, and together they climbed out of the basin of the tarn.

From the hilltop, they heard the flute more accurately. It sounded like its music had been warped by the desert sun.

The plains beyond the plateau looked flat and ruined to the horizons, all life hammered out of them; nothing green or bearable lifted its head from the upland dirt. Yet Glimmermere's water and the shape of the hills seemed to insist that life was still possible here, that in some stubborn way the ground was not entirely wasted.

However, the lower plains gave no such impression. Most of the river evaporated before it reached the bottom of Furl Falls; the rest disappeared within a stone's throw of the cliff. The sun flamed down at Linden as if it were calling her to itself. Before they reached the flat wedge of the plateau which contained Revelstone, she knew that her determination to stand by him would not prove easy. In the bottom of her heart lurked a black desire for the power to master the Sunbane, make it serve her. Every moment of the sun's touch reminded her that she was still vulnerable to desecration.

But by the time they rejoined Cail at the city's entrance, they could hear that the fluting came from the tip of the promontory overlooking the watchtower. By mute agreement, they walked on down the wedge; and at the Keep's apex they found Pitchwife. He sat with his legs over the edge, facing eastward. The deformation of his spine bent him forward. He appeared to be leaning toward a fall.

His huge hands held a flute to his mouth as if he were wrestling with it—as if he thought that by sheer obstinate effort he would be able to wring a dirge from the tiny instrument.

At their approach, he lowered the flute to his lap, gave them a wan smile of habit rather than conviction. "Earthfriend," he said; and his voice sounded as frayed and uncertain as the notes he had been playing. "It boons me to behold you again and whole. The Chosen has proven and reproven her worth for all to see—and yet has survived to bring her beauty like gladness before me." He did not glance at Linden. "But I had thought that you were gone from us altogether."

Then his moist gaze wandered back to the dry, dead terrain below him. "Pardon me that I have feared for you. Fear is born in doubt, and you have not merited my doubt." With an awkward movement, like suppressed violence, he indicated the flute. "The fault is mine. I can find no music in this instrument."

Instinctively, Linden went to stand behind the Giant, placed her hands on his shoulders. In spite of his sitting posture and crooked back, his shoulders were only a little below hers; and his muscles were so oaken that she could hardly massage them. Yet she rubbed at his distress because she did not know how else to comfort him.

"Everybody doubts," Covenant breathed. He did not go near the Giant. He remained rigidly where he was, holding his vertigo back from the precipice. But his voice reached out through the sun's arid heat. "We're all scared. You have the right." Then his tone changed as if he were remembering what Pitchwife had undergone. Softly, he asked, "What can I do for you?"

Pitchwife's muscles knotted under Linden's hands. After a moment, he said simply, "Earthfriend, I desire a better outcome."

At once, he added, "Do not mistake me. That which has been done here has been well done. Mortal though you are, Earthfriend and Chosen, you surpass all estimation." He let out a quiet sigh. "But I am not content. I have shed such blood— The lives of the innocent I have taken from them by the score, though I am no Swordmain and loathe such work. And as I did so, my doubt was terrible to me. It is a dire thing to commit butchery when hope has been consumed by fear. As you have said, Chosen, there must be a reason. The world's grief should unite those who live, not sunder them in slaughter and malice.

"My friends, there is a great need in my heart for song, but no song comes. I am a Giant. Often have I vaunted myself in music. 'We are Giants, born to sail, and bold to go wherever dreaming goes.' But such songs have become folly and arrogance to me. In the face of doom, I have not the courage of my dreams. Ah, my heart must have song. I find no music in it.

"I desire a better outcome."

His voice trailed away over the cliff-edge and was gone. Linden felt the ache in him as if she had wrapped her arms around it. She wanted to protest the way he seemed to blame himself; yet she sensed that his need went deeper than blame. He had tasted the Despiser's malice and was appalled. She understood that. But she had no answer to it.

Covenant was more certain. He sounded as strict as a vow as he asked, "What're you going to do?"

Pitchwife responded with a shrug that shifted Linden's hands from his shoulders. He did not look away from the destitution sprawling below him. "The First has spoken of this," he said distantly. The thought of his wife gave him no ease. "We will accompany you to the end. The Search requires no less of us. But when you have made your purpose known, Mistweave will bear word of it to Seareach. There Starfare's Gem will come if the ice and the seas permit. Should you fail, and those with you fall, the Search must yet continue. The knowledge which Mistweave will bear to Seareach will enable Sevinhand Anchormaster to choose the path of his service."

Linden looked at Covenant sharply to keep him from saying that if he failed there would be no Earth left for the Search to serve. Perhaps the journey the First had conceived for Mistweave was pointless; still Linden coveted it for him. It was clear and specific, and it might help him find his way back to himself. Also she approved the First's insistence on behaving as if hope would always endure.

But she saw at once that Covenant had no intention of denying the possibility of hope. No bitterness showed beyond his empathy for Pitchwife; his alloyed despair and determination were clean of gall. Nor did he suggest that Pitchwife and the First should join Mistweave. Instead, he said as if he were content, "That's good. Meet us in the forehall at noon, and we'll get started."

Then he met Linden's gaze. "I want to go look at Honninscrave's grave." His tone thickened momentarily. "Say good-bye to him. Will you come with me?"

In response, she went to him and hugged him so that he would understand her silence.

Together they left Pitchwife sitting on the rim of the city. As they neared the entrance to Revelstone, they heard the cry of his flute again. It sounded as lorn as the call of a kestrel against the dust-trammeled sky.

Gratefully, Linden entered the great Keep, where she was shielded from the desert sun. Relief filled her nerves as she and Covenant moved down into the depths of Revelstone, back to the Hall of Gifts.

Cail accompanied them. Beneath his impassivity she sensed a strange irresolution, as if he wanted to ask a question or boon and did not believe he had the right. But when they reached their goal, she forgot his unexplained emanations.

During Covenant's battle with Gibbon, and the rending of the Raver, she had taken scant notice of the cavern itself. All her attention had been focused on what was happening —and on the blackness which Gibbon had called up in her. As a result, she had not registered the extent to which the Hall and its contents had been damaged. But she saw the havoc now, felt its impact.

Around the walls, behind the columns, in the corners and distant reaches, much of the Land's ancient artwork remained intact. But the center of the cavern was a shambles. Tapestries had been cindered, sculptures split, paintings shredded. Cracks marked two of the columns from crown to pediment; hunks of stone had been ripped from the ceiling, the floor; the mosaic on which Gibbon had stood was a ruin. Centuries of human effort and aspiration were wrecked by the uncontainable forces Covenant and the Raver had unleashed.

For a moment, Covenant's gaze appeared as ravaged as the Hall. No amount of certainty could heal the consequences of what he had done—and had failed to do.

While she stood there, caught between his pain and the Hall's hurt, she did not immediately recognize that most of the breakage had already been cleared away. But then she saw Nom at work, realized what the Sandgorgon was doing.

It was collecting pieces of rock, splinters of sculpture, shards of pottery, any debris it was able to lift between the stumps of his forearms, and it was using those fragments meticulously to raise a cairn for Honninscrave.

The funerary pile was already taller than Linden; but Nom was not yet satisfied with it. With swift care, the beast continued adding broken art to the mound. The rubble was too crude to have any particular shape. Nevertheless Nom moved around and around it to build it up as if it were an icon of the distant gyre of Sandgorgons Doom.

This was Nom's homage to the Giant who had enabled it to rend Gibbon-Raver. Honninscrave had contained and controlled *samadhi* Sheol so that the Raver could not possess Nom, not take advantage of Nom's purpose and power. In that way, he had made it possible for Nom to become something new, a Sandgorgon of active mind and knowledge and volition. With this cairn, Nom acknowledged the Master's sacrifice as if it had been a gift.

The sight softened Covenant's pain. Remembering Hergrom and Ceer, Linden would not have believed that she might ever feel anything akin to gratitude toward a Sandgorgon. But she had no other name for what she felt as she watched Nom work.

Though it lacked ordinary sight or hearing, the beast appeared to be aware of its onlookers. But it did not stop until it had augmented Honninscrave's mound with the last rubble large enough for its arms to lift. Then, however, it turned abruptly and strode toward Covenant.

A few paces in front of him, it stopped. With its back-bent knees, it lowered itself to the floor, touched its forehead to the stone.

He was abashed by the beast's obeisance. "Get up," he muttered. "Get up. You've earned better than this." But Nom remained prostrate before him as if it deemed him worthy of worship.

Unexpectedly, Cail spoke for the Sandgorgon. He had recovered his *Haruchai* capacity for unsurprise. He reported the beast's thoughts as if he were accustomed to them.

"Nom desires you to comprehend that it acknowledges you. It will obey any command. But it asks that you do not command it. It wishes to be free. It wishes to return to its home in the Great Desert and its bound kindred. From the rending of the Raver, Nom has gained knowledge to unmake Sandgorgons Doom—to release its kind from pent fury and anguish. It seeks your permission to depart."

Linden felt that she was smiling foolishly; but she could not stop herself. Fearsome though the Sandgorgons were, she had hated the idea of their plight from the moment when Pitchwife had told her about it. "Let it go," she murmured to Covenant. "Kasreyn had no right to trap them like that in the first place."

He nodded slowly, debating with himself. Then he made his decision. Facing the Sandgorgon, he said to Cail, "Tell it, it can go. I understand it's willing to obey me, and I say it can go. It's free. But," he added sharply, "I want it to leave the *Bhrathair* alone. Those people have the right to live, too. And God knows I've already done them enough damage. I don't want them to suffer any more because of me."

Faceless, devoid of expression, the albino beast raised itself erect again. "Nom hears you," Cail replied. To Linden's percipience, his tone seemed to hint that he envied Nom's freedom. "It will obey. Its folk it will teach obedience also. The Great Desert is wide, and the *Bhrathair* will be spared."

Before he finished, the Sandgorgon burst into a run toward the doorway of the Hall. Eager for its future, it vanished up the stairs, speeding in the direction of the open sky. For a few moments, Linden felt its wide feet on the steps; their force seemed to make the stone Keep jangle. But then Nom passed beyond her range, and she turned from it as if it were a healed memory—as if in some unexpected way the deaths of Hergrom and Ceer and Honninscrave had been made bearable at last.

She was still smiling when Covenant addressed Cail. "We've got some time before noon." He strove to sound casual; but the embers in his eyes were alight for her. "Why don't you find us something to eat? We'll be in Mhoram's room."

Cail nodded and left at once, moving with swift unhaste. His manner convinced Linden that she was reading him accurately: something had changed for him. He seemed willing, almost eager, to be apart from the man he had promised to protect.

But she had no immediate desire to question the *Haruchai*. Covenant had put his arm around her waist, and time was precious. Her wants would have appeared selfish to her if he had not shared them.

However, when they reached the court with the bright silver floor and the cracked stone, they found Sunder and Hollian waiting for them.

The Stonedownors had rested since Linden had last seen them, and they looked better for it. Sunder was no longer slack-kneed and febrile with exhaustion. Hollian had regained much of her young clarity. They greeted Covenant and Linden shyly, as if they were uncertain how far the Unbeliever and the Chosen had transcended them. But behind their shared mood, their differences were palpable to Linden.

Unlike Sunder's former life, Hollian's had been one of acceptance rather than sacrifice. The delicate scars which laced her right palm were similar to the pale pain-lattice on his left forearm, but she had never taken anyone else's blood. Yet since that time her role had been primarily one of support, aiding Sunder when he had first attuned himself to Memla's *rukh* during the company's journey toward Seareach as well as in his later use of the *krill*. It was he, guilt-sore and vehement, who hated the Clave, fought it—and had been vindicated. He had struck necessary blows on behalf of the Land, showing himself a fit companion for Giants and *Haruchai*, Covenant and Linden. Now he bore himself with a new confidence; and the silver light seemed to shine

bravely in his eyes, as though he knew that his father would
have been proud of him.

Hollian herself was proud of him. Her open gaze and
gentle smile showed that she regretted nothing. The child
she carried was a joy to her. Yet Linden saw something
plainly unfinished in the eh-Brand. Her emanations were now
more complex than Sunder's. She looked like a woman who
knew that she had not yet been tested. And she wanted that
test, wanted to find the destiny which she wore about her like
the raven-wings of her lustrous hair. She was an eh-Brand,
rare in the Land. She wished to learn what such rareness
meant.

Covenant gave Linden a glance of wry rue; but he accepted
the untimely presence of the Stonedownors without protest.
They were his friends, and his surety included them.

In response to Covenant's greeting, Sunder said with abrupt
awkwardness, "Thomas Covenant, what is your purpose now?"
His recent accomplishments had not given him an easy
manner. "Forgive us that we intrude upon you. Your need for
rest is plain." His regard told Linden that her fatigue was
more obvious than Covenant's. "Should you elect to remain
here for any number of days, the choice would become you.
In times past"—his scowl was a mix of self-mockery and
regret—"I have questioned you, accusing you of every madness and all pain." Covenant made a gesture of dismissal; but
Sunder hastened to continue, "I do not question you now.
You are the Earthfriend, Illender and Prover of Life—and
my friend. My doubt is gone.

"Yet," he went on at once, "we have considered the Sunbane. The eh-Brand foretells its course. With Sunstone and
krill, I have felt its power. The quenching of Banefire and
Clave is a great work—but the Sunbane is not diminished.
The morrow's sun will be a sun of pestilence. It reigns still
upon the Land, and its evil is clear."

His voice gathered strength and determination as he spoke.
"Thomas Covenant, you have taught me the falsehood of the
Clave. I had believed the Land a gallow-fells, a punishing
place conceived by a harsh Master. But I have learned that
we are born for beauty rather than ill—that it is the Sunbane
which is evil, not the life which the Sunbane torments." His
gaze glinted keenly. "Therefore I find that I am not content.
The true battle is yet before us." He was not as tall as Cove-

nant; but he was broader and more muscular. He looked as
solid as the stone of his home. "Thus I ask, what is your
purpose now?"

The question distressed Covenant. His certainty could not
protect him from his own empathy. He concealed his pain;
but Linden saw it with her health-sense, heard it in the
gruffness of his reply. "You're not content," he muttered.
"Nobody's content. Well, you ought to be." Beneath the surface, he was as taut as a fraying bowstring. "You've done
enough. You can leave the Sunbane to me—to me and
Linden. I want you to stay here."

"Stay—?" The Graveler was momentarily too surprised to
understand. "Do you mean to depart from us?" Hollian placed
a hand on his arm, not to restrain him, but to add her concern to his.

"Yes!" Covenant snapped more strongly than necessary.
But at once he steadied himself. "Yes. That's what I want.
You're the future of the Land. There's nobody else. The
people the Clave let live are all too old or sick to do much,
or too young to understand. You two are the only ones left
who know what's happened, what it means. What the life of
the Land should be like. If anything happens to you, most of
the survivors won't even know the Clave was wrong. They'll
go on believing those lies because there won't be anybody
around to contradict them. I need you to tell them the truth.
I can't risk you."

Linden thought he would say, Please. *Please.* But Sunder's
indignation was vivid in the sharp light. "Risk, ur-Lord?" he
rasped as soon as Covenant stopped. "Is it risk you fear? Or
do you deem us unworthy to partake of your high purpose?
Do you forget who we are?" His hand gripped at the *krill*
wrapped and hidden within his jerkin. "Your world is other-
where, and to it you will return when your task is done. But
we are the Land. We are the life which remains. We will not
sit in safety while the outcome of that life is determined!"

Covenant stood still under Sunder's outburst; but the small
muscles around his eyes flinched as if he wanted to shout,
What's the matter with you? We're going to face Lord Foul!
I'm trying to spare you! Yet his quietness held.

"You're right," he said softly—more softly than Linden's
desire to defend him. "You are the life of the Land. And
I've already taken everything else away from you. Your

homes, your families, your identities—I've spent them all and let you bear the cost. Don't you understand? I want to give something back. I want you to have a *future*." The one thing he and Linden did not possess. "So your son will have at least that much chance to be born and grow up healthy." The passion underlying his tone reminded her that he had a son whom he had not seen for eleven years. He might have been crying, Let me do this for you! "Is safety such a terrible price to pay?"

Hollian appeared to waver, persuaded by Covenant's unmistakable concern. But Sunder did not. His anger was swept out of him; his resolution remained. Thickly, he said, "Pardon my unseemly ire. Thomas Covenant, you are my friend in all ways. Will you grant to me your white ring, that I may ward you from the extremity of the Land's plight?" He did not need to wait for Covenant's answer. "Neither will I cede to you the meaning of my life. You have taught me to value that meaning too highly."

Abruptly, he dropped his gaze. "If it is her wish, Hollian will abide here. The son she bears is ours together, but that choice must be hers." Then his eyes fixed Covenant squarely again. "I will not part from you until I am content."

For a moment, the Graveler and Covenant glared at each other; and Linden held her breath. But then Hollian broke the intensity. Leaning close to Sunder, grinning as if she meant to bite his ear, she breathed, "Son of Nassic, you have fallen far into folly if you credit that I will be divided from you in the name of simple safety."

Covenant threw up his hands. "Oh, hell," he muttered. "God preserve me from stubborn people." He sounded vexed; but his frown had lost its seriousness.

Linden gave a sigh of relief. She caught Hollian's glance, and a secret gleam passed between them. With feigned brusqueness, she said, "We're going to leave at noon. You might as well go get ready. We'll meet you in the forehall."

Allowing Covenant no opportunity to demur, she drew him into Mhoram's quarters and closed the door.

But later even through Revelstone's vital rock she felt the midday of the desert sun approaching; and her heart shrank from it. Sunder was right: the Sunbane had not been diminished. And she did not know how much more of it she could bear. She had stood up to it across the expanse of the North Plains. She had faced Gibbon-Raver, although his mere proximity had made the darkness in her writhe for release. But those exertions had pushed her to her limits. And she had had no sleep. The comfort of Covenant's love did many things for her, but it could not make her immune to weariness. In spite of the shielding Keep, a visceral dread seeped slowly into her.

Covenant himself was not impervious to apprehension. The mood in which he hugged her was complicated by a tension that felt like grief. When Cail called them to the forehall, Covenant did not hesitate. But his eyes seemed to avoid hers, and his hands fumbled as he buckled his belt, laced up his boots.

For a moment, she did not join him. She sat naked on Mhoram's bed and watched him, unwilling to cover his place against her breasts with the less intimate touch of her shirt. Yet she knew that she had to go with him, that everything she had striven for would be wasted if she faltered now. She said his name to make him look at her; and when he did so, she faced her fear as directly as she could.

"I don't really understand what you think you're going to do—but I suppose that doesn't matter. Not right now, anyway. I'll go with you—anywhere. But I still haven't answered my own question. Why me?" Perhaps what she meant was, *Why do you love me? What am I, that you should love me?* But she knew that if she asked her question in those terms she might not comprehend the reply. "Why was I chosen? Why did Gibbon keep insisting I'm the one—?" She swallowed a lump of darkness. "The one who's going to desecrate the Earth." *Even if I give in—even if I go crazy and decide I want to be like him after all. Where would I get that kind of power?*

Covenant met her gaze through the dim lantern-light. He stood straight and dear before her, a figure of dread and love and contradiction; and he seemed to know what she sought. Yet the timbre of his voice told her he was not certain of it.

"Questions like that are hard. You have to create your own answer. The last time I was here, I didn't know I was going to beat Foul until I did it. Then I could look back and say that was the reason. I was chosen because I had the capacity to do what I did—even though I didn't know it." He spoke quietly, but his manner could not conceal the implications of severity and hope which ran through his words. "I think you were chosen because you're like me. We're the kind of people who just naturally feel responsible for each other. Foul thinks he can use that to manipulate us. And the Creator—" For an instant, he reminded her strangely of the old man who had said to her, *You will not fail, however he may assail you. There is also love in the world.* "He hopes that together we'll become something greater than we would alone."

Severity and hope. Hope and despair. She did not know what would happen—but she knew how important it had become. Arising from the bed, she went to Covenant and kissed him hard. Then she donned her clothes quickly so that she would be ready to accompany him wherever he wanted to go.

In the name of his smile, she accepted everything.

While she hurried, Cail repeated his announcement that the Giants, *Haruchai*, and Stonedownors were waiting in the forehall. "We're coming!" Covenant responded. When she nodded, he opened the door and ushered her outward with a half humorous flourish, as if she were regal in his eyes.

Cail bowed to them, looking as much as his dispassion allowed like a man who wanted to say something and had almost made up his mind to say it. But Linden saw at a glance that he still had not found the right moment. She returned his bow because he, too, had become someone she could trust. She had never doubted his fidelity, but the native extravagance of his judgment had always made him appear dangerous and unpredictable. Now, however, she saw him as a man who had passed through repudiation and unworth to reach a crucial decision—a decision she hoped she would be able to comprehend.

Together, Covenant, Cail, and Linden left behind the bright silver aftermath of the Unbeliever's first encounter with the Clave. That radiance shining against her back gave her a pang of regret; it represented a part of him which had been lost. But he was frowning to himself as he strode forward, concentrating on what lay ahead. That was his answer to loss. And he did not need Cail's guidance to find his way through the involute Keep. For a sharp moment, she let the rue wash through her, experiencing it for both of them. Then she shrugged her attention back to his side and tried to brace herself for the Sunbane.

The forehall hardly resembled her memory of it. Its floor remained permanently pocked and gouged, awkward to walk; but the space was bright with torches, and sunlight reflected through the broken gates. The bodies of the dead had been cleared away; the blood of battle had been sluiced from the stone. And the wounded had been moved to more comfortable quarters. The improvement suggested that Revelstone might yet become habitable again.

Near the gates were gathered the people who had accompanied or fought for the Unbeliever and survived: the First of the Search with Pitchwife and Mistweave; Sunder and Hollian; Durris and Fole, Harn, Stell, and the rest of the *Haruchai*; the black Demondim-spawn; Findail the Appointed. Pitchwife hailed Covenant and Linden as if the prospect of leaving Revelstone had restored some portion of his good cheer; but the rest of the company stood silent. They seemed to wait for Covenant as if he were the turning point of their lives. Even the *Haruchai*, Linden sensed with a touch of quiet wonder. In spite of their mountain-bred intransigence, they were balanced on a personal cusp and could be swayed. As Covenant drew near, each of them dropped to one knee in mute homage.

The others had fewer questions to ask. Neither Vain nor Findail had any use for questions. And Covenant had already accepted the companionship of the First and Pitchwife, Hollian and Sunder. They only needed to know where they were going. The issues which had yet to be resolved belonged to the *Haruchai*.

But when Covenant had urged Cail's people back to their feet, it was the First who addressed him. In spite of battle and grief, she looked refreshed. Unlike her husband, she had found exigencies and purposes she understood, was trained for, in the test of combat. "Earthfriend," she said formally, a gleam in her hair and her voice, "you are well come. The quenching of Clave and Banefire and the freeing of Revelstone merit high pride, and they will be honored in song from Sea to Sea wherever our people still hold music in their hearts. None would gainsay you, should you choose to bide here in rest and restoration. It is fitting that the craft and vision of this Giant-wrought bourne should serve as accolade to that which you and the Chosen have accomplished.

"Yet," she went on without pausing, "I applaud the purpose which draws you away. From peril to loss across the world I have followed in your wake, and at last have been granted to strike a blow against evil. But our losses have been dire and sore, and one blow does not suffice. I desire to strike again, if I am able. And the Stonedownors have shown to us that the Sunbane remains, seeking the rapine of the Earth. The Search has not reached its end. Earthfriend, where do you go?"

Linden looked at Covenant. He was an upright self-contradiction, at once fearful and intrepid. He held his head high as if he knew that he was worthy of the Giants and *Haruchai*, the Graveler and the eh-Brand; and sunlight reflecting from the washed stone lit his clean face, so that he looked like the pure bone of the Earth. And yet his shoulders were rigid, knotted in the act of strangling his own weakness, his desire to be spared. Too much depended on him, and he had no health-sense for guidance.

Frail, invincible, and human, he met the First's gaze, looked past her to Cail and Durris and the injured *Haruchai*. Then he answered.

"When I was in Andelain, I met some of my old friends—the people who had faith in me, took care of me, loved me long before I could do any of those things for myself. Mhoram reminded me of a few lessons I should've already learned. Foamfollower gave me Vain. Bannor promised his people would serve me. And Elena," Elena his daughter, who had loved him in the same unbalanced way that she had hated Lord Foul, "told me what I'd have to do in the end. She said, 'When the time is upon you, and you must confront the Despiser, he is to be found in Mount Thunder—in Kiril Threndor, where he has taken up his abode.'" He swallowed thickly. "That's where I'm going. One way or another, I'm going to put an end to it."

Though he spoke quietly, his words seemed to ring and echo in the high hall.

The First gave a nod of grim, eager approval.

She started to ask him where Mount Thunder was, then

stopped. Durris had taken a step forward. He faced Covenant with an unwonted intensity gleaming from his flat eyes.

"Ur-Lord, we will accompany you."

Covenant did not hesitate. In a voice as unshakable as the *Haruchai*'s, he said, "No, you won't."

Durris lifted an eyebrow, but permitted himself no other sign of surprise. For an instant, his attention shifted as he conferred silently with his people. Then he said, "It is as you have claimed. A promise of service was given to you by Bannor of the Bloodguard among the Dead. And that service you have earned in our redemption from the compulsion and sacrifice of the Clave. Ur-Lord, we will accompany you to the last."

Pain twisted Covenant's mouth. But he did not waver. His hands were closed into fists, pressed against his thighs. "I said, no."

Again, Durris paused. The air was tight with suspense; issues Linden did not know how to estimate had come to a crisis. She did not truly comprehend Covenant's intent. The First moved as though she wanted to interpose some appeal or protest. But the *Haruchai* did not need her to speak for them. Durris leaned slightly closer to Covenant, and his look took on a hint of urgency. His people knew better than anyone else what was at stake.

"Thomas Covenant, bethink you." Obliquely, Linden wondered why it was Durris who spoke and not Cail. "The *Haruchai* are known to you. The tale of the Bloodguard is known to you. You have witnessed that proud, deathless Vow—and you have beheld its ending. Do not believe that we forget. In all the ages of that service, it was the grief of the Bloodguard that they gave no direct battle to Corruption. And yet when the chance came to Bannor—when he stood at your side upon Landsdrop with Saltheart Foamfollower and knew your purpose—he turned aside from it. You had need of him, and he turned aside.

"We do not judge him. The Vow was broken. But I say to you that we have tasted failure, and it is not to our liking. We must restore our faith. We will not turn aside again."

Shifting still closer to Covenant, he went on as if he wanted no one else to hear him, "Ur-Lord, has it become with you as it was the Kevin Landwaster? Is it your intent to be parted from those who would prevent you from the Ritual of Desecration?"

At that, Linden expected Covenant to flare out. She wanted to protest herself, deny hotly Durris' unwarranted accusation. But Covenant did not raise his voice. Instead, he lifted his half-hand between himself and Durris, turned it palm outward, spread his fingers. His ring clung like a manacle to what had once been his middle finger.

"You remember," he said, allowing himself neither sarcasm nor bitterness. "Have you forgotten why the Vow was broken?

"I'll tell you why. Three Bloodguard got their hands on a piece of the Illearth Stone, and they thought that made them powerful enough to do what they always wanted. So they went to Foul's Creche, challenged Corruption. But they were wrong. No flesh and blood is immune. Foul mastered them—the same way he mastered Kevin when Elena broke the Law of Death. He maimed them to look like me—like *this*"—he waved his half-hand stiffly—"and sent them back to Revelstone to mock the Bloodguard."

An outcry rose in him; but he held it down. "Are you surprised the Vow was broken? I thought it was going to break their hearts.

"Bannor didn't turn aside. He gave me exactly what I needed. He showed me it was still possible to go on living."

He paused to steady himself; and now Linden felt the meld of his certainty and power growing, felt him become palpably stronger.

"The fact is," he said without accusation, "you've been wrong all along. You've misunderstood your own doubt from the beginning. What it means. Why it matters. First Kevin, then the other Lords, then me—ever since your people first came to the Land, you've been swearing yourselves in service to ordinary men and women who simply can't be worthy of what you offer. Kevin was a good man who broke down when the pressure got to be worse than he could stand—and the Bloodguard were never able to forgive him because they pinned their faith on him and when he failed they thought it was their fault for not making him worthy, not preventing him from being human. Over and over again, you put yourselves in the position of serving someone who *has* to fail

you for the mere reason that he's human and all humans fail
at one time or another—and then you can't forgive him because his failure casts doubt on your service. And you can't
forgive yourselves either. You want to serve perfectly, and
that means you're responsible for everything. And whenever
something comes along to remind you you're mortal—like the
merewives—that's unforgivable too, and you decide you aren't
worthy to go on serving. Or else you want to do something
crazy, like fighting Foul in person."

Slowly, he lowered his hand; but the gaze he fixed on
Durris did not falter, and his clarity burned from his eyes.
"You can do better than that. Nobody questions your worth.
You've demonstrated it a thousand times. And if that's not
enough for you, remember Brinn faced the Guardian of the
One Tree and won. *Ak-Haru Kenaustin Ardenol.* Any one of
you would've done the same in his place. You don't need to
serve me anymore.

"And," he added carefully, "I don't need you. Not in the
way you think. I don't want you to come with me."

Durris did not retreat. But Linden sensed that he wished
to draw back, that Covenant's certain strength abashed him.
He seemed unable to deny the image Covenant painted—and
unwilling to accept its implications.

"Ur-Lord, what would you have us do?" he asked as if he
felt no distress. "You have given our lives to us. We must
make recompense. That is necessary." In spite of its in-
flexibility, his voice put the weight of *Haruchai* history into the
word, *necessary.* The extravagance and loyalty of his people
required an outlet. "The Vow of the Bloodguard was sworn
to meet the bounty and grandeur of High Lord Kevin and
Revelstone. It was not regretted. Do you ask such an oath
from us again, that we may preserve the meaning of our lives?"

"No." Covenant's eyes softened and blurred, and he put
his hand on Durris' shoulder as if he wanted to hug the
Haruchai. Linden felt pouring from him the ache of his appreciation. Bloodguard and *Haruchai* had given themselves
to him without question; and he had never believed that he
deserved them. "There's something else I want you to do."

At that, Durris' stance sharpened. He stood before the
Unbeliever like a salute.

"I want you to stay here. In Revelstone. With as many of

your people as you can get. For two reasons. To take care
of the wounded. The Land's going to need them. It's going to
need every man or woman who can possibly be persuaded to
face the future. And to protect the city. This is Revelstone,
Lord's Keep. It belongs to the Land—not to Corruption or
Ravers. I want it safe. So the future will have a place to center.
A place where people can come to learn about the past—
and see what the Land means—and make plans. A place of
defense. A place of hope. You've already given me everything Bannor promised and more. But I want you to do this,
too. For me. And for yourselves. Here you can serve something that isn't going to fail you."

For a long moment, Durris was silent while his mind
addressed his people. Then he spoke, and his dispassionate
voice thrilled Linden's hearing like a distant tantara of horns.

"Ur-Lord, we will do it."

In response, Covenant squeezed Durris' shoulder and tried
to blink the gratitude out of his eyes. Instinctively, Linden
put her arms around him, marveling at what he had become.

But when Durris withdrew to stand among the other
Haruchai, Cail came forward. His old scar showed plainly
on one arm; but he bore other hurts as well. With Brinn, he
had once demanded retribution against Linden, believing her
a servant of Corruption. And with Brinn, he had succumbed
to the song of the *merewives*. But Brinn had gone alone to
meet the Guardian of the One Tree; Cail had been left behind
to pay the price of memory and loss.

"Thomas Covenant," he said softly. "Earthfriend. Permit
me."

Covenant stared at him. A strange bleakness showed in
Cail's eyes.

"I have heard your words," said the *Haruchai*, "but they
are not mine to acknowledge or eschew. Since that time when
the white beauty and delusion of the *merewives* took me from
myself, I have not stood in your service. Rather have I followed the command placed upon me by *ak-Haru Kenaustin
Ardenol*. You have not forgotten." Covenant nodded, wary of
grief; but still Cail quoted, " 'Cail will accept my place at
your side until the word of the Bloodguard Bannor has been
carried to its end.' " Then he went on, "That I have done.
But it was not I who was proven against the Guardian of the

One Tree. In the stead of victory, I have met only the deaths of Giants and the doubt of my people. And this I have done, not solely because I was commanded, but also because I was promised. It was given to me that when the word of Bannor was fulfilled I would be permitted to follow my heart.

"Earthfriend, you have proclaimed that fulfillment. And I have served you to my best strength. I ask now that you permit me.

"Permit me to depart."

"Depart?" Covenant breathed. His open face showed that this was not what he had expected. He made an effort to pull himself out of his surprise. "Of course you can go. You can do whatever you want. I wouldn't stop you if I could. You've earned—" Swallowing roughly, he changed direction. "But you're needed here. Are you going home—back to your family?"

Without expression, Cail replied, "I will return to the *merewives*."

Covenant and the First reacted in simultaneous protest, but her hard voice covered his. "That is madness! Have you forgotten that you were scant moments from death? Almost Galewrath and I failed of your rescue. I will not see the life which I brought up from the deep cast away!"

But surprise and apprehension seemed to tighten Linden's percipience to a higher pitch, a keener penetration; and she saw Cail with sudden acuity, felt parts of him which had been hidden until now. She knew with the instantaneous certainty of vision that he did not intend to throw his life away, did not want death from the Dancers of the Sea: he wanted a different kind of life. A resolution for the inextricable desire and bereavement of his extreme nature.

She cut Covenant off, stopped the First. They glared at her; but she ignored their vehemence. They did not understand. Brinn had said, *The limbs of our women are brown from sun and birth. But there is also a whiteness as acute as the ice which bleeds from the rock of mountains, and it burns as the purest snow burns in the most high tor, the most wind-flogged col.* And from it grew a yearning which Cail could no longer bear to deny. Panting with the force of her wish to support him, give him something in return for his faithfulness, she rushed to utter the first words that came to her.

"Brinn gave his *permission*. Don't you see that? He knew what he was saying—he knew what Cail would want to do. He heard the same song himself. Cail isn't going to die."

But then she had to halt. She did not know how to explain her conviction that Brinn and Cail could be trusted.

"Thomas Covenant," Cail said, "I comprehend the value of that which you have granted to the *Haruchai*—a service of purity and worth. And I have witnessed Brinn's encounter with *ak-Haru Kenaustin Ardenol*, the great victory of our people. But the cost of that victory was the life of Cable Seadreamer. For myself I do not desire such worth.

"The song of the *merewives* has been named delusion. But is not all life a manner of dreaming? Have you not said that the Land itself is a dream? Dream or delusion, the music I have heard has altered me. But I have not learned the meaning of this change. Ur-Lord, I wish to prove what I have dreamed to its heart. Permit me."

Linden looked at Covenant, imploring him with her eyes; but he did not meet her gaze. He faced Cail, and conflicting emotions wrestled each other visibly across his mien: recognition of what Cail was saying; grief over Seadreamer; fear for the *Haruchai*. But after a moment he fought his way through the moil. "Cail—" he began. His throat closed as though he dreaded what he meant to say. When he found his voice, he sounded unexpectedly small and lonely, like a man who could not afford to let even one friend go.

"I heard the same song you did. The *merewives* are dangerous. **Be** *very* careful with them."

Cail did not thank the Unbeliever. He did not smile or nod or speak. But for an instant the glance he gave Covenant was as plain as a paean.

Then he turned on his heel, strode out of the forehall into the sunlight, and was gone.

Covenant watched the *Haruchai* go as if even now he wanted to call Cail back; but he did not do so. And none of the other *Haruchai* made any move to challenge Cail's decision. Slowly, a rustle like a sigh passed through the hall, and the tension eased. Hollian blinked the dampness out of her eyes. Sunder gazed bemusement and awe at the implications of Cail's choice. Linden wanted to show Covenant the gratitude Cail had neglected; but it was unnecessary. She saw that he

understood now, and his expression had softened. Behind his
sorrow over all the people he had lost lurked a wry smile
which seemed to suggest that he would have made Cail's choice
if she had been a Dancer of the Sea.

The First cleared her throat. "Earthfriend, I am no equal
for you. These determinations surpass me. In your place, my
word would have been that our need for the accompaniment
of the *Haruchai* is certain and immediate. But I do not question you. I am a Giant like any other, and such bravado
pleases me.

"Only declare swiftly where this Mount Thunder and
Kiril Threndor may be found, that Mistweave may bear the
knowledge eastward to Seareach. It may be that his path and
Cail's will lie together—and they will have need of each other."

Covenant nodded at once. "Good idea." Quickly, he described as well as he could Mount Thunder's location astride
the center of Landsdrop, where the Soulsease River passed
through the Wightwarrens and became the main source for
Sarangrave Flat and the Great Swamp. "Unfortunately," he
added, "I can't tell you how to find Kiril Threndor. I've been
there once—it's in the chest of the mountain somewhere—
but the whole bloody place is a maze."

"That must suffice," the First said. Then she turned to
Mistweave. "Hear you? If skill and courage may achieve it,
Sevinhand Anchormaster will bring Starfare's Gem to Seareach and The Grieve. There you must meet him. If we fail,
the fate of the Earth falls to you. And if we do not," she
continued less grimly, "you will provide for our restoration
Homeward." In a softer voice, she asked, "Mistweave, are
you content?"

Linden looked at Mistweave closely and was reassured.
The Giant who had sought to serve her and believed that he
had failed was injured and weary, his arm in a sling, bruises
on his broad face; but much of his distress had faded. Perhaps
he would never entirely forgot his self-doubt. But he had redeemed most of it. The spirit within him was capable of
peace.

She went to him because she wanted to thank him—and
wanted to see him smile. He towered over her; but she was
accustomed to that. Taking one of his huge hands in her
small grasp, she said up to him, "Sevinhand's going to be the

Master now. Galewrath'll be the Anchormaster." Deliberately, she risked this reference to Honninscrave's end. "Starfare's Gem will need a new Storesmaster. Someone who knows something about healing. Tell them I said you should have the job."

Abruptly, he loomed over her, and she was swept into the embrace of his uninjured arm. For an instant, she feared that he was hurt and weeping; but then his emotions came into better focus, and she returned his clasp as hard as she could.

When he set her down again, he was grinning like a Giant.

"Begone, Mistweave," the First muttered in a tone of gruff kindness. "Cail *Haruchai* will outdistance you entirely."

In response, he shouted a laugh. "Outdistance a Giant? Not while I live!" With a holla to Pitchwife and a salute to Covenant and Linden, he snatched up his sack of supplies and dashed for the tunnel under the watchtower as if he intended to run all the way to Landsdrop rather than let Cail surpass him.

After that, nothing remained to delay the company. The First and Pitchwife shouldered their packs. Sunder and Hollian lifted the bundles they had prepared for themselves. For a moment, Covenant looked around the stone of the forehall as though he feared to leave it, dreaded the consequences of the path he had chosen; but then his certitude returned. After saying a brief farewell to the *Haruchai*, and accepting their bows with as much grace as his embarrassment allowed, he turned his feet toward the sunlight beyond the broken gates. Vain and Findail took their familiar positions behind him— or behind Linden—as the company moved outward.

Gritting her teeth against the shock of the Sunbane on her bare nerves, Linden went back out into the desert sun.

THIRTEEN: The Eh-Brand

IT was worse than she had expected. It seemed worse than it had been that morning. Glimmermere's cleansing and Revelstone's protection appeared to have sharpened her health-sense, making her more vulnerable than ever to the rife ill of the Sunbane. The sun's heat felt as hard and heavy as stone. She knew it was not literally gnawing the flesh from her bones, not charring her bones to the malign blackness which she had inherited from her father. Yet she felt that she was being eaten away—that the Sunbane had found its likeness in her heart and was feeding on her.

During the long days when she and the quest had been away from the sun's corruption, she had groped toward a new kind of life. She had heard intimations of affirmation and had followed them urgently, striving to be healed. At one time, with the tale of her mother told for the first time and Covenant's arms about her, she had believed that she could say no forever to her own dark hungers. *There is also love in the world.* But now the desert sun flamed at her with the force of an execration, and she knew better.

In some ways, she was unable to share Covenant's love for the Land. She had never seen it healthy; she could only guess at the loveliness he ascribed to it. And to that extent he was alone in his dismay. *There's only one way to hurt a man who's lost everything. Give him back something broken.* Yet she was like the Land herself. The power tormenting it was the same might which demonstrated to her undefended nerves that she was not whole.

And she and her companions were on their way to confront Lord Foul, the source and progenitor of the Sunbane.

And they were only eight. In effect, they were only six: two Giants, two Stonedownors, Covenant and Linden. Vain and Findail could be trusted to serve no purposes but their own. With the sun burning against her face as it started its afternoon decline, she lost what little understanding she had ever had of Covenant's reasons for refusing the aid of the *Haruchai*. Their intransigent integrity at her side might have helped to keep the Sunbane out of her soul.

Mount Thunder lay to the east; but Covenant was leading the company west and south down through the dead foothills below the intricately wrought face of the Keep. His intent, he explained, was to join the watercourse which had once been the White River and follow it toward Andelain. That was not the most direct path, but it would enable the company to do what Sunder, Linden, and he had done previously—to ride the river during a sun of rain. Recollections of cold and distress made Linden shiver, but she did not demur. She favored any plan which might reduce the amount of time she had to spend exposed to the sun.

Above her rose the sheer, hard face of Revelstone. But some distance ahead, Furl Falls came tumbling down the side of the plateau; and its implications were comforting. Already, much of the potent water springing from the roots of Glimmermere had been denatured. Furl Falls was only a wisp of what it should have been. Yet it remained. Centuries of the Sunbane had not ruined or harmed the upland tarn. Through the brown heat and light of the sun, Furl Falls struck hints of bluelike sparks from the rough rock of the cliff.

To the south, the hills spread away like a frown of pain in the ground, becoming slowly less rugged—or perhaps less able to care what happened to them—as they receded from the promontory of the Westron Mountains. And between them wound the watercourse Covenant sought. Following what might once have been a road, he brought the company to an ancient stone bridge across the broad channel where the White River had stopped running. A trickle of water still stretched thinly down the center of the riverbed; but even that moisture soon vanished into a damp, sandy stain. The sight of it made Linden thirsty with empathy, although she had eaten and drunk well before leaving Mhoram's quarters.

Covenant did not cross the bridge. For a moment, he glared at the small stream as if he were remembering the

White River in full spate. Then, controlling his fear of heights with a visible effort, he found a way down into the riverbed. The last sun of rain had not left the channel smooth or clear, but its bottom offered an easier path than the hills on either side.

Linden, Sunder, and Hollian followed him. Pitchwife came muttering after them. Vain leaped downward with a lightness which belied his impenetrability; on his wooden wrist and left ankle, the heels of the Staff of Law caught the sun dully. Findail changed shape and glided gracefully to the river-bottom. But the First did not join the rest of the company. When Covenant looked back up at her, she said, "I will watch over you." She gestured along the higher ground of the east bank. "Though you have mastered the Clave, some caution is needful. And the exertion will ease me. I am a Giant and eager, and your pace gives me impatience."

Covenant shrugged. He seemed to think that he had become immune to ordinary forms of peril. But he waved his acceptance; and the First strode away at a brisk gait.

Pitchwife shook his head, bemused by his wife's sources of strength. Linden saw a continuing disquiet in the unwonted tension of his countenance; but most of his unhappiness had sunk beneath the surface, restoring his familiar capacity for humor. "Stone and Sea!" he said to Covenant and Linden. "Is she not a wonder? Should ever we encounter that which can daunt her, then will I truly credit that the Earth is lost. But then only. For the while, I will study the beauty of her and be glad." Turning, he started down the watercourse as if he wished his friends to think he had left his crisis behind.

Hollian smiled after them. Softly, Sunder said, "We are fortunate in these Giants. Had Nassic my father spoken to me of such beings, mayhap I would have laughed—or mayhap wept. But I would not have believed."

"Me neither," Covenant murmured. Doubt and fear cast their shadows across the background of his gaze; but he appeared to take no hurt from them. "Mhoram was my friend. Bannor saved my life. Lena loved me. But Foamfollower made the difference."

Linden reached out to him, touched her palm briefly to his clean cheek to tell him that she understood. The ache of the Sunbane was so strong in her that she could not speak.

Together, they started after Pitchwife.

The riverbed was a jumble of small stones and large boulders, flat swaths of sand, jutting banks, long pits. But it was a relatively easy road. And by midafternoon the west rim began casting deep shade into the channel.

That shade was a balm to Linden's abraded nerves—but for some reason it did not make her any better able to put one foot in front of another. The alternation of shadow and acid heat seemed to numb her mind, and the consequences of two days without rest or sleep came to her as if they had been waiting in the bends and hollows of the watercourse. Eventually, she found herself thinking that of all the phases of the Sunbane the desert sun was the most gentle. Which was absurd: this sun was inherently murderous. Perhaps it was killing her now. Yet it gave less affront to her health-sense than did the other suns. She insisted on this as if someone had tried to contradict her. The desert was simply dead. The dead could inspire grief, but they felt no pain. The sun of rain had the force of incarnate violence; the malign creatures of the sun of pestilence were a pang of revulsion; the fertile sun seemed to wring screams from the whole world. But the desert only made her want to weep.

Then she was weeping. Her face was pressed into the sand, and her hands scrubbed at the ground on either side of her head because they did not have the strength to lift her. But at the same time she was far away from her fallen body, detached and separate from Covenant and Hollian as they called her name, rushed to help her. She was thinking with the precision of a necessary belief, This can't go on. It has got to be stopped. Every time the sun comes up, the Land dies a little deeper. It has got to be stopped.

Covenant's hands took hold of her, rolled her onto her back, shifted her fully into the shadows. She knew they were his hands because they were urgent and numb. When he propped her into a sitting position, she tried to blink her eyes clear. But her tears would not stop.

"Linden," he breathed. "Are you all right? Damn it to hell! I should've given you a chance to rest."

She wanted to say, This has got to be stopped. Give me your ring. But that was wrong. She knew it was wrong because the darkness in her leaped up at the idea, avid for power. She could not hold back her grief.

Hugging her hard, he rocked her in his arms and murmured words which meant nothing except that he loved her.

Gradually, the helplessness faded from her muscles, and she was able to raise her head. Around her stood Sunder, Hollian, the First, and Pitchwife. Even Findail was there; and his yellow eyes yearned with conflicts, as if he knew how close she had come—but did not know whether he was relieved or saddened by it. Only Vain ignored her.

She tried to say, I'm sorry. Don't worry. But the desert was in her throat, and no sound came.

Pitchwife knelt beside her, lifted a bowl to her lips. She smelled *diamondraught*, took a small swallow. The potent liquor gave her back her voice.

"Sorry I scared you. I'm not hurt. Just tired. I didn't realize I was this tired." The shadow of the west bank enabled her to say such things.

Covenant was not looking at her. To the watercourse and the wide sky, he muttered, "I ought to have my head examined. We should've stayed in Revelstone. One day wouldn't have killed me." Then he addressed his companions. "We'll camp here. Maybe tomorrow she'll feel better."

Linden started to smile reassurance at him. But she was already asleep.

That night, she dreamed repeatedly of power. Over and over again, she possessed Covenant, took his ring, and used it to rip the Sunbane out of the Earth. The sheer violence of what she did was astounding; it filled her with glee and horror. Her father laughed blackness at her. It killed Covenant, left him as betrayed as her mother. She thought she would go mad.

You have committed murder. Are you not evil?

No. Yes. Not unless I choose to be. I can't help it.

This has got to be stopped. Got to be stopped. *You are being forged as iron is forged.* Got to be stopped.

But sometime during the middle of the night she awoke and found herself enfolded by Covenant's sleeping arms. For a while, she clung to him; but he was too weary to waken. When she went back to sleep, the dreams were gone.

And when dawn came she felt stronger. Stronger and calmer, as if during the night she had somehow made up her mind. She kissed Covenant, nodded soberly in response to the questioning looks of her friends. Then, while the Stone-downors and Giants defended themselves against the sun's first touch by standing on rock, she climbed a slope in the west bank to get an early view of the Sunbane. She wanted to understand it.

It was red and baleful, the color of pestilence. Its light felt like disease crawling across her nerves.

But she knew its ill did not in fact arise from the sun. Sunlight acted as a catalyst for it, a source of energy, but did not cause the Sunbane. Rather, it was an emanation from the ground, corrupted Earthpower radiating into the heavens. And that corruption sank deeper every day, working its way into the marrow of the Earth's bones.

She bore it without flinching. She intended to do something about it.

Her companions continued to study her as she descended the slope to rejoin them. But when she met their scrutiny, they were reassured. Pitchwife relaxed visibly. Some of the tension flowed out of the muscles of Covenant's shoulders, though he clearly did not trust his superficial vision. And Sunder, who remembered Marid, gazed at her as if she had come back from the brink of something as fatal as venom.

"Chosen, you are well restored," said the First with gruff pleasure. "The sight gladdens me."

Together, Hollian and Pitchwife prepared a meal which Linden ate ravenously. Then the company set itself to go on down the watercourse.

For the first part of the morning, the walking was almost easy. This sun was considerably cooler than the previous one; and while the east bank shaded the riverbottom, it remained free of vermin. The ragged edges and arid lines of the landscape took on a tinge of the crimson light which made them appear acute and wild, etched with desiccation. Pitchwife joined the First as she ascended the hillside again to keep watch over the company. Although Hollian shared Sunder's visceral abhorrence of the sun of pestilence, they were comfortable with each other. In the shade's protection, they walked and talked, arguing companionably about a name for their son. Initially, Sunder claimed that the child would grow up to be an eh-Brand and should therefore be given an eh-Brand's name; but Hollian insisted that the boy would take after his father. Then for no apparent reason they switched positions and continued contradicting each other.

By unspoken agreement, Linden and Covenant left the Stonedownors to themselves as much as possible. She listened to them in a mood of detached affection for a time; but gradually their argument sent her musing on matters that had nothing to do with the Sunbane—or with what Covenant hoped to accomplish by confronting the Despiser. In the middle of her reverie, she surprised herself by asking without preamble, "What was Joan like? When you were married?"

He looked at her sharply; and she caught a glimpse of the unanswerable pain which lay at the roots of his certainty. Once before, when she had appealed to him, he had said of Joan, *She's my* ex-*wife,* as if that simple fact were an affirmation. Yet some kind of guilt or commitment toward Joan had endured in him for years after their divorce, compelling him to accept responsibility for her when she had come to him in madness and possession, seeking his blood.

Now he hesitated momentarily as if he were searching for a reply which would give Linden what she wanted without weakening his grasp on himself. Then he indicated Sunder and Hollian with a twitch of his head. "When Roger was born," he said, overriding a catch in his throat, "she didn't ask me what I thought. She just named him after her father. And her grandfather. A whole series of Rogers on her side of the family. When he grows up, he probably won't even know who I am."

His bitterness was plain. But other, more important feelings lay behind it. He had smiled for Joan when he had exchanged his life for hers.

And he was smiling now—the same terrible smile that Linden remembered with such dismay. While it lasted, she was on the verge of whispering at him in stark anguish, Is *that* what you're going to do? Again? *Again?*

But almost at once his expression softened; and the thing she feared seemed suddenly impossible. Her protest faded. He appeared unnaturally sure of what he meant to do; but, whatever it was, it did not reek of suicide. Inwardly shaken, she said, "Don't worry. He won't forget you." Her attempt to console him sounded inane, but she had nothing else to offer. "It's not that easy for kids to forget their parents."

In response, he slipped an arm around her waist, hugged her. They walked on together in silence.

But by midmorning sunlight covered most of the riverbed, and the channel became increasingly hazardous. The rock-gnarled and twisted course, with its secret shadows and occasionally overhanging banks, was an apt breeding place for pestilential creatures which lurked and struck. From Revelstone Hollian had brought an ample store of *voure*; but some of the crawling, scuttling life that now teemed in the riverbottom seemed to be angered by the scent or immune to it altogether. Warped and feral sensations scraped across Linden's nerves. Everytime she saw something move, a pang of alarm went through her. Sunder and Hollian had to be more and more careful where they put their bare feet. Covenant began to study the slopes where the Giants walked. He was considering the advantages of leaving the channel.

When a scorpion as large as Linden's two fists shot out from under a rock and lashed its stinger at the side of Covenant's boot, he growled a curse and made his decision. Kicking the scorpion away, he muttered, "That does it. Let's get out of here."

No one objected. Followed mutely by Vain and Findail, the four companions went to a pile of boulders leaning against the east bank and climbed upward to join the First and Pitchwife.

They spent the rest of the day winding through the hills beside the empty riverbed. Periodically, the First strode up to a crest that gave her a wider view over the region; and her fingers rubbed the hilt of her longsword as if she were looking for a chance to use it. But she saw nothing that threatened the company except the waterless waste.

Whenever the hills opened westward, Linden could see the Westron Mountains sinking toward the horizon as they curved away to the south. And from the top of a rocky spine she was able to make out the distant rim of Revelstone, barely visible now above the crumpled terrain. Part of her yearned for the security it represented, for stone walls and the guardianship of *Haruchai*. Red limned the edges of the Land, made the desert hills as distinct as the work of a knife. Overhead, the sky seemed strangely depthless. Considered directly, it remained a pale blue occluded with fine dust; but the corners of her vision caught a hue of crimson like a hint of the Despiser's bloody-mindedness; and that color made the heavens look flat, closed.

Though she was defended by *voure*, she flinched internally at the vibrating ricochet of sandflies as big as starlings, the squirming haste of oversized centipedes. But when the First and Covenant started on down the far side of the spine, she wiped the sweat from her forehead, combed her hair back from her temples with her fingers, and followed.

Late in the afternoon, as shadows returned the sun's vermin to quiescence, the company descended to the watercourse again so that they could travel more easily until sunset. Then, when the light faded, they stopped for the night on a wide stretch of sand. There they ate supper, drank *metheglin* lightly flavored with *diamondraught*, hollowed beds for themselves. And Hollian took out her *lianar* wand to discover what the morrow's sun would be.

Without a word, Sunder handed her the wrapped *krill*. Carefully, as if Loric's blade still awed her, she parted the cloth until a clear shaft of argent pierced the twilight. Sitting cross-legged with the knife in her lap, she began to chant her invocation; and as she did so, she raised her *lianar* into the *krill*-gem's light.

From the wood grew shoots and tendrils of fine fire. They spread about her on the ground like creepers, climbed into the argence like vines. They burned without heat, without harming the wand; and their radiant filigree made the night eldritch and strange.

Her flame was the precise incarnadine of the present sun.

Linden thought then that Hollian would cease her invocation. A second day of pestilence was not a surprise. But the eh-Brand kept her power alight, and a new note of intensity entered her chant. With a start, Linden realized that Hollian was stretching herself, reaching beyond her accustomed limits.

After a moment, a quiet flare of blue like a gentle coruscation appeared at the tips of the fire-fronds.

For an instant, azure rushed inward along the vines, transforming the flames, altering the crimson ambience of the dark. Then it was quenched; all the fire vanished. Hollian sat with the *lianar* cradled in her fingers and the light of the *krill* on her face. She was smiling faintly.

"The morrow's sun will be a sun of pestilence." Her voice

revealed strain and weariness, but they were not serious. "But the sun of the day following will be a sun of rain."

"Good!" said Covenant. "Two days of rain, and we'll practically be in Andelain." He turned to the First. "It looks like we're not going to be able to build rafts. Can you and Pitchwife support the four of us when the river starts to run?"

In answer, the First snorted as if the question were unworthy of her.

Gleaming with pride, Sunder put his arms around Hollian. But her attention was fixed on Covenant. She took a deep breath for strength, then asked, "Ur-Lord, is it truly your intent to enter Andelain once again?"

Covenant faced her sharply. A grimace twisted his mouth. "You asked me that the last time." He seemed to expect her to renew her former refusal. "You know I want to go there. I never get enough of it. It's the only place where there's any Law left alive."

The *krill*-light emphasized the darkness of her hair; but its reflection in her eyes was clear. "You have told that tale. And I have spoken of the acquaintance of my people with the peril of Andelain. To us its name was one of proven madness. No man or woman known to us entered that land where the Sunbane does not reign and returned whole of mind. Yet you have entered and emerged, defying that truth as you defy all others. Thus the truth is altered. The life of the Land is not what it was. And in my turn I am changed. I have conceived a desire to do that which I have not done— to sojourn among my fears and strengths and learn the new truth of them.

"Thomas Covenant, do not turn aside from Andelain. It is my wish to accompany you."

For a long moment, no one spoke. Then Covenant said in a husky voice, "Thanks. That helps."

Softly, Hollian recovered the *krill*, let darkness wash back over the company. The night was the color of her hair, and it spread its wings out to the stars.

The next day, the red sun asserted its hold over the Land more swiftly, building on what it had already done. The company was forced out of the watercourse well before midmorning. Still they made steady progress. Every southward

league softened the hills slightly, and by slow degrees the going
became easier. The valleys between the rises grew wider; the
slopes, less rugged. And Hollian had said that the next day
would bring a sun of rain. Severely, Linden tried to tell herself that she had no reason to feel so beaten, so vulnerable to
the recurring blackness of her life.

But the Sunbane shone full upon her. It soaked into her as
if she had become a sponge for the world's ill. The stink of
pestilence ran through her blood. Hidden somewhere among
the secrets of her bones was a madwoman who believed that
she deserved such desecration. She wanted power in order to
extirpate the evil from herself.

Her percipience was growing keener—and so her distress
was keener.

She could not inure herself to what she felt. No amount
of determination or decision was enough. Long before noon,
she began to stumble as if she were exhausted. A red haze
covered her mind, blinding her to the superficial details of
the terrain, the concern of her friends. She was like the Land,
powerless to heal herself. But when Covenant asked her if she
wanted to rest, she made no answer and went on walking. She
had chosen her path and did not mean to stop.

Yet she heard the First's warning. Unsteady on her feet,
her knees locked, she halted with Covenant as the Giants
came back at a tense trot from a low ridge ahead of the
company. Distress aggravated Pitchwife's crooked features.
The First looked apprehensive, like iron fretted with rust.
But in spite of their palpable urgency, they did not speak for
a moment. They were too full of what they had seen.

Then Pitchwife groaned far back in his throat. "Ah, Earthfriend." His voice shuddered. "You have forewarned us of
the consequences of this Sunbane—but now I perceive that
I did not altogether credit your words. It is heinous beyond
speech."

The First gripped her sword as an anchor for her emotions.
"We are blocked from our way," she said, articulating the
words like chewed metal. "Perchance we have come blindly
upon an army of another purpose—but I do not believe it. I
believe that the Despiser has reached out his hand against us."

Trepidation beat the haze from Linden's mind. Her mouth
shaped a question. But she did not ask it aloud. The Giants

stood, rigid, before her; and she could see as clearly as language that they had no answer.

"Beyond that ridge?" asked Covenant. "How far?"

"A stone's throw for a Giant," the First replied grimly. "No more. And they advance toward us."

He glanced at Linden to gauge her condition, then said to the First, "Let's go take a look."

She nodded, turned on her heel and strode away.

He hurried after her. Linden, Sunder, and Hollian followed. Pitchwife placed himself protectively at Linden's side. Vain and Findail quickened their steps to keep up with the company.

At the ridgecrest, Covenant squatted behind a boulder and peered down the southward slope. Linden joined him. The Giants crouched below the line-of-sight of what lay ahead. Findail also stopped. Careful to avoid exposing themselves, Sunder and Hollian crept forward. But Vain moved up to the rim as if he wanted a clear view and feared nothing.

Covenant spat a low curse under his breath; but it was not directed at the Demondim-spawn. It was aimed at the black seethe of bodies moving toward the ridge on both sides of the watercourse.

As black as Vain himself.

The sight of them sucked the strength from Linden's limbs.

She knew what they were because Covenant had described them to her—and because she had met the Waynhim of Hamako's *rhysh*. But they had been changed. Their emanations rose to her like a shout, telling her precisely what had happened to them. They had fallen victim to the desecration of the Sunbane.

"Ur-viles," Covenant whispered fiercely. "Hell and blood!"

Warped ur-viles.

Hundreds of them.

Once they had resembled the Waynhim: larger, black instead of gray; but with the same hairless bodies, the same limbs formed for running on all fours as well as for walking erect, the same eyeless faces and wide, questing nostrils. But no longer. The Sunbane had made them monstrous.

Over the sickness in her stomach, Linden thought bleakly that Lord Foul must have done this to them. Like the Waynhim, the ur-viles were too lore-wise to have exposed themselves accidentally to the sun's first touch. They had been corrupted deliberately and sent here to block the company's way.

"Why?" she breathed, aghast. *"Why?"*

"Same reason as always," Covenant growled without looking away from the grotesque horde. "Force me to use too much power." Then suddenly his gaze flashed toward her. "Or to keep us out of Andelain. Exposed to the Sunbane. He knows how much it hurts you. Maybe he thinks it'll make you do what he wants."

Linden felt the truth of his words. She knew she could not stay sane forever under the pressure of the Sunbane. But a bifurcated part of her replied, Or maybe he did it to punish them. For doing something he didn't like.

Her heart skipped a beat.

For making Vain?

The Demondim-spawn stood atop the ridge as if he sought to attract the notice of the horde.

"Damnation!" Covenant muttered. Creeping back a short way from the rim, he turned to the Giants. "What're we going to do?"

The First did not hesitate. She gestured eastward along the valley below the ridge. "There lies our way. Passing their flank unseen, we may hope to outrun them toward Andelain."

Covenant shook his head. "That won't work. This isn't exactly the direct route to Andelain—or Mount Thunder, for that matter—but Foul still knew where to find us. He has some way of locating us. It's been done before." He glared at his memories, then thrust the past side. "If we try to get around them, they'll know it."

The First scowled and said nothing, momentarily at a loss for alternatives. Linden put her back to the boulder, braced her dread on the hard stone. "We can retreat," she said. "Back the way we came." Covenant started to protest; but she overrode him. "Until tomorrow. When the rain starts. I don't care how well they know where we are. They're going to have trouble finding us in the rain." She was sure of that. She knew from experience that the Sunbane's torrents were as effective as a wall. "Once the rain starts, we can ride the river right through the middle of them."

Covenant frowned. His jaws chewed a lump of bitterness. After a moment, he asked, "Can you do it? Those ur-viles aren't likely to rest at night. We'll have to keep going until dawn. And we'll have to stay right in front of them. So they won't have time to react when we try to get past them." He faltered out of consideration for her, then forced himself to say, "You're already having trouble just staying on your feet."

She gave him a glare of vexation, started to say, What choice have we got? I can do whatever I have to. But a black movement caught the edge of her sight. She turned her head in time to see Vain go striding down the slope to meet the ur-viles.

Covenant snapped the Demondim-spawn's name. Pitchwife started after Vain; the First snatched him back. Sunder hurried to the rim to see what would happen, leaving Hollian with a taut concentration on her face.

Linden ignored them. For the first time, she felt an emotion radiating from Vain's impenetrable form.

It was anger.

The horde reacted as if it could smell his presence even from this range. Perhaps that was how they knew where to find the company. A spatter of barking burst from the ur-viles; they quickened their pace. Their wide mass converged toward him.

At the foot of the slope, he halted. The ur-viles were no great distance from him now. In a few moments, they would reach him. As they moved, their barking resolved into one word:

"Nekhrimah!"

The word of command, by which Covenant had once compelled Vain to save his life. But Foamfollower had said that the Demondim-spawn would not obey it a second time.

For a moment, he remained still, as if he had forgotten motion. His right hand dangled, useless, from his wooden forearm. Nothing else marred his passive perfection. The scraps of his raiment only emphasized how beautifully he had been made.

"Nekhrimah!"

Then he raised his left arm. His fingers curved into claws. His hand made a feral, clutching gesture.

The leading ur-vile was snatched to the ground as if Vain had taken hold of its heart and ripped the organ apart.

Snarling furiously, the horde broke into a run.

Vain did not hurry. His good arm struck a sideward blow

through the air: two ur-viles went down with crushed skulls.
His fingers knotted and twisted: one of the approaching faces
turned to pulp. Another was split open by a punching movement that did not touch his assailant.

Then they were on him, a tide of black, monstrous flesh
breaking against his ebon hardness. They seemed to have no
interest in the company. Perhaps Vain had always been their
target. All of them tried to hurl themselves at him. Even the
ur-viles on the far bank of the river surged toward him.

"Now!" breathed the First eagerly. "Now is our opportunity! While they are thus engaged, we may pass them by."

Linden swung toward the Giant. The fury she had felt
from Vain whipped through her. "We can do that," she grated.
"As long as we leave him to die. Those are ur-viles. They
know how he was made. As soon as he kills enough of them
to get their attention, they're going to remember how to unmake him." She rose to her feet, knotted her fists at her sides.
"We've got to make him stop."

Behind her, she felt the violence of Vain's struggle,
sensed the blood of ur-viles spurting and flowing. They would
never kill him by physical force. He would reduce them one at
a time to crushed, raw meat. All that butchery—! Even the
abominable products of the Sunbane did not deserve to be
slaughtered. But she knew she was right. Before long, the
frenzy of the horde would pass; the ur-viles would begin to
think. They had shown that they were still capable of recognition and thought when they had used the word of command.
Then Vain would die.

Covenant appeared to accept her assertion. But he responded bitterly, "*You* stop him. He doesn't listen to me."

"Earthfriend!" the First snapped. "Chosen! Will you remain
here and be slain because you can neither redeem nor command this Vain? We must flee!"

That's right. Linden was thinking something different; but
it led to the same conclusion. Findail had moved to the ridgecrest. He stood watching the bloody fray with a particular
hunger or hope in his eyes. In *Elemesnedene*, the *Elohim* had
imprisoned Vain to prevent him from the purpose for which
he had been designed. But they had been thwarted because
Linden had insisted on leaving the area—and Vain's instinct
to follow her or Covenant had proved stronger than his bonds.

Now Findail seemed to see before him another means by which the Demondin-spawn could be stopped. And the answer was unchanged: flee so that Vain would follow.

But how? The company could not hope to outrun the ur-viles now.

"Perhaps it may be done," said Hollian, speaking so quietly that she could barely be heard over the savage din. "Assuredly it is conceivable. The way of it is plain. Is it not possible?"

Sunder turned back from the rim to gape at her. Inchoate protests tumbled together in him, fell voiceless.

"Conceivable?" Covenant demanded. "What're you talking about?"

Hollian's pale face was intense with exaltation or vision. Her meaning was so clear to her that she seemed beyond question.

"Sunder and I have spoken of it. In Crystal Stonedown Sivit na-Mhoram-wist titled me Sun-Sage—and that naming was false. But does not his very fear argue that such work is possible?"

Linden flinched. She had never done anything to earn the epithet the *Elohim* had given her. She feared even to consider its implications. Did Hollian think that she, Linden, could change the Sunbane?

But Sunder strode toward Hollian urgently, then stopped and stood trembling a few steps away. "No," he murmured. "We are mortal, you and I. The attempt would reave us to the marrow. Such power must not be touched."

She shook her head. "The need is absolute. Do you wish to lose the lives of the ur-Lord and the Chosen—the hope of the Land—because we dare not hazard our own?" He started to expostulate. Suddenly, her voice rose like flame. "Sunder, I have not been tested! I an unknown to myself. No measure has been taken of that which I may accomplish." Then she grew gentle again. "But your strength is known to me. I have no doubt of it. I have given my heart into your hands, and I say to you, it is possible. It may be done."

From beyond the ridge came harsh screams as Vain ripped and mangled the ur-viles. But the pace of their cries had diminished; he was killing fewer of them. Linden's senses registered a rippling of power in the horde. Some of the clamor had taken on a chanting cadence. The monsters were summoning their lore against the Demondim-spawn.

"Hellfire!" Covenant ejaculated. "Make sense! We've got to *do* something!"

Hollian looked toward him. "I speak of the alteration of the Sunbane."

Surprise leaped in his face. At once, she went on, "Not of its power or its ill. But of its course, in the way that the shifting of a stone may alter the course of a river."

His incomprehension was plain. Patiently, she added, "The morrow's sun will be a sun of rain. And the pace of the Sunbane increases as its power grows, ever shortening the space of days between the suns. It is my thought that perhaps the morrow's sun may be brought forward, so that its rain will fall upon us now."

At that, Linden's apprehension jerked into clarity, and she understood Sunder's protest. The strength required would be enormous! And Hollian was pregnant, doubly vulnerable. If the attempt ran out of control, she might rip the life out of more than one heart.

The idea appalled Linden. And yet she could think of no other way to save the company.

Covenant was already speaking. His eyes were gaunt with the helplessness of his alloyed puissance. Thoughts of warped black flesh and bloodshed tormented him. "Try it," he whispered. "Please."

His appeal was directed at Sunder.

For a long moment, the Graveler's eyes went dull, and his stature seemed to shrink. He looked like the man who had faced Linden and Covenant in the prison-hut of Mithil Stonedown and told them that he would be required to kill his own mother. If she had been able to think of any alternative at all—any alternative other than the one which horrified her —Linden would have cried out, You don't have to do this!

But then the passion that Covenant had inspired in Sunder's life came back to him. The muscles at the corners of his jaw bunched whitely, straining for courage. He was the same man who had once lied to Gibbon-Raver under extreme pain and coercion in an effort to protect the Unbeliever. Through his teeth, he gritted, "We will do it. If it can be done."

"Praise the Earth!" the First exhaled sharply. Her sword leaped into her hands. "Be swift. I must do what I may to aid the Demondim-spawn." Swinging into motion, she passed the rim and vanished in the direction of Vain's struggle.

Almost immediately, a roynish, guttural chorus greeted her. Linden felt the mounting power of the ur-viles fragment as they were thrown into frenzy and confusion by the First's onset.

But Sunder and Hollian had room in their concentration for nothing else. Slowly, woodenly, he placed himself before her. She gave him a smile of secret eagerness, trying to reassure him; he scowled in reply. Fear and determination stretched the skin of his forehead across the bones. He and Hollian did not touch each other. As formally as strangers, they sat down cross-legged, facing each other with their knees aligned.

Covenant came to Linden's side. "Watch them," he breathed. "Watch them hard. If they get into trouble, we've got to stop them. I can't stand—" He muttered a curse at himself. "Can't afford to lose them."

She nodded mutely. The clangor of battle frayed her attention, urged it away from the Stonedownors. Gritting her teeth, she forced herself into focus on Sunder and Hollian. Around her, the edges of the landscape throbbed with the sun's lambency, the hue of blood.

Sunder bowed his head for a moment, then reached into his jerkin and drew out his Sunstone and the wrapped *krill*. The *orcrest* he set down squarely between himself and Hollian. It lay like a hollow space in the dead dirt; its strange translucence revealed nothing.

Hollian produced her *lianar*, placed it across her ankles. A soft invocation began to sough between her lips as she raised her palms to Sunder. She was the eh-Brand: she would have to guide the power to its purpose.

Dread twisted Sunder's visage. His hands shook as he exposed the *krill*, let its light shine into his eyes. Using the cloth to protect his grip from the *krill*'s heat, he directed its tip at Hollian's palms.

Covenant winced as the Graveler drew a cut down the center of each of her hands.

Blood streaked her wrists. Her face was pale with pain, but she did not flinch. Lowering her arms, she let thick drops fall onto the orcrest until all its surface was wet. Then she took up her wand.

Sunder sat before her as if he wanted to scream; but somehow he forced his passion to serve him. With both fists, he gripped the handle of the *krill*, its tip aimed upward in front of his chest. The eh-Brand held her *lianar* likewise, echoing his posture.

The sun was almost directly above them.

Faintly, Linden heard the First cursing, felt an emanation of Giantish pain. Pieces of the ur-viles' power gathered together, became more effective. With a groan like a sob, Pitchwife tore himself from the Stonedownors and ran past the ridge to help his wife.

Sweating under the sun of pestilence, Linden watched as Sunder and the eh-Brand reached *krill* and *lianar* toward each other.

His arms shook slightly; hers were precise. Her knuckles touched his, wand rested against *krill*-gem, along a line between the bloodied *orcrest* and the sun.

And hot force stung through Linden as a vermeil shaft sprang from the Sunstone. It encompassed the hands of the Stonedownors, the blade and the wand, and shot away into the heart of the sun.

Power as savage as lightning: the keen might of the Sunbane. Sunder's lips pulled back from his teeth. Hollian's eyes widened as if the sheer size of what she was attempting suddenly appalled her. But neither she nor the Graveler withdrew.

Covenant's half-hand had taken hold of Linden's arm. Three points of pain dug into her flesh. On the Sandwall, for entirely different reasons, Cail had gripped her in that same way. She thought she could hear the First's sword hacking against distorted limbs, hideous torsos. Vain's anger did not relent. The strain of Pitchwife's breathing came clearly through the blood-fury of the ur-viles.

Their lore grew sharper.

But the scalding shaft of Sunbane-force had a white core. Argent blazed within the beam, reaching like the will of the Stonedownors to pierce the sun. It came from the gem of the *krill* and the clenched strength of Sunder's determination.

It pulled him so far out of himself that Linden feared he was already lost.

She started forward, wildly intending to hurl herself upon

him, call him back. But then the eh-Brand put forth her purpose; and Linden froze in astonishment.

In the heart of the gem appeared a frail, blue glimmer.

Sensations of power howled silently against Linden's nerves, scaled upward out of comprehension, as the blue gleam steadied, became stronger. Flickers of it bled into the beam and flashed toward the sun. Still it became stronger, fed by the eh-Brand's resolve. At first, it appeared molten and limited, torn from itself drop after drop by a force more compelling than gravity. But Hollian renewed it faster than it bled. Soon it was running up the beam in bursts so rapid that the shaft seemed to flicker.

Yet the aura around the sun showed no sign of alteration.

The Stonedownors chanted desperately, driving their exertion higher; but their voices made no sound. The incandescent beam absorbed their invocations directly into itself. Soundless force screamed across Linden's hearing. Something inside her gibbered, Stop them stop they'll kill themselves *stop!* But she could not. She could not tell the difference between their agony and the wailing in her mind.

The *krill*'s jewel shone blue. Constant azure filled the core of the shaft, hurled itself upward. Still the aura around the sun did not change.

The next instant, the power became too great.

The *lianar* caught fire. It burst in Hollian's hands, shedding a bright vehemence that nearly blinded Linden. The wood flared to cinders, burned the eh-Brand's palms to the bone. A cry ripped through her. The shaft wavered, faltered.

But she did not fall back. Leaning into the power, she closed her naked hands around the blade of the *krill*.

At her touch, the shaft erupted, shattering the Sunstone, shattering the heavens. The ground wrenched itself aside in a convulsion of pain, sent Linden and Covenant sprawling. She landed on him while the hills reeled. The air was driven from his lungs. She rolled off him, fought to get her feet under her. The earth quivered like outraged flesh.

Another concussion seemed to wipe everything else out of the world. It rent the sky as if the sun had exploded. Linden fell again, writhed on the heaving dirt. Before her face, the dust danced like shocked water, leaving fine whorls in the wake of the blast. The light faded as if the fist of the heavens had begun to close.

When she raised her head, she saw tremendous thunderheads teeming toward her from all the horizons, rushing to seal themselves over the sun's blue corona.

For an instant, she could not think, had forgotten how to move. There was no sound at all except the oncoming passion of the rain. Perhaps the battle beyond the ridge was over. But then awareness recoiled through her like a thunderclap. Surging in panic to her hands and knees, she flung her percipience toward the Stonedownors.

Sunder sat as if the detonation of earth and sky had not touched him. His head was bowed. The *krill* lay on the ground in front of him, its handle still partially covered. The fringes of the cloth were charred. His breathing was shallow, almost undiscernible. In his chest, his heart limped like a mauled thing from beat to beat. To Linden's first alarm, his life looked like the fading smoke of a snuffed wick. Then her health-sense reached deeper, and she saw that he would live.

But Hollian lay twisted on her back, her cut and heat-mangled palms open to the mounting dark. Her black hair framed the pale vulnerability of her face, pillowed her head like the cupped hand of death. Between her lost lips trickled a delicate trail of blood.

Scrambling wildly across the dirt, Linden dove for the eh-Brand, plunged her touch into Hollian and tried to call back her spirit before it fled altogether. But it was going fast; Linden could not hold it. Hollian had been damaged too severely. Linden's fingers clutched at the slack shoulders, tried to shake breath back into the lungs; but there was nothing she could do. Her hands were useless. She was just an ordinary woman, incapable of miracles—able to see nothing clearly except the extent of her failure.

As she watched, the life ran out of the eh-Brand. The red rivulet from her mouth slowed and stopped.

Power: Linden had to have power. But grief closed her off from everything. She could not reach the sun. The Earth was desecrated and dying. And Covenant had changed. At times in the past, she had tapped wild magic from him without his volition; but that was no longer possible. He was a new being, an alloy of fire and person. His might was inaccessible without possession. And if she had been capable of doing that to him, it would have taken time—time which Hollian had already lost.

The eh-Brand looked pitifully small in death, valiant and fragile beyond endurance. And her son also, gone without so much as a single chance at life. Linden stared blindly at the failure of her hands. The *krill*-gem glared into her face.

From all directions at once, the rain ran forward, hissing like flame across the dirt.

Drops of water splashed around her as Covenant took hold of her, yanked her toward him. Unwillingly, she felt the feral thrust of his pain. "I told you to watch!" he raged, yelling at her because he had asked the Stonedownors to take this risk in spite of his inability to protect them from the consequences. "I told you to *watch*!"

Through the approaching clamor of the rain, she heard Sunder groan.

He took an unsteady breath, raised his head. His eyes were glazed, unseeing, empty of mind. For an instant, she thought he was lost as well. But then his hands opened, stretching the cramps from his fingers and forearms, and he blinked several times. His eyes focused on the *krill*. He reached out to it stiffly, wrapped it back in its cloth, tucked it away under his jerkin.

Then the drizzle caught his attention. He looked toward Hollian.

At once, he lurched to his feet. Fighting the knots in his muscles, the ravages of power, he started toward her.

Linden shoved herself in front of him. Sunder! she tried to say. It's my fault. I'm so sorry. From the beginning, failure had dogged her steps as if it could never be redeemed.

He did not heed her. With one arm, he swept her out of his way so forcefully that she stumbled. A blood-ridden intensity glared from his orbs. He had lost one wife and son before he had met Linden and Covenant. Now they had cost him another. He bent over Hollian for a moment as if he feared to touch her. His arms hugged the anguish in his chest. Then, fiercely, he stooped to her and rose again, lifting her out of the new mud, cradling her like a child. His howl rang through the rain, transforming the downpour to grief: *"Hollian!"*

Abruptly, the First hove out of the thickening dark with Pitchwife behind her. She was panting hugely. Blood squeezed from the wide wound in her side where the lore of the ur-viles had burned her. Pitchwife's face was aghast at the things he had done.

Neither of them seemed to see Hollian. "Come!" called the First. "We must make our way now! Vain yet withholds the ur-viles from us. If we flee, we may hope that he will follow and be saved!"

No one moved. The rain belabored Linden's head and shoulders. Covenant had covered his face with his hands. He stood immobile in the storm as if he could no longer bear the cost of what he had become. Sunder breathed in great, raw hunks of hurt, but did not weep. He remained hunched over Hollian, concentrating on her as if the sheer strength of his desire might bring her back.

The First gave a snarl of exasperation. Still she appeared unaware of what had happened. Aggravated by her injury, she brooked no refusal. "Come, I say!" Roughly, she took hold of Covenant and Linden, dragged them toward the watercourse.

Pitchwife followed, tugging Sunder.

They scrambled down into the riverbed. The water racing there frothed against the thick limbs of the Giants. Linden could hardly keep her feet. She clung to the First. Soon the river rose high enough to carry the company away.

Rain hammered at them as if it were outraged by its untimely birth. The riverbanks were invisible. Linden saw no sign of the ur-viles or Vain. She did not know whether she and her friends had escaped.

But the lightning that tore the heavens gave her sudden glimpses around her. One of them revealed Sunder. He swam ahead of Pitchwife. The Giant braced him with one hand from behind.

He still bore Hollian in his arms. Carefully, he kept her head above water as if she were alive.

At intervals through the loud rain and the thunder, Linden heard him keening.

FOURTEEN: The Last Bourne

AT first, the water was so muddy that it sickened Linden. Every involuntary mouthful left sand in her throat, grit on her teeth. Rain and thunder fragmented her hearing. At one moment, she felt totally deaf; the next, sound went through her like a slap. Dragged down by her clothes and heavy shoes, she would have been exhausted in a short time without the First's support. The Swordmain's wound was a throbbing pain that reached Linden in spite of the chaos of water, the exertion of swimming. Yet the Giant bore both Covenant and the Chosen through the turmoil.

But as the water rose it became clearer, less conflicted—and colder. Linden had forgotten how cold a fast river could be with no sunlight on it anywhere. The chill leeched into her, sucking at her bones. It whispered to her sore nerves that she would be warmer if she lowered herself beneath the surface, out of the air and the battering rain. Only for a moment, it suggested kindly. Until you feel warmer. You've already failed. It doesn't matter anymore. You deserve to feel warmer.

She knew what she deserved. But she ignored the seduction, clung instead to the First—concentrated on the hurt in the Giant's side. The cleaner water washed most of the sand and blood from the burn; and the First was hardy. Linden was not worried about infection. Yet she poured her percipience toward that wound, put herself into it until her own side wailed as if she had been gored. Then, deliberately, she numbed the sensation, reducing the First's pain to a dull ache.

The cold frayed her senses, sapped her courage. Lightning and thunder blared above her, and she was too small to endure them. Rain flailed the face of the river. But she clinched herself to her chosen use and did not let go while the current bore the company hurtling down the length of the long afternoon.

At last the day ended. The torrents thinned; the clouds rolled back. Legs scissoring, the First labored across to the west bank, then struggled out of the water and stood trembling on the sodden ground. In a moment, Pitchwife joined her. Linden seemed to feel his bones rattling in an ague of weariness.

Covenant looked as pale as a weathered tombstone, his lips blue with cold, gall heavy on his features. "We need a fire," he said as if that, too, were his fault.

Sunder walked up the wet slope without a glance at his companions. He was hunched over Hollian as though his chest were full of broken glass. Beyond the reach of the river, he stumbled to his knees, lowered Hollian gently to the ground. He settled her limbs to make her comfortable. His blunt fingers caressed the black strands of hair from her face, tenderly combed her tresses out around her head. Then he seated himself beside her and wrapped his arms over his heart, huddling there as if his sanity had snapped.

Pitchwife unshouldered his pack, took out a Giantish firepot which had somehow remained sealed against the water. Next he produced a few fagots from his scant supply of firewood. They were soaked, and he was exhausted; but he bent over them and blew raggedly until they took flame from the firepot. Nursing the blaze, he made it hot enough to sustain itself. Though it was small and pitiable, it gave enough heat to soften the chill in Linden's joints, the gaunt misery in Covenant's eyes.

Then Pitchwife offered them *diamondraught*. But they refused it until he and the First had each swallowed a quantity of the potent liquor. Because of his cramped lungs and her injury, the Giants were in sore need of sustenance. After that, however, Linden took a few sips which ran true warmth at last into her stomach.

Bitterly, as if he were punishing himself, Covenant accepted the pouch of *diamondraught* from her; but he did not drink. Instead, he forced his stiff muscles and brittle bones toward Sunder.

His offer produced no reaction from the Graveler. In a

burned and gutted voice, Covenant urged, pleaded. Sunder did not raise his head. He remained focused on Hollian as if his world had shrunk to that frail compass and his companions no longer impinged upon him. After a while, Covenant shambled back to the fire, sat down, and covered his face with his hands.

A moment later, Vain appeared.

He emerged from the night into the campfire's small illumination and resumed at once his familiar blank stance. An ambiguous smile curved his mouth. The passion Linden had felt from him was gone. He appeared as insentient and unreachable as ever. His wooden forearm had been darkened and charred, but the damage was only superficial.

His left arm was withered and useless, like a congenital deformity. Pain oozed from several deep sores. Mottled streaks the color of ash marred his ebony flesh.

Instinctively, Linden started toward him, though she knew that she could not help him, that his wounds were as imponderable as his essential nature. She sensed that he had attacked the ur-viles for his own reasons, not to aid or even acknowledge the company; yet she felt viscerally that the wrong his sculptured perfection had suffered was intolerable. Once he had bowed to her. And more than once he had saved her life. Someone had to at least try to help him.

But before she reached him, a wide, winged shape came out of the stars like the plunge of a condor. Changing shapes as it descended, it landed lightly beside the Demondim-spawn in human form.

Findail.

He did not look at Covenant or Linden, ignored Sunder's hunched and single-minded grief; instead, he addressed Vain.

"Do not believe that you will win my heart with bravery." His voice was congested with old dismay, covert and unmistakable fear. His eyes seemed to search the Demondim-spawn's inscrutable soul. "I desire your death. If it lay within the permit of my Würd, I would slay you. But these comrades for whom you care nothing have again contrived to redeem you." He paused as if he were groping for courage, then concluded softly, "Though I abhor your purpose, the Earth must not suffer the cost of your pain."

Suddenly lambent, his right hand reached out to Vain's left shoulder. An instant of fire blazed from the touch, cast startling implications which only Linden could hear into the fathomless night. Then it was gone. Findail left Vain, went to stand like a sentinel confronting the moonlit prospect of the east.

The First breathed a soft oath of surprise. Pitchwife gaped in wonder. Covenant murmured curses as if he could not believe what he had seen.

Vain's left arm was whole, completely restored to its original beauty and function.

Linden thought she caught a gleam of relief from the Demondim-spawn's black eyes.

Astonishment stunned her. Findail's demonstration gave her a reason to understand for the first time why the *Elohim* believed that the healing of the Earth should be left to them, that the best choice she or Covenant could make would be to give Findail the ring and simply step aside from the doom Lord Foul was preparing for them. The restoration of Vain's arm seemed almost miraculous to her. With all the medical resources she could imagine, she would not have been able to match Findail's feat.

Drawn by the power he represented, she turned toward him with Sunder's name on his lips. *Help him. He doesn't know how to bear it.*

But the silhouette of the Appointed against the moon refused her before she spoke. In some unexplained way, he had aggravated his own plight by healing Vain. Like Sunder, he was in need of solace. His stance told her that he would deny any other appeal.

Pitchwife sighed. Muttering aimlessly to himself, he began to prepare a meal while the fire lasted.

Later that night, Linden huddled near Covenant and the fading embers of the fire with a damp blanket hugged around her in an effort to ward off the sky-deep cold and tried to explain her failure. "It was too sudden. I didn't see the danger in time."

"It wasn't your fault," he replied gruffly. "I had no right to blame you." His voice seemed to issue from an injury hidden within the clenched mound of his blanket—hidden and fatal. "I should've made them stay in Revelstone."

She wanted to protest his arrogation of responsibility. *Without them, we would all be dead. How else were we going to* get away from those ur-viles? But he went on, "I used to be afraid of power. I thought it made me what I hate—another Landwaster. A source of Despite for the people I care about. But I don't need power. I can do the same thing by just standing there."

She sat up and peered at him through the moon-edged night. He lay with his back to her, the blanket shivering slightly on his shoulders. She ached to put her arms around him, find some safe warmth in the contact of their bodies. But that was not what he needed. Softly, harshly, she said, "That's wonderful. You're to blame for everything. Next I suppose you're going to tell me you bit yourself with that venom, just to prove you deserve it."

He jerked over onto his back as if she had hit him between the shoulderblades. His face came, pale and wincing, out of the blanket. For a moment, he appeared to glare at her. But then his emanations lost their fierce edge. "I know," he breathed to the wide sky. "Atiaran tried to tell me the same thing. After all I did to her." Quietly, he quoted, " 'Castigation is a doom which achieves itself. In punishing yourself, you come to merit punishment.' All Foul has to do is laugh." His dark features concentrated toward her. "The same thing's true for you. You tried to save her. It wasn't your fault."

Linden nodded. Mutely, she leaned toward him until he took her into his embrace.

When she awoke in the early gray of dawn, she looked toward Sunder and saw that he had not moved during the night.

Hollian was rigid with death now, her delicate face pallid and aggrieved in the gloom; but he appeared unaware of any change, uncognizant of night or day—numb to anything except the shards of pain in his chest and her supine form. He was chilled to the bone, but the cold had no power to make him shiver.

Covenant roused with a flinch, yanked himself roughly out of his dreams. For no apparent reason, he said distinctly, "Those ur-viles should've caught up with us by now." Then he, too, saw Sunder. Softly, he groaned.

The First and Pitchwife were both awake. Her injury was still sore; but *diamondraught* had quickened her native toughness, and the damage was no longer serious. She glanced at the Graveler, then faced Covenant and Linden and shook her head. Her training had not prepared her to deal with Sunder's stricken condition.

Her husband levered himself off the ground with his elbow and crawled toward the sacks of supplies. Taking up a pouch of *diamondraught*, he forced his cramped muscles to lift him upright, carry him to the Graveler's side. Without a word, he opened the pouch and held it under Sunder's nose.

Its scent drew a sound like a muffled sob from the Stonedownor. But he did not raise his head.

Helpless with pity, Pitchwife withdrew.

No one spoke. Linden, Covenant, and the Giants ate a cheerless meal before the sun rose. Then the First and Pitchwife went to find stone on which to meet the day. In shared apprehension, Linden and Covenant started toward Sunder. But, by chance or design, he had seated himself upon an exposed face of rock. He needed no protection.

Gleaming azure, the sun crested the horizon, then disappeared as black clouds began to host westward.

Spasms of wind kicked across the gravid surface of the White River. Pitchwife hastened to secure the supplies. By the time he was finished, the first drizzle had begun to fall. It mounted toward downpour with a sound like frying meat.

Linden eyed the quick current of the White and shuddered. Its cold ran past her senses like the edge of a rasp. But she had already survived similar immersions without *diamondraught* or *metheglin* to sustain her. She was determined to endure as long as necessary. Grimly, she turned back to the problem of Sunder.

He had risen to his feet. Head bowed, eyes focused on nothing, he faced his companions and the River.

He held Hollian upright in his arms, hugging her to his sore breast so that her soles did not touch the ground.

Covenant met Linden's gaze. Then he moved to stand in front of Sunder. The muscles of his shoulders bunched and throttled; but his voice was gentle, husky with rue. "Sunder," he said, "put her down." His hands clenched at his sides. "You'll drown yourself if you try to take her with you. I can't lose you too." In the background of his words blew a wind of grief like the rising of the rain. "We'll help you bury her."

Sunder gave no response, did not look at Covenant. He

appeared to be waiting for the Unbeliever to get out of his way.

Covenant's tone hardened. "Don't make us take her away from you."

In reply, Sunder lowered Hollian's feet to the ground. Linden felt no shift in his emanations, no warning. With his right hand, he drew the *krill* from his jerkin.

The covering of the blade fell away, flapped out of reach along the wind. He gripped the hot handle in his bare fingers. Pain crossed his face like a snarl, but he did not flinch. White light shone from the gem, as clear as a threat.

Lifting Hollian with his left arm, he started down toward the river.

Covenant let him pass. Linden and the Giants let him pass. Then the First sent Pitchwife after him, so that he would not be alone in the swift, cold hazard of the current.

"He's going to Andelain," Covenant grated. "He's going to carry her all the way to Andelain. Who do you think he wants to find?"

Without waiting for an answer, he followed Pitchwife and the Graveler.

Linden stared after them and groaned, His Dead! The Dead in Andelain. Nassic his father. Kalina his mother. The wife and son he had shed in the name of Mithil Stonedown.

Or Hollian herself?

Sweet Christ! How will he stand it? He'll go mad and never come back.

Diving into the current, Linden went downriver in a wild rush with the First swimming strongly at her side.

She was not prepared for the acute power of the cold. As her health-sense grew in range and discernment, it made her more and more vulnerable to what she felt. The days she had spent in the Mithil River with Covenant and Sunder had not been this bad. The chill cudgeled her flesh, pounded her raw nerves. Time and again, she believed that surely *now* she would begin to wail, that at last the Sunbane would master her. Yet the undaunted muscle of the First's shoulder supported her. And Covenant stayed with her. Through the bludgeoning rain, the thunder that shattered the air, the lightning that ripped the heavens, his stubborn sense of purpose remained within reach of her percipience. In spite of

numbing misery and desperation, she wanted to live—
wanted to survive every ill Lord Foul hurled against her.
Until her chance came to put a stop to it.

Visible by lightning burst, Pitchwife rode the River a stroke
or two ahead of the First. With one hand, he held up the
Graveler. And Sunder bore Hollian as if she were merely
sleeping.

Sometime during the middle of the day, the White dashed
frothing and tumbling into a confluence that tore the travelers
down the new channel like dead leaves in the wind. Joined
by the Grey, the White River had become the Soulsease; and
for the rest of that day—and all the next—it carried the
company along. The rains blinded Linden's sense of direction.
But at night, when the skies were clear and the waning moon
rose over the pummeled wasteland, she was able to see that
the river's course had turned toward the east.

The second evening after the confluence, the First asked
Covenant when they would reach Andelain. He and Linden
sat as close as possible to the small heat of their campfire;
and Pitchwife and the First crouched there also as if even
they needed something more than *diamondraught* to restore
their courage. But Sunder remained a short distance away in
the same posture he had assumed the two previous nights
hunched over his pain on the sheetrock of the campsite with
Hollian outstretched rigidly in front of him as if at any
moment she might begin to breathe again.

Side by side, Vain and Findail stood at the fringes of the
light. Linden had not seen them enter the river, did not
know how they traveled the rain-scoured waste. But each
evening they appeared together shortly after sunset and
waited without speaking for the night to pass.

Covenant mused into the flames for a moment, then replied, "I'm a bad judge of distance. I don't know how far
we've come." His face appeared waxen with the consequences
of cold. "But this is the Soulsease. It goes almost straight to
Mount Thunder from here. We ought—" He extended his
hands toward the fire, put them too close to the flames, as if
he had forgotten the reason for their numbness. But then
his leper's instincts caused him to draw back. "It depends on
the sun. It's due to change. Unless we get a desert sun, the
river'll keep running. We ought to reach Andelain sometime
tomorrow."

The First nodded and went back to her private thoughts. Behind her Giantish strength and the healing of her injury, she was deeply tired. After a moment, she drew her long-sword, began to clean and dry it with the slow, methodical movements of a woman who did not know what else to do.

As if to emulate her, Pitchwife took his flute from his pack, shook the water out of it, and tried to play. But his hands or his lips were too weary to hold any music. Soon he gave up the attempt.

For a while, Linden thought about the sun and let herself feel a touch of relief. A fertile sun or a sun of pestilence would warm the water. They would allow her to see the sky, open up the world around her. And a desert sun would certainly not be cold.

But gradually she became aware that Covenant was still shivering. A quick glance showed her he was not ill. After his passage through the Banefire, she doubted that he would ever be ill again. But he was clenched around himself, knotted so tightly that he seemed feverish.

She put her hand over his right forearm, drew his attention toward her. With her eyes, she asked what troubled him.

He looked at her gauntly, then returned his gaze to the fire as if among the coals he might find the words he needed. When he spoke, he surprised her by inquiring, "Are you sure you want to go to Andelain? The last time you had the chance, you turned it down."

That was true. Poised at the southwest verge of the Hills with Sunder and Hollian, she had refused to go with Covenant, even though the radiance of health from across the Mithil River had been vivid to her bruised nerves. She had feared the sheer power of that region. Some of her fear she had learned from Hollian's dread, Hollian's belief that Andelain was a place where people lost their minds. But most of it had arisen from an encompassing distrust of everything to which her percipience made her vulnerable. The Sunbane had bored into her like a sickness, as acute and anguished as any disease; but as a disease she had understood it. And it had suited her: it had been appropriate to the structure of her life. But for that very reason Andelain had threatened her more intimately. It had endangered her difficult self-possession. She had not believed that any good could come of anything which had such strength over her.

And later Covenant had relayed to her the words of Elena among the Dead. The former High Lord had said, *I rue that the woman your companion lacked heart to accompany you, for you have much to bear. But she must come to meet herself in her own time. Care for her, beloved, so that in the end she may heal us all.* In addition, the Forestal had said, *It is well that your companions did not accompany you. The woman of your world would raise grim shades here.* The simple recollection of such things brought back Linden's fear.

A fear which had made its meaning clear in lust and darkness when Gibbon-Raver had touched her and affirmed that she was evil.

But she was another woman now. She had found the curative use of her health-sense, the access to beauty. She had told Covenant the stories of her parents, drawn some of their sting from her heart. She had learned to call her hunger for power by its true name. And she knew what she wanted. Covenant's love. And the end of the Sunbane.

Smiling grimly, she replied, "Try to stop me."

She expected her answer to relieve him. But he only nodded, and she saw that he still had not said what was in him. Several false starts passed like shadows across the background of his expression. In an effort to reach him, she added, "I need the relief. The sooner I get out of the Sunbane, the saner I'll be."

"Linden—" He said her name as if she were not making his way easier. "When we were in Mithil Stonedown—and Sunder told us he might have to kill his mother—" He swallowed roughly. "You said he should be allowed to put her out of her misery. If that was what he wanted." He looked at her now with the death of her mother written plainly in his gaze. "Do you still believe that?"

She winced involuntarily. She would have preferred to put his question aside until she knew why he asked it. But his frank need was insistent. Carefully, she said, "She was in terrible pain. I think people who're suffering like that have the right to die. But mercy killing isn't exactly merciful to the people who have to do it. I don't like what it does to them." She strove to sound detached, impersonal; but the hurt of the question was too acute. "I don't like what it did to me. If you can call what I did mercy instead of murder."

He made a gesture that faltered and fell like a failed assuagement. His voice was soft; but it betrayed a strange ague. "What're you going to do if something's happened to Andelain? If you can't get out of the Sunbane? Caer-Caveral knew he wasn't going to last. Foul's corrupted everything else. What'll we do?" His larynx jerked up and down like a presage of panic. "I can stand whatever I have to. But not that. Not that."

He looked so belorn and defenseless that she could not bear it. Tears welled in her eyes. "Maybe it'll be all right," she breathed. "You can hope. It's held out this long. It can last a little longer."

But down in the cold, dark roots of her mind she was thinking, If it doesn't, I don't care what happens. I'll tear that bastard's heart out. I'll get the power somewhere, and I'll tear his heart out.

She kept her thoughts to herself. Yet Covenant seemed to sense the violence inside her. Instead of reaching out to her for comfort, he withdrew into his certainty. Wrapped in decisions and perceptions she did not understand and could not share, he remained apart from her throughout the night.

A long time passed before she grasped that he did not mean to reject her. He was trying to prepare himself for the day ahead.

But the truth was plain in the sharp, gray dawn, when he rolled, bleak and tense, out of his blankets to kiss her. He was standing on an inner precipice, and his balance was fragile. The part of him which had been fused in the Banefire did not waver; but the vessel bearing that sure alloy looked as brittle as an old bone. Yet in spite of his trepidation he made the effort to smile at her.

She replied with a grimace because she did not know how to protect him.

While Pitchwife prepared a meal for the company, Covenant went over to Sunder. Kneeling behind the Graveler, he massaged Sunder's locked shoulders and neck with his numb fingers.

Sunder did not react to the gesture. He was aware of nothing except Hollian's pallid form and his own fixed purpose. To Linden's health-sense, his body ached with the weakness of inanition. And she felt the hot blade of the *krill* scalding his unshielded belly under his jerkin. But he seemed to draw strength from that pain as if it were the promise that kept him alive.

After a while, Covenant rejoined the two Giants and Linden. "Maybe he'll meet her in Andelain," he sighed. "Maybe she'll be able to get through to him."

"Let us pray for that outcome," muttered the First. "His endurance must fail soon."

Covenant nodded. As he chewed bread and dried fruit for breakfast, he went on nodding to himself like a man who had no other hope.

A short time later, the sun rose beyond the rim of the world; and the companions stood on the rainswept sheetrock to meet the daybreak.

It crested the horizon in a flaring of emerald, cast green spangles up the swift, broken surface of the River.

At the sight, Linden went momentarily weak with relief. She had not realized how much she had feared another sun of rain.

Warmth: the fertile sun gave warmth. It eased the vehemence of the current, softened the chill of the water. And it shone on her nerves like the solace of dry, fire-warmed blankets. Supported by the First, with Covenant beside her and Pitchwife and Sunder only a few short strokes away, she rode the Soulsease and thought for the first time that perhaps the river had not been gratuitously named.

Yet relief did not blind her to what was happening to the earth on either side of the watercourse. The kindness of the fertile sun was an illusion, a trick performed by the River's protection. On the banks, vegetation squirmed out of the ground like a ghoul-ridden host. Flailed up from their roots, vines and grasses sprawled over the rims of the channel. Shrubs raised their branches as if they were on fire; trees clawed their way into the air, as frantic as the damned. And she found that her own relative safety only accentuated the sensations pouring at her from the wild, unwilling growth. She was floating through a wilderness of voiceless anguish: the torment around her was as loud as shrieks. Tortured out of all Law, the trees and plants had no defense, could do nothing for themselves except grow and grow—and hurl their dumb hurt into the sky.

Perhaps after all the Forestal of Andelain was gone. How long could he bear to hear these cries and be helpless?

Between rising walls of agony, the river ran on toward the
east and Mount Thunder after a long southeastward stretch.
Slowly, Linden fell into a strange, bifurcated musing. She held
to the First's shoulder, kept her head above water, watched
the riverbanks pass, the verdure teem. But on another level
she was not aware of such things. Within her, the darkness
which had germinated at Gibbon's touch also grew. Fed by
the Sunbane, it twined through her and yearned. She remembered now as if she had never forgotten that behind the superficial grief and pain and abhorrence had lurked a secret glee
at the act of strangling her mother—a wild joy at the taste
of power.

In a detached way, she knew what was happening to her.
She had been too long exposed to Lord Foul's corruption. Her
command over herself, her sense of who she wanted to be, was
fraying.

She giggled harshly to herself—a snapping of mirth like the
sound of a Raver. The idea was bitterly amusing. Until now
it had been the sheer difficulty and pain of traveling under the
Sunbane which had enabled her to remember who she was.
The Despiser could have mastered her long ago by simply allowing her to relax.

Fierce humor rose in her throat. Fertility seemed to caper
along her blood, frothing and chuckling luridly. Her percipience sent out sneaky fingers to touch Covenant's latent fire as
if at any moment she would muster the courage to take hold
of it for herself.

With an effort of will, she pulled at the First's shoulder. The
Giant turned her head, murmured over the wet mutter of the
river, "Chosen?"

So that Covenant would not hear her, Linden whispered,
"If I start to laugh, hit me. Hold me under until I stop."

The First returned a glance of piercing incomprehension.
Then she nodded.

Somehow, Linden locked her teeth against the madness and
did not let it out.

Noon rose above her and passed by. From the truncated
perspective of the waterline, she could see only a short distance ahead. The Soulsease appeared to have no future. The
world contained nothing except tortured vegetation and despair. She should have been able to heal that. She was a doctor. But she could not. She had no power.

But then without transition the terrain toward which the company was borne changed. Beyond an interdict as precise as a line drawn in the Earth, the wild fertility ended; and a natural woodland began on both sides of the Soulsease.

The shock of it against her senses told her what it was. She had seen it once before, when she had not been ready for it. It rushed into her even from this distance like a distillation of all *vitrim* and *diamonddraught*, a cure for all darkness.

The First nudged Covenant, nodded ahead. Thrashing his legs, he surged up in the water; and his crow split the air: "Andelain!"

As he fell back, he pounded at the current like a boy, sent sun-glistered streams of spray arcing across the Soulsease.

In silence, Linden breathed, Andelain, Andelain, as if by repeating that name she might cleanse herself enough to enter among the Hills. Hope washed through her in spite of everything she had to fear. *Andelain.*

Brisk between its banks, the river ran swiftly toward the Forestal's demesne, the last bastion of Law.

As they neared the demarcation, Linden saw it more acutely. Here thronging, tormented brush and bracken, mimosas cracked by their own weight, junipers as grotesque as the dancing of demons, all stopped as if they had met a wall: there a greensward as lush as springtime and punctuated with peonies like music swept up the graceful hillslopes to the stately poplars and red-fruited elders that crowned the crests. At the boundary of the Forestal's reign, mute hurt gave way to *aliantha*, and the Sunbane was gone from the pristine sky.

Gratitude and gladness and relief made the world new around her as the Soulsease carried the company out of the Land's brokenness into Andelain.

When she looked behind her, she could no longer see the Sunbane's green aura. The sun shone out of the cerulean heavens with the yellow warmth of loveliness.

Covenant indicated the south bank. The First and Pitchwife turned in that direction, angling across the current. Covenant swam with all his strength; and Linden followed. The water had already changed from ordinary free-flowing cleanness to crystal purity, as special and renewing as dew. And when she placed her hands on the grass-rich ground to boost herself out of the river, she received a new thrill, a sensation of vibrancy as keen as the clear air. She had been exposed

to the Sunbane for so long that she had forgotten what the
Earth's health felt like.

But then she stood on the turf with all her nerves open and
realized that what she felt was more than simple health. It was
Law quintessenced and personified, a reification of the vitality
which made life precious and the Land desirable. It was an
avatar of spring, the revel of summer; it was autumn glory and
winter peace. The grass under her feet sprang and gleamed,
seemed to lift her to a taller stature. The sap in the trees rose
like fire, beneficent and alive. Flowers scattered color everywhere. Every breath and scent and sensation was sapid beyond
bearing—and yet they urged her to bear them. Each new exquisite perception led her onward instead of daunting her,
carried her out of herself like a current of ecstasy.

Laughter and weeping rose in her together and could not
be uttered. This was Andelain, the heart of the Land Covenant
loved. He lay on his face in the grass, arms outspread as if
to hug the ground; and she knew that the Hills had changed
everything. Not in him, but in her. There were many things
she did not understand; but this she did: the bale of the Sunbane had no power here. She was free of it here. And the Law
which brought such health to life was worth the price any
heart was willing to pay.

That affirmation came to her like a clean sunrise. It was the
positive conviction for which she had been so much in need.
Any price. To preserve the last beauty of the Land. Any price
at all.

Pitchwife sat on the grass and stared hungrily up the hillsides, his face wide with astonishment. "I would not have
credited—" he breathed to himself. "Not have believed—"
The First stood behind him, her fingertips resting on his shoulders. Her eyes beamed like the sun-flashes dancing on the gay
surface of the Soulsease. Vain and Findail had appeared while
Linden's back had been turned. The Demondim-spawn betrayed no reaction to Andelain; but Findail's habitual distress
had lightened, and he took the crisp air deep into his lungs as
if, like Linden, he knew what it meant.

Free of the Sunbane and exalted, she wanted to run—
wanted to stretch and bound up the Hills and tumble down
them, sport like a child, see everything, taste everything, race
her bruised nerves and tired bones as far as they would go into
the luxuriant anodyne of this region, the sovereign solace of

Andelain's health. She skipped a few steps away from the River, turned to call Covenant after her.

He had risen to his feet, but was not looking at her. And there was no joy in his face.

His attention was fixed on Sunder.

Sunder! Linden groaned, instantly ashamed that she had forgotten him in her personal transport.

He stood on the bank and hugged Hollian upright against his chest, seeing nothing, comprehending no part of the beauty around him. For a time, he did not move. Then some kind of focus came into his eyes, and he stumbled forward. Too weak now to entirely lift the eh-Brand's death-heavy form, he half dragged her awkwardly in front of him across the grass.

Ashen with hunger and exhaustion and loss, he bore her to the nearest *aliantha*. There he laid her down. Under its holly-like leaves, the bush was thick with viridian treasure-berries. The Clave had proclaimed them poison; but after Marid had bitten Covenant, *aliantha* had brought the Unbeliever back from delirium. And that experience had not been lost on Sunder. He picked some of the fruit.

Linden held her breath, hoping he would eat.

He did not. Squatting beside Hollian, he tried to feed the berries between her rigid lips.

"Eat, love." His voice was hoarse, veined and cracked like crumbling marble. "You have not eaten. You must eat."

But the fruit only broke on her teeth.

Slowly, he hunched over the pain of his fractured heart and began to cry.

Pain twisted Covenant's face like a snarl as he moved to the Graveler's side. But when he said, "Come on," his voice was gentle. "We're still too close to the Sunbane. We need to go farther in."

For a long moment, Sunder shook with silent grief as if at last his mad will had failed. But then he scooped his arms under Hollian and lurched, trembling, to his feet. Tears streamed down his gray cheeks, but he paid them no heed.

Covenant gestured to the Giants and Linden. They joined him promptly. Together, they turned to the southeast and started away from the River across the first hillsides.

Sunder followed them, walking like a mute wail of woe.

His need conflicted Linden's reactions to the rich atmosphere of Andelain. As she and her friends moved among the

Hills, sunshine lay like immanence on the slopes; balm filled the shade of the trees. With Covenant and the Giants, she ate *aliantha* from the bushes along their way; and the savor of the berries seemed to add a rare spice to her blood. The grass gave a blessing back to the pressure of her shoes, lifting her from stride to stride as if the very ground sought to encourage her forward. And beneath the turf, the soil and skeleton of Andelain were resonant with well-being, the good slumber of peace.

And birds, soaring like melody above the treetops, squabbling amicably among the branches. And small woodland animals, cautious of the company's intrusion, but not afraid. And flowers everywhere, flowers without number—poppy, amaryllis, and larkspur—snapdragon, honeysuckle, and violet —as precise and numinous as poetry. Seeing them, Linden thought that surely her heart would burst with pleasure.

Yet behind her Sunder bore his lost love inward as if he meant to lay her at the feet of Andelain itself and demand restitution. Carrying death into the arduously defended region, he violated its ambience as starkly as an act of murder.

Though Linden's companions had no health-sense, they shared her feelings. Covenant's visage worked unself-consciously back and forth between leaping eagerness and clenched distress. Pitchwife's eyes devoured each new vista, every added benison—and flicked repeatedly toward Sunder as if he were flinching. The First held an expression of stern acceptance and approval on her countenance; but her hand closed and unclosed around the handle of her sword. Only Vain and the Appointed cared nothing for Sunder.

Nevertheless the afternoon passed swiftly. Sustained by treasure-berries and gladness, and by rills that sparkled like liquid gem-fire across their path, Linden and her companions moved at Sunder's pace among the copses and hillcrests. And then evening drew near. Beyond the western skyline, the sun set in grandeur, painting orange and gold across the heavens.

Still the travelers kept on walking. None of them wanted to stop.

When the last emblazonry of sunset had faded, and stars began to wink and smile through the deepening velvet of the sky, and the twittering communal clamor of the birds subsided, Linden heard music.

At first it was music for her alone, melody sung on a pitch of significance which only her hearing could reach. It sharpened the star-limned profiles of the trees, gave the light of the low, waning moon on the slopes and trunks a quality of etched and lovely evanescence. Both plaintive and lustrous, it wafted over the Hills as if it were singing them to beauty. Rapt with eagerness, Linden held her breath to listen.

Then the music became as bright as phosphorescence; and the company heard it. Covenant drew a soft gasp of recognition between his teeth.

Swelling and aching, the melody advanced. It was the song of the Hills, the incarnate essence of Andelain's health. Every leaf, every petal, every blade of grass was a note in the harmony; every bough and branch, a strand of singing. Power ran through it—the strength which held back the Sunbane. But at the same time it was mournful, as stern as a dirge; and it caught in Linden's throat like a sob.

"Oh, Andelain! Forgive! For I am doomed to fail this war.
    I cannot bear to see you die—and live,
Foredoomed to bitterness and all the gray Despiser's lore.
    But while I can I heed the call
    Of green and tree; and for their worth,
I hold the glaive of Law against the Earth."

While the words measured out their sorrow and determination, the singer appeared on a rise ahead of the company— became visible like a translation of song.

He was tall and strong, wrapped in a robe as fine and white as the music which streamed from the lines of his form. In his right hand, he gripped a long, gnarled tree-limb as though it were the staff of his might. For he was mighty—oh, he was mighty! The sheer potency of him shouted to Linden's senses as he approached, stunning her not with fear but with awe. A long moment passed before she was able to see him clearly.

"Caer-Caveral," whispered Covenant. "Hile Troy." Linden felt his legs tremble as if he ached to kneel, wanted to stretch himself prostrate in front of the eldritch puissance of the Forestal. "Dear God, I'm glad to see you." Memories poured from him, pain and rescue and bittersweet meeting.

Then at last Linden discerned through the phosphorescence

and the music that the tall man had no eyes. The skin of his
face spread straight and smooth from forehead to cheek over
the sockets in which orbs should have been.

Yet he did not appear to need sight. His music was the
only sense he required. It lit the Giants, entrancing them
where they stood, leaving them with a glamour in their faces
and a cessation of all hurt in their hearts. It trilled and swirled
through Linden, carrying her care away, humbling her to silence. And it met Covenant as squarely as any gaze.

"You have come," the man sang, drawing glimmers of
melody from the greensward, spangled wreaths of accompaniment from the trees. "And the woman of your world with you.
That is well." Then his singing concentrated more personally
on Covenant; and Covenant's eyes burned with grief. Hile
Troy had once commanded the armies of the Land against
Lord Foul. But he had sold himself to the Forestal of Garroting Deep to purchase a vital victory—and the price had
been more than three millennia of service.

"Thomas Covenant, you have become that which I may no
longer command. But I ask this of you, that you must grant
it." Melody flowed from him down the hillside, curling about
Covenant's feet and passing on. The music tuned itself to a
pitch of authority. "Ur-Lord and Illender, Unbeliever and
Earthfriend. You have earned the valor of those names. Stand
aside."

Covenant stared at the Forestal, his whole stance pleading
for comprehension.

"You must not intervene. The Land's need is harsh, and its
rigor falls upon other heads as well as yours. No taking of
life is gentle, but in this there is a necessity upon me, which
you are craved to honor. This Law also must be broken." The
moon was poised above the Hills, as acute as a sickle; but its
light was only a pale echo of the music that gleamed like droplets of bright dew up and down the slope. Within the trunks
of the trees rose the same song which glittered on their
leaves. "Thomas Covenant," the Forestal repeated, "stand
aside."

Now the rue of the melody could not be mistaken. And
behind it shimmered a note of fear.

"Covenant, please," Caer-Caveral concluded in a completely different voice—the voice of the man he had once

been. "Do this for me. No matter what happens. Don't interfere."

Covenant's throat worked. "I don't—" he started to say. I don't understand. Then, with a wrench of will, he stepped out of the Forestal's way.

Stately and grave, Caer-Caveral went down the hillside toward Sunder.

The Graveler stood as if he did not see the tall, white figure, heard no song. Hollian he held upright against his heart, her face pressed to his chest. But his head was up: his eyes watched the slope down which Caer-Caveral had come. A cry that had no voice stretched his visage.

Slowly, like an action in a dream, Linden turned to look in the direction of Sunder's gaze.

As Covenant did the same, a sharp pang sprang from him.

Above the company, moonshine and Forestal-fire condensed to form a human shape. Pale silver, momentarily transparent, then more solid, like an incarnation of evanescence and yearning, a woman walked toward the onlookers. A smile curved her delicate mouth; and her hair swept a suggestion of dark wings and destiny past her shoulders; and she shone like loss and hope.

Hollian eh-Brand. Sunder's Dead, come to greet him.

The sight of her made him breathe in fierce, shuddering gasps, as if she had set a goad to his heart.

She passed by Covenant, Linden, and the Giants without acknowledging them. Perhaps for her they did not exist. Erect with the dignity of her calling, the importance of her purpose, she moved to the Forestal's side and stopped, facing Sunder and her own dead body.

"Ah, Sunder, my dear one," she murmured. "Forgive my death. It was my flesh that failed you, not my love."

Helpless to reply, Sunder went on gasping as if his life were being ripped out of him.

Hollian started to speak again; but the Forestal raised his staff, silencing her. He did not appear to move, to take any action. Yet music leaped around Sunder like a swirl of moonsparks, and the Graveler staggered. Somehow, Hollian was taken from him. She was enfolded tenderly in the crook of the Forestal's left arm. Caer-Caveral claimed her stiff death for himself. The song became keener, whetted by loss and trepidation.

Wildly, Sunder snatched the *krill* from its resting place against his burned belly. Its argent passion pierced the music. All reason was gone from him. Wracked for air, he brandished Loric's blade at the Forestal, mutely demanding that Hollian be given back to him.

The restraint Hile Troy had asked of Covenant made him shudder.

"Now it ends," fluted Caer-Caveral. The singing which conveyed his words was at once exquisitely beautiful and unbearable. "Do not fear for me. Though it is severe, this must be done. I am weary, eager of release and called to rest. Your love supplies the power, and none other may take the burden from you. Son of Nassic"—the music contained no command now, but only sorrow—"you must strike me."

Covenant flinched as if he expected Sunder to obey. The Graveler was desperate enough for anything. But Linden watched him with all her senses and saw his inchoate violence founder in dismay. He lowered the *krill*. His eyes were wide with supplication. Behind the mad obsession which had ruled him since Hollian's death still lived a man who loathed killing —who had shed too much blood and never forgiven himself for it. His soul seemed to collapse inward. After days of endurance, he was dying.

The Forestal struck the turf with his staff, and the Hills rang. "Strike!"

His demand was so potent that Linden raised her hands involuntarily, though it was not directed at her. Yet some part of Sunder remained unbroken, clear. The corners of his jaw knotted with the old obduracy which had once enabled him to defy Gibbon. Deliberately, he unbent his elbow, let the *krill* dangle from his weak hand. His head slumped forward until his chin rested on his chest. He no longer made any effort to breathe.

Caer-Caveral sent a glare of phosphorescence at the Graveler. "Very well," he trilled angrily. "Withhold—and be lost. The Land is ill-served by those who will not pay the price of love." Turning sharply away, he strode back through the company in the direction from which he had come. He still bore Hollian's physical form clasped in his left arm.

And the Dead eh-Brand went with him as if she approved. Her eyes were silver and grieving.

It was too much. A strangled cry tore Sunder's refusal. He could not let Hollian go; his desire for her was too strong. Raising the *krill* above his head in both fists, he ran at the Forestal's back.

Too late, Covenant shouted, "No!" and leaped after Sunder.

The Giants could not move. The music held them fascinated and motionless. Linden was not certain that they were truly able to see what was happening.

She could have moved. She felt the same stasis which enclosed the First and Pitchwife; but it was not strong enough to stop her. Her percipience could grasp the melody and make it serve her. With the slow instantaneousness of visions or nightmares, she knew she was able to do it. The music would carry her after Sunder so swiftly that he might never reach the Forestal.

Yet she did not. She had no way to measure the implications of this crisis. But she had seen the pain shining in Hollian's eyes, the eh-Brand's recognition of necessity. And she trusted the slim, brave woman. She made no effort to stop Sunder as he hammered the point of the *krill* between Caer-Caveral's shoulderblades with the last force of his life.

From the blow burst a deflagration of pearl flame which rent away immobility, sent Linden and the Giants sprawling, hurled Covenant to the grass. At once, all the music became fire and raced toward the Forestal, sweeping around him—and Sunder and Hollian with him—so that they were effaced from sight, consumed in an incandescent whirlwind that spouted into the heavens, reached like the ruin of every song toward the bereft stars. A cacophony of fear clashed and wept around the flame; but the flame did not hear it. In a rush of ascension, the blaze burned its hot, mute agony against the night as if it fed on the pure heart of Andelain, bore that spirit writhing and appalled through the high dark.

And as it rose, Linden seemed to hear the fundamental fabric of the world tearing.

Then, before the sight became unendurable, the fire began to subside. By slow stages, the conflagration changed to an ordinary fire, yellow with heat and eaten wood, and she saw it burning from the black and blasted stump of a tree trunk which had not been there when Caer-Caveral was struck.

Stabbed deep into the charred wood beyond any hope of

removal was the *krill*. Only the flames that licked the stump made it visible: the light of its gem was gone.

Now the fire failed swiftly, falling away from the stricken trunk. Soon the blaze was extinguished altogether. Smoke curled upward to mark the place where the Forestal had been slain.

Yet the night was not dark. Other illuminations gathered around the stunned companions.

From beyond the stump, Sunder and Hollian came walking hand-in-hand. They were limned with silver like the Dead; but they were alive in the flesh—human and whole. Caer-Caveral's mysterious purpose had been accomplished. Empowered and catalyzed by the Forestal's spirit, Sunder's passion had found its object; and the *krill* had severed the boundary which separated him from Hollian. In that way, the Graveler, who was trained for bloodshed and whose work was killing, had brought his love back into life.

Around the two of them bobbed a circle of Wraiths, dancing a bright cavort of welcome. Their warm loveliness seemed to promise the end of all pain.

But in Andelain there was no more music.

FIFTEEN: Enactors of Desecration

In the lush, untrammeled dawn of the Hills, Sunder and Hollian came to say farewell to Covenant and Linden.

Linden greeted them as if the past night had been one of the best of her life. She could not have named the reasons for this; it defied expectation. With Caer-Caveral's passing, important things had come to an end. She should have lamented instead of rejoicing. Yet on a level too deep for language she had recognized the necessity of which the Forestal had spoken. *This Law also*. Andelain had been bereft of music, but not of beauty or consolation. And the restoration of the Stonedownors made her too glad for sorrow. In a paradoxical way, Caer-Caveral's self-sacrifice felt like a promise of hope.

But Covenant's mien was clouded by conflicting emotions. With his companions, he had spent the night watching Sunder and Hollian revel among the Wraiths of Andelain—and Linden sensed that the sight gave him both joy aud rue. The healing of his friends lightened his heart; the price of that healing did not. And surely he was hurt by his lack of any health-sense which would have enabled him to evaluate what the loss of the Forestal meant to Andelain.

However, there were no clouds upon the Graveler and the eh-Brand. They walked buoyantly to the place where Linden and Covenant sat; and Linden thought that some of the night's silver still clung to them, giving them a numinous cast even in daylight, like a new dimension added to their existence. Smiles gleamed from Sunder's eyes. And Hollian bore herself with an air of poised loveliness. Linden was not surprised to perceive that the child in the eh-Brand's womb shared her elusive, mystical glow.

For a moment, the Stonedownors gazed at Covenant and Linden and smiled and did not speak. Then Sunder cleared his throat. "I crave your pardon that we will no longer accompany you." His voice held a special resonance that Linden had never heard before in him, a suggestion of fire. "You have said that we are the future of the Land. It has become our wish to discover that future here. And to bear our son in Andelain.

"I know you will not gainsay us. But we pray that you find no rue in this parting. We do not—though you are precious to us. The outcome of the Earth is in your hands. Therefore we are unafraid."

He might have gone on; but Covenant stopped him with a brusque gesture, a scowl of gruff affection. "Are you kidding?" he muttered. "I'm the one who wanted you to stay behind. I was going to ask you—" He sighed, and his gaze wandered the hillside. "Spend as much time here as you can," he breathed. "Stay as long as possible. That's something I've always wanted to do."

His voice trailed away; but Linden was not listening to its resigned sadness. She was staring at Sunder. The faint silver quality of his aura was clear—and yet undefinable. It ran out of her grasp like water. Intuition tingled along her nerves, and she started speaking before she knew what she would say.

"The last time Covenant was here, Caer-Caveral gave him the location of the One Tree." Each word surprised her like a hint of revelation. "But he hid it so Covenant couldn't reach it himself. That's why he had to expose himself to the *Elohim*, let them work their plots." The bare memory brought a tremor of anger into her voice. "We should never have had to go there in the first place. Why did Caer-Caveral give him that gift—and then make it such a secret?"

Sunder looked at her. He was no longer smiling. A weird intensity filled his gaze like a swirl of sparks. Abruptly, he said, "Are you not now companioned by the Appointed of the *Elohim*? How otherwise could that end have been achieved?"

The strangeness of the Graveler's tone snatched back Covenant's attention. Linden felt him scrambling after inferences; a blaze of hope shot up in him. "Are you—?" he asked. "Is that it? Are you the new Forestal?"

Instead of answering, Sunder looked to Hollian, giving her the opportunity to tell him what he was.

She met his gaze with a soft smile. But she answered quietly, kindly, "No." She had spent time among the Dead and appeared certain of her knowledge. "In such a transferral of power, the Law which Caer-Caveral sought to rend would have been preserved. Yet we are not altogether what we were. We will do what we may for the sustenance of Andelain—and for the future of the Land."

Questions thronged in Linden. She wanted a name for the alteration she perceived. But Covenant was already speaking.

"The Law of Life." His eyes were hot and gaunt on the Stonedownors. "Elena broke the Law of Death—the barrier that kept the living and the dead from reaching out to each other. The Law Caer-Caveral broke was the one that kept the dead from crossing back into life."

"That is sooth," replied Hollian. "Yet it is a fragile crossing withal, and uncertain. We are sustained, and in some manner defined, by the sovereign Earthpower of the Andelainian

Hills. Should we depart this region, we would not long endure among the living."

Linden saw that this was true. The strange gleam upon the Stonedownors was the same magic which had given Caer-Caveral's music its lambent strength. Sunder and Hollian were solid, physical, and whole. Yet in a special sense they had become beings of Earthpower—and they might easily die if they were cut off from their source.

Covenant must have understood the eh-Brand's words also. But he heard them with different ears than Linden's. As their implications penetrated him, his sudden hope went out.

That loss sent a pang through Linden. She had been concentrating too hard on Sunder and Hollian. She had not realized that Covenant had been looking for an answer to his own death.

At once, she reached out a hand to his shoulder, felt the effort he made to suppress his dismay. But the exertion was over in an instant. Braced on his certainty, he faced the Stonedownors. His tone belied the struggle he made to keep it firm.

"I'll do everything I can," he said. "But my time's almost over. Yours is just beginning. Don't waste it."

Sunder returned a smile that seemed to make him young. "Thomas Covenant," he promised, "we will not."

No good-byes were said. This farewell could not be expressed with words or embraces. Arm in arm, the Graveler and the eh-Brand simply turned and walked away across the bedewed grass. After a moment, they passed the crest of the hill and were gone.

Behind them, they left a silence that ached as if nothing would be able to take their place.

Linden stretched her arm over Covenant's shoulders and hugged him, trying to tell him that she understood.

He kissed her hand, then rose to his feet. As he scanned the bright morning, the untainted sun, the flower-bedizened landscape, he sighed, "At least there's still Earthpower."

"Yes," Linden averred, climbing erect to join him. "The Hills haven't changed." She did not know how else to comfort him. "Losing the Forestal is going to make a difference. But not yet." She was sure of that. Andelain's health still surged around her in every blade and leaf, every bird and rock. No disease or weakness was visible anywhere. And the shining sun had no aura. She thought that the tangible world had never held so much condensed and treasurable beauty. Like a prayer for Andelain's endurance, she repeated, "Not yet."

A grin of grim relish bared Covenant's teeth. "Then he can't hurt us. For a while, anyway. I hope it drives him crazy."

Linden breathed a secret relief, hoping that he had weathered the crisis.

But all his moods seemed to change as soon as he felt them. An old bleakness dulled his gaze; haggard lines marked his mien. Abruptly, he started toward the charred stump which had once been the Forestal of Andelain.

At once, she followed him. But she stopped when she understood that he had gone to say farewell.

He touched the inert gem of the *krill* with his numb fingers, tested the handle's coldness with the back of his hand. Then he leaned his palms and forehead against the blackened wood. Linden could hardly hear him.

"From fire to fire," he whispered. "After all this time. First Hamako. Then Honninscrave. Now you. I hope you've found a little peace."

There was no answer. When at last he withdrew, his hands and brow were smudged with soot like an obscure and contradictory anointment. Roughly, he scrubbed his palms on his pants; but he seemed unaware of the stain on his forehead.

For a moment, he studied Linden as if he sought to measure her against the Forestal's example. Again she was reminded of the way he had once cared for Joan. But Linden was not his ex-wife; she faced him squarely. The encompassing health of the Hills made her strong. And what he saw appeared to reassure him. Gradually his features softened. Half to himself, he murmured, "Thank God you're still here." Then he raised his voice. "We should get going. Where are the Giants?"

She gave him a long gaze, which Hollian would have understood, before she turned to look for the First and Pitchwife.

They were not in sight. Vain and Findail stood near the foot of the slope exactly as they had remained all night; but the Giants were elsewhere. However, when she ascended to the hillcrest, she saw them emerge from a copse on the far side of a low valley, where they had gone to find privacy.

They responded to her wave with a hail and a gesture eastward, indicating that they would rejoin her and Covenant in that direction. Perhaps their keen eyes were able to descry the smile she gave them, glad to see that they felt safe enough in Andelain to leave their companions unguarded.

Covenant came to her wearily, worn by strain and lack of sleep. But at the sight of the Giants—or of the Hills unfurled before him like pleasure rolling along the kind breeze—he, too, smiled. Even from this distance, the restoration of Pitchwife's spirit was visible in the way he hobbled at his wife's side with a gait like a mummer's capriole. And her swinging stride bespoke eagerness and a fondly remembered night. They were Giants in Andelain. The pure expanse of the Hills suited them.

Softly, Covenant mused, "They aren't people of the Land. Maybe *Coercri* was enough. Maybe they won't meet any Dead here." As he remembered the slain Unhomed—and the *caamora* of release he had given them in The Grieve—the timbre of his voice conveyed pride and pain. But then his gaze darkened; and Linden saw that he was thinking of Saltheart Foamfollower, who had lost his life in Covenant's former victory over the Despiser.

She wanted to tell him not to worry. Perhaps the battle for Revelstone had made Pitchwife familiar with despair and doom. Yet she believed that eventually he would find the song he needed. And the First was a Swordmain, as true as her blade. She would not lightly submit to death.

But Covenant had his own strange sources of surety and did not wait for Linden's answer. With his resolve stiffening, he placed his half-hand firmly in her clasp and drew her toward the east along a way among the Hills which would intersect the path of the Giants.

After a moment, Findail and Vain appeared behind them, following them as always in the direction of their fate.

For a while, Covenant walked briskly, his smudged forehead raised to the sun and the savory atmosphere. But at the first brook they encountered, he stopped. From under his belt, he drew a knife which he had brought with him from Revelstone. Stooping to the crisp water, he drank deeply, then soaked his ragged beard and set himself to shave.

Linden held her breath as she watched him. His grasp on the blade was numb; and fatigue made his muscles awkward. But she did not try to intervene. She sensed that this risk was necessary to him.

When he had finished, however, and his cheeks and neck were scraped clean, she could not conceal her relief. She knelt beside him, cupped water into her hands, and washed the soot from his forehead, seeking to remove the innominate implications of that mark.

An oak with a tremendous trunk spread its wide leaves over that part of the brook. Satisfied with Covenant's face, she pulled him after her and leaned back into the shade and the grass. The breeze played down the length of her legs like the sport of a lover; and she was in no hurry to rejoin the Giants.

But suddenly she felt a mute cry from the tree, a burst of pain which shivered through the ground, seemed to violate the very air. She whirled from Covenant's side and surged to her feet, trembling to find the cause of the oak's hurt.

The cry rose. For an instant, she saw no reason for it. Harm shook the boughs; the leaves wailed; muffled rivings ran through the heartwood. Around the oak, the Hills seemed to concentrate as if they were appalled. But she saw nothing except that Vain and Findail were gone.

Then, too swift for surmise, the Appointed came flowing out of the wood's anguish.

As he transformed himself from oak to flesh, his care-cut visage wore an unwonted shame. Vexed and defensive, he faced Linden and Covenant. "Is he not Demondim-spawn?" he demanded as if they had accused him unjustly. "Are not his makers ur-viles, that have ever served the Despiser with their self-abhorrence? And will you trust him to my cost? He must be slain."

At his back, the oak's hurt sharpened to screaming.

"You bastard!" Linden spat, half guessing what Findail had done—and afraid to believe it. "You're killing it! Don't you even care that this is Andelain?—the only place left that at least ought to be safe?"

"Linden?" Covenant asked urgently. "What—?" He lacked her percipience, had no knowledge of the tree's agony.

But he did not have to wait for an answer. A sundering pain like the blow of an axe split Linden's nerves; and the trunk of the oak sprang apart in a flail of splinters.

From the core of the wood, Vain stepped free. Unscathed, he left the still quivering tree in ruins. He did not glance at Findail or anyone else. His black eyes held nothing but darkness.

Linden stumbled to her knees in the grass and wrapped her arms around the hurt.

For a stunned moment, grief held the Hills. Then Covenant rasped, "That's terrific." He sounded as shaken as the dying boughs. "I hope you're proud of yourself."

Findail's reply seemed to come from a great distance. "Do you value him so highly? Then I am indeed lost."

"I don't give a good goddamn!" Covenant was at Linden's side. His hands gripped her shoulders, supporting her against the empathic force of the rupture. "I don't trust either of you. Don't you *ever* try anything like that again!"

The *Elohim* hardened. "I will do what I must. From the first, I have avowed that I will not suffer his purpose. The curse of Kastenessen will not impel me to that doom."

Swirling into the form of a hawk, he flapped away through the treetops. Linden and Covenant were left amid the wreckage.

Vain stood before them as if nothing had happened.

For a moment longer, the ache of the tree kept Linden motionless. But by degrees Andelain closed around the destruction, pouring health back into the air she breathed, spreading green vitality up from the grass, loosening the knotted echo of pain. Slowly, her head cleared. Sweet Christ, she mumbled to herself. I wasn't ready for that.

Covenant repeated her name; his concern reached her through his numb fingers. She steadied herself on the undergirding bones of the Hills and nodded to him. "I'm all right." She sounded wan; but Andelain continued to lave her in its balm. Drawing a deep breath, she pulled herself back to her feet.

Across the greensward, the sunshine lay like sorrow among the trees and shrubs, *aliantha* and flowers. But the shock of violence was over. Already, the distant hillsides had begun to smile again. The brook resumed its damp chuckle as though the interruption had been forgotten. Only the riven trunk went on weeping while the tree died, too sorely hurt to keep itself alive.

"The old Lords—" Covenant murmured, more to himself than to her. "Some of them could've healed this."

So could I, Linden nearly replied aloud. If I had your ring. I could save it all. But she bit down the thought, hoped it did not show in her face. She did not trust her intense desire for power. The power to put a stop to evil.

However, he lacked the sight to read her emotions. His own

grief and outrage blinded him. When he touched her arm and gestured onward, she leaped the brook with him; and together they continued among the Hills.

Unmarred except by the dead wood of his right forearm, Vain followed them. His midnight countenance held no expression other than the habitual ambiguity of his slight grin.

The day would have been one of untrammeled loveliness for Linden if she could have forgotten Findail and the Demondim-spawn. As she and Covenant left the vicinity of the shattered oak, Andelain reasserted all its beneficent mansuetude, the gay opulence of its verdure, the tuneful sweep and soar and flash of its birds, the endearing caution and abundance of its wildlife. Nourished by treasure-berries and rillwater, and blandished from stride to stride by the springy surf, she felt crowded with life, as piquant as the scents of the flowers, and keen for each new vista of the Andelainian Hills. After a time, the First and Pitchwife rejoined Linden and Covenant, appearing from the covert of an antique willow with leaves in their hair and secrets in their eyes. For greeting, Pitchwife gave a roistering laugh that sounded like his old humor; and it was seconded by one of his wife's rare, beautiful smiles.

"Look at you," Linden replied in mock censure, teasing the Giants. "For shame. If you keep that up, you're going to become parents whether you're ready for it or not."

A shade like a blush touched the First's mien; but Pitchwife responded with a crow. Then he assumed an air of dismay. "Stone and Sea forfend! The child of this woman would surely emerge bladed and bucklered from the very womb. Such a prodigy must not be blithely conceived."

The First frowned to conceal her mirth. "Hush, husband," she murmured. "Provoke me not. Does it not suffice you that one of us is entirely mad?"

"Suffice me?" he riposted. "How should it suffice me? I have no wish for loneliness."

"Aye, and none for wisdom or decorum," she growled in feigned vexation. "You are indeed shameful."

When Covenant grinned at the jesting of the Giants, Linden nearly laughed aloud for pleasure.

Yet she did not know where Findail had gone or what he would do next. And the death of the oak remained aching in

the back of her mind. Ballasted by such things, her mood did
not altogether lose itself in the analystic atmosphere. There
was a price yet to be paid for the passing of the Forestal, and
the destination of the company had not changed. In addition,
she had no clear sense of what Covenant hoped to achieve
by confronting the Despiser. Caer-Caveral had once said of
her, *The woman of your world would raise grim shades here.*
She relished Pitchwife's return to glee, enjoyed the new lightness which the badinage of the Giants produced in Covenant.
But she did not forget.

As evening settled around Andelain, she experienced a faint
shiver of trepidation. At night the Dead walked the Hills. All
of Covenant's olden friends, lambent with meanings and memories she could not share. The woman he had raped. And the
daughter of that rape, who had loved him—and had broken
the Law of Death in his name, trying as madly as hate to spare
him from his harsh doom. She was loath to meet those potent
revenants. They were the men and women who had shaped
the past, and she had no place among them.

Under a stately Gilden, the company halted. A nearby
stream with a bed of fine sand provided water for washing.
Aliantha were plentiful. The deep grass cushioned the ground
comfortably. And Pitchwife was a wellspring of good cheer,
of *diamondraught* and tales. While the satin gloaming slowly
folded itself away, leaving Linden and her companions uncovered to the darkness and the hushed stars, he described the
long Giantclave and testing by which the Giants of Home had
determined to send out the Search and had selected his wife
to lead it. He related her feats as if they were stupendous,
teasing her with her prowess. But now his voice held a hidden
touch of fever, a suggestion of effort which hinted at his more
fundamental distress. Andelain restored his heart; but it could
not heal his recollection of Revelstone and gratuitous bloodshed, could not cure his need for a better outcome. After a
time, he lapsed into silence; and Linden felt the air of the
camp growing tense with anticipation.

Across the turf, fireflies winked and wandered uncertainly,
as if they were searching for the Forestal's music. But eventually they went away. The company settled into a vigil. The
mood Covenant emitted was raw with fatigue and hunger. He,
too, appeared to fear his Dead as much as he desired them.

Then the First broke the silence. "These Dead," she began

thoughtfully. "I comprehend that they are held apart from their deserved rest by the breaking of the Law of Death. But why do they gather here, where all other Law endures? And what impels them to accost the living?"

"Companionship," murmured Covenant, his thoughts elsewhere. "Or maybe the health of Andelain gives them something as good as rest." His voice carried a distant pang; he also had been left forlorn by the loss of Caer-Caveral's song. "Maybe they just haven't been able to stop loving."

Linden roused herself to ask, "Then why are they so cryptic? They haven't given you anything except hints and mystification. Why don't they come right out and tell you what you need to know?"

"Ah, that is plain to me," Pitchwife replied on Covenant's behalf. "Unearned knowledge is perilous. Only by the seeking and gaining of it may its uses be understood, its true worth measured. Had Gossamer Glowlimn my wife been mystically granted the skill and power of her blade without training or test or experience, by what means could she then choose where to strike her blows, how extremely to put forth her strength? Unearned knowledge rules its wielder, to the cost of both."

But Covenant had his own answer. When Pitchwife finished, the Unbeliever said quietly, "They can't tell us what they know. We'd be terrified." He was sitting with his back to the Gilden; and his fused resolve gave him no peace. "That's the worst part. They know how much we're going to be hurt. But if they tell us, where will we ever get the courage to face it? Sometimes ignorance is the only kind of bravery or at least willingness that does any good."

He spoke as if he believed what he was saying. But the hardness of his tone seemed to imply that he had no ignorance left to relieve the prospect of his immedicable intent.

The Giants fell still, unable to deny his assertion or respond to it. The stars shone bleak rue around the scant sliver of the moon. The night grew intense among the Hills. Behind the comforting glow of its health and wholeness, Andelain grieved for the Forestal.

Terrified? Linden asked herself. Was Covenant's purpose as bad as that?

Yet she found it impossible to question him. Not here, with the Giants listening. His need for privacy was palpable to her.

And she was too restless to concentrate. She remained charged with the energy and abundance of the Hills; and the night seemed to breathe her name, urging her to walk off her nervous anticipation. Covenant's Dead were nowhere in evidence. Within the range of her percipience lay only the fine slumber and beauty of the region.

A strange glee rose in her: she wanted to run and caracole under the slight moon, tumble and roll and tumble again down the lush hillsides, immerse herself in Andelain's immaculate dark. Perhaps a solitary gambol would act as an anodyne for the other blackness which the Sunbane had nourished in her veins.

Abruptly, she sprang to her feet. "I'll be back," she said without meeting the eyes of her companions. "Andelain is too exciting. I need to see more of it."

The Hills murmured to her, and she answered, sprinting away from the Gilden southward with all the gay speed of her legs.

Behind her, Pitchwife had taken up his flute. At once broken, piercing, and sweet, its awkward tones followed her as she ran. They carried around her like the ghost-limbs of the trees, the crouching midnight of the bushes, the unmoonlit loom and pause of the shadows. He was trying to play the song which had streamed so richly from Caer-Caveral.

For a moment, he caught it—or almost caught it—and it went through her like loss and exaltation. Then she seemed to outrun it as she passed over a rise and sped downward again, deeper into the occult night of the Andelainian Hills.

The Forestal had said that she would raise grim shades here; and she thought of her father and mother. Unintentionally, without knowing what they were doing, they had bred her for suicide or murder. But now she defied them. Come on! she panted up at the stars. I dare you! For good or ill, healing or destruction, she had become stronger than her parents. The passion surging in her could not be named or confined by the harsh terms of her inheritance. She taunted her memories, challenging them to appear before her. But they did not.

And because they did not, she ran on, as heedless as a child —altogether unready for the door of might which opened suddenly against her, slapping her to the ground as if she were not strong or real enough to be noticed by the old puissance emerging from it.

A door like a gap in the first substance of the night, as abrupt and stunning as a detonation, and as tall as the heavens. It opened so that the man could stride through it. Then it closed behind him.

Her face was thrust into the grass. She fought for breath, strove to raise her head. But the sheer force of the presence towering over her crushed her prostrate. His bitter outrage seemed to fall on her like the wreckage of a mountain. Beneath his ire, he was so poignant with ruin, so extreme in the ancient and undiminished apotheosis of his despair, that she would have wept for him if she had been able. But his tremendous wrath daunted her, turned her vulnerability against herself. She could not lever her face out of the turf to look at him.

He felt transcendently tall and powerful. For an instant, she believed that he could not be aware of her, that she was too small for his notice. Surely he would pass by her and go about his fell business. But almost immediately her hope failed. His regard lit between her shoulderblades like the point of a spear.

Then he spoke. His voice was as desolate as the Land under a desert sun, as twisted and lorn as the ravages of a sun of pestilence. But anger gave it strength.

"Slayer of your own Dead, do you know me?"

No, she panted. *No.* Her fingers gouged into the loam as she struggled to shift her abject posture. He had no right to do this to her. Yet his glare impaled her, and she could not move.

He replied as if her resistance had no meaning:

"I am Kevin. Son of Loric. High Lord of the Council. Founder of the Seven Wards. And enactor of the Land's Desecration by my own hand. I am Kevin Landwaster."

In response, she was able to do nothing except groan, Dear God. Oh, dear God.

Kevin.

She knew who he was.

He had been the last High Lord of Berek's lineage, the last direct inheritor of the Staff of Law. The wonder and munificence of his reign in Revelstone had won the service of the Bloodguard, confirmed the friendship of the Giants, advanced the Council's dedication to the Earthpower, given beauty and purpose to all the Land. And he had failed. Tricked and defeated by the Despiser, he had proved himself unequal to the Land's defense. By his own mistakes, the object of his love and service had been doomed. And because he had understood that doom, he had fallen into despair.

Madly, he had conceived the ploy of the Ritual of Desecration, believing that Lord Foul would thereby be undone— that the price of centuries of devastation for the Land would purchase the Despiser's downfall. Therefore they had met in Kiril Threndor within the heart of Mount Thunder, mad Lord and malign foe. Together, they had set in motion the dire Ritual.

But in the end it was Kevin who fell while Lord Foul laughed. Desecration had no power to rid the world of Despite.

Yet that was not the whole tale of his woe. Misled by the confusion of her love and hate, the later High Lord, Elena, daughter of Lena and Covenant, had thought that the Landwaster's despair would be a source of irrefusable might; and so she had selected him for her breaking of the Law of Death, had rent him from his natural grave to hurl him in combat against the Despiser. But Lord Foul had turned the attempt against her. Both she and the Staff of Law had been lost; and Dead Kevin had been forced to serve his foe.

The only taste of relief he had been granted had come when Thomas Covenant and Saltheart Foamfollower had defeated the Despiser.

But that victory was now three millennia past. The Sunbane was rampant upon the Land, and Lord Foul had found the path to triumph. Kevin's dismay and wrath poured from him in floods. His voice was as hard as a cable under terrific stress.

"We are kindred in our way—the victims and enactors of Despite. You must heed me. Do not credit that you may exercise choice here. The Land's need admits no choice. You must heed me. *Must!*"

The word hammered and echoed and pleaded through her. *Must.* He had not come to appall her, meant her no harm. Rather, he approached her because he had no other way to reach out among the living, exert himself against the Despiser's machinations.

Must.

She understood that. Her fingers relaxed their grasp on the grass; her senses submitted to his vehemence. *Tell me what it is*, she said as if she had no more need to choose. *Tell me what I should do.*

"You will not wish to heed me. The truth is harsh. You will seek to deny it. But it will not be denied. I have borne horror upon my head and am not blinded by the hope which refuses truth. You must heed me."

Must.

Yes.

Tell me.

"Linden Avery, you must halt the Unbeliever's mad intent. His purpose is the work of Despite. As I have done before him, he seeks to destroy that which he loves. He must not be permitted.

"If no other means suffice, you must slay him."

No! In a rush of trepidation, she strove against his power—and still she had no strength to raise her head. *Slay him?* Goaded by his gaze, her heart labored. *No! You don't understand. He wouldn't do that.*

But his voice came down on her back like a fall of stone.

"No. It is you who do not understand. You have not yet learned to comprehend the cunning of despair. Can you think that I allowed my fellow Lords to guess my purpose when I had set my heart to the Ritual? Have you been granted the gift of such sight, and are you yet unable to see? When evil rises in its full power, it surpasses truth and may wear the guise of good without fear of discovery. In that way was I brought to my own doom.

"He walks the path which his friends among the Dead have conceived for him. But they also do not comprehend despair. They were redeemed from it by his brave mastery of the Despiser—and so they see hope where there is only Desecration. Their vision of evil is incomplete and false."

He gathered force in the night, became as shattering as a shout of disaster.

"It is his intent to place the white ring into Lord Foul's hand.

"If you suffer him to succeed, the term of our grief will be slight, for all Earth and Time will be lost.

"You must halt him."

Repeating until all the Hills replied, *Must. Must.*

After a moment, he left her. The door of his power closed behind him. But she did not notice his departure. For a long time, she went on staring blindly into the grass.

SIXTEEN: "Andelain! forgive!"

LATER, it started to rain.

Drizzling lightly, clouds covered the stars and the moon. The rain was as gentle as the touch of springtime, as clean and kind and sad as the spirit of the Hills. It fed the grass, blessed the flowers, garlanded the trees with droplets. In no way did it resemble the hysterical fury of the sun of rain.

Yet it closed the last light out of the world, leaving Linden in darkness.

She lay outstretched on the turf. All will and movement were gone from her. She had no wish to lift her head, to stir from her prostration. The crushing weight of what she had learned deprived her of the bare desire to breathe. Her eyes accepted the rain without blinking.

The drizzle made a quiet stippling noise on the leaves and grass, a delicate elegy. She thought that it would carry her away, that she would never be asked to move again. But then she heard another sound through the spatter of drops: a sound like the chime of a small, perfect crystal. Its fine note conveyed mourning and pity.

When she looked up, she saw that Andelain was not altogether dark. A yellow light shed streaks of rain to the grass. It came like the chiming from a flame the size of her palm which bobbed in the air as if it burned from an invisible wick.

And the dancing fire sang to her, offering her the gift of its sorrow.

One of the Wraiths of Andelain.

At the sight, pain seized her heart, brought her to her feet. That such things would be destroyed! That Covenant meant to sacrifice even Wraiths and Andelain on the altar of his despair, let so much lorn and fragile beauty be ripped out of life! Instinctively, she knew why the flame had come to her.

"I'm lost in this rain," she said. Outrage rose behind her clenched teeth. "Take me back to my people."

The Wraith bobbed like a bow; perhaps it understood her. Dancing and guttering, it moved away through the drizzle. Droplets crossed its light like falling stars.

She followed it without hesitation. Darkness crowded around her and through her; but the flame remained clear.

It did not mislead her. In a short time, it guided her to the place where she had left her companions.

Under the Gilden, the Wraith played for a moment above the huge, sleeping forms of the First and Pitchwife. They were not natives of the Land. Unappalled by personal revenants, they slumbered as if they had been unable to refuse the peace of the Hills.

The flitting flame limned Vain briefly, sparked the rain beading on his black perfection so that he seemed to wear an intaglio of glisters. His ebon orbs watched nothing, admitted nothing. His slight smile appeared to have no meaning.

But Covenant was not there.

The Wraith left her then as if it feared to go farther with her. It chimed away into the dark like a fading hope. Yet when her sight adjusted to the cloud-closed night, she caught a glimpse of what she sought. In a low hollow to the east lay a soft glow of pearl.

She moved in that direction, and the light became brighter.

It revealed Thomas Covenant standing among his Dead.

His wet shirt clung to his torso. Rain-dark hair straggled across his forehead. But he was oblivious to such things. And he did not see Linden coming. All of him was concentrated on the specters of his past.

She knew them by the stories and descriptions she had heard of them. The Bloodguard Bannor resembled Brinn too closely to be mistaken. The man in the grave and simple robe had dangerous eyes balanced by a crooked, humane mouth: High Lord Mhoram. The woman was similarly attired because she also was a former High Lord; and her lucid beauty was marred—or accentuated—by a prophetic wildness that echoed Covenant's: she was Elena, daughter of Lena. And the Giant with laughter and certainty and grief shining from his gaze was surely Saltheart Foamfollower.

The power they emanated should have abashed Covenant, though it was not on the same scale as Kevin's. But he had no percipience with which to taste their peril. Or perhaps his ruinous intent called that danger by another name. His whole body seemed to yearn toward them as if they had come to comfort him.

To shore up his resolve, so that he would not falter from the destruction of the Earth.

And why not? In that way they would be granted rest from the weary millennia of their vigil.

Must, Linden thought. The alternative was altogether terrible. Yes. Her clothes soaked, her hair damp and heavy against her neck, she strode down into the gathering; and her rage shaped the night.

Covenant's Dead were potent and determined. At one time, she would have been at their mercy. But now her passion dominated them all. They turned toward her and fell silent in mingled surprise, pain, refusal. Bannor's face closed against her. Elena's was sharp with consternation. Mhoram and Foamfollower looked at her as if she cast their dreams into confusion.

But only Covenant spoke. "Linden!" he breathed thickly, like a man who had just been weeping. "You look awful. What's happened to you?"

She ignored him. Stalking through the drizzle, she went to confront his friends.

They shone a ghostly silver that transcended moonlight. The rain fell through their incorporeal forms. Yet their eyes were keen with the life which Andelain's Earthpower and the breaking of the Law of Death made possible for them. They stood in a loose arc before her. None of them quailed.

Behind her, Covenant's loss and love and incomprehension poured into the night. But they did not touch her. Kevin had finally opened her eyes, enabled her to see what the man she loved had become.

She met the gazes of the Dead one by one. The flat blade of Mhoram's nose steered him between the extremes of his vulnerability and strength. Elena's eyes were wide with speculation, as if she were wondering what Covenant saw in Linden. Bannor's visage wore the same dispassion with which Brinn had denounced her after the company's escape from *Bhrathairealm*. The soft smile that showed through Foamfollower's jutting beard underscored his concern and regret.

For a fraction of a moment, Linden nearly faltered. Foamfollower was the Pure One who had redeemed the *jheherrin*. He had once walked into lava to aid Covenant. Elena had been driven into folly at least in part by her love for the man who had raped her mother. Bannor had served the Unbeliever as faithfully as Brinn or Cail. And Mhoram—Linden and Covenant had embraced in his bed as if it were a haven.

But it had not been a haven. She had been wrong about that, and the truth appalled her. In her arms in Mhoram's bed, Covenant had already decided on desecration—had already become certain of it. *It is his intent to place the white ring into Lord Foul's hand.* After he had sworn that he would not. Anguish surged up in her. Her cry ripped fiercely across the rain.

"Why aren't you *ashamed*?"

Then her passion began to blow like a high wind. She fanned it willingly, wanted to snuff out, punish, eradicate if she could the faces silver-lit and aghast in front of her.

"Have you been dead so long that you don't know what you're doing anymore? Can't you remember from one minute to the next what matters here? This is *Andelain*! He's saved your souls at least once. And you want him to destroy it!

"You." She jabbed accusations at Elena's mixed disdain and compassion. "Do you still think you love him? Are you that arrogant? What good have you ever done him? None of this would've happened if you hadn't been so eager to rule the dead as well as the living."

Her denunciation pierced the former High Lord. Elena tried to reply, tried to defend herself; but no words came. She had broken the Law of Death. The blame of the Sunbane was as much hers as Covenant's. Stricken and grieving, she wavered, lost force, and went out, leaving a momentary afterglow of silver in the rain.

But Linden had already turned on Bannor.

"And *you*. You with your bloody self-righteousness. You promised him service. Is that what you call *this*? Your people are sitting on their hands in Revelstone when they should be *here*! Hollian was killed because they didn't come with us to fight those ur-viles. Caer-Caveral is dead and it's only a matter of time before Andelain starts to rot. But never mind that. Aren't you satisfied with letting Kevin ruin the Land once?" She flung the back of her hand in Covenant's direction. "They should be here to *stop him*!"

Bannor had no answer. He cast a glance like an appeal at Covenant; then he, too, faded away. Around the hollow, the darkness deepened.

Fuming, Linden swung toward Foamfollower.

"Linden, no," Covenant grated. "Stop this." He was close to fire. She could feel the burning in his veins. But his demand did not make her pause. He had no right to speak to her. His Dead had betrayed him—and now he meant to betray the Land.

"And *you*. Pure One! You at least I would've expected to care about him more than this. Didn't you learn anything from watching your people die, seeing that Raver rip their brains out? Do you think desecration is *desirable*?" The Giant flinched. Savagely, she went on, "You could've prevented this. If you hadn't given him Vain. If you hadn't tried to make him think you were giving him hope, when what you were really doing was teaching him to surrender. You've got him believing he can afford to give in because Vain or some other miracle is going to save the world anyway. Oh, you're Pure all right. Foul himself isn't that Pure."

"Chosen—" Foamfollower murmured, "Linden Avery—" as if he wanted to plead with her and did not know how. "Ah, forgive. The Landwaster has afflicted you with this pain. He does not comprehend. The vision which he lacked in life is not supplied in death. The path before you is the way of hope and doom, but he perceives only the outcome of his own despair. You must remember that he has been made to serve the Despiser. The ill of such service darkens his spirit. Covenant, hear me. Chosen, forgive!"

Shedding gleams in fragments, he disappeared into the dark.

"Damnation!" Covenant rasped. "Damnation!" But now his

curses were not directed at Linden. He seemed to be swearing at himself. Or at Kevin.

Transported out of all restraint, Linden turned at last to Mhoram.

"And you," she said, as quiet as venom. "*You.* They called you 'seer and oracle.' That's what I've heard. Everytime I turn around, he tells me he wishes you were with him. He values you more than anyone." Her anger and grief were one, and she could not contain them. Fury that Covenant had been so misled; tearing rue that he trusted her too little to share his burdens, that he preferred despair and destruction to any love or companionship which might ease his responsibilities. "You should have told him the truth."

The Dead High Lord's eyes shone with silver tears—yet he did not falter or vanish. The regret he emitted was not for himself: it was for her. And perhaps also for Covenant. An aching smile twisted his mouth. "Linden Avery"—he made her name sound curiously rough and gentle—"you gladden me. You are worthy of him. Never doubt that you may justly stand with him in the trial of all things. You have given sorrow to the Dead. But when they have bethought themselves of who you are, they will be likewise gladdened. Only this I urge of you: strive to remember that he also is worthy of you."

Formally, he touched his palms to his forehead, then spread his arms wide in a bow that seemed to bare his heart. "My friends!" he said in a voice that rang, "I believe that you will prevail!"

Still bowing, he dissolved into the rain and was gone.

Linden stared after him dumbly. Under the cool touch of the drizzle, she was suddenly hot with shame.

But then Covenant spoke. "You shouldn't have done that." The effort he made to keep himself from howling constricted his voice. "They don't deserve it."

In response, Kevin's *Must!* shouted through her, leaving no room for remorse. Mhoram and the others belonged to Covenant's past, not hers. They had dedicated themselves to the ruin of everything for which she had ever learned to care. From the beginning, the breaking of the Law of Death had served only the Despiser. And it served him still.

She did not turn to Covenant. She feared that the mere shape of him, barely discernible through the dark, would make her weep like the Hills. Harshly, she replied, "That's why you did it, isn't it. Why you made the *Haruchai* stay behind. After what Kevin did to the Bloodguard, you knew they would try to stop you."

She felt him strive for self-mastery and fail. He had met his Dead with an acute and inextricable confusion of pain and joy which made him vulnerable now to the cut of her passion. "You know better than that," he returned. "What in hell did Kevin say to you?"

Bitter as the breath of winter, she rasped, " 'I'll never give him the ring. Never.' How many times do you think you said that? How many times did you promise—?" Abruptly, she swung around, her arms raised to strike out at him —or to ward him away. "You incredible bastard!" She could not see him, but her senses picked him precisely out of the dark. He was as rigid and obdurate as an icon of purpose carved of raw granite hurt. She had to rage at him in order to keep herself from crying out in anguish. "Next to you, my father was a hero. At least he didn't *plan* to kill anybody but himself." Black echoes hosted around her, making the night heinous. "Haven't you even got the guts to go on living?"

"Linden." She felt intensely how she pained him, how every word she spat hit him like a gout of vitriol. Yet instead of fighting her he strove for some comprehension of what had happened to her. "What did Kevin say to you?"

But she took no account of his distress. He meant to betray her. Well, that was condign: what had she ever done to deserve otherwise? But his purpose would also destroy the Earth—a world which in spite of all corruption and malice still nurtured Andelain at its heart, still treasured Earthpower and beauty. Because he had given up. He had walked into the Banefire as if he knew what he was doing—and he had let the towering evil burn the last love out of him. Only pretense and mockery were left.

"You've been listening to Findail," she flung at him. "He's convinced you it's better to put the Land out of its misery than to go on fighting. I was terrified to tell you about my mother because I thought you were going to hate me. But this is worse. If you hated me, I could at least hope you might go on fighting."

Then sobs thronged up in her. She barely held them back.

"You mean everything to me. You made me live again when I might as well have been dead. You convinced me to keep trying. But you've decided to give up." The truth was as plain as the apprehension which etched him out of the wet dark. "You're going to give Foul your ring."

At that, a stinging pang burst from him. But it was not denial. She read it exactly. It was fear. Fear of her recognition. Fear of what she might do with the knowledge.

"Don't say it like that," he whispered. "You don't understand." He appeared to be groping for some name with which to conjure her, to compel acquiescence—or at least an abeyance of judgment. "You said you trusted me."

"You're right," she answered, grieving and weeping and raging all at once. "I don't understand."

She could not bear any more. Whirling from him, she fled into the rain. He cried after her as if something within him were being torn apart; but she did not stop.

Sometime in the middle of the night, the drizzle took on the full force of a summer storm. A cold, hard downpour pelted the Hills; wind sawed at the boughs and brush. But Linden did not seek shelter. She did not want to be protected. Covenant had already taken her too far down that road, warded her too much from the truth. Perhaps he feared her—was ashamed of what he meant to do and so sought to conceal it. But during the dark night of Andelain she did him the justice of acknowledging that he had also tried to protect her for her own sake—first from involvement in Joan's distress and the Land's need, then from the impact of Lord Foul's evil, then from the necessary logic of his death. And now from the implications of his despair. So that she would be free of blame for the loss of the Earth.

She did him that justice. But she hated it. He was a classic case: people who had decided on suicide and had no wish to be saved typically became calm and certain before taking their lives. Sheer pity for him would have broken her heart if she had been less angry.

Her own position would have been simpler if she could have believed him evil. Or if she had been sure that he had lost his mind. Then her only responsibility would have been to stop him at whatever cost. But the most terrible aspect of her dilemma was that his fused certainty betrayed neither madness nor malice to her health-sense. In the grip of an intent which was clearly insane or malign, he appeared more than ever to be the same strong, dangerous, and indomitable man with whom she had first fallen in love. She had never been able to refuse him.

Yet Kevin had loved the Land as much as anyone, and his protest beat at her like the storm. *When evil rises in its full power, it surpasses truth and may wear the guise of good without fear.*

Evil or crazy. Unless she fought her way into him, wrestled his deepest self-conceptions away from him and looked at them, she had no way to tell the difference.

But once before when she had entered him, trying to bring him back from the silence imposed on his spirit by the *Elohim*, he had appeared to her in the form of Marid—an innocent man made monstrous by a Raver and the Sunbane. A tool for the Despiser.

Therefore she fled him, hastened shivering and desperate among the Hills. She could not learn the truth without possessing him. And possession itself was evil. It was a kind of killing, a form of death. She had already sacrificed her mother to the darkness of her unhealed avarice for the power of death.

She did not seek shelter because she did not want it. She fled from Covenant because she feared what a confrontation with him would entail. And she kept on walking while the storm blew and rushed around her because she had no alternative. She was traveling eastward, toward the place where the sun would rise—toward the high crouched shoulders and crown of Mount Thunder.

Toward Lord Foul.

Her aim was as grim as lunacy—yet what else could she do? What else but strive to meet and outface the Despiser before Covenant arrived at his crisis? There was no other way to save him without possessing him—without exposing herself and him and the Land to the hot ache of her capacity for blackness.

That's right, she thought. I can do it. I've earned it.

She knew she was lying to herself. The Despiser would be hideously stronger than any Raver; and she had barely survived the simple proximity of *samadhi* Sheol. Yet she persisted. In spite of the night, and of the storm which sealed

away the moon and the stars, she saw as clearly as vision
that her past life was like the Land, a terrain possessed by
corruption. She had let the legacy of her parents denude her
of ordinary health and growth, had allowed a dark desire to
rule her days like a Raver. In a sense, she had been possessed
by hate from the moment when her father had said to her,
You never loved me anyway—a hatred of life as well as of
death. But then Covenant had come into her existence as he
had into the Land, changing everything. He did not deserve
despair. And she had the right to confront the Despite which
had warped her, quenched her capacity for love, cut her
off from the vitality of living. The right and the necessity.

Throughout the night, she went on eastward. Gradually,
the storm abated, sank back to a drizzle and then blew away,
unveiling a sky so star-bedizened and poignant that it seemed
to have been washed clean. The slim curve of the moon
setting almost directly behind her told her that her path
was true. The air was cold on her sodden clothes and wet
skin; her hair shed water like shivers down her back. But
Andelain sustained her. Opulent under the unfathomable
heavens, it made all things possible. Her heart lifted against
its burdens. She kept on walking.

But when she crossed a ridge and met the first clear sight
of the sunrise, she stopped—froze in horror. The slopes and
trees were heavy with raindrops; and each bead caught the
light in its core, echoing back a tiny piece of daybreak to
the sun, so that all the grass and woods were laced with
gleams.

Yellow gleams fatally tinged by vermilion.

The sun wore a halo of pestilence as the Sunbane rose over
the Hills.

It was so faint that only her sight could have discerned it.
But it was there. The rapine of the Land's last beauty had
begun.

For a long moment, she remained still, surprised into her
old paralysis by the unexpected swiftness with which the
Sunbane attacked Andelain's residual Law. She had no power.
There was nothing she could do. But her heart scrambled for
defenses—and found one. Her friends lacked her Land-bred
senses. They would not see the Sunbane rising toward them;
and so the Giants would not seek stone to protect themselves.

They would be transformed like Marid into creatures of destruction and self-loathing.

She had left them leagues behind, could not possibly return to warn them in time. But she had to try. They needed her.

Abandoning all other intents, she launched herself in a desperate run back the way she had come.

The valley below the ridge was still deep in shadow. She was racing frenetically, and her eyes were slow to adjust. Before she was halfway down the hillside, she nearly collided with Vain.

He seemed to loom out of the crepuscular air without transition, translated instantly across the leagues. But as she reeled away from him, staggered for balance, she realized that he must have been trailing her all night. Her attention had been so focused on her thoughts and Andelain that she had not felt his presence.

Behind him in the bottom of the valley were Covenant, the First, and Pitchwife. They were following the Demondim-spawn.

After two nights without rest, Covenant looked haggard and febrile. But determination glared from his strides. He would not have stopped to save his life—not with Linden traveling ahead of him into peril. He did not look like the kind of man who could submit to despair.

But she had no time to consider his contradictions. The sun was rising above the ridge. "The Sunbane!" she cried. "It's here! Find stone!"

Covenant did not react. He appeared too weary to grasp anything except that he had found her again. Pitchwife stared dismay at the ridgecrest. But the First immediately began to scan the valley for any kind of rock.

Linden pointed, and the First saw it: a small, hoary outcropping of boulders near the base of the slope some distance away. At once, she grabbed her husband by the arm and pulled him at a run in that direction.

Linden glanced toward the sun, saw that the Giants would reach the stones with a few moments to spare.

In reaction, all her strength seemed to wash out of her. Covenant was coming toward her, and she did not know how to face him. Wearily, she slumped to the grass. Everything she had tried to define for herself during the night had been lost. Now she would have to bear his company again, would have to live in the constant presence of his wild purpose. The Sunbane was rising in Andelain for the first time. She covered her face to conceal her tears.

He halted in front of her. For a moment, she feared that he would be foolish enough to sit down. But he remained standing so that his boots would ward him against the sun. He radiated fatigue, lamentation, and obduracy.

Stiffly, he said, "Kevin doesn't understand. I have no intention of doing what he did. He raised his own hand against the Land. Foul didn't enact the Ritual of Desecration alone. He only shared it. I've already told you I'm never going to use power again. Whatever happens, I'm not going to be the one who destroys what I love."

"What difference does that make?" Her bitterness was of no use to her. All the severity with which she had once endured the world was gone and refused to be conjured back. "You're giving up. Never mind the Land. There're still three of us left who want to save it. We'll think of something. But you're abandoning yourself." Do you expect me to forgive you for that?

"No." Protest made his tone ragged. "I'm not. There's just nothing left I can do for you anymore. And I can't help the Land. Foul took care of that long before I ever got here." His gall was something she could understand. But the conclusion he drew from it made no sense. "I'm doing this for myself. He thinks the ring will give him what he wants. I know better. After what I've been through, I *know* better. He's wrong."

His certainty made him impossible to refute. The only arguments she knew were the ones she had once used to her father, and they had always failed. They had been swallowed in darkness—in self-pity grown to malice and hosting forth to devour her spirit. No argument would suffice.

Vaguely, she wondered what account of her flight he had given the Giants.

But to herself she swore, I'm going to stop you. Somehow. No evil was as great as the ill of his surrender. The Sunbane had risen into Andelain. It could never be forgiven.

Somehow.

* * *

Later that day, as the company wended eastward among the Hills, Linden took an opportunity to drift away from Covenant and the First with Pitchwife. The malformed Giant was deeply troubled. His grotesque features appeared aggrieved, as if he had lost the essential cheer which preserved his visage from ugliness. Yet he was plainly reluctant to speak of his distress. At first, she thought that this reluctance arose from a new distrust of her. But as she studied him, she saw that his mood was not so simple.

She did not want to aggravate his unhappiness. But he had often shown himself willing to be pained on behalf of his friends. And her need was exigent. Covenant meant to give the Despiser his ring.

Softly, so that she would not be overheard, she breathed, "Pitchwife, help me. Please."

She was prepared for the dismal tone of his reply, but not for its import. "There is no help," he answered. "She will not question him."

"She—?" Linden began, then caught herself. Carefully, she asked, "What did he say to you?"

For an aching moment, Pitchwife was still. Linden forced herself to give him time. He would not look at her. His gaze wandered the Hills morosely, as if already they had lost their luster. Without her senses, he could not see that Andelain had not yet been damaged by the Sunbane. Then, sighing, he mustered words out of his gloom.

"Rousing us from sleep to hasten in your pursuit, he announced your belief that it is now his intent to destroy the Land. And Gossamer Glowlimn my wife will not question him.

"I acknowledge that he is the Earthfriend—worthy of all trust. But have you not again and again proven yourself alike deserving? You are the Chosen, and for the mystery of your place among us we have been accorded no insight. Yet the *Elohim* have named you Sun-Sage. You alone possess the sight which proffers hope of healing. Repeatedly the burdens of our Search have fallen to you—and you have borne them well. I will not believe that you who have wrought so much restoration among the Giants and the victims of the Clave have become in the space of one night mad or cruel. And you have withdrawn trust from him. This is grave in all sooth. It must be questioned. But she is the First of the Search. She forbids.

"Chosen—" His voice was full of innominate pleading, as if he wanted something from her and did not know what it was. "It is her word that we have no other hope than him. If he has become untrue, then all is lost. Does he not hold the white ring? Therefore we must preserve our faith in him— and be still. Should he find himself poised on the blade-edge of his doom, we must not overpush him with our doubt.

"But if he must not be called to an accounting, what decency or justice will permit you to be questioned? I will not do it, though the lack of this story is grievous. If you are not to be equally trusted, you must at least be equally left in silence."

Linden did not know how to respond. She was distressed by his troubled condition, gratified by his fairness, and incensed by the First's attitude. Yet would she not have taken the same position in the Swordmain's place? If Kevin Landwaster had spoken to someone else, would she not have been proud to repose her confidence in the Unbeliever? But that recognition only left her all the more alone. She had no right to try to persuade Pitchwife to her cause. Both he and his wife deserved better than that she should attempt to turn them against each other—or against Covenant. And yet she had no way to test or affirm her own sanity except by direct opposition to him.

Even in his fixed weariness and determination, he was so dear to her that she could hardly endure the acuity of her desire for him.

A fatigue and defeat of her own made her stumble over the uneven turf. But she refused the solace of Pitchwife's support. Wanly, she asked him, "What are you going to do?"

"Naught," he replied. "I am capable of naught." His empathy for her made him acidulous. "I have no sight to equal yours. Before the truth becomes plain to me, the time for all necessary doing will have come and gone. That which requires to be done, you must do." He paused; and she thought that he was finished, that their comradeship had come to an end. But then he gritted softly through his teeth, "Yet I say this, Chosen. You it was who obtained Vain Demondim-spawn's escape from the snares of *Elemesnedene*. You it was who made possible our deliverance from the Sandhold. You it was who procured safety for all but Cable Seadreamer from the Worm of the World's End, when the

Earthfriend himself had fallen nigh to ruin. And you it was who found means to extinguish the Banefire. Your worth is manifold and certain.

"The First will choose as she wishes. I will give you my life, if you ask it of me."

Linden heard him. After a while, she said simply, "Thanks." No words were adequate. In spite of his own baffled distress, he had given her what she needed.

They walked on together in silence.

The next morning, the sun's red aura was distinct enough for all the company to see.

Linden's open nerves searched the Hills, probing Andelain's reaction to the Sunbane. At first, she found none. The air had its same piquant savor, commingled of flowers and dew and treesap. *Aliantha* abounded on the hillsides. No discernible ill gnawed at the wood of the nearby Gildens and willows. And the birds and animals that flitted or scurried into view and away again were not suffering from any wrong. The Earthpower treasured in the heart of the region still withstood the pressure of corruption.

But by noon that was no longer true. Pangs of pain began to run up the tree trunks, aching in the veins of the leaves. The birds seemed to become frantic as the numbers of insects increased; but the woodland creatures had grown frightened and gone into hiding. The tips of the grass-blades turned brown; some of the shrubs showed signs of blight. A distant fetor came slowly along the breeze. And the ground began to give off faint, emotional tremors—an intangible quivering which no one but Linden felt. It made the soles of her feet hurt in her shoes.

Muttering curses, Covenant stalked on angrily eastward. In spite of her distrust, Linden saw that his rage for Andelain was genuine. He pushed himself past the limits of his strength to hasten his traversal of the Hills, his progress toward the crisis of the Despiser. The Sunbane welded him to his purpose.

Linden kept up with him doggedly, determined not to let him get ahead of her. She understood his fury, shared it: in this place, the red sun was atrocious, intolerable. But his ire made him appear capable of any madness which might put an end to Andelain's hurt, for good or ill.

Dourly, the Giants accompanied their friends. Covenant's

best pace was not arduous for Pitchwife; the First could have
traveled much faster. And her features were sharp with
desire for more speed, for a termination to the Search, so that
the question which had come between her and her husband
would be answered and finished. The difficulty of restraining
herself to Covenant's short strides was obvious in her. While
the company paced through the day, she held herself grimly
silent. Her mother had died in childbirth; her father, in the
Soulbiter. She bore herself as if she did not want to admit
how important Pitchwife's warmth had become to her.

For that reason, Linden felt a strange, unspoken kinship
toward the First. She found it impossible to resent the Swordmain's attitude. And she swore to herself that she would
never ask Pitchwife to keep his promise.

Vain strode blankly behind the companions. But of Findail
there was no sign. She watched for him at intervals, but he
did not reappear.

That evening, Covenant slept for barely half the night:
then he went on his way again as if he were trying to steal
ahead of his friends. But somehow through her weary slumber
Linden felt him leave. She roused herself, called the Giants
up from the faintly throbbing turf, and went after him.

Sunrise brought an aura of fertility to the dawn and a
soughing rustle like a whisper of dread to the trees and
brush. Linden felt the leaves whimpering on their boughs, the
greensward aching plaintively. Soon the Hills would be reduced to the victimized helplessness of the rest of the
Land. They would be scourged to wild growth, desiccated to
ruin, afflicted with rot, pummeled by torrents. And that
thought made her as fierce as Covenant, enabled her to keep
up with him while he exhausted himself. Yet the mute pain
of green and tree was not the worst effect of the Sunbane.
Her senses had been scoured to raw sensitivity: she knew that
beneath the sod, under the roots of the woods, the fever of
Andelain's bones had become so argute that it was almost
physical. A nausea of revulsion was rising into the Earthpower of the Hills. It made her guts tremble as if she were
walking across an open wound.

By degrees, Covenant's pace became labored. Andelain
no longer sustained him. More and more of its waning
strength went to ward off the corruption of the Sunbane. As
a result, the fertile sun had little superficial effect. A few

trees groaned taller, grew twisted with hurt; some of the shrubs raised their branches like limbs of desecration. All the birds and animals seemed to have fled. But most of the woods and grass were preserved by the power of the soil in which they grew. *Aliantha* clung stubbornly to themselves, as they had for centuries. Only the analystic refulgence of the Hills was gone—only the emanation of superb and concentrated health—only the exquisite vitality.

However, the sickness in the underlying rock and dirt mounted without cessation. That night, Covenant slept the sleep of exhaustion and *diamondraught*. But for a long time Linden could not rest, despite her own fatigue. Whenever she laid her head to the grass, she heard the ground grinding its teeth against a backdrop of slow moans and futile outrage.

Well before dawn, she and her companions arose and went on. She felt now that they were racing the dissolution of the Hills.

That morning, they caught their first glimpse of Mount Thunder.

It was still at least a day away. But it stood stark and fearsome above Andelain, with the sun leering past its shoulder and a furze of unnatural vegetation darkening its slopes. From this distance, it looked like a titan that had been beaten to its knees.

Somewhere inside that mountain, Covenant intended to find Lord Foul.

He turned to Linden and the Giants, his eyes red-rimmed and flagrant. Words yearned in him, but he seemed unable to utter them. She had thought him uncognizant of the Giants' disconsolation, offended by her own intransigent refusal; but she saw now that he was not. He understood her only too well. A fierce and recalcitrant part of him felt as she did, fought like loathing against his annealed purpose. He did not want to die, did not want to lose her or the Land. And he had withheld any explanation of himself from the Giants so that they would not side with him against her. So that she would not be altogether alone.

He wished to say all those things. They were plain to her aggrieved senses. But his throat closed on them like a fist, would not let them out.

She might have reached out to him then. Without altering any of her promises, she could have put her love around him. But horror swelled in the ground on which they stood, and it snatched her attention away from him.

Abhorrence. Execration. Sunbane and Earthpower locked in mortal combat beneath her feet. And the Earthpower could not win. No Law defended it. Corruption was going to tear the heart out of the Hills. The ground had become so unstable that the Giants and Covenant felt its tremors.

"Dear Christ!" Linden gasped. She grabbed at Covenant's arm. "Come on!" With all her strength, she pulled him away from the focus of Andelain's horror.

The Giants were aghast with incomprehension; but they followed her. Together, the companions began to run.

A moment later, the grass where they had been standing erupted.

Buried boulders shattered. A large section of the greensward was shredded; stone-shards and dirt slashed into the sky. The violence which broke the Earthpower in that place sent a shock throughout the region, gouged a pit in the body of the ground. Remnants of ruined beauty rained everywhere.

And from the naked walls of the pit came squirming and clawing the sick, wild verdure of the fertile sun. Monstrous as murder, a throng of ivy teemed upward to spread its pall over the ravaged turf.

In the distance, another eruption boomed. Linden felt it like a wail through the ground. Piece by piece, the life of Andelain was being torn up by the roots.

"Bastard!" Covenant raged. "Oh, you bastard! You've crippled everything else. Aren't you content?"

Turning, he plunged eastward as if he meant to launch himself at the Despiser's throat.

Linden kept up with him. Pain belabored her senses. She could not speak because she was weeping.

SEVENTEEN: Into the Wightwarrens

EARLY the next morning, the company climbed into the foothills of Mount Thunder near the constricted rush of the Soulsease River. Covenant was gaunt with fatigue, his gaze as gray as ash. Linden's eyes burned like fever in their sockets; strain throbbed through the bones of her skull. Even the Giants were tired. They had only stopped to rest in snatches during the night. The First's lips were the color of her fingers clinching the hilt of her sword. Pitchwife's visage looked like it was being torn apart. Yet the four of them were united by their urgency. They attacked the lower slopes as if they were racing the sun which rose behind the fatal bulk of the mountain.

A desert sun.

Parts of Andelain had already become as blasted and ruinous as a battlefield.

The Hills still clung to the life which had made them lovely. While it lasted, Caer-Caveral's nurture had been complete and fundamental. The Sunbane could not simply flush all Earthpower from the ground in so few days. But the dusty sunlight reaching past the shoulders of Mount Thunder revealed that around the fringes of Andelain—and in places across its heart—the damage was already severe.

The vegetation of those regions had been ripped up, riven, effaced by hideous eruptions. Their ground was cratered and pitted like the ravages of an immedicable disease. The previous day, the remnants of those woods had been overgrown and strangled by the Sunbane's feral fecundity. But now, as

383

the sun advanced on that verdure, every green and living thing slumped into viscid sludge which the desert drank away.

Linden gazed toward the Hills as if she, too, were dying. Nothing would ever remove the sting of that devastation from her heart. The sickness of the world soaked into her from the landscape outstretched and tormented before her. Andelain still fought for its life and survived. Much of it had not yet been hurt. Leagues of soft slopes and natural growth separated the craters, stood against the sun's arid rapine. But where the Sunbane had done its work the harm was as keen as anguish. If she had been granted the chance to save Andelain's health with her own life, she would have taken it as promptly as Covenant. Perhaps she, too, would have smiled.

She sat on a rock in a field of boulders that cluttered the slope too thickly to admit vegetation. Panting as if his lungs were raw with ineffective outrage, Covenant had stopped there to catch his breath. The Giants stood nearby. The First studied the west as if that scene of destruction would give her strength when the time came to wield her blade. But Pitchwife could not bear it. He perched himself on a boulder with his back to the Andelainian Hills. His hands toyed with his flute, but he made no attempt to play it.

After a while, Covenant rasped, "Broken—" There was a slain sound in his voice, as if within him also something vital were perishing. "All that beauty—" Perhaps during the night he had lost his mind. " 'Your very presence here empowers me to master you. The ill that you deem most terrible is upon you.' " He was quoting Lord Foul; but he spoke as if the words were his. " 'There is despair laid up for you here—' "

At once, the First turned to him. "Do not speak thus. It is false."

He gave no sign that he had heard her. "It's not my fault," he went on harshly. "I didn't do any of this. None of it. But I'm the cause. Even when I don't do anything. It's all being done because of me. So I won't have any choice. Just by being alive, I break everything I love." He scraped his fingers through the stubble of his beard; but his eyes continued staring at the waste of Andelain, haunted by it. "You'd think I wanted this to happen."

"No!" the First protested. "We hold no such conception.

You must not doubt. It is doubt which weakens—doubt which corrupts. Therefore is this Despiser powerful. *He* does not doubt. While you are certain, there is hope." Her iron voice betrayed a note of fear. "This price will be exacted from him if you do not doubt!"

Covenant looked at her for a moment. Then he rose stiffly to his feet. His muscles and his heart were knotted so tightly that Linden could not read him.

"That's wrong." He spoke softly, in threat or appeal. "You need to doubt. Certainty is terrible. Let Foul have it. Doubt makes you human." His gaze shifted toward Linden. It reached out to her like flame or beggary, the culmination and defeat of all his power in the Banefire. "You need every doubt you can find. I want you to doubt. I'm hardly human anymore."

Each flare and wince of his eyes contradicted itself. Stop me. Don't touch me. Doubt me. Doubt Kevin. Yes. No. Please.

Please.

His inchoate supplication drew her to him. He did not appear strong or dangerous now, but only needy, appalled by himself. Yet he was as irrefusable as ever. She touched her hand to his scruffy cheek; her arms hurt with the tenderness of her wish to hold him.

But she would not retreat from the commitments she had made, whatever their cost. Perhaps her years of medical training and self-abnegation had been nothing more than a way of running away from death; but the simple logic of that flight had taken her in the direction of life, for others if not for herself. And in the marrow of her bones she had experienced both the Sunbane and Andelain. The choice between them was as clear as Covenant's pain.

She had no answer for his appeal. Instead, she gave him one of her own. "Don't force me to do that." Her love was naked in her eyes. "Don't give up."

A spasm of grief or anger flinched across his face. His voice sank to a desert scraping in the back of his throat. "I wish I could make you understand." He spoke flatly, all inflection burned away. "He's gone too far. He can't get away with this. Maybe he isn't really sane anymore. He isn't going to get what he wants."

But his manner and his words held no comfort for her. He

might as well have announced to the Giants and Vain and the ravaged world that he still intended to surrender his ring.

Yet he remained strong enough for his purpose, in spite of little food, less rest, and the suffering of Andelain. Dourly, he faced the First and Pitchwife again as if he expected questions or protests. But the Swordmain held herself stern. Her husband did not look up from his flute.

To their silence, Covenant replied, "We need to go north for a while. Until we get to the river. That's our way into Mount Thunder."

Sighing, Pitchwife gained his feet. He held his flute in both hands. His gaze was focused on nothing as he snapped the small instrument in half.

With all his strength, he hurled the pieces toward the Hills.

Linden winced. An expostulation died on the First's lips. Covenant's shoulders hunched.

As grim as a cripple, Pitchwife raised his eyes to the Unbeliever. "Heed me well," he murmured clearly. "I doubt."

"Good!" Covenant rasped intensely. Then he started moving again, picking a path for himself among the boulders.

Linden followed with old cries beating against her heart. *Haven't you even got the guts to go on living? You never loved me anyway.* But she knew as surely as vision that he did love her. She had no means by which to measure what had happened to him in the Banefire. And Gibbon's voice answered her, taunting her with the truth. *Are you not evil?*

The foothills of Mount Thunder, ancient Gravin Threndor, were too rugged to bear much vegetation. And the light of the desert sun advanced rapidly past the peak now, wreaking dissolution on the ground's residual fertility. The company was hampered by strewn boulders and knuckled slopes, but not by the effects of the previous sun. Still the short journey toward the Soulsease was arduous. The sun's loathsome corruption seemed to parch away the last of Linden's strength. Heatwaves like precursors of hallucination tugged at the edges of her mind. A confrontation with the Despiser would at least put an end to this horror and rapine. One way or the other. As she panted at the hillsides, she found herself repeating the promise she had once made in Revelstone—the promise she had made and broken. *Never. Never again.* Whatever happened, she would not return to the Sunbane.

Because of her weakness, Covenant's exhaustion, and the difficulty of the terrain, the company did not reach the vicinity of the River until midmorning.

The way the hills baffled sound enabled her to catch a glimpse of the swift water before she heard it. Then she and her companions topped the last rise between them and the Soulsease; and the loud howl of its rush slapped at her. Narrowed by its stubborn granite channel, the river raced below her, white and writhing in despair toward its doom. And its doom towered over it, so massive and dire that the mountain filled all the east. Perhaps a league to Linden's right, the river flumed into the gullet of Mount Thunder and was swallowed away—ingested by the catacombs which mazed the hidden depths of the peak. When that water emerged again, on the Lower Land behind Gravin Threndor, it would be so polluted by the vileness of the Wightwarrens, so rank with the waste of charnals and breeding-dens, the spillage of forges and laboratories, the effluvium of corruption, that it would be called the Defiles Course—the source of Sarangrave Flat's peril and perversion.

For a crazy moment, Linden thought Covenant meant to ride that extreme current into the mountain. But then he pointed toward the bank directly below him; and she saw that a roadway had been cut into the foothills at some height above the River. The River itself was declining: six days had passed since the last sun of rain; and the desert sun was rapidly drinking away the water which Andelain still provided. But the markings on the channel's sheer walls showed that the Soulsease virtually never reached as high as the roadway.

Along this road in ages past, armies had marched out of Mount Thunder to attack the Land. Much of the surface was ruinous, cracked and gouged by time and the severe alternation of the Sunbane, slick with spray; but it was still traversable. And it led straight into the dark belly of the mountain.

Covenant gestured toward the place where the walls rose like cliffs to meet the sides of Mount Thunder. He had to shout to make himself heard, and his voice was veined with stress. "That's Treacher's Gorge! Where Foul betrayed Kevin and the Council openly for the first time! Before they knew what he was! The war that broke Kevin's heart started there!"

The First scanned the thrashing River, the increasing constriction of the precipitate walls, then raised her voice through the roar. "Earthfriend, you have said that the passages of this mountain are a maze! How then may we discover the lurking place of the Despiser?"

"We won't have to!" His shout sounded feverish. He looked as tense and strict and avid as he had when Linden had first met him—when he had slammed the door of his house against her. "Once we get in there, all we have to do is wander around until we run into his defenses. He'll take care of the rest. The only trick is to stay alive until we get to him!"

Abruptly, he turned to his companions. "You don't have to come! I'll be safe. He won't do anything to me until he has me in front of him." To Linden, he seemed to be saying the same things he had said on Haven Farm. *You don't know what's going on here. You couldn't possibly understand it. Go away. I don't need you.* "You don't need to risk it."

But the First was not troubled by such memories. She replied promptly, "Of what worth is safety to us here? The Earth itself is at risk. Hazard is our chosen work. How will we bear the songs which our people will sing of us, if we do not hold true to the Search? We will not part from you."

Covenant ducked his head as though he were ashamed or afraid. Perhaps he was remembering Saltheart Foamfollower. Yet his refusal or inability to meet Linden's gaze indicated to her that she had not misread him. He was still vainly trying to protect her, spare her the consequences of her choices—consequences she did not know how to measure. And striving also to prevent her from interfering with what he meant to do.

But he did not expose himself to what she would say if he addressed her directly. Instead, he muttered, "Then let's get going." The words were barely audible. "I don't know how much longer I can stand this."

Nodding readily, the First at once moved ahead of him toward an erosion gully which angled down to the roadway. With one hand, she gripped the hilt of her longsword. Like her companions, she had lost too much in this quest. She was a warrior and wanted to measure out the price in blows.

Covenant followed her stiffly. The only strength left in his limbs was the stubbornness of his will.

Linden started after him, then turned back to Pitchwife. He still stood on the rim of the hill, gazing down into the river's rush as if it would carry his heart away. Though he was half again as tall as Linden, his deformed spine and grotesque features made him appear old and frail. His mute aching was as tangible as tears. Because of it, she put everything else aside for a moment.

"He was telling the truth about that, anyway. He doesn't need you to fight for him. Not anymore." Pitchwife lifted his eyes like pleading to her. Fiercely, she went on, "And if he's wrong, I can stop him." That also was true: the Sunbane and Ravers and Andelain's hurt had made her capable of it. "The First is the one who needs you. She can't beat Foul with just a sword—but she's likely to try. Don't let her get herself killed." *Don't do that to yourself. Don't sacrifice her for me.*

His visage sharpened like a cry. His hands opened at his sides to show her and the desert sky that they were empty. Moisture blurred his gaze. For a moment, she feared he would say farewell to her; and hard grief clenched her throat. But then a fragmentary smile changed the meaning of his face.

"Linden Avery," he said clearly, "have I not affirmed and averred to all who would hear that you are well Chosen?"

Stooping toward her, he kissed her forehead. Then he hurried after the First and Covenant.

When she had wiped the tears from her cheeks, she followed him.

Vain trailed her with his habitual blankness. Yet she seemed to feel a hint of anticipation from him—an elusive tightening which he had not conveyed since the company had entered *Elemesnedene.*

Picking her way down the gully, she gained the rude shelf of the roadway and found her companions waiting for her. Pitchwife stood beside the First, reclaiming his place there; but both she and Covenant watched Linden. The First's regard was a compound of glad relief and uncertainty. She welcomed anything that eased her husband's unhappiness—but was unsure of its implications. Covenant's attitude was simpler. Leaning close to Linden, he whispered against the background of the throttled River, "I don't know what you said to him. But thanks."

She had no answer. Constantly, he foiled her expectations. When he appeared most destructive and unreachable, locked away in his deadly certainty, he showed flashes of poignant kindness, clear concern. Yet behind his empathy and courage lay his intended surrender, as indefeasible as despair. He contradicted himself at every turn. And how could she reply without telling him what she had promised?

But he did not appear to want an answer. Perhaps he understood her, knew that in her place he would have felt as she did. Or perhaps he was too weary and haunted to suffer questions or reconsider his purpose. He was starving for an end to his long pain. Almost immediately, he signaled his readiness to go on.

At once, the First started along the crude road toward the gullet of Mount Thunder.

With Pitchwife and then Vain behind her, Linden followed, stalking the stone, pursuing the Unbeliever to his crisis.

Below her, the Soulsease continued to shrink between its walls, consumed by the power of the Sunbane. The pitch of the rush changed as its roar softened toward sobbing. But she did not take her gaze from the backs of the First and Covenant, the rising sides of the gorge, the dark bulk of the mountain. Off that sun-ravaged crown had once come creatures of fire to rescue Thomas Covenant and the Lords from the armies of Drool Rockworm, the mad Cavewight. But those creatures had been called down by Law; and there was no more Law.

She had to concentrate to avoid the treachery of the road's surface. It was cracked and dangerous. Sections of the ledge were so tenuously held in place that her precipience felt them shift under her weight. Others had fallen into the Gorge long ago, leaving bitter scars where the road should have been. Only narrow rims remained to bear the company past the gaps. Linden feared them more on Covenant's behalf than on her own: his vertigo might make him fall. But he negotiated them without help, as if his fear of height were just one more part of himself that he had already given up. Only the strain burning in his muscles betrayed how close he came to panic.

Mount Thunder loomed into the sky. The desert sun scorched over the rocks, scouring them bare of spray. The noise of the Soulsease sounded increasingly like grief. In spite of her fatigue, Linden wanted to run—wanted to pitch herself into the mountain's darkness for no other reason than to get out from under the Sunbane. Out of daylight into the black catacombs, where so much power lurked and hungered.

Where no one else would be able to see what happened when the outer dark met the blackness within her and took possession.

She fought the logic of that outcome, wrestled to believe that she would find some other answer. But Covenant intended to give Lord Foul his ring. Where else could she find the force to stop him?

She had done the same thing once before, in a different way. Faced with her dying mother, the nightmare blackness had leaped up in her, taking command of her hands while her brain had detached itself to watch and wail. And the darkness had laughed like lust.

She had spent every day of every year of her adulthood fighting to suppress that avarice for death. But she knew of no other source from which she might obtain the sheer strength she would need to prevent Covenant from destruction.

And she had promised—

Treacher's Gorge narrowed and rose on either side. Mount Thunder vaulted above her like a tremendous cairn that marked the site of buried banes, immedicable despair. As the river's lamentation sank to a mere shout, the mountain opened its gullet in front of the company.

The First stopped there, glowering distrust into the tunnel that swallowed the Soulsease and the roadway. But she did not speak. Pitchwife unslung his diminished pack, took out his firepot and the last two fagots he had borne from Revelstone. One he slipped under his belt; the other he stirred into the firepot until the wood caught flame. The First took it from him, held it up as a torch. She drew her sword. Covenant's visage wore a look of nausea or dread; but he did not hesitate. When the First nodded, he started forward.

Pitchwife quickly repacked his supplies. Together, he and Linden followed his wife and Covenant out of the Gorge and the desert sun.

Vain came after them like a piece of whetted midnight, acute and imminent.

Linden's immediate reaction was one of relief. The First's torch hardly lit the wall on her right, the curved ceiling above her. It shed no light into the chasm beside the roadway. But to her any dark felt kinder than the sunlight. The peak's clenched granite reduced the number of directions from

which peril could come. And as Mount Thunder cut off the
sky, she heard the sound of the Soulsease more precisely.
The crevice drank the River like a plunge into the bowels of
the mountain, carrying the water down to its defilement. Such
things steadied her by requiring her to concentrate on them.

In a voice that echoed hoarsely, she warned her companions away from the increasing depth of the chasm. She
sounded close to hysteria; but she believed she was not. The
Giants had only two torches. The company would need her
special senses for guidance. She would be able to be of use
again.

But her relief was shortlived. She had gone no more than
fifty paces down the tunnel when she felt the ledge behind
her heave itself into rubble.

Pitchwife barked a warning. One of his long arms swept
her against the wall. The impact knocked the air from her
lungs. For an instant while her head reeled, she saw Vain
silhouetted against the daylight of the Gorge. He made no
effort to save himself.

Thundering like havoc, the fragments of the roadway bore
him down into the crevice.

Long tremors ran through the road, up the wall. Small
stones rained from the ceiling, pelted after the Demondim-
spawn like a scattering of hail. Linden's chest did not contain
enough air to cry out his name.

Torchlight splayed across her and Pitchwife. He tugged her
backward, kept her pressed to the wall. The First barred
Covenant's way. Sternness locked her face. Sputtering flames
reflected from his eyes. "Damnation," he muttered. "Damnation!" Little breaths like gasps slipped past Linden's teeth.

The torch and the glow of day beyond the tunnel lit Findail
as he melted out of the roadway, transforming himself from
stone to flesh as easily as thought.

He appeared to have become leaner, worn away by pain.
His cheeks were hollow. His yellow eyes had sunk into his
skull; their sockets were as livid as bruises. He was rife with
mortification or grief.

"You did that," Linden panted. "You're still trying to kill
him."

He did not meet her gaze. The arrogance of his people
was gone from him. "The Würd of the *Elohim* is strict and

costly." If he had raised his eyes to Linden's, she might have
thought he was asking for understanding or acceptance. "How
should it be otherwise? Are we not the heart of the Earth
in all things? Yet those who remain in the bliss and blessing
of *Elemesnedene* have been misled by their comfort. Because
the *clachan* is our home, we have considered that all questions
may be answered there. Yet it is not in *Elemesnedene* that
the truth lies, but rather in we who people the place. And
we have mistaken our Würd. Because we are the heart, we
have conceived that whatever we will must perforce transcend
all else.

"Therefore we do not question our withdrawal from the
wide Earth. We contemplate all else, yet give no name to what
we fear."

Then he did look up; and his voice took on the anger of
self-justification. "But I have witnessed that fear. Chant and
others have fallen to it. Infelice herself knows its touch. And
I have participated in the binding to doom of the Appointed.
I have felt the curse of Kastenessen upon my head." He was
ashamed of what he had done to Vain—and determined not
to regret it. "You have taught me to esteem you. You bear the
outcome of the Earth well. But my peril is thereby increased.

"I will not suffer that cost."

Folding his arms across his chest, he closed himself off
from interrogation.

In bafflement, Covenant turned to Linden. But she had no
explanation to offer. Her percipience had never been a match
for the *Elohim*. She had caught no glimpse of Findail until
he emerged from the roadway, still knew nothing about him
except that he was Earthpower incarnate, capable of taking
any form of life he wished. Altogether flexible. And dangerously unbound by scruple. His people had not hesitated to
efface Covenant's mind for their own inhuman reasons. More
than once, he had abandoned her and her companions to
death when he could have aided them.

His refusals seemed innumerable; and the memory of them
made her bitter. The pain of the tree he had slaughtered in
his last attempt on Vain's life came back to her. To Covenant,
she replied, "He's never told the truth before. Why should
he start now?"

Covenant frowned darkly. Although he had no cause to

trust Findail's people, he appeared strangely reluctant to judge them, as if instinctively he wanted to do them more justice than they had ever done him.

But there was nothing any of the company could do about Vain. The river-cleft was deep now—and growing sharply deeper as it advanced into the mountain. The sound of the water diminished steadily.

The First gestured with her touch. "We must hasten. Our light grows brief." The fagot she held was dry and brittle; already half of it had burned away. And Pitchwife had only one other brand.

Swearing under his breath, Covenant started on down the tunnel.

Linden was shivering. The stone piled imponderably around her felt cold and dire. Vain's fall repeated itself across her mind. Her breathing scraped in her throat. No one deserved to fall like that. In spite of Mount Thunder's chill atmosphere, sweat trickled uncertainly between her breasts.

But she followed Covenant and the First. Bracing herself on Pitchwife's bulky companionship, she moved along the roadway after the wavering torch. She stayed so close to the wall that it brushed her shoulder. Its hardness raised reminders of the hold of Revelstone and the dungeon of the Sandhold.

Findail walked behind her. His bare feet made no sound.

As the reflected light from the mouth of the gullet faded, the darkness thickened. Concentrated midnight seemed to flow up out of the crevice. Then a gradual bend in the wall cut off the outer world altogether. She felt that the doors of hope and possibility were being closed on all sides. The First's torch would not last much longer.

Yet her senses clung to the granite facts of the road and the tunnel. She could not see the rim of the chasm; but she knew where it was exactly. Pitchwife and Findail were also explicit in spite of the dark. When she focused her attention, she was able to read the surface of the ledge so clearly that she did not need to stumble. If she had possessed the power to repulse attack, she could have wandered the Wightwarrens in relative safety.

That realization steadied her. The inchoate dread gnawing at the edges of her courage receded.

The First's brand started to gutter.

Beyond it, Linden seemed to see an indefinable softening of

the midnight. For a few moments, she stared past the First
and Covenant. But her percipience did not extend so far.
Then, however, the Swordmain halted, lowered her torch; and
the glow ahead became more certain.

The First addressed Covenant or Linden. "What is the
cause of that light?"

"Warrenbridge," Covenant replied tightly. "The only way
into the Wightwarrens." His tone was complex with memories.
"Be careful. The last time I was here, it was guarded."

The leader of the Search nodded. Placing her feet softly,
she moved forward again. Covenant went with her.

Linden gripped her health-sense harder and followed.

Gradually, the light grew clear. It was a stiff, red-orange
color; and it shone along the ceiling, down the wall of the
tunnel. Soon Linden was able to see that the roadway took a
sharp turn to the right near the glow. At the same time, the
overhanging stone vaulted upward as if the tunnel opened into
a vast cavern. But the direct light was blocked by a tremendous boulder which stood like a door ajar across the
ledge. The chasm of the river vanished under that boulder.

Cautiously, the First crept to the edge of the stone and
peered beyond it.

For an instant, she went rigid with surprise. Then she
breathed a Giantish oath and strode out into the light.

Advancing behind Covenant, Linden found herself in a
high, bright cavity like an entryhall to the catacombs.

The floor was flat, worn smooth by millennia of use. Yet
it was impassable. The cleft passed behind the boulder, then
turned to cut directly through the cavern, disappearing finally
into the far wall. It was at least fifty feet wide, and there were
no other entrances to the cavity on this side. The only egress
lay beyond the crevice.

But in the center of the vault, a massive bridge of native
stone spanned the gulf. Warrenbridge. Covenant's memory
had not misled him.

The light came from the crown of the span. On either side
of it stood a tall stone pillar like a sentinel; and they shone
as if their essential rock were afire. They made the entire
cavern bright—too bright for any interloper to approach
Warrenbridge unseen.

For an instant, the light held Linden's attention. It reminded her of the hot lake of graveling in which she and the

company had once almost lost their lives. But these emanations were redder, angrier. They lit the entrance to the Wightwarrens as if no one could pass between them in hope or
peace.

But the chasm and the bridge and the light were not what
had surprised the First. With a wrench, Linden forced herself
to look across the vault.

Vain stood there, at the foot of Warrenbridge. He seemed
to be waiting for Covenant or Linden.

Near him on the stone sprawled two long-limbed forms.
They were dead. But they had not been dead long. The blood
in which they lay was still warm.

A clench of pain passed across Findail's visage and was
gone.

The First's torch sputtered close to her hand. She tossed
its useless butt into the chasm. Gripping her longsword in both
fists, she started onto the span.

"Wait!" Covenant's call was hoarse and urgent. At once,
the First froze. The tip of her blade searched the air for perils
she could not see.

Covenant wheeled toward Linden, his gaze as dark as
bloodshed. Trepidation came from him in fragments.

"The last time—it nearly killed me. Drool used those pillars—that rocklight—I thought I was going to lose my mind."

Drool Rockworm was the Cavewight who had recovered the
Staff of Law after the Ritual of Desecration. He had used it
to delve up the Illearth Stone from the roots of Mount Thunder. And when Covenant and the Lords had wrested the Staff
from Drool, they had succeeded only in giving the Illearth
Stone into Lord Foul's hold.

Linden's percipience scrambled into focus on the pillars.
She scrutinized them for implications of danger, studied the
air between them, the ancient stone of Warrenbridge. That
stone had been made as smooth as mendacity by centuries of
time, the pressure of numberless feet. But it posed no threat.
Rocklight shone like ire from the pillars, concealing nothing.

Slowly, she shook her head. "There's nothing there."

Covenant started to ask, "Are you—?" then bit down his
apprehension. Waving the First ahead, he ascended the span
as if Warrenbridge were crowded with vertigo.

At the apex, he flinched involuntarily; his arms flailed,
grasping for balance. But Linden caught hold of him. Pitch-

wife put his arms around the two of them. By degrees, Covenant found his way back to the still center of his certitude, the place where dizziness and panic whirled around him but did not touch him. In a moment, he was able to descend toward the First and Vain.

With the tip of her sword, the First prodded the bodies near the Demondim-spawn. Linden had never seen such creatures before. They had hands as wide and heavy as shovels, heads like battering rams, eyes without pupil or iris, glazed by death. The thinness of their trunks and limbs belied their evident strength. Yet they had not been strong enough to contend with Vain. He had broken both of them like dry wood.

"Cavewights," Covenant breathed. His voice rattled in his throat. "Foul must be using them for sentries. When Vain showed up, they probably tried to attack him."

"Is it possible"—the First's eyes glared in the rocklight—"that they contrived to send alarm of us ere they fell?"

"Possible?" growled Covenant. "The way our luck's going, can you think of any reason to believe they didn't?"

"It is certain." Findail's unexpected interpolation sent a strange shiver down Linden's spine. Covenant jerked his gaze to the Appointed. The First swallowed a jibe. But Findail did not hesitate. His grieving features were set. "Even now," he went on, "forewarning reaches the ears of the Despiser. He savors the fruition of his malign dreams." He spoke quietly; yet his voice made the air of the high vault ache. "Follow me. I will guide you along ways where his minions will not discover you. In that, at least, his intent will be foiled."

Passing through the company, he strode into the dark maze of the Wightwarrens. And as he walked the midnight stepped back from him. Beyond the reach of the rocklight, his outlines shone like the featureless lumination of *Elemesnedene.*

"*Damn* it!" Covenant spat. "Now he wants us to trust him."

The First gave a stern shrug. "What choice remains to us?" Her gaze trailed Findail down the tunnel. "One brand we have. Will you rather trust the mercy of this merciless bourne?"

At once, Linden said, "We don't need him. I can lead us. I don't need light."

Covenant scowled at her. "That's terrific. Where're you going to lead us? You don't have any idea where Foul is."

She started to retort, I can find him. The same way I found

Gibbon. All I need is a taste of him. But then she read him
more clearly. His anger was not directed at her. He was angry
because he knew he had no choice. And he was right. Until
she felt the Despiser's emanations and could fix her health-
sense on them, she had no effective guidance to offer.

Swallowing her vexation, she sighed, "I know. It was a bad
idea." Findail was receding from view; soon he would be out
of sight altogether. "Let's get going."

For a moment, Covenant faced her as though he wanted to
apologize and did not know how because he was unable to
gauge the spirit of her acquiescence. But his purpose still
drove him. Turning roughly, he started down the tunnel after
the Appointed.

The First joined him. Pitchwife gave Linden's shoulder a
quick clasp of comradeship, then urged her into motion.

Vain followed them as if he were in no danger at all.

The tunnel went straight for some distance; then side passages began to mark its walls. Glowing like an avatar of
moonlight, Findail took the first leftward way, moved into a
narrow corridor which had been cut so long ago that the rock
no longer seemed to remember the violence of formation. The
ceiling was low, forcing the Giants to stoop as the corridor
angled upward. Findail's illumination glimmered and sheened
on the walls. A vague sense of peril rose behind Linden like
a miasma. She guessed that more of the Despiser's creatures
had entered the tunnel which the company had just left. But
soon she reached a high, musty space like a disused mustering-
hall; and when she and her companions had crossed it to a
larger passage, her impression of danger faded.

More tunnels followed, most of them tending sharply downward. She did not know how the Appointed chose his route;
but he was sure of it. Perhaps he gained all the information he
needed from the mountain itself, as his people were said to
read the events of the outer Earth in the peaks and cols of
the Rawedge Rim which enclosed *Elemesnedene*. Whatever
his sources of knowledge, however, Linden sensed that he was
leading the company through delvings which were no longer
inhabited or active. They all smelled of abandonment, forgotten death—and somehow, obscurely, of ur-viles, as if this section of the catacombs had once been set apart for the products

of the Demondim. But they were gone now, perhaps forever. Linden caught no scent or sound of any life here.

No life except the breathing, dire existence of the mountain, the sentience too slow to be discerned, the intent so immemorially occluded and rigid that it was hidden from mortal perception. Linden felt she was wandering the vitals of an organism which surpassed her on every scale—and yet was too time-spanning and ponderous to defend itself against quick evil. Mount Thunder loathed the banes which inhabited it, the use to which its depths were put. Why else was there so much anger compressed in the gutrock? But the day when the mountain might react for its own cleansing was still centuries or millennia away.

The First's bulk blocked most of Findail's glow. But Linden did not need light to know that Vain was still behind her, or that Covenant was nearly prostrate on his feet, frail with exhaustion. Yet he appeared determined to continue until he dropped. For his sake, she called Findail to a halt. "We're killing ourselves like this." Her own knees trembled with strain; weariness throbbed in her temples. "We've got to rest."

Findail acceded with a shrug. They were in a rude chamber empty of everything except stale air and darkness. She half expected Covenant to protest; but he did not. Numbly, he dropped to the floor and leaned his fatigue against one wall.

Sighing to himself, Pitchwife rummaged through the packs for *diamondraught* and a meal. Liquor and food he doled out to his companions, sparing little for the future. The future of the Search would not be long, for good or ill.

Linden ate as much as she could stomach, but only took a sip of the *diamondraught* so that she would not be put to sleep. Then she turned her attention to Covenant.

He was shivering slightly. Findail's light made him look pallid and spectral, ashen-eyed, doomed. His body seemed to draw no sustenance from the food he had consumed. Even *diamondraught* had little effect on him. He looked like a man who was bleeding internally. On Kevin's Watch, he had healed the wound in his chest with wild magic. But no power could undo the blow which had pierced him back in the woods behind Haven Farm. Now his physical condition appeared to be merging with that of the body he had left behind, the torn flesh with the knife still protruding from its ribs.

He had told her this would happen.

But other signs were missing. He had no bruises to match the ones he had received when Joan had been wrested from him. And he still had his beard. She clung to those things because they seemed to mean that he was not yet about to die.

She nearly cried out when he raised the knife he had brought from Revelstone and asked Pitchwife for water.

Without question, Pitchwife poured the last of the company's water into a bowl and handed it to the Unbeliever.

Awkwardly, Covenant wet his beard, then set the knife to his throat. His hands trembled as if he were appalled. Yet by his own choice he conformed himself to the image of his death.

Linden struggled to keep herself from railing at his self-abnegation, the surrender it implied. He behaved as if he had indeed given himself up to despair. It was unbearable. But the sight of him was too poignant; she could not accuse or blame him. Wrestling down her grief, she said in a voice that still sounded like bereavement, "You know, that beard doesn't look so bad on you. I'm starting to like it." Pleading with him.

His eyes were closed as if in fear of the moment when the blade would slice into his skin, mishandled by his numb fingers. Yet with every stroke of the knife his hands grew calmer.

"I did this the last time I was here. An ur-vile knocked me off a ledge. Away from everyone else. I was alone. So scared I couldn't even scream. But shaving helped. If you'd seen me, you would've thought I was trying to cut my throat in simple terror. But it helps." Somehow, he avoided nicking himself. The blade he used was so sharp that it left his skin clean. "It takes the place of courage."

Then he was done. Putting the knife back under his belt, he looked at Linden as if he knew exactly what she had been trying to say to him. "I don't like it." His purpose was in his voice, as hard and certain as his ring. "But it's better to choose your own risks. Instead of just trying to survive the ones you can't get out of."

Linden hugged her heart and made no attempt to answer him. His face was raw—but it was still free of bruises. She could still hope.

Gradually, he recovered a little strength. He needed far more rest than he allowed himself; but he was noticeably more stable as he climbed erect and announced his readiness.

The First joined him without hesitation. But Pitchwife looked toward Linden as if he wanted confirmation from her. She saw in his gaze that he was prepared to find some way to delay the company on Covenant's behalf if she believed it necessary.

The question searched her; but she met it by rising to her feet. If Covenant were exhausted, he would be more easily prevented from destruction.

At once, her thoughts shamed her. Even now—when he had just given her a demonstration of his deliberate acquiescence to death, as if he wanted her to be sure that Kevin had told her the truth—she felt he deserved something better than the promises she had made against him.

Mutely, Findail bore his light into the next passage. The First shouldered her share of the company's small supplies, drew her longsword. Muttering to himself, Pitchwife joined her. Vain gazed absently into the unmitigated dark of the catacombs. In single file, the questors followed the Appointed of the *Elohim* onward.

Still his route tended generally downward, deeper by irregular stages and increments toward the clenched roots of Mount Thunder; and as the company descended, the character of the tunnels changed. They became more ragged and ruinous. Broken gaps appeared in the walls, and from the voids beyond them came dank exhalations, distant groaning, cold sweat. Unseen denizens slithered away to their barrows. Water oozed through cracks in the gutrock and dripped like slow corrosion. Strange boiling sounds rose and then receded.

With a Giant's unfear of stone and mountains, Pitchwife took a rock as large as his fist and tossed it into one of the gaps. For a long time, echoes replied like the distant labor of anvils.

The strain of the descent made Linden's thighs ache and quiver.

Later, she did hear anvils, the faint, metallic clatter of hammers. And the thud of bellows—the warm, dry gusts of exhaust from forges. The company was nearing the working heart of the Wightwarrens. Sourceless sounds made her skin crawl. But Findail did not hesitate or waver; and gradually the noise and effort in the air lessened. Moiling and sulfur filled the tunnel as if it were a ventilation shaft for a pit of brimstone. Then they, too, faded.

The tremendous weight of the mountain impending over her made Linden stoop. It was too heavy for her. Everywhere around her was knuckled stone and darkness. Findail's light was ghostly, not to be trusted. Somewhere outside Mount Thunder, the day was ending—or had already ended, already given the Land its only relief from the Sunbane. But the things which soughed and whined through the catacombs knew no relief. She felt the old protestations of the rock like the far-off moaning of the damned. The air felt as cold, worn, and dead as a gravestone. Lord Foul had chosen an apt demesne: only mad creatures and evil could live in the Wightwarrens.

Then, abruptly, the wrought passages through which Findail had been traveling changed. The tunnel narrowed, became a rough crevice with a roof beyond the reach of Linden's percipience. After some distance, the crevice ended at the rim of a wide, deep pit. And from the pit arose the fetor of a charnal.

The stench made Linden gag. Covenant could barely stand it. But Findail went right to the edge of the pit, to a cut stair which ascended the wall directly above the rank abysm. Covenant fought himself to follow; but before he had climbed a dozen steps he slumped against the wall. Linden felt nausea and vertigo gibbering in his muscles.

Sheathing her blade, the First lifted him in her arms, bore him upward as swiftly as Findail was willing to go.

Cramps knotted Linden's guts. The stench heaved in her. The stair stretched beyond comprehension above her; she did not know how to attempt it. But the gap between her and the light—between her and Covenant—was increasing at every moment. Fiercely, she turned her percipience on herself, pulled the cramps out of her muscles. Then she forced herself upward.

The fetor called out to her like the Sunbane, urged her to surrender to it—surrender to the darkness which lurked hungrily within her and everywhere else as well, unanswerable and growing toward completion with every intaken breath. If she let go now, she would be as strong as a Raver before she hit bottom; and then no ordinary death could touch her. Yet she clung to the rough treads with her hands, thrust at them with her legs. Covenant was above her. Perhaps he was already safe. And she had learned how to be stubborn. The mouth of the old man whose life she had saved on Haven

Farm had been as foul as this; but she had borne that putrid halitus in order to fight for his survival. Though her guts squirmed, her throat retched, she fought her way to the top of the stair and the well.

There she found Findail, the First, and Covenant. And light —a different light than the Appointed emitted. Reflecting faintly from the passage behind him, it was the orange-red color of rocklight. And it was full of soft, hot boiling, slow splashes. A sulfurous exudation took the stench from the air.

Pitchwife finished the ascent with Vain behind him. Linden looked at Covenant. His face was waxen, slick with sweat; vertigo and sickness glazed his eyes. She turned to the First and Findail to demand another rest.

The *Elohim* forestalled her. His gaze was shrouded, concealing his thoughts. "Now for a space we must travel a common roadway of the Wightwarrens." Rocklight limned his shoulders. "It is open to us at present—but shortly it will be peopled again, and our way closed. We must not halt here."

Linden wanted to protest in simple frustration and helplessness. Roughly, she asked the First, "How much more do you think he can take?"

The Giant shrugged. She did not meet Linden's glare. Her efforts to refuse doubt left little room for compromise. "If he falters, I will carry him."

At once, Findail turned and started down the passage.

Before Linden could object, Covenant shambled after the Appointed. The First moved protectively ahead of the Unbeliever.

Pitchwife faced Linden with a grimace of wry fatigue. "She is my wife," he murmured, "and I love her sorely. Yet she surpasses me. Were I formed as other Giants, I would belabor her insensate rather than suffer this extremity." He clearly did not mean what he was saying; he spoke only to comfort Linden.

But she was beyond comfort. Fetor and brimstone, exhaustion and peril pushed her to the fringes of her self-control. Fuming futilely, she coerced her unsteady limbs into motion.

The passage soon became a warren of corridors; but Findail threaded them unerringly toward the source of the light. The air grew noticeably warmer; it was becoming hot. The boiling sounds increased, took on a subterranean force which throbbed irrhythmically in Linden's lungs.

Then the company gained a tunnel as broad as a road; and the rocklight flared brighter. The stone thrummed with bottomless seething. Ahead of Findail, the left wall dropped away; acrid heat rose from that side. It seemed to suck the air out of Linden's chest, tug her forward. Findail led the company briskly into the light.

The road passed along the rim of a huge abyss. Its sheer walls were stark with rocklight; it blazed heat and sulfur.

At the bottom of the gulf burned a lake of magma.

Its boiling made the gutrock shiver. Tremendous spouts reached massively toward the ceiling, then collapsed under their own weight, spattering the walls with a violence that melted and reformed the sides.

Findail strode down the roadway as if the abyss did not concern him. But Covenant moved slowly, crouching close to the outer wall. The rocklight shone garishly across his raw face, made him appear lunatic with fear and yearning for immolation. Linden followed almost on his heels so that she would be near if he needed her. They were halfway around the mouth of the gulf before she felt his emanations clearly enough to realize that his apprehension was not the simple dread of vertigo and heat. He recognized this place: memories beat about his head like dark wings. He knew that this road led to the Despiser.

Linden dogged his steps and raged uselessly to herself. He was in no shape to confront Lord Foul. No condition. She no longer cared that his weakness might lessen the difficulty of her own responsibilities. She did not want her lot eased. She wanted him whole and strong and victorious, as he deserved to be. This exhausting rush to doom was folly, madness.

Gasping at the heat, he reached the far side of the abyss, moved two steps into the passage, and sagged to the floor. Linden put her arms around him, trying to steady herself as well as him. The molten passion of the lake burned at her back. Pitchwife was nearly past the rim. Vain was several paces behind.

"You must now be swift," Findail said. He sounded strangely urgent. "There are Cavewights nigh."

Without warning, he sped past the companions, flashed back into the rocklight like a striking condor.

As he hurtled down the roadway, his form melted out of humanness and assumed the shape of a Sandgorgon.

Fatal as a bludgeon, he crashed headlong against the Demondim-spawn.

Vain made no effort to evade the impact. Yet he could not withstand it. Findail was Earthpower incarnate. The shock of collision made the road lurch, sent tremors like wailing through the stone. Vain had proved himself stronger than Giants or storms, impervious to spears and the na-Mhoram's *Grim*. He had felt the power of the Worm of the World's End and had survived, though that touch had cost him the use of one arm. He had escaped alone from *Elemesnedene* and all the *Elohim*. But Findail hit him with such concentrated might that he was driven backward.

Two steps. Three. To the last edge of the rim.

"Vain!" Covenant thrashed in Linden's grasp. Frenzy almost made him strong enough to break away from her. *"Vain!"*

Instinctively, Linden fought him, held him.

Impelled by Covenant's fear, the First charged past Pitchwife after the Appointed.

Vain caught his balance on the lip of the abyss. His black eyes were vivid with intensity. A grin of relish sharpened his immaculate features. The iron heels of the Staff of Law gleamed dully in the hot rocklight.

He did not glance away from Findail. But his good arm made a warding gesture that knocked the First backward, stretched her at her husband's feet, out of danger.

"Fall!" the Appointed raged. His fists hammered the air. The rock under Vain's feet ruptured in splinters. "Fall and die!"

The Demondim-spawn fell. With the slowness of nightmare, he dropped straight into the abyss.

At the same instant, his dead arm lashed out, struck like a snake. His right hand closed on Findail's forearm. The Appointed was pulled after him over the edge.

Rebounding from the wall, they tumbled together toward the center of the lake. Covenant's cry echoed after them, inarticulate and wild.

Findail could not break Vain's grip.

He was *Elohim*, capable of taking any form of the living Earth. He dissolved himself and became an eagle, pounded the air with his wings to escape the spouting magma. But Vain clung to one of his legs and was borne upward.

Instantly, Findail transformed himself to water. The heat threw him in vapor and agony toward the ceiling. But Vain clutched a handful of essential moisture and drew the Appointed back to him.

Swifter than panic, Findail became a Giant with a great-sword in both fists. He hacked savagely at Vain's wrist. But Vain only clenched his grip and let the blade glance off his iron band.

They were so close to the lava that Linden could barely see them through the blaze. In desperation, Findail took the shape of a sail and rode the heat upward again. But Vain still held him in an unbreakable grasp.

And before he rose high enough, a spout climbed like a tower toward him. He tried to evade it by veering; but he was too late. Magma took both *Elohim* and Demondim-spawn and snatched them down into the lake.

Linden hugged Covenant as if she shared his cries.

He was no longer struggling. "You don't understand!" he gasped. All the strength had gone out of him. "That's the place. Where the ur-viles got rid of their failures. When something they made didn't work, they threw it down there. That's why Findail—" The words seized in his throat.

Why Findail had made his final attempt upon the Demondim-spawn here. Even Vain could not hope to come back from that fall.

Dear Christ! She did not understand how the *Elohim* saw such an extravagant threat in one lone creation of the ur-viles. Vain had bowed to her once—and had never acknowledged her again. He had saved her life—and had refused to save it. And after all this time and distance and peril, he was lost before he found what he sought. Before she understood—

He had gripped Findail with the hand that hung from his wooden forearm.

Other perceptions demanded her attention, but she was slow to notice them. She had not heeded the Appointed's warning. Too late, she sensed movement in the passage which had led the company to this abyss.

Along the rim of the pit, a party of Cavewights charged into the rocklight.

At least a score of them. Upright on their long limbs, they were almost as tall as Pitchwife. They ran with an exaggerated, jerky awkwardness, like stick-figures; but their strength was unmistakable: they were the delvers of the Wightwarrens. The red heat of lava burned in their eyes. Most of them were armed with truncheons; the rest carried battle-axes with wicked blades.

Still half stunned by the force of Vain's blow, the First reeled to her feet. For an instant, she wavered. But the company's need galvanized her. Her longsword flashed in readiness. Roaring, "Flee!" she faced the onset of the Cavewights.

Covenant made no effort to move. The people he loved were in danger, and he had the power to protect them—power he dared not use. Linden read his plight immediately. The exertion of will which held back the wild magic took all his strength.

She fought herself into motion. Summoning her resolve, she began to wrestle him down the tunnel.

He seemed weightless, almost abject. Yet his very slackness hampered her. Her progress was fatally slow.

Then Pitchwife caught up with her. He started to take Covenant from her.

The clangor of battle echoed along the passage. Linden spun and saw the First fighting for her life.

She was a Swordmain, an artist of combat. Her glaive flayed about her, at once feral and precise; rocklight flared in splinters off the swift iron. Blood spattered from her attackers as if by incantation rather than violence, her blade the wand or scepter by which she wrought her theurgy.

But the roadway was too wide to constrict the Cavewights. Their reach was as great as hers. And they were born to contend with stone; their blows had the force of granite. Most of her effort went to parry clubs which would have shattered her arms. Step by step, she was driven backward.

She stumbled slightly on the uneven surface, and a truncheon flicked past her. On her left temple, a bloody welt seemed to appear without transition. The Cavewight that hit her pitched into the abyss, clutching his slashed chest. But more creatures crowded after her.

Linden looked at Pitchwife. He was being torn apart by conflicting needs. His eyes ached whitely, desperate and suppliant. He had offered her his life. Like Mistweave.

She could not bear it. He deserved better. "Help the First!" she barked at him. "I'll take care of Covenant!"

Pitchwife was too frantic to hesitate. Releasing the Unbeliever, he sped to the aid of his wife.

Linden grabbed Covenant by the shoulders, shook him
fiercely. "Come on!" she raged into his raw visage. "For God's
sake!"

His struggle was terrible to behold. He could have effaced
the Cavewights with a simple thought—and brought down the
Arch of Time, or desecrated it with venom. He was willing to
sacrifice himself. But his friends! Their peril rent at him. For
the space of one heartbeat, she thought he would destroy
everything to save the First and Pitchwife. So that they would
not die like Foamfollower for him.

Yet he withheld—clamped his ripped and wailing spirit in
a restraint as inhuman as his purpose. His features hardened;
his gaze became bleak and desolate, like the Land under the
scourge of the Sunbane. "You're right," he muttered softly.
"This is pathetic."

Straightening his back, he started down the tunnel.

She clinched his numb half-hand and fled with him into
darkness. Cries and blows shouted after them, echoed and
were swallowed by the Wightwarrens.

As the reflected rocklight faded, they reached an intersection. Covenant veered instinctively to the right; but she took
the leftward turning because it felt less traveled. Almost at
once, she regretted her choice. It did not lead away from the
light. Instead, it opened into a wide chamber with fissures
along one side that admitted the shining of the molten lake.
Sulfur and heat clogged the air. Two more tunnels gave access
to the chamber; but they did not draw off the accumulated
reek.

The roadway along the rim of the abyss was visible through
the fissures. This chamber had probably been intended to allow Mount Thunder's denizens to watch the road without being seen.

The First and Pitchwife were no longer upon the rim. They
had retreated into the tunnel after Linden and Covenant. Or
they had fallen.

Linden's senses shrilled an alarm. Too late: always too late.
Bitterly, she wheeled to face the Cavewights that thronged into
the chamber from all three entrances.

She and her companions must have been spotted from this
covert when they first made their way past the abyss. And the

brief time they had spent watching Vain and Findail had given the Cavewights opportunity to spring this trap.

In the tunnel Linden and Covenant had used, the First and Pitchwife appeared, battling tremendously to reach their friends. But most of the Cavewights hurried to block the Giants' way. The Swordmain and her husband were beaten back.

Pitchwife's inchoate cry wrung Linden's heart. Then he and the First were forced out of sight. Cavewights rushed in pursuit.

Brandishing cudgels and axes, the rest of the creatures advanced on Covenant and Linden.

He thrust her behind him, took a step forward. Rocklight limned his desperate shoulders. "I'm the one you want." His voice was taut with suppression and wild magic. "I'll go with you. Leave her alone."

Rapt and grim, the Cavewights gave no sign that they heard him. Their eyes smoldered.

"If you hurt her," he gritted, "I'll tear you apart."

One of them grabbed him, manacled both his wrists in a huge fist. Another raised his club and leveled a crushing blow at Linden's head.

She ducked. The truncheon whipped through her hair, almost touched her skull. Launching herself from the wall, she dodged toward Covenant.

The Cavewights seemed slow, awkward. For a moment, they did not catch her.

Somehow, Covenant twisted his wrists free. He snatched his knife from his belt, began slashing frenetically about him. A Cavewight howled, hopped back. But the blade was deep in the creature's ribs, and Covenant's half-hand failed of its grip; the knife was ripped from him.

Weaponless, he spun toward Linden. His face stretched as if he wanted to cry out, *Forgive*—!

The Cavewights surrounded him. They did not use their cudgels or axes: apparently, they wanted him alive. With their fists, they beat him until he fell.

Linden tried to reach him. She was avid for power, futile without it. Her arms and legs were useless against the Cavewights. They laughed coarsely at her struggles. Wildly, she groped for Covenant's ring with her health-sense, tried to take hold of it. The infernal air choked her lungs. Bottomless and hungry through the fissures came the boiling of the molten lake. Vain and Findail had fallen. The First and Pitchwife were lost. Covenant lay like a sacrifice on the stone. She had nothing left.

She was still groping when a blow came down gleefully on the bone behind her left ear. At once, the world turned over and sprawled into darkness.

EIGHTEEN: No Other Way

THOMAS Covenant lay face down on the floor. It pressed like flat stone against his battered cheek. Bruises malformed the bones of his visage. Though he wanted nothing but peace and salvation, he had become what he was by violence—the consequences of his own acts. From somewhere in the distance arose a throaty murmuring, incessant and dire, like a litany of invocation, dozens of voices repeating the same word or name softly, but with different cadences, at varying speeds. They were still around him, the people who had come to bereave him. They were taunting his failure.

Joan was gone.

Perhaps he should have moved, rolled over, done something to soften the pain. But the effort was beyond him. All his strength was sand and ashes. And he had never been physically strong. They had taken her from him without any trouble at all. It was strange, he reflected abstractly, that someone who had as little to brag of as he did spent so much time trying to pretend he was immortal. He should have known better. God knew he had been given every conceivable opportunity to outgrow his arrogance.

Real heroes were not arrogant. Who could have called

Berek arrogant? Or Mhoram? Foamfollower? The list went on and on, all of them humble. Even Hile Troy had finally given up his pride. Only people like Covenant himself were arrogant enough to believe that the outcome of the Earth depended on their purblind and fallible choices. Only people like himself. And Lord Foul. Those who were capable of Despite and chose to refuse it. And those who did not. Linden had told him any number of times that he was arrogant.

That was why he had to defeat Lord Foul—why the task devolved on him alone.

Any minute now, he told himself. Any minute now he was going to get up from the floor of his house and go exchange himself for Joan. He had put it off long enough. *She* was not arrogant—not really. She did not deserve what had happened to her. She had simply never been able to forgive herself for her weaknesses, her limitations.

Then he wanted to laugh. It would have done him a world of good to laugh. He was not so different from Joan after all. The only real difference was that he had been summoned to the Land while it was still able to heal him—and while he was still able to know what that meant. He was sane—if he *was* sane—by grace, not by virtue.

In a sense, she actually was arrogant. She placed too much importance on her own faults and failures. She had never learned to let them go.

He had never learned that lesson either. But he was trying. Dear God, he was trying. Any minute now, he was going to take her place in Lord Foul's fire. He was going to let everything go.

But somehow the floor did not feel right. The murmurous invocation that filled his ears and his lungs and his bones called on a name that did not sound like the Despiser's. It perplexed him, seemed to make breathing difficult. He had forgotten something.

Wearily, he opened his eyes, blinked at the blurring of his vision, and remembered where he was.

Then he thought that surely his heart would fail. His bruises throbbed in his skull. He had received them from Cavewights, not from Joan's captors. He did not have long to live.

He lay near the center of a large cave with rough walls and a ragged ceiling. The air smelled thickly of rocklight,

which burned from special stones set into the walls at careless
intervals. The cave was crudely oval in shape; it narrowed at
both ends to dark, unattainable tunnels. The odor of the rocklight was tinged with a scent of ancient moldering—rot so old
that it had become almost clean again.

It came from a large, high mound nearby. The heap looked
like a barrow, as if something revered had been buried there.
But it was composed entirely of bones. Thousands of skeletons
piled in one place. Most of them had been set there so long
ago that they had decomposed to fine gray dust, no longer of
interest even to maggots. But the top of the mound was more
recent. None of the skeletons were whole: all had been either
broken in death or dismembered afterward. Even the newer
ones had been cleaned of flesh. However, a few of them still
oozed from the marrow.

They were not human bones, or ur-vile. Cavewight, then.
Apparently, the creatures that the First and Pitchwife had
slain had already been added to the mound.

The murmuring went on without let, as if dozens or hundreds of predators were growling to themselves. He felt that
sound like the touch of panic in his vitals. Some name was
being repeated continuously, whispered or muttered at every
pitch and pace; but he could not distinguish it. Heat and
sound and rocklight squeezed sweat from the sore bones of
his head.

He was surrounded by Cavewights. Most of them squatted
near the walls, their knees jutting at their ears, their hot eyes
glowing. Others appeared to be dancing about the mound,
storklike and graceless on their long legs. Their hands attacked the air like spades. They all murmured and murmured,
incantatory and hypnotic. He had no idea what they were
saying, or how much longer he would be lulled, snared.

He was afraid—so afraid that his fear became a kind of
lucidity. Not afraid for himself. He had met that particular
terror in the Banefire and burned it to purity. These creatures
were only Cavewights, the weak-minded and malleable chil-
dren of Mount Thunder's gutrock, and Lord Foul had mastered them long ago. They could hardly hope to come between
Covenant and the Despiser. Though the way to it was hard,
his purpose was safe.

But in a small clear space against one wall sat Linden. He

saw her with the precision of his fear. Her right shoulder
leaned on the stone. With her arms, she hugged her knees to
her chest like a lorn child. Her head was bowed; her hair had
fallen forward, hiding her face. But the side of her neck was
bare. It gleamed, pale and vulnerable, in the red-orange illumination.

Black against the pallor, dried blood marked her skin. It
led in a crusted trail from behind her left ear down to the
collar of her shirt.

She, too—! A tremor of grief went through him. She, too,
had been made to match the physical condition of the body
she had left behind in the woods behind Haven Farm.

They did not have much time left.

He would have cried out, if he had possessed the strength.
Not much time—and to spend it like this! He wanted to hold
her in his arms, make her understand that he loved her—that
no death or risk of ruin could desecrate what she meant to
him. Lena had once tried to comfort him by singing, *The soul
in which the flower grows survives.* He wanted—

But perhaps the blow she had been struck had been harder
than either of them had realized, and she also was about to
die. Killed like Seadreamer because she had tried to save him.
And even if she did not die, she would believe that she had
lost him to despair. In Andelain, Elena had told him to *Care
for her. So that in the end she may heal us all.* He had failed
at that as at so many other things.

Linden. He tried to say her name, but no sound came. A
spasm of remorse twisted his face, made his bruises throb.
Ignoring the pain, the fathomless ache of his exhaustion, he
levered his elbows under him and strove to pry his weakness
off the stone.

A rough kick pitched him onto his back, closer to the
mound of bones. Gasping, he looked up into the leer of a
Cavewight.

"Be still, accursed!" the creature spat. "Punishment comes.
Punishment and apocalypse! Do not hasten it."

Cavorting grotesquely on his gangly limbs, he resumed his
muttering and danced away.

Covenant wrestled for breath and squirmed onto his side to
look toward Linden again.

She was facing him now, had turned toward him when the

Cavewight spoke. Her visage was empty of blood, of hope. The gaze she cast at him was stark with abuse and dumb pleading. Her hands clasped each other uselessly. Her eyes seemed as dark and hollow as wounds.

She must have looked like that when she was a child, locked in the attic with her father while he died.

He fought for his voice, croaked her name through the manifold invocation of the Cavewights. But she did not appear to hear him. Slowly, she dropped her head, lowered her gaze to the failure of her hands.

He could not go to her. He hardly knew where he might find enough strength to stand. And the Cavewights would not let him move. He had no way to combat them except with his ring—the wild magic he could not use. He and she were prisoners completely. And there was no name that either of them might call upon for rescue.

No name except the Despiser's.

Covenant hoped like madness that Lord Foul would act quickly.

But perhaps Lord Foul would not act. Perhaps he permitted the Cavewights to work their will, hoping that Covenant would once again be forced to power. Perhaps he did not understand—was incapable of understanding—the certainty of Covenant's refusal.

The throaty chant of the Cavewights was changing: the incessant various repetitions were shifting toward unison. One creature started a slightly sharper inflection, a more specific cadence; and his immediate neighbors fell into rhythm with him. Cavewight by Cavewight, the unison spread until the invoked name took Covenant by surprise, jolted alarm through him.

He knew that name.

Drool Rockworm.

More than three millennia ago, Drool Rockworm of the Cavewights had recovered the lost Staff of Law—and had conceived a desire to rule the Earth. But he had been too unskilled in lore to master what he had found. In seduction or folly, he had turned to the Despiser for knowledge. And Lord Foul had used the Cavewight for his own purposes.

Drool Rockworm.

First he had persuaded Drool to summon Covenant, luring

the Cavewight with promises of white gold. Then he had snatched Covenant away, sent the Unbeliever instead to the Council of Lords. And the Lords had responded by challenging Drool's power. Sneaking into the Wightwarrens, they had taken the Staff from him, had called down the Fire-Lions of Mount Thunder to destroy him.

Thus armed, they had thought themselves victorious. But they had only played into the Despiser's hands. They had rid him of Drool, thereby giving him access to the terrible bane he desired—the Illearth Stone. And from that time forward the Cavewights had been forced to serve him like puppets.

Drool Rockworm.

The name vibrated like acid in the air. The rocklight throbbed. All the Cavewights held themselves still. Their laval eyes focused on what they were invoking.

Beside Covenant, an eerie glow began to leak from the mound of bones. Sick red flames licked like swampfire around the pile. Fragments of bone seemed to waver and melt as if they were passing into hallucination.

Suddenly, he no longer believed that these creatures served the Despiser.

Drool Rockworm!

"Covenant." Linden's voice reached between the beats of the name. She had come out of herself, drawn by what the Cavewights were doing. "There's something—" Fiercely, she struggled to master her despair. "They're bringing it to life."

Covenant winced in dismay. But he did not doubt her. The Law that protected the living had been broken. Any horror might now be summoned past the barrier of death, given the will—and the power. The mound squirmed with fires and gleamings like a monstrous cocoon, decay and dust in the throes of birth.

Then one of the Cavewights moved. He strode across the chant toward Covenant. "Rise, accursed," he demanded. His eyes were as feral as his grin. "Rise for blood and torment."

Covenant stared whitely up at him, did not obey.

"Rise!" the creature raged. With one spatulate hand, he grabbed Covenant's arm and nearly dislocated it yanking him to his feet.

Covenant bit down panic and pain. "You're going to regret this!" He had to shout to make himself heard. The invocation pounded in his chest. "Foul wants me! Do you think you can defy him and get away with it?"

"Ha!" barked the Cavewight as if he were close to ecstasy. "We are too wily! He does not know us. We have learned. Learned. Him so wise." For an instant, all the voices shared his contempt. *Drool Rockworm!* "He is blind. Believes we have not found you." The creature spat wildness instead of laughter.

Then he wrenched Covenant around to face the mound. Linden groaned Covenant's name. He heard a thud as one of the creatures silenced her. His arm was gripped by fingers that knew how to break stone.

Flames began to writhe like ghouls across the mound, casting anguish toward the roof of the cave.

"Witness!" the Cavewight grated. "The Wightbarrow!"

The invocation took on a timbre of lust.

"We have served and served. Forever we have served. Chattel. Foder. Sacrifice. And no reward. Do this. Do that. Dig. Run. Die. No reward. None!

"Now he pays. Punishment and *apocalypse!*"

The Cavewights' virulence staggered Covenant. The muscles of his arm were being crushed. But he shut his mind to everything else. Groping for a way to save Linden's life if not his own, he protested hoarsely, "How? He's the Despiser! He'll tear your hearts out!"

But the Cavewights were beyond fear. "Witness!" Covenant's captor repeated. "See it. Fire. Life! The Wightbarrow of Drool Rockworm!"

Drool Rockworm, hammered the chant. *Drool Rockworm!*

"From the dead. We have learned. Bloodshed. Sunbane. Law broken. The blood of the accursed!" He almost capered in his exultation. "You!"

His free hand clasped a long spike of rock like a dagger.

In litany, he shouted, "Blood brings power! Power brings life! Drool Rockworm rises! Drool takes ring! Ring crushes Despiser! Cavewights are free! Punishment and apocalypse!"

Brandishing his spike at Covenant's face, he added, "Soon. You are the accursed. Bringer of ruin. Your blood shed upon the Wightbarrow." The side of the spike stroked Covenant's stiff cheek. "Soon."

Covenant heard Linden pant as she struggled for breath,

"Bones—" He winced, expecting her to be hit again. But still she tried to make him hear her. "The bones—"

Her voice was congested with effort and intention; but he had no idea what she meant.

The flames worming through the mound made his skin crawl; yet he could not look away from them. Perhaps everything he had decided or understood was false, Foul-begotten. Perhaps the Banefire had been too essentially corrupt to give him any kind of trustworthy *caamora*. How could he tell? He could not *see*.

The pain in his arm made his head reel. The rocklight seemed to yell orange-red heat, stoking the fire in the Wight-barrow. He had lost the First and Pitchwife and Vain, had lost Andelain itself. Now he was about to lose his life and Linden and everything because there was no middle ground, no wild magic without ruin. She was whispering his name, but it no longer made any difference.

His balance drifted, and he found himself staring emptily at the stone on which he barely stood. It was the only part of the floor that had been purposefully shaped. The Cavewight had placed him in the center of a round depression like a basin. Its shallow sides had been rubbed smooth and polished until they reflected rocklight around him like burnished metal.

From between his feet, a narrow trough led straight under the mound. A trough to channel his blood toward what remained of Drool Rockworm's bones. Fire rose hungrily toward the ceiling.

Abruptly, the invocation was cut off, slashed out of the air as if by the stroke of a blade. Its sudden cessation seemed to leave him deaf. He jerked up his head.

The spike was poised to strike like a fang at the middle of his chest. He planted his feet, braced himself to try to twist away, make one last effort for life.

But the blow did not fall. The Cavewight was not looking at him. None of the creatures were looking at him. Around the cave, they surged upright in outrage and fear.

An instant later, he recovered his hearing as the clamor of battle resounded past the Wightbarrow.

Into the cave charged the First and Pitchwife.

They were alone; but they attacked as if they were as potent as an army.

Surprise made them momentarily irresistible. She was
battered and weary; but her longsword flashed in her hands
like red lightning, hit with the force of thunder. The Cavewights went down before her like wheat in a storm. Pitchwife
followed at her back with a battle-axe in each hand and
fought as if he were not wounded and scarcely able to draw
breath. Bright galls scored her sark where the mail had
deflected blows; his dripped blood where cudgels had crushed
it into his flesh. Exertion sheened their faces and limbs.

The Cavewights moiled against them in frenzy.

The creatures were too frantic to fight effectively. They
hampered each other, blocked their own efforts. The First
and Pitchwife were halfway to the Wightbarrow before the
sheer pressure of numbers stopped them.

But there the impetus of combat shifted. Desperation
rallied the Cavewights. And the widening of the cave allowed
the Giants to be surrounded, assailed from all sides. Their
attempted rescue was valiant and doomed. In moments, they
would be overwhelmed.

Sensing their opportunity, the creatures became less wild.
Their mountain-delving strength dealt out blows which forced
the First and Pitchwife back-to-back, drove them to fight
defensively, for bare survival.

Covenant's captor faced him again. The Cavewight's laval
eyes burned flame and fury. Rocklight gleamed on his spike
as he cocked his arm to stab out Covenant's life.

Hoarse with panic and insight, Linden yelled, "The bones!
Get the bones!"

At once, one of the creatures hit her so hard that she
sprawled into the basin at Covenant's feet. She lay there,
stunned and twisted. He feared her back had been broken.

But the Cavewights understood her if he did not. A sound
like a wail shrilled across the combat. They fought with
redoubled fever. The spike aimed at Covenant wavered as
the Cavewight looked fearfully toward the fray.

Covenant could not see the First or Pitchwife through the
fierce press. But suddenly her shout sprang at the ceiling—
the tantara of a Swordmain summoning her last resources:
"Stone and Sea!"

And the throng of Cavewights seemed to rupture as if she
had become a detonation. Abandoning Pitchwife, she crashed

past the creatures, shed them from her arms and shoulders
like rubble. In a spray of blood, she hacked her way toward
the Wightbarrow.

Pitchwife could have been slain then. But he was not. His
assailants hurled themselves after the First. His axes bit into
their backs as he followed her.

The wailing scaled into a shriek when she reached the
mound.

Snatching up a bone, she whirled to face her attackers. The
bone shed flame like a fagot; but her Giantish fingers bore
the pain and did not flinch.

Instantly, all the creatures froze. Silence seized their cries;
horror locked their limbs.

Pitchwife wrenched one axe out of the spine of a Cavewight, raised his weapons to parry blows. But none came. He
was ignored. Retching for air, he thrust through the crowd
toward the First. No one moved.

He limped to her side, dropped one axe, and grasped
another burning bone. The paralysis of the Cavewights
tightened involuntarily. Their eyes pleaded. Some of them
began to shiver in chill panic.

By threatening the mound, the First and Pitchwife endangered the only thing which had given these creatures
the courage to defy Lord Foul.

Covenant struggled against his captor, tried to reach Linden.
But the Cavewight did not release him, seemed oblivious to
his efforts—entranced by fear.

Stooping, the First wiped the blood from her glaive on the
nearest body. Then she sheathed the longsword and took up
a second bone. Fire spilled over her hands, but she paid it
no heed. "Now," she panted through her teeth. "Now you
will release the Earthfriend."

The Cavewight locked his fingers around Covenant's arm
and did not move. A few creatures at the fringes of the press
shifted slightly, moaned in protest.

Abruptly, Linden twitched. With a jerk, she thrust herself
out of the basin. When she got her feet under her, she
staggered and stumbled as if the floor were tilting. Yet
somehow she kept her balance. Her eyes were glazed with
anger and extremity. She had been pushed too far. Half
lurching, she passed behind Covenant.

Among the Cavewights crouching there, she found a loose truncheon. It was almost too heavy for her to lift. Gripping its handle in both hands, she heaved it from the floor, raised it above her head, and brought it down on the wrist of the creature holding Covenant.

He heard a dull snapping noise. The Cavewight's fingers were torn from his arm.

The creature yowled. Madly, he cocked the spike to stab it down at Linden's face.

"Hold!" The First's command rang through the cave. She thrust one foot into the mound, braced herself to kick dust and fragments across the floor.

The Cavewight froze in renewed terror.

Slowly, she withdrew her foot. A faint sigh of relief soughed around the walls of the cave.

Pain lanced through Covenant's elbow, knifed into his shoulder. For a moment, he feared that he would not be able to stand. The clutch of the Cavewight had damaged his arm; the blood pounding back into it felt like acid. The cave seemed to roar in his ears. He heard no other sound except Pitchwife's harsh respiration.

But he had to stand, had to move. The Giants deserved better than this from him. Linden and the Land deserved better. He could not afford such weakness. It was only pain and vertigo, as familiar to him as an old friend. It had no power over him unless he was afraid—unless he let himself be afraid. If he held up his heart, even despair was as good as courage or strength.

That was the center, the point of stillness and certainty. Briefly, he rested. Then he let the excruciation in his arm lift him out of the basin.

Linden came to him. Her touch made his body totter; but inwardly he did not lose his balance. She would stop him if he proved himself wrong. But he was not wrong. Together, they moved toward the Giants.

Pitchwife did not look up from his gasping. His lips were flecked with red spittle; his exertions had torn something in his chest. But the First gave Covenant and Linden a nod of greeting. Her gaze was as grim as a hawk's. "You gladden me!" she muttered. "I had not thought to behold you again alive. It is well that these simple creatures do not glance often behind them. Thus we were able to follow when we had foiled our pursuers. What dire rite do they seek to practice against you?"

Linden answered for Covenant, "They're trying to bring an old leader back from the dead. He's buried under there somewhere." She grimaced at the Wightbarrow. "They want Covenant's blood and the ring. They think this dead leader'll free them from Foul. We've got to get out of here."

"Aye," growled the First. Her eyes assayed the Cavewights. "But they are too many. We cannot win free by combat. We must entrust ourselves to the sanctity of these bones."

Covenant thought he smelled the faint reek of charring flesh. But he had no health-sense, could not tell how seriously the Giants' hands were being hurt.

"My husband," the First gritted, "will you lead us?"

Pitchwife nodded. A moment of coughing brought more blood to his lips. Yet he rallied. When he raised his head, the look in his eyes was as fierce as hers.

With a bone flaming like a brand in one hand, an axe in the other, he started toward the nearer mouth of the cave.

At once, a snarl sharpened the air, throbbing from many throats. A shiver ran through the Cavewights. The ones farthest from the Wightbarrow advanced slightly, placed themselves to block Pitchwife's path. Others tightened their hands on their weapons.

"No!" Linden snapped at Pitchwife. "Come back!"

He retreated. When he reached the mound, the Cave-wights froze again.

Covenant blinked at Linden. He felt too dizzy to think. He knew he ought to understand what was happening. But it did not make sense.

"What means this, Chosen?" the First asked like iron. "Are we snared in this place for good and all?"

Linden replied with a look toward Covenant as if she were begging him for courage. Then, abruptly, she wrapped her arms around her chest and strode away from the mound.

The First breathed a sharp warning. Linden's head flinched from side to side. But she did not stop. Deliberately, she moved among the Cavewights.

She was alone and small and vulnerable in their midst. Her difficult bravery was no defense; any one of them could have felled her with one blow. But none of them reacted. She squeezed between two of them, passed behind a poised cluster, walked halfway to the cavemouth. Their eyes remained fixed on the First and Pitchwife—on the bones and the Wightbarrow.

As she moved, she raised her head, grew bolder. The vindication of her percipience fortified her. Less timorously, she made her way back to her companions.

Rocklight burned in Covenant's eyes. The First and Pitchwife stared at Linden. Grimly, she explained, "They won't move while you threaten the mound. They need it. It's their reason—the only answer they've got." Then she faltered; and her gaze darkened at the implications of what she was saying. "That's why they won't let us take any of the bones out of here."

For one moment—a piece of time as acute as anguish—the First looked beaten, overcome by everything she had already lost and would still be required to lose. Honninscrave and Seadreamer had been dear to her. Pitchwife was her husband. Covenant and Linden and life were precious. Her sternness broke down, exposing a naked hurt. Both her parents had given their lives for her, and she had become what she was by grief.

Yet she was the First of the Search, chosen for her ability to bear hard decisions. Almost at once, her visage closed around itself. Her hands knotted as if they were hungry for the fire of the bones.

"Then," she responded stiffly, "I must remain to menace this mould, so that you may depart." She swallowed a lump of sorrow. "Pitchwife, you must accompany them. They will have need of your strength. And I must believe that you live."

At that, Pitchwife burst into a spasm of coughing. A moment passed before Covenant realized that the malformed Giant was trying to laugh.

"My wife, you jest," he said at last. "I have found my own reply to doubt. The Chosen has assigned me to your side. Do not credit that the song which the Giants will sing of this day will be sung of you alone."

"I am the First of the Search!" she retorted. "I command—"

"You are Gossamer Glowlimn, the spouse of my heart." His mouth was bloody; but his eyes gleamed. "I am proud of you beyond all endurance. Demean not your high courage with foolishness. Neither Earthfriend nor Chosen has any need of my accompaniment. They are who they are—and will not fail. I am sworn to you in love and fealty, and I will remain."

She glared at him as if she were in danger of weeping openly. "You will *die*. I have borne all else until my heart breaks. Must I bear *that* also?"

"No." Around Covenant, the rock seemed to spin and fade as if Mount Thunder itself were on the verge of dissolution; but he clung to the center of his mortality and stood certain, an alloy in human flesh and bone of wild magic and venom, life and death. "No," he repeated when the First and Pitchwife met his gaze. "There's no reason for either of you to die. It won't take long. Kiril Threndor can't be very far from here. All I have to do is get there. Then it'll be over, one way or the other. All you have to do is hang on until I get there."

Then Pitchwife did laugh, and his face lifted with gladness. "There, my wife!" he chortled. "Have I not said that they are who they are? Accept that I am with you, and be content." Abruptly, he dropped his axe, drew out his last fagot and lit it from the Wightbarrow, handed the sputtering wood to Linden. "Begone!" he gleamed, "ere I become maudlin at the witnessing of such valor. Fear nothing for us. We will hold and hold until the mountain itself is astonished, and still we will hold. Begone, I say!"

"Aye, begone," growled the First as if she were angry; but her tears belied her tone. "I must have opportunity to instruct this Pitchwife in the obedience which is his debt to the First of the Search."

Covenant wanted words, but none came to him. What could he have said? He had made his promises long ago, and they covered everything. He rubbed the heels of his hands into his eyes to clear his sight. Then he turned toward Linden.

If he had spoken, he would have asked her to stay with the Giants. He had never forgotten the shock of her intervention in the woods behind Haven Farm. And he had not loved her then. Now everything was multiplied to the acuteness of panic. He did not know how he might preserve the bare shreds and tatters of dignity—not to mention clear courage or conviction—if she accompanied him.

But the look of her silenced him. She was baffled and perceptive, frightened and brave; terrified of Cavewights and Lord Foul, and yet avid for a chance to stand against them; mortal, precious, and irrefusable. Her face had lost its imposed severity, had become in spite of wear and strain as soft as her mouth and eyes. Yet its underlying structure remained precise, indomitable. The sad legacy of her parents had led her to what she was—but the saddest thing about her was that she did not understand how completely she had transformed that legacy, had made of herself something necessary and admirable. She deserved a better outcome than this. But he had nothing else to offer her.

She held his gaze as if she wanted to match him—and feared she could not. Then she tightened her grip on her torch and stepped out among the clenched Cavewights.

She had read them accurately: any threat to the Wight-barrow outweighed all other considerations. When Covenant left the First and Pitchwife, a raw muttering aggravated the rocklight. Several Cavewights shifted their positions, raised their weapons. But the First poised one foot to begin scattering the mound; and the creatures went rigid again. Covenant let weakness and fear and pain carry him like hope toward the mouth of the cave.

"Go well, Earthfriend," the First breathed after them, "hold faith, Chosen," as if she had become impervious to doubt. Pitchwife's faint chuckling was torn and frayed; but it followed Covenant and Linden like an affirmation of contentment.

Barely upright on his feet, Covenant made his way past the Cavewights. Their eyes flamed outrage and loss at him; but they did not take the risk of striking out. The cave narrowed to a tunnel at its end, and Linden began to hurry. He did his best to keep up with her. The vulnerable place between his shoulderblades seemed to feel the Cavewights turning to hurl their truncheons; but he entrusted himself to the Giants, did not look back. In a moment, he left the rocklight behind. Linden's torch led him back into the darkness of the catacombs.

At the first intersection, she turned as if she knew where she was going. Covenant caught up with her, put his hand on her arm to slow her somewhat. She acceded, but continued to bear herself as though she were being harried by unseen wings in Mount Thunder's immeasurable midnight. As her senses hunted the way ahead for peril or guidance, she began to mutter—to herself or to him, he could not tell which.

"They're wrong. They don't know enough. Whatever they

brought back from the dead, it wasn't going to be Drool Rockworm. Not just another Cavewight. Something monstrous.

"Blood brings power. They had to kill someone. But what Caer-Caveral did for Hollian can't be done here. It only worked because they were in Andelain. And Andelain was intact. All that concentrated Earthpower. Concentrated and clean. Whatever those Cavewights resurrected, it was going to be abominable."

When he understood that she was not talking about the Cavewights and Drool—that she was trying to say something else entirely—Covenant stumbled. His throbbing arm struck the wall of the passage, and he nearly lost his balance. Pain made his arm dangle as if it were being dragged down by the inconceivable weight of his ring. She was talking about the hope which he had never admitted to himself—the hope that if he died he, too, might be brought back.

"Linden—" He did not wish to speak, to argue with her. They had so little time left. Fire gnawed up and down his arm. He needed to husband his determination. But she had already gone too far in his name. Swallowing his weakness, he said, "I don't want to be resurrected."

She did not look at him. Roughly, he went on, "You're going to go back to your own life. Sometime soon. And I won't get to go with you. You know it's too late to save me. Not back there. Where we come from, that kind of thing doesn't happen. Even if I'm resurrected, I won't get to go with you.

"If I can't go with you"—he told her the truth as well as he could—"I'd rather stay with my friends. Mhoram and Foamfollower." Elena and Bannor. Honninscrave. And the wait for Sunder and Hollian would not seem long to him.

She refused to hear him. "Maybe not," she rasped. "Maybe we can still get back in time. I couldn't save you before because your spirit wasn't there—your will to live. If you would just stop giving up, we might still have a chance." Her voice was husky with thwarted yearning. "You're bruised and exhausted. I don't know how you stay on your feet. But you haven't been *stabbed* yet." Her gaze flashed toward the faint scar in the center of his chest. "You don't have to die."

But he saw the grief in her eyes and knew that she did not believe her own protestation.

He drew her to a halt. With his good hand, he wrested his

wedding band from its finger. His touch was cold and numb, as if he had no idea what he was doing. Fervent and silent as a prayer, he extended the ring toward her. Its unmarred argent cast glints of the wavering torchlight.

At once, tears welled in her eyes. Streaks of reflected fire flowed down the lines which severity and loss had left on either side of her mouth. But she gave the ring no more than a glance. Her gaze clung to his countenance. "No," she whispered. "Not while I can still hope."

Abruptly, she moved on down the passage.

Sighing rue and relief like a man who had been reprieved or damned and did not know the difference—did not care if there were no difference—he thrust the ring back into place and followed her.

The tunnel became as narrow as a mere crack in the rock, then widened into a complex of junctions and chambers. The torch barely lit the walls and ceiling; it revealed nothing of what lay ahead. But from one passage came a breeze like a scent of evil that made Linden wince; and she turned that way. Covenant's hearing ached as he struggled to discern the sounds of pursuit or danger. But he lacked her percipience; he had to trust her.

The tunnel she had chosen angled downward until he thought that even vertigo would not be strong enough to keep him upright. Darkness and stone piled tremendously around him. The torch continued to burn down. It was half consumed already. Somewhere beyond the mountain, the Land lay in day or night; but he had lost all conception of time. Time had no meaning here, in the lightless unpity of Lord Foul's demesne. Only the torch mattered—and Linden's pale-knuckled grasp on the brand—and the fact that he was not alone. For good or ill, redemption or ruin, he was not alone. There was no other way.

Without warning, the walls withdrew, and a vast impression of space opened above his head. Linden stopped, searched the dark. When she lifted the torch, he saw that the tunnel had emerged from the stone, leaving them at the foot of a blunt gutrock cliff. Chill air tingled against his cheek. The cliff seemed to go straight up forever. She looked at him as if she were lost. The scant fire made her eyes appear hollow and brutalized.

A short distance from the tunnel's opening rose a steep

slope of shale, loam, and refuse—too steep and yielding to
be climbed. He and Linden were in the bottom of a wide
crevice. Something high up in the dark had collapsed any
number of millennia ago, filling half the floor of the chasm
with debris.

Memories flocked at him out of the enclosed night: recogni-
tions ran like cold sweat down his spine. All his skin felt
clammy and diseased. This looked like the place— The place
where he had once fallen, with an ur-vile struggling to bite
off his ring and no light anywhere, nothing to defend him
from the ambush of madness except his stubborn insistence
on himself. But that defense was no longer of any use. Kiril
Threndor was not far away. Lord Foul was close.

"This way." Linden gestured toward the left, along the
sheer wall. Her voice sounded dull, half stupefied by the
effort of holding onto her courage. Her senses told her things
that appalled her. Though his own perceptions were fatally
truncated, he felt the potential for hysteria creep upward in
her. But instead of screaming she became scarcely able to
move. How virulent would Lord Foul be to nerves as vulnerable as hers? Covenant was at least protected by his numbness.
But she had no protection, might as well have been naked.
She had known too much death. She hated it—and ached to
share its sovereign power. She believed that she was evil.

In the unsteady torchlight, he seemed to see her already
falling into paralysis under the pressure of Lord Foul's
emanations.

Yet she still moved. Or perhaps the Despiser's will coerced
her. Dully, she walked in the direction she had indicated.

He joined her. All his joints were stiff with pleading. Hang
on. You have the right to choose. You don't have to be
trapped like this. Nobody can take away your right to
choose. But he could not work the words into his locked
throat. They were stifled by the accumulation of his own
dread.

Dread which ate at the rims of his certainty, eroded the
place of stillness and conviction where he stood. Dread that
he was wrong.

The air was as damp and dank as compressed sweat. Shivering in the chill atmosphere, he accompanied Linden along
the bottom of the chasm and watched the volition leak out
of her until she was barely moving.

Then she stopped. Her head slumped forward. The torch hung at her side, nearly burning her hand. He prayed her name, but she did not respond. Her voice trickled like blood between her lips:

"Ravers."

And the steep slope beside them arose as if she had called it to life.

Two of them: creatures of scree and detritus from the roots of the mountain. They were nearly as tall as Giants, but much broader. They looked strong enough to crush boulders in their massive arms. One of them struck Covenant a stone blow that scattered him to the floor. The other impelled Linden to the wall.

Her torch fell, guttered and went out. But the creatures did not need that light. They emitted a ghastly lumination that made their actions as vivid as atrocities.

One stood over Covenant to prevent him from rising. The other confronted Linden. It reached for her. Her face stretched to scream, but even her screams were paralyzed. She made no effort to defend herself.

With a gentleness worse than any violence, the creature began to unbutton her shirt.

Covenant gagged for breath. Her extremity was more than he could bear. Every inch of him burned for power. Suddenly, he no longer cared whether his attacker would strike him again. He rolled onto his chest, wedged his knees under him, tottered to his feet. His attacker raised a threatening arm. He was battered and frail, barely able to stand. Yet the passion raging from him halted the creature in midblow, forced it to retreat a step. It was a Raver, sentient and accessible to fear. It understood what his wild magic would do, if he willed.

His half-hand trembling, he pointed at the creature in front of Linden. It stopped at the last buttons. But it did not turn away.

"I'm warning you." His voice spattered and scorched like hot acid. "Foul's right about this. If you touch her, I don't care what else I destroy. I'll rip your soul to atoms. You won't live long enough to know whether I break the Arch or not."

The creature did not move. It seemed to be daring him to unleash his white gold.

"Try me," he breathed on the verge of eruption. "Just try me."

Slowly, the creature lowered its arms. Backing carefully, it retreated to stand beside its fellow.

A spasm went through Linden. All her muscles convulsed in torment or ecstasy. Then her head snapped up. The dire glow of the creatures flamed from her eyes.

She looked straight at Covenant and began to laugh.

The laughter of a ghoul, mirthless and cruel.

"Slay me then, groveler!" she cried. Her voice was as shrill as a shriek. It echoed hideously along the crevice. "Rip my soul to atoms! Perchance it will pleasure you to savage the woman you love as well!"

The Raver had taken possession of her, and there was nothing in all the world that he could do about it.

He nearly fell then. The supreme evil had come upon her, and he was helpless. *The ill that you deem most terrible.* Even if he had groveled entirely, abject and suppliant, begging the Ravers to release her, they would only have laughed at him. Now in all horror and anguish there was no other way— could be no other way. He cried out at himself, at his head to rise, his legs to uphold him, his back to straighten. Seadreamer! he panted as if that were the liturgy of his conviction, his fused belief. Honninscrave. Hamako. Hile Troy. All of them had given themselves. There was no other way.

"All right," he grated. The sound of his voice in the chasm almost betrayed him to rage; but he clamped down his wild magic, refused it for the last time. "Take me to Foul. I'll give him the ring."

No way except surrender.

The Raver in Linden went on laughing wildly.

NINETEEN: Hold Possession

SHE was not laughing.

Laughter came out of her mouth. It sprang from her corded throat to scale like gibbering up into the black abyss. Her lungs drew the air which became malice and glee. Her face was contorted like the vizard of a demon—or the rictus of her mother's asphyxiation.

But she was not laughing. It was not Linden Avery who laughed.

It was the Raver.

It held possession of her as completely as if she had been born for its use, formed and nurtured for no other purpose than to provide flesh for its housing, limbs for its actions, lungs and throat for its malign joy. It bereft her of will and choice, voice and protest. At one time, she had believed that her hands were trained and ready, capable of healing—a physician's hands. But now she had no hands with which to grasp her possessor and fight it. She was a prisoner in her own body and the Raver's evil.

And that evil excoriated every niche and nerve of her being. It was heinous and absolute beyond bearing. It consumed her with its memories and purposes, crushed her independent existence with the force of its ancient strength. It was the corruption of the Sunbane mapped and explicit in her personal veins and sinews. It was the revulsion and desire which had secretly ruled her life, the passion for and against death. It was the fetid halitus of the most diseased mortality condensed to its essence and elevated to the transcendence of prophecy, promise, suzerain truth—the definitive commandment of darkness.

All her life, she had been vulnerable to this. It had thronged into her from her father's stretched laughter, and she had confirmed it by stuffing it down her mother's abject throat. Once, she had flattered herself that she was like the Land under the Sunbane, helplessly exposed to desecration. But that was false. The Land was innocent.

She was *evil*.

Its name was *moksha* Jehannum, and it brought its past with it. She remembered now as if all its actions were her own. The covert ecstasy with which it had mastered Marid— the triumph of the blow that had driven hot iron into Nassic's human back (and the rich blood frothing at the heat of the blade)—the cunning which had led *moksha* to betray its possession of Marid to her new percipience, so that she and Covenant would be condemned and Marid would be exposed to the perverting sun. She remembered bees. Remembered the apt mimesis of madness in the warped man who had set a spider to Covenant's neck. She might as well have done those things herself.

But behind them lay deeper crimes. Empowered by a piece of the Illearth Stone, she had mastered a Giant. She had named herself Fleshharrower and had led the Despiser's armies against the Lords. And she had tasted victory when she had trapped the defenders of the Land between her own forces and the savage forest of Garroting Deep—the forest which she hated, had hated for all the long centuries, hated in every green leaf and drop of sap from tree to tree—the forest which should have been helpless against ravage and fire, would have been helpless if some outer knowledge had not intervened, making possible the interdict of the Colossus of the Fall, the protection of the Forestals.

Yet she had been tricked into entering the Deep, and so she had fallen victim to the Deep's guardian, Caerroil Wildwood. Unable to free herself, she had been slain in torment and ferocity on Gallows Howe, and her spirit had been sorely pressed to keep itself alive.

For that reason among many others, *moksha* Jehannum was avid to exact retribution. Linden was only one small morsel to the Raver's appetite. Yet her possessor savored the pleasure her futile anguish afforded. Her body it left unharmed for its own use. But it violated her spirit as fundamentally as rape. And it went on laughing.

Her father's laughter, pouring like a flood of midnight from the old desuetude of the attic; a throng of nightmares in which she foundered; triumph hosting out of the dire cavern and plunge which had once been his frail mouth. *You never loved me anyway.* Never loved him—or anyone else. She had not mustered the bare decency to cry aloud as she strangled her mother, drove that poor sick woman terrified and alone into the last dark.

This was what Joan had felt, this appalled and desperate horror which made no difference of any kind, could not so much as muffle the sound of malice. Buried somewhere within herself, Joan had watched her own fury for Covenant's blood, for the taste of his pain. And now Linden looked out at him as if through *moksha* Jehannum's eyes, heard him with ears that belonged to the Raver. Lit only by the ghoulish emanations of the creatures, he stood in the bottom of the crevice like a man who had just been maimed. His damaged arm dangled at his side. Every line of his body was abused with need and near-prostration. The bruises on his face made his visage appear misshapen, deformed by the pressures building inside him, where the wild magic was manacled. Yet his eyes gleamed like teeth, focused such menace toward the Ravers that *moksha* Jehannum's brother had not dared to strike him again.

"Take me to Foul," he said. He had lost his mind. This was not despair: it was too fierce for despair. It was madness. The Banefire had cost him his sanity. "I'll give him the ring."

His gaze lanced straight into Linden. If she had owned a voice, she would have cried out.

He was smiling like a sacrifice.

Then she found that she did not have to watch him. The Raver could not require consciousness of her. Its memories told her that most of its victims had simply fled into mindlessness. The moral paralysis which had made her so accessible to *moksha* Jehannum would protect her now, not from use but from awareness. All she had to do was let go her final hold upon her identity. Then she would be spared from witnessing the outcome of Covenant's surrender.

With glee and hunger, the Raver urged her to let go. Her consciousness fed it, pleased it, sharpened its enjoyment of her violation. But if she lapsed, it would not need exertion to master her. And she would be safe at last—as safe as she had once been in the hospital during the blank weeks after her father's suicide—relieved from excruciation, inured to pain— as safe as death.

There were no other choices left for her to make.

She refused it. With the only passion and strength that remained to her, she refused it.

She had already failed in the face of Joan's need—been stricken helpless by the mere sight of Marid's desecration. Gibbon's touch had reft her of mind and will. But since then she had learned to fight.

In the cavern of the One Tree, she had grasped power for the first time and had used it, daring herself against forces so tremendous—though amoral—that terror of them had immobilized her until Findail had told her what was at stake. And in the Hall of Gifts— There *samadhi* Sheol's nearness had daunted her, misled her, tossed her in a whirlwind of palpable ill; she had hardly known where she stood or what she was doing. But she had not been stripped of choice.

Not, she insisted, careless of whether the Raver heard her. Because she had been needed. By all her friends. By Covenant before the One Tree, if not in the Hall of Gifts. And because she had experienced the flavor of efficacy, had gripped it to her heart and recognized it for what it was. Power: the ability to make choices that mattered. Power which came from no external source, but only from her own intense self.

She would not give it up. Covenant needed her still, though the Raver's mastery of her was complete and she had no way to reach him. *I'll give him the ring.* She could not stop him. But if she let herself go on down the blind road of her paralysis, there would be no one left to so much as wish him stopped. Therefore she bore the pain. *Moksha* Jehannum crowded every nerve with nausea, filled every hearbeat with vitriol and dismay, shredded her with every word and movement. Yet she heeded the call of Covenant's fierce eyes and flagrant intent. Consciously, she clung to herself and refused oblivion, remained where the Raver could hurt her and hurt her, so that she would be able to watch.

And try.

"Will you?" chortled her throat and mouth. "You are belatedly come to wisdom, groveler." She raged at that epithet: he did not deserve it. But *moksha* only mocked him more trenchantly. "Yet your abasement has been perfectly prophesied. Did you fear for your life among the Cave-wights? Your fear was apt. Anile as the Dead, they would have slain you—and blithely would the ring have been seduced from them. From the moment of your summoning, all hope has been folly! All roads have led to the Despiser's triumph, and all struggles have been vain. Your petty—"

"I'm sick of this," rasped Covenant. He was hardly able to stay on his feet—and yet the sheer force of his determination commanded the Ravers, sent an inward quailing through them. "Don't flatter yourselves that I'm going to break down here." Linden felt *moksha*'s trepidation and shouted at it, Coward! then gritted her teeth and gagged for bare life as its fury crashed down on her. But Covenant could not see what was happening to her, the price she paid for defiance. Grimly, he went on, "You aren't going to get my ring. You'll be lucky if he even lets you live when he's finished with me." His eyes flashed, as hard as hot marble. "Take me to him."

"Most assuredly, groveler," *moksha* Jehannum riposted. "I tremble at your will."

Tearing savagery across the grain of Linden's clinched consciousness, the Raver turned her, sent her forward along the clear spine of the chasm.

Behind her, the two creatures—both ruled now by *moksha*'s brother—set themselves at Covenant's back. But she saw with the senses of the Raver that they did not hazard touching him.

He followed her as if he were too weak to do more than place one foot in front of the other—and too strong to be beaten.

The way seemed long: every step, each throb of her heart was interminable and exquisite agony. The Raver relished her violation and multiplied it cunningly. From her helpless brain, *moksha* drew images and hurled them at her, made them appear more real than Mount Thunder's imponderable gut-rock. Marid with his fangs. Joan screaming like a predator for Covenant's blood, wracked by a Sunbane of the soul. Her mother's mouth, mucus drooling at the corners—phlegm as rank as putrefaction from the rot in her lungs. The incisions across her father's wrists, agape with death and glee. There was no end to the ways she could be tortured, if she refused to let go. Her possessor savored them all.

Yet she held. Stubbornly, uselessly, almost without reason, she clung to who she was, to the Linden Avery who made promises. And in the secret recesses of her heart she plotted *moksha* Jehannum's downfall.

Oh, the way seemed long to her! But she knew, had no defense against knowing, that for the Raver the distance was short and eager, little more than a stone's throw along the black gulf. Then the dank light of Covenant's guards picked out a stairway cut into the left wall. It was a rude ascent, roughly hacked from the sheer stone immemorially long ago and worn blunt by use; but it was wide and safe. The Raver went upward with strong strides, almost jaunty in its anticipation. But Linden watched Covenant for signs of vertigo or collapse.

His plight was awful. She felt his bruises aching in the bones of his skull, read the weary limp of his pulse. Sweat like fever or failure beaded on his forehead. An ague of exhaustion made all his movements awkward and imprecise. Yet he kept going, as rigid of intent as he had been on Haven Farm when he had walked into the woods to redeem his ex-wife. His very weakness and imbalance seemed to support him.

He was entirely out of his mind; and Linden bled for him while *moksha* Jehannum raked her with scorn.

The stairway was long and short. It ascended for several hundred feet and hurt as if it would go on forever without surcease. The Raver gave her not one fragment or splinter of respite while it used her body as if she had never been so healthy and vital. But at last she reached an opening in the wall, a narrow passage-mouth with rocklight reflecting from its end. The stairs continued upward; but she entered the tunnel. Covenant followed her, his guards behind him in single file.

Heat mounted against her face until she seemed to be walking into fire; but it meant nothing to *moksha*. The Raver was at home in dire passages and brimstone. For a while, all the patients she had failed to help, all the medical mistakes she had made beat about her mind, accusing her like furies. In the false name of life, she was responsible for so much death. Perhaps she had employed it for her own ends. Perhaps she had introduced pain and loss to her victims, needing them to suffer so that she would have power and life.

Then the passage ended, and she found herself in the place where Lord Foul had chosen to wield his machinations.

Kiril Threndor. Heart of Thunder.

Here Kevin Landwaster had come to enact the Ritual of Desecration. Here Drool Rockworm had recovered the lost Staff of Law. It was the dark center of all Mount Thunder's ancient and fatal puissance.

The place where the outcome of the Earth would be decided.

She knew it with *moksha* Jehannum's knowledge. The Raver's whole spirit seemed to quiver in lust and expectation.

The cave was large, a round, high chamber. Entrances gaped like mute cries, stretched in eternal pain, around its circumference. The walls glared rocklight in all directions. They were shaped entirely into smooth, irregular facets which cast their illumination like splinters at Linden's eyes. And that sharp assault was whetted and multiplied by a myriad keen reflections from the chamber's ceiling. There the stone gathered a dense cluster of stalactites, as bright and ponderous as melting metal. Among them swarmed a chiaroscuro of orange-red gleamings.

But no light seemed to touch the figure that stood on a low dais in the middle of the time-burnished floor. It rose there like a pillar, motionless and immune to revelation. It might have been the back of a statue or a man; perhaps it was as tall as a Giant. Even the senses of the Raver saw nothing certainly. It appeared to have no color and no clear shape or size. Its outlines were blurred as if they transcended recognition. But it radiated power like a shriek through the echoing rocklight.

The air reeked of sulfur—a stench so acrid that it would have brought tears to her eyes if it had not given such pleasure to her possessor. But under that rank odor lay a different scent, a smell more subtle, insidious, and consuming than any brimstone. A smell on which *moksha* fed like an addict.

A smell of attar. The sweetness of the grave.

Linden was forced to devour it as if she were reveling.

The force of the figure screamed into her like a shout

poised to bring down the mountain, rip the vulnerable heart of the Land to rubble and chaos.

Covenant stood a short distance away from her now, dissociating his plight from hers so that she would not suffer the consequences of his company. He had no health-sense. And even if his eyes had been like hers, he might not have been able to discern what was left of her—might not have seen the way she cried out to have him beside her. She knew everything to which he was blind, everything that could have made a difference to him. Everything except how in his battered weakness he had become strong enough to stand there as though he were indefeasible.

With *moksha*'s perceptions, she saw the two creatures and the Raver which controlled them leave the chamber. They were no longer needed. She saw Covenant look at her and form her name, trying mutely to tell her something that he could not say and she could not hear. The light flared at her like a shattered thing, stone trapped in the throes of fragmentation, the onset of the last collapse. The stalactites shed gleams and imminence as if they were about to plunge down on her. Her unbuttoned shirt seemed to let attar crawl across her breasts, teasing them with anguish. Heat closed around her faint thoughts like a fist.

And the figure on the dais turned.

Even *moksha* Jehannum's senses failed her. They were a blurred lens through which she saw only outlines that dripped and ran, features smeared out of focus. She might have been trying to gauge the figure past the high, hot intervention of a bonfire. But it resembled a man. Parts of him suggested a broad chest and muscular arms, a patriarchal beard, a flowing robe. Tall as a Giant, puissant as a mountain, and more exigent than any conflagration of bloodshed and corruption, he turned; and his gaze swept Kiril Threndor—swept her and Covenant as if with a blink he could have brushed them out of existence.

His eyes were the only precise part of him.

She had seen them before.

Eyes as bitter as fangs, carious and cruel; eyes of deliberate force, rabid desire; eyes wet with venom and insatiation. In the woods behind Haven Farm, they had shone out of the blaze and pierced her to the pit of her soul, measuring and disdaining every aspect of her as she had crouched in fright.

They had required paralysis of her as if it were the first law of her existence. When she had unlocked her weakness, run down the hillside to try to save Covenant, they had fixed her like a promise that she would never be so brave again, never rise above her mortal contradictions. And now with infinitely multiplied and flagrant virulence they repeated that promise and made it true. Reaching past *moksha* Jehannum to the clinched relict of her consciousness, they confirmed their absolute commandment.

Never again.

Never.

In response, her voice said, "He has come to cede his ring. I have brought him to your will," and chortled like a burst of involuntary fear. Even the Raver could not bear its master's direct gaze and sought to turn that baleful regard aside.

But for a moment Lord Foul did not look away. His eyes searched her for signs of defiance or courage. Then he said, "To you I do not speak." His voice came from the rocklight and the heat, from the reek of attar and the chiaroscuro of the stalactites—a voice as deep as Mount Thunder's bones and veined with savagery. Orange-red facets glittered and glared in every word. "I have not spoken to you. There was no need—is none. I speak to set the feet of my hearers upon the paths I design for them, but your path has been mine from the first. You have been well bred to serve me, and all your choices conduce to my ends. To attain that which I have desired from you has been a paltry exercise, scarce requiring effort. When I am free"—she heard a grin in the swarming reflections—"you will accompany me, so that your present torment may be prolonged forever. I will gladly mark myself upon such flesh as yours."

With her mouth, the Raver giggled tense and sweating approval. The Despiser's gaze nailed dismay into her. She was as abject as she had ever been, and she tried to wail; but no sound came.

Then she would have let go. But Covenant did not. His eyes were midnight with rage for her; his passion refused to be crushed. He looked hardly capable of taking another step —yet he came to her aid.

"Don't kid yourself," he snapped like a jibe. "You're already beaten, and you don't even know it. All these threats are just pathetic."

Assuredly he was out of his mind. But his sarcasm shifted the Despiser toward him. Linden was left to the cunning tortures of her possessor. They slashed and flayed at her, showed her in long whipcuts all the atrocities an immortal could commit against her. But when Lord Foul's gaze left her, she found that she was still able to cling. She was stubborn enough for that.

"Ah," the Despiser rumbled like the sigh of an avalanche, "at last my foeman stands before me. He does not grovel—but groveling has become needless. He has spoken words which may not be recalled. Indeed, his abasement is complete, though he is blind to it. He does not see that he has sold himself to a servitude more demeaning than prostration. He has become the tool of my Enemy, no longer free to act against me. Therefore he submits himself, deeming in his cowardice that here the burden of havoc and ruin will pass from him." Soft laughter made the rocklight throb; mute shrieks volleyed from the walls. "He is the Unbeliever in all sooth. He does not believe that the Earth's doom will at last be laid to his charge.

"Thomas Covenant"—he took an avid step forward—"the spectacle of your puerile strivings gives me glee to repay my long patience, for your defeat has ever been as certain as my will. Were I to be foiled, the opportunity belonged to your companion, not to you—and you see how she has availed herself of it." With one strong, blurred arm, he made a gesture toward Linden that nearly unseated her reason. Again, he laughed; but his laughter was devoid of mirth. "Had she seduced you of the ring—ah, then would I have been tested. But therefore did I choose her, a woman altogether unable to turn aside from my desires.

"You are a fool," he went on, "for you have known yourself doomed, and yet you have come to me. Now I require your soul." The heat of his voice filled Linden's lungs with suffocation. *Moksha* Jehannum shivered, hungry for violence and ravage. The Despiser sounded unquestionably sane—but that only made him more terrible. One of his hands—a bare smear across the Raver's sight—seemed to curl into a fist; and Covenant was jerked forward, within Lord Foul's reach. The walls spattered light like sobs, as if Mount Thunder itself were appalled.

As soft as the whisper of death, the Despiser said, "Give the ring to me."

Linden believed that she would have obeyed in Covenant's place. The command of that voice was absolute. But he did not move. His right arm hung at his side. The ring dangled as if it were empty of import—as if his numb finger within the band had no significance. His left fist closed and unclosed like the aggrieved labor of his heart. His eyes looked as dark as the loneliness of stars. Somehow, he held his head up, his back straight—upright in conviction or madness.

"Talk's cheap. You can say anything you want. But you're wrong, and you ought to know it. This time you've gone too far. What you did to Andelain. What you're doing to Linden—" He swallowed acid. "We aren't enemies. That's just another lie. Maybe you believe it—but it's still a lie. You should see yourself. You're even starting to look like me." The special gleam of his gaze reached Linden like a gift. He was irremediably insane—or utterly indomitable. "You're just another part of me. Just one side of what it means to be human. The side that hates lepers. The poisonous side." His certainty did not waver at all. "We are one."

His assertion made Linden gape at what he had become. But it only drew another laugh from the Despiser—a short, gruff bark of dismissal. "Do not seek to bandy truth and falsehood with *me*," he replied. "You are too inane for the task. Lies would better serve the trivial yearning which you style love. The truth damns you here. For three and a half millennia I have mustered my will against the Earth *in your absence*, groveler. I am the truth. *I.* And I have no use for the sophistry of your Unbelief." He leveled his voice at Covenant like the blade of an axe. Fragments of rocklight shot everywhere but could not bring his intense form into any kind of focus. "Give the ring to me."

Covenant's visage slackened as if he were made ill by the necessity of his plight. But still he withheld submission. Instead, he changed his ground.

"At least let Linden go." His stance took on an angle of pleading. "You don't need her anymore. Even you should be satisfied with how much she's been hurt. I've already offered her my ring once. She refused it. Let her go."

In spite of everything, he was still trying to spare her.

Lord Foul's response filled Kiril Threndor. "Have done, groveler." Attar made the Raver ecstatic, wracked Linden. "You weary my long patience. She is forfeit to me by her own acts. Are you deaf to yourself? You have spoken words which can never be recalled." Concentrated venom dripped from his outlines. As distinct as the breaking of boulders, he demanded a third time, "Give the ring to me."

And Covenant went on sagging as though he had begun to crumble. All his strength was gone. He could no longer pretend to hold himself upright. One by one, his loves had been stripped from him: he had nothing left. After all, he was only one ordinary man, small and human. Without wild magic, he was no match for the Despiser.

When he weakly lifted his half-hand, began tugging the ring from his finger, Linden forgave him. *No choice but to surrender it.* He had done everything possible, everything conceivable, had surpassed himself again and again in his efforts to save the Land. That he failed now was cause for grief, but not for blame.

Only his eyes showed no collapse. They burned like the final dark, the last deep midnight where no Sunbane shone.

His surrender took no more than three heartbeats. One to raise his hand, take hold of the ring. Another to pull the band from his finger as if in voluntary riddance of marriage, love, humanity. A third to extend the immaculate white gold toward the Despiser.

But extremity and striving made those three moments as long as agony. During them, Linden Avery pitted her ultimate will against her possessor.

She forgave Covenant. He was too poignant and dear to be blamed. He had given everything that her heart could ask of him.

But she did not submit.

Gibbon had said, *The principal doom of the Land is upon your shoulders.* Because no one else had this chance to come between Covenant and his defeat. *You are being forged as iron is forged to achieve the ruin of the Earth.* Forged to fail here. *Because you can* see.

Now she meant to determine what kind of metal had been made of her.

Gibbon-Raver had also told her she was evil. Perhaps that was true. But evil itself was a form of power.

And she had become intimately familiar with her possessor. From the furthest roots of its past, she felt springing its contempt for all things that had flesh and could be mastered—a contempt born of fear. Fear of any form of life able to refuse it. The Forests. Giants. The *Haruchai*. It was unquenchably hungry for immortal control, for the safety of sovereignty. All refusals terrified it. The logic of its failures led inexorably to death. If it could be refused, then it could also be slain.

She had no way to understand the lost communal mind of the Forests. But Giants and *Haruchai* were another question. Though *moksha* Jehannum ripped and shrieked at her, she picked up the strands of what she knew and wove them to her purpose.

The Giants and *Haruchai* had always been able to refuse. Perhaps because they had not suffered the Land's long history of Ravers, they had not learned to doubt their autonomy. Or perhaps because they used little or no outward expressions of power, they comprehended more fully that true choice was internal. But whatever the explanation, they were proof against possession where the people of the Land were not. They believed in their capacity to make choices which mattered.

That belief was all she needed.

Moksha was frantic now, savage and brutal. It assailed every part of her that was able to feel pain. It desecrated her as if she were Andelain. It made every horrifying memory of her life incandescent before her: Nassic's murder and Gibbon's touch; the lurker of the Sarangrave; Kasreyn's malign cunning; Covenant bleeding irretrievably to death in the woods behind Haven Farm. It poured acid into every wound which futility had ever inflicted upon her.

And it argued with her. She could not choose: she had already made the only choice that signified. When she had accepted the legacy of her father and stuffed it in handsful of tissue down her mother's throat, she had declared her crucial allegiance, her definitive passion—a passion in no way different than her possessor's. Despite had made her what she was, a lost woman as ravaged as the Land, and the Sunbane dawning in her now would never set.

But the sheer intensity of her hurt made her lucid. She saw

the Raver's lie. Only once had she tried to master death by destroying life. After that, all her striving had gone to heal those who suffered. Though she had been haunted and afraid, she had not been cruel. Suicide and murder were not the whole story. When the old man on Haven Farm had collapsed in front of her, the stink issuing from his mouth had sickened her like the foretaste of Despite; but she had willingly breathed and breathed that fetor in her efforts to save him.

She was evil. Her visceral response to the dark might of her tormentors gave her the stature of a Raver. And yet her instinct for healing falsified *moksha*.

That contradiction no longer paralyzed her. She accepted it.

It gave her the power to choose.

Squalling like a butchered thing, the Raver fought her. But she had entered at last into her true estate. *Moksha* Jehannum was afraid of her. Her will rose up in its shackles. Tested the iron of her possessor's malice. Took hold of the chains.

And broke free.

Lord Foul had not yet grasped the ring. There was still an instant of space between his hand and Covenant's. Rocklight yowled desire and triumph from the walls.

Linden did not move. She had no time to think of that. Motionless as if she were still frozen, she hurled herself forward. With her Land-born health-sense, she sprang into Covenant, scrambled toward the fiery potential of his wedding band.

Empowered by wild magic, she drew back his hand.

At that, rage swelled Lord Foul: he sent out a flood of fury which should have washed her away. But she ignored him. She was sure that he would not touch her now—not now, while she held possession of Covenant and the ring. She was suddenly strong enough to turn her back upon the Despiser himself. The necessity of freedom protected her. The choice of surrender or defiance was hers to make.

In the silent privacy of his mind, she faced the man she loved and took all his burdens upon herself.

He could not resist her. Once before, he had beaten back her efforts to control him. But now he had no defense. With his own strength, she mastered him as completely as ever the *Elohim* or Kasreyn had mastered him.

No evil! she breathed at him. Not this time. Her previous

attempt to possess him had been wrong, inexcusable. She had read in him his intent to risk the Banefire, and she had reacted as if he meant to commit suicide. Instinctively, she had tried to stop him. But then his life and the risk had been his alone. She had had no right to interfere.

Now, however, he surrenderd the Earth as well as himself. He was not simply risking his own life: he was submitting all life to certain destruction. Therefore she had the responsibility to intervene. The responsibility and the right.

The *right*! she cried. But he made no answer. Her will occupied him completely.

She seemed to meet him where they had met once before, when she had surrendered herself to save him from the silence of the *Elohim*—in a field of flowers, under an inviolate sky, a clean sun. But now she recognized that field as one of the rich leas of Andelain, bordered by hills and woods. And he was no longer young. He stood before her exactly as he stood before the Despiser—altogether untouchable, his face misshaped by bruises he did not deserve, his body nearly prostrate with exhaustion, the old knife-cut in the center of his shirt gaping. His eyes were fixed on her, and they flamed hot midnight, the final extremity of the heavens.

No smile in the world could have softened his gaze.

He stood there as if he were waiting for her to search him, catechize him, learn the truth. But she failed to close the gulf between them. She ran and ran toward him, aching to fling her arms around him at last; but the field lay as still as the sunlight, and his eyes shone darkness at her, and all her strength brought her no nearer. She knew that if she reached him she would understand—that the vision or despair which he had found in the Banefire would be communicated to her —that his certainty would become comprehensible. He was certain, as sure as white gold. But she could not approach him. He met her appeal with the indefeasible *Don't touch me* of leprosy or ascension, apotheosis.

His refusal made grief well up in her like the wail of a lost child.

Then she wanted to turn and hurl all her newfound force at the Despiser, wanted to call up white fire and scourge him from the face of the Earth. *Some infections have to be cut out. Why else do you have all that power?* She could do it. He had hurt Covenant so deeply that she was no longer able to reach him. In her anguish she was greedy for fire. She possessed him heart and limb—and his left hand held the ring, gripped it on the brink of detonation. She was capable of that. If no other hope remained, and she could not touch her love, then let it be she who fought, she who ravaged, she who ruled. Let Lord Foul learn the nature of what he had forged!

Yet Covenant's gaze held her as if she were sobbing, too weak to do anything except weep. He said nothing, offered her nothing. But the purity of his regard did not let her turn. How could he speak, do anything other than repudiate her? She had taken his will from him—had dehumanized him as thoroughly as if she were a Raver and relished his helplessness. And yet he remained human and desirable and stubborn, as dear as life to her. Perhaps he was mad. But was she not something worse?

Are you not evil?

Yes. Beyond question.

But the black flame in his eyes did not accuse her of evil. He did not despise her in any way. He only refused to be swayed.

You said you trusted me.

And who was she to believe him wrong? If doubt was necessary, why should it be doubt of him rather than of herself? Kevin Landwaster had warned her, and she had felt his honesty. But perhaps after all he did not understand, was blinded by the consequences of his own despair. And Covenant remained before her in sunshine and flowers as if the beauty of Andelain were the ground on which he took his stand. His darkness was as lonely as hers. But hers was like the lightless cunning and violence of the Wightwarrens; his resembled the heart of the true night, where the Sunbane never shone.

Yes, she said again. She had known all along that possession in every guise was evil; but she had tried to believe otherwise, both because she wanted power and because she wanted to save the Land. Destruction and healing: death and life. She could have argued that even evil was justified to keep the white ring out of Lord Foul's grasp. But now she was truly weeping. Covenant had said, *I'm going to find some other answer.* That was the only promise which mattered.

Deliberately, she let him go—let love and hope and power

go as if they were all one, too pure to be possessed or desecrated. Locking her cries in her throat, she turned and walked
away across the lea. Out of sunshine into attar and rocklight.

With her own eyes, she saw Covenant lift the ring once
more as if his last fears were gone. With her own ears, she
heard the savage relief of Lord Foul's laughter as he claimed
his triumph. Heat and despair seemed to close over her like
the lid of a coffin.

Moksha Jehannum tried to enter her again, cast her down.
But the Raver could not touch her now. Grief crowded
upward in her, thronged for utterance. She was hardly aware
of *moksha*'s failure.

The Despiser made Kiril Threndor shudder:

"Fool!"

He was crowing over Linden, not Covenant. His eyes bit a
trail of venom through her mind.

"Have I not said that all your choices conduce to my ends?
You serve me absolutely!" The stalactites threw shards of
malice at her head. "It is you who have accorded the ring to
me!"

He raised one hand like a smear across her sight. In his
grasp, the band began to blaze. His shout gathered force
until she feared it would shatter the mountain.

"Here at last I hold possession of all life and Time forever!
Let my Enemy look to his survival and be daunted! Freed of
my gaol and torment, I will rule the cosmos!"

She could not remain upright under the weight of his
exaltation. His voice split her hearing, hampered the rhythm
of her heart. Kneeling on the tremorous stone, she gritted her
teeth, swore to herself that even though she had failed at
everything else she would at least breathe no more of this
damnable attar. The walls threw argent in carillon from all
their facets. The Despiser's power scaled toward apocalypse.

Yet she heard Covenant. Somehow, he kept his feet. He
did not shout; but every word he said was as distinct as
augury.

"Big deal. I could do the same thing—if I were as crazy
as you." His certainty was unmatched. "It doesn't take power.
Just delusion. You're out of your mind."

The Despiser swung toward Covenant. Wild magic effaced
the rocklight, made Kiril Threndor scream white fire. "Groveler, I will teach you the meaning of my suzerainty!" His

whole form rippled and blurred with ecstasy, violence. Only his carious eyes remained explicit, as cruel as fangs. They seemed to shred the substance from Covenant's bones. "I am your *Master!*"

He towered over Covenant; his arms rose in transport or imprecation. In one fist, he held the prize for which he had craved and plotted. The searing light he drew from the ring should have blinded Linden entirely, scorched her eyes out of their sockets. But from *moksha* Jehannum she had learned how to protect her senses. She felt that she was peering into the furnace of the desecrated sun; but she was still able to see.

Able to see the blow which Lord Foul hammered down on Covenant as if the wild magic were a dagger.

It made Mount Thunder lurch, snapped stalactites from the ceiling like a rain of spears which narrowly missed Linden. It slapped Covenant to the floor as if all his limbs had been broken. For an instant, a convulsion of lightning writhed over him. Power and coruscation like the immaculate silver-white of the ring clamored through him, shrilled along the lines of his form. She tried to yell; but the air in her lungs had given out.

When the blow passed, it left white flame spouting from the center of his chest.

The wound bled argent: all his blood was ablaze. Fire fountained from his gaping hurt, spat gouts and plumes of numinous and incandescent deflagration, untainted by any darkness or venom. During that moment, he looked like he was still alive.

But it was transitory. The fire faded rapidly. Soon it flickered and failed. His blasted husk lay on the floor and did not move again.

Too stunned to cry out, Linden hugged her arms around herself and keened in the marrow of her bones.

But Lord Foul went on laughing.

Like a ghoul he laughed, a demon of torment and triumph. His lust riddled the mountain; more stalactites fell. From wall to wall, a crack sprang through the chamber; and shattered stones burst like cries from the fissure. Kiril Threndor shrieked argent. The Despiser became titanic with white fire.

"Ware of me, my Enemy!" His shout deafened Linden in spite of her instinctive self-protection. She heard him, not with her overwhelmed ears, but with the tissues and vessels of her lungs. "I hold the keystone of Time, and I will reave it to rubble! Oppose me if you dare!"

Fire mounted around him, whipped higher and higher by his fierce arms. The ring raged like a growing sun in his fist. Already, his power dwarfed the Banefire, outsized every puissance she had ever witnessed, surpassed even the haunted faces of her nightmares.

Yet she moved. Crawling across the agonized lurch and shudder of the stone, she wrestled her weak body toward Covenant. She could not help him. She could not help herself. But she wanted to hold him in her embrace one more time. To ask his forgiveness, though he would never be able to hear her. Lord Foul had become so tremendous that only the edges of his gathering cataclysm were still discernible. She crept past him as if she were ignoring him. Battered and aggrieved of body and soul, she reached Covenant, sat beside him, lifted his head into her lap, and let her hair fall around his face.

In death, his visage wore a strange grimace of relief and pain. He looked like a man who was about to laugh and weep at the same time.

At least I trusted you, she replied. Whatever else I did wrong. I trusted you in the end.

Then anguish seized her heart.

You didn't even say good-bye.

None of the people who had died while she loved them had ever said good-bye.

She did not know how it was possible to continue breathing. Lord Foul's attar had become as intense as the light. The destruction he purposed tore a howl through the stone. Kiril Threndor became the stretched mouth of the mountain's hurt. Her mere flesh seemed to fray and dissolve in the proximity of such power. His blast was nearly ready.

Instinctively, almost involuntarily, she looked up from Covenant's guilt and innocence, impelled by an inchoate belief that there should be at least one witness to the riving of Time. While her mind lasted, she could still watch what the Despiser did, still send her protest to hound him into the heavens.

A maelstrom swept around him and grew as if he meant to break the Earth by consuming it alive. His fire was so extreme that it pulsed through the mountain, made all of Mount Thunder pound. But gradually he pulled the flame into himself, focused it in the hand that held the ring. Too bright to be beheld, his fist throbbed like the absolute heart of the world.

With a terrible cry, he hurled his globe-splitting power upward.

An instant later, his exaltation changed to astonishment and rage.

Somewhere in the rock which enclosed Kiril Threndor, his blast shattered. Because it was aimed at the Arch of Time, it was not an essentially physical force, though the concussion of its delivery nearly reft Linden of consciousness. It did no physical damage. Instead, it burst as if it had struck a midnight sky and snapped. In a fathomless abyss, ruptured fragments of fire shot and blazed.

And the hot lines of light spread like etchwork, merged and multiplied swiftly, took shape within the bulk of the mountain. From wild magic and nothingness, they created a sketch of a man.

A man who had placed himself between Lord Foul and the Arch of Time.

The outlines gained substance and feature as they absorbed the Despiser's attack.

Thomas Covenant.

He stood there inside Mount Thunder's gutrock, a specter altogether different than the ponderous stone. All which remained of his mortal being was the grimace of power and grief that marked his countenance.

"No!" the Despiser howled. *"No!"*

But Covenant replied, "Yes." He had no earthly voice, made no human sound. Yet he could be heard through the clamor of tormented stone, the constant repercussions of Lord Foul's fury. Linden listened to him as if he were as clear as a trumpet. "Brinn showed me the way. He beat the Guardian of the One Tree by sacrificing himself, letting himself fall. And Mhoram told me to 'Remember the paradox of white gold.' But for a long time I didn't understand. I'm the paradox. You can't take the wild magic away from me." Then he seemed to move forward, concentrating more intensely on the Despiser. His command was as pure as white fire. "Put down the ring."

"Never!" Lord Foul shouted instantly. Might leaped in him, wild for use. "I know not what chicane or madness has brought you before me from the Dead—but it will not avail! You have once cast me down! I will not suffer a second debasement! *Never!* The white gold is mine, freely given! If you combat me, Death itself will not ward you from my wrath!"

Something like a smile sharpened the specter's acute face. "I keep telling you you're wrong. I wouldn't dream of fighting you."

Lord Foul's retort was a bolt that sizzled the air like frying meat. Power fierce enough to blow off the crown of the peak sprang at Covenant, raging for his immolation.

He did not oppose it, made no effort to resist or evade the attack. He simply accepted it. The clench of pain between his brows showed that he was hurt; but he did not flinch. The blast raved and scourged into him until Linden feared that even a dead soul could not survive it. Yet when it ended he had taken it all upon himself. Bravely, he stood forth from the fire.

"I'm not going to fight you." Even now, he seemed to pity his slayer. "All you can do is hurt me. But pain doesn't last. It just makes me stronger." His voice held a note of sorrow for the Despiser. "Put down the ring."

But Lord Foul was so far gone in fury and frustration that he might have been deaf. "No!" he roared again. No fear hampered him: he was transported to the verge of absolute violence.

"No!"

"NO!"

And with every cry he flung his utterest force against the Unbeliever.

Blast after blast, faster and faster. Enough white power to bring Mount Thunder down in rubble, cast it off Landsdrop into the ruinous embrace of Sarangrave Flat. Enough to leave the One Tree itself in ash and cinders. Enough to shatter the Arch of Time. All Lord Foul's ancient puissance was multiplied and channeled by the argent ring. He struck and struck, the unanswerable knell of his hunger adumbrating through Kiril Threndor until Linden's mind reeled and her life almost stopped, unable to support the magnitude of his rage. She clung to Covenant's body as if it were her last anchor and fought to endure and stay sane while Lord Foul strove to rip down the essential definition of the Earth.

But each assault hit nothing except the specter, hurt nothing except Covenant. Blast after blast, he absorbed the power of Despite and fire and became stronger. Surrendering to their savagery, he transcended them. Every blow elevated him from the mere grieving spectation of the Dead in Andelain, the ritualized helplessness of the Unhomed in *Coercri*, to the stature of pure wild magic. He became an unbreakable bulwark raised like glory against destruction.

At the same time, each attack made Lord Foul weaker. Covenant was a barrier the Despiser could not pierce because it did not resist him; and he could not stop. After so many millennia of yearning, defeat was intolerable to him. In accelerating frenzy, he flung rage and defiance and immitigable hate at Covenant. Yet each failed blow cost him more of himself. His substance frayed and thinned, denatured moment by moment, as his attacks grew more reckless and extravagant. Soon he had reduced himself to such evanescence that he was barely visible.

And still he did not stop. Surrender was impossible for him. If he had not been limited and confined by the mortal Time of his prison, he would have gone on forever, seeking Covenant's eradication. For a while, his form guttered and wailed as complete fury drove him to the threshold of banishment. Then he failed and went out.

Though she was stunned and stricken, Linden heard the faint metallic clink of the ring when it fell to the dais and rolled to a stop.

TWENTY: The Sun-Sage

SLOWLY, silence settled like dust back into Kiril Threndor. Most of the rocklight had been extinguished, but pieces still flared along the facets of the walls, giving the chamber an obscure illumination. Without the cloying scent of attar, the brimstone atmosphere smelled almost clean. Holes gaped in the ceiling where many of the stalactites had hung. Long tremors still rumbled into the distance, but they were no longer dangerous. They subsided like sighs as they passed beyond Linden's percipience.

She sat cross-legged near the dais, with Covenant's head in her lap. No breath stirred his chest. He was already growing cold. The capacity for peril which had made him so dear to her had gone out. But she did not let him go. His face wore a grimace of defeat and victory—a strange fusion of commandment and grace—that was as close as he would ever come to peace.

She did not look up to meet the argent gaze of his revenant. She did not need to see him bending over her as if his heart bled to comfort her. The simple sense of his presence was enough. In silence, she bowed over his body. Her eyes streamed at the beauty of what he had become.

For a long moment, his empathy breathed about her, clearing the last reek from the air, the taste of ruin from her lungs. Then he said her name softly. His voice was tender, almost human, as if he had not passed beyond the normal strictures of life and death. "I'm sorry." He seemed to feel that it was he who needed her forgiveness, rather than she who ached for his. "I didn't know what else to do. I had to stop him."

I understand, she answered. You were right. Nobody else could've done it. If she had possessed half his comprehension, a fraction of his courage, she might have tried to help him. There had been no other way. But she would have failed. She was too tainted by her own darkness for such pure sacrifices.

Nobody else, she repeated. But any moment now she was going to begin sobbing. She had lost him at last. When the true grief started, it might never stop.

Yet he had already passed beyond compassion into necessity. Or perhaps he felt the hurt rising in her and sought to answer it. As gentle as love, he said, "Now it's your turn. Pick up the ring."

The ring. It lay at the edge of the dais perhaps ten feet from her. And it was empty—devoid of light or power—an endless silver-white band with no more meaning than an unused manacle. Without Covenant or Lord Foul to wield it, it had lost all significance.

She was too weak and lorn to wonder why Covenant wanted her to do something about his ring. If she had been given some reason to hope that his spirit and his flesh might be brought back to each other, she would have obeyed him. No frailty or incomprehension would have prevented her from obeying him. But those questions had already been answered. And she had no desire to let his body out of her embrace.

"Linden." His emanations were soft and kind; but she felt their urgency growing. "Try to think. I know it's hard—after what you've been through. But try. I need you to save the Land."

She could not look up at him. His dead face was all that remained to her, all that held her together. If she raised her head to his unbearable beauty, she would be lost as well. With her fingertips, she stroked the gaunt lines of his cheek. In silence, she said, I don't need to. You've already done it.

"No," he returned at once. "I haven't." Every word made his tension clearer. "All I did was stop him. I haven't healed anything. The Sunbane is still there. It has a life of its own. And the Earthpower's been too badly corrupted. It can't recover by itself." His tone went straight into her heart. "Linden, please. Pick up the ring."

Into her heart, where a storm of lamentation brewed. Instinctively, she feared it. It seemed to rise from the same source which had given birth to her old hunger for darkness.

I can't, she said. Gusts and rue tugged through her. You know what power does to me. I can't stop hurting the people I want to help. I'll just turn into another Raver.

His spirit shone with comprehension. But he did not try to answer her dread, to deny or comfort it. Instead, his voice took on a note of harsh exigency.

"I can't do it myself. I don't have your hands—can't touch that kind of power anymore. I'm not physically alive. And I can be dismissed. I'm like the Dead. They can be invoked— and they can be sent away. Anybody who knows how can make me leave." He appeared to believe he was in that danger. "Even Foul could've done it, if he hadn't tried to use wild magic against me.

"Linden, think." His sense of peril burned in the cave. "Foul isn't dead. You can't kill Despite. And the Sunbane will bring him back. It'll restore him. He can't get past me to break the Arch. But he'll be able to do anything he wants to the Land—to the whole Earth.

"Linden!" The appeal broke from him. But at once he coerced himself to quietness again. "I don't mean to hurt you. I don't want to demand more than you can do. You've already done so much. But you've got to understand. You're starting to fade."

That was true. She recognized it with a dim startlement like the foretaste of a gale. His body had become harder and heavier, more real—or else her own flesh was losing definition. She heard winds blowing like the ancient respiration of the mountain. Everything around her—the rocklight, the blunt stone, the atmosphere of Kiril Threndor—sharpened as her perceptions thinned. She was dwindling. Slowly, inexorably, the world grew more quintessential and necessary than anything her trivial mortality could equal. Soon she would go out like a snuffed candle.

"This is the way it usually works," Covenant went on. "The power that called you here recoils when whoever summoned you dies. You're going back to your own life. Foul isn't dead—but as far as your summons goes, he might as well be. You'll lose your last chance." His demand focused on her like anger. Or perhaps it was her own diminishment that made him sound so fiercely grieved. "Pick up the ring!"

She sighed faintly. She did not want to move; the prospect of dissolution struck her as a promise of peace. Perhaps she would die from it—would be spared the storm of her pain. That hurt cut at her, presaging the wind which blew between the worlds. She had lost him. Whatever happened now, she had lost him absolutely.

Yet she did not refuse him. She had sworn that she would put a stop to the Sunbane. And her love for him would not let her go. She had failed at everything else.

She was in no hurry. There was still time. The process leeching her away was slow, and she retained enough percipience to measure it. Groaning at the ache in her bones, she unbowed her back, lowered his head tenderly to her thighs. Her fingers fumbled stiffly, as if they were no longer good for anything; but she forced them to serve her—to rebutton her shirt, closing at least that much protection over her bare heart. In her nightmare, she had used her shirt to try to stanch the bleeding. But she had failed then as well.

At that moment, a voice as precise as a bell rang in her mind. She seemed to recognize it, though it could not be him, that was impossible. Nothing had prepared her for his desperation.

—Avaunt, shade! Your work is done! Urge me no more dismay!

Commands clamored through the chamber; revocations thronged against Covenant. Instantly, his specter frayed and faded like blown mist. His power was gone. He had no way to refuse the dismissal.

Crying Linden's name in supplication or anguish, he dissolved and was effaced. His passing left trails of argent across her vision. Then they, too, were gone. There was nothing left of him to which she might cling.

At once, the bell rang again, clarion and compulsory. It was so close to frenzy that it nearly deafened her.

—Chosen, withhold! Do not dare the ring!

In the wake of the clangor, Findail and Vain entered Kiril Threndor, came struggling forward as if they were locked in mortal combat.

But the battle was all on one side. Findail thrashed and twisted, fought wildly; Vain simply ignored him. The *Elohim* was Earthpower incarnate, so fluid of essence that he could turn himself to any conceivable form. Yet he was unable to break the Demondim-spawn's grip. Vain still clasped his wrist. The black creation of the ur-viles remained adamantine and undaunted.

Together, they moved toward the ring. Findail's free hand clawed in that direction. His mute voice was a tuneless clatter of distress.

—He has compelled me to preserve him! But he must not be suffered! Chosen, withhold!

Now Vain resisted Findail, exerted himself to hold the *Elohim* back. But in this Findail was too strong for him. Fighting like hawks, they strove closer and closer to the dais.

Then Linden thought that she would surely move. She would go to the ring and take it, if for no other reason than because she trusted neither the Appointed nor his ebon counterpart. Vain was either unreachable or utterly violent.

Findail showed alternate compassion and disdain as if both were simply facets of his mendacity. And Covenant had tried to warn her. The abrupt brutality of his dismissal drew anger from her waning heart.

But she had waited too long. The mounting winds blew through her as if she were a shadow. Covenant's head had become far more real than her legs; she could not shift them. The ceiling leaned over her like a distillation of itself, stone condensed past the obduracy of diamond. The snapped fragments of the stalactites were as irreducible as grief. This world was too much for her. In the end, it surpassed all her conceptions of herself. Flashes of rocklight seemed to leave lacerations across her sight. Findail and Vain struggled and struggled toward the ring; and every one of their movements was as acute as a catastrophe. Vain wore the heels of the Staff of Law like strictures. She was fading to extinction. Covenant's dead weight held her helpless.

She tried to cry out. But she was too insubstantial to make any sound which Mount Thunder might have heard.

Yet she was answered. When she believed that she had wasted all hope, she was answered.

Two figures burst from the same tunnel which had brought her to Kiril Threndor. They entered the chamber, stumbled to a halt. They were desperate and bleeding, exhausted beyond endurance, nearly dead on their feet. Her longsword was notched and gory; blood dripped from her arms and mail. His breathing retched as if he were hemorrhaging. But their valor was unquenchable. Somewhere, Pitchwife found the strength to gasp urgently, "Chosen! The ring!"

The sudden appearance of the Giants defied comprehension. How could they have escaped the Cavewights? But they were *here*, alive and half prostrate and willing. And the sight of them lifted Linden's spirit like an act of grace. They brought her back to herself in spite of the gale pulling her away.

Findail was scarcely a step from the ring. Vain could not hold him back.

But the Appointed did not reach it.

Linden grasped Covenant's wedding band with the thin remains of her health-sense, drew fire spouting like an affirmation out of the metal. It was her ring now, granted to her in love and necessity; and the first touch of its flame restored her with a shock at once exquisitely painful and glad, ferocious and blessed. Suddenly, she was as real as the stone and the light, as substantial as Findail's frenzy, Vain's intransigence, the Giants' courage. The pressure thrusting her out of existence did not subside; but now she was a match for it. Her lungs took and released the sulfur-tinged air as if she had a right to it.

With white fire, she repelled the *Elohim*. Then, as kindly as if he were alive, she slid her legs from under Covenant's head.

Leaving him alone there, she went to take the ring.

For an instant, she feared to touch it, thinking its flame might burn her. But she knew better. Her senses were explicit: this blaze was hers and would not harm her. Deliberately, she closed her right fist around the fiery band.

At once, argent flame ran up her forearm as if her flesh were afire. It danced and spewed to the beat of her pulse. But it did not consume her, took nothing away from her: the price of power would be paid later, when the wild magic was gone. Instead, it seemed to flow into her veins, infusing vitality. The fire was silver and lovely, and it filled her with stability and strength and the capacity for choice as if it were a feast.

She wanted to shout aloud for simple joy. This was power, and it was not evil if she were not. The hunger which had dogged her days was only dark because she had feared it, denied it. It had two names, and one of them was life.

Her first impulse was to turn to the Giants, heal the First and Pitchwife of their hurts, share her relief and vindication with them. But Vain and Findail stood before her—the Appointed held by the clench of Vain's hand—and they demanded her attention.

The Demondim-spawn was looking at her: a feral grin shaped his mouth. Rough bark unmarked by lava or strain enclosed his wooden forearm. But Findail could not meet her gaze. The misery of his countenance was now complete. His eyes were blurred with tears; his silver hair straggled to his shoulders in strands of pain. He sagged against Vain as if all his strength had failed. His free hand clutched at his companion's black shoulder like pleading.

Linden had no more anger for them. She did not need it. But the focus of Vain's midnight eyes baffled her. She knew intuitively that he had come to the cusp of his secret purpose

—and that somehow its outcome depended on her. But even white gold did not make her senses sharp enough to read him. She was sure of nothing except Findail's fear.

Clinging to Vain's shoulder, the Appointed murmured like a child, "I am *Elohim*. Kastenessen cursed me with death— but I am not made for death. I must not die."

The Demondim-spawn's reply was so unexpected that Linden recoiled a step. "You will not die." His voice was mellifluous and clean, as perfect as his sculpted flesh—and entirely devoid of compassion. He neither dismissed nor acknowledged Findail's fear. "It is not death. It is purpose. We will redeem the Earth from corruption."

Then he addressed Linden. Neither deference nor command flawed his tone. "Sun-Sage, you must embrace us."

She stared at him. "Embrace—?"

He did not respond: his voice seemed to lapse as if he had uttered all the words he had been given and would never speak again. But his gaze and his grin met her like expectation, an unwavering and inexplicable certainty that she would comply.

For a moment, she hesitated. She knew she had little time. The pressure which sought to recant her summoning continued to grow. Before long, it would become too potent to be resisted. But the decision Vain required of her was crucial. Everything came together here—the purpose of the ur-viles, the plotting of the *Elohim*, the survival of the Land—and she had already made too many bad choices.

She glanced toward the Giants. But Pitchwife had no more help to give her. He sat against the wall and wrestled with the huge pain in his chest. Crusted blood rimmed his mouth. And the First stood beside him, leaning on her sword and watching Linden. She held herself like a mute statement that she would support with her last strength whatever the Chosen did.

Linden turned back to the Demondim-spawn.

For no sufficient reason, she found that she was sure of him. Or perhaps she had become sure of herself. White fire curled up and down her right arm, plumed toward her shoulder, accentuated the strong rush of her life. He was rigid and murderous, blind to any concerns but his own. But because he had been given to Covenant by Foamfollower—

because he had bowed to her once—because he had saved her life—and because he had met with anger the warping of his makers—she did what he asked.

When she put her arms around his neck and Findail's, the *Elohim* flinched. But his people had Appointed him to this peril, and their will held. At the last instant, he raised his head to meet his personal Würd.

In that instant, Linden became a staggering concussion of power which she had not intended and could not control.

But the blast had no outward force: it cast no light or fire, flung no fury. It might have been invisible to the Giants. All its energy was directed inward.

At the two strange beings hugged in her arms.

> *Wild magic graven in every rock,*
> *contained for white gold to unleash or control—*
> *gold, rare metal, not born of the Land,*
> *nor ruled, limited, subdued*
> *by the Law, with which the Land was created—*
> *and white—white gold—*
> *because white is the hue of bone:*
> *structure of flesh,*
> *discipline of life.*

Filled with white passion, her embrace became the crucible in which Vain and Findail melted and were made new.

Findail, the tormented *Elohim*: Earthpower incarnate. Amoral, arrogant, and self-complete, capable of everything. Sent by his people to redeem the Earth at any cost. To obtain the ring for himself if he could. And if he could not, to pay the price of failure.

This price.

And Vain, the Demondim-spawn: artificially manufactured by ur-viles. More rigid than gutrock, less tracible than bone. Alive to his inbred purpose and cruelly insensate to every other need or value or belief.

In Linden's clasp, empowered by wild magic, their opposite bodies bled together. While she held them, they began to merge.

Findail's fluid Earthpower. Vain's hard, perfect structure. And between them, the old definition forged into the heels of the Staff of Law. The *Elohim* lost shape, seemed to flow through the Demondim-spawn. Vain changed and stretched toward the iron bands which held his right wrist and left ankle.

His forearm shed its bark, gleamed like new wood. And the wood grew, spread out across the transformation, imposed its form upon the merging.

When she understood what was happening, Linden poured herself into the apotheosis. Wild magic supplied the power, but that was not enough. Vain and Findail needed more from her. Vain had been so perfectly made that he attained the stature of natural Law, brought to beauty all the long self-loathing of the ur-viles. But he had no ethical imperative, no sense of purpose beyond this climax. Findail's essence supplied the capacity for use, the strength which made Law effective. But he could not give it meaning: the *Elohim* were too self-absorbed. The transformation required something which only the human holder of the ring could provide.

She gave the best answer she had. Fear and distrust and anger she set aside: they had no place here. Exalted by white fire, she shone forth her passion for health and healing, her Land-born percipience, the love she had learned for Andelain and Earthpower. By herself, she chose the meaning she desired and made it true.

In her hands, the new Staff began to live.

Living Law filled the bands of lore; living power shone in every fiber of the wood. The old Staff had been rune-carved to define its purpose. But this Staff was alive, almost sentient: it did not need runes.

As her fingers closed around the wood, she was swept away in a flood of possibility.

Almost without transition, her health-sense became as huge as the mountain. She tasted Mount Thunder's tremendous weight and ancientness, felt the slow, wracked breathing of the stone. Cavewights scurried like motes through the unmeasured catacombs. Far below her, two Ravers cowered among the banes and creatures of the depths. Somewhere above them, the few surviving ur-viles watched Kiril Threndor in a reflective pool of acid and barked vindication at Vain's success. Spouting lava cast its heat onto her bare cheek. A myriad passages, dens, offal-pits, and charnels ached emptily and stank because the river which should have run through Treacher's Gorge was dry, supplied no water to wash the Wightwarrens. At the peak, Fire-Lions crouched, waiting in eternal immobility for the invocation to life.

And still her range increased. Wild magic and Law carried her outward. Before she could clarify half her perceptions, they reached beyond the mountain, went out to the Land.

The sun was rising. Though she stood in Kiril Threndor as if she were entranced, she felt the Sunbane dawn over her.

It was insanely intense. She had become too vulnerable: it stabbed along her nerves like the life-thrust of a hot knife, pierced her heart with venom like a keen fang. At once, she snatched herself back toward shelter—recoiled as if she were reeling to the cave where the Giants watched her in wide astonishment and Covenant lay dead upon the floor.

A fertile sun. Visceral fever gripped her. Sunder and Hollian had abhorred the sun of pestilence more than any other. But for Linden the fertile sun was the worst. It was ill beyond bearing, and everything it touched became a sob of anguish.

Echoes of her fire licked the walls. One long crack marked the floor. Something precious had been broken here. The First and Pitchwife stared at her as if she had become wonderful.

She had so little time left. She needed time, needed peace and rest and solace in which to muster courage. But the pressure of her dismissal continued to build. And the Staff of Law multiplied that force. Summons and return acted by rules which the Staff affirmed. Only her fist on the ring and her grip on the clean wood—only her clenched will—held her where she was.

She knew what she would have to do.

The prospect appalled her.

But she had already borne so much, and it would all be rendered meaningless if she faltered now. She did not have to fail. This was why she had been chosen. Because she was fit to fulfill Covenant's last appeal. It was too much—and yet it was hardly enough to repay her debts. Why should she fail? The mere thought that she would have to let the Sunbane touch her and touch her made her guts writhe, sent nausea beating down her veins. Horror raised mute cries of protest. In a sense, she would have to become the Land—to expose herself as fully as the Land to the Sunbane's desecration. It would be like being locked again in the attic with her dying father while dark glee came hosting against her—like enduring again her mother's abject blame until she was driven to the point of murder. But she had survived those things. She had found her way through them to a life worthy of more respect than she had ever given it. And the old man whose life she had saved on Haven Farm had given her a promise to sustain her.

Ah, my daughter, do not fear. You will not fail, however he may assail you. There is also love in the world.

Because she needed at least one small comfort for herself, she turned to the Giants.

They had not moved. They had no eyes to see what was happening. But indomitability still shone in the First's face. No grime or bloodshed could mar her iron beauty. She looked as acute as an eagle. And when he met Linden's gaze, Pitchwife grinned as if she were the last benison he would ever need.

With the Staff of Law and the white ring, Linden caressed the fatigue out of the First's limbs, restored her Giantish strength. The rupture in Pitchwife's lungs Linden effaced, healing his respiration. Then, so that she would be able to trust herself later, she unbent his spine, restructured the bones in a way that allowed him to stand straight, breathe normally.

But after that she had no more time. The wind between the worlds keened constantly across the background of her thoughts, calling her away. She could not refuse it much longer.

Be true.

Deliberately, she opened her senses and went by her own choice back out into the Sunbane.

Its power was atrocious beyond belief; and the Land lay broken under it—broken and dying, a helpless body slain like Covenant in her worst nightmare, the knife driven by an astonishing violence which had brought up more blood than she had ever seen in her life. And from that wound corruption welled upward.

Nothing could stop it. It ate at the ground like venom. The wound grew wider with every sunrise. The Land had been stabbed to its vitals. Murder spewed across the sodden hillsides, clogged the dry riverbeds, gathered and reeked in every

hollow and valley. Only the heart of Andelain remained un-
ruined; but even there the sway of slaughter grew. The very
Earth was bleeding to death. Linden had no way to save herself from drowning.

That was the truth of the Sunbane. It could never be
stanched. She was a fool to make the attempt.

But she held wild magic clenched like bright passion in her
right fist; and her left hand gripped the living Staff. Both were
hers to wield. Guided by her health-sense—by the same vulnerability which let the Sunbane run through her like a riptide,
desecrating every thew of her body, every ligament of her will
—she stood within her mind on the high slopes of Mount
Thunder and set herself to do battle with perversion.

It was a strange battle, weird and terrible. She had no op-
ponent. Her foe was the rot Lord Foul had afflicted upon the
Earthpower; and without him the Sunbane had neither mind
nor purpose. It was simply a hunger which fed on every form
of nature and health and life. She could have fired her huge
forces blast after blast and struck nothing except the ravaged
ground, done no hurt to anything not already lost. Only scant
moments after dawn, green sprouts of vegetation stretched
like screams from the soil.

And beyond this fertility lurked rain and pestilence and
desert in erratic sequence, waiting to repeat themselves over
and over again, always harder and faster, until the foundations of the Land crumbled. Then the Sunbane would be free
to spread.

Out to the rest of the Earth.

But she had learned from Covenant—and from the Raver's
possession. She did not attempt to attack the Sunbane. Instead, she called it to herself, accepted it into her personal
flesh.

With white fire she absorbed the Land's corruption.

At first, the sheer pain and horror of it excruciated her
hideously. One shrill cry as hoarse as terror ripped her throat,
rang like Kevin's despair over the wide landscape below her,
echoed and echoed in Kiril Threndor until the Giants were
frantic, unable to help her. But then her own need drove her
to more power.

The Staff flamed so intensely that her body should have
been burned away. Yet she was not hurt. Rather, the pain she

had taken upon herself was swept from her—cured and cleansed, and sent spilling outward as pure Earthpower. With Law she healed herself.

She hardly understood what she was doing: it was an act of exaltation, chosen by intuition rather than conscious thought. But she saw her way now with the reasonless clarity of joy. It could be done: the Land could be redeemed. With all the passion of her thwarted heart, all the love she had learned and been given, she plunged into her chosen work.

She was a storm upon the mountain, a barrage of determination and fire which no eyes but hers could have witnessed. From every league and hill and gully and plain of the Land, every slope of Andelain and cliff of the peaks, every southern escarpment and northern rise, she drew ruin into herself and restored it to wholeness, then sent it back like silent rain, analystic and invisible.

Her spirit became the medicament that cured. She was the Sun-Sage, the Healer, Linden Avery the Chosen, altering the Sunbane with her own life.

It fired green at her like the sickness of emeralds. But she understood intimately the natural growth and decay of plants. They found their Law in her, their lush or hardy order, their native abundance or rarity; and then the green was gone.

Blue volleyed thunderously at her head, then lost the Land as she accepted every drop of water and flash of violence.

The brown of deserts came blistering around her, scorched her skin. But she knew the necessity of heat—and the restriction of climate. She felt in her bones the rhythm of rise and fall, the strict and vital alternation of seasons, summer and winter. The desert fire was cooled to a caress by the Staff and emitted gently outward again.

And last, the red of pestilence, as scarlet as disease, as stark as adders. It swarmed against her like a world full of bees, shot streaks of blood across her vision. In spite of herself, she was fading, could not keep from being hurt. But even pestilence was only a distortion of the truth. It had its clear place and purpose. When it was reduced, it fit within the new Law which she set forth.

Sun-Sage and ring-wielder, she restored the Earthpower and released it upon the wracked body of the Land.

She could not do everything. Already, she had made herself faint with self-expenditure, and the ground sprawling below her to the horizons reeled. She had nothing left with which she might bring back the Land's trees and meadows and crops, its creatures and birds. But she had done enough. She knew without questioning the knowledge that seeds remained in the soil—that even among the wrecked treasures of the Waynhim were things which might yet produce fruit and young—that the weather would be able to find its own patterns again. She saw birds and animals still flourishing in the mountains to the west and south, where the Sunbane had not reached: they would eventually return. The people who stayed alive in their small villages would be able to endure.

And she saw one more reason for hope, one more fact that made the future possible. Much of Andelain had been preserved. Around its heart, it had mustered its resistance—and had prevailed.

Because Sunder and Hollian were there.

In their human way, they contained as much Earthpower as the Hills; and they had fought. Linden saw how they had fought. The loveliness of what they were—and of what they served—was lambent about them. Already, it had begun to regain the lost region.

Yes, she breathed to herself. Yes.

Across the wide leagues, she spoke a word to them that they would understand. Then she withdrew.

She feared the dismissal would take her while she was still too far from her body to bear the strain. As keen as a gale, the wind reached toward her. Too weary even to smile at what she had accomplished, she went wanly back through the rock toward Kiril Threndor and dissolution.

When she gained the cave, she saw in the faces of the Giants that she had already faded beyond their perceptions. Grief twisted Pitchwife's visage; the First's eyes streamed. They had no way of knowing what had happened—and would not know it until they found their way out of the Wight-warrens to gaze upon the free Land. But Linden could not bear to leave them hurt. They had given her too much. With her last power, she reached out and placed a silent touch of victory in their minds. It was the only gift she had left.

But it, too, was enough. The First started in wonder: unexpected gladness softened her face. And Pitchwife threw back his head to crow like a clean dawn, "Linden Avery! Have I not said that you are well Chosen?"

The long wind pulled through Linden. In moments, she would lose the Giants forever. Yet she clung to them. Somehow, she lasted long enough to see the First pick up the Staff of Law.

Linden still held the ring; but at the last moment she must have dropped the Staff beside the dais. The First lifted it like a promise. "This must not fall to ill hands," she murmured. Her voice was as solid as granite: it nearly surpassed Linden's hearing. "I will ward it in the name of the future which Earthfriend and Chosen have procured with their lives. If Sunder or Hollian yet live, they will have need of it."

Pitchwife laughed and cried and kissed her. Then he bent, lifted Covenant into his arms. His back was strong and straight. Together, he and the First left Kiril Threndor. She strode like a Swordmain, ready for the world. But he moved at her side with a gay hop and caper, as if he were dancing.

There Linden let go. The mountain towered over her, as imponderable as the gaps between the stars. It was heavier than sorrow, greater than loss. Nothing would ever heal what it had endured. She was only mortal; but Mount Thunder's grief would go on without let or surcease, unambergrised for all time.

Then the wind took her, and she felt herself go out.

Out into the dark.

Restoration

TWENTY-ONE: "To Say Farewell"

BUT when she was fully in the grip of the wind, she no longer felt its force. It reft her from the Land as if she were mist; but like mist she could not be hurt now. She had been battered numb. When the numbness passed, her pain would find its voice again and cry out. But that prospect had lost its power to frighten her. Pain was only the other side of love; and she did not regret it.

Yet for the present she was quiet, and the wind bore her gently across the illimitable dark. Her percipience was already gone, lost like the Land: she had no way to measure the spans of loneliness she traversed. But the ring—Covenant's ring, *her* ring—lay in her hand, and she held it for comfort.

And while she was swept through the midnight between worlds, she remembered music—little snatches of a song Pitchwife had once sung. For a time, they were only snatches. Then their ache brought them together.

> My heart has rooms that sigh with dust
> And ashes in the hearth.
> They must be cleaned and blown away
> By daylight's breath.
> But I cannot essay the task,
> For even dust to me is dear;
> For dust and ashes still recall,
> My love was here.

I know not how to say Farewell,
   When Farewell is the word
That stays alone for me to say
   Or will be heard.
But I cannot speak out that word
   Or ever let my loved one go:
How can I bear it that these rooms
   Are empty so?

I sit among the dust and hope
   That dust will cover me.
I stir the ashes in the hearth,
   Though cold they be.
I cannot bear to close the door,
   To seal my loneliness away
While dust and ashes yet remain
   Of my love's day.

The song made her think of her father.

He came back to her like Pitchwife's voice, sprawling there in the old rocker while his last life bled away—driven to self-murder by the possession of Despite. His loathing of himself had grown so great that it had become a loathing of life. It had been like her mother's religion, only able to prove itself true by imposing itself upon the people around it. But it had been false; and she thought of him now with regret and pity which she had never before been able to afford. He had been wrong about her: she had loved him dearly. She had loved both her parents, although she had been badly misled by her own bitterness.

In a curious way, that recognition made her ready. She was not startled or bereft when Covenant spoke to her out of the void.

"Thank you," he said gruffly, husky with emotion. "There aren't enough words for it anywhere. But thanks."

The sound of his voice made tears stream down her face. They stang like sorrow on her cheeks. But she welcomed them and him.

"I know it's been terrible," he went on. "Are you all right?"

She nodded along the wind that seemed to rush without motion around her as if it had no meaning except loss. I

think so. Maybe. It doesn't matter. She only wanted to hear
his voice while the chance lasted. She knew it would not
last long. To make him speak again, she said the first words
that occurred to her.

"You were wonderful. But how did you do it? I don't have
any idea how you did it."

In response, he sighed—an exhalation of weariness and
remembered pain, not of rue. "I don't think I did it at all. All
I did was *want*. The rest of it—

"Caer-Caveral made it possible. Hile Troy." An old longing
suffused his tone. "That was the 'necessity' he talked about.
Why he had to give his life. It was the only way to open
that particular door. So that Hollian could be brought back.
And so that I wouldn't be like the rest of the Dead—unable
to act. He broke the Law that would've kept me from oppos-
ing Foul. Otherwise I would've been just a spectator.

"And Foul didn't understand. Maybe he was too far gone.
Or maybe he just refused to believe it. But he tried to ignore
the paradox. The paradox of white gold. And the paradox of
of himself. He wanted the white gold—the ring. But I'm the
white gold too. He couldn't change that by killing me. When
he hit me with my own fire, he did the one thing I couldn't
do for myself. He burned the venom away. After that, I was
free."

He paused for a moment, turned inward. "I didn't know
what was going to happen. I was just terrified that he would
let me live until after he attacked the Arch." Dimly, she remembered the way Covenant had jibed at Lord Foul as if
he were asking for death.

"We aren't enemies, no matter what he says. He and I are
one. But he doesn't seem to know that. Or maybe he hates
it too much to admit it. Evil can't exist unless the capacity to
stand against it also exists. And you and I are the Land—in
a manner of speaking, anyway. He's just one side of us. That's
his paradox. He's one side of us. We're one side of him.
When he killed me, he was really trying to kill the other
half of himself. He just made me stronger. As long as I accepted him—or accepted myself, my own power, didn't try to
do to him what he wanted to do to me—he couldn't get past
me."

There he fell silent. But she had not been listening to him

with any urgency. She had her own answers, and they sufficed. She listened chiefly to the sound of his voice, cared only that he was with her still. When he stopped, she groped for another question After a moment, she asked him how the First and Pitchwife had been able to escape the Cavewights.

At that, a note like a chuckle gleamed along the wind. "Ah, that." His humor was tinged with grimness; but she treasured it because she had never heard him come so close to laughter. "That I'll take credit for.

"Foul gave me so much power. And it made me crazy to stand there and not be able to touch you. I had to do something. Foul knew what the Cavewights were doing all along. He let them do it to put more pressure on us. So I made something rise out of the Wightbarrow. I don't know what it was—it didn't last long. But while the Cavewights were bowing, the First and Pitchwife had a chance to get away. Then I showed them how to reach you."

She liked his voice. Perhaps guilt as well as venom had been burned out of it. They shared a moment of companionship. Thinking about what he had done for her, she almost forgot that she would never see him alive again.

But then some visceral instinct warned her that the darkness was shifting—that her time with him was almost over. She made an effort to articulate her appreciation.

"You gave me what I needed. I should be thanking you. For all of it. Even the parts that hurt. I've never been given so many gifts. I just wish—"

Shifting and growing lighter. On all sides, the void modulated toward definition. She knew where she was going, what she would find when she got there; and the thought of it brought all her hurts and weaknesses together into one lorn outcry. Yet that cry went unuttered back into the dark. In mute surprise, she realized that the future was something she would be able to bear.

Just wish I didn't have to lose you.

Oh, Covenant!

For the last time, she lifted her voice toward him, spoke to him as if she were a woman of the Land:

"Farewell, beloved."

His response came softly, receding along the wind. "There's no need for that. I'm part of you now. You'll always remember."

At the edge of her heart, he stopped. She was barely able to hear him.

"I'll be with you as long as you live."

Then he was gone. Slowly, the gulf became stone against her face.

Light swelled beyond her eyelids. She knew before she raised her head that she had come back to herself in the ordinary dawn of a new day.

The air was cool. She smelled dew and springtime and cold ash and budding trees. And blood that was already dry.

For a long moment, she lay still and let the translation complete itself. Then she levered her arms under her.

At once, a forgotten pain labored in the bones behind her left ear. She groaned involuntarily, slumped again to the stone.

She would have been willing to lie still while she persuaded herself that the hurt did not matter. She was in no hurry to look at her surroundings. But as she slumped, unexpected hands came to her shoulders. They were not strong in the way she had learned to measure strength; but they gripped her with enough determination to lift her to her knees. "Linden," a man's care-aged voice breathed. "Thank God."

Her eyes were slow to focus; her sight seemed to come back from a great distance. She was conscious of the dawn, the blurred gray stone, the barren hollow set like a bowl of death into the heart of the green woods. But gradually she made out Covenant's form. He was stretched on the rock nearby, within the painted triangle of blood. The light stroked her dear face like a touch of annunciation.

From the center of his chest jutted the knife which had made everything else necessary.

The man holding her repeated her name. "I'm so sorry," he murmured. "I never should've gotten you into this. We shouldn't have let him keep her. But we didn't know he was in this much danger."

Slowly, she turned her head and met the alarmed and wearied gaze of Dr. Berenford.

His eyes seemed to wince in their sockets, making the heavy pouches under them quiver. His old moustache drooped over his mouth. The characteristic wry dyspepsia of his tone was gone; it failed him here. Almost fearfully, he asked her the same question Covenant had asked. "Are you all right?"

She nodded as well as the pain in her skull allowed. Her voice scraped like rust in her throat. "They killed him." But no words were adequate to her grief.

"I know." He urged her into a sitting position. Then he turned away to snap open his medical bag. A moment later, she smelled the pungence of antiseptic. With reassuring gentleness, he parted her hair, probed her injury, began to cleanse the wound. But he did not stop talking.

"Mrs. Jason and her three kids came to my house. You probably saw her outside the courthouse the first day you were here. Carrying a sign that said, 'Repent.' She's one of those people who thinks doctors and writers just naturally go to hell. But this time she needed me. Got me out of bed a few hours ago. All four of them—" He swallowed convulsively. "Their right hands were terribly burned. Even the kids."

He finished tending her hurt, but did not move to face her. For a while, she stared sightlessly at the dead ash of the bonfire. But then her gaze returned to Covenant. He lay there in his worn T-shirt and old jeans as if no cerements in all the world could give his death dignity. His features were frozen in fear and pain—and in a kind of intensity that looked like hope. If Dr. Berenford had not been with her, she would have taken Covenant into her arms for solace. He deserved better than to lie so untended.

"At first she wouldn't talk to me," the older man went on. "But while I drove them to the hospital, she broke down. Somewhere inside her, she had enough decency left to be horrified. Her kids were wailing, and she couldn't bear it. I guess none of them knew what they were doing. They thought God had finally recognized their righteousness. They all had the same vision, and they just obeyed it. They whipped themselves into a tizzy killing a horse to get the blood they used to mark his house. They weren't sane anymore.

"Why they picked on him I don't know." His voice shook. "Maybe because he wrote 'unChristian' books. She kept talking about 'the maker of desecration.' When he was forced to offer himself for sacrifice, the world would be purged of sin. Retribution and apocalypse. And Joan was his victim. She couldn't be rescued any other way." His bitterness mounted. "What a wonderful idea. How could they resist it?

They thought they were saving the world when they put their hands in that fire.

"They didn't snap out of it until you interrupted them."

Linden understood his dismay, his anger. But she had passed the crisis. Without turning, she said, "They were like Joan. They hated themselves—their lives, their poverty, their ineffectuality." Like my parents. "It made them crazy." She yearned with pity for the people who had done this to Covenant.

"I suppose so," Dr. Berenford sighed. "It wouldn't be the first time." Then he resumed, "Anyway, I left Mrs. Jason in Emergency and got the Sheriff. He didn't exactly believe me —but he came out to Haven Farm anyway. We found Joan. She was asleep in the house. When we woke her up, she didn't remember a thing. But she looked like she had her mind back. I couldn't tell. At least she wasn't violent anymore.

"I made the Sheriff take her to the hospital. Then I came looking for you."

Again he swallowed at his distress. "I didn't want him with me. I didn't want him to think you were responsible for this."

At that, she looked toward him in wonder. His concern for her—his desire to spare her the conclusions which the Sheriff might draw from finding her alone with Covenant's body—touched the spring of something new in her; and it opened as if it were blossoming. His face had sagged under the weight of his baffled care; he appeared reluctant to meet her gaze. But he was a good man; and when she looked at him she saw that Covenant's spirit was not dead. Without knowing it, he showed her the one true way to say Farewell.

She placed her hand on his shoulder. Softly, she said, "Don't blame yourself. You couldn't have known what would happen. And he got what he wanted most. He made himself innocent." Then she leaned on him so that she could rise to her feet.

The sunlight felt warm and kind to her weariness. Above the bare slopes of the hollow stood trees wreathed in the new green of spring, buoyant, ineffable, and clean. In this world also there was health to be served, hurts to be healed.

When the older man joined her, she said, "Come on. We've got work to do. Mrs. Jason and her kids weren't the only ones. We have a lot more burned hands to take care of."

After a moment, Dr. Berenford nodded. "I'll tell the Sheriff where to find him. At least we can make sure he gets a decent burial."

"Yes," she answered. The sun filled her eyes with brightness. Together, she and her companion started up the barren hillside toward the trees.

With her right hand, Linden Avery kept a sure hold on her wedding ring.

Here ends
The Second Chronicles of Thomas Covenant.

Glossary

ak-Haru: a supreme *Haruchai* honorific

aliantha: treasure-berries

Amith: a woman of Crystal Stonedown

Anchormaster: second-in-command aboard a Giantship

Andelain, the Hills of: a region of the Land free of the Sunbane

Appointed, the: an *Elohim* chosen to bear a particular burden;
Findail

Arch of Time, the: symbol of the existence and structure of
time

arghule/arghuleh: ferocious ice-beasts

Atiaran: former woman of Mithil Stonedown; mother of Lena

Bahgoon: character in a Giantish tale

Banefire, the: fire by which the Clave wields the Sunbane

Bannor: former Bloodguard

Berek Halfhand: ancient hero; the Lord-Fatherer

Bern: *Haruchai* lost to the Clave

Bhrathair, the: a people who live on the verge of the Great
Desert

Bhrathairealm: the land of the *Bhrathair*

Bloodguard: former servants of the Council of Lords

Brinn: *Haruchai*; former protector of Covenant, now Guardian
of the One Tree

caamora: Giantish ordeal of grief by fire

Cable Seadreamer: a Giant; member of the Search; brother
of Honninscrave; possessed by the Earth-Sight; slain at the
One Tree

477

Caer-Caveral: Forestal of Andelain; formerly Hile Troy

Caerroil Wildwood: former Forestal of Garroting Deep

Cail: *Haruchai*; former protector of Linden Avery; now protector of Covenant

Cavewights: evil earth-delving creatures living within Mount Thunder

Ceer: *Haruchai*; slain in *Bhrathairealm*

Celebration of Spring, the: the Dance of the Wraiths of Andelain on the dark of the moon in the middle night of Spring

Center Plains, the: a region of the Land

Chant: one of the *Elohim*

Chosen, the: title given to Linden Avery

clachan, **the:** demesne of the *Elohim*

Clave, the: the rulers of the Land

Coercri: The Grieve; former home of the Giants in Seareach

Colossus of the Fall, the: ancient stone figure formerly guarding the Upper Land

Corruption: *Haruchai* name for Lord Foul

Council of Lords: former rulers of the Land

Courser: beast of transport made by the Clave by the power of the Sunbane

croyel: mysterious creatures which bargain for power

Crystal Stonedown: village of the Land; home of Hollian

Dancers of the Sea, the: *merewives*

Daphin: one of the *Elohim*

Dawngreeter: highest sail on the foremast of a Giantship

Dead, the: specters of those who have died

Defiles Course: a river of the Land

Demondim, the: spawners of ur-viles and Waynhim

Demondim-spawn: Vain

Despiser, the: Lord Foul

Despite: evil

dhurng: a Waynhim

diamondraught: Giantish liquor

Dolewind, the: wind blowing to the Soulbiter

dromond: a Giantship

Drool Rockworm: former Cavewight

During Stonedown: home of Hamako; former village destroyed by the *Grim*

Durris: *Haruchai*

Earthfriend: title given to Berek Halfhand, then to Covenant

Earthpower, the: source of all power in the Land

Earth-Sight: Giantish ability to perceive distant dangers and needs

eh-Brand: one who can use wood to read the Sunbane; Hollian

Elemesnedene: home of the *Elohim*

Elena: former High Lord; daughter of Lena and Covenant

Elohim, the: a faery people first met by the wandering Giants

Enemy: Lord Foul's term of reference for the Creator

Far Woodhelven: a village of the Land

Findail: one of the *Elohim*; the Appointed

Fire-Lions: fire-flow of Mount Thunder

First of the Search, the: leader of the Giants who follow the Earth-Sight

Fleshharrower: former Giant-Raver; *moksha* Jehannum

Foamkite: *tyrscull* belonging to Honninscrave and Seadreamer

Fole: *Haruchai*

Forestal: a protector of the forests of the Land

Foul's Creche: the Despiser's former home; destroyed by Covenant

Furl Falls: waterfall at Revelstone

Gallows Howe: place of execution in Garroting Deep

Garroting Deep: a former forest of the Land

ghramin: a Waynhim

Giants: a seafaring people of the Earth

Giantclave: Giantish conference

Giantfriend: title given to Covenant

Giantship: stone sailing vessel made by Giants

Giant Woods: a forest of the Land

Gibbon: the na-Mhoram; leader of the Clave

Gilden: a maplelike tree with golden leaves

Glimmermere: a lake on the upland above Revelstone

Gossamer Glowlimn: a Giant; the First of the Search

Graveler: one who uses stone to wield the Sunbane; Sunder

graveling: fire-stones

Gravin Threndor: Mount Thunder

Great Desert, the: a region of the Earth; home of the *Bhrathair* and the Sandgorgons

Great Swamp, the: a region of the Land

Grey River, the: a river of the Land
Grieve, The: *Coercri*
Grim, **the:** destructive storm sent as a curse by the Clave
Grimmand Honninscrave: a Giant; Master of Starfare's Gem; member of the Search; brother of Cable Seadreamer
Guardian of the One Tree, the: mystical figure warding the approach to the One Tree; also *ak-Haru Kenaustin Ardenol*

Halfhand: title given to Covenant as well as to Berek
Hall of Gifts, the: large chamber in Revelstone devoted to artworks of the Land
Hamako: former Stonedownor adopted by Waynhim
Harn: *Haruchai*; protector of Hollian
Haruchai, **the:** a people who live in the Westron Mountains
Hearthcoal: a Giant; cook of Starfare's Gem; wife of Seasauce
Heft Galewrath: a Giant; Storesmaster of Starfare's Gem
Herem: a Raver
Hergrom: *Haruchai*; slain in *Bhrathairealm*
High Lord: former leader of the Council of Lords
Hile Troy: a man formerly from Covenant's world who became a Forestal
Hollian: daughter of Amith; eh-Brand formerly of Crystal Stonedown
Home: homeland of the Giants
Hotash Slay: flow of lava formerly protecting Foul's Creche

Illearth Stone, the: green stone; a source of evil power
Illender: title given to Covenant
Infelice: reigning leader of the *Elohim*
Isle of the One Tree, the: location of the One Tree

Jehannum: a Raver; also known as *moksha*
jheherrin: living by-products of Lord Foul's misshaping

Kalina: wife of Nassic; mother of Sunder; former woman of Mithil Stonedown
Kasreyn of the Gyre: a thaumaturge; former power in *Bhrathairealm*
Kastenessen: one of the *Elohim*; former Appointed
Keep of the na-Mhoram: Revelstone
Kemper, the: chief minister of *Bhrathairealm*; Kasreyn

Kemper's Pitch: highest level of the Sandhold

Kenaustin Ardenol: a figure of *Haruchai* legend; paragon and measure of all *Haruchai* virtues

Kevin Landwaster: son of Loric; former Lord; enactor of the Ritual of Desecration

Kevin's Watch: mountain lookout near Mithil Stonedown

Kiril Threndor: Heart of Thunder; chamber of power within Mount Thunder

krill, **the:** knife of power formed by Loric

Land, the: a focal region of the Earth

Landsdrop: great cliff separating the Upper and Lower Lands

Landsverge Stonedown: a village of the Land

Landwaster: title given to Kevin

Law, the: the natural order

Law of Death, the: separation of the living from the dead

Law of Life, the: separation of the dead from the living

Lena: former woman of Mithil Stonedown; daughter of Atiaran; mother of Elena

lianar: wood of power used by an eh-Brand

Lord-Fatherer, the: title given to Berek

Lord Foul: the Despiser

Lords, the: former rulers of the Land

Lord's Keep: Revelstone

Loric Vilesilencer: son of Damelon; father of Kevin; former Lord

Lower Land, the: region east of Landsdrop

lurker of the Sarangrave: a swamp-monster

Marid: a man of Mithil Stonedown; Sunbane victim

Master: Clave-name for Lord Foul

Master, the: captain of a Giantship

master-rukh: iron triangle in Revelstone which feeds and reads all other *rukhs*

Memla: a former Rider of the Clave

merewives: the Dancers of the Sea

metheglin: a beverage; mead

Mhoram: former High Lord

Mistweave: a Giant

Mithil River: a river of the Land

Mithil Stonedown: a village of the Land

moksha: a Raver; also known as Jehannum
Mount Thunder: a peak at the center of Landsdrop

na-Mhoram, the: leader of the Clave
na-Mhoram-in: highest rank of the Clave
na-Mhoram-wist: middle rank of the Clave
Nassic: a former man of Mithil Stonedown; father of Sunder, inheritor of the Unfettered One's mission to welcome Covenant
Nicor: great sea-monsters; said to be offspring of the Worm of the World's End
Nom: a Sandgorgon
North Plains, the: a region of the Land
Northron Climbs, the: a region of the Land

One Forest, the: ancient sentient forest which once covered most of the Land
One Tree, the: mystic tree from which the Staff of Law was made
Old Lords, the: the Lords of the Land prior to the Ritual of Desecration
orcrest: Sunstone; a stone of power, used by a Graveler

pitchbrew: a beverage combining *diamondraught* and *vitrim*, conceived by Pitchwife
Pitchwife: a Giant; member of the Search; husband of Gossamer Glowlimn
Prover of Life: title given to Covenant
Pure One, the: redemptive figure of *jheherrin* legend; Saltheart Foamfollower

Ramen: a people of the Land; tenders of the Ranyhyn
Ranyhyn: the great horses; formerly inhabited the Plains of Ra
Ravers: Lord Foul's three ancient servants
Rawedge Rim, the: mountains around *Elemesnedene*
Reader: a member of the Clave who tends and uses the *master-rukh*
Revelstone: mountain-city of the Clave
rhysh: a community of Waynhim
rhyshyshim: a gathering of *rhysh*; a place in which such gathering occurs
Rider: a member of the Clave

ring-wielder: *Elohim* term of reference for Covenant
Ritual of Desecration: act of despair by which Kevin Land-waster destroyed much of the Land
rocklight: light emitted by glowing stone
rukh: iron talisman by which a Rider wields power

sacred enclosure: former Vespers hall in Revelstone; now site of the Banefire and the *master-rukh*
Saltheart Foamfollower: former Giant
Salttooth: jutting rock in the harbor of Home
samadhi: a Raver; also known as Sheol
Sandhold, the: castle of the rulers of *Bhrathairealm*
Sandgorgon: a monster of the Great Desert
Sandgorgons Doom: imprisoning storm created by Kasreyn to trap the Sandgorgons
Sandwall, the: great wall defending *Bhrathairealm*
Sarangrave Flat: a region of the Lower Land
Search, the: quest of the Giants for the wound in the Earth seen by the Earth-Sight
Seareach: a region of the Land; formerly inhabited in Giants
Seasauce: a Giant; cook of Starfare's Gem; husband of Hearthcoal
Seven Wards, the: collection of knowledge hidden by Kevin
Sevinhand: a Giant; Anchormaster of Starfare's Gem
Sheol: a Raver; also known as *samadhi*
Shipsheartthew: the wheel of a Giantship
Sivit: a Rider
soothtell: ritual of prophecy practiced by the Clave
Soulbiter, the: dangerous ocean of Giantish legend
Soulsease River, the: a river of the Land
South Plains, the: a region of the Land
Staff of Law, the: a tool of power formed by Berek from the One Tree
Starfare's Gem: Giantship used by the Search
Stell: *Haruchai*; former protector of Sunder
Stonedown: a village of the Land
Stonedownor: inhabitant of a Stonedown
Stonemight Woodhelven: a village of the Land
Storesmaster: third-in-command aboard a Giantship
Sunbane, the: a power arising from the corruption of nature by Lord Foul
Sunder: son of Nassic; former Graveler of Mithil Stonedown

Sun-Sage, the: title given to Linden Avery by the *Elohim*; one who can affect the progress of the Sunbane
Sunstone: *orcrest*
Swordmain/Swordmainnir: Giant trained as a warrior

thronehall, the: the Despiser's former seat in Foul's Creche
Toril: *Haruchai* lost to the Clave
Treacher's Gorge: river-opening into Mount Thunder
treasure-berries: *aliantha*; a nourishing fruit
Trothgard: a region of the Land
tyrscull: a Giantish training vessel for apprentice sailors

Unbeliever, the: title given to Covenant
Unhomed, the: former Giants of Seareach
upland: plateau above Revelstone
Upper Land, the: region west of Landsdrop
ur-Lord: title given to Covenant
ur-viles: spawn of the Demondim; creatures of power; creators of Vain
ussusimiel: nourishing melon grown by the people of the Land

Vain: Demondim-spawn; bred by the ur-viles for a secret purpose
vitrim: nourishing fluid created by Waynhim
voure: a plant-sap which wards off insects; a medicine for Sunbane-sickness
Vow, the: Bloodguard oath of service to the Lords
vraith: a Waynhim

Warrenbridge: bridge leading to the catacombs under Mount Thunder
Waynhim: spawn of the Demondim; opposed to ur-viles
Weird of the Waynhim, the: Waynhim concept of doom, destiny, or duty
Westron Mountains: mountains bordering the Land
white gold: a metal of power not found in the Earth
White River, the: a river of the Land
Wightbarrow, the: cairn under which Drool Rockworm is buried
Wightwarrens: catacombs; home of the Cavewights under Mount Thunder

wild magic: the power of white gold; considered the keystone of the Arch of Time

Woodhelven: a village of the Land

Worm of the World's End, the: mystic creature believed by the *Elohim* to have formed the foundation of the Earth

Wraiths of Andelain: creatures of living light which inhabit Andelain

Würd of the Earth, the: term used by the *Elohim* to suggest variously their own nature, the nature of the Earth, and their ethical compulsions; could be read as Word, Worm, or Weird

About the Author

Born in 1947 in Cleveland, Ohio, Stephen R. Donaldson made his publishing debut with the first Covenant trilogy in 1977. Shortly thereafter he was named best New Writer of the Year and given the prestigious John W. Campbell Award. He graduated from the College of Wooster (Ohio) in 1968, served two years as a conscientious objector doing hospital work in Akron, then attended Kent State University where he received his M.A. in English in 1971. Donaldson now lives in New Mexico.